TRIPLE JEOPARDY: *THREE NOVELS*

TRIPLE JEOPARDY includes three novels by a master of detective fiction, and two of them feature the admirable Colonel Anthony Gethryn.

WARRANT FOR X: considered by Alexander Woollcott "the best detective story in any language."

ESCAPE: "a memorable adventure in breathlessness."

THE POLFERRY RIDDLE: a clever twist to the classic "locked room" mystery.

Scene: England

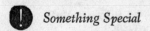 Something Special

TRIPLE JEOPARDY:

THREE NOVELS

PHILIP MacDONALD

Published for the Crime Club by
DOUBLEDAY & COMPANY, INC.
Garden City, New York
1962

All of the characters in this book
are fictitious, and any resemblance
to actual persons, living or dead,
is purely coincidental.

WARRANT FOR X

CHAPTER I

The fact that Sheldon Garrett was an American makes it comprehensible that, although a widely travelled and widely read person, it was not until his thirty-fourth birthday that he made acquaintance with any of the work of Mr. G. K. Chesterton. This birthday fell, in the year with which we are concerned, upon a September Friday and coincided happily enough with the first night of the London production of his play, *Wise Man's Holiday*. It being clear by 11:45 P.M. that the play was going to be a success, the party given after the show by Brooks-Carew was a decisively alcoholic affair. It is instructive to think that had it not been, Sheldon Garrett would not have spent the most of Saturday reading the *Napoleon of Notting Hill* and would not, therefore, have been himself in the vicinity of Notting Hill upon Sunday afternoon. For, if Brooks-Carew's drinks had been fewer and smaller, neither Sheldon Garrett nor Manvers, of the *Telegram*, would have reached that solemn stage of insobriety which led them, neither knowing the other from Adam or even Eve, to a ponderous literary discussion conducted in Brooks-Carew's bathroom; and then Garrett, looking over the Savoy bookstall on the following night, would not have purchased a cheap edition of what is, after all, perhaps the best of all Mr. Chesterton's good work.

He read from one o'clock upon Sunday morning until, at just before five, he had finished with the histories of Adam Wayne and Auberon. And then he slept, to wake at the awkward hour of 1 P.M. This tardiness necessitated the mendacious cancellation of a luncheon appointment and, further, left the liar with nothing to do in London upon a grey autumnal Sunday afternoon. He lunched in belated solitude and in his own sitting room. Over the meal he dipped again into *Napoleon*—and by half-past three was descending from a scarlet omnibus opposite the depressing façade of Notting Hill underground station.

He then walked—led, as it were, by Chance and Chesterton. At first unable to reconcile even the Sunday afternoon quietude of the main thoroughfare with the brave sombreness of the streets down which Adam Wayne had walked and wondered, he found himself, by a lucky turn to his left, at once in an atmosphere where indeed the railings were like spears.

London was very grey that day and, summertime having undergone its annual destruction three days before, the blue dimness of early evening soon began to blend with the steely light which had been all that told of a sun somewhere above smooth, unending clouds.

He had, he thought, been walking for some thirty minutes before he glanced at his watch and found, not without surprise, that it was a little more than double that time since he had alighted from the bus. He was in some sort of Ladbrookish square whose tall, grey-fronted, be-pillared houses frowned down with ugly and angular dignity upon an iron-surrounded oval of bright green grass and dusty, dark green bushes.

The place seemed dead and Garrett felt himself on a sudden very tired and—yes!—faintly afraid. He did up the top button of his overcoat, squared his admirable shoulders and set off at a brisk pace designed to assure himself that he was moving somewhere of set purpose.

He was unashamedly relieved when, coming to a side turning, he met another wayfarer in this dead place of glowering brick—a grimy man who carried over his shoulder a slender, laden sack.

They met almost face to face, so that the sack bearer was forced to step aside.

"Evening!" said Sheldon Garrett, who felt the need for speech.

"Eh?" said the sack bearer.

"Er," said Sheldon Garrett and hastily produced a cigarette case. "Got a match?"

The sack bearer searched in pockets with his right hand, balancing his sack with his left. Without a word he produced matches and proffered them.

"Thanks!" said Garrett and lit a cigarette which he did not want. He held out the still-open case. "Have one?"

The sack bearer shook his head. Garrett closed the case, put it back in his pocket and returned the box of matches.

"Thanks," he said.

The sack bearer returned box to pocket, shifted his burden from the left shoulder to the right, took a step sideways to avoid his accoster and marched off into the gathering gloom.

Young Garrett looked after him, feeling a violent and ridiculous urge to run in pursuit and—as he had seen in English newspaper reportings—"commit assault with intent to do grievous bodily harm." But Mr. Sheldon Garrett, traveller and man of substance and author of the successful play, *Wise Man's Holiday,* merely threw away a newly lighted cigarette and strode off in the opposite direction.

Now it was really dark. Behind curtains lights began to show in windows which hitherto had been blankly frowning eyes and every here and there, on high, the distorted rectangles of street lamps sent out feeble yellow radiance. Garrett tried to remember the course of his meanderings and came to the conclusion that if he kept bearing to his right he would once more reach the thoroughfare along whose bosom he had been borne from the Savoy and the haunts of men. He turned to his right and was in a street which was like many others along which he had walked. Halfway down it he saw a boy with a dog but he did not speak to the boy. He came to the end of the street and found forward progress barred. He turned left—and it seemed to him that he was in the same street yet again. He saw a woman with a dog. He did not speak to the woman. He walked on, unconsciously both lengthening and quickening his stride rather in the way in which a man lost in the bush will lengthen and quicken his stride before allowing his mind to tell him that he doesn't know, after all, where he is.

He turned to his right. And now he was clearly in a different street. It was narrower and the houses which lined it, although they, too, frowned, were shorter and dingier and behind their railings (which did not look in the least like spears) seemed to give out into the chill dank air an abstract miasma of decay. Onto a low wall dividing the pavement along which he walked from the dark shadows of the houses behind it jumped a long, gaunt cat. It stared at him with shiny yellow eyes and was gone.

He became aware now of physical as well as spiritual discomfort. His legs ached and his feet were resenting the pounding of paving stones. The chill air stung his face but beneath his clothes his body was uncomfortably warm.

He came to a turning upon his right and took it and found himself, by means of one of those sulky conjuring tricks which London so often performs, in a different world. Gone was the sense of decay. Now there surrounded him, like an uncomfortable cloak, that air of chilly, black-gloved rectitude which, owing to the lingering slaughter of the English language, must be expressed in the word "respectability." The houses were neat. The brass of letter boxes and knockers shone bright. The very street lamps seemed to have cleaner panes to their windows. The railings, though certainly not spears again, were yet frigid guardians of a privacy which needed no guard.

And then, though direfully discreet, came small shops, all but the last having barred doors and blank, shaded windows which offered nothing save unfriendliness.

Garrett strode on; but at the next corner suddenly halted. For the last shop was not, strictly speaking, a shop at all. Over its door hung a lantern encased in fancifully patterned wrought iron which tried to look old. And behind the glass panes of the lantern shone a yellow light and on the panes of the lantern appeared the words, in tortured Gothic script, Ye Willow-Pattern Tea Shoppe.

"Ah!" said Garrett aloud.

Most untraditionally he liked tea. And he was tired and footsore and too hot for more walking and his throat was parched. He pressed the handle of the muslin-curtained door and from somewhere in dim recesses came the tinkle of a mournful bell.

2

Inside the place was dimly lighted and larger than he had expected. Along one wall were ranged, to face each other, high-backed settles of deal stained to look like oak. On the walls were hanging plates and dishes of cheap earthenware painted to look like willow pattern. Such light as there was came from a central hanging lamp of brass designed to look as if it were old and from a few weakly powered and faintly pink bulbs held to the walls by iron brackets which tried to look like candlesticks. Ye Willow-Pattern Tea Shoppe was, in other words, own brother to a hundred other Tea Shoppes.

It was empty. For a moment Garrett looked about him, considering flight, but then there appeared—silently and as if by some dreary magic—the usual handmaiden. She was tall and willowy and fatigued. She was clad in the sort of long and shapeless garment which invariably goes with Tea Shoppes and had about her, as inevitably, an air of aggressive gentility. She did not speak to Garrett; she merely looked at him with a glitter of pince-nez.

Garrett said: "Tea. Could I have some tea, please?" and presently found himself seated, to face the door, in the last and darkest of the booths made by the settles.

He ordered China tea and, because it seemed expected of him, scones and jam. The neophyte drifted silently away to be lost in the shadows at the far end of the room. There came to Garrett's ears the sound of a door opening and shutting and then, from somewhere presumably behind this door, a faint chinking of china. He lit a cigarette and disposed himself as comfortably as the unfriendly settle would let him. He found himself still too warm and rose and took off his overcoat and put this down with his hat upon the settle facing him.

He had finished his cigarette when his tea came. Strangely enough it was good. He drank two cups and ate two pieces of one tasteless scone. He poured himself the third cup and lit another cigarette and sat back in his corner and wondered what he was thinking about and found that he did not know.

The street door opened with a faint squeaking followed by the dim tinkling of the bell. It closed again and the bell stopped ringing and Garrett heard footsteps and the voices of women. He was sitting in the angle formed by the wall and the back of his booth and he did not move. He felt, indeed, vaguely annoyed at the intrusion in the way that a man does when suddenly aroused from the pleasant state of musing heavily upon nothing. He heard another faint sound from the door in the black shadows at the far end of the shop and then, a moment later, another murmur of voices as the languid ancilla spoke with the newcomers. Then there came a sudden marching of feet and persons disposed themselves in the booth immediately next to his. He still had not moved forward, so that he did not see them nor they him; but his ears told him that there were two.

Followed murmurs, rustles, the clearing of a throat, clatters as umbrellas were laid down and creakings as bodies were disposed upon the deal seats. The neophyte came, swimming for a moment across Garrett's little field of vision, then departed with orders. The voice that gave the order was beyond doubt a woman's; but it was curiously deep and had in its tone a decisive and masculine quality which interested Garrett despite himself.

His cigarette had been finished before the new entry and now he idly debated with himself as to whether the trouble of reaching to a hip pocket for his case were worth the dubious solace of more tobacco. He decided that it was not and thereby irretrievably involved himself.

He looked at the watch upon his wrist. Its hands stood at twenty minutes to six. He had not realized that it was so late. He must be back at the Savoy and changing by half-past six. Without otherwise moving he put a hand to his breast pocket for his notecase, remembering that he had no change. He pulled out the soft leather wallet with fingers so idle that the thing slipped from them, struck softly against his knee and slid noiselessly to the floor. He bent to retrieve it. His groping hand did not find it at first, so that he was forced to sink to one knee and continue his fumbling over a wider area.

Curiously—because he was not particularly endeavouring to be quiet—it so happened that over the whole of this operation he made no noise at all.

His searching fingers had just found the edge of the wallet when there came to his ear, echoing curiously by reason of his nearness to the floor, the sound of voices from the next booth. The first voice was the deep one but the second voice was its very antithesis: high pitched yet soft; youthful yet pleasantly modulated; delightful yet somehow strange in accent to Garrett's ear. And it managed to convey, without tremolo, a suggestion of fear.

The first voice said: "I told you so. Not a soul in the place."

The second voice said: "Except the waitress . . . and . . . did you look in the booth behind me?"

The deep voice said: "Not a soul, I tell you! Don't be——"

The gentle voice said: "I'll look . . . just to make sure. . . . There's no harm . . ." It died away. Like the other voice it had not whispered and yet, like the other voice, it somehow conveyed to Garrett's ear a suggestion of furtiveness. The wallet now in his fingers, he remained—quite why he could not have told you at the moment—utterly immobile. He even held his breath. He heard through the pounding of the blood through his ears the sounds of someone rising; then a scraping upon the boards and then, following the sound of this one seating herself again, the second or gentle voice. It said:

"No. There isn't anybody." It was noticeably louder. It was, also, *surer*.

The deep voice said: "What did I tell you! Never talk secrets in a private house. Never talk secrets in a public park. If you must talk secrets, talk 'em in a teashop."

A muffled bubble of laughter, not conveying much of mirth, came from the other throat and the gentle voice said: "You do say such *things!*"

"What I say," said the deep voice, "always means something. . . . Now then, miss, what's your answer? Are you going to see it through? Or not?"

The gentle voice said: "I—I—can't make up my mind. It sort of frightens me. I—you see—I——"

To the ears of Sheldon Garrett, conscious not only of the slightly ludicrous indignity of his position but of certain views of his own upon eavesdroppers, came the sound of the service door opening and a faint rattling which told of the bearing of a laden tray. In one swift movement, cleverly noiseless, he was up from the floor and in his seat again.

The deep voice said in a harsh, savage half whisper which only just carried to Garrett's ear:

"Shut up!" And then, in a louder and commendably natural tone: "Good! Here's our tea!"

It came and its bearer went. Sheldon Garrett found himself relieved that not once did the languid servitor so much as glance in his direction. He sat back and played with the notecase, telling himself mendaciously that he was about to go. But he played with a deliberate absence of sound. And he did not go. Nor did he move.

The deep voice said roughly: "Now she's gone! Take that moony look off your face and answer up. On or off?"

"I—I—I tell you I'm . . ." stammered the gentle voice.

"Don't tell me you're afraid. You said that before."

"But I . . . but I . . ."

"You sound like a gramophone record that's stuck. I told you last time, and I'm telling you again today, that there's nothing to be afraid of!"

The gentle voice said after a noticeable pause:

"But I *am* afraid! Sometimes I want to do it and then I think perhaps that if I do terrible things will happen to me. Because after all it's—it's not *right!*" The words had come fast this time: only once, and that towards the end of the sentence, had there been any of the hesitation of the previous periods. But the speed had been the speed of agitation.

There followed a silence, broken by the chinking of china as, probably, the spout of a teapot clinked against a cup edge. Garrett took opportunity to remonstrate with himself. Why should he sit here, in deliberate hiding, and listen to the confidences of two women who imagined themselves alone? Why, because he was a stranger to London and had found a part of London which was inimical as the jungle, should he have this queer sense of disaster to come? Why, even if he were weak minded enough to allow climate and surroundings so to impress him, should he imagine that what was probably the beginning of some sordid discussion, abortive in all senses of the word, was a dark and hideous sidelight upon some facet of abomination? Why, in short, did he not cough and rattle crockery and get to his feet and stamp towards the door and pay his bill and go away from here? . . .

Four whys, and not an answer. He sat still.

The deep voice said—and it was harsher even than before: "So you're *frightened!* Frightened of doing something which couldn't possibly get you into any trouble! Frightened of living in comfort for a while and then getting a lump of money which'll keep you in a damn sight more than comfort for the rest of your life if you live to be a hundred! *Frightened!*" The voice suddenly altered its tone; with its next words it kept all the harshness but seemed to take on a sort of musing quality most unpleasing to the ear; a quality which was in itself a threat. It said: "Well, I'll have to go back and tell Evans. I don't suppose he'll like it, with you knowing all about things. But there we are."

"Oh!" said the gentle voice suddenly, itself on a new note. "Don't talk like that! I—I—I didn't say I wouldn't. I was just saying that I was——"

"Frightened! I know. Well, forget it and don't be a silly fool. Think of that money. God knows, you must want money or you'd never——"

"You don't understand! Of course I want the money!" The gentle voice was lower now; but still, by leaning a little forward, Sheldon Garrett could catch its words. "And I know *I* shan't get into trouble—at least if everything is as you and he said it would be . . . but it isn't that at all! It's—it's—well, I might get fond . . ." Here the gentle voice dropped so low that for the first time Garrett could not hear its words; only a little murmur reached his ear at the end of this sentence.

"You make me tired!" The deep voice was contemptuous. "Nobody's going to hurt it."

The note of sneering ire seemed to sting the owner of the gentle voice into some loss of temper herself. She said with a rather astonishing acerbity in her soft tones:

"Well, suppose they don't. It's still . . . not right! And anyhow, what about *him!*" The gentle voice paused on an upward and, as it were, temporarily triumphant inflection.

"Eh?" said the harsh voice quickly, and even in the tone of this one ejaculation Garrett could detect a sudden and intense interest. "What you talking about?"

"You know very well what I'm talking about. Suppose I *was* willing to take the position and then do what I'm told and then get the money. That's all right. But it doesn't mean that on top of that I'm willing to be mixed up in what's nothing more nor less than——"

Garrett did not hear the end of this sentence for the excellent reason that it was never finished. Instead of words there came a sudden violent creaking of the settle; a soft thud as something struck the edge of the table; a rattling of overturned crockery.

And then a whispered little scream of protest—from the gentle voice. It said:

"Oh, *don't!* You're hurting!"

Another creaking as someone resumed a seat. Then the deep voice again. It said in a tone much lower than it had used before and with a slowness which gave to it—at least to Garrett's ear—a quality of increased menace:

"You must be crazy!"

A little stifled sound which might be a sob. And then:

"You're rough! You hurt my wrist."

"Damn your wrist!"

Two stifled sounds, definitely sobs.

"You're—you're—horrible today!"

"You're mad today. . . . Will you tell me, *now*, what crazy bee's buzzing round in your bonnet?"

"I—I—I didn't mean anything. . . ."

"You don't say!"

"Don't look at me like that! You know I—I—why, you know I wouldn't ever—ever *say* anything."

The deep voice said: "You might not get the chance! . . . And don't sit there and snivel! Tell me, *now,* what crazy idea you've got in your head. *And* where you got it from. Come on, now!"

"I—I—oh dear! . . . I didn't mean anything. . . . It was something I heard the other——"

The deep voice interrupted in a savage half whisper. "Something you *heard?*" said the deep voice on a note of restrained fury. "Where did you hear it? When? What was it? Come on, tell me now or we'll go straight round and see Evans." The words came very fast and the voice was so low that Garrett only just caught them.

"The last time I was at the house. I was in the parlour there; and you and——"

"Keyhole work, eh!" said the deep voice. There was a muffled note to its clearness now, as if the words had been said without the speaker opening her teeth.

"No! No! I wasn't listening. Really I wasn't! I mean, not on purpose. I went over to that corner table there by the door to get a paper and the other man was talking very loud. I couldn't help hearing. I——"

"What—did—you—hear?"

"Please don't look at me like that. I didn't hear anything, really. I mean it wasn't—wasn't sort of definite. It only gave me a sort of idea and then when I was thinking . . . I suppose I'm really very stupid. . . ."

"You are! Go on."

"Well, I—I—when you got angry at me just now I was very silly and got sort of angry too. And then—well, I suppose I said more than I really meant. But I didn't say anything really. Did I?"

The harsh voice said: "You *should* be good for the job. You're just like a kid yourself. But sometimes kids get silly ideas. And very often kids wag their tongues a lot too much."

"I didn't mean to say anything, really I didn't. It was just that I got angry a little because I thought you were angry at me."

"Hmm! It doesn't matter what you meant to say. What does matter is what you think."

"I don't think anything. Really I don't. . . . I—I was just being silly." There was a dreadful note of eagerness in the soft voice.

The deep voice said less harshly: "That's all right, then—*if* you're on."

"You mean if I——"

"If you take the job. *And* do exactly as you're told. And remember, for your own damn fool sake, that nobody—is—going—to—get—hurt."

Pause.

The gentle voice said then with a tremulous but definite decision: "I'll do it."

The deep voice laughed; a musical and paradoxical sound at once genial and humourless. "You may seem a fool but you're a sensible girl really. That amount of money, *and* a possible extra cut, isn't bad for a few months work. Especially when the work's what *they'd* call a cinch."

The gentle voice said: "How long will it be?"

"You know enough not to ask silly questions like that. I can tell you how long it *won't* be. It won't be longer than six months."

"But it might be shorter. Do say it might be shorter."

The harsh voice chuckled again. "It not only *might* be shorter, it probably will be. And a damn sight shorter. . . . Here, let's get out of this."

Sheldon Garrett stiffened in his corner. Instinctively he drew his body back, pressing it against the wall and the back of his settle as if he would merge himself into the wood and plaster. To his strained ears the sound of a teaspoon rattling against a cup in traditional demand for attention sounded loud as gunfire. He started. Behind his right shoulder the deal boards creaked. He sat motionless, holding his breath and expecting every moment sounds from the other side of the far partition which would tell that his presence had been heard.

But it had not. The teacup was rattled again, furiously. In answer to it came first the creaking of the service door and then, more languid than ever, the genteel servitor. For a moment she crossed Garrett's line of vision again but again she did not look at him. He heard her beside the next booth; heard the harsh voice ask the amount owing and heard the mincing tones which answered her. . . .

And here Garrett made a mistake. He sat where he was. From behind the thin partition he could hear the chinking of money. Then came the inevitable "Thenk yew" of all Olde Tea Shoppes and the scraping bustle of departure.

Ancilla drifted once more away. Feminine heels clattered on the boards as his two neighbours went towards the door. Careful to be silent, Garrett leaned swiftly forward, propping his body on a hand placed at the very outside edge of his settle. He caught one glimpse of them as they opened the door. Their backs were as unlike as their voices—one short and solid and square, very erect, with a subtle suggestion of unperverted masculinity about it; the other tall, slender and with that charm which makes a man want to see the face.

They looked, somehow, just as he had imagined they would look. The short thick one—Deep Voice evidently—was clad in some dark, "respectable" clothing (the strange words *sub fusc* flooded into Garrett's mind). But the tall slim Gentle Voice had subdued touches of colour about her. Her hat, certainly, was red; and the fur about her neck was of a delightful blue-y grey. And he thought there had been a coloured belt to the dark overcoat.

He jerked himself back into hiding as they reached the door and one of them set fingers to its handle.

The bell clinked dismally as the door opened and then was silent as it shut behind the outgoers. Its opening brought with it, for a flash of time, a ghostly eddy of cold, dank air.

Garrett jumped to his feet, knocking the table with his knee so that cup and saucer and teapot rattled violently in the dusty silence. He was out of the booth and reaching for his coat and struggling into it in one continuous movement. He became aware, without time for surprise, that his heart was thudding as if he had been running. It is to be believed—though he is not quite sure upon the point himself—that in this dim sanctuary of the drear he even shouted for his bill. But no answer came and the service door did not creak and already the two women whose course he knew he must follow had been gone for many seconds.

He rammed on his hat, fumbled in his pocket, remembered that he had no change and in two bounds was at the door. He wrenched it open and plunged into outer air.

3

For a moment, with a most curious mixture of relief and disappointment, he thought he had lost them. And then, by the grace of God and a street lamp under which they passed, he saw them. They were to his right as he stood with his back to the door. They were some thirty yards away. There was no mistaking the backs.

He set off in pursuit. He wanted to run but restrained himself, for the sound of running feet in this brick solitude might well make his quarry turn to look. By dint of long and furious strides he was soon at a reasonable distance. The night was very still and he could hear the murmur of the women's voices as they talked ahead of him. He crossed the road lest they should have any feeling of pursuit. He walked along upon the far pavement only a few yards behind them.

But by having crossed the road he very nearly lost them again. For suddenly they went into a narrow, dark-mouthed turning to their right; a turning which, from his far side of the street, he had neither seen nor suspected. He plunged after them, again barely restraining himself from running.

It was an alleyway between two houses into which they had gone—probably, Garrett thought with dim memories of the peculiarities of English law, some ancient right of way which must be preserved. It was a dark narrow place with high walls and the tapping of their heels was flung back to him twentyfold by dismal, long-drawn echoes. He walked like Agag. He had lost way and was now some fifteen yards behind. He would have liked to shorten this distance but with the necessity here for tiptoed progress he could not.

The gloom lessened. At the far end of the alleyway there were lights and from the direction of the lights a steadily increasing rumble of traffic.

Garrett diagnosed a main road. Fearful lest once in a busy thoroughfare he should lose the quarry, he threw part of discretion to the winds and ran with loping but still tiptoed strides until he was only some twenty-five feet behind them.

They did not look round. He could hear their voices plainly now; could even catch some of the words. It was the deep voice which was speaking.

He caught a mumble and then one or two half words and then, quite clearly:

". . . if he can see you tomorrow. Then we can go ahead. You should be there in under a fortnight."

The end of this sentence brought the women to the end of the alleyway. They turned to their right and were, therefore, for a few seconds hidden from Garrett's eyes. He covered the last yards that he had to travel in leaping strides.

He emerged from the mouth of the alleyway like a halfback getting away from the scrum. His right shoulder caught a man's chest and his left arm a woman's ribs. Even as he recovered himself he glared wildly to his right; then breathed relief. Not only were they in sight, but they were stationary.

"Reely!" said the woman he had struck. But she sniffed and passed on. Garrett raised his hat to a departing back. He began to say:

"You must pardon me, mad . . ." but was cut short by his other victim.

This was a burly person in neckerchief and corduroy. He said, catching Garrett by the shoulder and swinging him round:

"'Ere, 'ere! Wot's the bleedin' 'urry?"

"So sorry! So sorry!" Garrett said feverishly. He stared anxiously over his victim's shoulder. . . . Yes: they were still there. They were pretending to look into a shop window but probably they were still talking. If only he could be behind them, listening. Then he might . . .

"I said, wot's the bloody 'urry?" The hoarse voice recalled him to himself. He said desperately: "I'm very sorry. I was trying to catch a friend of mine."

Over the man's shoulder he saw his quarry moving; and moving away from him! He looked for the first time closely at his interlocutor, gauging the man's age as ten years more than his and his weight at only a few pounds more. He said briskly:

"I've apologized. I'm busy. Get the hell out of it!" He wrenched his shoulder free from the calloused hand which still held it, put his own right hand flat against the spotted neckerchief—and thrust. The attacked staggered back, to come with a resounding thud against the end of the alley wall. He coughed and gasped and then lurched forward.

But his adversary was gone. Threading syncopated way across the bus-ridden road were the short, square, swaggering back and the slim, tall, very feminine back, and close behind them, twice narrowly missing death, went Sheldon Garrett.

The women reached the far curb. A violent hooting and a hoarse cry made Garrett leap back. A vast omnibus surged between him and the pavement. He ran round its tail and reached the curb. There were many people upon the pavement. They were all bent, it seemed to him, upon obstructing him. And they all were surging towards a great arched doorway. He reared himself to the full of his height and looked wildly over as many heads as he could. Ah! There they were. He had caught sight of the red hat. He began to plough his way through the crowd, heedless of glares and objurgation, and found himself in what he had sufficient knowledge of London to know was the booking hall of an underground station.

Ah! There was the slim back beneath the red hat. It was before a ticket machine. He moved towards it.

Ah! There was the square back, beside the other one. They moved away, walking towards a corner where showed the grilled gates of four lifts.

Garrett followed; then remembered that he must have a ticket before he could pass the man at the door of what he called the elevator.

In his own land he would have chanced the possibility of pushing by a ticket clipper, thrusting a note into the man's hand, but, rightly or wrongly, he decided that a servant of London Railways was unlikely to permit this. He pulled out his notecase and ran wildly back, bumping oncoming passengers, towards the window of the booking office. Mercifully no one was at it. He slammed down a note, shouted, "Piccadilly Circus," snatched the yellow pasteboard shot towards him and ran off without his change.

As he crossed the hall people were still streaming into what he knew was the first liftful. He sighed relief and ran on, reaching the doors of the entrance to the lift behind a last thin rank.

Over a fat, seal-covered shoulder he peered into the packed interior.

Thank God! There they were, still with their backs towards him.

The man before him moved forward, had his ticket clipped and stepped in.

Garrett moved forward but was held back by a blue official arm. In his ear a hoarse cry sounded. "Next lift, please!" and across his face, barely an inch from it, shot the extending grille of the lift gate as it shut with a roaring clang.

"God damn the luck to hell!" said Sheldon Garrett.

With a gargantuan sigh the lift descended. Hopelessly he went to the next and, when it was full, descended to tubular warrens which for a long and entirely fruitless while he searched. . . .

4

Despondent, he came up to ground level again and pushed his way out to the street and found a taxi and gave its driver vague orders. Eventually—perhaps half an hour later—he entered for the second time Ye Willow-Pattern Tea Shoppe. He stood just inside the door and waited. The service door creaked. Ancilla floated drearily towards him. As she drew near a spasm of something like human feeling flitted across her face beneath the pince-nez. But before she could speak Garrett had his notecase out. He said hurriedly:

"I left without paying my check."

A spasm which might have been a smile had crossed the woman's pale lips at the sight of the notecase, but at Garrett's speech this was replaced by something like a frown. She said:

"Cheque? Ay'm afraid we cannot . . ."

Garrett said: "I beg your pardon. I meant my *bill*. I had tea here. I rushed out without paying, so I thought I'd . . ." He let his speech tail off but he took from the wallet a ten-shilling note and proffered it.

It was taken, with an action most genteel, from between his fingers. The woman said:

"Ay'm mech oblayged, Ay'm sewer."

Garrett, though he did not understand a word of this, took it correctly enough to be thanks. He hurried on to his purpose. He said, with a laugh which he meant to be genial but which frightened his own ears by its appalling artificiality:

"Very strange thing! Those two ladies who sat in the booth next to mine . . ."

"Booth?" Ancilla repeated.

Garrett repressed an urgent desire to take the thin neck between his hands and squeeze. He turned and pointed. He said: "At the next table."

"Oh yais. Ay believe Ay remember. Two ladies. Yais."

Garrett smiled. He would like to have risked the jovial laugh again but feared it. He said, still smiling:

"I knew them. But I didn't realize it until I saw them go. I suppose I must have been thinking of something else. When I saw them go, and recognized them—or rather, one of them—I had to run after them."

Ancilla said: "Ay quate understand. . . . Bay the way, one of your friends left a glev. . . . Ay wonder . . ."

Garrett's heart leapt. So he *was* going to find something tangible. But what was it? He said:

"I beg your pardon!"

Ancilla said: "One of your friends—one left a glev."

"Indeed!" said Garrett, hoping that time would show.

It did. Ancilla swam away from him, was lost in dim shadows near the service door and swam back.

"Oh!" said Garrett. "A glove."

Ancilla said. "Yais. One of your friends mest hev dropped it."

She handed it to him. Garrett took it. He did not want to betray too much interest so folded it with as careless an air as he could manage and thrust it into a side pocket. It was a very ordinary glove, for a very ordinary-sized hand. It was of black kid and had white stitching on the backs of the hands and white mother-of-pearl buttons.

"Thank you!" said Garrett and then, carried away by a passion for his part: "Doris *will* be glad to have it back."

"Deon't mention it," Ancilla said. "Gled to hev been of service, Ay'm sewer. . . . End yewer bill—one and nane." She looked down at the note in her fingers. "Ay will procure change."

She melted away from Garrett's sight. So soon as she had gone he took the glove from his pocket and turned it this way and that. He wished that he were Dr. Thorndyke—and then, with an excitement such as he had not felt for years, felt suddenly, if not like Dr. Thorndyke, at least like Inspector French.

For as he held the glove in his hand, feeling its cheap texture, he felt something else. In the palm of the glove it was.

With fingers which he noted with surprise to be not quite steady he searched it.

He found a bus ticket and a little slip of paper.

CHAPTER II

He was very late for dinner. After it he spoke for a moment with a pacified hostess. He said:

"It was unpardonable. But a most curious affair was the cause of it. I'm certain I overheard two people planning a—well, a crime. I—"

"*Terribly* interesting!" his hostess said. "How *fascinating*! I'm so frightfully keen on criminology, aren't you! So—so *real*! I wish Roger were here. You and he really ought to get together. Yes, you and Roger would have such a *lot* in common. . . . Oh, you *must* meet Adela properly, you and she were so far apart at dinner. . . . Adela! Adela! Come over here a minute. . . . Adela Pomfret, you know. Written all *sorts* of things, including that thing everybody was *raving* about last year or something; that thing, Mr. Somebody's Whatd'youcallit or something. . . . Oh, Adela darling, I thought you and Mr. Sheldon should talk to each other. The bad man was so late there were no proper introductions before dinner. Mr. Sheldon's an expert on criminology, aren't you, Mr. Sheldon? And *have* you seen his play at the Apollo, *Fools Rush In?* Of course you have. . . . Now I *must* go and talk to Tommy. . . ."

Mr. Sheldon Garrett looked at Miss Adela Pomfret. She was shaped like a tarantella dancer but her face was that of an egocentric and ill-tempered horse. He said:

"My name's Garrett. Sheldon Garrett. . . ."

She nodded. "I know. And the play's called *Wise Man's Holiday*. I haven't seen it."

"Er—yes," Garrett said. "Or no, I should say."

"I never go to the theatre!" said Adela Pomfret. "I never read. I hardly ever go out. I am not interested in criminology. Have you heard Pandomano's lectures? I don't suppose so. No. Do I see drinks on that table over there? You could get me one."

"Certainly," said Garrett and bowed and left her and was at pains not to return.

He was introduced to a man whose name he did not catch; a tall, heavily built person with a face which seemed made for a K.C.'s wig. They chatted. After a while Garrett said:

"What would you do if you knew some sort of a—well, crime was going to be committed and——"

The heavy face gave forth sonorous laughter. "Tell the criminals how to do it, make sure there was a loophole and get briefed for the defence. What d'you think of that? Eh? What?"

Garrett screwed his face into a polite semblance of mirth. He said after due protraction of the spasm:

"I meant it seriously, though. If you *knew* that a serious crime was going to be committed——"

"What sort of a crime?" said Vaughan Critchley, who was indeed a K.C. "Murder? Arson? Rape? Criminal libel? Theft? Blackmail? Treason? Fraud? Abduction? . . . There are many."

"Yes," Garrett said with an iron patience. "I know there are a lot of headings under the word 'crime.' I——"

He was interrupted. His hostess was at his elbow. Words came from her. They seemed to say:

"Oh, there you are, Mr. Sheldon. . . . Vaughan, do you know Mr. Garrett Sheldon? Oh, of course . . . I see you do. I heard what you were saying, Mr. Sheldon. . . . Vaughan, do you know that Mr. Sheldon's an expert criminologist? . . . You two should have a lot in common. . . . Oh, I must go and talk to Adela. . . . I'll leave you to your talk . . . so interesting. . . ."

It seemed to Garrett that Vaughan Critchley's eyes rested upon him with something of disfavour. Vaughan Critchley said:

"So you're interested in criminology?"

Garrett shook his head. "No," he said firmly. "Not at all."

"Oh," said Vaughan Critchley and then, catching sight of an acquaintance over Garrett's shoulder: "How are you, Morris? I've been wanting to see you for the past week. I——"

Sheldon Garrett withdrew himself. So soon as he decently could he went to his hostess and made adieu. She said:

"So awfully glad you could come. . . . Lovely having you. . . . Do hope I shall see more of you. . . . I should love you to meet Roger. You and he would have such a lot in common. . . . You must dine with us quietly sometime; then you and Roger can have a real heart-to-heart talk. Roger's awfully keen on criminology too. . . . Good-bye, Mr. Sheldon, good-bye. I haven't seen your play yet but I've made up my mind that I'm going to at the very earliest possible moment. . . . Good-bye. . . . And do give my love to Maureen."

Garrett went out into the air. His temper was bad; his head ached; and he wondered, savagely, who on God's earth or below it Maureen could be.

He considered the hour—eleven-thirty—and bed. But he foresaw sleeplessness and thought of the club to which, by Brooks-Carew's efforts, he had been elected a visiting member.

2

He entered the club, having walked there, at exactly midnight. It was nearly empty. He made his way to the big bar whose windows overlook the river. Two men were there—Jack, the bartender, and one member who sat upon a high stool with his head in his hands.

Garrett ordered a whiskey and soda and, as he was drinking it, looked more closely at his one fellow drinker. He saw with delight that this was a man he knew, being none other than Jamieson Phipps, journalist and playwright and political firebrand.

Garrett went over and announced himself. Phipps took one hand from his head and looked up. For a moment he stared blankly and then a smile split his round pale moon of a face. He waved to a stool. He said:

"Siddown. Glad see you."

"And I," Garrett said, "am glad to see you. Very glad indeed! It seems to me that, although I know I'm wrong, you're the only person of sense in this city. That's the sort of day I've spent."

"Too bad," said Phipps. "Too bad. Have a drink?" He made a sign to the bartender.

Garrett was looking at the floor. He suddenly said, without raising his eyes: "Look here, Phipps, I want your advice. . . . I want you to tell me, seriously, what you'd do in this place—London, I mean—if you had reason to know that a really serious—well, crime was going to be committed but you didn't know against whom?"

The bartender put down two glasses: in front of Garrett a whiskey and soda, in front of Phipps a tumbler half full of something darker. Phipps turned his head towards Garrett. He said: "Whassay?"

Garrett looked down at the floor again. He was trying to get muddled thoughts in order. He said after a pause:

"Let's put it another way. If you heard two men, that you couldn't see, talking about a serious crime they were going to commit and then you followed them and lost touch with them without seeing their faces, what would you do?"

Phipps turned fully round upon his stool. He looked squarely at Garrett. His eyes were screwed up as if in concentration of thought. He stretched out a hand for his glass and picked it up and drank. With his round, thin-haired, pale-faced head and his long and very thin body he looked, as he perched upon the stool with his heels over its topmost rail and his long arms hanging down at his sides, like an intellectual hobgoblin.

Garrett looked at him, awaiting an answer.

"What would I do?" said Phipps suddenly in a great voice so many times exceeding in volume his previous mutterings that both Garrett and the bartender jumped. "I'll show you what I'd do."

Slowly he unfolded his legs and lowered them to the ground and stood, revealing himself as even longer and more emaciated than Garrett had remembered him. He bellowed:

"I'll tell you what I'd do. I'd—I'd—I'd sing a song of sixpence, a pocket full of rye . . ."

On the word "rye" his voice went up to a cracked shriek and now, while Garrett stared in aghast astonishment and the bartender scurried for the gate at the end of the bar, Jamieson Phipps threw up his hands, gurgled twice and fell as a tree falls.

Garrett, staring in incredulous wonder, saw the white-coated bartender kneel beside the prostrate body. The man said:

"If you'll just help me, sir . . ."

They picked him up and laid him upon a sofa. He was surprisingly and even a little pathetically light.

"He's been on that stool," said the barman, "ever since eleven this morning—except for one or two little trips like. Brandy, it's been. But I *was* hopin' *this* time he wouldn't get like this!"

"Good *Lord!*" said Garrett.

"I've been wondering, sir," the barman said, "whether it was something you said to him that upset him like."

Garrett smiled. The smile started as a light twist of his mouth but ended in a gust of laughter which struck even his own ears as almost maniacal. . . .

3

He was back at the Savoy by a few minutes after one. He entered the lift frowning and preoccupied. He came out of the lift smiling and intent upon a purpose. He had achieved an idea, and a good idea. As he almost ran along the softly carpeted corridor to his little suite he joyously cursed himself for a fool. There was one man who would tell him what to do; tell him at once whether he was being a quixotic fool or a normal being—and a man, moreover, who most certainly would not be in bed at this time and would not mind being called even if he were.

He opened his door and slammed it behind him, hurrying into his sitting room. He looked in his notebook and found a number and asked for it.

There was a long pause, broken by the voice of the hotel operator. It said: "There doesn't seem to be any answer from your number, sir."

"Try again," said Garrett and waited.

Another and longer pause and then, just as he had given up hope, an answer. A man's voice; a very sleepy voice.

"Bill!" said Garrett.

The voice said: "Beg pardon, sir. Do you want Mr. Akehurst?"

"Yes!" said Garrett.

The telephone said: "I'm sorry, sir, but Mr. Akehurst is away. He is in Vienna."

"Hell!" said Sheldon Garrett and then: "When's he coming back?"

The telephone said: "The time of his return, sir, is uncertain. This is Mr. Akehurst's valet speaking, sir. Is there anything I can do?"

"No!" said Garrett and slammed back the receiver.

4

He got to bed at a quarter to two. He tried to read but could not. He put out the light and tried to go to sleep and thought that he could not but did.

He then dreamed. Unpleasantly. He was running down a long narrow street. Upon each side of him rotting houses of grey brick reared themselves up like skyscrapers. None of their windows was lighted and the man-made canyon was dark save for a whitish effulgence which seemed to come from the low walls separating pavement from mouldering garden. In front of him, as he ran, were two other figures. From behind him, as he ran, came the sound of other running feet. He did not look round but he knew that these feet belonged to an enemy of whom he stood in deadly fear; an enemy who carried over his shoulder like a vanquished enemy a long slender sack. Before him the hurrying figures ran on. Behind him the pursuing feet drew nearer. His whole being was absorbed with a desire to reach some sanctuary which he felt he did not know now but would know so soon as he should set eye upon it. And then, immediately, he saw it. It was upon a corner. It was a small place. It was surrounded by Chinese paper lanterns. He ran towards its entrance, cringing as he came into the light of the lanterns. He plunged through a door and was in temporary safety. It was a vast hall in which he found himself, but a hall which he seemed to know. Over the floor of it were scattered, higgledy-piggledy, little eating booths, each containing a table. He plunged into one in a far dark corner like a frightened rabbit diving into its hole. He crawled under the little table and made himself small and lay there panting, his heart thudding as if it would break its way out of his body through his throat. And then the others came. And they crowded into all the other booths which were all around him. There seemed to be hundreds of them, all talking at once and all talking in whispers. But he could hear their whispers and he knew what they were saying, even when some of the words were inaudible because of the thumping of his heart in his ears. They were talking about him. His name was like an obligato to the rise and fall of their hissing voices. They were going to do something to him. But that was not all. There was suddenly another note introduced into the sibilant choir. They were going to do things to him. That was bad. But they were also going to hurt someone else; someone whom he was suddenly surprised to find mattered to him more than himself. Who was it? The name was clear enough in their whisperings but, although he could hear it, it was as if it was in another language and he could not translate it. Not that that made any difference. It did not. That they were going to hurt *her*—so it was a woman!—was much worse than that they were going to hurt him. And then, like a thunderous bass to the foul music, came yet another name. And that was the worst of all, because if they were going to hurt this one then it would not only be worse than hurting himself but worse than hurting "her." He wanted to get up and shout. He wanted to crawl out from his silly little hiding place and defy them. His mind felt suddenly as strong as God's mind, but when he tried to make his body obey it would not, but lay there cringing and trembling as before. And then he was conscious of something new: he was conscious that somewhere in one of these places near him—perhaps in another little hiding place near his own—there was Someone Else; Someone Else who did not know him or the others, the whisperers; Someone Else who *could* help him against them. But would he? *Would he?* . . .

He waked, sweating. The bedclothes were on the floor. All the muscles in his body were quivering and his throat was parched. He got up and switched on lights and drank water and roughly made his bed again. But there was no more sleep for him.

CHAPTER III

Sheldon Garrett moved abruptly in his chair; so abruptly that his elbow, which had been resting upon the table, knocked over his coffee cup. A waiter came hurrying and busied himself with repairing damage.

"By God, I *will!*" said Sheldon Garrett.

The waiter stared. "Beg pardon, sir!"

Garrett started. He looked down at the white napkin which the waiter was spreading over the brown stain. He said:

"Sorry! Very clumsy of me! Don't know what I was thinking about!"

Which was a lie.

2

He took a taxi from a rank in the Strand. For some reason, which he admitted to himself was foolish, he did not want to give his destination in the hearing of the Savoy hall porter. It was a salmon-colored taxi, very smart.

"Where to, sir?" said the driver, who, astonishingly, was not only as smart as his taxi but was civil.

Garrett said: "Scotland Yard, please. And as quick as you can."

"Lost Property Office, sir?" The driver was brisk.

"No," said Garrett.

"Which entrance then, sir?"

Garrett got into the cab and slammed the door behind him. He leaned out of the window and spoke. He said:

"I don't know. Any one."

3

"It won't be Inspector Michaelson that you need after all, sir!" said the sergeant.

Garrett looked at his watch. "Who then?" he said, it is to be feared a little shortly.

The sergeant smiled ruefully. "Sorry to have kept you waiting, sir, but Inspector Andrews will be free in a very few minutes."

4

Detective Inspector Andrews looked past his visitor and out of the window. His visitor, looking at him, thought that he detected certain twitchings about Detective Inspector Andrews' mouth which might denote the beginnings of a smile.

"And that, sir," said Andrews at last, "is all that you have to tell me?"

Garrett moved uneasily in his chair. He said irritably:

"Yes. Isn't it enough?"

"In one sense, yes sir. In another, no." Andrews looked at a pad upon which, during Garrett's recital, he had from time to time been scribbling. He said with a briskness which seemed to presage dismissal: "Now let me see. I think we have everything. The address of the shop. Your description of these two women. Your own address and particulars. And the clerk has shorthand notes of what you recollect of the conversation in the shop." He looked up at Garrett. "That all?"

"Yes!" said Garrett firmly. As he spoke it seemed to him that the folded glove in his pocket and two small pieces of paper in his wallet were smouldering.

Andrews rose. In this small hutch of a room whose walls—and even part of whose floor—were covered with dusty, orange-covered files, he seemed disproportionately large; like a Saint Bernard who has outgrown his kennel.

Garrett, a sudden feeling of furious obstinacy surging over him, sat where he was. Behind him a door opened and a voice said:

"I want to see you when you get a minute, Andrews."

Andrews looked from the door to Garrett; from Garrett to the door. He said to the door:

"Shan't be long," and then waited.

But still Garrett did not move. He crossed one leg over the other and folded his hands upon his lean stomach and looked up at the towering policeman. He said after a pause:

"What are you going to do about it?"

Andrews put up a hand and rubbed reflectively at his long, smooth-shaven chin. He said heavily after a heavy pause:

"That, Mr. Garrett, is for my superiors to say. You understand that all —er—matters of this kind I make a written report about."

"When?" said Garrett.

The eyes of Detective Inspector Andrews opened more widely. He said:

"The report will be on my superior's desk this evening."

"Good!" said Garrett. "I'll call tomorrow at noon." He rose and with his rising the little cubbyhole of a room seemed suddenly filled with men beyond its capacity. Somehow Andrews slid round him to the door and held it open. He said:

"Don't bother to do that, sir. We'll communicate with you if——"

Garrett turned on the threshold. "It won't be any trouble. I'll call tomorrow at noon."

He turned on his heel and walked away down a stone-floored corridor. As he walked he took himself to task. His tone, he knew, had been wrong. But he had not been able to help it. Telling his halting story to the flat, expressionless face of the man he had just left, he had felt a fool—and there is nothing that makes a man more angry. More, having felt a fool, he had proceeded to justify the feeling by behaving like one. He twitched his shoulders angrily and walked out of the Yard itself and thence onto the Embankment.

5

At nine forty-five upon the following morning Chief Detective Inspector Horler came to the following passage in a report from one of his inspectors. He read:

2. *Thomas Sheldon Garrett.* This man called here this afternoon and was interviewed. He is an American citizen visiting this country on a six months guest permit. His passport is in order. He states that he is of independent means and also a writer of dramatic works. A dramatic piece of his, entitled *Wise Man's Holiday,* is now showing at the Apollo Theatre. He is residing at the Savoy Hotel, Strand. He states that on Sunday last, the eighteenth inst., he was walking in the neighbourhood of Notting Hill. At about five-twenty he entered a teashop on the corner of Houston and Wilberforce streets, W.3 (name of teashop: Ye Willow-Pattern Tea Shoppe). He was served with tea, being on his entry the only customer. At five thirty-five approx. two women entered the shop and sat at a near-by table. He did not see them, owing to the disposition of the furnishings. He states that he then overheard a conversation between these two women (who were unaware of his presence for the reason given above) which seemed to him to denote that they were discussing some criminal undertaking involving possibly the abduction of a child and the execution of bodily harm upon some other person. When questioned as to what led him to suppose this, he stated, "The general tone of the conversation." Questioned further, he stated that one of the women seemed in fear of the other, who was threatening her by references to a man named Evans. Asked whether he could give any of the conversation verbatim, he endeavoured to do so. Notes of what he said were taken but are not included here as they did not seem to indicate anything serious. In fact, there was nothing in his statement which could not be explained by ordinary circumstances. Upon this being pointed out to him he grew excited and lost his temper.

I am of the opinion that there is nothing in this. The man being both a writer and a stranger to this country, it seems likely that he has let his imagination run away with him.

A frown creased the usually cheerful face of Chief Detective Inspector Horler. For a moment he regarded this paragraph with narrowed eyes; then shrugged broad shoulders; then went on to the end of the report; then turned back again to its second paragraph.

He said something under his breath and touched a bell. Five minutes later he was reading:

THOMAS SHELDON GARRETT
Statement re Alleged Conversation
in Willow-Pattern Tea Shoppe.

The women came in. They couldn't see me or I them. I knew there were two because of their voices. They sat in the next booth. The waitress came and they ordered their tea and she went away to get it. They had very different voices, so it was easy to tell which one was speaking. One had a deep harsh voice and the other a high soft voice. As soon as the waitress had gone away the one with the deep voice said something and the other one got nervous about whether anyone could hear them. The one with the deep voice told her that there was nobody in the place but all the same one of them made sure by looking over into my booth—the only booth they couldn't have seen into. As it happened I had dropped my wallet just at this minute and was under the table looking for it when this was going on. I heard them sit down again and then one of them said that there wasn't anybody. There was something very strange about the way they were talking— the deep voice bullying and the other frightened—and both being so particular about not being overheard. I got back into my seat without making any noise and, as it were, against my will, settled down to listen. There was something so underhanded and—"furtive" is the only word I can think of— about them that I was deeply interested right from the start. When were settled down again the first thing that happened was that the one with the deep harsh voice asked the other whether she had made up her mind. She apparently hadn't because she said she was frightened and then —I think I can remember her exact words here—she said: "I want to do it but I can't help thinking that if I do terrible things will happen to me; because when all's said and done it's not *right!*" I should say that at some time just about here their tea came and they stopped talking. I was frightened that the waitress would speak to me and thus give my presence away but luckily she didn't. As soon as she went away they went on. And now the bullying one seemed to get angry. She said she was disgusted with the other for being frightened! She wanted to know what there was to be frightened about when there was no danger and a lot of money coming if whatever they were talking about was put through properly. Then she seemed to put on the screw a bit by pretending she'd accepted no for an answer and saying that she supposed she'd "have to go and tell Evans." I think I can remember some more of her exact words here. She said: "He won't like it with you knowing everything." This mention of Evans seemed to put the other woman into a real panic. She began to stall and say she hadn't meant anything and—let me think—and it was then, I believe, that they went into a real fight, because the one with the deep voice said something that seemed to get under the other's skin and *she* got angry too. She said something like this: "Of course I want the money and I know there won't be any trouble but that's not it! The trouble is that I might get *fond* . . ." and then the other one interrupted her and she said something that gives the cue to the whole thing. She said: "You make me sick. Nobody's going to hurt it." Please mark the "it." And then the other one—the gentle voice—she got madder still and said: "Even suppose they didn't. It's still wrong." And then she said, right on top of that: "Anyhow, what about *him!*" She accented the "him" strongly so that I could tell that this "him" wasn't the same as the "it." And I should say, too, that she said this in a voice I can only describe as being heavy with threat; she said it as if she were playing a trump the other woman didn't know anything about. It certainly scared the other one, who said—damn roughly: "What are you talking about?" And the gentle one, still mad, said something like: "You know what I'm talking about! If I did take the position and follow instructions and then get paid that would be all right if that was all there was to it. But I'm not going to be mixed up in what amounts to . . ." and then, before she could say the last word, the other one must have reached over the table and grabbed at her because she gave a little sort of scream and said: "Don't! You're hurting me." The other one told her she must be crazy and demanded to know what fool idea she'd got hold of. It was obvious that the gentle one had acquired some knowledge she wasn't supposed to have. It was equally obvious that she wished she hadn't said anything but was so terrified by the other woman and references to this Evans that at last she admitted to having heard something not intended for her "the last time she was at the house." She said she'd been waiting in the parlour while the other woman and some other people were in a room and she'd accidentally overheard something they were saying. She said "the other man was talking very loud" and she couldn't help but hear. She then tried to make things better for herself by saying that she hadn't heard anything *definite* but it was obvious that she had, though she was too frightened to say what it was. That seemed to be her crisis, as it were, because after that, and after some more bullying by the other one, she surrendered completely. It was clear that she was so frightened of the other woman and "Evans" that she wasn't going to give them any more trouble. By the end of the conversation she had agreed to do anything they wanted. She was then congratulated by the other, who again referred to easy money or something of the sort. And—oh yes!—the other woman dinned it into her that—I remember the exact words—"that nobody was going to get hurt." I can only tell you, about that remark, that it was said in such a way as to convince me that it meant the very reverse. That was all they said in the shop. They then paid their bill and went out, still without seeing me. Then, as I've told you, I followed them. On the way to the subway station where I lost them I caught one more bit of talk. It was from the boss woman—the deep voice. She said something about if someone could see the other woman tomorrow they could get on with things. And then she said—I remember these words: "You should be there in under a fortnight." That's all, I think. Oh, wait though, there *was* something else. At one stage—it was after the one with the soft voice had got really docile—

she asked how long everything would take, and then the boss one said it couldn't be longer than six months but would probably be "a damn sight shorter." And that *is* all.

Horler set down the sheets. He stared at them for a moment; then picked up a desk telephone.

6

Chief Detective Inspector William Horler looked genially across his table at Mr. Thomas Sheldon Garrett. The geniality of the look must go down to Horler's credit, for he had spent, of a busy day, nearly two hours with his visitor; a time not made lighter by his visitor's manner.

Horler tilted back his chair, rested his elbows upon its arms and placed the tips of ten broad fingers nicely together. He said:

"So you see, Mr. Garrett, when we examine your statement piecemeal the way we have this afternoon we find that there's absolutely nothing to act upon. No definite statement of any kind was made by either of these women and—at least so far as you can tell us—neither of them said anything that couldn't refer to—er—perfectly ordinary matters. What I think——"

Sheldon Garrett twisted in his chair. "But, look here! *I* heard that conversation. I *know* that there was some—something devilish that those two women and the man they were talking about were going to do. I don't think I'm quite a lunatic, and I'm absolutely *sure*——"

"One moment, Mr. Garrett, one moment!" Horler's voice was unexpectedly loud and he held up a vast hand for silence. Behind him Garrett's mind could see, ranged in orderly, passive ranks, the ratepayers of Great Britain.

"I must ask you to understand, Mr. Garrett"—the voice was normal again—"that this matter has been very fully considered. Possibly even more fully considered than if you had been a native of this country. We like to do all we can for strangers and above all we like to show that we're grateful to those who try to assist us in our duties. On the other hand, you must allow us the superior knowledge and experience. We're extremely obliged to you for bringing to our notice what you thought was the planning of a criminal action. . . ."

Sheldon Garrett stood up. It is to be regretted that he said, "Nerts!"

Chief Detective Inspector Horler rose. He said politely: "I beg your pardon!"

Garrett said: "Nothing! Nothing! Sorry if I seem rude, but this business, and trying to explain it to you people, has got me a bit edgy."

Horler came out from behind his table. He said:

"Believe me, I quite understand, Mr. Garrett. And, if I may say so, I appreciate the spirit in which you have come here. But I'd like to put it to you that you're worrying yourself needlessly. Between you and me, I shouldn't be a bit surprised but what one of the women had got into a scrape of some kind—you know the sort of thing—and the other was trying to help her out of it. That would explain the—what you called 'furtiveness' of the conversation. But nothing criminal. I don't think that for a moment. And, if I may say so, I've had a great deal of experience at this game. I can smell a crime ten miles away and I get no scent here." He laughed with heartiness. "Not a trace of scent."

"I see," said Garrett dully.

CHAPTER IV

Avis Bellingham let herself into her flat. She did this, as indeed she did everything, with little noise. Her maid, therefore, did not hear her. She put down a small parcel and her gloves and her bag upon the small table in the small hall. She crossed the hall and went into her drawing room. It was evening and the room was dark save for a fire which sent little flickers of light softly over pleasant furnishings. She took off her coat and threw it over the arm of a chair. She took off her hat and put it on top of the coat. There was a mirror over the mantelpiece and to the left of the mirror a light switch. She crossed to the fire and stood before the mirror and pressed the switch and two soft lights above and to the sides of the mirror sprang into life. She looked into the mirror and put her hands to her hair.

But she saw something in the mirror as well as her own reflection. Her hands dropped to her sides and she turned and stared, her eyes even larger than nature had made them.

"My God!" said Avis Bellingham and for a moment continued to stare.

She was looking down at a large, low chair which stood to the right of the fireplace, half in and half out of the soft light cast by the right-hand lamp. This chair should have been empty. There was no excuse for it being filled. And yet it was. And, astonishingly, by the body of a man. Dark-trousered legs sprawled out into the light; but above the waist the body was in shadow, merging its darkness into the darkness of the enveloping chair.

Avis Bellingham moved. She crossed the room towards the door but did not go through it. Instead she pressed the light switch beside the jamb and the lights inside the bowl which hung from the middle of the ceiling sprang into life.

She stood where she was, looking towards the chair. She could see now that its occupant was lying back. One arm was crooked across his face, hiding not only this but all the head. Still he did not move. Crazy and unpleasing thoughts shot unbidden across the surface of her mind. She repressed them and concentrated her gaze upon the chair. Was the body motionless? Or was there a slight movement which told of breathing? . . .

"This is absurd!" said Avis Bellingham and found her voice strange in her own ears. Again she was forced to apply the curb to imagination fed by bookish memory.

And then the man stirred—a definite movement; a movement which, even in its inconsequentiality, put dread imaginings to ludicrous flight. Consumed now by the relatively pleasant sensation of curiosity, she moved across the room again. She stood in front of the chair and once more stared down at it and its occupant.

"Hey!" she said.

The arm came down; but the eyes in the now revealed face were still closed in deep sleep. The man twisted in the chair and a thick, somnolent voice came from him. It said:

"Lot o' saps! *Is* some way! Must be!"

"*Tom!*" said Avis Bellingham. A smile of pleasure curved her large and charming mouth. She bent down and set a hand to the sleeper's shoulder and shook it.

Thomas Sheldon Garrett awoke. He sat bolt upright, his arms stretched out upon the arms of the chair. He looked once wildly round the charming little room and found it strange. He rubbed a hand across his eyes and looked up at the woman.

He shot to his feet. He said, seeming and feeling like a small boy caught jam-handed:

"Avis! I—I—how—they said—I hope you——"

She went on smiling at him. She said: "Sit down. And stop making noises."

Twenty minutes later she looked at him over the rim of a glass. He was no longer tousled but from beneath sleek blond hair his face looked at her, haggard and drawn. She said:

"Finish that drink and get yourself another. And then tell me."

Garrett laughed; a laugh which she did not remember. He rose and obeyed her and came back and sat once more to face her. He said:

"Tell you all about what?"

"Everything. What are you doing in London? How long have you been here? Why haven't you been to see me before? How did you get in? And, much more important, what's the trouble?"

"I'm in London because Brooks-Carew has been fool enough to do a play of mine. . . ."

"Tom! And I never knew! But I *won't* read the papers."

"I've been here two weeks. I haven't been to see you before because—as you might guess—I didn't know you were here. I found out yesterday, accidentally, from Dorothy Brooks-Carew. When I got here this afternoon your maid said you were out so I gave her a long hard-luck story and got in. I didn't mean to go to sleep but I did mean to see you—even if I waited here a couple of days. . . . That's all, isn't it?"

"No sir, thank you, sir. It's not even the beginning! What's the *matter?*"

"Should I only come to see you because there's something the matter?"

"Don't be a donkey. But there *is* something!"

"What makes you think that way?"

"You ought to be beaten. You're more like a small boy than any small boy ever was. Sit back, relax, sip at your goblet of some amber-coloured fluid and—tell me what's the matter! In order to avert further procrastination on your part I'll tell you that you look, though distinguished as ever, like hell. You're nervous, you're jumpy, you've lost weight, you've got that reversed look about your eye which tells of an idée fixe . . . and, finally, you haven't been sleeping. . . ."

Garrett said: "Haven't been *sleeping!*" and laughed.

"*And* your laugh's about the worst imitation of one that I ever heard. . . . Don't be silly, Tom! Tell me!"

Sheldon Garrett looked at his hostess. For a long moment his eyes were caught in the great blue pools of her eyes. There flowed into him, like salving oil upon an angry wound, a sense of sudden ease; the relaxation of a strain whose tension he had not known until it was lessened. He said:

"You're right. But then I suppose you always are. There *is* something— only I'm beginning to think it's so damn silly that perhaps I'm going hay-wire. But it's got me, though I tried not to let it. When I'd done everything I could about it and got nowhere I told myself to forget it. But I didn't succeed. Not a bit. It's been eating with me and trying to sleep with me and making me behave so oddly that everybody's thinking I'm qualified for a lunatic asylum. And I can't get rid of it. . . ."

"Tom! Will you stop beating round all these bushes!"

"Listen!" said Garrett and began. . . .

2

"And that," said Garrett thirty minutes later, "is what's the matter. Now say I'm a fool with an overheated imagination! Tell me the world goes on much better when people mind their own business! Tell me that by going to Scotland Yard I've done everything possible! Tell me to forget the whole thing! Show me—oh, so reasonably!—that I read into a conversation a lot of stuff that wasn't there! Tell me——"

Avis Bellingham stood up. "What I do tell you," she said, "is to shut up!" She went to the door. With her fingers on its handle she turned. She said: "Wait here. And be good." She opened the door.

"Here! Wait a minute!" Garrett jumped to his feet. "What you going to do?"

"Telephone," said Avis.

He crossed the room towards her. "About—about my—idée fixe?"

She pulled a face at him. "Don't be egotistic!" she said and was gone.

She was with him again after five minutes or less. She was smiling and there was a sparkle in the blue eyes. She looked at her watch and then at Garrett. She said:

"It's half-past six. How long to go and put on a dinner jacket and get back here?"

He looked at her curiously. "Forty-five minutes. Why?"

"You're dining out. With me. So hurry!"

"But I . . ."

"But nothing! You—are—dining—out—with me!"

"Oh," said Garrett, "I see."

CHAPTER V

The taxi bumped and jolted. Garrett said, breaking a silence:

"And where are we going?"

"Didn't I tell you? How stupid of me!" She did not look at him. "To some great friends of mine. You'll like them. I hope they'll like you. I——"

"The name?" said Garrett.

"Gethryn. Lucia Gethryn and her husband."

"Oh!" said Garrett in a different tone. And then: "You don't mean Lucia Gethryn and her husband. You mean Anthony Gethryn and his wife!" He leant forward in his seat with hand outstretched to tap upon the driver's window.

But gloved fingers, surprisingly strong, caught his wrist and a voice said softly:

"Don't be a fool, Tom!"

He dropped his hand and turned in his seat and stared through the dimness at a profile which said:

"And, if you *must* be a fool, don't be an ill-mannered one!"

He said: "Sorry, Avis! But I won't be dragged into a busy man's home as a poor sap with a bug in his head and——"

She said: "I don't like to think that coming out with me is being *dragged*. And at the moment Anthony's not a busy man."

"But . . ."

She drew a deep breath. "*And* I've said nothing about your bug! Nor will I until you tell me." She looked at him without turning her head. "And I thought it wouldn't do your bug any harm for you to know the one man who might——"

"Stop!" said Garrett. "I'm sorry. And you're a darling."

"That's better," said Avis Bellingham.

2

"Something tells me," said Lucia Gethryn, "that the hostess now collects the women with her eye. Come on, Avis!"

Garrett opened the door for them. As he shut it, and before he turned back towards the table, the left eye of Anthony Gethryn closed momentarily. Spencer Hastings[1] nodded.

Garrett came back to the table and sat. The port went round. There was desultory talk. Hastings began the inside story of the informal cabinet meet-

[1] See Footnote on page 47.

ing which had led, two days before, to the abrupt resignation of the foreign secretary.

Upstairs in the drawing room Avis Bellingham and the friend who was her hostess sat and smoked and stared at a fire of logs.

Lucia said: "I smoke too many of these things. I like him. But why did you say he wasn't much to look at?"

Avis lit another cigarette. "I wonder whether the stories are over yet?"

Lucia said: "They don't, not much anyhow. In fact, not nearly as much as we do."

"That's not what I mean," said Avis Bellingham.

Lucia said: "I know."

Avis said: "D'you think they've got to it yet? . . . Lucia, you didn't tell Anthony . . . ?"

Lucia said: "Of course I did! At least I told him that Mr. Garrett wanted advice about something. I even said a bit more. . . ."

"*Lucia!* You *promised.*"

"*But* I also told him that you thought it best not to let Mr. Garrett know that you'd said anything at all about it."

"Oh!" said Avis Bellingham and then, after a pause: "How's the heir?"

Lucia smiled. "Magnificent. He asked after you yesterday, at great length. So you've got two fervent admirers at least; and at the moment both under the same roof. Must be nice."

Avis Bellingham said: "Alan's adorable."

Downstairs Hastings filled his glass and pushed the decanter, to complete its circle, towards Garrett. He said to his host:

"But that doesn't say that, theoretically, the whole basis of police work is wrong. . . ."

"Of course it's wrong," said Anthony Gethryn. "But then, it never could be right. Because in no state of civilization will there ever be enough public wealth to establish the only sort of police that a Utopian would tolerate."

Hastings said: "That sounds clever. Unfortunately it doesn't mean anything."

Anthony grinned. "Put in simple words for the young, Spencer, what I mean is that the ideal police force is not an organization for the apprehension and punishment of criminals but an organization for the *prevention* of crime."

Garrett started. He looked sharply from his host to his fellow guest—but neither was looking at him.

Hastings said: "A foul idea! The only way it could be run would be to make every man a spy on his neighbour. We haven't much privacy left as it is; for God's sake, let's be alone sometimes—even if it leads to rape and murder."

"Thereby," said Anthony, "giving Spencer Hastings—and the rest of Fleet Street—a continued and lucrative existence."

Garrett stared at his host. "Look here!" he said suddenly and loudly.

"D'you *mean* what you're saying? Or are you just taking the thin end of an argument?"

"He doesn't know," said Hastings.

Anthony said: "It's a theory; but a sound one. Unfortunately, however, progress is the enemy of sense."

Garrett still stared at him. "But you *do* mean that you believe that crime should be prevented rather than punished?"

"Naturally," said Anthony. "Don't you?"

Hastings said: "Deprive man of his time-honoured occupation of shutting stable doors after horses have been stolen and you take a good deal of the salt away from his daily food."

"Yes! Yes!" Garrett said. "I see all that." He spoke hastily and with a lack of politeness most foreign to him. And he did not look at the man to whom he was speaking but continued to gaze at his host. He said suddenly, his eyes narrowing: "Did Avis Bellingham say anything to you? About me, I mean?"

Anthony's slight stare of bewilderment was admirable. He said:

"Sorry! I don't quite understand."

"All I meant," said Garrett, "was—well, skip that! I was just going to say: It's most extraordinary that we should get on a topic like this. Because only a few days ago I ran right into a living example of it. I . . . But perhaps it'd bore you. You must get your belly full of crime and criminals."

Spencer Hastings laughed.

Anthony said: "I was born suspecting the doctor, I shall die indicting the priest. Go on."

3

Garrett came to the end of his story. He smiled, more than a little wryly. He said:

"So I suppose I'm crazy, or at least feeble minded."

Anthony smiled. It was a preoccupied smile and the crease which had come between his eyes did not leave. He said:

"Only if you go on thinking so. . . . Who did you see at the Yard, the second time?"

"Man called Horler," said Garrett. "Chief Detective Inspector Horler."

Anthony said: "Not a bad fellah. Find him a bit short on imagination?"

Garrett said: "If he'd got any he certainly hid it someplace. But he was very civil, which I'm afraid I wasn't."

Anthony said slowly: "And you never once saw even a profile of either of those women?"

Garrett shook his head. "Not even half a cheek. I saw 'em from the back first, last and all the time. If it hadn't been for that goddam elevator I'd——" He broke off, lifting his shoulders in a small, helpless gesture.

Anthony seemed absorbed in the little puddle of dark wine at the bottom of his glass. He said without looking up:

"And you didn't hear where either of them booked to?"

Garrett stared at him. "Booked?"

"When you got to the tube station you weren't close enough behind them at the ticket office to hear where they took tickets for?"

"Oh!" said Garrett. "Sorry. They didn't get tickets at the window. They got them out of one of those machines."

Anthony looked up sharply. "Both out of the same machine?"

Garrett nodded. "Yes. Why?"

"If you went back to the station could you point out the particular machine?"

"Yes," said Garrett.

Anthony said: "That helps. Or might."

Garrett looked at him. "I don't see how."

Spencer Hastings said: "Nor, with all due respect to Master Mind, do I. What you mean, I take it, is that if Garrett showed you the machine you would at least know within half-a-dozen stations where they went to."

"Magnificent!" murmured Anthony.

"But," said Hastings, "you wouldn't know whether any of the stations represented the district either of 'em lived in. One doesn't always go home after tea—even in Notting Hill. Particularly on a Sunday."

Garrett looked at his host. But Anthony's gaze was still down bent and he did not raise it and no sound came from him.

Garrett said: "I hadn't thought of that. . . ." His voice trailed off into silence but he was conscious of a vast relief, for here at last were intelligent men who were not treating him like a frightened small boy who must be humoured but were actually applying their minds to this business which obsessed his own.

Still Anthony did not speak nor raise his head. But Hastings said:

"It's like Sawing through a Woman."

"Eh!" said Garrett.

"Or the rope trick," Hastings said. "I mean, it's damned interesting but impossible to work out."

"Oh!" said Garrett.

"Think!" said Spencer Hastings. "Think! In greater London there are roughly eight million people. There is nearly, I believe, a two-to-one preponderance of women. That gives us at least five million women. . . . God, what a thought! . . . And out of these five million you've got to find two backs. . . ."

"And two voices," Garrett said. "Don't forget that." His tone was heavy.

Hastings said: "That's not really a help. It's like Sawing through a Woman again. You know there must be two women in the box but you can't see how the devil they got in there."

"*Backs!*" said Anthony suddenly. He lifted his head and looked at Garrett. "Ordinary backs? No shoulder higher than other shoulders? No humps? No limps? No odd gaits? No real peculiarity of dress?"

Garrett shook his head.

"Wait!" Hastings leaned forward suddenly, nearly upsetting his glass. "They might go back to that tea place again."

Garrett smiled without mirth. "No one in their senses would. . . . And, anyway, they hadn't up to yesterday. I went back there."

Anthony looked at him. He said slowly:

"You're pretty sure about this, aren't you, Garrett? I mean, sure there was what you'd call dirt in it?"

Garrett said: "I *know* there was! I've told you, very badly, what they said. But there was more—far more—in the way they said it."

The other men looked at him curiously. They saw that his face was suddenly pale and that there were new lines in it.

Anthony said as if to himself: "If only there were *something* else!"

Garrett moved suddenly in his chair. He looked first at his host and then at his fellow guest. He was frowning in concentration. His eyes seemed to be trying to push vision beyond faces. He suddenly stood up and they stared at him, surprised by the suddenness of the movement. He leaned his hands upon the table and again looked at them both. He said:

"You're interested in this—this thing. That's plain. But how far is your interest going? Is it academic only? Or is it—*real?*"

He hesitated a little; then added in a different tone: "I know I'm being the worst kind of nuisance. But I want a real answer to that."

Spencer Hastings spoke first. He said: "You want the truth, I gather. My interest, so far, is purely academic. It's got to be—because I say that your problem's impossible to solve."

Anthony said: "I'm interested. And not academically. It's time somebody's old governess joined this party to tell us there's no such word as 'can't' in the dictionary."

"Right!" said Garrett. He put a hand to his breast pocket and took out a wallet. He laid this on the table and flipped it open and from it took, with great care, two envelopes. From the first and larger envelope he drew a woman's black kid glove; from the second, two small pieces of paper. He said:

"Here are the only things I didn't tell you about. As far as I can see they don't make matters any easier, but they are 'something else', and you were asking for that."

Anthony pushed back his chair and rose and walked round the table to stand beside his guest. He looked at the exhibits with his head cocked to one side. Garrett said:

"When I went back to the teashop just after I'd lost the women in that subway station I pretended I knew them. The waitress swallowed the story and told me that one of the women—she didn't know which—had dropped a glove. She said would I take it and I did. Inside the palm of the glove were those bits of paper."

"Hmm!" Anthony grunted and pulled his chair towards him and sat. He picked up the glove by its extreme edge and looked at it and laid it down.

He bent over the two scraps of paper, flipping them towards him by their edges.

Spencer Hastings rose and sauntered round the table and stood by Anthony's right shoulder. Anthony said without looking up:

"Show these to anyone at the Yard?"

Garrett shook his head. "No. Not when I saw what sort of reception my story was going to have."

Hastings peered over Anthony's shoulder. "One cheap glove; best bargain-basement style. One numbered bus ticket. One—what's that—oh, one shopping list. *Very* enlightening! All you've got more, Garrett, is handwriting. Problem: if there are five million women in London how can you find one when you've never seen her face, you don't know where she lives, you're not even sure she's a Londoner, *but* you've heard her voice and seen her handwriting and know she knows a man called Evans? The answer, I'm afraid, is nohow!"

Tea
Slt Bttr.
P. ons.
gt. Shrmps
1/2 lb. Ssgls
Matches
L Lamb.
1 lb Str

"Why her own handwriting?" Anthony spoke without looking up. "Might be her mother's. Or anyone's."

"The glove," said Garrett. "Is there any way of analyzing . . . ?"

Spencer Hastings laughed. "Shades of Thorndyke!"

Anthony said: "You mean, have the dirt extracted from it and examined and see what combinations you get. That's been done. It works, too, *if* you're lucky enough to have subjects which belong, for instance, to someone who lives with a starch factory behind him, a flour mill in front of him and a pencil manufacturer's at the end of his road. But it *doesn't* work if the owner of your subject's just an ordinary person living in an ordinary neighbourhood with ordinary soot and ordinary mud and ordinary dust."

Hastings said: "Anthony, you can't do it! What's the matter with you? Can't you see——"

Garrett said: "You don't *have* to discourage him, do you?" His voice was harsh.

Hastings looked at him quickly; then smiled. He said:

"I'm sorry. Didn't mean to be a wet blanket. But, anyhow, you can't stop Carlton Howe[2] when his nose is to the trail."

Garrett said: "It's I who ought to apologize. I'm——"

Anthony said: "For God's sake, shut up! Both of you." His elbows were on the table now and his chin was propped on his hands. Immediately in front of him, now tidily arranged, were the little scrap of paper which was the shopping list, then the bus ticket and then, half full of air and thus rather horribly caricaturing life, the black glove of cheap kid.

There was silence in the room for a long moment while six eyes gazed at the little miscellany upon the table edge; and then Anthony pushed back his chair and stood. He said, looking at Garrett:

"That ticket machine. Did you notice the value? . . . I mean, was it a twopenny machine? Or a fourpenny? Or——"

Garrett said: "Couldn't say. You see, I was——"

Anthony said: "But if we go there now you can point it out to me?"

"Yes," said Garrett. . . .

4

"But how long will they be?" said Lucia Gethryn.

Spencer Hastings smiled. "Anthony's driving. They've been gone five minutes. They'll be back before I want another drink."

Three minutes after this Garrett opened eyes whose lids for the last mile of his journey had been screwed tight shut. He sighed a small sigh of relief and turned down his collar and got out and stood on the pavement and found himself facing the arched entrance to Leinster Terrace underground station. Anthony joined him and they walked through the archway and into the booking hall. It was almost deserted.

Garrett pointed. "That one," he said.

They walked towards the machines and now Garrett saw that at the top of his choice was a large plaque bearing the sign "3d." and underneath this a printed list of stations. This list, he saw with disappointment, was a long one. He said:

"Seem to get everywhere in the world from here."

Anthony did not answer. He took out a pen and a small red notebook and began to write rapidly. He finished writing and put pen and book away. "Come on!" he said and started with long strides for the street.

But once on the pavement he did not make for the car. He halted and looked about him. He said:

[2] See *The White Crow*.

"Just a minute. There should be one somewhere here."

Garrett wondered what the "one" might be and then saw, as Anthony moved towards it, a flat-capped, blue-uniformed figure standing with broad back to a tobacconist's window. As they drew close he read, up on the badge above the cap peak, the words "London General Omnibus Company."

CHAPTER VI

Anthony Gethryn and his wife were alone. Through the library windows came faintly to their ears the sound of the starter of Hastings' car mingled with a grinding of gears from the taxi in which were Garrett and Avis Bellingham.

Lucia sat upon a corner of the big writing table and looked across the room at her husband.

"And now," she said, "perhaps you'll tell me what it's all about."

Anthony crossed the room and stood to face her. He said:

"Young American, solitary, hears two women, unaware of his presence, talking in a teashop. For him the conversation, being largely allusive, is vague in detail and indefinite in statement; but is sinister in purport, tone and atmosphere. It conveys definite impression that there is a scheme afoot which will make money through a child and may also bring injury to a male adult. The only name mentioned is that of an ally and is the disconcertingly ubiquitous one of Evans. Young American decides to make himself able to identify the women and unobtrusively follows them when they leave the shop. They get to Leinster Terrace tube station and he loses 'em, never having managed to see their faces. He goes back to the teashop and has his first piece of luck, getting one of the women's gloves, inside which are a bus ticket and a scrap of paper bearing a pencilled shopping list. These leave him no wiser. After much thought and abortive search for advice he goes to Scotland Yard, which, not unnaturally, is civil but unimpressed. The thing gets on his mind but there seems nothing he can do about it until he finds a charming friend who knows us. Finish."

A small and worried frown creased Lucia's white forehead. "But . . ." she began.

"And here," said her husband, interrupting, "we have exhibits A, B and C." He went to the front of the table and opened its centre drawer and took out the glove, the bus ticket and the scrap of buff-coloured paper. He said, half to himself:

"Here are some things and some very pretty things. Now who is the owner of these very pretty things?"

Lucia got to her feet and came round the edge of the table and stood beside him and put her hand upon his shoulder. She said:

"Listen, darling! I'm—I'm worried."

Anthony raised his head sharply to look at her but he did not speak. She said after a pause:

"That's a very nice man and this thing seems to have eaten right into his mind. To you it's just a new sort of puzzle—new because instead of being asked to find out who *did* something you're being asked to find out who's *going to do* something. And—and . . ."

"Well?" said Anthony. He looked at her with the beginnings of a smile pulling down one corner of his mouth. She said:

"It's—it's . . . Oh, damn! It's just that I can't help thinking you've given the boy too much encouragement. Didn't you see how different he looked when he left—after you'd told him to come to lunch tomorrow and hinted that you might be further ahead? You *must* have seen. And I just thought it wasn't . . ."

Anthony said: "All right, Officer, I'll talk!" All vestige of the smile had left his face. "I liked Garrett. And you know what I think about Avis. In any case I'd help any friend of hers. But in this business I'm not being actuated by friendship. . . . If you go up our stairs, madam, to the third floor and open the second door on your right, what do you find?"

Lucia stared at him.

"The night nursery, of course."

"And in a corner there's a natty small bed, isn't there? And what's in the natty small bed?"

"What *are* you talking about, Anthony?"

"What's in the natty small bed? Answer me!"

Lucia said: "Alan, you fool!"

Anthony said: "Yes. And, thanks to God and despite the treasury, I'm a moderately rich man. Suppose, then, that when we left this room, in about an hour, we walked together up to the third floor and opened the second door on the right, very quietly so as not to wake the occupant of the natty small bed. And suppose we found the french windows on to the balcony there wide open and the natty small bed entirely empty. And suppose that, earlier in the evening, downstairs here, we'd heard some sound from above but hadn't thought anything of it. And suppose——"

"Stop! Will you stop!" Lucia was white faced and her breath came quick.

"Suppose . . ." began Anthony again and then put his hands upon his wife's shoulders. Beneath his touch he could feel her body shaking. He kissed her and smiled and said:

"Sorry. But I wanted to make you understand. I believe, not only what Garrett heard, but what he felt and feels. And if this is a long business I want you to understand it because you've got to feel like that too. You see, my dear, you didn't hear him tell his story after dinner. He told it damn badly but it was the more convincing for that."

Lucia stood on tiptoe and returned the caress of a moment ago. And then, turning, she was gone from under his hands and crossing the room. Her gait showed desire for haste cloaked by simulation of leisure.

Anthony stood where he was, looking at an open door. There came to his ears a series of soft, swift, ascending sounds.

2

Lucia came softly down the stairs. She was smiling but behind her upon the third floor the nursery door stood wide. She reached the foot of the stairs and crossed the hallway and went into the library.

Anthony, seated before the writing table, did not turn as she came in. She crossed the room and stood beside him. Now the glove and the bus ticket and the scrap of paper were at one side of the table, their place taken by two maps, one overlapping the other—a folded map of the Central London Underground Railway System and a bus chart headed, "Route 19H."

"Anthony!" said his wife and he turned his head to look up at her.

"I've been thinking!" she said. "Those things don't happen in England."

"Everything happens in England," said her husband.

The dark head was shaken. "No. Not kidnapping."

"It has," Anthony said. "And it will again."

"It's American!" said his wife. "It's American!"

"And England," said Anthony, "in common with the rest of the world, is becoming more Americanized every day. In the main not a bad thing. Very clean. In some specific instances like this . . ." He shrugged.

"These women," Lucia said. "Were they American?"

"Don't think so. Why should they be?"

"But, Anthony, are you seriously trying to tell me that you believe that this might be—well, a sort of beginning to a kidnapping whatd'youcallit?"

"Racket, d'you mean?"

"Yes. . . . But, after all, why should it be kidnapping at all? Did these women say anything about *stealing* a child?"

"How can you make money—big money—through a child unless you kidnap it? I could think of other things but I'd rather not . . . and anyhow, they wouldn't fit."

Lucia pondered. "What I don't see is why this worries Sheldon Garrett so much. After all, it's not even his own country. And even, according to him, the women didn't say anything *definite*. Why doesn't he just forget it? Or are all playwrights public spirited?"

"I'll tell you," Anthony said. "I got it out of him on the way back from Leinster Terrace. He has a sister with a child. And she married Barry Hendricksen——"

Lucia interrupted. "Hendricksen! Not . . . ?"

"Yes," said Anthony.

"But they got the boy back, didn't they? Not that it wasn't terrible, but I mean, it wasn't like that awful Lindbergh thing."

Anthony smiled at her. "If you'd wait a minute, woman!" His smile went. "It was only given out to the world that the child was sent back after the third ransom payment. What was omitted from the news was the fact that when it came back it left half its mind behind it."

Lucia stared at him, the colour ebbing from her face. Her lips opened as if to speak but no sound came from them. Her husband turned his chair and once more stared down at the maps. He said almost briskly:

"Now watch ye and wait, for ye know not at what hour the Answer cometh. . . . Two feminine voices; two feminine backs; one feminine glove; one feminine shopping list; one neuter bus ticket; the knowledge that both women booked from the threepenny machine at Leinster Terrace . . . Problem: find the owner of the glove."

Lucia perched herself upon the arm of the chair and, one hand upon his right shoulder, looked down over his left at the maps. She said:

"It's impossible! You can't do it! . . . Oh! And you forgot that one of the voices knew a man called Evans."

Anthony said: "There's no such word as 'can't', missie, in the English language. Listen! We discard the voices as being useless. Likewise we discard Evans and the glove. Contrariwise we hang on, first of all, to the bus ticket plus the knowledge of that threepenny machine." He opened a drawer and took from it a pencil and with the pencil made a ring round one of the black dots upon the railway map. He said:

"That's Goldhawk Market. And it's the last station but one of the longest possible threepenny rides from Leinster Terrace, going west. Why do I choose it when I could choose any of sixteen other stations reachable for threepence from Leinster Terrace? The answer to this minor problem is to be found in exhibit B." He pointed to the bus ticket. "See what I mean?"

Lucia said: "I don't and you know I don't. I've——"

" 'Ush, 'ush! I will have 'ush. Why do I choose Goldhawk Market, I say? I choose it because the owner of the glove took a threepenny ticket from Leinster Terrace station and in the glove was found this ticket from an L.G.O.C. bus on the 19H route."

"But . . ." Lucia began.

" 'Ush again! This bus ticket, although it hasn't got any names on it, has numbers. And it is a twopenny ticket punched at Number 5. Now the western end of the 19H route is Gunnersbury. Station 1, which by no means strangely coincides with the beginning, is the Bald-Faced Stag in Iron Lane, Gunnersbury. Station 2 is the junction of Goldhawk Road and Jennifer Street. Station 3 . . . but why bother you with all this professional detail. Let it suffice to say that, being twopenn'orth and having been punched at Station 5, the ticket must have been bought by someone boarding the bus between the Goldhawk Road–Jennifer Street junction and the Shepherd's Bush Empire and intending to get off at the Notting Hill point. We thus have a good presumptive knowledge of the district where the owner of the glove lives. . . ."

"Why?" said Lucia quickly and drawing a deep breath. "She might live in Hampstead and 've been driven out to Richmond by a cousin to see an aunt and then driven back as far as Shepherd's Bush and then have got on a bus to Notting Hill to meet the other woman and then have been going out to supper with a friend *anywhere* on the threepennyworth from Leinster Terrace. . . ."

Anthony looked at her. "The Eighth Wonder," he said. "Reba the Reasoning Woman . . . We are going, madam—we've got to go—by probabilities; and I say, taking the threepenny train ticket in conjunction with the bus ticket, that it is eminently probable that the owner of the glove lives—or has constant association with someone who does live—within a radius of half a mile from a point midway between the Shepherd's Bush Empire and the joining point of Jennifer Street and the Goldhawk Road. . . ." His voice tailed off and he muttered as if to himself: "And he said these didn't help."

Lucia said: "Well, they don't much, do they? It's really just as impossible in that radius of yours as it is in the whole of London. I mean, to find a woman you've never even seen properly. Needles get lost in haystacks; I shouldn't think the size of a haystack would——"

"If you lost a thimble in a forty-acre field," said Anthony, "and God came down on a cloud and told you it was in the middle acre, you'd be nearer finding that thimble than you were at first? . . . And hold your jaw, woman!"

He pushed away the maps and picked up the glove and the dirty little scrap of paper and set them before him on the blotting pad. He said:

"Three little articles belonging to Who. One gave a message and now there are Two."

"Whimsical, aren't you?" said his wife.

Anthony did not answer. He had turned away from her again. He propped his elbows on the edge of the writing table and dropped his head into cupped hands. . . .

3

The hands of the clock upon the table stood at a few moments after one. Lucia had long since gone to bed but her husband still sat and stared down at a piece of buff paper and a black right-hand glove. The smoke from his pipe hung above him in a blue cloud. Neither his head nor his body moved but the green eyes were alive. . . .

"Hell!" said Anthony suddenly and thrust back his chair and stood and stretched his long body. He began to walk up and down the big room; from balcony windows to door and back again. His pipe went out and he did not relight it. He went on walking—and his brain went on behaving like a squirrel on a treadmill.

He halted. He found himself opposite the writing table again and once more staring down at the paper and the glove. He took himself to task and opened a drawer and dropped into it the glove and the scrap of paper and the bus ticket. He locked the drawer and walked across the room and switched out the lights and began to make his way upstairs.

4

He was in his dressing room. As she had not called to him, he knew that upon the far side of the inner door Lucia slept. He pulled on pyjamas and stood for a moment motionless while his unruly mind insisted upon giving him, yet again, an orderly résumé of L'affaire Garrett.

Odd thing to happen to an American on a Sunday afternoon in Notting Hill. Odd thing for this kind of an American to be in Notting Hill at all, Sunday or no Sunday. . . .

"My *God!*" said Anthony Gethryn aloud. He tore open the wardrobe door and reached a long arm into its dark interior and snatched at a dressing gown. Pulling it on as he went, he left the room and ran downstairs. He opened the library door and switched on the lights and made for the writing table with long strides. He unlocked the drawer and opened it and took out the little scrap of buff paper.

CHAPTER VII

The telephone rang, and went on ringing.

It waked Thomas Sheldon Garrett from the first real sleep he had achieved since the night of Saturday, the seventeenth. He raised himself on an elbow and muttered thick curses and reached out a groping hand. He opened his eyes and his gaze fell, even as his fingers closed over the telephone, upon the travelling clock beside it. The time was ten minutes to eight.

He lifted the receiver and held it to his ear and growled.

The telephone said: "Garrett? Gethryn here."

"Oh!" said Garrett, anger leaving him.

The telephone said: "Sorry to wake you. Can you change that lunch appointment to breakfast?"

2

"Did I wake you?" said the telephone.

"Yes," said Spencer Hastings bitterly. "Get to hell! What d'you want?"

"Dyson," said the telephone. "And Flood."

"They're busy," said Hastings, now not so much himself as editor and half owner of *The Owl*.[1]

[1] *The Owl* is a weekly review of which Colonel Gethryn is half proprietor. His friend, Spencer Hastings, is half proprietor and editor. *The Owl*, besides its ordinary weekly edition, runs "special" editions whenever there is "scooped" any news sufficiently exciting to warrant these. In connection with the specials a special staff is employed. Description of the paper and its methods was first given in *The Rasp*. Dyson and Flood, who are the mainstay of the criminal side

"What on?" said the telephone.

The editor said: "Eh—oh—I——"

The telephone said: "Come out of the manger. I need 'em."

"Right!" Hastings was fully awake now. "What's on?"

"You should know," said the telephone.

"Good Lord!" Hastings was astonished. "You don't mean——"

The telephone interrupted. "So if you'd have 'em sent down as soon as they get to the office I'd be glad. G'bye."

3

Garrett stood before the writing table in Anthony's library. Upon the blotter there was now spread an inch-scale sectional map whose centre was the green of Shepherd's Bush. Anthony tapped with a forefinger upon a spot somewhat to the left of this. He said:

"I chose a point roughly halfway between the bus stop here and Gold-hawk Market, which is *here*. I then took a compass and used this spot as the centre and drew a half-inch or half-mile circle." He looked at the studiously blank face of his guest and a little smile twitched momentarily at the corner of his mouth.

Garrett said with a stolidity of tone which did him credit: "I'm afraid I don't see we've got much further—except, purely presumptively, to narrow our search to a mile-wide circle of what seems to be a very densely populated part of this city. And as we still don't know—and how could we if you come to think of it?—what the woman looks like or what she's called . . ."

He let his voice trail off into silence and Anthony's smile became a laugh.

"I'm afraid I don't see the joke," said Garrett stiffly.

"There isn't one," said Anthony. "I apologize. But I'm pleased with myself. I've got something we can get any number of teeth into. And it's not only a new fact, it's also corroborative of *this* district"—he tapped the map with a forefinger, right on the inch-wide circle—"being the right one."

Garrett said: "Go on! Go on!"

Without speaking Anthony opened the centre drawer of the table. His right hand went into it and came away bearing a six-inch square of white cardboard. Garrett, looking with puzzled eye, saw that in the centre of this was neatly pasted the yellow, irregularly edged slip of paper which bore the shopping list.

"You said your exhibits would tell us nothing," said Anthony and pointed to the list. "But *that*, my lad, shouts information!"

"Eh!" said Garrett and frowned and picked up the cardboard gingerly. He stared at the paper pasted to it. He said:

"But it's just a shopping list. We all——"

Anthony interrupted. "Read it out. And construe."

---

of the paper's "special" department, first worked with Anthony Gethryn in the case of Daniel Bronson described in *The Noose*.

Garrett held the cardboard nearer to his eyes. He said hesitantly: " 'Tea.' That's easy. Then 'one slt. bttr.' I didn't know what that meant until you told me, salt butter. 'P.ons.' I remember you or Hastings said that was pickled onions. The next means a quart of shrimps. Then one half pound of sausages; then matches; then a leg of lamb and one pound of—of—I can't remember what you said, something——"

"Suet," said Anthony and grinned.

"That's it!" Garrett looked from the cardboard to Anthony's face and then back. He studied the list again, his lips moving as he repeated each item to himself. He said at last:

"Sorry, I don't see."

Anthony said: "I don't blame you. In your enlightened country any sort of foodstuff can be bought on Sunday. Here the only shops which are open on Sunday are sweetstuff shops, occasional chemists, what you'd call delicatessens and tobacconists. There are some others, of course, but they don't matter here. . . . *Now* look!"

Garrett obeyed; only to glance up again after a moment. He shook his head and lifted his shoulders. He said:

"It's no use! I see what you mean but I don't see what the effect is. You mean that there are some things on the list—I suppose butter and meat and suet—that she couldn't have bought that day. But I still . . ."

Anthony said: "You're getting close. But the real point isn't so much the impossibility of buying certain things on Sunday; it's this—that whoever wrote this list *knew that impossibility.* A shopping list written on a scrap of paper torn from a magazine and thrust into a glove isn't a shopping list for the morrow; it is, almost inevitably, a shopping list for the same day and the same trip for which the glove is put on—because no woman, under normal circumstances, carries anything in a glove which isn't for immediate use. In other words we can assume that the woman of the glove was going to translate the list into commodities before returning home. We know that she put the list into her glove on Sunday and that therefore this was Sunday shopping—a fact borne out by all the list except the last two entries, for only those are impossible of Sunday purchase. She can't have been ignorant of the fact that it was Sunday, because such ignorance, in this still Sabbatical town, is impossible even to a half-witted child. Therefore this is, on all heads, a Sunday list. Therefore lamb and suet—particularly the first, are intruders and unbelievable intruders. Follow?"

Garrett nodded but between the eyes which were fixed upon Anthony was still a frown compounded of bewilderment and disbelief. He said:

"It sounds all right. But lamb and suet are there!"

"That," said Anthony, "is where you're wrong. They are *not* there!" He opened the middle drawer of the table again and from it took a reading glass. He said: "Take that and have another look."

"Listen!" Garrett said. "If you think I lived with that thing for days and didn't look at it under a glass you must be——" He checked himself. "You must think I'm dumber than I am! If what you're trying to tell me is that the last two items on the list weren't written at the same time as the others, or were written with a different pencil, you can save yourself the trouble." His tone showed him almost beyond pretence of civility. "I didn't happen to mention it when I gave it to you because I thought anyone could see it with half an eye."

Anthony looked at him. "I see. How d'you account for it then?"

Garrett said: "I thought it was simple. I thought it meant that at some period the owner of the list suddenly remembered the meat and the suet and added them on."

"And that roughness in those entries," said Anthony. "You can see what I mean with the naked eye, but better under the glass."

Garrett stared at him. "Written on a rough surface. Against a wall, maybe. Or on anything which wasn't smooth."

"Say a handbag?"

Garrett laughed; a harsh little sound. "No. I've *thought* about this business, you know! Not a handbag. Because if she'd had a handbag she'd have put the list into that and not into her glove."

"Possibly," said Anthony softly, "someone else's handbag. And, also possibly, in a moving vehicle. If you look carefully you'll see that the letters —especially the *m* in 'lamb' and the *b* just before 'St'—are shakily made."

Now Garrett did look, bending over the card on the table and using the glass. He said grudgingly:

"It's possible." He straightened and turned once more to face his host. "But it doesn't alter anything. It merely means that she may have written this in a train or a bus or a car."

"And on a Sunday?" Anthony's tone was meek.

"I don't . . ." began Garrett and then checked himself. His right hand rubbed reflectively at the back of his head. He said in a sudden little burst of words:

"Look here, *will* you tell me what you're driving at?"

Anthony smiled. "Sorry. I love to be mysterious and reveal all in the last chapter. . . . Let's recapitulate. First, the day the woman put this in her glove was Sunday. Second, the last two items on the list are the only ones not purchasable on Sunday. Third, she has no foreign accent and therefore knows the Sunday shopping laws. Fourth, she added the last two items to this Sunday shopping list in a moving vehicle and so had to press the paper upon a rough surface which, as there is nothing in a tube train or bus which will fill the bill, was most probably the outside of a woman's handbag. Fifth, she carried no handbag herself or she would not have put the list in her glove. . . . Add those five points together and I think you'll agree that the last two entries do *not* refer to a leg of lamb and a pound of suet. As a corollary to all that I'll add this—that once it had dawned on me that the last two lines were not what they seemed it also dawned upon me that, if they had been, they'd have been most curious. Because legs of lamb don't fit at all with the sort of larder that goes in for half pounds of salt butter and small quantities of pickled onions. Further, it's unlikely that this sort of larder would buy, at one and the same time, sausages and lamb."

Garrett had picked up the card again and was looking at it. When he spoke his excitement was audible. He said:

"But what *are* these last two things?"

Anthony said: "Think. Our woman who (a) has no bag with her, (b) is unlikely to be buying legs of lamb and (c) wouldn't try to buy a leg of lamb on a Sunday, takes a bus to Notting Hill and while in the bus writes something at the bottom of her shopping list, using *someone else's* bag to write upon. But, since it cannot be shopping which she is adding to her shopping list, why should she write at all in the bus? Because it is some-thing which she has suddenly thought of, and wants to remember, which has been brought to her attention while on the bus. Now, bearing all that farrago in mind, consider the actual words that she wrote. 'L. Lamb' and 'I Lb. St.' We thought, because we saw it in conjunction with a shopping list, that these last meant leg of lamb and one pound of suet. I maintain that what they really mean is: Miss, or Mrs., Lucy, or Letitia or Lettice or Lulu or Lola or what the L you like, Lamb, who lives at Number 1 'Lb.' Street."

"Great *God!*" said Garrett.

"You see," Anthony said, "it all fits. The bus, the bag and the Lamb. . . . If you write something, on the only bit of paper you have, when you're on a bus, and you put the paper on a bag that you've had to borrow, I think it's a reasonable seventy-five-out-of-a-hundred chance that you're writing down the address of someone you've met in that bus. Now what sort of someone? It *might* be an acquaintance made during the bus ride but you're only having a twopenny ride and that doesn't seem long enough to get to the address-writing stage: it's more probable, therefore, that the address is that of a friend of other days and the same sex whom you've just met again."

"God!" said Garrett again. "It's grand. It doesn't matter a damn, Gethryn, whether it was a sudden woman acquaintance, a man she picked up or an old friend of either sex! It doesn't matter if it was a hermaphrodite! *Who-ever* it was is going to be able to tell us *something*. If we——"

Anthony grinned. "Hold your horses! What sort of a street d'you think 'Lb.' stands for?"

Garrett stared at him. "I wouldn't know that. You have damn funny street names anyway." Anxiety took the place of irritation in his tone. "Do you mean you can't . . ."

"I mean," said Anthony, "that I can't see Lb. as an abbreviation for any word likely to be the name of any London street. And if those two letters are Lb. we've got the devil of a job in front of us because it'd mean that we're dealing with an abbreviation which is unreasonable. I haven't yet looked through the London Directory but I'll bet you a pound to a dollar there aren't more than two streets beginning with *l* and ending *b*. And *no* street which *begins* with Lb. . . ."

"Hell," said Garrett, and two words more.

"Quite," said Anthony. "But look again through the glass at those two letters before the St. of 'street.' When our minds were on shopping we naturally saw Lb. But now I want to think that *b* is really another *l*."

Garrett snatched up the glass and bent again over the card. He said almost at once:

"It might be! It might quite easily be. . . . Damn it, it's *got* to be. . . ."

"Zeal, all zeal, Mr. Easy!" Anthony crossed to the table and sat upon its edge. "But let's take it as a double *l* for a minute. And let's take something else. This isn't unassailable logic but I think it's fair presumption. If Miss X meets Miss Lamb on a bus near Miss X's home or place of constant visiting and writes Miss Lamb's address down in such extremely abbreviated form, it argues, both by reason of this extreme abbreviation and by reason of the coincidence of meeting on the bus, that Miss Lamb is living in the same neighbourhood as Miss X. If Miss Lamb were living in quite another district it would not only make the coincidence of their meeting on this bus far greater, but it would also tend, I think, to make Miss X write down the address more fully. I say, therefore, that our first step is to enlarge the circle which I've drawn on that map and then look inside it for all streets beginning with a double *l*."

"But look here," said Garrett and then was cut short by sounds from outside the door—the closing of another door; men's feet upon parquet flooring; a rap upon the door of the room in which they were.

Anthony smiled. "Reinforcements," he said and then, raising his voice: "Come in!"

"Don't worry, we'll go right in."

The door opened to admit two men. The first was tall and thin and stooping and was clad in a stained and dirty raincoat from beneath which there came down two shapeless cylinders of ancient, maculate grey flannel. He carried a tortured bundle of greenish-grey felt which might have been a hat and around his neck was a woollen muffler of the colour of wholemeal bread. From the folds of this protruded a head like that of an eagle with a sense of humour and lank black hair. A pair of the largest horn-rimmed glasses which Garrett had ever seen bestrode the fierce beak, enlarging dark eyes which were at once heavy lidded and alert.

The second visitor was as different from the first as well could be; a youngish-looking man, clad with beautiful ease in brown, rich tweed, with a round and smooth and freshly coloured face, very sleek blond hair, rather prominent light blue eyes and a trim solidity of body which made him seem shorter than his real height—in short, what would have been a picture of healthy, pleasant, rather fatuous young English manhood save for the lines about the mouth and the gleam of tired and doubting humour in the light blue eyes.

"I want you two," said Anthony, "to meet Mr. Sheldon Garrett. Garrett, Mr. Dyson; Mr. Flood."

In that order the first man nodded his eagle's head; the second came forward and held out his hand and clasped Garrett's and shook it firmly.

"Dyson and Flood," said Anthony, "are going to help us." He looked at the two. "At least I think they are. Anything interesting on?"

Dyson shook his head, drawing down the corners of his wide, thin-lipped mouth. Flood said:

"There isn't anything interesting. Not any more."

"Sit down," said Anthony. "And I'll change your minds."

They sat, Dyson collapsed into a corner of the big leathern sofa chair with one hand hiding his spectacles, Flood neatly upright in a high-backed chair. Anthony addressed them. He was brief and lucid and extremely careful of details—but he came at last to the end. He surveyed his visitors and said:

"*Now* is there anything interesting? Have a drink?"

"Yes," said Dyson without taking his hand away from his face. "And yes."

Flood said: "So the first step is Ll Street? . . . Thanks, I believe I will."

4

Dyson took a glass from his lips. "Need a street directory," he said. Flood nodded.

"All done," said Anthony. "We've got five alternatives on the Ll line. Lloyd Street. Llewellyn Street and Llowndes Street—though what a name like that's doing down there is puzzling—and Lowell Street and Laval Street."

Dyson's collapsed length seemed suddenly to have received, from source unknown, a revivification; at one moment he had been lying back collapsed, at the next he was on his feet.

Flood rose too. He took out a linen handkerchief and neatly wiped his mouth and put the handkerchief away again. Dyson looked at him. Without a word they went towards the door, opened it and were gone. It shut behind them.

Garrett looked at his host with raised brows.

Anthony said: "We'll hear. . . . Come and meet my son."

CHAPTER VIII

A small neat motorcar with bright blue paint and gleaming fittings turned into the Hammersmith end of Lloyd Street. It hesitated at the corner, slid along the left-hand curb and then, after a moment, shot directly across the road and repeated the performance. Seeming to regain sanity, it crossed to its proper side and purred easily down the street. At the farthermost end it stopped and there emerged from it a young man in admirable clothes of brown tweed. He looked this way and that along the street and then up at the door of the first house; a door which once had been green but which

now was of an indeterminate putty colour flecked by streaks of grey where
time and weather had entirely removed its paint.

The young man ran up the steps. He looked upon each side of the door
for a bell and, finding none, put his hand to a knocker of wrought iron
which hung by only one screw. A hollow sound came and he waited. After
a minute he knocked again; then again waited. He inclined his head towards the door and seemed to be listening. He straightened himself and
knocked with considerable force, this time using the side of a gloved fist.

No sound had come from behind it but the door was suddenly opened
with a violence which sent its inner handle crashing against the wall of the
passage. Flood blinked and saw that there stood framed in the doorway a
short square man clad in blue trousers too large for him and grey shirt too
small. The trousers were held neither by belt nor braces, and their nether
ends hung down in a series of elephantine folds. The shirt, buttonless, gaped
across a rufus-thatched chest and its sleeves were rolled up over a pair of ab-
normally muscled forearms. In the left hand was an open book whose large
print afforded to Flood's quick eye a surprising glimpse of Latin verse. From
the massive shoulders rose a short thick neck almost wholly hidden by the
ragged edge of a bright red beard, and from beneath bushy brows of the
same improbable colour two fierce little eyes shot fire.

With effort Flood kept upon his face the smile which he had prepared.
He said:

"Is Mrs. Lamb in?"

Through the beard came a deep and distant voice.

"No!" it said.

Flood tried again, still smiling. "Miss Lamb, then?"

"No!"

Flood eased his aching mouth. He said with impressive courtesy: "Do I
address Mr. Lamb?"

"No!"

Flood persevered. "Perhaps you can tell me," he said, "when Mrs. or Miss
Lamb *will* be in?"

"No!" This time the sound was a bellow.

Flood stood his ground though many a man would have recoiled. But
he no longer smiled. He said:

"Haven't you *any* idea?"

Flames seemed to dart from beneath the beetling red brows. The beard
moved, this time enough to show teeth of extreme whiteness. From between
them came one word.

"No!"

Flood, with the feeling of one who plays spillikens with shreds of am-
monal, stuck to his tank. But he, too, became monosyllabic.

He said: "Why?"

The figure in the doorway moved. It took a step back and lifted a right
hand as big as a cluster of plantains and set it to the edge of the door. The

hirsute head was suddenly thrust forward and the bearded lips opened once more. From them came a roar.

"Because they don't live here!"

Then a shattering crash which made Flood fear for the very walls of the dilapidated house and he was left staring once more at the maculate, putty-coloured door.

2

A postman came down the steps of Number 9 Lowell Street. As he reached the pavement a large and loud and mud-splashed motorcycle slid up the gutter beside him.

"Oy!" said its rider and propped himself with one foot on the curb.

The postman stared into a pair of vast horn-rimmed spectacles. "Beg pardon!" he said.

"Where's Number 1?" said the rider. "Or did they pull it down?"

"Number 1 Lowell Street?" The postman pondered. "That's the Red Lion at the corner. Y'see, they don't——" He was left staring, his ears ringing with the explosions of an exhaust which did not comply with regulations. . . .

In the Red Lion's public bar, a lady of contours ministered with Olympian condescension to four casuals who sipped and chatted and were at ease. The scent of beer was over all and there was peace—which, with brutal lack of warning, was suddenly shattered.

"Mercy on us!" The goddess put a hand to the amplitudes of her bosom. "What's that?"

A thin man smiled beneath a moustache. "Like Vimy!" he said.

The swing doors crashed inwards and there marched up to the bar a tall and thin and stooping form wrapped in a stained raincoat. Beneath a hat of age showed horn-rimmed spectacles astride a fierce nose.

"Bitter!" said Mr. Francis Dyson and put down money.

The goddess served him. He picked up the glass and put it to his mouth and set it down empty. He said:

"Thanks! Name of Lamb?"

"Eh?" said the goddess.

Mr. Dyson repeated himself.

"Paget," said the goddess. "And the Christian name is Doris. Though what it's got to do with *you*, young man . . ." Her voice trailed off into silence, for Mr. Dyson was already halfway to the door.

"*Well!*" said Miss Paget, and the door swung shut behind Mr. Dyson's going.

There was no other customer in the Lion's saloon bar when Mr. Dyson entered.

"Bitter!" said Mr. Dyson and put down money and received his glass.

"Thanks!" he said and drank and put the glass down, empty. "Name of Lamb?"

He spoke to a large and corpulent and genial male whose every action and circumstance proclaimed him landlord.

Across the darkly gleaming mahogany of the bar this one looked benevolently at Mr. Dyson. He said:

"No sir. The name's Prescott. Alf Prescott. . . . No sir, there's no one 'ere of the name o' Lamb. There's the Blue Eagle in the Finchley Road, now! That's——"

He found himself regarding Mr. Dyson's departing back.

3

Llewellyn Street is very small, very shy and very neat. It contains, in all, twenty-two houses. It hides itself discreetly between the noisy bustle of Gunnersbury High Road on the one side and the clangour of the railway on the other. It is surrounded by other small and narrow streets which are of different character, being as untidy and blatant as Llewellyn Street is quiet and reserved. Something of an anomaly, Llewellyn Street, but an anomaly curiously common in the sprawling unreason of London.

The houses in Llewellyn Street are small, square brick boxes—but each is separated from the pavement by a narrow, railed-off strip and it is with these strips that the street expresses itself. Some are flagged with stone; some actually green with growing grass; some bright with neatly rolled gravel round which grow shrubs and even flowers. To come into Llewellyn Street, as Flood came in his little blue car, from the neighbouring squalor of Pettifer Road is to please the senses—both by contrast and intrinsic merit.

Flood, driving slowly along the curb and peering out at the neat doorways, saw a brass-knockered 21 and then a white-painted 19. He increased the pressure of his right foot and the little car shot forward, to stop at last before the corner house.

Flood wriggled out onto the pavement. He looked with pleasure at Number 1 and walked towards its little iron gate, between which and the white steps leading up to the door was a patch of vivid green grass. He passed through the gate and in two strides was at the white steps. He mounted them and pressed a bell whose surrounding brasswork gleamed gold in the sunshine.

From the other side of the neat door came the crisp tinkling of a bell; the sound of the opening of some interior door; quick footsteps.

The door opened. Flood raised his hat and smiled, this time without difficulty. He was faced by a young woman in pleasing accord with Llewellyn Street in general and Number 1 in particular. She was tall enough; and slim enough without angularity; and owned very blue eyes which looked straight into Flood's from a round face of cheerful comeliness. And the hair of her neat small head reflected the warm goldness of the sunshine.

"Miss Lamb?" said Flood in his best manner.

The blue eyes opened a thought wider; but they continued to rest without displeasure upon the visitor.

"That's me," she said. And her voice was good match for face and figure and the whiteness of her teeth when she smiled.

"Good!" said Flood with a heartiness easy of achievement. He thought quickly, rejecting two prepared stories and adapting a third in the space of a second. He said with a nice blend of camaraderie and diffidence:

"My name's Aston. Charles Aston. Of Aston, Sparks and Aston. I'm the second Aston. We're solicitors. . . ."

The blue eyes lost something of their friendliness. "What d'you *want?*" said the mouth beneath them.

Flood hastened to repair damage. "Don't think for a moment that there's anything unpleasant about my visit, Miss Lamb." His tone was judiciously chosen. "But if you *could* give me just five minutes of your time you might be able to do us a great service and—er . . ." The ingenuous junior partner of the mythical firm of Aston, Sparks and Aston became suitably embarrassed. "And—er—and what I mean is, the firm would be only too glad to— in fact . . ." Mr. Aston lost his thread and fumbled for a notecase.

The blue eyes of Miss Lamb were cleared of suspicion.

"You mean," said Miss Lamb, "you might make it worth me while?"

Young Mr. Aston was grateful. He laughed heartily. "Exactly! . . . Exactly!"

Miss Lamb, her attractive head upon one side, went through a short parade of consideration. " 'Specs you better step in," she said at last. She stood aside and young Mr. Aston, removing an admirable brown hat, passed through the door.

"In here," said Miss Lamb and ushered young Mr. Aston into a small bright room completely filled with furniture.

"Jest a minute," said Miss Lamb and was gone, closing the door behind her.

Mr. Aston threaded short-stepped way between two occasional tables, a rocking chair and a harmonium. He stood before a crowded mantelshelf and looked with awe upon a glass case beneath which sea shells were cemented upon crimson plush. From some recess of the little house voices came to his ear—the sharp but pleasing tones of Miss Lamb blending with a lower but still feminine rumble which was beyond doubt maternal.

Miss Lamb came back. "Jest tellin' Mother," she said crisply. "Sit down. Make yourself atome!"

Mr. Aston made himself at home upon the edge of a chair of alarming discomfort. Miss Lamb arranged herself to face him. She folded her hands in her lap and looked at him.

"Now!" she said.

Mr. Aston began his story. It was, he could promise Miss Lamb, a rather curious combination of circumstances which had brought him here. A sort of coincidence. Miss Lamb was, in fact, a godsend, if she might be called that without offence—and Mr. Aston was sure she might. And so on and so on. . . .

"But coming to the point," said Mr. Aston in suddenly professional tones, "do you recollect, Miss Lamb, travelling upon a Number 19H omnibus upon Sunday, the eighteenth of this month?"

"Quite the lawyer, aren't we!" said Miss Lamb. "Now, let's see. Sunday the eighteenth; that'd be a fortnight ago come next Sunday."

"That's it!" said Mr. Aston eagerly. "On a 19H, going east."

"East!" said Miss Lamb. "I don't take no truck with compasses and such. . . ."

"Towards Notting Hill," said Mr. Aston. "Surely you remember!"

"Yes!" said Miss Lamb. "Yes, I do. I was—but that's neither here nor there."

"The point is this," said Mr. Aston impressively. "Do you remember, Miss Lamb, meeting someone on that bus?"

"Aha!" said Miss Lamb. "*Now* I see what you're after." She regarded Mr. Aston with something like suspicion. She said slowly:

"Suppose I was to say that any of my friend's business was no business of mine. Suppose I was to say that I didn't——"

"My dear lady," said Mr. Aston. "I don't want you to suppose for a moment that you'll be doing anybody at all any harm by helping me." He smiled a candid, boyish smile which produced its answer upon the face of his hostess.

"In fact," continued Mr. Aston, "I can solemnly assure you, Miss Lamb, that you'll be doing your friend a good service. Now, you *do* remember meeting a friend on that bus, don't you?"

A moment or so passed before Miss Lamb answered—a moment during which, though she kept her gaze upon Mr. Aston's face, she seemed to be considering other things than Mr. Aston. And then the look of abstraction left the blue eyes and she became decisive. She said:

"There don't seem any harm in you. . . . Yes, I remember well enough riding on the bus and I remember meeting Janet. Couldn't very well forget. Y'see, we useter be great chums and I hadn't seen her for nigh on a couple of years. What about it?"

"This is excellent!" said Mr. Aston with enthusiasm. "Splendid! Now, Miss Lamb, I'll tell you exactly why I want to get in touch with your friend and you'll see where you'll be doing her a good turn. And—er"—Mr. Aston coughed—"possibly yourself as well."

Miss Lamb regarded him, her blue eyes entirely friendly. "Get it off your chest," she said.

4

Anthony Gethryn was deep in the largest of his library chairs. His long legs were crossed and fragrant clouds of cigar smoke hung round him. Through half-closed lids his eyes surveyed the nervous prowlings of his guest.

"Sit down, man!" he said, "and take it easy. We'll hear soon."

"Sorry!" said Sheldon Garrett and laughed. He threw himself into a chair and looked at his host. "This thing's got right under my skin." He jumped up and resumed his pacing. He said:

"D'you *really* think those two'll get anything?"

Anthony held up a finger for silence and cocked his head towards the door. The sound of footsteps came faintly from outside it; and then a knock and then White, who said, "Mr. Flood, sir." And then Flood himself.

He came slowly across the room, his face expressionless. He nodded to Garrett and walked over to the big writing table and took a cigarette from a box and lit it.

"Well?" said Anthony.

Flood's hand went to a side pocket and came away with an envelope in its fingers. He looked at the envelope and read aloud:

"Miss Janet Murch, care of Lady Ballister, 27 Roxburne Gardens, S.W. 7."

Garrett started forward. "Do you mean . . . ?"

"Look for yourself," said Flood and handed over the envelope.

Garrett looked at it, reading the words that Flood had read; words written in a round, schoolgirlish script.

"The address," said Flood, "of the owner of the glove."

"My God!" said Garrett and sat down.

"Turn it over," said Flood.

Garrett twisted the paper in his fingers. Upon the back was written in the same script: "Mrs. Bellows, 148A Iron Court, Stockholm Lane." He read the words aloud.

"J. Murch's aunt," Flood said. "And Stockholm Lane's right on the 19H route. And the shopping list 'd be for Aunt Bellows."

"Great!" said Garrett and smiled broadly. "*Great!*"

Anthony looked at Flood. "Was it Llowndes? Or Lloyd?"

"Llewellyn," said Flood. "Second shot. Heard from Dyson?" A smile threatened to divide his face.

Anthony shook his head.

"He'll call," said Flood and went on smiling.

Garrett said: "Who's L. Lamb?"

Flood said: "Girl. Name's Letty. Pretty. Early twenties. Good sort. Used to work with Janet Murch about three years ago. On the bus was the first time they'd met since then."

Garrett frowned. "Doesn't sound like what we're after, if it's true."

Anthony said: "My good Garrett, you didn't think we'd bagged both birds with the first rock, did you!"

"Well . . ." Garrett shrugged. "It was possible."

Anthony smiled. "But damned unlikely. The women you heard talking hadn't just met, had they? They knew each other's addresses without writing 'em down, didn't they?"

Garrett nodded. "I was just dumb, I guess."

Flood said: "Lamb's all right. All aboveboard. And she wasn't in any teashop on Sunday: I checked up to make sure."

Anthony stood up and stretched his long body. "Lamb's out. We concentrate on Murch." He looked at Flood. "Where's that she's working?"

Flood said: "Janet's doing well. *Very* superior. She works for Major General Sir Charles Ballister—you know, big bug in the War Office."

Anthony went over to the writing table and from the shelves above it pulled down the red bulk of Who's Who. Garrett looked at Flood.

"How in the world did you do it?" he said.

Flood grinned. He told of Mr. Charles Aston's call upon Miss Lamb. "When she heard that the firm of Aston, Sparks and Aston were looking for Janet Murch in order to pay Janet Murch a legacy Letty was only too glad to help—*and* get the couple of quid which the junior partner thought was an adequate reward for helping his firm."

"Here we are," said Anthony from behind Who's Who. " 'Ballister. Major General Sir Charles Montague. b. 1870' . . . Blah. . . . 'm. 1910 Alice, e.d. of Mr. and Mrs. Fenton of Stoke Poges' . . . Blah . . . blah . . . *and* blah . . . 'one s. two d.' . . . blah . . . blah . . . 'address 27 Roxburne Gardens S.W. 7.' " He closed the book with a slam. "And there, in a manner of speaking, we all are." He looked at Flood. "Would they know at the *Owl* office?"

Flood looked at him. "Such as?"

"Age of children," Anthony said. "All three."

"Use the phone?" Flood said.

Anthony nodded.

"Look here," said Garrett, suddenly staring at Flood. "What I don't see is, how in the world you got the woman's name."

Flood smiled, not without complacence. "Letty gave it to me. The Christian name right away. I had a few nasty moments because I couldn't get her round to saying the surname without giving away that I didn't know it. She kept Janeting and made it a bit tough for poor Mr. Aston. . . " He smiled reminiscently. "But poor Mr. Aston has a bad hand; sprained the tendons of his thumb and first finger. Too bad! But Letty didn't mind writing Janet's address on that envelope."

"Oh!" said Garrett and laughed. "Pretty good."

" 'One s. and two d.,' " Anthony murmured. "I could bear to know their ages."

"Sorry!" said Flood and went round the table and picked up the telephone. He was busy with it, cryptically, for a few minutes. He hung up the receiver and came back to the middle of the room. He said:

"Son thirteen; just gone to Charterhouse. One daughter, nine; second daughter, seven."

There was silence for a long moment. Anthony looked at the end of his cigar, Flood down at the floor and Garrett from one face to the other.

Garrett tried to keep silence; but could not. He was at once elated and obsessed with desire for action. He said, looking at Anthony:

"It's easy now. Isn't it?"

Anthony continued to look at the end of his cigar. He said: "Maybe. Nice delicate approach shot required." He put the cigar back in his mouth and went over to the table and sat upon it and reached for the telephone.

CHAPTER IX

Anthony Gethryn walked up the six shallow steps which led, between the pillars of a portico, to the gleaming front door of Number 27 Roxburne Gardens. As he reached the topmost step the door opened and a man came out. He was a little man who accorded ill with front doors in Roxburne Gardens; a little man in dark nondescript clothes and an ill-brushed bowler hat a size too small. He had a large head whose pale sharp face was undistinguished in its foxy outline but whose carriage was peculiar in a sideways tilt which implied its habitual averting from any and every eye.

He passed Anthony and ran down the steps with a quick pattering. Behind him the door started to close and then, with a jerk, opened widely to show a portly manservant whose impeccable mask regarded Anthony with the prescribed blend of doubt, deference and inquiry.

"Lady Ballister," said Anthony. "She expects me. Mr. Gethryn."

The man stood aside. "If you would come in, sir. . . ."

In a spacious but cheerless hall Anthony removed his hat. It was taken from him with a correct murmuring and he followed the portly back down the length of the hallway and into a library.

"If you would wait here, sir, I will inform her ladyship. . . ." The door shut discreetly and Anthony was alone.

He likes strange rooms. They interest him; and this room was no exception to rule. Very much a library. A few pieces of gleaming silver. Many hundreds of books, probably unread and certainly uninteresting. A businesslike writing desk of an ugliness quite supreme. Leather chairs whose invitation was in inverse ratio to their apparent size and comfort. A small fire glowing redly in an ugly grate. A pair of curtained french windows behind which could be sensed the usual grey Kensingtonian garden. A steel engraving of moorland and cattle; a surprisingly good water colour of a brigantine before the wind; a stiff, awkward bazaar scene in oils; a Sergeantesque portrait of a woman whose original might have been beautiful; a very bad hunting scene. On the writing table a large photograph, in a silver frame, of a woman who might be the original of the portrait. On the mantel, between two pieces of Benares brasswork, a photograph of three children—a lanky, bespectacled boy awkwardly posed between two round-faced and younger girls . . .

The door opened and there came towards Anthony the original of the portrait and the photograph. She was tall and moved well, though with a certain suppression of grace. "All my people are service people," thought Anthony and moved forward to meet her, manœuvring so that the light from the curtained french windows fell upon her face. It was a good face; better by far than that which artist or camera had shown him. He put her down, with an eye aided by memory of the Who's Who entry, as in her early forties. There was no trace of grey in the dark hair but there were deep lines from the corners of the nostrils to the mouth. She was very pale, with a sort of luminous greyish pallor possibly natural but possibly impermanent and recently caused.

She said in a voice so low that it gave the impression of determination to subdue unsteadiness:

"Colonel Gethryn? I—I had a message from Edith Carisbrooke . . ."

Anthony bowed and held out his hand. He said:

"Sorry to bother you like this but I'm sure you'll understand. . . ."

His hand remained outstretched. Its insistence could not be denied, and a slim, long-fingered hand was put within its grasp; a very cold hand which seemed to be shaking a little.

Anthony released it. It was clear to him that he was supposed to speak next and so he did not speak and there was a moment of silence, uncomfortably protracted.

"I'm afraid I didn't quite understand Edith," said the woman at last. "She wasn't clear what it was that you wanted." Her mouth barely opened for the words.

Anthony laughed. "I was afraid you might be fogged. It's purely a domestic matter, but perhaps all the more important for that." He was genially fatuous. "Really, my wife should be seeing you. But she's in bed with a chill. Dreadful weather, this. . . . What I'm going to bother you about is the vitally important question of nursemaids. My son's nurse is leaving us. She's going to get married—awkward woman!" His laugh was a masterpiece. "And both my wife and myself, Lady Ballister, are almost morbidly careful about nurses. Now Edith Carisbrooke was talking to my wife the other day and happened to mention what an extremely good nursemaid you had for your two little girls. And so . . ."

He allowed his sentence to dissolve. He wanted once more to force those lips to make words; to watch the lips to see whether they would not at last defeat the will behind them and obviously tremble. He waited and wondered—and she spoke and the lips did tremble. She said:

"Oh! . . . A nursemaid? Yes, I see. Yes . . . Yes, Janet *is* very good." She stopped. She seemed to think that she had answered.

Half-formed ideas in Anthony's mind were forced into dissolution. It was plain enough that his hostess was agitated; had received, recently, a shock. But since it was plain that her mind was not on the conversation—and therefore not upon children—that shock was foreign to Colonel Gethryn's business. He said:

"What I really wanted, Lady Ballister, was a few words with this excellent nurse of yours. Really, Edith Carisbrooke was so impressive about her that we wondered whether the girl could put us on to a good thing, as it were. Very odd request, I know! But I always say, you can't be too careful!"

From beneath thin dark brows, eyes which were clouded with other thoughts regarded him. The brows bent themselves together, as if in effort at concentration, and a light came into the eyes beneath them.

"Talk to Janet?" said Alice Ballister. "Oh! . . . I see what you mean. You wish to interview my nurse."

Anthony nodded. "Yes. That's the idea. See if she's got a sister as good as she is, what? Ha!"

"I'm sorry," said the woman, "but Janet has left."

"Oh!" said Anthony. He experienced some trouble in maintaining pose. "I see. . . ." He pulled himself together and achieved heartiness once more. "That's too bad! Too bad! So Edith Carisbrooke was wrong, what?"

"No!" said the low voice. "Janet was an excellent nurse. Excellent!" The voice showed the straining of the mind for concentration. "I'd no fault to find with her. She gave notice herself a few days ago. She left yesterday. I tried to persuade her to stay; offered her more wages. But her mind seemed made up. . . ."

The voice died away. The pallor of the face was increased, as if fatigue had been piled upon horror.

"Too bad!" said Colonel Gethryn again. "Better job, I suppose. Or what she thought was a better job. Damn ungrateful, the servant class!" He was all sympathetic indignation.

The woman put up a hand to her forehead and drew long fingers across her brow as if to ease pain. She said:

"I've no idea." There was a desperate under-ring to the muttered voice; it was as if she were preparing herself for one effort which must be the last. She said in a louder tone than any she had used:

"I'm sorry I can't help you. I haven't even got her address."

"Thanks. Thanks!" Colonel Gethryn was taking his cue. He made the beginnings of a movement towards the door. "So sorry I've had to give you this trouble for nothing."

Her mouth made effort to twist itself into a smile. Murmurs came from it. She moved doorwards with Colonel Gethryn.

They stood a moment in the hall. From recesses appeared the portly manservant, bearing Colonel Gethryn's hat. Colonel Gethryn took it and bowed over it to his hostess. He said:

"Thanks again! And again apologies for having bothered you."

The woman stared at him with clouded eyes. She said:

"I'm sorry I couldn't be of more use." And then with a last attempt at courtesy: "If it's any use to you I know of a very good agency. Janet came to me from there." Once more the hand went to her brow and drew long fingers across it. "It's called the—the KJB. It's not far from here. In Brabazon Road, behind the Naval Museum. I—I can't remember the number but . . ." Once more the voice died away with the passing of effort.

"Very kind of you!" said Colonel Gethryn. "Very kind!" He bowed again and through more apologies got himself to the door and out. He ran down the steps. Drawn up to the pavement, two houses away, was his car. He went to it with long strides and seated himself behind the wheel and beside Thomas Sheldon Garrett. The air was thick with the smoke of Garrett's cigarettes.

"Get anything?" said the smoker with eagerness. "Did you see her? Do you think . . . ?"

Anthony shook his head. "Check!" he said.

2

And "Check!" he said again, twenty-five minutes later, when the long black car stood at the curb outside the grocery shop which stands at the corner of Stockholm Lane and Iron Court.

"Hell!" said Garrett. "Why?"

Anthony settled himself behind the wheel. "Because Mrs. Bellows, who is Martha Bellows and the aunt of our Miss Murch, is no longer in residence."

A frown creased Garrett's forehead and there came back into his face something of the look which it had worn when Avis Bellingham had taken him to dine in Stukeley Gardens.

Anthony looked at him. "I said *check,* not checkmate. Remember KJB."

Garrett shrugged. "The agency. That's unlikely to be of much use." He put a cigarette between his lips but forgot to light it.

Anthony started the car, slipping into first gear and beginning to thread careful way through the narrow and encumbered unpleasantness of Stockholm Lane.

Garrett made a motion with his head towards the place from which they had come. "Wasn't there *anyone* there? Anyone who could tell——"

Anthony interrupted. "There were many and they could all tell. But not much. Iron Court's what you'd call a tenement. Martha had a two-room. At the beginning of last week, on Tuesday, Martha told her neighbour, Mrs. Pettigrew, that she'd 'had a letter' and was going away. Mrs. Pettigrew says that Martha was much excited. The letter, it seems, had had money in it. The letter, Mrs. Pettigrew was inclined to think, had come from *relations.* It certainly entailed a visit to Scotland. Martha packed her traps, put her trunk in charge of the caretaker and went off with two bags in a taxi. The taxi stuck in the Pettigrew throat: taxis are rare in Iron Court." He fell silent, intent upon nosing the car out of Stockholm Lane and into the wider but no less grim thoroughfare of the Goldhawk Road.

"No address?" said Garrett. "No knowledge of even the part of Scotland?"

Anthony shook his head. "None so far. A sprinkling of ten-shilling notes and a day's work might produce something. But I say KJB first." He sent a sidelong glance at his passenger. "Cheer up. All good runs have a check or two."

Garrett smiled with noticeable effort. "I know," he said and fell silent.

The black car swung in and out of traffic. It reached Hammersmith Broadway; checked; swung round the circle and shot along the easier way of the broad Hammersmith Road, past St. Paul's School and Olympia; over the humpbacked bridge at Addison Road and so swiftly to the broad Kensington ways and the grey, ugly shapes of the museums. It swung left; then right; then left again and was in a narrow cul-de-sac whose eastern end was dominated by the looming bulk of the Naval Museum and whose northern and southern sides were lined with small Victorian houses of a shabby gentility.

The car slowed. Its driver looked out of the near side window while it crept up the northern side of the street. The car stopped. It was opposite the fourth house from the end. Over the door hung a neat sign in white letters upon a black board.

"Third hole," said Anthony and pointed.

Garrett, craning his neck to look out of the window, saw the board and read what was on it—KJB DOMESTIC AGENCY.

Anthony got out of the car and went to the door beneath the sign and pressed the button on the jamb. From within the house came the sound of a bell; but no other sound followed. He pressed again and waited, looking up at the sign. After a moment he looked at his watch and went slowly back to the car. He opened the door and once more sat beside his passenger. He said briefly:

"Sorry. Closed for the evening."

3

Brabazon Street, in bright, early morning sunshine, wore its shabbiness with cheerful defiance; there was about it a this-is-the-way-I-am-and-if-you-don't-like-it-you-can-go-to-the-devil sort of air which was not offensive but friendly. It was a place impossible to any city but London and seemed to know this. It held itself, with a kind of gamecock perkiness, secure in the protection of the grey skirts of the museum. It was clean despite dilapidation and the windows of some of the little houses were brightly curtained and on the southern side a front door had been newly painted bright red. At the end of the cul-de-sac, just beneath the museum wall, two trees amazingly lifted their grace from the roadway and beneath the brown-gold of their branches a small white dog and a large orange-hued cat gambolled in amity.

Garrett, who had come by tube to Brompton Road station, turned into the open end of Brabazon Street as the museum clock chimed the quarter-hour before ten. He had, despite the disappointments of the day before, slept very well; the fast, short walk from the station had warmed him. He liked the morning; he liked the sunshine; he liked Brabazon Street—and he was aware of a pleasant excitement within him. Yesterday he had watched while other men worked upon this business which, after all, was his; his by right of discovery, by right of insistence, by right of anxiety and determination and devotion. But now, today, he was at work upon it while the others waited for what news *he* should bring *them!*

He lengthened his stride and swung the stick which seemed so natural to his hand in London and began to whistle, with soft and tuneful incongruity, "The Sidewalks of New York."

He came to the door, halfway down the northern side of the street, over which hung the black-and-white signboard. Beneath this he paused for a moment, making unostentatious parade of reading what it might say and in his mind running over the lines which his side of any coming interview must take.

He turned to the door and found that this morning it stood open. The word ENTER, neatly lettered in ink upon a square of white card, was tacked upon the right of the doorway. He obeyed it, to find himself in a dark, narrow hallway which smelt, not unpleasantly, of soap and linoleum and floor polish. Facing him and the front door, past the foot of stairs which ran up to his left, was another door, having an upper half of ground glass upon which, in black letters, were the words: INQUIRIES: PLEASE STEP IN.

Again he obeyed. As he pushed open the glass door a bell tinkled above his head. He closed the door and looked about him and found himself in a thin room which stretched the width of the little house. It had a french window at the back, through which came sunlight and suggestions of a tidy little gravelled garden. It was barely furnished with filing cabinets, two typewriting tables and a few chairs. It was very clean. Upon one of the cabinets stood a vase of bright flowers. The walls were distempered a clear, primrose yellow and in a bright-barred grate a small fire blazed gaily. In the back wall of the room, at the opposite end from the french window, was another glass-topped door bearing in black letters the word MANAGER. At the typewriting table nearer to this door sat a neat and round-faced girl. She looked up as Garrett came in and flashed up at him a friendly but well-modulated smile.

Garrett cleared his throat. "Nursemaids," he said. "I—er—wanted to inquire . . ."

She rose and came out from behind her table and shifted the position of one of the chairs by half an inch. She said:

"If you'd sit down? I'll see if Mr. Hines is free."

Garrett sat looking about him at the bare, cheerful little room. To his American eye it was so little like an office—and yet so very definitely an office—that he found it of interest. The girl had disappeared through the door marked MANAGER. From behind it came a murmur of voices and then, through it, the girl again. She held the door open and looked across the room at Garrett.

He rose and crossed the room and found himself in another. It was smaller but by contrast almost luxurious. From behind a flat-topped mahogany table a little man rose and bobbed his head jerkily in greeting. He might have served as a model for one of the Cheeryble brothers. He waved to a chair with courteous gestures.

"Nursemaids," said Garrett. "I wanted to inquire about one." He warmed to his work. "You see, I'm an American staying in London. My wife and small daughter are joining me next week and I have strict orders to get the best nursemaid procurable."

"Exactly! Exactly!" said the little man behind the table. "If I may say so, Mr.—Mr.——" Through the glittering spectacles a pair of bright brown eyes regarded Garrett with inquiry.

"Schumacher," said Garrett easily. "Leslie Schumacher."

"And you want a nursemaid, Mr. Schumacher?" The little man rubbed his hands. "If I may say so you couldn't have come to a better place. . . . Now let me see! Let me see!" He reached out a neat white hand and pulled towards him a fat black ledger and opened it and began to turn its pages. From his lips there came a cheerful little humming sound.

"Just a moment," said Garrett. "I should explain . . ."

The eyes behind the glasses twinkled at him. "I'm sure, Mr. Schumacher, that we shall be able to satisfy you."

Garrett smiled. He liked the little creature. He said:

"It's like this, Mr. Hines. I'm not after *any* nursemaid. I want a particular nursemaid—if you follow me."

"You mean . . . ?" The small round head was cocked to one side.

"Just what I say," said Garrett. "You have on your books a particular young woman whom I'm very anxious to get. Her name's Murch. Janet Murch."

The mouth of Mr. Hines pursed itself and a frown of concentration creased his smooth brow. "Murch?" said Mr. Hines as if to himself. "Murch?"

"Janet Murch," said Garrett firmly.

"The name is familiar, Mr. Schumacher. Definitely familiar." The head was nodded decisively and a white thumb ran down the indented index letters of the ledger and flipped it open again.

"Murch?" said Mr. Hines. "Murch . . . Murch . . . Ah!" His forefinger stopped at the bottom of a page. "Here we are. Murch. . . . Yes . . . hmmm . . . Yes . . . hmmm. Now in service with Lady Ballister. Wife of one of our most famous soldiers, Mr. Schumacher. I very much fear——"

Garrett frowned. A sinking sensation attacked his stomach. He said a little sharply:

"But she isn't. She gave Lady Ballister notice some time ago and left just recently. I thought . . ."

The eyes behind the spectacles regarded him with wonder. "Left? A position like that! Are you sure, Mr. Schumacher? I——"

"If I wasn't sure," said Garrett shortly, "I shouldn't be here."

"Tsck-tsck!" Mr. Hines was perturbed. He pressed a bell upon his desk and after a moment the door opened and the round-faced girl stood at Garrett's elbow. She was given orders and departed.

She was back again in thirty seconds, bearing a card from an index-system drawer. She laid this before her employer, who studied it and frowned and made little cheeping noises.

"Nothing here! Nothing here!" said Mr. Hines and pushed the card away from him and sat back and regarded his acolyte. He said: "Murch has not telephoned, Miss Burns? You have not heard from her at all?"

The girl shook her head. "Nothing, Mr. Hines."

The little man was perturbed. "Curious!" he said. "Curious! Did you say . . . ?" He looked inquiry and again the girl shook her head.

"No, Mr. Hines. Murch paid all the commission due as early as last

March. There would have been another payment to come on the third of December."

"Tsck!" said Mr. Hines. "Tsck! Tsck!" His plump little hand waved the girl away. He looked across the table at Garrett with a glance of real concern. He said: "I am sorry, Mr. Schumacher. Very sorry indeed. But these things will happen. Every now and then girls leave us. . . . Now, if you will allow me, I think I can find you exactly what you require even though Janet Murch is no longer in our hands. . . ." Once again he pulled the ledger towards him and began running a forefinger down its columns.

"I'm sorry," said Garrett. "But I really do want Janet Murch."

Mr. Hines looked up from the ledger. He raised plump shoulders and spread his hands. From behind the glittering glasses his soft brown eyes looked at Garrett sadly. He said:

"Once more I must apologize, Mr. Schumacher, but you heard what my secretary told me. Murch has thrown up a very good position without consulting us and, moreover, has not come back to us. We must therefore strike Murch from our books!" His kindly little mouth closed in a firm line.

Garrett shifted in his chair. "You mean that you can't even give me her address?"

"We-ll . . ." The tone was doubtful.

Garrett hastened to remedy tactlessness. He said hurriedly:

"Of course I should insist upon your taking a fee for the information." His left hand made a suggestive gesture towards his right breast pocket. "Should we say . . ."

"Tsck-tsck!" said Mr. Hines again but this time with a different intonation. "Very handsome of you, I'm sure! But really, Mr. Schumacher, might I suggest that we try and get you something else. We have many good girls on our books. Excellent girls. I do not wish to boast in any way but I think I may say that, particularly in the nursemaid line, we can do better for you than any similar establishment in London. I can say that with no fear of contradiction." Once more he turned to the still open ledger. "Now for instance, I see, purely by chance, that we have here—momentarily disengaged——"

Garrett interrupted "I'm sorry. But I *do* want Janet Murch."

The little man closed the ledger with a slam. He smiled a defeated but friendly smile. "Janet Murch's address? Very well, Mr. Schumacher." He pressed a bell and the round-faced girl came again and was bidden to bring back Murch's card and returned immediately with it. Mr. Hines adjusted pince-nez. He picked up the card and cleared his throat. He said:

"Murch's address, Mr. Schumacher, is care of Mrs. Bellows, 148A Iron Court, Stockholm Lane, W." He laid down the card and over it beamed at his visitor.

But Garrett did not answer the smile. Once more there had come to him that feeling of emptiness. Once more he was at a dead end. He said after a moment during which Mr. Hines gazed at him with concern:

"That won't do. I got that address from Lady Ballister. Yesterday. I went there but failed to get in touch with Janet Murch. Mrs. Bellows is her aunt and Mrs. Bellows left two or three days ago and the rooms have been given up."

"Tsck! Tsck!" said Mr. Hines and then, "Dear me!" He mused for a moment, placing his elbows upon the arms of his chair and the tips of his outspread fingers together. He said at last over the finger tips:

"Really, Mr. Schumacher, I don't want to appear pressing—it is a motto of KJB never to press a client—but I would like to suggest, especially in view of all the circumstances, that you let us try and provide you with some other young woman. Murch really seems to have been behaving in a most curious way and I think that perhaps someone *steadier* . . ."

Garrett shook his head. "No. I must try and get in touch with the Murch woman." He pulled himself together. "I'll go off and see what I can do." With effort he smiled across the table at the plumpness of Mr. Hines. "You've been very kind." He rose. "More than kind." He got himself to the door, followed by exclamations of distress from the little man. With his fingers upon the handle he turned. "Of course," he said with effort, "if I have to give up Murch I'll come back to you."

He closed the door firmly and a moment later was out again in Brabazon Street. But now, although the sun still shone, it seemed only a cheerless and dirty little backwater.

CHAPTER X

Mr. Sheldon Garrett walked rapidly across the Savoy lounge. His step was springing and his pace was rapid and a wide smile of welcome was upon his face; but Avis Bellingham, looking up from the chair in which she had been awaiting him, saw that the face itself was bloodless and drawn and that the smiling eyes were strangely glittering. She held up a hand to him and he took it in both his own and bent over it and raised it to his lips. The eyes of Mrs. Bellingham widened a little.

"Here we are!" said Mr. Sheldon Garrett. "Here we are! Here we are!" His tone was louder than was normal with him; and he still retained the gloved hand.

"Tom!" said Avis Bellingham and stared at him. "You're tight!"

He released the hand. He made a gesture in the grand manner. "You mock one," he said, "who has this day stared into the jaws of death."

Mrs. Bellingham continued to regard him with gravity. "I should like some lunch," she said.

They walked side by side out of the lounge and into the grillroom and Garrett went on talking. He was still in speech as they sat at his corner table and it was in a froth of words that he ordered their meal.

Avis Bellingham looked at the cocktails. She said: "I think I should have yours as well." Her tone was light enough but there was a faint frown between the eyes which still looked, with something puzzled in them, at her host.

"Beautiful," said Sheldon Garrett, "you can have as much to drink as you like; but you cannot have my drink. No!" He drained his glass and set it down. "You see, darling, I am a shattered wreck! A bundle of nerves! Only an hour since, almost did I embrace the Grim Reaper——"

She said sharply: "Tom! What on earth are you talking about?"

He waved a hand towards windows through which showed, instead of the daylight which the hour should have brought, only a greyish-yellow vapor.

"Fog," he said. "London fog. The motorist's enemy, the doctor's friend, the stand-by of the American novelist. Observe Sheldon Garrett himself, at a few moments short of noon, clutching his stout staff, whistling to his dogs and plunging out into the perpetual night. Observe him making slow but valiant way across the Strand and then, by devious and dingy ways, coming at last to the theatre——"

"What theatre?" said Avis Bellingham.

Garrett stared. "What theatre! There's only one theatre. The rest are mere mumming booths. *The* theatre is that where Sheldon Garrett's masterpiece is now showing." He lifted the glass which the waiter had just filled and drank and set it down again nearly empty.

"We left our hero battling through the fog. We battle with him as he swings along, insouciant, and comes at last to the little alleyway down which he must plunge in order to reach the stage door of the one and only theatre. Does he gain the entrance without untoward incident? He does not—because Death tries to bar the way! Over the stage door is a scaffolding where large men in unseemly trousers have for weeks been endeavouring to replace three bricks and a beam. Today the large men were not working, for fog is bad for their chests. But during their absence something untoward happened upon the scaffolding—so much so that our hero, singing a snatch of Touranian melody, is just about to pass beneath the scaffolding when there comes from above him a tearing, rending, avalanche-like sound and there swiftly descends, from a height of about thirteen feet, an enormous balk of timber! . . . Any ordinary man would inevitably have been annihilated. Not so, however, our hero: light-footed as a chamois, he let out a piercing shriek and jumped. The timber struck the place where he had been, knocking off his hat in the process and—yes indeed!—splitting the flagstone upon which it fell. . . . If you like this story please tell your friends. There will be another adventure of Sheldon Garrett in our next issue. . . ."

Avis Bellingham looked from her own empty plate to Garrett's full one. "Will you please eat?" she said.

Garrett picked up knife and fork. "And that," he said with bitterness, "is all the reaction I get." But he began to eat and was at last silent.

Avis put her elbows on the table and her chin in her hands and stared at him. She said after a moment:

"I know what's the matter with you. I mean, as well as being tight."

Garrett set down knife and fork. "I am *not* tight! I never get tight! And there's nothing the matter with me."

"Eat!" she said. "I *think,* Thomas, that something's gone wrong with your—your puzzle. I've been with you nearly an hour and you haven't mentioned it. And I don't think that just because something nearly fell on you you'd drink so much in the morning."

Garrett looked at her in silence. He was smiling but the smile was awry. "There's nothing wrong with my 'puzzle' as you call it; nothing wrong at all! How could there be when the whole affair's in the capable hands of Colonel Gethryn? No, nothing's wrong at all—nothing beyond the fact that although we know the woman's name we can't find out where she is or get hold of anyone who can tell us anything! No, there's nothing wrong! And even if there was, why should I care? Like Mehitabel, my motto is Toujours gai!"

For the first time the half-searching, half-puzzled look left the blue eyes of Mrs. Bellingham. "Oh, Tom," she said, "I'm so sorry! But it's probably only a temporary check; and Anthony Gethryn's hands *are* capable. More than capable. Once he's started something like this he doesn't stop. I'll bet you he's doing something now, at this minute!"

The smile left Garrett's face. "What he's doing at this minute is to wait. That's all he can do. We've got one line and one line only. Somewhere in Scotland—*maybe*—there's an old aunt of the Murch woman. Gethryn's got lines out for her. . . ." He put the smile back upon his face. "They won't catch her of course. But what the hell if they don't! Toujours gai!"

2

They had coffee in the sitting room of Garrett's suite. Outside the windows the fog pressed, grey-yellow and heavy, unabashed by the lights within.

"Have some brandy?" said Garrett and from a cupboard brought two great bubbles of glass and a dust-smeared bottle.

His guest shook her head.

"It's good, darling!" said Garrett. He poured a liberal dark gold splash into each glass.

Avis Bellingham sat straight. She said:

"I don't want brandy. Nor do you."

Garrett sat upon the edge of the table. He took his glass in cupped hands and began gently to swirl its contents. He looked at her over the glass. He said:

"How wrong you are! But you look adorable like that: so few women can be angry and wrong *and* lovely all in one expression!" He lifted the glass and sniffed at its bouquet and put it to his lips.

"I don't *think,*" said Avis Bellingham, "that I like you like this." Her mouth was smiling but her eyes were not. "I can only hope that whoever it was was wrong about in vino veritas. . . ." She leant forward. "Tom, do please be nice!"

"Nice?" said Garrett. "*Nice!* What a word! But I know what you mean. Haven't I been nice? Am I not now nice? Shall I not go on being nice? Nice, forsooth!" He drained his glass and set it down and picked up the other. He said:

"*Nice!*" and then, raising the second glass: "A toast; a toast! Your husband, God blast—I mean, bless him!"

She started. The smile that she had been striving to keep upon her face was wiped away. She looked at Garrett with a gaze he found it difficult to meet. She said with an odd inflection:

"That's the first time you've mentioned George. D'you know that, Tom? And since that evening you paid your first visit to the flat, we've——"

He took the glass from his lips and interrupted. "Let us not speak of the man! He cramps my style! Whenever I look at you his wraith rises gibbering before me! Whenever I follow the rustle of your skirts, my heart pounding, I feel him dogging my very footsteps! I am like one who turns no more his head, because he knows a Frightful Fiend doth close behind him tread! . . . That's apt! . . . How I dislike the man! My New England conscience gives him a power which my libido refutes! I am on the horns of a Dilemma—see under Zoo. I am a poor thing and not even mine own. My heart is yours to tread and I dare not—durst not!—put it beneath your number fives!"

"Tom!" said his visitor sharply. "Shut up!"

He reached behind him for the bottle upon the table and splashed more brandy into his glass and lifted the glass and drank.

"And that," said Avis, "is *not* the way to drink good brandy! If you must wallow, at least do it like a gentleman!" Her words came fast and her pallor was a match for his.

He set down the glass and dropped upon one knee before her in transpontine humility. He said, tripping a little over his words:

"Pour scorn upon me! Vilify me! Ridicule my hopeless passion! I love it, I'm a masochist!" He reached out his hands towards her in traditional supplication. "I love you, madame! I——"

Avis Bellingham got to her feet. Her face was very white and the blue eyes blazed fire through a sheen which glittered. She said:

"Damn you! I hate you!"

Garrett was left staring at a door, the echo of its slamming ringing in his ears.

3

Anthony Gethryn picked up his telephone.

"When you get him," said Lucia, "ask him to dinner."

Anthony spoke into the telephone; then over his shoulder. "They're getting him." He waited.

Lucia said: "And I *won't* ask Avis."

Anthony turned again. "Why not?"

"Fog!" said his wife. "*And* they're in love but aren't sure of it—at least, *he* isn't for some reason."

Anthony said: "Wrong, aren't you?" And then into the telephone: "Ah, that you, Garrett? . . . Gethryn here. . . . Dine this evening? . . . Yes, do. There's nothing yet but there might be. . . . What? . . . Yes, if the fog's still on, come by tube. Strand to Knightsbridge. When you get out of the station . . ." He gave explicit directions and rang off and turned his chair to look across at his wife. He said:

"Sound picture of dramatist in dumps!"

And that was at five minutes past five.

4

It was a quarter to seven when Garrett left the Savoy, coming through the centre swing door and out into the court. The fog was worse; the air was chill and there was no breath of wind. The lights from the lamps and the windows of the hotel and the portico of the little theatre did not diminish obscurity; they merely thinned the greyish-yellow curtain of vapor, misleading men who had thought light means vision.

A cold and acrid stinging of his nose and throat made Garrett pull his muffler up about his mouth. He thrust his hands deep into the pockets of his overcoat and walked slowly along towards the lights of the Strand—yellow nimbuses behind the veil. He passed the portico of the theatre and, keeping close to the wall, reached the broad pavement of the Strand and turned left along it. His progress was now easier. The roadway, indeed, was crowded, with long lines of monstrous shapes crawling nose to tail westward and eastward but the pavement was almost bare of pedestrians. Counting the corners carefully and only twice having to halt to avoid collision with other humans, he got safely into John Street and then, by brushing the railings of the houses with his left shoulder, came with creditable speed down the hill and at last into Villiers Street and across it to the Strand tube station.

He found the booking office and bought his ticket and plunged beneath the surface of the earth. He experienced for the first time that sense of gratitude to the makers of the underground railway which is no uncommon feeling for a Londoner. The tubular, tiled warrens were brightly lit and evenly temperatured, and a man could see so far as his eyes would let him. And here, too, were men and women—many men and women—who were real and sure stepping, not dim and furtive and blundering wraiths.

At the end of the corridor leading to his platform Garrett found himself walking with small shuffling steps by reason of the pressure of his fellow creatures. He had a mental vision of a town beneath the earth; of men living, with the common sense and security of badgers, beneath the surface of an unfriendly world only to be entered in adventure.

He came out of the corridor and onto the platform. It was black with people. Of inclination and by reason of pressure behind him he went forward. In front of him was a little clear space at the edge of the platform. Beside him men and women were converging on it. He marked out the clear space for himself and with two long strides was there. He hoped that when the train came in it would have the grace so to arrange its length that there was a door immediately in front of him. Idly he glanced up and to his right at the hanging electric signboard. It would, he felt, be in keeping with this bad day if the next train proved to be omitting Knightsbridge from its halts; but when the letters of the sign sprang into life he saw that in this small thing at least he was lucky.

He waited. . . . From afar came the beginnings of a rumbling roar. . . . He was aware of a shifting and milling of the crowd about him. More people were flooding in from the corridors to the platforms. . . . He foresaw with a dim, subconscious foreboding that if there were no door opposite him when the train came in he would have a struggle to get to one. From the back of his mind there suddenly pushed its way forward to the front the barbed wish to be going, on this same train whose roaring was now louder, to a station which would lead him, not to the house in Stukeley Gardens, but to the great building of grey stone which contained, vividly real among a hundred unrealities, Avis' little house. . . .

In a crescendo of demoniac noise the train burst from the enclosing sheath of its tunnel. With a scarcely perceptible slackening of speed it slid shrieking into the station, its rows of lighted windows bulging out over the edge of the platform. Garrett, head turned towards its onrush, again speculated, with a corner of his mind, on the problem of doors.

There was a stirring among the crowd; a murmur; a preparatory shuffling. It was like a beast who rises from sleep and stands and stretches and makes ready for movement.

And then, as the two gleaming lights on the front of the train were almost level with him, there came from behind him, as it were, from *within* the general movement, a violent flurry: a short harsh cry; a little clattering; a sudden violent blow upon his shoulders and back. His toes were almost at the edge of the platform. There was nothing between him and the yawning trough along whose floor ran the rails. And right upon him, as he felt himself impelled downwards into that trough, was the front of the oncoming monster.

He does not know to this day—nor do the people who were round him —how his mind conveyed to his body, in such an infinitesimal fraction of time, the message which made him, with a racking of every muscle and sinew in him, resist the impulsion of his own weight. But somehow, semi-miraculously, he twisted himself upon the balls of his feet and threw himself backwards and sideways. His arms flung themselves out. His hands clutched at the soft fur of an animal. He slipped to one knee. He felt the wind of the passing of the first carriage of the train. His ears were filled with the screeching of brakes. His eyes saw nothing save a black mist; a mist which had counterpart in his mind and did not clear until he found himself sitting in a corner seat of a long carriage crammed with humanity. All the seats were filled and down the centre of the long car men and women supported themselves against the swaying and bumping of the train by gripping leather loops depending from steel rods. He did not know how he had got in or how he had come to be seated. He looked down at his hands. In one of them was a tuft of greyish fur. He brushed it off with the other and saw that both were shaking and that upon the left was a long graze from which red blood oozed. He pulled out a handkerchief with the right hand and began to dab at the wound. Hearing came back to him. He was conscious that there was an excited muttering of voices all about him; from the seat next to his; from above, where two men clung to straps and swayed with the motion of the train. He turned his head, finding a curious difficulty in the movement. Beside him there sat, overflowing the seat arm between them, a large woman of middle age. Her face, which was round and by all laws should have been highly coloured, was grey and drawn. She was wrapped in a coat made from the beautiful fur of grey squirrels. She was talking stridently, shouting to make herself heard above the roaring of the train. She was talking, upwards, to the two men—one long and cadaverous, the other short and sanguine. They were talking too. All three of them were talking; all shouting their words; all trying to drown the noise, not only of the train, but of each other's voices.

He began to catch scraps of the talk. . . . *"Miraculous!"* . . . *"Somebody dropped a stick; first thing I know I was falling forward!"* . . . *"You must have pushed him right in the back!"* . . . *"Thought nothing could stop him from going!" "Good thing I'm not one of these thin women!"* . . . *"Nearly a terrible accident!"* . . . *"Nobody seemed to see it!"* . . . *"All's well that ends well, thank goodness! . . ."*

"I say!" said Garrett and was astonished to hear his voice as a strange croaking sound. "I say!"

The woman turned to him a face into which the colour was creeping back. It was a pleasant and good-natured face. She said:

"Feeling better? That's good! You're a *very* lucky man!"

Garrett looked fixedly at a place upon the sleeve of the grey coat. Near the shoulder was a bare patch. He remembered the fur upon his hand. He said:

"If it hadn't been for you I'd have been over."

She laughed, showing admirable teeth. She said: "I was saying, it's a good thing I'm not one of the thin sort! If I'd weighed a couple of stone less you wouldn't be here. . . ."

"Your coat," said Garrett. "I . . ."

"Don't pay any attention. It's old *and* insured!" Once more the friendly, chuckling laugh.

Garrett felt better. "What happened?" he said.

Now the two strap-hanging men joined the talk again.

"It was me who pushed you," said the tall cadaverous one.

"But he was pushed from the back," said his round and sanguine companion. "I was standing just beside *you*." He looked at Garrett. "Somebody somewhere behind this gentleman dropped a stick and it seemed to me like as if he made a grab for it and lost his balance and bumped into this gentleman and this gentleman, of course, bumped into you. . . . *Phoo!* That was a narrow squeak, that was!"

5

Garrett walked up the corridor towards the lifts of Knightsbridge station. He was annoyed with his legs. They felt unsure of themselves. As he walked he brooded. A bad day! Filthy weather! Balks of timber which fall near a man! Fools on crowded platforms who drop sticks and nearly push a man in front of a train! The obvious necessity of buying a grey squirrel coat—outsize! A permanent feeling of sick disappointment concerned with the blindness of the trails which had seemed so certain to lead to Janet Murch. Horrible memories concerning the little son of his sister, who was Barry Hendricksen's wife. . . . All these—and something else; something which persisted in thrusting itself to the front of his consciousness against orders. Something to do with a fool of a man who lets disappointment and weather and unpleasing adventure lead him to unprecedented consumption of alcohol; a fool of a man who behaves like a boorish and conceited schoolboy to the loveliest woman in the world!

A crammed lift bore him upwards and he came out into the little arcade of Knightsbridge station where there struck him once more the foul and acrid reek of the fog. It was even thicker here than it had been in the Strand. The highway was choked with lines of stationary vehicles whose lights only seemed to increase their helplessness. The red flares of policemen's torches stung the yellow veil. There was sound but it was muffled and unreal. This city aboveground was dead and full of useless ghosts; only below ground were there light and comfort and purposeful movement. . . .

He took three steps away from the arcade entrance and the fog closed about him. He pulled up his muffler over his nose and mouth and buttoned the collar of his overcoat tight and pulled down the brim of his black soft hat. He held his hand out before his face: at arm's length he could not see it. He halted. He thought of the warm, well-lighted warrens below his feet and half decided to plunge back into them.

A groping woman bumped into him; murmured half-scared apologies; veered off and was lost.

"Come *on!*" said Garrett to himself. He groped his way along, making his mind blank save for the purpose of this journey. He must keep on this pavement. Then second on the right. Then on until the first cross street. Then turn, cross the road and go down the continuation of this cross street and he would be in Stukeley Gardens. Then up to the first angle of the Gardens and immediately across to Number 19A.

He groped his way onward. He made one false turn but was lucky enough to bump into a policeman. He was put right and retraced his steps and this time found his turning. He came down to the cross street, fumbled his way across the road and was in Stukeley Gardens. He walked faster now. Either the fog was thinner or the bare pavement and the guide of the Garden railings made progress easier. He reached the first corner of the square, pushed himself away from the friendly iron, turned to his left and walked out into the road.

He shuffled across the roadway, his smarting eyes trying to pierce the yellow murk. Soon he must come to the curb—and if he came to the curb without seeing it he might fall. He did not want to fall. His whole aching body rebelled against the very idea of falling. He saw the curb. He sighed relief and lifted his foot and stepped up onto the pavement.

A faint sound came from behind him. And then something fell with dreadful, crushing force upon the back of his head.

Behind his eyes came a sudden burst of bright yellow flame and then darkness. A grunting sound burst from his throat and he pitched forward onto his face and twisted once and lay still.

6

White came out of the baize door at the end of Colonel Gethryn's hall. He crossed to the chest of Breton oak which stood against the right-hand wall, near the front door. He hoped that there were no letters. But there were—four of them. All stamped and addressed and crying for the dark maw of a pillar box.

White sighed. In his square, clean-shaven face the lips moved in the shape of a round and military oath. He picked up the letters and opened the front door and grimaced at the fog. He turned up the collar of his coat and went carefully down the steps and along the flagged pathway to the gate. He frowned as he went and screwed up his eyes against the sting of the fog and blew through closed lips as if he were grooming a horse. He came to the gate and opened it and stepped out onto the pavement. He thought with distaste of the hundred yards which separated him from the pillar box at the corner. He shut the gate behind him and turned to his right and began the walk.

He had not gone more than five yards before he stumbled. His right foot had met something soft and heavy.

"What the 'ell!" said White and stooped to see.

The body was lying on its face. It was crumpled, with one arm flung out straight beside its head and one leg twisted beneath it. It might, from the attitude, have been devoid of life. But White thought not: he had seen many dead men.

He knelt. The cold dampness of the flags was chill against his knees. With a grunt he turned the body over. It was heavy. The yellow fog was all round them, pressing down upon the consciousness like a foul blanket. White stooped lower. He could not see anything of the face save a white oval blur but he put his ear to the blur and felt little gasps of warm breath come from between the lips. He straightened himself, still on his knees, and fumbled in his pocket for matches. He found one and struck it. Shielding the little flame with his hand, he bent once more over the face. He started. The flame flickered but he saved it. He bent again.

"Kor bloody swop me!" said White. He stood up and threw away the dead match and for a moment strained his eyes uselessly against the fog this way and that. He gave up trying to see and instead, for another moment, tried to hear. But there was nothing to hear. He made up his mind and stooped over the body and caught one of its arms and, twisting his thick solidity, got beneath it to apply the fireman's lift. . . .

CHAPTER XI

At five minutes to nine the fog was thicker than ever but at seven minutes past nine there was no fog. A gentle easterly breeze had swept it from every crevice of the city. Now a black, star-encrusted sky arched over the world.

Mrs. Bellingham sat in her drawing room. It was orderly; it was softly but adequately lighted and the fire glowed red and the book which was open upon Mrs. Bellingham's knee was by a man who can write and was a book to whose reading Mrs. Bellingham had been looking forward for weeks. And Mrs. Bellingham wore a favourite gown and had cigarettes within reach and had dined lightly but with excellence.

She should, therefore, have been content. But the book, though open, remained unread and the cigarettes tasted of nothing but smoke and the pleasant redness of the fire did not glow for her eyes and even the gown felt as if it sat awkwardly upon her body.

She looked over the book and into the fire with eyes which saw neither. There were little lines about her mouth which generally were not there. And her head was held too consciously erect and there was a look of pain somewhere in the blue depths of the unseeing eyes. . . .

There came to her ears the sound which told of pressure upon the bell of the outer door. She started, almost violently. The book slid from her knees and lay unheeded upon the carpet by her feet.

She took herself to task. It was plain to her that she had been *listening*. It was also plain to her that the sound she had expected was not that of the doorbell but that of the telephone. At the back of her mind there had been, ever since she had reached home, the thought of the telephone. . . .

The bell rang again, insistently reminding her that her maid was out. She got to her feet and crossed to the door and opened it and went out into her little hall. Through the ground glass of the upper half of the outer door she could see a man's shadow. In defiance of the stern orders of her mind her heart jumped. She crossed to the door and put fingers to its latch and opened it.

The original of the shadow raised his hat.

"*Anthony!*" said Avis Bellingham.

2

Anthony Gethryn stood with his back to Mrs. Bellingham's drawing-room fire. He looked at Mrs. Bellingham, noting the whiteness of her face. He said:

"You heard what I was saying. There's no danger." His tone was sharp.

The lids which had veiled the blue eyes were raised slowly. The blue eyes looked up and met the steady stare of the green. She said:

"You're sure? There can't be——"

Anthony interrupted. "No, there can't. He's unconscious but there's no possibility of his dying." His tone was intentionally brutal.

Her tongue came out and moistened her lips. She said with difficulty: "How . . . what . . . Have they any idea how . . ."

Anthony said: "Blow on the back of the head. No bruises. Fairly advanced concussion. No means of telling how it happened. Might have been a fall —but he was lying on his face when White found him and it seems improbable that after a blow like that he'd have turned over. Possibly struck by something projecting from a car." He looked down at the woman. "Dozens of ways it might have happened," he said slowly. There was a slight emphasis on the fifth word of the sentence.

Avis Bellingham sat upright. She said: "I—I'm afraid I've been silly. But —but it was rather a shock. I——"

Again Anthony interrupted. "What you need is a drink. Thank you, I'll have one too. Don't move; I can find it." He reached the door in three strides and was gone.

He returned quickly, carrying a tray upon which were decanter and siphon and glasses. His hostess smiled at him as he set the tray upon a table near the fire. She said:

"Is there anything you're bad at?"

Anthony poured whiskey. "Golf and letter writing," he said and added soda water to whiskey and put a full glass into her hand. "Drink that."

She sipped.

"Drink!" said Anthony.

She drank and took the glass from her mouth and smiled up at him. She said:

"I'm all right. Give yourself one—and then tell me what you think."

Again Anthony busied himself over the tray. He said:

"About accident to prominent playwright?"

She nodded.

He took his stand before the fire and lifted his glass and drank.

"It's possible," he said at last, "that it *was* an accident."

From the depths of the big chair Avis Bellingham stared up at him. She said, her eyes widening:

"I don't . . . Has he said anything?"

Anthony shook his head. "He's unconscious. He'll probably remain so for quite a while." He was looking at her keenly. "What else do you know?"

She said: "What I was going to say was . . . that it's—it's sort of odd——"
She stopped. White teeth bit her lower lip and a frown of concentration
came between her eyes. She said:

"I lunched with Tom today. At the Savoy. He—he—he told me about an
accident he'd had this morning——" Again she broke off.

"This morning?" said Anthony. "Tell me."

She said: "He went out before lunch. It was foggy. He went to the
theatre to see George Brooks-Carew. Builders have been doing repairs over
the stage door. They weren't working today but as Tom went into the stage
door something happened to the scaffolding and a great beam fell and
nearly hit him. It might have killed him." Her voice was deliberately flat.

"And then?" said Anthony.

She stared at him. "I was only thinking . . . that's *two* accidents in one
day. It's—it's rather frightening, somehow."

"You think, don't you?" said Anthony. He put a hand to his pocket and
brought it away bearing a thin wallet of blue morocco leather bound with
gold. Upon the outer side were the small stamped initials T.S.G. He said:

"This was all he had in his pocket. There's ten pounds in it; some cards
of his own; a driving licence—American; and this." He opened the wallet
and put his fingers into one of its compartments and brought them away
bearing a woman's visiting card. He took a step away from the fire and
held the card before her eyes. She read: Mrs. Claude Kenealy, 97 Stockbrook Road, Richmond, Surrey. In the bottom left-hand corner there was a
pencilled telephone number—Richmond-0246.

"Know her?" said Anthony.

Avis shook her head.

There was silence. Anthony, after regarding the card for a moment, put
it back into the wallet and returned the wallet to his pocket. He said:

"You saw it was crumpled. When I found it it was bent double. It had
been shoved into the wallet in a hurry. Rest of the wallet shows neatness. . . . In the circumstances a call to Richmond-0246 is indicated."

She looked at him intently. "I don't know what you're driving at."

"Nor do I," said Anthony. "But we'll find out." He crossed to a corner
table and sat by it and lifted the receiver from the telephone and worked
the dial. Avis twisted in her chair to watch him.

"Hello!" said Anthony. "Richmond-0246? . . . Is Mrs. Kenealy there?
Oh, I see! This is a friend of Mr. Sheldon Garrett speaking. Mr. Garrett has
met with an accident and——" He was cut short by a perfect flood of talk
from the telephone. The metallic cackle rang in Avis' ears. She rose and
crossed the room and went swiftly to the table and stood by Anthony. He
said into the telephone as she reached him:

"I see. . . . No, it wasn't anything to do with that. . . . He was coming
to dine with me and he met with this accident just outside my house. . . .
What? Oh! Martin; Theodore Martin. I live in South Kensington. . . . Yes.
. . . Yes. . . . Yes, I'm afraid it was a nasty accident. . . . Must have been

hit by a car which didn't stop in the fog. You know what these motorists are! . . ."

Again Avis was forced to listen to a cackling outburst from the receiver at her visitor's ear. Again she could not distinguish a word. Unconsciously she put a hand upon Anthony's shoulder; a hand whose fingers dug painfully.

"I see," said Anthony to the telephone. "Most extraordinary thing! . . . Yes, obviously his unlucky day! . . . Yes. . . . Yes. . . . I'm afraid I don't quite understand. . . . Oh, I see! Yes, I'll tell him. . . . Yes, by all means —my number's Flaxman-00123. . . . Yes. . . . Thank you. . . . Thank you. . . . Yes. . . . Goodnight. . . ."

He replaced the receiver firmly. He turned in his chair and looked up at his hostess. He said, smiling:

"What long, strong fingers you have, Grandmamma!"

Avis Bellingham looked down at the hand which had been digging into his shoulder. She said, taking it away:

"Oh, I'm sorry! . . . What was that, Anthony? I couldn't get a word. I didn't——"

Anthony rose. He rubbed at his shoulder and smiled at her. He said:

"That? That was another oddity in a maze of oddities. Curiouser and curiouser! Mrs. Claude Kenealy says that she met Mr. Garrett for the first time this evening. On the Piccadilly railway. She hadn't known him before. She was standing beside him on the westbound platform when somebody slipped in the crowd behind him, just as the train was coming in, and very nearly pushed him in front of the train. . . ."

"God!" said Mrs. Bellingham.

"Quite," said Anthony, "but by an effort which Mrs. Kenealy thinks miraculous Mr. Sheldon Garrett saved himself. In saving himself he was forced to clutch at Mrs. Kenealy. In clutching he damaged her fur coat. They travelled together as far as Knightsbridge, where Mr. Garrett got out. Mrs. Kenealy insists that the damage to her fur coat doesn't matter but Mr. Garrett—always the gentleman—insisted that it did and exchanged cards with Mrs. Kenealy. Two men witnessed the near accident but Mrs. Kenealy doesn't know who they are. As far as she knows Mr. Garrett—who seemed shaken, but who in the circumstances was marvellously self-contained—did not exchange names and addresses with them. Mrs. Kenealy was definite in the assertion that neither of these two men was the person who originally caused the near accident. Mrs. Kenealy thought that Mr. Garrett was a most prepossessing young man, though American. She wishes very much to be informed of his progress. . . . So I gave her the number of Mr. Theodore Martin who lives in South Kensington. It's actually the private number of a fellow called Gethryn. Message ends."

Avis sank into a chair. She said, and seemed to have some difficulty in saying it:

"That's *three!* In one day! And—and——" Her voice shook but she mastered it. "Isn't that—isn't that—well, queer?"

Anthony went back to the mantelpiece and retrieved his glass. He said:

"I don't think so. *Accidents* are queer; but if, in one day in London, when you are deeply interested in a business more than queer, you meet with three happenings, any one of which might cause your death, they cannot be accidents. Therefore they are not queer. At least, not queer in the sense in which you mean. For there's nothing irrational in desiring the obliteration of a person and setting out to cause that obliteration."

She stared at him but she said: "I knew you were going to say that. At least, I knew you were going to say that these things weren't accidents . . . that *someone* was trying to—to kill him. But . . ." Her voice trailed off into silence.

Anthony smiled down at her; a reassuring smile. "But you didn't know that I was going to suggest that the attempts were anything to do with Miss Murch, et omnes?"

She nodded without speaking.

"They must be," said Anthony. "Listen!"

3

And "Listen!" said Anthony an hour later into a telephone at the other end of which was Lucas.[1]

"I shall be in your office," said Anthony, "at nine forty-five tomorrow. Ack emma."

"Go to hell!" said the telephone sleepily.

At twenty minutes past ten upon the following morning Sir Egbert Lucas sat back in his chair and turned his head to look at Superintendent Pike. They both looked at the long and lean and recumbent form in the armchair beneath that window which, it is popularly supposed, has the best river view in all Scotland Yard.

There was a silence which Lucas broke. He said:

"Very interesting, Gethryn! A pretty story! A little forced, perhaps, but who can help that nowadays with so many people writing these things?" He was all irony. "But what, exactly, d'you think *we* can do?"

Superintendent Pike looked at Colonel Gethryn—but said nothing.

A voice came from the armchair. "It isn't so much what I expect, Lucas; it's what I hope."

Lucas smiled sourly. "Still the master of persiflage! Elucidate."

Anthony sat up. "I was hoping that for once you'd exercise your real function—or what should be your real function—and help me to shut a stable door before a horse is stolen."

---

[1] Sir Egbert Lucas, K.C.B., etc., assistant commissioner of police and head of the C.I.D. Lucas is an old friend of Anthony Gethryn. It was through his acquaintance with Lucas that Anthony brought the difficult Hood case (recorded in *The Rasp*) to such a satisfactory conclusion; and his successful working with the police throughout all his other cases has been greatly helped by the friendship.

Superintendent Pike continued silent; but he also continued to stare with speculative eyes at Colonel Gethryn.

Lucas lit a cigarette. Through smoke he said:

"I'm sorry but I can't see any door that wants shutting. I can see an over-heated imagination at work; but that's all. I——" A telephone upon his desk rang shrill. "Just a minute!" He picked up the receiver and spoke into it and listened. He said:

"What's that? . . . Who? . . . How do you spell it? . . . Oh! . . ." There was surprise in the last ejaculation. "Who's the divisional surgeon? . . . Oh yes. Good man! . . . What did you say? . . . Yes. . . . Yes. . . . That's something to be thankful for, anyhow. Well, get on to Andrews and get all the detail done and have the usual report sent. . . ." He put back the receiver and looked once more at Anthony. "Sorry!" he said. "But that was business."

Pike looked at him with an eyebrow inquiringly cocked.

Lucas said: "No bother. Suicide. There'll be a fuss, though. It was old Ballister's wife. Personally, no suicide in *his* family would surprise me. I once sat——"

He broke off to stare across the table at the suddenly risen form of his visitor. "What's the matter?" he said.

Anthony came up to the far side of the table and leant his hands upon it and stared across it at its owner. His face was devoid of expression but yet there was about him a certain tensity which a moment before had not been there. Superintendent Pike continued to stare, now with a deep frown between his brows.

"Alice Ballister?" said Anthony. "Wife of Charles Montague Ballister, major general et al?"

"Yes," said Lucas.

"When?" said Anthony.

"Found this morning," said Lucas. "An hour ago, to be precise. Divisional surgeon says she may have been dead three hours. Definitely suicide."

Anthony sat himself sideways upon the desk. He said:

"Well, well! And that's that! Now, Police, you'll *have* to help me with my stable door."

Lucas sat back in his chair. He said with rude clarity:

"What in the name of God are you talking about?"

Anthony said: "Alice Ballister was the employer of Sheldon Garrett's Janet Murch. I saw her myself."

The right hand of Superintendent Pike began to rub reflectively at his lantern-shaped lower jaw.

"What!" said Lucas. And then: "Must be a coincidence."

"You," said Anthony, "are one of these survivals who live by the application of old wives' tales; the sort of man who thinks that an albino can divine gold and that a right-footed sock from a left-handed man will cure the staggers! Coincidence my eye!" He looked down at Lucas with an air blent of tolerance and irritation. He said after a pause:

"Listen! You obviously need the whole thing again—only this time including the unfortunate Ballister woman. . . . Are you ready? We're off! A man hears two women talking. He is convinced they are planning a crime or crimes, part and parcel of which is the kidnapping of a child. He is a stranger to this town and country and has difficulty in finding anyone to believe he isn't just a scaremonger with a hypersensitive imagination. But he gets help at last and he and his helpers find that the only clue he had leads them to a friend of one of the women whom he heard but never properly saw. From the friend they get the woman's name—Janet Murch—and the information that Murch is working in the household of General Ballister. Helper Gethryn—by unprincipled use of a common acquaintance—calls upon Lady Ballister and asks to interview Janet Murch. But Janet Murch has left the Ballister service, of her own accord! Lady Ballister cannot tell Gethryn Janet Murch's address but she does tell Gethryn that she got Janet Murch in the first place through the KJB Domestic Agency of 14 Brabazon Road, South Kensington. Gethryn leaves with this information—and also with the knowledge, acquired by his observant eye and receptive personality, that, at the time of the interview at least, Alice Ballister is a harassed and extremely frightened woman. He does not—why should he?—associate this harassment and fear with the subject of his own search but merely files it in his encyclopedic brain for future reference, noting also the fact that as he entered the Ballister house a nasty little man, most unlikely to have been a social visitor, was leaving the house. Armed with the one piece of fresh Murch information—to wit, the address of the agency—he goes back to Mr. Sheldon Garrett. They decide that the next step is to go to the address of Janet Murch's aunt, furnished previously to another helper by Janet Murch's friend. But when they get there the aunt is flown! She has, most inconsiderately and indefinitely and suddenly, departed for Scotland —in great excitement and a taxicab. The next morning Garrett visits the KJB Domestic Agency—under the nom de guerre of Leslie Schumacher, a visiting and parental American in search of Janet Murch, said to be the world's champion nursemaid. The manager of the agency—a certain Hines —is cheerful and obliging but he cannot help his prospective client because Janet Murch has severed her connection with the agency. Mr. Hines endeavours, naturally enough, to induce Mr. Schumacher to let KJB procure him another nursemaid but Mr. Schumacher, also naturally enough, will not commit them to this course. This was on Saturday. On the following Monday Mr. Sheldon Garrett—about his own business—visits, in the fog, the theatre where his play is running. He then meets with the *accident* of the stage door which you will remember. In the evening he sets out to dine with Gethryn and is first nearly pushed under a tube train and then hit by a mysterious something—which I'll bet you a quarter's income to a sixpence was a sandbag—on the back of the head on his way to Gethryn's house. The next day Gethryn comes to Scotland Yard to tell his story and to use what appears to be an entirely mythical influence. After he has told it the would-be satiric gibberings of the assistant commissioner of Metropolitan Police are interrupted by a telephone call which announces the death, apparently by suicide, of Lady Alice-in-brackets Ballister."

He broke off, looking from one of his listeners to the other. He said:

"And that's that. And more than enough."

Lucas said: "It looks odd. I'll agree to that. But then, anything *can* look odd." He turned his glance on the third of the trio. "What do you say, Pike?"

Pike did not look up as he answered. He seemed to be regarding the tip of one of his shining boots. He said:

"I agree with both, sir, as you might say. What I mean: I see that the way Colonel Gethryn looks at it, it's a very queer business and one that could do with looking into and ought to be looked into. On the other hand, I know what *you* mean, sir. . . . It might just be coincidence."

"Yes, and again no," murmured Anthony. "Pike, you ought to be in the Foreign Office!"

Lucas said: "It's all conjecture." His tone was peevish. "What's more, it's not even complete conjecture. You want us to stop somebody from doing something but you don't know who's going to do it or what they're going to do. . . . Damn it all, Gethryn, it makes about as much sense as Lewis Carroll."

"That's saying a lot," said Anthony. "But you're not even right at that."

Pike said: "Gosh! I wonder whether . . ." He looked hard at Anthony. "You mean to suggest, sir, that Lady Ballister didn't commit suicide?"

Anthony shook his head. "No. It's a possibility, of course. But then . . ." He turned to Lucas. "Who was the divisional surgeon?"

"Latrobe," said Lucas.

Anthony said: "In that case it's a hundred to one that it was suicide." He looked at Pike again. "And it fits much better that way."

"Really?" Lucas was ironic again. "What fits what? What do you mean, 'fits'?"

Anthony said: "You remarked just now that I wanted you to try and stop an unknown human quantity from committing an unknown crime quantity and didn't know either of the quantities. Right?"

Lucas nodded.

Anthony said: "You meant, in other words, that I had no case against anyone. Right?"

Lucas nodded.

Anthony said: "I say that two cases lie. The first is against the absent Janet Murch. The second is against the present KJB Agency."

"Charges?" said Lucas. "Do you want me to find Janet Murch and put her in the dock on the charge of being such a good servant that her leaving caused the suicide of her mistress? Or do you want——"

Anthony interrupted. "What I do want is absolute 'ush! . . . Rex versus Janet Murch: Janet Murch is overheard talking about a possible crime which entails a new job along the nursemaid line. She gives up her nursemaid job, voluntarily, with Lady Ballister. She does not leave any address with Lady Ballister. She does not go and stay at her only other known address and the other owner of that address, the aunt, also leaves mysteriously. Reasonable inference—Janet Murch has taken up a nefarious job: we have indications that she was going to and her behaviour strengthens and colours them. After Janet's leaving Lady Ballister commits suicide. A man attempting to trace Janet Murch is nearly killed three times almost immediately following his inquiries. Presumption: That Janet Murch and/or her associates are unpleasant and criminal persons with whom the police should make acquaintance."

Lucas and Pike exchanged a glance. Lucas frowned and picked up a pencil from his desk and began to draw horses' heads upon a blotting pad.

Anthony said: "Rex versus the KJB Domestic Agency. The KJB Domestic Agency furnish Janet Murch to Lady Ballister. Janet Murch leaves Lady Ballister. Lady Ballister commits suicide. The KJB Domestic Agency are approached in regard to Janet Murch and cause the attempted murder of the inquirer. Presumption——"

"Whoa!" said Lucas; and Pike stirred in his chair.

"Yes?" said Anthony politely.

Lucas said: "Even if we assume that the three—er—adventures of Mr. Garrett yesterday were not coincidental accidents but deliberate attempts to murder him we cannot assume that the attempts necessarily had anything to do with this agency."

"Well, well!" said Anthony and looked from Lucas' face to Pike's.

Pike nodded. He murmured: "That seems right enough, sir."

"And why?" said Anthony.

Lucas repressed a movement of irritation. He began to draw again.

Pike said after a moment: "Because although Mr. Garrett did go and ask about this Murch at this agency there's plenty of other people, according to your own story, sir, who've been approached about Murch and who *might*'ve been the people who were trying to do away with Mr. Garrett."

"No," said Anthony.

Pike stuck to his guns. "But surely, sir! F'rinstance, there's this friend of Janet Murch—the one that gave her address in the first place. And there's all the other people who were asked while you were trying to find the address——"

Anthony said: "I triumph; but it's a cheap triumph because I may not have explained properly. The attempts on Garrett *must* have been made by KJB, or by those in association with it, because none of the other inquiries were made by him. Further, no one of the other persons questioned can have associated Garrett with the inquiries because (a) they never saw the inquirers more than once, (b) were given—where names were used at all— false names *and* (c) had no means whatsoever of following the inquirers. You can take that from me as being not supposition but fact. How different with Garrett and KJB. He goes into their office, having walked from South Kensington station. He gives a false name and inquires about Janet Murch. He will not take any other answer but Murch. He walks away and it is a simple matter to follow him back to the Savoy, inquire from a servant, entirely unsuspiciously, who he is and find out, not only that he is not Mr. Leslie Schumacher, but that he is unmarried. How simple, too, to follow the KJB line of reasoning when they have this information. Thomas Sheldon Garrett is a young American playwright. He has been in London for only a few weeks. Under a false name and on a false premise he is trying to find out how he can get in touch with Janet Murch. Though possible, it is very highly improbable that he needs a nursemaid—so wherein lies his anxiety? Janet Murch is engaged in nefarious business; why is anybody so interested in her? They talk it over and talk it over. They come to the conclusion that there is a possibility that Garrett has in some way come into possession of knowledge which has made him suspicious concerning the doings of Janet Murch. Anyone snooping about Janet Murch at the moment is most undesirable. It can do no harm to try and eliminate this sole snooper, providing the elimination is done in such a way as not to bring any suspicion to bear upon the eliminators. . . .''

"Wait!" said Lucas. "You're now trying to get us to believe that this KJB Agency is behind the Murch affair."

Anthony looked at him. "Oh, my dear fellow! Because I gave you two separate cases I didn't mean that the two affairs weren't bound up."

Lucas grunted.

Pike said: "If there's anything, sir, it's something big. They were taking a chance on this Mr. Garrett."

"*Big!*" said Anthony and laughed.

Lucas threw down his pencil. He leaned back in his chair and looked at Anthony. He said:

"I still don't see what we can do. If you want me to say that you've convinced me that there's something going on that oughtn't to be going on I will say it. But—what can we do?"

Anthony stood up. "I'll tell you," he said. "But later. . . . Good-bye and thanks for bearing with me."

Two men were left staring at a closed door. Lucas sighed and picked up his pencil and began upon another horse's head. He said without looking up:

"I suppose he's right. Damn him!"

CHAPTER XII

Big Ben was sounding the first stroke of noon when Anthony nosed his car out of the Whitehall entrance to Scotland Yard. It was six minutes past the hour when he pulled it up in Stukeley Gardens and jumped out and slammed its door behind him. Half a minute later he was seated at the writing table in the library. And then bodily activity ceased while his mind raced, swiftly but orderly tabulating those things which he must do. . . .

The door opened softly and Lucia came in. He looked at her and smiled and reached for the telephone and began to dial a number. She crossed the room and stood by his chair. He turned to speak to her but immediately was checked by an answer from the telephone. He said into the mouthpiece:

"Hello. . . . Dyson? . . . Gethryn here. . . ."

Dyson said: "Everything going by the book. We were all set just after ten. We missed one, while Harris was getting things fixed. But we caught all the others. He says the light's good. Any further orders?"

"No," said Anthony. "Carry on."

Dyson hung up his receiver and turned. He was in a small room whose furnishings proclaimed it as coming under the head "bed-sitting." There was a couch against one wall, spread with an orange-hued cover which incompletely disguised its nocturnal purposes; then a wardrobe of white-painted deal, one armchair, two ordinary chairs, a Jubilee chiffonier, a table and an insecure-seeming bookcase containing old periodicals and a nearly complete set of the works of Bulwer-Lytton. These were the normal trappings; but today there were more—a tripod of black wood and bright steel, set up in the one large window, and atop of it was what seemed a black rectangular box. Behind the tripod knelt a man. In a chair beside him, reading a pink paper, sat Flood.

Dyson came across the room and stood close behind the kneeling man and looked out through the window onto the cheerful, sunlit little stretch of Brabazon Road, South Kensington.

In the library of 19A Stukeley Gardens Anthony Gethryn twisted in his chair and looked up at his wife and saw that she was smiling.

She said: "He's been conscious. Nurse says that he suddenly came round and spoke to her. That was just after you'd gone out. He was in pain, so she gave him the injection that Doctor Holmes left. He's sleeping now."

"Good," said Anthony. "I could bear to see Avis."

Lucia stood up. "I've phoned her already. Nurse said he'd sleep for five hours at least. . . . But all the same I——"

Anthony said: "I do perceive here a divided duty. . . . Bring her in here as soon as she comes!" He smiled up at his wife again and reached once more for the telephone. "And now, woman, stand not upon the order of thy going." Once more he began to dial—the same number as before.

"Quite the Napoleon!" Lucia pulled a face at him and dropped a kiss upon the top of his head and was gone.

Anthony got his number. He said into the telephone:

"Mr. Flood, please. . . . Hello, that you, Flood? . . . Yes. . . . Yes. . . . I've got Lucas to take notice, *because* Lady——"

"Ballister has killed herself," said the telephone. "I saw that. I wondered——"

Anthony interrupted: "Don't, you're right. Here's your job: Shove a discreet paragraph into as many of this evening's papers as you can to the effect that Mr. Thomas Sheldon Garrett, distinguished young American playwright and author of *Wise Man's Holiday*, et cetera, so on and blah, had a severe fall in the street (locale unmentioned) yesterday. He was found by Samaritans and is now lying—concussed, unconscious and seriously ill—in the nursing home of Doctor Travers Hoylake in Welbeck Street. Pitch it in as strong as you can. Give a definite impression that it's most unlikely that he'll live. . . . No visitors allowed of course. . . . That's all you've got to worry about. I've already fixed things with Hoylake and the nursing home will know what to do if there are any calls. Repeat, will you?"

The telephone cackled briefly.

"Right!" said Anthony. He put back the receiver and rose and crossed to a far corner of the room and stood looking down, with distaste, at a small table upon which stood a typewriter. After a moment he sat before the machine and put paper in it and began with great speed, considering the use of only one finger upon each hand, to type. . . .

He sat back after thirty minutes and sighed relief. He picked up the five pages and put them into order and scanned them. He read:

DEAR LUCAS: Belated apologies for my intolerable manners this morning. But I had—or thought I had—to be rude before you would really give me your attention.

I know you well enough to be sure that your last remark to me meant that you were going to play. Therefore I send you this:

We know that the KJB Domestic Agency is not the innocent affair which it seems. However, so far, we have nothing which would be sufficiently concrete in the minds of the ordinary muttonheaded British jury (and the D.P.P. if it comes to that) to bring a charge against KJB and those behind it. Therefore, do not let us make the frightful mistake of warning them. This, as it is, is an upside-down case and must therefore be treated with upside-down methods. Whatever KJB (and those behind it) may have already done must be left for the moment, for we cannot stop that; but if we play our cards properly we may stop whatever they are going to do. Below I list some general and some particular lines for us to follow:

A. GENERAL

1. Do not by any overt act let anyone know, in connection with the Ballister case or otherwise, that there is any curiosity upon the part of the police in regard to KJB.

2. Exercise your "influence" with the coroner to see that the above applies to him too.

3. To effect (1) and (2) above properly, insure that the routine inquiry at the Ballister house is handled by someone who knows what we are really after and *not* by some intelligent and pushful peeler who *might* stumble upon something accidentally.

4. Above all do not let any official body, under any pretence or for any reason, go anywhere near the KJB office.

B. PARTICULAR

1. Put a good man on to Travers Hoylake's nursing home in Welbeck Street and follow anyone who calls there to ask after Garrett. (Garrett is still in my house. He is recovering. But, following my policy of not frightening KJB at all, I am having a notice put in this evening's papers to the effect that Garrett is in the nursing home, unconscious, and is not expected to recover, his injuries being due to a *fall*.)

2. Get in touch with Hoylake (who knows what's required) and tell him who his operator is to call at the Yard directly she receives any telephonic inquiries at all for Mr. Garrett. Also, if possible, arrange with the Exchange to keep a record of the numbers from which calls about Garrett to the nursing home are made.

3. Put a good man onto Miss Letitia Lamb, of Number 1 Llewellyn Street. He should not approach her personally but should find out, if possible, whether she is as innocent of entanglement with KJB and/or Janet Murch as her name and appearance (*vide* Flood) would appear. Has she a good record? Has she ever been in any way connected with undesirable persons, employment or happenings? (A purely precautionary measure, this. I feel sure Lamb is all right; but we must double-check.)

4. The same in regard to Mrs. Claude Kenealy, of 97 Stockbrook Road, Richmond, Surrey—the woman whose bulk and fur coat, she says, saved Garrett from a tubular death.

5. Try and find the present whereabouts of Mrs. Bellows, of 148A Iron Court, Stockholm Lane. This is the reputed aunt of Janet Murch. A few days before we obtained this address through Lamb Mrs. Bellows went suddenly and excitedly and mysteriously to Scotland—or said that she was going to Scotland. I have had rough inquiries made at the possible departure stations and also in the neighbourhood but these have got nowhere.

6. Get someone (I hope it is Pike) who has been in on the official inquiry into the Ballister suicide to tell me about and/or present to me all the concrete collected evidence in the matter. As soon as possible.

7. Have a search made in Records (if you haven't already) for Janet Murch. (It will probably be abortive but should be done.)

8. Ditto for Evans—the man used as a threat in the conversation which Garrett overheard in Notting Hill teashop and which started the affair. There will, of course, be thousands of Evanses but it might be well worth while to see if any of these have been connected with any nefarious doings in any way bound up with the domestic agency business in general or domestic service in particular.

9. Similar inquiries about the KJB Agency itself, though these are almost certain to be abortive.

10. Send me as soon as you can (if possible by White, who will bring

this to you) the reports of Garrett's two interviews at the Yard with Andrews and Horler on the nineteenth and twentieth of last month.

11. Try and find out, very discreetly, who the man was that left Ballister's house just before I saw Lady Ballister—i.e. at about three o'clock on Friday, the thirtieth of last month. What's his name and business? Whom did he see? Had he ever been to the house before? (I have no specific reason for wanting to know about this man except my favourite one of general oddity.)

12. If—but only if—you have a very good man making the Ballister routine inquiries get him to find out, without giving away interest in the concern, how many servants in the house within the last year came from KJB.

Thank you kindly, sir. Bear with me and get the quickest action possible.

Anthony came to an end of his reading and rose and took the sheets to the writing table and signed the last of them and pressed a bell.

2

Sheldon Garrett opened his eyes, for the second time this day, upon surroundings which were strange. The room was full of the grey-blackness of dusk about to turn to night but this melancholy pall was shot through with red and cheerful and flickering reflections which told of a large fire. He was barely conscious of his body. His eyes told him that he was in a bed but he did not feel the mattress beneath him nor the clothes above him. He was numb and glad to be so. . . .

He stared at the ceiling. His eyes saw what they looked at but they seemed heavy and sluggish and unwilling to move when his half-benumbed mind ordered them. But his ears were preternaturally sensitive. There came to them magnifications of every sound. . . . A very faint, very muffled rumbling of traffic. . . . A very loud, very sharp crackling of hot coals. . . . The creaking of wood as a body shifted its position in a chair. . . . A very faint sound of voices from somewhere beneath him in this house. . . . And then, imperiously imposing itself atop of all these sounds, the crackle of starched linen. . . .

His mind ordered his muscles to raise his head from the pillow and turn it to his right. But no movement resulted—only a stab of pain which, starting at the base of his skull, sent fiery fingers to every nerve in the whole of him. . . .

A mist came over his sight and he was dimly conscious that sweat had broken out all over him. He lay still. . . .

Preceded by a louder crackling of starched linen, there swam into his vision the upper half of a white-clothed woman. She bent over him, putting a dry hand, hard surfaced yet softly fleshed, upon his sweating forehead. Flickering rays from the fire struck sparks of light from the panes of glass which hid her eyes. She said:

"And how are we feeling?" Her voice was soft and devoid of all humanity.

He said, thick and low:

"Bit sick, eh? . . . Head hurts. . . . Where's this?" The words were not so much reflections of his thought as essays in the difficult exercise of speech.

She took the uncomfortable hand away from his forehead and straightened herself with another rustling and stood looking down at him. She said something; but his mind, wrapped up in its own affairs, did not trouble to interpret the words. He said:

"Mrs. Bellingham? . . . Where's she? . . . What house is this? . . . Call up Colonel Gethryn. . . ." The effort of so many words brought out beads of cold sweat upon his face. But he went on. "Colonel Gethryn . . . The number's—I can't remember. . . . Mrs. Bellingham—St. John-4383. . . . She'll tell . . ."

Another crackling of linen as once more she bent over him. Her mouth pursed itself and there came from it a *sshushing* sound. She said:

"Don't talk now! You'll only hurt yourself if you do. Lie quiet and everything will be all right!" She picked up his right hand, which lay outside the bedclothes. Her fingers fumbled for his pulse and, holding the wrist, she looked at a watch upon her own.

3

"You're sure," said Anthony, "that these are all we need to worry about?" He tapped with pencil butt upon the paper which lay upon the writing table before him. He looked across at the big chair in which his visitor sat.

Avis Bellingham nodded. "I don't think there can be any more. I used to know the whole family."

Anthony chewed the end of his pencil for a moment; then began to write. He came to an end and read aloud:

" 'Pay no attention reports seriousness of illness stop Perfectly all right stop Business reasons stop Telephoning by end of week love Tom.' "

He sat back in his chair and looked at his visitor. "All right?" he said.

She nodded again. She said: "If—do you really think he'll be able to telephone . . . I mean, that he'll be——"

Anthony smiled at her. "Of course. He'll——" A knock upon the door interrupted him. "Come in," he said.

The nurse made rustling entry. She stood just within the doorway and folded her hands and ranged her spectacles upon Anthony. She said:

"I am sorry to disturb you, Colonel Gethryn, but Mr. Garrett has awakened. He is in pain but I cannot give him another injection until Doctor Holmes has been. I endeavoured to find Mrs. Gethryn but I am told that she is out. I must keep Mr. Garrett quiet, however, and he keeps on asking me to 'call up' Colonel Gethryn or someone called Avis. He keeps saying this latter name." She was silent for a moment while the eyes behind the glittering glasses flickered momentarily towards Colonel Gethryn's visitor, who had made a sudden movement but who now was still again. She said: "I could only keep Mr. Garrett quiet by promising to go. . . ."

Anthony had listened enough. "Quite," he said, "quite! This is Mrs. Bel-

lingham, whom Mr. Garrett wants to see." He looked with deliberately
expressionless face at Avis. "If you wouldn't mind going up . . . ?"

Mrs. Bellingham rose with admirable slowness to her feet. There was
more colour than usual in her face. She looked at Anthony and smiled and
moved towards the nurse and the door. She said:

"Good afternoon, Nurse. . . . If I can be of any help . . ."

Anthony turned his chair back to face the table and picked up the draft
cablegram and reached for the telephone.

4

The opening of the door sounded in Garrett's ears like a battery of artillery. But he had learned; he did not try to raise his head. He lay still and
his breath came faster.

And then Avis was bending over him.

He looked up at her without moving his head. Slowly his eyes focused
their sight so that every detail of her face was clear. Her eyes were very
blue and very soft and they shone. Her lips moved as if she were going to
speak but no sound came from them. They remained parted a little, so that
behind the redness of their lovely curve he could see the whiteness of her
teeth. He smiled, now heedless of the pain which the stretching even of
these few muscles sent stabbing through his head. He was going to speak;
to say her name at least—but he found, suddenly, that he was seized by a
childlike and painful constriction of the breath. The smile stayed upon his
face but, unbidden, smarting moisture came into his heavy eyes. . . .

Then a starchy rustling; a bump; and the unctuous, unnecessary voice of
the nurse.

"Why don't you sit down, Mrs. Bellingham? And make yourself at home.
But you mustn't let him talk too much or I shall be getting into trouble with
Doctor Holmes." She had set down a chair behind Avis and was patting its
back invitingly.

Avis sat. She did not take her eyes off the drawn face on the pillow.

Another rustling and the nurse stood beside her and herself bent over the
pillow. She put her hand again upon the patient's head and held it there a
moment. She said, drawing it away:

"Well, the excitement of a visitor doesn't seem to have done you any
harm. But you must be good!" She wagged a distressingly roguish forefinger.
"You mustn't be a bad boy and spoil this nice surprise I got for you!"

Garrett's lips moved, shaping themselves into a soundless and deplorable
word. Avis choked. She took out a handkerchief and pressed it to her lips.
She felt a strange desire to giggle and weep at the same time.

"And now," said the fat voice, "I'll leave you to yourselves." Once more
the forefinger was raised in coy admonition. "But very little talking, mind!"

The starched linen creaked again and she was gone, to settle herself once
more, with a determinedly tactful back towards the bed, in her chair by the
fire.

Garrett's sluggish eyes moved themselves in her direction. Once more his lips soundlessly formed a fearful word.

"Don't!" said Avis Bellingham in a choked voice. "Please don't, Tom!"

And then, suddenly, all desire for laughter left both their minds and again they stared at each other.

Garrett spoke first. From between his barely moving lips came thick words:

"Crack on the head. . . . Don't know how long here. . . . I wanted to say sorry for lunch the other day. . . ." A groping look came into his heavy eyes. "When was it? . . . Seems . . ."

She leaned nearer to him. She said:

"It was on Monday, Tom. Yesterday. And there's absolutely nothing——"

The thick, guttural voice interrupted her. "There is! . . . Behaved badly. . . . Too many drinks. . . ." His voice was laboured and each successive word came with more difficulty. She interrupted him, leaning forward and putting a hand upon the clothes which covered his shoulder. She said:

"Don't, Tom! It's all right; it's perfectly all right!"

His lips moved again. " 'Tisn't all right. . . . Very bad! . . . Fooled about things I—I—really meant . . ." The voice died away and his tongue came out in effort to moisten the lips which seemed so unmanageable.

"Oh!" said Avis Bellingham softly. "I——" She seemed to check herself, closing her mouth tightly so that further words should not escape.

There was a silence.

"I don't know . . ." began Garrett slowly and painfully—and then was interrupted.

A voice came to their ears from across the room. It was fat and efficient and obviously gloving iron in velvet. It said:

"Not too much talking for the patient, please!"

Garrett moved heavy eyes slightly in the direction of the voice. But this time his lips did not move; they were too tired to waste effort.

Avis leant closer to him. She smiled at him and it was as if an Olympian balm had been poured over his hurts. She said through the smile:

"I'll do it for you." And her lips moved soundlessly to form a word.

Garrett started to grin, checking the wideness of the smile only just in time to stop another stab of that agonizing pain. And then his smile went and he said with a curious sharpening of tone and words:

"How's the—what did you call it?—the *riddle*? Been having . . ." His brows creased themselves into a slow and painful frown and a cloud came over his eyes. "Been having . . . sort of dreams. . . . Barry and Edna and—and——"

Mrs. Bellingham stopped him. She said in an imperious whisper:

"You mustn't talk! And don't think about that sort of thing! It's not going to happen! . . . I've just been with Anthony. This is his house, you know. He's very busy. Very. I'll tell you tomorrow, or he will. But lots of things have happened."

A light came into the languid eyes of the head upon the pillow and from the heavy lips came an eager croaking. It said:

"Found Murch?"

Avis said: "Sssh! I'm not going to tell you any details but you've got to believe me. All *sorts* of things are happening!"

Garrett said in a voice suddenly louder: "Please tell me——" And then with a determined crackling the nurse was at the bedside once more. She said in a voice from which everything save authority had gone:

"That'll do! No more now!"

CHAPTER XIII

There was amazement in the Gethryn household: its master not only appeared at the breakfast table but appeared bathed and shaven and clothed for the day. His son's joy and surprise were eagerly voiced; his wife's greetings satiric. He did not bow before the storm; he helped himself to food and sat down and began placidly to eat. He said:

"I'm a busy man. Great matters hang upon my every word and action." He drank coffee. "I might justly be likened to the spider."

His wife looked at him with interest. "You've got that secret look on, Anthony! And you're excited about something."

He put down his knife and fork. "I say nothing, though I could say much. I will only say that in future I should be known as Semloh, the Upside-Down Detective." He reached for the paper and opened it and from behind it said: "When you come to think of it I *am* a spider—a subtle spider who doth sit in middle of his web which spreadeth wide."

"I don't like spiders," said his son. "But their webs are pretty."

Anthony lowered the paper. He made the face which never failed to draw a crescendo peal of laughter from his son. He said, looking at his wife:

"No brighter nor skilful thread than mine, my cabbage. If aught do touch the utmost thread of it I feel it instantly on every side."

He finished his breakfast to ribald chaff from his family. He left them and went into his study and busied himself in thought.

At ten o'clock his expected visitor arrived. It was Pike, lantern faced and smiling and alert. He refused refreshment, took tobacco and sat in the big armchair close to Anthony's desk. He produced from his pocket a large and official-seeming envelope, and from the envelope a heterogeneous collection of paper bound with elastic. He said: "Well, sir?" and grinned.

"Well to you!" said Anthony and blew smoke rings.

Pike said: "I'll start, then. We did have the divisional plain-clothes inspector on the Ballister business, sir, but as soon as Mr. Lucas got your letter yesterday lunchtime he took him off. He asked me whether I'd go and I jumped at the chance, as you might say." He put his hand again to his breast pocket and brought it away bearing this time some folded sheets of typescript. He unfolded them and pressed out the creases upon his knee. He looked up at Anthony. "A copy of your letter, sir. How'd it be if I was to answer all the points right now?"

Anthony ceased to blow smoke rings. "All?" he said. "It would be magnificent. Can do?"

Pike smiled, not without pleasant traces of self-satisfaction. "Yes sir. Ready? . . . Taking the first paragraph of your letter, Mr. Lucas told me first of all to say that he hadn't taken any offence when you were there. Second, I was to say that of course we were going into it. Third, I was to say that he quite saw your point about not warning this KJB lot. . . . And now I can get down to your numbered points. Under the heading 'General', and taking them in order, I can tell you that *nobody* is going to get any idea that we're a bit interested in KJB. Second, we've sent Mr. Sparkes—you know him, sir!—to talk to the coroner—and *that's* all right: he won't show any interest in KJB. Third—well, I *hope* that's answered by my having charge of the inquiries personally. Fourth, I've taken good care that nobody in any way connected with the police is going anywhere near the KJB office."

He turned over a page of manuscript, sat back more comfortably, cleared his throat and began again. He said:

"Now, sir, for your heading 'Particular.' . . . One: I've put a very good man—you remember Howells?—onto the nursing home in Welbeck Street. He's an extra porter there now, in uniform and all. There's another man outside and if anybody comes to ask for Mr. Garrett, Howells will tell him and he'll do the necessary following. . . . Two: I've been onto Doctor Hoylake personally and told him his operator must call extension 232 at the Yard when she receives any telephonic inquiry for Mr. Garrett. I'm afraid, though, that we can't arrange with the Exchange for a record of numbers calling. This automatic business has beaten us in that way."

"Progress!" said Anthony. "Ourobboros!"

Pike stared politely. "Sir?"

"Swalloweth itself," said Anthony. "Go on."

Pike said: "I've put Dixon—I don't think you know him, but he's a good man—onto this young woman, Lamb. He's got some more work to do but I saw him this morning before I came here and I should say that from what he's got already there's no possibility of *her* being mixed up in this business at all. We've looked for her in Records and she doesn't appear there—nor anyone of the name. He's been into antecedents, as you might say, and everything's well aboveboard. . . . Now for Four: Last night I went after Mrs. Claude Kenealy myself. You can take it from me, sir, that *she's* all right."

He looked at Anthony with one eyebrow cocked.

"If you say so, Pike," said Anthony and meant it.

Pike beamed. "Thank you, sir. Number Five: Mrs. Bellows—I've got nothing to report on yet. We sent a man from Hammersmith Division down to

Iron Court and he reports that she was very well liked in the neighbourhood. Very respectable body. All bills paid and that sort of thing. Lived there for quite a while. She told the neighbours she was going to visit relatives in Scotland. No address given. We may have some more on this later when we've been properly round King's Cross and St. Pancras. But at present I've got to confess we're nowhere."

He paused for a moment and tapped the bundle of papers on his knee. "In Number Six you asked for all the concrete evidence in the Ballister business. Here it is, sir, and we'll come to it in a minute. . . . In Number Seven you asked us to search Records for Janet Murch. We've done so and haven't got anything—as you expected. In Number Eight you asked for a similar search about Evans." He laughed. "You were right about there being thousands of them, sir; *but* we haven't got any one of 'em who we can in any way hitch up with domestic service. . . . And it's the same for Number Nine—the KJB Agency. No record at all, and a very high-class character in the trade, as you might say. Number Ten was a request for the reports of Mr. Garrett's interviews at the Yard." He tapped the breast pocket again. "I've got those here. . . ."

He cleared his throat and shifted his position. Over the sheets of paper which he held he glanced at Anthony, noting, with a little smile, that Anthony's eyes were half closed. He said:

"With Number Eleven, sir, I can give you something definite. This man you saw leaving the house when you called on Lady Ballister on that Friday: I've found out about him. The butler knew about it. The man was a representative for some firm of central heating engineers. Lady Ballister had some idea of having central heating installed in the general's country residence— that's in Bucks, near Aylesbury—and this man was trying to interest her in his firm's system. I put a casual question to the old general about this, sir, and he confirmed it. They don't remember the name of the firm but if you want particularly to know I dare say we can find out. The man's been to the house on several other occasions: the butler thinks four. His name was Mr. Smithers. . . ."

For the first time during the recital Anthony interrupted. He said:

"Good name. Not so obvious as Smith."

Pike looked at him, frowning. "Beg pardon, sir."

Anthony said: "It doesn't matter. What about Twelve?"

Pike smiled. He said: "Maybe I've been too egoistic, as you might say, about this, sir. What you said was if we had a good man on the job he was to make inquiry about how many of the servants in the Ballister house, within the last twelve months, were from KJB. I took the liberty of assuming that I'd fill your bill and put out some discreet feelers—very discreet! I'm sure I didn't arouse any suspicion and anyway, sir, in a manner of speaking, there weren't any to arouse. Because why? Because none of the present servants in the house come from the KJB Agency! I checked on them. There are five all told, including the new nursemaid who took Murch's place. Four of them come from another agency and the fifth privately. But,

sir, not only Janet Murch came from KJB within the year, but one other—a
housemaid by the name of Dillson—Doris Dillson. She came in February
last. She left at the beginning of May, discharged for impertinence. . . .
And that, sir, I think covers, as far as we can at the moment, all the matters
in your report."

Pike sighed and sat back, relaxed. His small bright brown eyes searched
Anthony's face.

Anthony came to life. He said:

"Sometimes I agree with American novelists when they ascribe super-
human powers to Scotland Yard."

Pike smiled widely. He picked from his knee the elastic-bound bundle
of papers. He leant forward in his chair and proffered them to Anthony. He
said:

"Here's what you asked for, sir, in your Number Six: the stuff from the
Lady Ballister effects."

Anthony took the bundle and put it down upon the table and turned
his chair and undid the elastic band. He found the stubs of five cheque-
books; a passbook; an envelope, opened, addressed in a sprawling hand to
"Charles"; a little red morocco-bound book marked "Diary."

He spread these out upon the table and looked round at Pike.

"That all?" he said.

Pike nodded. "Yes sir, except for something else which I couldn't bring
and which I'll tell you about when you're ready."

"Hmmh!" grunted Anthony and bent over the collection.

Pike lit a cigarette and looked at his watch. The hands stood at eleven
o'clock. . . .

2

The clock over the Naval Museum was sounding the last stroke of eleven
when there came out of Number 14 Brabazon Road a young woman in the
blue cloak and blue-streamered bonnet of a nursemaid. Drawn up to the
wall almost underneath the KJB signboard was a perambulator. The nursemaid bent over the perambulator and peered at its occupant, who, securely
tucked beneath his covers, slept, red faced and peaceful. With care not to
make the process jerky the nursemaid eased the pram away from the wall,
cautiously turned it and set off briskly towards the end of Brabazon Road
and the main thoroughfare of Emperor's Gate. She was a slender-ankled,
brisk young woman carrying her becoming uniform with an air and wearing
upon her lavishly powdered and nicely formed face a look of supreme if
unsympathetic competence.

She had not gone more than halfway between the door of Number 14
and the end of Brabazon Road when there emerged from Number 11, upon
the other side of the street, a brisk young man in the dark cap and blue overalls of a mechanic. His overalls were fairly clean but his hands bore the
black marks of his calling and in the right was a small leather tool bag.
He turned sharply to his left as he reached the pavement and strode,

whistling shrilly, towards Emperor's Gate. The pretty nursemaid and her perambulator were moving fast but the mechanic was moving faster. As the nursemaid reached Emperor's Gate and turned to her right she was barely ten yards ahead.

The mechanic ceased to whistle. Having reached Emperor's Gate, he turned to the right, too, crossed the mouth of Brabazon Road and went on his way, more slowly. It was a way which seemed to coincide with that of the nurse and the perambulator. . . .

She reached the top of Emperor's Gate and turned left along the broad road which divides Kensington Gardens from the brown masses of the houses which front it. Sometimes twenty, sometimes only ten, yards behind her came the mechanic. The maid and the perambulator took the third turning on their left. So, a few seconds afterwards, did the mechanic. As he turned the corner he looked upwards, as if in doubt of his whereabouts, at the street plate. He read the words, "Pierpont Gardens" and strode on.

At Number 17 the nurse halted. The mechanic was then opposite Number 11. He dropped his bag and the catch sprang open and his tools spilled themselves about the pavement. He swore roundly and stooped to collect them. He seemed in no hurry about the work.

Outside Number 17 the nurse busied herself. She took a strap from the foot of the perambulator and hitched its wheel to the area railings. She removed the covers from the still-sleeping occupant, gathered him into her arms and mounted the steps to the front door.

The mechanic collected the last of his tools from the gutter. He fastened the catch of his bag and continued upon his path. He was now merely strolling. He arrived opposite Number 17 just as the door shut behind a flutter of blue. He looked up at the number above the door. He put his bag between his feet and made great play of consulting a card which he drew from the pocket of his overalls. Then, whistling, he marched to the area gate of Number 17, pushed it open and ran, still whistling, down the steps and pounded upon the tradesmen's door. . . .

3

Anthony pushed away the last of the little books of cheque stubs. He opened an envelope marked, "Letter Written by Lady Ballister (Deceased) to Husband." He read:

My dear Charles,

You must not think too harshly of me for what I am going to do and what I shall have done by the time you read this. I have told you, I think, of my headaches. But I have never told you how frightful they were. They have been periodic and getting steadily worse. And they have done things to my brain. I have kept myself under iron control, thinking that perhaps they would pass; but they never have! And *now* I know what is the matter: *I am going insane!*

I can bear neither the thought of being a thankless burden to you and to our dear children nor, for myself, of being a witless thing!

I am going to end it. I can only hope that you will forgive your loving wife,

Alice.

Anthony turned in his chair and looked at Pike. He said:

"And exhibit Three, that you couldn't bring?"

"Exhibit Three, sir," Pike said, "was a lot of charred paper in the grate of Lady Ballister's room. The fragments were analyzed. The report was— very thick paper on thin pasteboard, with one highly glazed surface."

Anthony shrugged. "Whatever that means, a bonfire's in order. It all fits, doesn't it?" He flicked a finger at the cheque stubs. "A woman spends about thirty-five pounds a month for years; then suddenly draws large cheques to Self, increasing in amount from a hundred to five hundred, every few weeks. She burns papers and kills herself, leaving an overwritten letter which doesn't ring at all true. It's all according to Cocker."

Pike nodded, his long face lugubrious. "Meaning the lady's suicide was caused by blackmail, sir? Yes sir."

Anthony looked at him. "What's the matter, Pike? Blackmail fits."

Pike said slowly: "What you want it all to mean, sir, is that this KJB Agency was behind the blackmail. Am I right?"

"Shades of Dupin!" said Anthony and grinned. "Pike, you're no police-man; you've got too much imagination."

"Am I right though, sir?" Pike was insistent.

Anthony said: "You are indeed! I was wondering when you'd make the sum of KJB plus Murch, plus KJB plus Ballister come out as KJB equalling blackmail." He looked at Pike and found no lightening of the gloom in the long face. "What I'm wondering now, Pike, is why you're so sad about it all."

Pike twisted uneasily in his chair. "For a whole heap of reasons, sir. And they make a pretty muddle in a man's head, if I may say so. First, there's——"

Anthony interrupted. "Hold those horses, Pike; they're getting away with you. Your only trouble's this: you feel—probably rightly—that however much we probe we won't be able to fix this Ballister blackmail on KJB and that, therefore, probing will only warn them that they're under suspicion and give them a chance to cover up l'affaire Murch so that we'll *never* get at it."

"That's it, sir. That's just it." Pike was animated. "You see——"

Again Anthony cut him short. "Wait. That's just half your worry. The second half's this: if we don't probe this Ballister case how are we going to get hold of anything at all against KJB which will serve as a handle for us in the forthcoming Murch business?" He surveyed Pike with benignity. "There you are. Your trouble in a nutshell. No fee."

Pike lost himself in frowning thought. After a moment he smiled, a little ruefully. He said:

"You're right, sir. That's all there was to it. But it's plenty, at that, when you come to look at it."

"So don't," said Anthony.

Pike stared. "Beg pardon, sir?"

"Don't come to look at it. Don't look at it. Don't consider it at all. Cancel the Ballisters, poor people. And incidentally, please Sir Charles, who certainly would fight tooth and nail to rebut all evidence of blackmail."

Pike got to his feet. He was fidgety, a most unusual state for him. He said vehemently:

"But then we've got *nothing* to work on from this KJB end. We——"

Anthony said: "Preserve absolute calm. We want KJB. First—forgetting the Ballisters—we need to prove to ourselves that KJB is nasty but without frightening KJB into being nice. Then we want to catch KJB red handed. Yes?"

Pike stopped the jerky walk with which he had been pacing from desk to window. He said almost savagely:

"All right, sir; I'll forget the Ballister case. That puts us back to where you said we weren't to go near KJB or do anything at all about them!"

Anthony nodded. "Exactly."

Pike almost glared at him. He said in a voice which came near to a shout: "Then we can't do *anything!*"

"Exactly," said Anthony again. "You can't." There was the slightest extra emphasis on the pronoun.

"Eh?" said Pike sharply. And then: "Do you mean to tell me, sir, that you've got somebody onto KJB yourself?"

Anthony nodded.

"Oh!" said Pike. His face was expressionless but he stood still and very straight.

Anthony said: "Don't collect umbrage. Remember that I came in on this *after* Scotland Yard had refused to listen to Mr. Garrett. Therefore I had to be unorthodox. Stay to lunch and I'll show you the results."

CHAPTER XIV

Pike stayed. They lunched at one and after the meal went into the drawing room. They talked, but not at all of the matter uppermost in their minds.

At a quarter past three they were joined by Flood. He nodded to Anthony and grinned at Pike and shook hands.

Pike said with a sound akin to a sniff:

"I'm not surprised!" But he smiled.

Flood looked at Anthony. "All ready," he said.

They moved towards the door, Anthony leading.

Pike said: "And where's our Mr. Dyson?"

"Busy," said Flood. "Quite the bee!"

They went downstairs and into the library once more. Heavy curtains were drawn over the windows and the centre lights were on. Over the book-shelves at the end of the room nearer the door was hung a white sheet. At the other end of the room, by the french windows, stood a cinematographic projector. Beside it was a small, bald-headed man with the appearance and manner of the skilled worker. A few feet in front of the projector, facing the sheet, were three chairs.

"Walk up!" said Flood. "Walk up! See the Wonderful Movin' Pitchers! The most sensational fillum of the century! Man Huntin' in the Kensington Wilds!"

"Shut up!" said Anthony and sat himself upon the middle chair and motioned Pike to one side of him and Flood to the other. He turned and looked over his shoulders at the man by the projector. "Ready when you are," he said.

There was a click and the lights went out. There was a whirring sound from the projector and then a broad swathe of white light illuminating the sheet.

"Modern Detective Methods!" said Flood beneath his breath. "Collecting Clues with the Camera!"

Pike grunted. He settled himself in his chair and dug his hands into his pockets and stared at the sheet.

Upon it there appeared a picture. It occupied the centre third of the sheet. It had, apparently, been taken from very close to its subject. It showed bricks—the mortar between them considerably crumbled—surrounding the dark and rectangular mouth of an open doorway. At the top of the picture, in the middle, hung something which looked like a batten of wood. Upon the right-hand jamb of the doorway, not quite halfway down the picture, appeared a card, enlarged upon the sheet to vast dimensions, upon which was lettered in black the word ENTER.

Anthony said: "Pike, you're looking at what is technically called a close-up of the front doorway of Number 14 Brabazon Road, South Kensington. That thing at the top is the base of the KJB signboard. Although the angle of the picture indicates that the camera was higher than its subject, it looks as if it had been close. Actually, however, it was in a first-floor window of Number 11 on the other side of the street—with a special telescopic lens on it——"

He broke off. There had come a sudden darkening of the picture and for an instant the little scene had been blotted out by a dark mass which had appeared on the left-hand side and then swept over. But at once the mass moved and diminished as it went away from the camera. It was the back of a man in the cap and high-collared coat of a chauffeur. The back vanished into the doorway and was swallowed up in the dark maw.

A flicker . . . and then, this time coming out of the dark mouth of the doorway, a figure again. The same figure, this time viewed from the front. The chauffeur's cap was at a jaunty angle. The bright buttons on the dark uniform coat glinted in the sunshine. Every feature of the clean-shaven, square-cut, hard yet youthful face was absolutely clear. The figure halted for a moment. The thin lips pursed themselves into what must have been a jaunty whistling and then hands were raised while big gauntleted gloves were drawn onto them. Then, giantlike, the figure surged forward. . . . The head was lost, the coat filled the screen. . . . Once more the doorway was untenanted. . . .

"Stop!" said Anthony over his shoulder.

A whirring and a click. The blade of light from the projector was cut off. Another click and the centre lights of the room went up.

Anthony looked at Flood.

Flood turned over the pages of a small red notebook in his hand. He read: "Fourth October—that's yesterday. Ten forty-one A.M. Second visitor. Drove up in Rolls-Royce saloon, Number GW-8439Y. Time between entering and departing—seven minutes. Unable to follow owing to car. Car belongs to Lord Charles Montfort, 34 Lennox Street and Bickleigh Towers, Hertfordshire. Chauffeur's name Thompson. Been in service with Montfort four months. Finish."

Pike grunted.

"Right!" said Anthony over his shoulder.

Once more the centre lights went out and, following the whirring noise, the beam of the projector came again and once more the doorway was upon the screen.

The next figure, which showed first back and then face, was a woman. She was fat and middle aged and dressed, with a certain neatness, in the manner of a past decade of domestic service. Once more, at Anthony's order, the film was stopped and the room lights came on. Once more Flood read from his little book. He said:

"Yesterday again. . . . In fact, all these are yesterday's because today's won't be developed in time. . . . Third visitor. Eleven-three A.M. Time between entering and departing fifteen minutes. Not chosen as suitable for following."

"Right!" said Anthony again, over his shoulder. . . .

This time it was a nursemaid clothed in a uniform which seemed to be not quite large enough for her. The back was enormous, the face almost nauseatingly maternal. . . . Flood read:

"Fourth visitor. Eleven-thirty A.M. Time between entering and departing —seven minutes. Followed. She was alone. Walked back to Emperor's Gate and took a bus to corner of Morden Gardens and Fulham Road. Entered Number 9 Morden Gardens by servants' entrance. Ascertained to be nursemaid to the three children of Mrs. Charles Frampton. Been in place for seven months. No known prospect of leaving."

The next was a girl as small and trim as the last occupant of the screen had been stout and untidy. She was bareheaded and wore a dark coat which covered the white apron and black clothes of the parlourmaid. . . .

Flood read: "Fifth visitor. Twelve-five P.M. Time between entering and departing, nine minutes. Followed. Walked round the corner into Emperor's Gate and entered Number 98. Ascertained to be parlourmaid in household of Count Feralli. Been in place for two months. No known prospect of leaving."

"Right!" said Anthony again . . . and the process went on.

2

It was over. The library was normal again and the sheet taken down and the little man and the projector gone.

Pike said, speaking for the first time since the film had come to an end: "That's very interesting, sir." He looked at Anthony with puzzled eyes: "But I must confess I don't see where it gets us. Particularly as I understand Mr. Garrett hasn't seen the pictures."

Anthony said: "He'll see them tomorrow."

"And you think . . ." Pike began.

Anthony interrupted. "No. I'd bet that he won't recognize any of these backs."

"Oh!" said Pike and then, in a tone frankly bewildered, "Then I *don't* see what you're driving at, sir. I suppose the pictures might be useful—but only if we ever got to the point where we could *act* in regard to KJB. And we're a long way off that."

Anthony said: "Consider, Pike, and you'll find that those pictures *do* advance our knowledge." He looked at Flood. "Correct me if I go wrong. . . . Yesterday there visited KJB thirteen persons. Four of these were in uniform and all of these four were followed and/or inquired into. In all cases we find that the persons are in good work, are not under notice and have not given notice. Four out of thirteen . . . let's see . . . that's over thirty per cent. Now I maintain that if KJB were only the respectable little business which it proclaims itself it would be impossible for it to have, in one day, thirty per cent of uniformed visitors *not* wanting jobs." He looked at Flood. "For further information we will apply to Agent X-13. He will tell us what happened today; the pictures won't be ready until tomorrow."

Flood grinned. He looked at Pike with a twinkle in his eyes. He said: "I've got the details up to two-thirty this afternoon." He put a hand to his pocket and brought the little red notebook out again and opened it. "From nine forty-five this morning until two-thirty this afternoon there were fourteen visitors, seven of 'em in uniform."

"Fifty per cent today," said Anthony.

Flood said: "We followed four but missed t'others. They overlapped, you see. The four were a couple of parlourmaidish sorts, a footman——"

Anthony interrupted: "Footman?"

Flood said: "Something of the sort. Had a soft hat and light overcoat, but underneath a livery suit with metal buttons. You'll see tomorrow."

"Go on," said Anthony.

"And the fourth was another nursemaid. She had a perambulator with a kid in it. I did her. Works in Number 17 Pierpont Gardens, South Kensington. Name's Jessie Brice. Very popular with the other servants. Been in the place six months and no one's heard anything about her leaving."

"Next?" said Anthony.

Flood said: "I only did one. Dyson had the others. Mine was the man. Works for Sir Harry Goodenough—that's the big steel man. Been in the place two months. Seems set. No discoverable question of him leaving. . . . Now Dyson's two women. One was a Fulham job—cook. The other was lady's maid to Nona Moon. Both been at the jobs three months. No talk of going."

Anthony looked at Pike. "So there!" he said. "On two ordinary days over forty per cent of the visitors to KJB are uniformed, in work and seem to have no prospect of being out of work. Why, then, do they go there? Normally servants only visit agencies to get jobs! When they're in work they try and forget the agency, often to the point of forgetting to pay."

Pike rubbed reflectively at his lower jaw. "Yes sir. Put like that, it's odd." He spoke slowly. "But it still doesn't get us anywhere. All we can say is, as I see it, that it's another queer thing to add to our list of queer things about KJB. It certainly doesn't give what I think we want—something we can take action on."

Anthony smiled. "Wait, Pike, wait!"

Pike pulled down one side of his mouth in a half-rueful smile. He said: "You're up to something, sir, I can see that. I suppose you can't tell me what it is."

"God forbid!" said Anthony. "You're too respectable. And you're paid to uphold the law as she is rather than as she ought to be."

"Antiquated," said Flood and shook his head solemnly. "Antiquated."

Pike glared at him. "As for you, you've probably broken the law a dozen times in the last six hours on these inquiries. And as for your friend Dyson——"

"Messrs. Flood and Dyson," said Flood with dignity, "are citizens of unimpeachable virtue. You're referring to two mechanics from the gas company."

Pike looked at Anthony again. "So you won't tell me what you're up to, sir."

Anthony said: "You wouldn't countenance it. And the commissioner would have a fit. Into your private ear, though, I'll whisper two little words. French words. Agents provocateurs!"

CHAPTER XV

At 10:30 A.M. on the morning of Friday, the seventh of October, Miss Rose Parfitt was being taxi-borne from the heights of St. John's Wood towards Waterloo Station. Upon Miss Parfitt's round and homely face was a broad smile like that of a child suddenly elated by an unexpected treat. In Miss Parfitt's bag was a five-pound note which she had not earned and beside the driver of the taxi was Miss Parfitt's trunk of yellow tin. Miss Parfitt was entering upon an unexpected and therefore doubly delightful holiday.

At 10:45 A.M. Miss Ada Brent entered the vestibule of Lords' Mansions, St. John's Wood. Behind her trailed a taxi driver bearing a trunk which might have been sister to that of Miss Rose Parfitt. Miss Ada Brent was of an age somewhere between twenty-five and thirty. She was of good figure and pretty, with a rather lavishly powdered face. She was neatly but soberly dressed in black.

Miss Brent had a few words with the commissionaire, who then superintended the setting down of Miss Brent's trunk and watched Miss Brent with approving eye while she paid the taxi driver.

"Fourteen A, is it?" said Miss Brent and made play with her large dark eyes.

The commissionaire said that it was 14A; that Miss . . . ?

"Brent," said Miss Brent and smiled.

"Ah!" said the commissionaire boldly and in military fashion twirled his fierce moustache and smiled. "Mine's Stubbs. Sergeant Stubbs. Eric Stubbs."

Miss Brent smiled, showing pretty teeth between very red lips.

"You'll see to my box then?" said Miss Brent and was assured and got herself to the lift and was raised rapidly to the sixth floor.

2

"I don't think you'll find it a hard place," said Mrs. Bellingham. "The man at the agency spoke very highly of you and, judging by your references, I think we'll suit each other admirably." She smiled. "I consider myself very lucky to get you on such short notice."

"Yes madam," said Miss Brent and allowed herself a civil answering smile which did not touch her eyes. "Thank you, madam."

She was then shown her room and made acquainted with her duties. She superintended the arrival of her trunk and in a space of time remarkably short was busy about her new employment, neatly and becomingly clad in black serge and white linen. . . .

She proved deft and quick and efficient and automatically courteous. She was even a good cook when occasion arose. She was, in fact, a far better servant in every way than the holiday-making Miss Parfitt. But, to a remarkable and sometimes almost abashing degree, she "knew her place." Round-faced Miss Parfitt made friends with her employers where she could and where she could not was unhappy and left them. Not so Miss Ada Brent, who never spoke unless she were spoken to and then from the wooden and soulless visage of the copybook servant. . . .

3

At seven o'clock upon the morning of the third day of her employment Miss Ada Brent switched off the bell of her alarm clock, got herself out of bed, bathed herself, dressed herself and set, with exemplary dispatch and efficiency, about her labours. By half-past eight the flat, except for the bedroom of her mistress, was ready to face the day. At nine o'clock punctually Miss Brent knocked upon her mistress's door and was bidden to enter and did so, bearing with her a tray upon which were coffee and croissants and a morning paper. . . .

Two hours later Miss Brent closed the front door behind her mistress. She was happy in the knowledge that her work was done; that her mistress would not be returning until after dinner; that she was not to wait up; that there was little chance of any of these arrangements going wrong; that all she had to do in the way of labour was to answer the telephone.

Miss Brent walked demurely along the narrow little passage and into her gleaming kitchen and sat down with her hands folded in her lap. Her face was masklike as ever. Upon a shelf over the stove, where Miss Brent could see it without turning her head, was a clock. There was silence in the flat and Miss Brent remained motionless and the minute hand of the clock moved with steady imperceptibility. . . .

It reached fifteen minutes past eleven—and a change came over Miss Brent. She always allowed a quarter of an hour, and now this one had flown. She rose and plucked the cap from her head and threw it onto the table and ran her hands through her charming mane of black hair and, whistling cleverly a melody of the moment, passed out of the kitchen and down the passage and into the drawing room. From a silver box upon the mantelshelf she took a cigarette. Lighting it, she wandered out of this room and into the dining room. Here, from a decanter and siphon upon the sideboard, she helped herself to a whiskey and soda. Glass in one hand, cigarette in the other, she sauntered back into the drawing room and sat herself down by the telephone and crossed admirably stockinged legs and lifted the receiver and worked the dial. She said after due pause:

"Harry in? . . . Well, wake him up. . . . Tell him it's Miss Brent. . . . Don't bloody well argue with me; you don't know who you're talking to. . . ." She scowled at the telephone; then smiled; then alternately sipped and smoked and composed herself to wait.

The telephone cackled.

"That you, sweetie?" said Miss Brent. "Listen, the bitch is out. The whiskey's good. I might be persuaded, if you promise *not* to behave like a gentleman, to ask you up for a visit this afternoon. . . ."

The telephone cackled excitedly.

"Listen!" said Miss Brent. "Cut that out! Until this afternoon! *Then* tell it to me!"

The telephone cackled, less exuberantly.

"No, I can't," said Miss Brent firmly. "No. You come at two-thirty—and not a minute sooner. . . . Yes, of course I've done my work. That's nothing to do with it. . . . Now listen, baby! Either you come when I invite you or you don't come at all! You don't want to get me wild, do you? Two-thirty and not a minute before. . . . And *don't* use the lift; walk straight in and come up the stairs. . . . Fourteen A. . . . S'long, ducky! And keep yourself good till this afternoon. . . ."

Miss Brent slammed back the receiver. For a moment she sat staring in apparently pleasant contemplation at the telephone; then rose and threw the end of her cigarette into the fire and finished her drink.

Whistling again, she took her glass out into the kitchen, rinsed it beneath the tap, dried it and took it back to its proper place in the dining room. And then she ceased whistling and there came over her whole demeanour a sudden change. Where she had been deliberately and pleasurably idling, she now was brisk and definite. She walked back into the drawing room with a gait as different from her hip-swaying stroll of a minute before as it was from the quick-stepped, demure walk of her servitude. Now she moved with a long and free and purposeful stride.

She went directly to the small writing desk in the corner of the drawing room. She pulled out the chair before the desk and sat herself down and began to search, obviously with some definite object, in the pigeonholes of the desk. The contents of some pigeonholes she passed over after a cursory glance but those of others she took out and set upon the blotting pad and methodically examined. It was notable that when she had finished each examination and put the papers back everything was not only in its proper relation, but the whole bore exactly the same appearance as before she had disturbed it.

She finished the pigeonholes and sat back and glowered at the desk. She said aloud:

"God damn it!" And then, on a sudden note of excitement: "Oh, p'r'aps . . ."

She opened the blotter. It was a parchment-bound thing of some sixty or seventy sheets and in the middle was what she sought—the letter over which her mistress had seemed to be so busy upon the night before but which, every indication had told Miss Brent, had not been completed.

And here it was! Seven sheets of it! And stopped in mid-paragraph. . . .

"*Bloody* fool!" said Miss Brent with ineffable scorn.

She began to read. Her eyebrows raised themselves after the first five lines of reading and when the avid eyes had devoured every line of the closely written pages she sat back in her chair and blew out her cheeks and there came from her pursed red lips a long subdued whistle of astonishment.

"And if that's not *hot!*" said Miss Brent.

4

It was on Tuesday, the eleventh of October—two days, that is, after Miss Brent had read the half-finished letter which had so much astonished her— that Mrs. Bellingham's maid answered a ring from the front doorbell, held colloquy with the ringer and then sought her mistress in the drawing room.

"If you please, madam?" said Miss Ada Brent.

Mrs. Bellingham set down her book. "Yes, Brent?"

"A man's called, madam. He says he wants to see you on very important business."

Mrs. Bellingham frowned. "See me? On important business?" She thought for a moment; then shook her head. "Did he give his name?"

"Yes madam. Jenks, madam."

"Jenks?" Mrs. Bellingham smiled. "I don't know anybody called Jenks, Brent."

"He said, madam, that I was to tell you that the business was very, very important."

Mrs. Bellingham shrugged her shoulders. "Possibly wants to sell me something. Tell him to go away, Brent. . . . Half a minute! What does he look like?"

Miss Ada Brent considered for a moment; then gave a ghost of a sniff; then said:

"Ordinary, madam. . . . Excuse me, madam, but I don't think he'll go away. I tried to tell him you couldn't see him unless he'd state his business. But he was very—well, insistent!"

Mrs. Bellingham made a gesture of irritation. "All right, Brent. All right, show him in."

"In here, madam?"

"Yes, yes." Mrs. Bellingham stood and closed her book and put it down upon a table and waited, facing the door.

The door opened. Miss Ada Brent came through it first and held it open and looked, with a sort of expressionless disapproval, at the figure which followed her. When it was well into the room she closed the door and could be heard walking back towards her kitchen.

Mrs. Bellingham faced her visitor. She saw a small man of indeterminate age whose clothes were as undistinguished as his appearance. He looked, indeed, like any lower-grade clerk beside whom one sits in bus or tube; but Mrs. Bellingham had observant eyes and saw, after a moment of scrutiny, that there emerged two peculiarities from this molecule of the ordinary: first, that the head, thinly covered with sparse sandy hair, was very large for the meagre body; second, that this head was carried with a peculiar sideways tilt which seemed to enable its owner to study faces without meeting the eyes in them with his own.

He carried a faintly dusty-looking bowler hat in his left hand and underneath his left arm was held, clamped to his side, a thin buff envelope of the largest size.

"Well," said Mrs. Bellingham, who stood with her back to the light which streamed from the four windows at the end of the pretty room.

The visitor bowed with a little sideways ducking of his head. He said: "Mrs. Bellingham, I believe?"

Mrs. Bellingham inclined her head.

"My name is Jenks," said her visitor. His voice was in keeping with his appearance: flat, monotonous and flavoured strongly with the pinched vowels and strident inflections of the City.

Mrs. Bellingham appeared to be studying him. "Yes, Mr. . . . Jenks? And what do you want?"

Mr. Jenks coughed. He murmured: "With your permission," and laid his hat, with a gesture which told of its worth to him, upon the arm of a chair. He took the envelope from beneath his arm and held it in both hands before him. He said:

"I represent a firm of—er—photographers, Mrs. Bellingham." He took two small steps towards her, still holding the envelope in both hands. His head seemed to be carried more than ever to one side and it looked, suddenly, monstrously large. It seemed to Mrs. Bellingham, who had difficulty in not recoiling, that suddenly he was reptilian.

"I am not interested in photography," said Mrs. Bellingham sharply. "I'm afraid you're wasting your time!"

The large head of the visitor was shaken from side to side; an unpleasing gesture as it remained tilted the whole time. He said:

"I think you will be interested in these photographs, Mrs. Bellingham."

He undid the clipped flap of the envelope and withdrew from it, slowly, two large square pieces of what appeared to Mrs. Bellingham, who could only see their backs, to be thin sheets of pasteboard.

He was now standing very close to her, after an advance which had been somehow imperceptible; and Mrs. Bellingham did now, indeed, step back. She said, more sharply still and on a higher note:

"I don't know what you're talking about. And I don't like your manners. Please go."

Mr. Jenks advanced again, this time with an open step. It became patent to Mrs. Bellingham, all at once, that his face was not ordinary as it had at first seemed, but was vulpine—and with a peculiarly dead-white skin. He said:

"I'm not guessing, Mrs. Bellingham. I *know* that you'll be interested in these photographs which my firm has taken." He suddenly turned the pasteboard sheets so that the face of the top one was beneath Mrs. Bellingham's eye.

She saw that the foremost sheet was glossy and that it contained what were apparently reproductions of two photographs, one higher than the other, of line upon line of a script which was familiar to her.

"Recognize the writing, eh?" said Mr. Jenks and held his hand higher.

Mrs. Bellingham did recognize the writing, and for the best of reasons. Her eyes widened and she drew in her breath with a sharp hiss. Her hand shot out but Mr. Jenks, with the air and balance of one playing a familiar game, put the things behind his back.

"No!" said Mr. Jenks. "That's naughty now!" . . .

5

Upon the following day, Wednesday, Mr. Jenks was again in the drawing room of Mrs. Bellingham and talking with its owner. He noted, with businesslike satisfaction, that Mrs. Bellingham seemed of the pallor appropriate to the interview and that the hand which kept raising the cigarette holder to her mouth was trembling.

Mr. Jenks laid his hat, this time without request for permission, in the same place that he had set it yesterday and from beneath his left arm, with yesterday's gesture, took a large envelope. He looked at Mrs. Bellingham and did not bow. He said with a most unpleasing affectation of heartiness:

"Good morning, good morning! And how are we this morning! Good girl, eh?"

Mrs. Bellingham did not speak. She was staring at him as if he were indeed a reptile. She continued to stare while Mr. Jenks went through curious evolutions which had not been part of yesterday's programme. He went past Mrs. Bellingham to the windows behind her and lifted each of the four long curtains which hung in folds beside every window. He peered behind each and dropped it and at last was satisfied. He went back to the centre of the room and stood, his big head more on one side than ever, while his eyes darted glances this way and that about the room. He crossed to the big sofa which stood diagonally athwart a corner and peered behind and underneath it. Satisfied again, he rose and, humming, crossed to the door and opened it and looked out.

He came back to take up his stand again before Mrs. Bellingham. He said, still with the noxious simulation of heartiness:

"Well, everything's nice and aboveboard! Glad to see you're a good girl. . . . Now then, let's get down to business!" He took the envelope from beneath his arm and opened it and took out the two prints which it contained. He said:

"Now then. I hope you remember what I told you yesterday. My principal's very particular about these things and never likes to handle checks—so if you'll just give me the money I'll hand over these!" He waved the prints in his right hand with a horridly jocular little movement.

Mrs. Bellingham was holding, tightly clenched in her left hand, a silk bag. Now she undid this and slowly produced from it a thick packet of treasury notes bound with an elastic band. She kept her eyes fixed, with a wide stare of fear and horror, upon the tilted face of Mr. Jenks. She made a motion as if to give him the packet; then snatched her hand back. She said, in a voice which was very different from the voice which she had used upon his first appearance:

"You're sure it's all right if I give you this two hundred now and you give me those prints——" She broke off, her throat working.

Her visitor said: "That's perfectly right. Then in thirty days from now I'll 'ave the pleasure of calling upon you again with the next lot of prints. Then you'll pay me for those . . . and so on, through all five prints, until we reach the sixth payment—which, you mustn't forget, is double, Mrs. B.—and *then* you get the negatives!"

Mrs. Bellingham opened her mouth as if to speak but no words came from it. Her tongue came out and moistened her lips and she tried again. She said at last:

"But—but—suppose I *can't* pay every time."

Mr. Jenks raised a monitory finger. He said:

"Now, now! We went into all that yestiddy. Business, Mrs. B., is business! You pay for these photographs on the date we arrange. If you don't . . ." Mr. Jenks paused. For a moment his head straightened from its usual tilt and he looked squarely into Mrs. Bellingham's blue eyes. He said: "If you don't . . . *then*, business being business, my principal will be reluctantly forced to send copies of these photographs to—well, you know who. . . ."

Mrs. Bellingham gasped. She said in a high-pitched voice:

"All right! All right! Now take this and give me those. Take it, I tell you, and give those to me!"

With his left hand Mr. Jenks took the packet of notes but with his right he held the photographs behind him. He said:

"Now don't be alarmed, you're going to have these, Mrs. B., but, business being business, I must count this little lot first."

He turned and went to the writing table at the far side of the room and set down the photographs and put the packet of notes on top of them and flicked it over with a rapid, practised forefinger.

Mrs. Bellingham stood where she was, staring across at him.

Mr. Jenks finished counting and got to his feet. He picked up the packet of notes and put them in a pocket and buttoned his shapeless coat firmly about him. He picked up the photographs and walked back across the room to Mrs. Bellingham and held them out to her and she took them in a slow and doubtful hand. He stepped back. He said:

"There you are! All square and aboveboard! You pay, we deliver the goods!"

Mrs. Bellingham stared down at the sheets of pasteboard in her hand. Without looking up she said in a voice so low as to be almost a whisper:

"Go! Please go!"

"*Certainly!*" said Mr. Jenks. "*Certainly!*" He stood for a moment regarding her, with his left cheek almost touching his shoulder; then turned on his heel and went across the room and picked up his hat and marched towards the door. Just before he reached it he turned again. He raised his voice and said:

"Don't forget, Mrs. B., I'll be round to see you again on the twelfth of next month."

Mrs. Bellingham did not answer.

Mr. Jenks turned, with his hand outstretched to open the door.

But it was opened for him. Mr. Jenks took three quick little gliding steps backwards and stood, staring, as if his feet were clamped to the floor. . . .

Mrs. Bellingham sat upon the arm of a chair and lit a cigarette.

Three men came through the open door towards him. One was a large and ponderous person in clothes which were very plain. One was a smaller, brisk young man with an air of authority and an excellent, if sober, taste in dress. One was a less emphatic edition of the first and carried with some ostentation a pencil and a reporter's notebook.

A sound came from the mouth of Mr. Jenks but it was not a word.

The second and authoritative young man walked smartly up to Mr. Jenks and tapped him on the shoulder. He said:

"I have a warrant here for your arrest upon a charge of blackmail."

CHAPTER XVI

Although only early afternoon, all the curtains of the library of 19A Stukeley Gardens were drawn and over the bookcase at the far end from the french windows there once more hung the sheet which served as cinematograph screen. In the shadows a small bald-headed man was packing tripod and projector into their neat containers.

Sheldon Garrett frowned at the now blank whiteness of the sheet. He was pale with the pallor of one who has spent recent days upon a sickbed and in the thinness of his face new lines seemed to have etched themselves deeply. He shook his head and a small sound came from his lips. Avis Bellingham, beside him, put an unobtrusive hand upon his arm. He turned his head and looked at her but did not speak.

The operator left the room, a black case in each hand. The door closed behind him; to be immediately opened again by their host, who surveyed them upon their chairs with amusement.

"You look," he said, "like two children in the ninepennies."

Garrett did not smile. He said:

"Even in dime seats one ought to get something for the money."

Anthony looked at him. "Meaning that you're no forrader. You didn't expect to be, did you?"

Garrett lifted his shoulders.

Avis said: "You've seen it four times, Tom. If the woman *had* been there you'd have recognized her at once. So——"

Garrett said: "I know, I know! I'm just a goddam fool!"

Anthony said: "I've come to cheer you." He put a hand to his breast pocket and brought it away holding a thin packet of neatly folded quarto sheets. "You might like to read this. Possible cure for those Bayswater Blues." He put the sheets into Garrett's hand. He said:

"Copy of letter to Lucas, delivered at noon. But before you read it the time has come, the sleuthhound said, to tell you many things—the first being that I am now in a position to report that, beyond the flock of social and friendly inquiries for you at Travers Hoylake's nursing home, where you're still supposed to be, there have been four anonymous telephone calls—in each case in a man's voice and emanating from various untraceable call boxes. Second, a young woman called in person this afternoon—a mysterious beauty of whom you will hear more in our next thrilling instalment. Further, you will doubtless be glad to hear that the police have at last succeeded in attaching a line to the elusive Mrs. Bellows, aunt to Janet Murch. . . ."

Garrett got to his feet. A wide smile took many of the new lines from his face. He said:

"Where is she? Have they got anything out of her? Does she know where Murch is? I always knew that if——"

Anthony smiled. "All zeal, Mr. Easy! Hold your horses. So far they only have one end of the line on the old lady, the end that begins in St. Pancras; the other appears to be in a little Midlothian village called Brodie; we shall know for certain by this evening." He pointed to the sheets in Garrett's hands. "Now get to it." He wandered across to the writing table and sat upon its edge and lit a cigarette.

Avis Bellingham moved closer to Garrett. She looked over his shoulder and with him read:

MY DEAR LUCAS: This for your files. It is a condensed record of my recent nefarious (and, of course, unsanctioned) activities in the matter of the KJB Domestic Agency and of the steps which today led to the arrest of Arthur Jenks or Smithers, Eustace Hines and Bella Barnes. With the kind and courageous co-operation of Mrs. George Bellingham the following series of events was brought about:

1. Mrs. Bellingham gave her maid a holiday.

2. Mrs. Bellingham informed the KJB Agency that she was without a maid and ordered another immediately.

3. Having been supplied with one (Ada Brent), Mrs. Bellingham, soon enough after Brent's employment, copied out—as if it were original—a letter drafted by me purporting to be for no less a person than Lord ——,[1] who is actually an acquaintance of hers and therefore (if any suspicion were aroused in the KJ Bosoms) would not look like a trap. (This letter, had it been genuine, would have been the very apotheosis of blackmailing tools, consisting as it did of nearly a thousand words of red-hot and by no means soulful passion.)

4. Having given Brent ample opportunity to find this letter, Mrs. Bellingham informed me, whereupon I had Brent's movements carefully checked, finding that she visited KJB in the evening, on Monday, the tenth instant, after closing hours. She was admitted and remained in the house for twenty minutes.

5. On the morning of Tuesday, the eleventh instant, Mrs. Bellingham was visited by a man giving the name of Jenks. He did not tell her from whom he came but proceeded to blackmail her by selling to her a photostatic copy of the letter mentioned above. Mrs. Bellingham, admirably simulating a thoroughly blackmailable woman, was then blackmailed—by instalments, as it were—Mr. Jenks arranging to call for the money on the morrow.

[1] For obvious reasons this illustrious name has to be omitted from the text.

6. Having made the above arrangements, Mrs. Bellingham notified me and I in turn got in touch with Pike.

7. This morning, acting on my advice, Mrs. Bellingham sent Ada Brent out upon an errand which would take her a couple of hours—and when Mr. Jenks called to receive his first payment he was overheard by means of a dictaphone and subsequently arrested by Detective Sergeant Sharples.

8. Brent returned to Lords' Mansions at exactly the moment when Jenks was being brought out in custody. She was in a taxi; she was seen and recognized by Detective Officer Manners, who had had the job of following her before. I also saw her, having just arrived at Lords' Mansions myself to fetch Mrs. Bellingham. Brent did not get out of the taxi. Neither Manners nor myself gave any indication of having seen her. She has, naturally enough, not returned to Mrs. Bellingham's, but she has been followed. Dyson was with me and, obtaining another taxi, managed to keep hers in sight.

I should also put it on record that I have asked you, and you have agreed, not to take any steps to arrest Ada Brent but to have her watched. I understand that one of Pike's men relieved Dyson shortly after noon and that, therefore, we can assume that Brent will be kept under continual observation.

And there, with an initialled signature, the letter ended. But Garrett, even after he had read it, remained with gaze down bent upon the last page. Avis eyed him with concern, for his pallor had given way to a dull red flush spreading from collar to forehead. She saw his eyes close and a little grimace which told of pain distort his face. She said something and moved closer to him but he held her off with outstretched hand as he looked at Anthony with furious eyes. He said:

"Take a bit too much on your own shoulders, don't you?"

"Why, Tom!" said Avis in astounded dismay.

Anthony said quietly: "Don't know what you mean."

Garrett's lips drew back a little from his teeth. "Just this: you might've got Avis hurt by these bastards! That's all! I suppose you didn't think of that! Next time try your tricks with a policewoman or some of your own family!"

"*Tom!*" said Avis Bellingham; and then was silent at a sign from Anthony, who said:

"Take it easy, Garrett. And get it straight." His tone was sober but free from anger or even tension. "You think I put Avis in danger because——"

Garrett interrupted, taking a step nearer to Anthony. His voice was harsh and his words came fast. "I know you put Avis in danger! Didn't these gorillas try and get me? Hadn't they been following me? Wasn't it likely they'd seen me with Avis and checked up on her? And then you go and get her to hire a maid through them to work a trap! Don't you see, they might've got onto it and——"

"Shut up!" said Anthony with a sudden force that made Avis jump.

Garrett glared but was silent. Unconsciously he put a hand up to his head.

"Listen," said Anthony in ordinary tone. "It *was* possible that they might connect Avis with you—*but,* if they did, all they had to do was to refuse the bait. *And* it was only a maid she engaged. *And* Dyson and Flood were in the next flat, always one of 'em there, all the time——"

"Anthony!" said Avis Bellingham. "You didn't tell me that!"

"*And,*" said Anthony, ignoring her, "the minute KJB took the bait it was perfectly certain that Avis wasn't in danger." He grinned suddenly. "So be good."

Garrett sat down suddenly upon the back of a chair. His hand was still at his head. He said after a moment:

"You're right. And I'm what's known here as a B.F. Sorry, Gethryn." Avis frowned upon him. "You ought to be ashamed of yourself, Tom!"

"Head hurts," he said. "Very pathetic case."

She smiled at him then and pulled round another chair and made him sit in it and perched herself upon its arm. He looked his thanks and spoke to Anthony. He said:

"Have to hand it to you. You're an ingenious devil!"

Anthony touched his forehead. "Thank 'ee kindly, sir."

"We oughtn't to be long now," said Garrett. "Ought we?"

Anthony lifted his shoulders. "Quien sabe?"

"What I'm thinking," said Avis suddenly, "is how sorry I am for all the poor people who've really been blackmailed. Just think what they'll go through when this case comes on!"

Anthony shook his head. "Not nearly as much as you think. We have a habit of conducting trials for blackmail without publishing the names of the blackmailees; and another habit—carried as far as is possible—of legally forgetting the errors of the blackmailees. I'll hazard a guess that the only real mud stirred up will be for Jenks and Company." He stood up. "And now, children, I leave you."

Avis looked at him. "Wait a minute! Why do we have to wait for that second instalment about the beautiful visitor at the nursing home?"

Anthony smiled at her. "Because I belong to the Detective's Union; motto: Never tell."

Avis did not smile. She said: "Well, I think it's horrid of you!" Her gaze flickered for a moment towards Garrett.

Anthony said: "Among my nobler qualities, however, is that of admitting when I'm wrong. I will now, therefore, tell you that the beautiful unknown who called at noon today at the nursing home and inquired after the progress of Mr. Thomas Sheldon Garrett was none other than Miss Ada Brent!"

They stared at him wide eyed.

"And what d'you know about *that!*" said Garrett after a pause. "What's it mean, anyway?"

Anthony walked towards the door. "God knows," he said, "and *He* won't split."

2

There was silence in the room of Sir Egbert Lucas. Lucas looked at Pike; Pike at Lucas. They did not speak. A telephone bell rang and Lucas with impatient gesture picked up the receiver. He said after a moment:

"Send him in."

Pike looked inquiry and was answered by an affirmative nod. They waited.

The door opened and through it came the long and elegant person of Colonel Anthony Gethryn. He sat upon the arm of a chair and looked from one frowning face to the other. He said:

"Problem picture. After John Collier. Police, what ails you?"

"Cheerful, aren't you?" Lucas was sour.

"Why not? Our affair marches. Or doesn't it?"

"*Marches!*" said Lucas and barked a laugh without mirth.

"Obstacles," said Anthony, offensively oracular, "are made to be overcome."

Lucas looked at him. "Oh, quite! And all is for the best in this best of all possible worlds! And so on ad infinitum and ad nauseam! What you think you're——"

Anthony interrupted. "Whoa! And tell me why woe there is."

"Pike will," said Lucas, and fell to drawing horses' heads.

Pike cleared his throat. "What Sir Egbert means," he said, "is that we've come to what you might call a dead end; a blind alley, as you might say."

Anthony said: "Might, but won't. Elucidate."

"Try French," said Lucas with bitterness. "Cul-de-sac, Gethryn!"

"Irritable," said Anthony. "Peevish. Snaps. Refuses food. A pinch of sulphur in the drinking water works wonders." He looked at Pike. "Am I seriously to understand that you can't make a case against KJB and Company? After all the trouble I've taken?"

Pike stared, "Oh, *that's* all right, sir! Our trouble is that, after netting this lot, we can't get any further with what I might call the Murch affair."

Anthony stood up. Once more he looked from one to the other of the two men. He said:

"History in the making. Tableau Number 14, English Policemen at Last Interested in Shutting Stable Doors. . . ."

"Shut up!" said Lucas savagely.

Anthony sat down. "Sorry. Seriously, though, what's the matter? Won't any of the birds sing?"

The point of Lucas' pencil broke and he threw it down on his desk with a little clatter. "That's just it!" he said. "Damn you, Gethryn: you get us all stewed up about this case and just when it begins to be interesting we're forced back to where we started."

"No," said Anthony. "No. At the beginning of the case it wasn't a case at all." Once more he looked at Pike. "What did Hines say?"

Lucas answered him. "Nothing. Wouldn't make a statement; insisted on getting his solicitors first. And the solicitors, my lad, are none other than Dunkle and Abrahams. And Hines is getting Dunkle himself!"[2]

Anthony whistled. "And Jenks? No statement from him?"

Pike said: "A long one, sir. But——"

"All hot air," said Lucas. "Two thousand words meaning abracadabra."

Anthony pulled at his lower lip. "H'mm! What about the office girl—Barnes?"

Pike shook his head. "Nothing, sir. For the very good reason that she doesn't know anything."

Lucas looked at Anthony. "Pike's dead sure of that. He wants to let her go; but I think we'd better have her up and then get her remanded."

"That young woman, sir, has no more to do with any crooked business than—than the Archbishop of Canterbury." Pike's tone was resolute.

Anthony said: "Pike knows."

Lucas said: "If I let her go I'll put a man on her." He scribbled a line or two on a memorandum form and pressed a bell and gave it to the secretary who came in answer. Pike smiled at Anthony.

The secretary went and there was silence in the room for a long moment.

"I sometimes long," said Lucas meditatively, "for the—ah—wider questioning powers of my American colleagues."

Anthony grinned. "I'd love to see you giving Master Smithers-Jenks what I believe is known as the 'works.' I can see it all. Scene One: An Underground Cell in Scotland Yard. Characters: Police Captain Egg Lucas; Snipe Jenks. Uniforms by Office of Works. The piece of hose piping used in this scene supplied by Messrs. Dunlop."

Pike, shocked, studied the shining toecaps of his boots.

"But why the despair?" said Anthony. "You've had plenty of prisoners who wouldn't talk at first. They will later—after we've got on to Mother Bellows and——"

Lucas interrupted. "Show him that wire, Pike."

Pike got to his feet and crossed to Lucas' table and took from a tray upon it a pink telegraph form. In silence, his long face seeming more lantern shaped than ever, he handed these to Anthony.

Anthony read:

A.C.I. SCOTLAND YARD—LONDON | NO TRACE ANYONE BY NAME BELLOWS IN BRODIE STOP NO RESIDENT THERE THAT NAME AND SO FAR NO RECORD ANY RESIDENT HAVING CONNECTION THAT NAME STOP IN CIRCUMSTANCES YOUR DESCRIPTION BELLOWS NOT DETAILED ENOUGH STOP IF FURTHER CO-OPERATION DESIRED AMPLIFY DESCRIPTION

S MACFARLAND
SUPT MIDLOTHIAN

[2] For many years this firm of lawyers has been a thorn in the flesh of English justice: and they do not act for petty evildoers.

"H'mm!" said Anthony and again pulled at his lower lip.

"And now," said Lucas with relish, "to quote a line from your friend Sheldon Garrett's play: 'How do you like them onions?' "

Anthony shook his head. "Not so well. What've you done?"

Pike said: "Sent a man down to Iron Court to get the fullest description we can. See if he can get a photograph; all that. As soon as he gets back I'll send MacFarland another wire."

"You know what we *should* do." Lucas' tone was reflective. "Take in this Brent woman and see whether *she's* got anything to say."

Anthony shook his head. "Not unless the third degree's come to town. Listen, Lucas: that woman, imagining herself free, is the only chance we have to get something on the Murch line quickly." He looked at Pike. "I hope to God you've got a good man on her."

"The best I've got, sir."

Lucas said: "I still think we ought to take her in. How do we know she'll lead us to anything? What she'll probably do——"

Anthony interrupted. "She's already done something, Lucas. About a half-hour before your men took over from Dyson our Miss Brent called at Travers Hoylake's nursing home, asking for news of Garrett." He looked from Lucas to Pike and back again. "You'd have got that from your own men tonight but I thought I'd be first with the news." He surveyed Lucas' expression with pleasure. "And how, if I may ask you, do you like *them* onions?"

3

Miss Ada Brent, walking briskly, came out of the arcade of Knightsbridge station. She was first of the attenuated little crowd which had left the same underground train. Miss Brent turned to her right and, evenly maintaining her pace, pursued her way. About ten yards behind her, separated from her by other pedestrians, came a man whose size and clothes, gait and features, colouring and manner were so ordinary as to render him—as indeed they had on many an eventful occasion—practically invisible.

Miss Brent bore, except in feature, no resemblance to the quondam maid of Mrs. George Bellingham. Admirably, though perhaps in some subtle details oversmartly, dressed in severely cut and laudably tailored clothes, she was a sight to give pleasure to the eye of any young man and to arouse hope in the breast of those of their elderly brethren who like their women dominant. But, on this morning at least, Miss Brent did not so much as note the many glances cast at her. The V-shaped lines of a frown drew her slender brows together; the corners of her mouth were down turned and about her eyes was a fixed look telling of concentrated thought which was difficult or unpleasing or both. Miss Brent looked worried; could not, indeed, have looked more worried even had she known that, at the moment when she turned into Stukeley Gardens, she was the subject of a conversation then taking place in the office of the active head of the Criminal Investigation Department.

Miss Brent slackened her pace. So, behind her, did the apotheosis of the ordinary, Detective Officer C. D. Fields. Although melting, as it were, into the townscape and not by look or action deviating from his paradoxically intense normality, he kept his attention upon Miss Brent and neither saw nor noticed—as why should he?—that behind him, at a distance approximately equal to his own from Miss Brent, came another man. . . .

Miss Brent was looking at the numbers upon the stone pillars of the gateways. She came to Number 19A; hesitated; seemed for a moment about to pass—and then, with a squaring of her slim shoulders, set a hand to the latch of the gate, thrust it open and marched up the path leading to the steps and the front door.

4

It was a quarter to four in the afternoon when Miss Brent set her fingers to the doorbell of Anthony Gethryn's house.

Ten minutes earlier, in Lucas' office, Anthony had got to his feet and said: "I'll be off. Pike, be a good fellah and call me if there's anything new. See you both in the morning."

"Where're you going?" Lucas' tone was not free of suspicion.

"Home," said Anthony and smiled. "Only home."

Pike said: "I'm sorry, sir. I was hoping you'd come with me to have a look around Hines's house and Jenks's place."

Anthony looked at him. "Haven't they been gone over yet?"

Pike said reproachfully: "You know me better than that, sir. Search warrants were out before one o'clock, and a couple of men have been in each place ever since. But I was going to go round now and see what they'd found. Or missed."

Lucas said: "I wish all the department were as keen on everything as Pike always is on your affairs."

Pike looked at Anthony: "You might as well come along, sir."

"I suppose," said Anthony, "I might."

And so it was that instead of reaching his house at the moment when Miss Ada Brent was talking to White, Anthony, with Pike beside him, was changing the whole course of this history by driving through Hyde Park on his way to the solemn wastes of Bayswater.

5

At ten minutes to four Avis Bellingham sat in the bay window of Lucia Gethryn's drawing room.

Lucia bent forward and laid a hand upon the arm of her friend. She said: "Avis, I think that for an intelligent woman you're a perfect idiot. Why don't you tell him?"

"I can't!" said Avis Bellingham.

Lucia said almost angrily: "That's the most ridiculous thing I've ever heard!"

Avis shook her head. "No, it isn't. Don't you understand? It's a sort of new angle on the 'love me for myself alone' idea."

"But he doesn't *know!*"

"Exactly. But suppose I told him and then found that he didn't—didn't——" Avis cut herself short. "What's the use of talking about it anyway!" She turned her head and looked out of the window and down across the front garden to the broad straight sweep of Stukeley Gardens.

Lucia said: "Listen to me! I think that if you don't tell——"

She was brought to an abrupt stop. The whole pleasing frame of Avis Bellingham had suddenly stiffened and now her right hand grasped Lucia's arm with fingers which dug painfully into the flesh.

Lucia said, staring: "What's the matter?"

Avis was looking straight down into the garden, her eyes wide with astonishment. She said as if to herself:

"It's—it's *impossible!* What on *earth* . . ." She stared fixedly down.

"What *is* it?" Lucia bent forward and herself looked down. She saw beneath her, walking slowly along the path from door to gate, the slim and smartly dressed figure of a woman. She said:

"Who is it? Tell me."

"My *God!*" said Avis and leapt to her feet and ran. She wrenched open the door with such force that the handle crashed against the inner wall. She ran for the stairs and started up them. As she ran she shouted breathlessly: "Tom! Tom!"

6

Not Anthony nor Pike nor the men who had been in each place before them found anything in the small shabby house of Mr. Hines or the soulless, cheap flat of Mr. Jenks which might not have been there and these places sheltered humdrum and law-abiding persons.

It is no matter for wonder, therefore, that Anthony, upon returning to Stukeley Gardens at a little after six-thirty, should revile with lurid and choicely patterned cursings the ill luck which had led him to miss the phenomenon of Miss Brent's visit to his house.

White, with discreetly composed face masking his admiration of what he afterwards described to friends as "No more an' no less than an epic", maintained discreet silence.

"And why the frostbitten hell," said Anthony, "nobody had enough sense to try and get in touch with me immediately is more than I can understand."

White coughed: "Excuse me, sir, that was suggested, but after the mistress and Mr. Garrett and Mrs. Bellingham had read the note the young lady left, sir, the decision was took to wait till you returned."

"Note!" said Anthony. "Where's Mrs. Gethryn?"

"In the drawing room, sir," said White—and was alone, watching the long legs of his master take the first flight of stairs three at a time.

7

The note, written in a curiously small, neat script, said:

Dear Sir:

Knowing you are interested re Arthur Jenks and therefore re a great deal more which I could tell you about, I think you might find it worth your while for us to have a quiet talk. Shall give you a ring re this later.

A. Brent.

"My God!" said Anthony and looked from the face of his wife to the face of Avis Bellingham.

"What is it? What is it?" The two women spoke in unison. Dark eyes and blue searched Anthony's face.

"*Re!*" said Anthony.

His wife said: "Beast! I thought you'd found something."

Avis Bellingham said: "What does it *mean*, Anthony? Her coming here like that!"

Her host lifted his shoulders: "Search me!"

Lucia said: "Haven't you *any* idea?"

Anthony looked at her. "Plenty. Not tidy, though. Either of you women see her?"

Lucia laughed. "I should think we did. I thought Avis had gone mad. We were sitting on the window seat there——"

"Exchanging confidences," said Avis, "all girlish."

Lucia said: "And suddenly Avis grabbed my arm and pointed down into the garden. I didn't know who it was. I only saw a girl. But Avis went hurtling out of the room and up the stairs like a mad horse. . . ."

Avis said: "I went to get Tom. I dragged the poor boy out of bed and got him to the windows just in time to get a good look at the back of Miss Brent. I had an idea, you see, Anthony. I thought it was brilliant! I thought that perhaps——"

"Miss Brent might be alias Murch!" said Anthony and smiled at her. "You think, don't you?"

Avis shrugged with a disconsolate lifting of her shoulders. "Not to much avail. As far as Tom knows—Miss Brent is Miss Brent. Her back certainly isn't the back of either of the teashop women. Not a bit like, Tom said. He was almost cross with me."

"He was, was he!" said Anthony; then broke off as the door opened to admit a White who exhibited unwonted signals of excitement.

"Sir!" said White. "A young woman, sir. On the telephone, sir. Gave the name of Brent, sir. Seems to——" He never finished his sentence. He saw, for the second time within a half-hour, how quickly his employer could move.

In 19A Stukeley Gardens there are several telephones but the nearest to the drawing room is upon the little table in the alcove at the foot of the stairs. It was, therefore, to this that Anthony ran. Above him, at the head of the

flight, White and Lucia and Avis Bellingham crowded, listening un-
ashamed. Anthony's voice came up to them clearly. They heard:

"Yes, speaking. . . . No: there's no nonsense—this is Anthony Gethryn.
. . . Yes. . . . Yes. . . . They told me that you'd called. I am sorry I wasn't
in. . . . Yes, I certainly could, or would you rather come here? . . . I see.
Give me the address then. . . . No, you needn't be in the least alarmed. I
assure you that if I say I won't tell the police I mean it! . . . Thank you.
You flatter me. . . . Are you speaking from home? Oh, you haven't a tele-
phone—very wise! . . . One-six-three Swinburne House. . . . Yes; yes I do.
Near Sloane Square. Yes. . . . Nine forty-five, then. . . . Good-bye."

The receiver clicked back upon its base.

CHAPTER XVII

There is a certain sedate and not uncomely cheerfulness about Sloane
Square; but in the environs to the southeast this quality is stillborn at best;
and in Daisy Street, which sullenly and most efficaciously belies its name, it
has not been, is not and never will be existent.

A long narrow strip of dirty greyness flanked by frowning boxes of brick
in which, presumably and unreasonably, certain human beings have their
habitation, Daisy Street, born, as it were, out of nothing, culminates fittingly
in the giant and frowning and prisonlike bulk of Swinburne House. Swinburne House is monument to the memory of a certain Joseph Hardcastle
who—perhaps self-consciously influenced by his surname—inflicted upon a
patient city half-a-dozen grim barracks known collectively as the Hardcastle
Improved Homes for Workmen. Naturally enough, no member of the labouring classes has ever been known to inhabit a Hardcastle Home; the
grim stone warrens—each with its hundreds of flats—are populated by all
manner of other types of person. Here are clerks and harlots, typists and
chorus men; Nonconformist pastors and drunken pressmen; earnest female
students; frivolous male students; struggling young doctors; lachrymose wid-
ows; parsimonious Eurasian demibarristers; retired merchant seamen; ele-
mentary schoolmistresses; and all the other thousand and one odds and ends
of that drab gallimaufry known as the lower middle class.

If Daisy Street by day—even in rare sunshine—is grey and desolate re-
minder of the calculating bitterness of civilization, by night its hopelessness
is abysmal. It is not clean enough nor rich enough to give any promise of
hope; not poor enough nor dirty enough to achieve the lurid colourings of
adventurous poverty. There is little enough life in Daisy Street during the
hours of daylight—except when the flood of City workers from Swinburne
House surges up its length to catch their morning train and down its length
to snatch their evening meal—but at night, save for belated and momentarily
high-living inhabitants of Swinburne House and an occasional empty taxi,

there is no life at all. And so it was empty and dead and dark as the long black car of Anthony Gethryn nosed into it from Sloane Square. Upon the windshield of the car a fine drizzle had begun to settle and through the open window on the driving side came gusts of that soft yet painfully penetrating cold wind in which London winters seem diabolically to specialize.

"God-forsaken place!" said Anthony over his shoulder.

Dyson grunted.

Flood said: "Beats Poplar!" He peered out of the window. "Where's the place?"

"Here," said Anthony and slid the car to the left-hand curb and switched off the engine.

The three climbed out into the wet dim silence. The sound of the car doors slamming was like artillery. Anthony shivered, turning up the collar of his dinner jacket to protect the silk.

Dyson said: "Ought to have worn a coat," and buried his chin in the upturned collar of the oil-stained burberry which shrouded his own lank form. Flood tilted back his head to look up from under down-drawn hat brim at the lowering bulk of Swinburne House. He said:

"Looks like Dartmoor."

Anthony led the way, across the black and faintly shining surface of the road, to the frowning archway of the side entrance. He halted beneath the arch, peering out across the dark wastes of the concrete square around whose four sides rose the dismal walls of Mr. Hardcastle's memorial to ugliness.

Dyson said: "What's the number?"

"One-six-three." Anthony moved nearer to the far mouth of the little tunnel.

Dyson said: "Across, to the right. Fourth entrance on the far side."

"Datas!" Flood said. "The Man Who Forgets Nothing."

"Come on!" said Anthony and, head down, walked with long strides through the archway and out into the drizzle-swept darkness of the court-yard.

The sound of three pairs of feet rang out with a muffled echo sent back fourfold by the towering, window-pierced walls. There was no other sound.

They came to the far side of the rectangle and passed along it to the fourth doorless entrance. Over this, as over its fellows, there glimmered a feeble yellow gaslight encased in a lantern of dirty glass and cheap wrought iron. Dyson said:

"One-six-three'll be on the fourth floor."

Anthony said: "Thanks. You two wait here. And be inconspicuous." His voice was pitched low.

Flood said: "What about coming with you? We could go up to the next landing and wait. We'd be nearer."

"Too near," said Anthony. "If Brent's genuine you might scare her out of usefulness."

Dyson said: "If it's a trap we're too far away here."

"You stay put!" said Anthony and was gone.

"Theirs not to reason why . . ." murmured Flood.

Dyson grunted.

They stood looking into the darkness of the entrance. To their ears came back the sound of Anthony's feet on the stone stairs.

2

Beneath Anthony's shoes the shallow stone treads were hard and the iron of the baluster rail was cold beneath his fingers. It was very dark in Swinburne House. Upon each landing was only one light; a gas jet which flared and flickered and did little else. Upon the stretches of unkind stairway was no light at all.

Anthony went on climbing. He passed the second and then the third landing, seeing little and hearing nothing save the sound of his own footsteps. He achieved the fourth landing and—if Dyson were right—the end of his climbing. He went down the little corridor towards the door over which the gas jet flared and by its meagre flame saw the number beneath it to be 167. One-six-three, then, should be upon the same side, two doors off.

It was. He peered at the door and found a small brass knocker and a bell-push. He put his thumb to the bell and pressed. From somewhere behind the door came a steady, tinny tinkling.

He waited. His ear anticipated movement from within but none came. He set his thumb to the bell again and again pressed and still was rewarded only by the burring tinkle. He took the little brass knocker between finger and thumb and with it beat a smart tattoo upon the door. There was no result save the sound itself and a devitalized echo.

"Hell!" said Anthony Gethryn and without hope tried the handle which projected below the yale lock. Surprisingly it turned in his fingers and the door gave.

There came over his lean face a new expression, curiously blent of wariness and not unpleasant anticipation. He lifted his right leg and with the sole of its foot thrust at the door. It swung inwards. He stood facing the rectangle of absolute darkness which showed where it had been. His arms hung loosely at his sides; his head was thrust a little forward in the attitude of one who listens for the faintest of faint sounds.

But no sound came. He took a step forward and stretched out a long arm and hooked its fingers round the doorjamb. They found a switch and pressed it and the rectangle was black no longer.

He went through the doorway. His eyes darted glances this way and that. He stood in a minute hallway. Facing him was an inner door. He opened it, repeating the procedure he had just now followed. Now light came from beneath a shade of distressing pinkness. It showed him a small room and plethora of unpleasing furniture whose coverings had a leering daintiness.

He threaded his way through the maze towards a door which stood ajar. He found a light switch and pressed it and passed through and was in a bedroom as unbeautifully spartan as the living room had been distressfully ornate. But, like the living room, it had no living occupant save himself. He looked about him at the furnishings. A single iron bed; a cheap chest of drawers with handles of white-chipped enamel; a tin washstand; a dilapidated towel horse; a wooden chair; across the corner by the window a green curtain dependent from a crookedly set brass rail. And, occupying nearly all the floor space, a large cabin trunk of good make and in excellent condition.

He went to the hanging curtain and pulled it aside and found clothes; many clothes—all a woman's; all good; some even beautiful. He probed among them and found nothing else. He turned back to the trunk and opened it. It was filled, to nearly a quarter of its capacity, with more clothes, obviously recently packed. He let the lid fall and stood straight and looked about him for a moment and then in two strides was back in the living room. Upon the other side of the window was another door still. He went to it and threw it open.

This time he did not have to grope for a switch. There was light already— from a single, unshaded bulb hanging from the ceiling.

He was in the narrow, cramped strip of a room which served this habitation as kitchen. And he saw, for the first time since his entrance to the flat, signs of humanity.

His eyes widened. He took two paces forward and stared down. He said aloud:

"*God Almighty!*"

3

Detective Sergeant Joseph Mather (C.I.D.) felt in his pockets for the new packet of cigarettes which should be somewhere on his person. He could not find it—for the excellent reason that it was not there. He cursed thickly beneath his breath, for the night now loomed long and black ahead of him. Outside the dark, cheerless shelter of the doorway in which he stood the drizzle was increasing to a steady fine rain beneath which the dark macadam surface of Daisy Street glistened unpleasantly. The rain did not come into the doorway but the wind—ever increasing in power and coldness —decisively did.

An all-night job and nothing to smoke! Sergeant Mather thrust his hands deeper into the side pockets of his frieze coat and tucked his chin down into his upturned collar. He glowered. He hated himself, his calling, Miss Ada Brent and Sir Walter Raleigh. He knew these jobs. Nothing would happen for the whole of a night whose every succeeding hour seemed double the length of its predecessor. And at the end of the night, in a cold and grey and probably rainy dawn, he would be relieved by another unfortunate and go back with a headache, a vile temper, a cold in the head and nothing to report.

It is to be regretted that Sergeant Mather said, aloud, a Chaucerian word. Perhaps he would have said more had his attention not been suddenly arrested by the sound of brisk footsteps which came from the courtyard of Swinburne House, whose arched entrance was immediately facing his lair.

These were beyond doubt a man's footsteps and therefore, in this particular job, not likely to be of official interest to Mather. But Mather was bored and disgruntled and ready for any distraction. He moved nearer to the mouth of the doorway and peered across the road towards the arch.

The owner of the feet came out and was for a fleeting instant visible beneath one of Daisy Street's few lamps. He turned to his left—and became simultaneously invisible and really interesting.

For as he passed out of the faint nimbus of light he ceased to walk and began to run. The sound of his feet—fast, long-striding feet—was a strange tattoo in the desolate silence.

Mather thought: "Bloody queer! Wonder what he's up to?" A fleeting wish crossed his mind that he were once more P.C. (M.X. 4321) Joseph Mather and in uniform. If he were still that Joseph Mather he could give himself something to do and keep himself warm by following the runner. But Detective Sergeant Joseph Mather (C.I.D.) must stay where he was, tobaccoless and futile, and watch a rabbit hole to see that one particular doe did not come out without being observed.

The sound of the runner's feet grew fainter; changed to the sound of walking feet; died away. Automatically Mather looked at his watch, seeing that its hands stood at ten minutes to ten.

Once more, now that there was no outside interest, his hands went to his pockets before his mind remembered that the shining, brand-new packet of twenty cigarettes was not there.

Again his lips formed the old word and again a wave of anger swept over his six feet and thirteen stone of solidity. To wrench his thoughts from tobacco he deliberately forced into ascendency the official part of his mind, trying to concentrate upon this very dull matter of Ada Brent. . . . But perhaps it wasn't so dull after all. There must be something unusual to it for the super to have put a sergeant on the job: after all, it *was* one of Colonel Gethryn's do's. . . .

He began to feel less injured. He even smiled to himself at the thought that only a few minutes ago he, unseen, had watched Colonel Gethryn and those two journalist blokes get out of the car which stood at the curb only a few yards from him and go into Swinburne House. . . .

Perhaps something might even happen tonight, thought Mather; for what else could those three be doing in a place like this if their visit weren't somehow tied up with Ada Brent? He felt better.

4

Flood stirred uneasily. He said: "How long's he been?"

Dyson grunted. "You're like an old woman!"

"I don't . . ." began Flood; then checked himself as there came to their ears, echoing curiously down the dark cold shaft of the stairway, a shrill whistle of three notes; a sound which they knew.

Dyson was first at the foot of the stairs. From a side pocket in the old burberry he pulled a bulbous electric torch and in the wavering white circle of its light began to take the stairs two at a time. On the last flight Flood caught him.

They saw Anthony's long figure standing just beneath the gas jet on the fourth landing. They went to him and he waved them through the open doorway of Number 163. He said:

"Don't kick up a row," and led the way into the living room and turned to face them under the pink light.

"Bird gone?" said Flood.

Anthony looked at him. "Yes," he said, "and no. Look!" He turned to the door of the kitchen and pushed it open and stood to one side.

Flood stopped on the threshold. He stared.

"*Christ!*" he whispered.

Dyson pushed by him and took two steps and was close to the sink at the end of the room and looking down at what was huddled beneath it. He said nothing but the lips beneath his beaklike nose pursed themselves and there came from between them a soft, long-drawn-out whistle. Flood said suddenly:

"Look out for your shoes, man!"

5

Mr. Arnold Pike, a pipe between his teeth and a whiskey and soda at his elbow, bent happily over a chess table which stood before the fire in his living room. He had left Scotland House at seven-thirty—almost a half holiday for him—had shopped successfully; dined well; exchanged blue serge and shining black footgear for aged tweed and slippers, and now was waiting with placid expectation the arrival of an old friend and older opponent in the greatest of all games.

The bell of a telephone rang shrill. Mr. Arnold Pike started, turning to stare at the instrument with a look comically compound of apprehension and annoyance. He thrust back his chair and rose. The bell continued to peal.

Mr. Arnold Pike, of 78 Poindexter Mansions, lifted the receiver and made the usual noises.

"*What!*" said Superintendent Arnold Pike of the Criminal Investigation Department.

"You heard," snarled the telephone. "Dyson here. Speaking from Swinburne House. Porter's lodge. Ada Brent's dead. Gethryn found her. . . ."

Pike said: "Murdered?"

The telephone said: "Utterly. Listen: Gethryn's up there. Flood's gone out to find your sleuth. Gethryn says come right away."

"Right!" said Pike and slammed down the receiver; then immediately lifted it again to call Whitehall-4000 and give crisp orders.

That was at five minutes past ten.

6

At thirty-two minutes past ten Superintendent Arnold Pike came out of the kitchen of Number 163 Swinburne House. In the pink light of the living room his face showed very pale.

Anthony looked at him. "Well?" he said.

The corners of Pike's mouth twitched downwards. "It takes a good bit to upset me, sir. But *that* does! Whoever did that must be the worst sort of madman."

Anthony said: "Meet Mr. Evans? Or don't you agree?"

Pike rubbed reflectively at his lower jaw. "You do jump, sir, don't you?" He murmured apology and went to the further door and through it, to return after a moment followed by two men in very plain clothes. The first carried a long thin case of japanned tin; the second a tripod and two large cases of black leather. Pike pointed to the kitchen door.

"In there," he said.

The softly heavy footsteps of the pair crossed the little room. The man with the tin case opened the kitchen door; halted with a jerk; drew a little hissing breath between his teeth and went in. His companion followed stolidly. The door closed behind them.

Pike looked at Anthony. "Now, sir?"

Anthony said: "While you and I were abortively searching the kennels of Jenks and Hines this afternoon Miss Ada Brent called at my house. . . ."

"*What!*" said Pike.

Anthony said: "Quite. Hearing I wasn't there, she left a note. Here it is."

Pike's small brown eyes were glittering. He took the paper from Anthony's hand and read avidly.

Anthony said: "She telephoned. She wouldn't come to the house. Asked me to call here at nine forty-five. On condition that I wouldn't tell the police. So I didn't. But, having a nasty suspicious nature, I brought Dyson and Flood along. Up here I couldn't get an answer. But, oddly enough, the door was on the latch. When I'd looked in the kitchen I sent Dyson to phone you and Flood to find the Yard man on Brent."

Pike said: "That's Mather. He's a good man. Where is he, sir?"

"Out," said Anthony. "Wild-goose hunting."

Pike's eyes narrowed. "Meaning, sir?"

Anthony said: "At ten minutes to ten—that's a few minutes after Flood and Dyson and I came here—Mather saw a man walk out of this catafalque into Daisy Street. He turned left and began to run like hell. Mather's official instincts were sufficiently aroused for him to note the time. A few minutes later Flood found Mather and brought him up here. Mather told me and I sent him out on a necessary goose chase. Agree?"

Pike nodded: "Of course, sir. Did he get a look at this man?"

Anthony lifted his shoulders. "For a split second. No use. Medium height; dark overcoat; ordinary build."

"H'mm!" Pike bent his head in his habitual gesture of thought; then raised it sharply as if offended by the sight of the battered brogues upon his feet. "He might have been running for a train; Sloane Square's up that way."

Anthony said: "And trains leave it every five minutes. Going both ways."

For the first time since he had been in this place Pike smiled. "He *might*'ve been running for a Hounslow, sir."

Anthony grinned. "Or exercise. Or a woman. Or just joie de vivre."

There was a small silence, broken only by the loud metallic ticking of a china clock and muffled stirrings from behind the kitchen door. Pike was the first to speak. He said:

"There's one chance. People are liable to notice a man running."

"Quite," said Anthony. "But he stopped running, Mather says, when he couldn't have been more than halfway up Daisy Street. Which was empty."

Pike shrugged his shoulders. "Well, we'll see." He looked about the room with little darting glances, his eyes resting at last upon the small writing desk. Upon its flap were some half-a-dozen tidy little piles of paper. He said: "Been busy, sir?"

Anthony nodded. "Yes; no result. Nothing but junk anyone might have."

Pike said slowly: "What time did you say it was, sir, when you and Flood and Dyson came here?"

Anthony said: "Say nine forty-two. That's near enough."

"And Mather saw this man come out at nine-fifty; eight minutes later?"

Anthony nodded. "Quite. And we didn't pass anyone in the courtyard. And I didn't pass anyone on the stairs. And Dyson and Flood stood in the doorway all the time and nobody came out of this block."

Pike said: "So it comes to this, sir: if the man Mather saw *was* the murderer he must have left this flat and this block before you got here and then hidden somewhere until after you'd passed."

"There are a thousand and one corners to this place," said Anthony. "Perhaps he was inside one of the flats in another block. As a visitor—or even a tenant."

Pike said quickly: "You said *Evans* just now, sir. D'you mean . . . ?"

Anthony shook his head. "I'm afraid not. Dyson went through the list in the porter's lodge. There's no tenant called Evans."

Pike said: "Look here, sir. If he'd only just——"

Anthony interrupted. "If you're going to suggest that he was in this flat until he heard me coming and then got out some other way—fire escape, for instance—you're wrong. I've been round the windows. There's only one that even a cat could get out by. It's in the bedroom and leads on to the fire escape; but there's undisturbed dust an eighth of an inch thick all round it."

Pike's brows drew themselves together in a deep frown. He pulled at his lower lip and looked down at the tips of his shoes. He said after a pause:

"When you found—*that*, sir"—he jerked his thumb towards the kitchen door—"how long would you say—well, it had been like that?"

Anthony said: "I'm no doctor. And even if I were I couldn't give you any definite time. But if you want a guess, no more than fifteen minutes at the outside. Some of the blood hadn't even begun to dry. . . . Where's the divisional surgeon? And who?"

"You know him, sir—Hancock. He'll be here any minute." Pike was still looking down at his shoes; still pulling at his lower lip with his finger and thumb.

The kitchen door opened and the two plain-clothes men came out, closing it behind them. The one of the tin case was first; his round face, glistening with sweat, showed pallid in the pink light. Behind him, stolid, the photographer bore his tripod and cases. Pike looked at them. He said:

"All through? How many photos, Harris?"

"Dozen, sir," said the man with the tripod. "Not counting the prints for Johnson."

Pike looked at the other. "Any luck, Johnson?"

The man patted at his forehead with a large handkerchief. "As a guess, sir, no. Plenty of prints, but seems like they're all"—he gulped—"all hers."

From just outside the room came the cracked, burring tinkle of the doorbell. Pike said:

"That'll be Doctor Hancock."

7

Charles Grandison Hancock, M.R.C.S., L.R.C.P., was bending over a steaming tin basin which stood on a corner of the gate-legged table beneath the pink light of the living room. His work over, he was vigorously washing his hands. A strong odour of disinfectant rose about him.

Anthony came out of the bedroom with Pike behind him. Hancock looked up and nodded and bent once more over the basin. Anthony sniffed at the air. He said after a moment:

"Smells good—in here."

Pike said: "Anything special, Doctor?"

Hancock began to dry his hands. "Depends what you mean. Specially messy job."

Pike said: "Looks almost like the work of a madman."

"Who's sane?" said Anthony.

Hancock nodded. He looked at Pike. "If the man who did it is mad you wouldn't notice it if you saw him. Very tidy. Until I saw that overall and those gloves lying under the sink there I was thinking he must have been saturated in blood."

Pike said: "Any indication that he's had surgical experience, as you might say?"

Hancock shook his head. "No knowledge shown beyond the ordinary. Anyone knows that if you slit a throat and rip a stomach you'll kill. Any surgically trained person would be tidier."

"Probably," said Anthony. "Not certain."

Hancock smiled, showing a flash of white teeth beneath the small black moustache. "Still the stickler," he said.

Pike said: "Listen, Doctor. What I want to know——"

Hancock interrupted. "I know, I know. Time of death. Not more than a couple of hours; not less than—say three quarters."

Pike cocked an eyebrow at him. "Nothing more definite, Doctor?"

Hancock shook his head. "Not from me, nor from anyone else who knows his job." He crossed the room towards his bag, dropped his towel into it, snapped the bag shut and stood up. "If there's nothing else . . ." he said and made brisk adieux and was gone.

Anthony looked at Pike. "Good example," he said. "Let's follow it."

Pike looked at his watch. He said: "I can't go yet, sir. Stephens and another man are coming down from the Yard. I've got to give 'em orders."

Anthony nodded. The tinny sound of the front doorbell rang sharply.

"There they are, sir," said Pike and went out into the little hallway to admit two solemn, solid men.

And that was at eleven-twenty.

CHAPTER XVIII

Thomas Sheldon Garrett could not sleep. Through his still sore head thoughts were racing willy-nilly. It was as though behind his forehead he had two treadmills of thought, both entirely different, both discomforting and, though so entirely different, each about a woman. . . .

"God damn it all to hell!" said Thomas Sheldon Garrett aloud and sat up in bed and stretched out an arm and switched on a light and began to grope in the miscellany of his bedside table.

He was searching for the little red box of opiate pills which, until this moment, he had determined not to use. It was not upon the table. In one movement he threw back his coverings, swung his legs to the floor and stood up.

He was rewarded by a giddiness so severe as to make him sit abruptly. His head whirled and his heart pounded and he felt a desire to vomit. He sat very still and little by little the seizure left him. He stood up slowly and began to cross the room towards a tall chest of drawers. He could see the red box leering at him from beside his cigarette case. And then, as he drew opposite the window, he heard the sound of a car coming to a stop before the house. Its doors slammed and he heard men's voices which he knew.

He realized, suddenly, that he did not want to go to sleep—and presently, clad in grey flannels and a sweater pulled over his pyjamas, was passing from his room to the head of the third flight of stairs.

He went down slowly and, as he went, heard voices. He crossed the hall and opened the library door and thrust his head round it. He said, a difficult smile creasing his drawn face:

"Any objection if I come in?"

And that was at eleven thirty-five.

2

"To sum up," said Anthony at one minute to midnight, "the state of the case is thuswise: Miss Ada Brent, an intimate associate of the Moriarty we are up against and whom, for want of a better name, I shall call Evans——"

"Are you sure?" said Garrett in excitement.

Anthony lifted his shoulders. "Don't get excited and don't get misled! We're not actually as near as that to Murch. I mean, we don't *know* that the murderer calls himself Evans and we don't *know,* whether he calls himself Evans or not, that he's the same man whose name was used as a threat to Murch. But everything in this unusual business points to one directing mind; therefore it's more than likely that the owner of this directing mind would be the threat."

Pike said: "No doubt, of course, he *might*——"

Anthony interrupted: "Don't be so subjunctive, Pike! If I want to call our Napoleon Evans, let me call him Evans."

Pike grinned: "Have it your own way, sir."

Garrett said: "How d'you know Brent was an intimate of—of Evans?"

Anthony said: "The proof of the pudding is in the eating. Wait for another slice and see what you get. Now then: Miss Ada Brent, an intimate associate of Evans and therefore more than the usual KJB blackmail operative, nevertheless takes on an ordinary operative's job in the case of Mrs. Bellingham. Why she does this we don't know but needn't worry about. What we do know is that Miss Brent sees confederate Jenks under arrest. She also sees that connected with the arrest is one Anthony Gethryn, whom she recognizes because—despite all his efforts—his photograph has frequently appeared in newspapers. Being quick witted, she does not get out of the taxi from which she sees all this but directs the driver to go on. Later, in at least temporary safety, she thinks things over and comes to a decision, one of the effects of which is to tell us what we have already stated, namely, that she is a confidante of Evans. She decides that she had best save her own skin by double-crossing Evans—not by going to the police, who can only turn her into king's evidence and get her a reduced sentence, but by going to the Gethryn man. He is not an official policeman but he does have the ear of authority. With him she can bargain."

Garrett said: "Wait a minute! I don't follow you. How does all this prove that she's an intimate of the Big Shot's?"

Anthony smiled. "Special allowances made for recently cracked heads. Because, my good Garrett, her decision to talk—whatever the reason behind it—must mean that she knew something *more* than the general KJB blackmail activities. Brent was, you must admit, obviously a young person of shrewdness. Therefore when she sees Jenks arrested for blackmail she knows either that (1) by degrees the police will find out all about the blackmail and KJB, in which case she has nothing to bargain *with;* or she knows that (2) Jenks, Hines and Company are so well protected by and/or afraid of Evans that they will inculpate no one but themselves."

"Ye-es." Garrett's tone was doubtful. "It's *probable.* . . ."

Anthony said: "Think, man, think! Just like that it's so probable as to be almost certain. But it's *sure* when you add to this hyper-probability the facts (a) that Miss Ada Brent called at Travers Hoylake's nursing home this afternoon and asked for you and (b) that the second and third lines of Miss Brent's note to me read something like this: 'Knowing you are interested re Arthur Jenks and *consequently re a great deal more which I could tell you about.*' "

Garrett put his elbows on his knees and dropped his head into his hands. He said:

"Of course! Of course! I'm sorry."

There was a small silence, broken by Pike. He said slowly, looking at Anthony:

"Seems to me, sir, that whenever we think we've got anywhere in this case we come to a blind alley, as you might say. What do we know now about the Murch angle, as you might call it, that we didn't know at the beginning?"

"We know it's there," said Garrett without lifting his head.

"And we know it's big," said Anthony.

"Big!" said Pike. "It's more than that, sir. But what I mean is, where are we?"

Anthony grinned. "You mean, where's Murch. Oh, where is Janet, what is she, that we poor swine can't find her?"

Pike did not smile. "Lady Ballister might've helped us: she's dead. This Brent was going to help us: she's dead. And we don't look like finding this Aunt——"

Garrett said: "If only you people had put Brent in jail!"

Anthony looked at Pike. "And *that's* what Lucas'll say. But if we had, Garrett, she wouldn't've talked. She'd have taken her chance with Jenks and Hines. Turning king's evidence would only have got her a reduced sentence. That wouldn't have appealed. She'd've gambled, that girl."

Garrett raised his head. He stared first at Anthony; then at Pike. He said: "Shan't we get Evans or whoever he is through this murder?"

Pike said: "If painstaking work will do it, Mr. Garrett, we shall. Two of my best men are in Swinburne House now, trying to get any line on Brent— habits, friends, anything. But——"

"You're not very sure," Garrett said.

Pike looked at him. "You don't want what Colonel Gethryn calls jam, do you, sir? . . . Well then, my personal feeling—my private opinion, as you might say—is that we'll get the murderer; but that it'll take us time. And plenty of it!"

"And in that time the—the Murch affair will probably be finished." Garrett was despondent.

Anthony said: "That's if we regard the murderer as our only line on Murch."

"You know," said Garrett, "what we've got to do is get hold of the old

Bellows dame. . . . We've *got* to! Don't you see that some hellish thing's going to be done?" His words were coming fast now; he sat bolt upright for the first time. "It was bad enough at the beginning. Now it's worse. At the start we just *smelt* crime—now we *know*; and know it's something bad enough to make the people behind it try to kill me and then butcher one of their own gang. And we sit here and gab and——"

Pike interrupted. He said stiffly:

"You can rest assured that the department——"

Anthony said: "Don't get official, Pike. This is Mr. Garrett's case. If it hadn't been for him . . ."

Garrett looked at Pike and essayed a smile. "Sorry, Superintendent. Didn't mean to knock. But this thing's got me. You see, I know, personally, what kidnapping means." His voice dropped; he looked down at the floor between his slippered feet. "It's—it's . . ." He checked himself. "But skip that! Just remember that this bunch tried to bump *me* off!" A hand went up to the back of his head.

Pike said earnestly: "Believe me, Mr. Garrett, I understand your feelings."

Anthony said: "Tomorrow's tasks: One: put more men onto the Brent murder. Two: ginger Midlothian about Mother Bellows. Three: go over Brent's chattels at——"

Garrett started. "For God's sake, haven't you——" He cut himself short. "Sorry, Gethryn!"

Anthony smiled. "We're not as bad as that. As far as the flat's concerned, Pike and I have been over everything—and found that it comes to nothing. What I was talking about was the trunk or what not she must have left at Avis'. We haven't got round to that yet."

Pike said: "It's being fetched tomorrow morning, sir."

Garrett said: "I don't suppose there'd be anything in it. She'd hardly take——" He broke off, staring at Anthony.

Anthony had got to his feet. A sudden frown was drawing his brows together and, although he was motionless, all ease had dropped from him. His face seemed leaner than ever and beneath the frowning brows the curiously green eyes were blazing.

Garrett said: "What's the matter?"

"What's Avis' number? Quick!"

Garrett stared, his eyes widening.

"Quick!" said Anthony. Now he was at the writing table, his hand outstretched for the telephone.

Garrett said: "St. John-4383." He found himself on his feet.

Anthony was working the dial. He said, his voice coming over the whirring little cackle of sound:

"We ought to be shot, Pike! He was running because he was in a hurry."

The dialing ceased. Pike, too, was now standing. Garrett went to Anthony's side and clutched his shoulder. He said:

"What's happened, Gethryn? Explain, for God's sake!"

"Wait!" said Anthony.

There was silence. Through it came, even to the ears of Garrett and Pike, a soft, intermittent purring from the telephone which told of a bell ringing at the other end.

Anthony listened. The purring went on. Then his face lightened. The purring had stopped, with a click which told of the removal of the far receiver.

"Hullo!" said Anthony. "Hullo!"

There was no answer.

He said: "Hullo! Hullo, there!" His voice was rising.

Garrett said: "Here, give it to me!" He snatched the instrument from Anthony's hand and put it to his mouth and shouted into it.

There was no answer.

Anthony looked at his watch. The time was twenty past midnight.

Garrett was shouting into the telephone. "Hello! *Hello!*"

Anthony said: "Shut up a minute, Garrett! P'r'aps she's out and someone else took off the receiver."

Garrett said: "Talked to her this evening. She was going to bed early. And there's the maid. Why shouldn't *she* answer if she goes to the phone!" He shouted again into the receiver.

Pike looked at Anthony. "Got another phone, sir?"

Anthony nodded. "Private line. My dressing room. Know the way?"

Pike was gone.

Garrett was shouting: *"Hello! Hello!"*

Anthony caught him by the left shoulder and swung him round and snatched the receiver and slammed it back on its hook. He said:

"Waste of time. Pike's onto Hampstead Police now. I'm going."

In three strides he was at the door. He wrenched it open and was gone.

3

It had stopped raining and the sky was clear; but the wind was now stronger and colder. And the engine of the Voisin was cold.

Anthony cursed and adjusted the choke and trod again upon the starter. The engine coughed; stuttered; burst into low, full-throated life.

The near-side front door was snatched open. Gasping, Garrett scrambled into the car.

"Damn fool!" said Anthony. "You're ill!" But he leaned over and clutched at the still open door and slammed it shut. He said:

"Hold tight!"

The black car shot down the length of Stukeley Gardens and swung right, with a pull which sent Garrett's body lurching against Anthony's shoulder, into the broad stream of Knightsbridge itself.

Garrett pulled himself upright. The needle on the speedometer jerked to fifty . . . sixty. . . . Past Garrett's painfully straining eyes flashed the bulk of the Hyde Park Hotel. He shouted:

"The Park, man! The Park!"

But by the time the words had left his mouth the car was nearing the yellow nimbus of light opposite St. George's Hospital which guides the belated to the coffee stall known as the Junior Turf. Anthony said out of the corner of his mouth:

"Park's shut."

The coffee stall was passed; then the double gates of the Corner. The Voisin swung left into Park Lane. Garrett was hurled against the door at his left shoulder. He pushed himself upright. He said, almost shouted:

"What d'you think's happened! Tell me!"

Anthony was driving almost on the crown of the empty road. On the left the black railings of the Park streamed by. On the right loomed the dark mass of Dorchester House. From the turning just past it there suddenly shot out, right across the Voisin's path, a yellow taxicab.

Garrett involuntarily closed his eyes. A short breath hissed between his teeth and his right arm came up to guard his head. He felt the car swing violently under him and once more was thrown against the door. His ears were filled with the screaming of tortured tires. Suddenly, beneath him, came a bump which straightened his body and threw it off the seat. Then a lurching twist to the right, another bump—and once more smooth progression.

Garrett became aware of the arm across his eyes. With a little unreasonable pang of shame he took it down. He heard Anthony's voice. It said:

"Close one! Lucky the curb wasn't high."

And now they swung left, between the Marble Arch and the Park itself and were on the broad straight thoroughfare to Notting Hill Gate.

The needle on the speedometer dial touched seventy and passed it; the engine began to give out that low humming note which she achieves at high speeds. Then, as Lancaster Gate drew near, Anthony's foot was transferred from accelerator to brake. Garrett said:

"For God's sake, Gethryn! Tell me what you think has happened."

"Hold tight!" said Anthony.

Garrett clutched at the window and held himself steady while—it seemed on two wheels—the car swung right into Westbourne Terrace. Anthony's foot came down again upon the accelerator. In the comparative darkness of the terrace his headlights cut a white swathe. Garrett said:

"For God's sake, Gethryn! D'you think that devil has——"

The rasping, two-noted blare of the Voisin's klaxon drowned his next two words. They were approaching, at fifty miles per hour, the last cross street before the Marylebone Road, and across the blackness of the macadam, from the right-hand mouth of the cross street, was shining a single approaching headlight. Steering obliquely to his left, Anthony slammed his right foot down. The car seemed to throw itself forward. It flashed with an actually safe but apparently perilous yard to spare across the path of the owner of the headlight—a motor-police cycle and sidecar.

The Voisin roared on; but from behind her came the sudden and infuriated wail of a police siren.

"We're off!" said Anthony.

Over the Canal Bridge . . . then right . . . then left . . . then right again and up to Westbourne Grove. . . . Left and on the straight again. . . . The needle on the speedometer hovered over the eighty mark. . . . The two-noted klaxon blared continuously. Behind, the police siren screamed its rage. . . . A bad tenth of a second with a van without a taillight. . . . A worse fifth with a careless or legally minded taxi driver. . . .

Then the long wall of the Lords . . . a squealing of brakes. . . . A sliding to the curb opposite the entrance to Lords' Mansions.

Anthony thrust himself out of the car, slamming its door behind him, the siren rang once more in his ears and he was bathed in the white flood of a single headlight. A deep, irate voice shouted at him. Coming through the sound of the voice was that of the far door of the Voisin slamming and those of men's footsteps as Garrett came round the front of the car at a stumbling run and two bulky, dark-clad, flat-capped forms detached themselves from cycle and sidecar and ran for their quarry.

Anthony, already halfway up the flagged walk which joins the portico of Lords' Mansions to the pavement, shouted back over his shoulder. To Garrett's ears, in which the blood pounded with a sound like the hammer of Thor, came two words: ". . . explain . . . card . . ." And at Garrett's feet, which persisted paradoxically in feeling as if they were made of lead and yet treading upon air, something landed with a little soft plop.

4

The flat of Mrs. George Bellingham is upon the second floor of Lords' Mansions. Anthony, knowing that there was no lift attendant after eleven at night, took to the stairs. As he reached the first landing he heard from beneath the sound of the swing doors and heavily shod feet running along the tiled vestibule.

He passed no one in his ascent and there was no one upon the second landing. He ran down it and with long strides to Avis' door. It was smugly closed. Behind its ground-glass, curtained upper half no light showed. He tried its handle but it did not give. With his left hand he beat a sharp tattoo with the knocker; with his right thumb he pressed the bellpush. But he did not wait for answer; knock and ring had not been appeal but admonition. His hands came away from knocker and bell. In one movement they had unbuttoned and ripped off his dinner jacket. He dropped it over his right hand, clenched this into a fist and wrapped about it, in a thick bundle, the soft black cloth and softer black silk. He thrust with a short stabbing punch at the pane of glass nearest to the lock. The tinkling crackle of the breaking glass mingled with the sound of heavy boots racing up the stairs.

He shook the coat from his arm and it fell and lay like a black stain upon the carpet. He thrust his shirt-sleeved left arm with swift caution through the broken pane and groped with long fingers and found the knob of the lock and turned it.

The door opened. He thrust his way into the darkness of the little hall.

Inside, the memory of his only two visits to this place serving him well, he reached for the wall to the left of the door and found a light switch and pressed it. Above his head a softly shaded amber light jumped into life and flooded down upon a scene of perfect order. Nothing was out of place. To his right the drawing-room door stood closed; and closed, too, were all the other doors in the corridor which stretched away to the left.

The heavy running feet pounded close outside. The door creaked again and there came a fresh little tinkle of broken glass as it moved. Anthony swung round. He saw a policeman but not the policeman he had expected, for here was no motorcyclist but a helmeted sergeant with beads of sweat glistening on a round and red but shrewd-eyed face. Anthony sighed relief. He said sharply:

"From Hampstead Station? Superintendent Pike's orders?"

A hand went up to the helmet in salute. "Yes, sir. Colonel Gethryn?" The voice was jerky from recent exertion.

Anthony said: "Yes. Look in all the rooms on the right. Watch your step!"

Again the hand went to the helmet in salute. Anthony made for the drawing-room door and threw it open. The room was dark. He reached his arm round the door for a light switch and found it after groping. Into view sprang another scene of complete and charming order. He turned and went back into the hall. From the first door upon the right—that of the dining room—the uniformed figure of the sergeant came out. He looked towards Anthony and said:

"All right in there, sir."

"Get on! Get on!" said Anthony and himself ran to the first door upon the left.

What room this led to he did not know. He threw it open. It was dark like the drawing room. He reached his arm round the doorjamb but this time his groping fingers found no switch. He took a step forward, then checked himself. To his ear had come two sounds—or rather, one group of sounds and one particular sound. From outside the flat two or three more pairs of heavy running feet; from inside the flat, in the sergeant's briskly hoarse voice, words whose shape he did not catch but whose tone brought him back into the passage in a leap and sent him running towards the second door upon the right. This stood open and light streamed from it.

He was at it in two strides. A hand on the jamb, he swung into the room.

He saw the sergeant kneeling beside an inert, prostrate bundle which he saw, as he took a step forward, to be that of a woman.

She was lying on her back. She was fully dressed for the street in clothes of cheap but tidy black. A round blob of a face, the eyes closed, was pallidly upturned to the ceiling. The arms were flung wide. One leg was twisted underneath the body. Behind the head, still somehow attached to a mass of untidy but incongruously beautiful brown hair, was a hat of grey-black felt. From the right ear a thin chain dangled, at its end a pair of pince-nez from which broken glass had fallen to the floor and lay in small glittering stars upon the carpet.

The sergeant turned his head and looked up at Anthony. He said:

"She's alive, all right, sir. Had a bad crack on the head though." He pointed to a place on the forehead where a blue bruise lay like a shadow.

From outside came the creaking of the front door again; footsteps; a murmur of male voices; then Garrett's, which shouted:

"Gethryn! Gethryn!"

"Here!" called Anthony.

The sergeant, still on his knees, turned and pointed to the corner of the room farthest from the door. He said:

"Look there, sir!"

But Anthony was already looking. Pulled out from the corner, its lid gaping, was a tin trunk and all around it, in appalling disarray, lay what had obviously been its contents. The sergeant said:

"Someone in a hurry, sir?"

Anthony turned back to the door. He said over his shoulder:

"Put her on the bed. Then go through the rest of the house and come back to her."

He went through the door and swung to the left and was brought into collision with a large blue-clad man in the gaiters and gauntlets and flatcap of the motor police.

" 'Ere!" said a bass rumble. "What's *your* business?" A gloved hand which seemed in itself to weigh a stone clamped itself upon Anthony's shirt-clad left shoulder.

Anthony's feet did not move; nor did his body. But his right arm came up and across, and its open, rigid hand brought its edge down in a short snapping blow upon blue-covered biceps. . . .

"*Urch!*" The rumble was, almost comically, now more baritone than bass.

"Out of my way!" said Anthony and thrust with a shoulder and was past.

The narrow corridor and the slightly widening rectangle which formed the little entrance hall seemed full of men. Under the amber light stood another motorcyclist constable. His thumbs were hooked into his belt and his feet planted wide apart and beneath the visor of his cap his long, boyish face showed blank and gaping and bewildered. Beside him, just entered, was a man in shirt and trousers; hair tousled from sleep. He, too, was gaping. From the doorway of the first room into which the sergeant had looked came Sheldon Garrett. He saw Anthony and stopped. He swayed and leant against the doorjamb. He said:

"Avis! She there?" His voice was harsh and laboured. He made a gesture towards the farther part of the corridor.

Anthony shook his head. "Hold on!" he said and stepped past Garrett into the room. A woman's bedroom, delightful as its owner.

But its owner was not there.

The room bore signs of recent occupancy. There was no counterpane upon the bed. Upon its left-hand side was a pillow which still bore the impression of a head, and blankets and sheets were thrown back. It was a bed which recently had been inhabited.

Anthony took Garrett's arm and drew him into the room and thrust him gently backwards into a chair. The edge of the seat took the man behind the knees and he sat. Anthony said:

"Answer my questions."

"Yes," said Garrett. His voice was flat and dead and seemed to come from somewhere deep within him. He looked at Anthony with eyes which seemed to be set inches back in his skull.

Anthony said: "She told you she was going to bed early. When was that?"

The flat voice said: "Around eight-thirty. She said she was going to bed right away."

Anthony said: "There's a woman knocked out along there—in the maid's room. Short. Fat. Middle thirties. Sunday-go-to-meeting clothes. Lots of brown hair. Glasses. That the skivvy?"

"Yes. Name's Parfitt." Garrett stared unwinkingly.

Anthony said: "One more question. Is this Parfitt's usual evening off?"

Garrett put a hand up to his head, passing it in a squeezing movement across his forehead. Then, suddenly, he jumped to his feet. He said:

"What the hell am I doing, sitting here like a dummy!" He turned and took a quick step towards the door.

Anthony caught him by the shoulder and swung him round. "Damn you! Do as I say! This Parfitt's usual day off?"

"Yes," said Garrett. "And now, damn *you,* let me go!" He wrenched his shoulder free.

Anthony became aware that the murmur of voices from the passage had suddenly ceased. Now one voice spoke, a crisp, authoritative voice which he knew.

Pike was in the passage. Behind him were the gaping motorcyclist and the man in shirt and trousers. Before him were the other motorcyclist, still rubbing ruefully at his right arm and, in the doorway of the servant's room, the sergeant. Pike was holding in his hands the thin morocco pocketbook which Anthony had thrown at Garrett's feet outside the building. Pike was saying:

"Lot of dunderheads! You *saw* this!" He waved the pocketbook at the arm-rubbing giant. "Inside it are Colonel Gethryn's own card *and* his special card from the commissioner! . . . Now get busy." He pointed at the arm-rubber. "Go get a doctor for the woman, quick!" He turned to the man in shirt and trousers. "What're you? Caretaker? Yes. . . . Get out into the corridor and wait. Don't go away." He turned on the gaping motorcyclist; then on the sergeant. Definite, brief orders came from him in a steady stream. . . .

Garrett came out of the bedroom, turned to his right and, pushing past the staring sergeant, blundered down the passage.

Anthony came out of the bedroom. He looked at Pike.

"Good man!" he said.

And that was at twelve forty-five.

CHAPTER XIX

By fifteen minutes past one much information had been brought to Pike in Avis Bellingham's dining room. He collated it—and found himself possessed of nothing. No one had seen Mrs. Bellingham since seven in the evening, when she had come in. No one had seen or heard any visitor to Mrs. Bellingham's flat. The caretaker, communicating over the telephone with Sergeant Stubbs, the day commissionaire, had discovered that Rose Parfitt had been seen to leave Lords' Mansions at half-past four in the afternoon but beyond this no one knew anything about Miss Parfitt, who still lay unconscious upon her bed, though now with a doctor tending her.

And no one of the dozen or more friends of Mrs. Bellingham to whom Garrett had telephoned had seen or heard of Mrs. Bellingham since the morning.

Pike, frowning, sent subordinates upon yet more errands of investigation, in none of which he had an instant's faith. In the servant's bedroom Dr. Harold Porteous bent over the inanimate person of Rose Parfitt, while behind him, in the corner by Ada Brent's open trunk, Anthony Gethryn knelt and probed ceaselessly into its past and present contents.

In the drawing room Sheldon Garrett, a white-faced automaton, sat with a telephone list before him and steadily called number after number. . . .

2

At precisely twenty minutes past one Avis Bellingham drove her car into the garage of Lords' Mansions, backed it neatly into place, left it and entered the building by the basement door. She had, indeed, gone to bed before eight o'clock. But by eight-thirty she had realized that she was wrong in assuming that bed was the place in which to think. She had, accordingly, risen at eight thirty-five and gone, in lone innocence, to a cinematograph theatre and thence, with an acquaintance encountered in the lobby after the show, for a drink at the Berkeley.

At twenty-two minutes past one she halted to face the front door of her flat and saw the broken pane of glass by its lock. The fingers which had been fumbling in her bag for a key withdrew themselves, for she saw that the door was not latched. Bewilderment making her eyes even larger than was their habit, she pushed at the door with a tentative little thrust. It gave. She became conscious of a murmur of male voices from the direction of her dining room. She frowned. She squared her slim shoulders beneath their covering of soft grey fur and marched into her little hallway. The voices from her left were clearer now. Her ear seemed to detect a familiar tone but before her mind could dwell upon this familiarity and name its owner she heard, through the half-open door of her drawing room, the rattle of a telephone dial and then the voice of Sheldon Garrett. It said:

"Mrs. Marshall? I'm sorry to disturb you but it's imperative that I should know whether Avis Bellingham . . ."

Avis Bellingham stared at the drawing-room door. The voice droned on. She did not hear all its words but the flat, deliberately emotionless tone made clear to her puzzled mind the fact that Tom thought that something had happened to her. . . .

She hurried to the drawing-room door and through it. Garrett sat with his back to her at the little table which bore the telephone. He was saying:

"You're *certain?* You see——"

Avis put a hand on his shoulder.

"Tom!" she said.

Garrett turned. As he turned he got to his feet. The light chair upon which he had been sitting fell to the carpet with a soft crash. In his hand the telephone cackled in agitation. His eyes, dark rimmed in an ashen face, widened in a stare of unbelief. The blood suddenly rushed darkly to his face; only to drain from it as quickly as it had come.

"Tom!" said Avis Bellingham again and took a step towards him and put a hand upon his arm.

There came an odd, constricted feeling into Garrett's throbbing and so recently maltreated head; his ears were filled with a roaring sound and everything in the sight of his staring eyes began to whirl about him.

He took a step towards the vision which had spoken to him. The telephone, cackling no longer, somehow slipped from his hand. It hit the leg of the table with a crash. He took another step forward and felt himself falling. . . .

3

He felt something wet and cold on his forehead and something wet and burning on his tongue. He opened his eyes but the light sent a stab of pain through his eyeballs into his head and he closed the lids again. There was a confused rumbling of voices all about him. He lay still and fought with his mind and steadied it until his hearing cleared. He heard, first, a man's voice which he did not know: a deep, slow voice with precise enunciation. It was saying:

". . . not to be wondered at. If the concussion, as you say, was serious, then all this excitement and agitation would be bound to leave——"

And then Avis' voice. "But, Doctor, there's no real damage, is there? I mean this won't——" Her voice broke off.

Then the deep, precise voice again. "Madam, there is nothing which cannot be rectified by that best of all specifics, a day in bed."

Then Avis again, only this time with a slightly different sound, as if her head were turned in another direction: "Anthony! Why did you let him——"

Then another well-known voice. "What was I to do, throw him out of the car? If I hadn't brought him he'd either have gone off his head waiting or——"

Garrett said without opening his eyes:

"Or done something equally damn silly. I'm—I'm all right now."

Cautiously he raised his eyelids, veiling sight with their lashes so that the light did not send that stabbing pain back into his head. He looked up into Avis' face, now as white as his own, and saw eyes which were blue pools of pity and perhaps something else.

He closed his own eyes and felt soft hands on his forehead.

4

At twenty-five minutes to two the doctor pronounced Rose Parfitt as able to answer questions—"as few as possible, you understand, gentlemen, *please!*"

Rose Parfitt was luxurious in her mistress's bed, but shaken and nervous and filled with a feeling of pity for Rose Parfitt. Pike and Anthony surveyed her with compassion and friendliness and determination.

"Now, Rose," said Anthony, "we want your help."

"Y-yes sir." Brown eyes looked up at him from beneath snowy bandaging.

"And we don't want to bother you"—Anthony's tone was nicely blent of sympathy and command—"but we must know whether you saw the person who struck you."

"O-oh, sir!" The voice trembled and the sore head moved a little. "O-oh, sir!" Words ceased and a whimpering began.

Anthony sat upon the edge of the bed and picked up a pudgy, work-roughened hand and patted it. He jerked his head in an infinitesimal gesture and Pike withdrew softly from the Parfitt field of sight.

"Now, now," said Anthony. "We know how you feel, Rose. But you've got to be a brave girl and help us."

The eyes fixed themselves upon his with almost canine worship. She said:

"Y-yes sir. I—I did see 'im. For a flick of a second like. I—I come in all unexpectin' like an' goes along to my room an' opens the door an'—an'—o-oh!" Once more she began to whimper.

Anthony patted the fat hand again. "That's a good girl, Rose. That's a brave girl. Now take your time and tell us and we'll go away and the doctor'll give you something to give you a good sleep."

"Y-yes sir. Well, I opened me door an' thinks, 'ow did the light come to be on? An' then I 'ears a movement and out from behind the door comes a man an' 'e 'as something in 'is 'and an' ups with it an' 'its me." The voice began to falter; then grew stronger again as Anthony resumed the patting. "An' that's all, sir."

Anthony said: "Thank you, Rose. Thank you very much. We'll soon be out of here now. Just tell us what this man looked like. Just anything that you remember, however little it is. Anything."

The head moved a little. "There—there wasn't anything, sir. An' it was only the flick of a second before—before——"

Anthony patted. "I know. I know. Tell you what, Rose, I'll ask some questions. Then you won't have so much talking to do. Good idea, that, isn't it? . . . Now, was he a tall man?"

"No sir."

"Was he short?"

"No sir."

"I see—medium. Was he heavily built?"

"N-no sir. About—about medium, sir."

"I see. Did he have light clothes or dark?"

"Dark, sir. Oh, an' I remember 'e 'ad an overcoat on."

"Hat on, too, Rose?"

Her eyes flickered shut while she thought. "N-o sir. No, 'e didn't."

"Good girl, Rose. What colour was his hair?"

"No special colour, sir. Sort of—sort of—*medium.*"

"I see. Now I'm nearly finished, Rose, so think hard for this one. Do you remember anything particular about his face? Anything at all, Rose?"

The eyes regarded him pitifully; then once more were closed in a not undramatic struggle for thought. She said at last:

"No sir. Not anything at all, sir."

"Did he wear glasses?"

"No sir. 'Is face was—was—sort of *medium,* sir. I'm sorry, sir, but it doesn't seem like there was anything about 'im *to* remember, sir. I—I don't even know as I should know 'im again if I was to see 'im, sir. I——"

"It's all right, Rose. It's all right." Anthony patted the hand again and stood up. He looked at the hovering doctor and nodded and bade Rose good night and went out with Pike at his heels.

In the passage they looked at each other.

"Nothing there, sir." Pike drew down the corners of his mouth.

"*Medium!*" said Anthony. "Well—back to the luggage." He led the way to Parfitt's own room and once more stood over the open trunk which had been Ada Brent's and looked down at it and the surrounding litter. Pike said:

"It's all very well, sir, but we aren't getting anywhere." He pointed to the trunk. "You've been through it already."

"Very perfunctory search," said Anthony and knelt. "If at first you don't succeed, Pike, pry, pry, pry again!" His head and shoulders were now so deep in the great box of tin that his voice came hollow and booming.

Pike said: "Can't see how we'll get anywhere this way, sir. We know this man—this Evans—came here to look for something. But we don't know what he came to look for—and either he found it and took it away with him or he didn't find it. But in any case we're none the wiser."

"Wait!" said Anthony and got to his feet, holding in his right hand a little collection of papers clasped together at their corner by a fastener of bent wire. He said:

"Taffy was a Welshman: Evans is a thief. Evans came to this house and stole . . . Let's see whether we can't find out what he did steal!" His long fingers turned over the papers, disclosing a cheap dressmaker's bill for fourteen and elevenpence; a receipt from the KJB Agency for nine shillings; a printed notice from the Hammersmith branch of the Carnegie Library to the effect that the return of a work apparently entitled *Lady Wickmansworth's Folly* was much to be desired; a picture post card, with no message on it, of a particularly dreary stretch of the front of Torquay and an advertisement of bathing suits torn from a Sunday paper.

Pike frowned. Had his companion been any other person than Anthony Gethryn he would have sniffed. But he went on looking. Anthony had ceased to flick the papers over and now something was visible that had been hidden before—a small, jagged-edged piece of paper, wedged under the clip.

"Ah!" said Pike and made a movement with his hand.

"Yes," said Anthony. He slipped the clip sideways and delicately picked out the scrap. It was of cheap, coarse paper; the sort of paper which will take only printer's ink or pencil. It was about an inch along its top, half an inch wide at its broadest and tapered down to a point where the tear ended. At the right-hand edge of the top was a mark in print—possibly the down-stroke of a capital letter.

"Here is a thing," said Anthony. "And a very pretty thing!" He turned his head to look at Pike. "What the hell is it? I should know. It tells me that I know. But I'm damned if I do."

Pike took the scrap between finger and thumb and looked at it this way and that and finally held it up to the light. He said at last:

"In such a hurry that he tore it." He looked at Anthony. "That's about the first bad slip he's made, sir."

"It's only a slip if we find out, quickly, what this is." Anthony's finger pointed to the morsel of paper.

Pike said: "Some sort of cheap notice. In the morning, sir, we'll get Summers onto it. He'll find out."

Anthony groaned. "That's too late." He looked at Pike and a sudden gleam came into the green eyes. He said softly:

"You know, we're not thinking. Because we're hurrying Evans, we mustn't let him hurry us. Think, bobbie, think!"

Pike said, smiling a little:

"Thinking won't do much good, sir; not at this juncture, as you might say. What I mean, sir: *after* Summers has found out what this is"—he waved the scrap of paper— *"then's* the time to start thinking. Until then— well, we *might* hear something from Scotland about the Bellows woman."

Anthony did not seem to be listening. A frown was drawing his eyes together. He said in the voice of a man talking to himself:

"Vile paper which could only take pencil or print . . . A form of some kind . . ."

Pike looked at him intently: he knew this voice; he said nothing. Anthony said:

"Intrinsically of no possible value. But he did one murder and half another to get it . . . it's extremely important to him but it can't be in *itself*. Ergo, it *stands* for something important."

Pike's small brown eyes were bright now, like a bird's. He said:

"By gosh! A safety-deposit ticket, by jing!" The schoolboy oaths—a trick of his when excited—rang with all the brazen fervour of profanities. Again he held the slip to the light.

Anthony took it from his fingers. "Possibly, yes. But the vile quality of the paper is much more——"

"By *cripes!*" said Pike. "Cloakroom ticket! 'Scuse me, sir!" He brushed past Anthony and reached the door in two strides and was gone.

Anthony followed leisurely. By the time he crossed the threshold of the drawing room Pike was already talking on the telephone, to the Yard. On the sofa lay Garrett, his head propped by cushions; on one of the arms to face him sat Avis Bellingham. There was more colour now in Garrett's face and he wore the sheepish look of a man who has been so supposedly feminine as to faint.

Pike was saying to the telephone: ". . . yes. Now: get men on this right away! Understand? At *once!* Inside an hour I want a specimen cloakroom ticket from every railway company with stations in London."

Garrett looked at Anthony. "Cloakroom ticket?"

"Baggage check," said Anthony. "That's what Evans took from Brent's trunk . . . I think."

Pike said to the telephone: "*I* know they're shut. But I want a specimen from every line inside an hour. I'll be in my office by then." The tone, most definitely, was a superintendent's.

Anthony grinned. "They'd better get 'em!" he said to no one in particular.

5

It was some minutes after three when Anthony, once more in his own house, answered a telephone whose ringing was insistent.

Pike's voice came to him. "We've done it, sir!" The tone was one of sternly suppressed elation.

"Congratulations!" said Anthony. "What is it?"

"A corner off a London and Great Eastern cloakroom ticket," said the telephone.

Anthony said: "And so . . . ?"

The telephone spoke at length.

"Yes," said Anthony. "Yes. Neat arrangement. Very good indeed, Pike. . . . There's one thing, though. Make absolutely sure that each man understands that he's not to arrest the person presenting the ticket. Just follow him, and then——"

The telephone interrupted. "I made sure of that already, sir. One man inside; one out. They follow the person presenting the ticket; they don't take any further steps without calling here."

"Good!" said Anthony and meant it.

CHAPTER XX

Despite the needlecraft of his mother his father's trousers were still too large for James Widgery, which explains why, at a quarter of nine on the morning of Thursday, the thirteenth of October, James fell heavily to the pavement at the corner of a street in Lambeth.

The morning was cold, with a grey sky and an east wind which hurt. And the pavement was hard. James Widgery, for all his thirteen years, began to weep.

A hand came from nowhere in particular and helped James to his feet. He continued to blubber and looked up at the owner of the hand and saw a man and heard a voice which said:

"Hurt yourself, sonny?"

James, who had stopped blubbering, began to blubber afresh. He scented consolatory copper.

"Not 'arf!" said James through tears.

The gloved hand of James's rescuer went into the pocket of his overcoat. It came out again holding a silver coin which glittered.

James, having caught his breath, produced heart-rending sobs.

"You could earn this," the man said. "And another. They might make you feel better."

"Gotter go t' school," said James Widgery but without conviction.

2

James Widgery did not go to school. Instead he appeared—at nine thirty-five upon this cold, grey morning—outside the entrance to the East Dulwich station of the London and Great Eastern Railway. One hand was busy in holding up the trousers of Albert Widgery; the other was firmly clutched about a small slip of paper in the right-hand pocket of these trousers.

He looked up at the sooty façade of the station; then made his way through the central archway into the dingy, acrid-smelling booking hall. To his right was a line of ticket windows. To his left, upon the far side of a heterogeneous row of telephone booths and slot machines, there showed a lighted recess over which appeared the word, in great yellow letters, Cloakroom.

Towards this James strode as manfully as he could in his hampering garments. He halted with his chin only a few inches above the outer edge of the counter and whistled between his teeth to attract the attention of the sallow-faced man behind it. He produced from the right-hand pocket of the trousers a hot and grimy paw and threw down its content upon the dirty, polished wood.

The luggage clerk surveyed James without approval. His nose wrinkling, he picked up the crumpled paper slip and unfolded it. He looked at it for a long moment with a lack of facial expression wholly admirable in the circumstances. He said sourly to James:

"Jest a minute," and was gone, disappearing behind baggage-filled racks.

3

At exactly twenty minutes to ten James Widgery, still holding up his trousers with his left hand, but now carrying in his right a flat leather portfolio of a certain quiet elegance, made his way across the station courtyard towards the bus stop outside the railings. He whistled as he walked. There was in him—despite the certainty of a thrashing for having played truant from school—a great glow of satisfaction, for did there not repose in his pocket a whole half crown? And would there not, when he had delivered the little bag to the gentleman, be another added to it!

Five whole shillings! James caught his breath and ceased to whistle and passed out of the courtyard and took his stand on the curb to await a west-bound bus.

As he did so a young and burly man came out of the station and strolled, with every appearance of leisure, over the way taken by James. As he walked he read, absorbedly, a *Racing Special*.

A bus came. James climbed inside it and, finding it practically empty, ensconced himself luxuriously in a front seat. He congratulated himself that, having still twopence of his mother's shopping money in his pocket, he need not, as yet, break the half crown. He sat forward, the bag balanced on his bony knees, and looked out of the window with the alert curiosity of the gamin. He did not know—nor would he have cared if he had—that the man who had just entered the bus and was now seated by the door reading a racing paper was what his father would have termed a "busy."

The bus began to move—and just as it did so another passenger swung himself aboard; a large, thick-looking man in blue serge. James Widgery did not know—nor would he have cared if he had—that here was yet another "busy."

4

Strictly speaking, the fare from the East Dulwich station of the L. & G.E.R. to Piccadilly Circus is fivepence. Wise, however, to the ways of conductors, James made the journey for less than half of this sum. At Swan and Edgar's he alighted and, after dealing with the refractory trousers, dived like a rabbit down the more southerly of the stairways to the tube station. Close on his heels, but exhibiting no interest in him, came the two men of the bus trip.

Although the time was not yet ten-thirty in the morning there were, as always in this great underground clearinghouse of humanity, many people hurrying this way and that, upward and downward, round and about—with all the fussy speed and apparent aimlessness of ants. James Widgery, at the foot of the stairway, turned to his right and, swinging the incongruous portfolio, began to walk briskly round the circle. Behind him Detective

Officers Frawley and King quickened their steps. Though not now attempting to conceal their companionship, they did not speak, each occupied in keeping in view the small, red, capless head of their quarry.

James moved through the thin crowd with the speed and precision of an eel—and, slipping behind a newspaper kiosk to avoid the oncoming surge of a crowd of uniformed schoolgirls, was momentarily lost to the eyes of King and Frawley.

"Where the hell . . . ?" said King, blowing out his cheeks.

Frawley said: "Right there! Behind that newspaper stall!" He saw the boy again as he spoke.

King stopped dead in his tracks. A puzzled frown, showing the beginnings of alarm, creased his bucolic face. He said urgently: "Come *on!*"

James Widgery was standing still, looking about him with quick dartings—strangely reptilian—of his red head. His face was agonized, the mouth half open, the eyes glaring as they shot their glances in every direction.

And James Widgery was empty handed.

CHAPTER XXI

James Widgery stood upon the soft grey carpet in the room of Sir Egbert Lucas in Scotland House. He felt afraid and important and dirty. He had, it seemed to him, been answering questions for countless hours but the clock upon the mantel showed only eleven-thirty.

There were several men in the room and they all, at one time or another, spoke to James Widgery. At intervals they tried to persuade him to sit down but this he would not do—so they went on questioning him as he stood. Though asked in many ways, and with plethora of subsidiaries, the questions came down, really, to two: What was the man like who had given James the job and the half crown? And what was the appearance of the person who had snatched the leather portfolio from him in Piccadilly Circus station?

James said, many times, with as much variation as was allowed by his vocabulary, that the man who gave him the job and the half crown wasn't tall and wasn't short; wasn't smart and wasn't shabby; wasn't dark and wasn't fair; wasn't thin and wasn't fat—was, in short, medium.

He was obviously attempting, with effort which brought sweat to his young brow, to tell the truth—both when he said what had gone before and when, in reply to the second question, he averred that he'd no more idea than the man in the moon who it was—or what—that had grabbed the bag away from him at his appointed meeting place with the first man. One minute the bag was in his hand; the next it was gone, pulled away from behind like. When he'd whipped round there had been so many people he couldn't tell and none of them *seemed* to have the bag. . . .

At ten to twelve they let him go, the tall man who had questioned him most following him to the door and giving him a florin.

James Widgery clattered down a stone staircase and out of this history, while Anthony Gethryn went back into Lucas' room.

2

In an office three floors below two large and sheepish men bore, with assumed stolidity, the imprecations of Chief Detective Inspector Horler.

"In Frawley's case," said Horler, wiping his forehead, "there *might* be some excuse! He's only been on this job for six months. . . . But as for *you*, King"—he jerked his head round to glare at his objective—"all I can say is—the only thing I can say—well, if this sort o' thing's going to go on, *you* won't!"

Detective Officer King played with his hat.

Detective Officer Frawley said in a very small voice:

"Excuse me, sir . . ."

"And what's more," said Horler, "if anything of the same sort happens again I'll have to send you up direct to the super."

King said, clearing his throat:

"Very sorry, sir!"

Frawley said in a still smaller voice:

"Excuse me, sir, but I've——"

"It's not as if it was a *difficult* job!" Horler was plaintive now. "Just tabbing a little kid!"

King said: "With all joo respect, sir, it might of 'appened to anyone. This boy, 'e just ducks be'ind a newspaper stall and ain't out of sight more than twenty seconds at the very most but juring them seconds *someone* comes up and snatches this bag right out of 'is 'and. Not seein' the boy, it's on'y natural that Frawley and meself didn't see 'oo snatched the bag from 'im——"

Horler interrupted: "That's enough! There's no excuse!"

Frawley coughed. He said in an ingratiating whisper:

"Excuse me, sir, but——"

Horler said: "That'll do! Excuses only make the thing worse! Now get out, both of you! And for the love of all that's holy, don't fluff like that again!"

"Yes sir!" said King smartly and turned towards the door.

But Frawley stood his ground. Frawley said:

"Excuse me, sir, but——"

Horler, who was now opening a blue-covered file upon his desk, looked up with a savage jerk of his head. He said:

"Get *out!*"

The young and cherubic face of Detective Officer James Davenport Frawley lost much of its ruddy glow. He said with a sort of hurried meekness:

"Yes sir. Thank you, sir." And obeyed.

3

In Lucas' room was a haze of tobacco smoke through which were visible Lucas himself, Anthony, Pike and a pale-faced Garrett. Lucas' voice, giving to Pike in more polished periods what Horler had just finished giving to King and Frawley, was the only sound.

Lucas came to an end, drew a deep breath and sat back in his chair.

Pike said: "Yes sir. I know, sir. If I'm not mistaken Horler will be dealing with the men right now, sir."

"Which," said Garrett bitterly, "is a hell of a lot of satisfaction!"

Anthony uncurled himself from the depths of Lucas' biggest chair and stretched. He said:

"Children! Children!"

Garrett said: "Shut up! I'm sick of all this suavity! All I can think of is that an hour ago we were on the point of getting our man and that *now* we're further away from him than we ever were! And just because somebody puts a couple of utterly incompetent flat feet on a job which should have been done by your best men! That's rude and I know it but I'm not going to apologize!" He was sitting very straight in his chair. His eyes blazed angrily, shooting challenging glances from one to another of the Englishmen.

Lucas looked at him, not too pleasantly; but was silent. Pike looked at the floor or, perhaps, at the tips of his brightly polished shoes.

" 'Tis true, 'tis pity," Anthony murmured. "And all we can do is to hope for Bellows."

The bell of a telephone on the desk blared imperiously. Lucas lifted the receiver and spoke. He said:

"Lucas speaking. . . . Yes. . . . What? . . . Yes, read it out." He took a pad of paper and a pencil and began to scribble as the telephone stuttered into his ear. He said quietly as he finished writing:

"Thanks. . . . Yes, I'll tell him." With exaggerated care he put the receiver back upon its hook. He pulled the pad upon which he had been writing towards him and looked at his companions. A smile in which there was little mirth crossed his face. He said slowly:

"Pike, that was from your office. A wire has just come in from Mac-Farland, of Midlothian. I'll read it to you. It says: 'Reference your AC-42 and my reply stop Body answering description Mrs. Bellows found on moor near Kinmarnock stop Death due strangulation medical opinion three days ago post-mortem today stop Further information follows MacFarland.' "

There was a long silence.

"And that," said Anthony, "is that! You've got to admit they're thorough."

Sheldon Garrett stood up. He was very white and looked like a man tired out. He walked across to a small table by the door and took his hat from it. He said with his fingers on the door handle:

"That finishes us, doesn't it? If they'd trailed the boy properly they'd've caught the man or someone who could have led us to him. But they didn't.

And now this poor old woman's been killed too. . . . And so we've just got to say that he's won." He paused for a moment and looked at Lucas. He said rather hesitantly:

"If I've been overofficious and uncivil I can only apologize."

He opened the door and went out, closing it quietly behind him.

After a moment's stillness Pike sighed and got to his feet and wandered over to a window. He said without turning:

"I can't help sympathizing with Mr. Garrett, if you know what I mean."

4

Downstairs in the small waiting room allocated to plain-clothes men of their division Officers Frawley and King were in mid-conversation, the former loquacious, the latter staring open mouthed.

". . . so when he said 'Get out'," Frawley was saying, "I got."

It is to be regretted that the reply of Detective Officer King is not printable. But it resulted in Frawley's immediate return to Horler's office.

5

Upstairs in Lucas' room its tenant spoke. He had listened to Pike and then to Anthony without a word. Now he said suddenly:

"I don't know what's got into you fellows. Because, for the moment, we've let this unknown quantity of a murderer get away you seem to think we've failed utterly. But really all we've had's a setback. A few days ago we didn't know anything about our man except what you'd guessed. But now it's very different: we've got two starting points to work from—the murders of the girl Brent and the old woman Bellows. Scotland Yard, you know, *has* been known to catch murderers!" He sat back in his chair and looked at Anthony.

But Anthony shook his head. "It's no good, Lucas. Specious enough, but signifying nothing." His tone was flat and sombre.

Lucas became indignant. "Meaning that this fellow's too clever for us?"

Anthony opened his eyes. "No. Meaning simply that Master Evans is too far ahead of us. We had an object in this thing, you know. We wanted to stop a crime—possibly involving kidnapping—in committing which a woman called Murch was involved, working under a man called Evans. We wanted, for once, to shut a stable door before a horse was stolen. This morning, through that cloakroom ticket, we *had* a chance of doing it. But that chance was, quite literally, snatched away from us. Possibly you will catch Mr. Evans and hang him! But unless something uncomfortably like a miracle happens you won't do it until after he's done whatever it is we've been trying to stop him from doing. . . . E. & O.E., that's the situation. Ask Pike if he doesn't agree."

Pike, his long, lantern-shaped face lugubrious, looked at Lucas. He said: "I'm afraid Colonel Gethryn's right, sir."

"Colonel Gethryn," said Lucas bitterly, "always is! According to you."

Anthony slowly uncoiled himself and got to his feet and flung his arms wide and stretched. He said:

"Well . . . what about some lunch? I suggest that, wrapped in sackcloth and reeking in ash, we visit a pub and eat tepid mutton and watery boiled potatoes. Then we might toast each other in coffee essence and lukewarm water, thereby signifying the unflattering end of that epic tale, *The Up-side-Down Murder Mystery.*"

Lucas looked at him. "Very whimsical! And what the hell is upside down?"

Anthony said: "Basically, your fallacious idea that a police force is for the purpose of punishing effected crime rather than preventing projected crime. Secondarily and consequentially, this 'case' itself, because instead of discovering a crime which *has been committed* and trying to find out who did it, we've discovered that a crime *is going to be committed* and are trying to find out not only who's going to do it, but what it is that he's going to do!"

Lucas said: "Well, I'll be damned!"

Anthony smiled. "Oh, my prophetic soul. . . . Of course, my dear fellah, I'm only theorizing. And theory's far more difficult than practice—a truism amply illustrated here. In an ordinary 'case'—shades of Quiller-Couch!—there's only one *essential* unknown quantity to be proved: who did it? But in this instance there are two essential unknown quantities to be proved: (a) what's going to be done, *and* (b) who's going to do it? . . . In the first example—Police Work As It Is—fifty people would be a very high number of possible suspects; but in this business the most modest computation of possible suspects is the population of Greater London which is, I believe, about eight million. . . . All of which goes to explain why you're very wise to stick to the ancient and well-established conviction that you're here to *shut* the stable doors."

Anthony drew a deep breath. He turned and walked across the room and took his hat from where it lay upon a chair.

Lucas looked at his back and said:

"Extremely entertaining! As to the concrete value of the speech, however, I won't venture to comment."

Anthony turned. "Don't worry. I'll be on the air again next Friday at two-fifteen, probably speaking from Daventree."

"Correct pronunciation," said Lucas nastily, "is Daintry. . . . Where're you going?"

Anthony halted, his hand upon the doorknob. "To find Garrett. He really oughtn't to've gone alone. He should be in bed." Once more his voice was flat and sombre. He opened the door and was gone, closing it behind him.

Lucas and Pike looked at each other in silence. Outside the window a leaden-grey sky hung over the river and the city. Inside the room there was grey discomfort. Pike said at last:

"Well, sir . . . I'd better get busy."

Lucas said heavily: "Yes. On the usual lines. Who did you put onto the Brent affair?"

"Murchison, sir. Shall I take over?"

"Yes," said Lucas slowly. "Perhaps you'd better."

Pike made a move towards the door; then hovered. He said:

"Too bad about those men, sir."

Lucas lifted his shoulders. "Spilt milk, Pike."

Pike rubbed at his long chin. "Sort of feel as if I'd let Colonel Gethryn down . . . if you follow me, sir."

Lucas said bitterly: "I'm ahead of you. But I still say 'spilt milk.' . . . Now cut off and get some lunch."

"Yes sir," said Pike gloomily and made for the door.

"And, Pike!" said Lucas suddenly in what doubtless was meant for a cheerful tone.

Pike turned. "Yes sir?"

"You never know; we *may* have a bit of luck!"

Pike tried to smile. "Thank you, sir. We need it." He turned again towards the door, which before he could reach it was flung suddenly open, narrowly missing his face.

Anthony stood on the threshold. He said:

"Ran into Horler as I was going out. He's on the way up. Says it's something new."

There appeared in the open doorway behind him the figures of Horler and Detective Officer Frawley.

Lucas looked at them as Anthony stepped aside. He said irritably:

"Come in! Come in!"

Horler came into the room with Frawley, a large and crimson-faced and youthful shadow, at his heels.

"Who's this?" snapped Lucas and looked at Frawley.

Anthony shut the door and stood leaning against it.

Horler cleared his throat. "Thought I'd better come right up, sir. This is D.O. Frawley, who was at Dulwich station cloakroom this morning."

"Oh," said Lucas and looked again at Frawley, who sweated.

Horler said: "Yes sir. But when I had him and the other man in my office just now to tell 'em—to reprimand them, sir, Frawley omitted to tell me something that he's just told, and in the circumstances, sir——"

"For God's sake!" said Lucas. "Get it off your chest!"

Horler said: "Well, sir, Frawley here acted in excess of his orders, which were the same as those given to all the men in all the other cloakrooms—to follow anyone notified as having presented a cloakroom ticket with the left-hand corner torn off."

Lucas flung himself back in his chair. He said between his teeth:

"*Will* you tell me what he did?"

At the tone Frawley wilted visibly; but Horler, who knew his Lucas, went stolidly on.

"Yes sir," said Horler. "When the clerk brought the ticket round to where

Frawley was sitting in the back office of the cloakroom, sir, Frawley got the notion, seeing that the bag was a small one, that he might exceed his orders by opening the bag, if it was unlocked, and making a list of what it contained."

Anthony came away from the door. He said:

"Three cheers for Frawley! Where's the list?"

Lucas, disregarding this most unofficial interruption, transferred a steely gaze from Horler to Frawley, who quivered.

Lucas said: "Well, Frawley?"

James Davenport Frawley tried to speak and found that no words came. He coughed and tried again but, instead of the well-modulated tone which he had intended to produce, emitted a sort of roaring squeak. Appalled by this strange sound, he swallowed. He said at last in a hoarse whisper which fortunately was audible:

"Here's the list, sir." He took from his pocket a folded piece of slightly begrimed paper.

"Oh," said Lucas. "Let's look!" His tone was noticeably less barbed.

With growing courage but still profusely sweating, Frawley advanced towards the desk, treading the carpet as if it were eggshell. He laid the paper down before Lucas, snatching his hand away as if the blotter were red hot.

Lucas lifted the soiled sheet and opened it. Almost simultaneously Anthony and Pike reached his shoulders.

They read, written in round and childish hand, the following words:

> One gent's cap. Dk. brown.
>   (Maker's name cut out)
> One gent's cap. Bk. and white check.
>   (Maker's name cut out)
> One travelling chess set.
> Six gent's hkfs.
> One pr. tort.-rimmed glasses.
>   (With plain glass)
> One pr. gent's leather gloves.
> Three pkts. £1 treasury notes.
>   (About £100 in each pkt.
>   Bound with paper tape. Notes
>   not new. On binding of one
>   packet pencil notation—
>   "L 10-5 A 10-11")

Lucas looked up at last. "All right, Frawley," he said. "Thanks. Good work."

Frawley made gratified noises.

Lucas looked at Horler. "All right. Thanks."

Horler made a movement towards the door, shepherding Frawley before him. As they reached it Lucas spoke again. He said:

"Oh, Frawley!"

Frawley turned. "Yes sir?"

Lucas said: "Another time, don't lose sight of your man!"

Horler opened the door and, pushing Frawley before him, went out. The door closed behind them.

Lucas looked at Pike, who was looking at his shoes; then at Anthony, who had picked the paper from the desk and was scanning it. Lucas said:

"Well . . . 'fraid it doesn't get us much further."

Anthony said without taking his eyes from the paper in his hand:

"Illuminating bagful! Nothing like changing the headgear in case you're followed. Nothing like horn rims to change the expression. Nothing like playing chess to take your mind off bigger schemes." He was mumbling, speaking more than half to himself. "Nothing like having a few quid in your pocket."

Pike said: "Wonder what he wrote the note numbers down for if they were old ones?"

Now Anthony did look up from the paper. He shook his head. "These aren't note numbers. That's what makes 'em interesting."

Pike grew suddenly alert. "On to something, sir?"

Anthony shrugged: "God knows! And, as I'm fond of remarking, *He* won't split. I could bear to know what these figures *mean*. That's all."

"Let's look!" said Lucas and took the paper from Anthony's hand and once more himself studied it. He read aloud:

"L ten hyphen five A ten hyphen eleven . . . no, they're not note numbers. They might be anything. Want to send 'em to a cipher expert?"

Anthony shook his head. "I don't think it's a cipher. It keeps being about to mean something and then doesn't. . . . Blast it!"

CHAPTER XXII

It was a quarter to one when Garrett rang the front doorbell of 19A Stukeley Gardens. He had left Scotland Yard a full forty minutes earlier; but the taxi which clattered away just as White opened the door had borne him, not direct from Westminster, but by roundabout way of St. John's Wood in general and Lords' Mansions in particular.

He reflected as he stepped through the door which White held open for him that if he had had any sense whatever in his aching head he would have telephoned Avis before going so fruitlessly to her flat. He could have saved time this way and, more than possibly, quite a deal of this feeling of nausea and malaise which held his over-driven body in thrall.

White took his hat and helped him out of his coat. Garrett said to him:

"Seen Mrs. Bellingham this morning, White?" His tone reeked of the casual.

White looked at him with some concern.

"Yes sir," said White.

A little colour came to Garrett's cheeks.

"For a few minutes, sir," said White.

"Oh," said Garrett with what he meant for indifference. He felt tired again and sick and his head was swimming.

White said: "Mrs. Bellingham went out with Mrs. Gethryn, sir. About half an hour ago. They said something about shopping, sir."

"Oh," said Garrett again. And then with a determined smile: "Tell you what: I think I could take a scotch highball."

"Pardon, sir?" White cocked his head to one side.

Garrett said: "Sorry, whiskey and soda. With a bit of ice."

White looked at him. "What you *should* 'ave, sir," said White, "is a glass of sherry and a nice cup of soup."

"Pr'aps you're right." Again Garrett essayed a smile. "I'll be in the library." He turned and went slowly across the hall.

The library was empty but a fire blazed in the grate and the big leather sofa was plumply inviting. He sank into its depths and closed his eyes.

White came in with a tray upon which were a decanter, a glass, a bowl which steamed and a gleaming little toast rack, half full. Garrett opened his eyes and murmured thanks and closed his eyes again.

White set down the tray upon a small table which he lifted to the side of the sofa. He said:

"Your soup, sir. And sherry." In his tone was some reflection of the qualities which had once made him—so Anthony Gethryn has often been heard to say—the best sergeant in the allied armies.

Garrett drank the soup, ate two pieces of toast and lingered over a glass and a half of the sherry.

White picked up the tray and left the room and Garrett let his head drop back upon the soft leather.

He fell, slowly and floatingly, down into a deep black cavern. It was soft and warm and enticing in its utter restfulness. It was death, his mind told him dimly, and he welcomed it and felt, through his absolute relaxation, a small pang of triumph that death was so exactly as he had, alive, always imagined it would be.

He lay in divine, barely conscious torpor. He was dead and knew it and was happy. Then with a sudden and searing stab vivid consciousness returned. He was sitting. He was bound to the thing which was serving him as a chair. It felt like metal but although there was no movement from it he knew sickeningly that it had life. He thought: I wish it wasn't so *dark*—and thus became aware of the frightful quality of this darkness and tried to scream. He racked himself with the effort but no sound came from his swelling throat. He strained at his bonds and they grew tighter. The frightful certainty that life—though of a form unknown—was in these bonds clutched at his entrails. A wave of terror shook him almost to nausea—and was forgotten as a voice, quite close to him, came to his ears. It was a child's voice, shrill and shaky with fear. It said one word which went through him like a sword.

"*Don't!*" it said.

Garrett made a tremendous effort. He must get free and help the child. But his foul bonds grew tighter yet—and something like a huge hand clamped down upon his shoulder and shook it, gently, yet with the power of God. . . .

2

The hand which was shaking him turned, suddenly and happily, into the normal and long-fingered and entirely real hand of Anthony Gethryn.

Garrett rubbed at his eyes and sat up, wallowing with joy in all the matter-of-factness of the room and the reassuring existence of other men cast in the same mould as himself.

Anthony and Pike looked down at him, noting the greenish tinge of his colouring and the great beads of sweat which stood out upon his forehead. Anthony said:

"Damn fool! You ought to be in bed."

Pike nodded.

"O.K. in a minute," said Garrett and mopped at his forehead. "Had a ghastly dream!"

Anthony smiled. "All about hobgoblins and a futile police force and Sheldon Garrett struggling to prevent some disaster from happening and failing. Something of that sort?"

Garrett stared at him through narrowed eyes.

"Something," he said.

"Well, don't dream any more!" said Anthony. "Just listen. After you left the Yard we had a bit of luck. We got a list of what was in that bag!"

"Go on!" Garrett began to get to his feet. "Go *on!*"

"Sit down!" said Anthony. "On a paper in the bag was a pencilled note—some letters and figures. At first we couldn't make them out, then I realized what they were. Pike still isn't convinced, so——" He broke off, taking from his pocket a small notebook and pencil. Opening the book, he scrawled some figures on it and held it under Garrett's eyes. He said:

"Oblige the Court by saying, at once, what those figures convey to you. Don't stop to think!"

Garrett said, staring perplexedly:

"Tenth of October."

Anthony turned to Pike. "And there, sir, I rest my case!"

Pike rubbed at his chin. He smiled and said:

"It's a bit of luck and no mistake!"

"If somebody," said Garrett, "doesn't tell me what all this is about I shall commit something or other."

Anthony looked at him with contrition. "Sorry," he said. He took from his pocket a slip of paper and put it into Garrett's hand. "Here's the puzzle."

Garrett read what was written: "L 10-5 A 10-11."

Anthony said: "Right from the beginning those figures meant something that I knew—but I couldn't think what it was. I thought of dates but they didn't make sense. I was just giving the whole thing up when the register turned somewhere and I realized that they *were* dates, but written as Americans write dates, with the number of the month first instead of second."

Pike said, half to himself: "So our man's a Yank!"

Anthony shook his head. "Not necessarily. For instance——"

Garrett said: "What the hell does it matter whether he's an American or an Irishman or an Eskimo!"

Anthony looked at him. "Nothing. Only I think that Pike, knowing that whatever we're trying to stop is probably in part kidnapping, wants to feel assured that the patent isn't being infringed by an Englishman."

Pike smiled a little wryly.

Garrett was studying the slip of paper. He said without looking up: "Suppose these things *are* dates—so what?"

Anthony said: "Oh, my dear fellah! One: assume that the figures mean the fifth and the eleventh of October, this present month; two: realize that even though Evans himself may not be an American these dates are stated in an American manner. Throw into saucepan and stir well and see what 'L' and 'A' *must* mean!"

Garrett shouted: "Leave and arrive!"

Pike looked up sharply.

Anthony smiled. "Exactly! The steps are easy. Kidnapping equals American; American dates with six days between them equals a voyage across the Atlantic."

Garrett, the pain in his head momentarily forgotten, jumped to his feet. "My God!" he said. His eyes blazed with excitement. "But what're we going to *do!*"

Then, as suddenly as it had come, the light died out of his face. A frown drew his brows together and he dropped down to sit once more upon the sofa. He said:

"What the hell am I getting so het up about! We haven't got anything really; not a thing!"

Anthony looked at him but did not speak. Pike said:

"You're wrong there, Mr. Garrett. You're wrong there!"

Anthony walked over to the fireplace and pressed the bell beside it and kicked the flickering logs into a blaze.

Garrett said to Pike: "Well, *I* can't see it!"

Anthony came across the room and stood by the sofa and looked down at its occupant. He seemed about to speak but broke off as the door opened.

"You rang, sir?" said White.

Anthony nodded. "Bring some whiskey. And a siphon and glasses. Oh yes, *and* ice. And when a man comes from the Green Star Line bring him straight in here."

"Yes sir," said White and was gone.

Garrett looked at Anthony. "Well, what is there?" There was weary challenge in his voice. "Pr'aps I *am* a fool—I've certainly gotten into the way of behaving like one—but I fail to understand why we should all make whoopee because there's a note in our man's bag which *may* refer to a ship sailing from New York to Southampton or vice versa! It doesn't necessarily mean a thing!"

Anthony grinned. "Because it ain't got that swing. Not the way you put it. Try this instead: Eliminating all but essentials, we have (1) the hypothesis that Janet Murch, under the direction of X (Evans-for-short), is to take part in the commission of a crime or crimes of which the whole or part is probably kidnapping; (2) the certain knowledge, lately acquired, that X-Evans *is* a dangerous criminal; and (3) the certain knowledge that X-Evans, or a confederate, noted down figures which *might* refer to the voyage of a ship across the Atlantic." He paused for a moment and looked steadily at Garrett. "Right?" he said.

Garrett, lying back against the arm of the sofa, nodded but did not speak. His eyes were fixed on Anthony's face.

"Thuslywise," said Anthony, speaking slowly now, "we come to (4) the certain knowledge that—*if* we find that a ship left New York on the fifth of this month, arrived here on the eleventh and carried a child, of wealthy parents, whose nursemaid answers to the description of Janet Murch—we have such an overwhelmingly presumptive case that we can act on it."

Garrett stood up.

Pike chuckled. "And prevent a stable door from opening, sir." He rubbed his hands and a wide smile split his long face.

Anthony bowed with courtliness. "I thank you, Superintendent!"

Garrett said slowly: "That's right enough! . . . By God, it *is* right! I got all muddled." He put an unconscious hand to his throbbing head. He said quickly: "It's the thirteenth. That boat's been in two days!"

"Hold your horses!" said Anthony. "Evans has been pretty busy for the last two days."

Garrett said: "Yes. Yes, he has. But *now* . . . we've got to hurry!" His dream came back to him with a dreadful clarity. He sweated.

Pike looked at him curiously.

Anthony said: "Zeal, all zeal, Mr. Easy!" He took Garrett by the arm and gently pushed him down onto the sofa. "Everything, in the words of Mrs. Eddy, is going to be all right!"

The door opened and a parlourmaid came in with a laden tray which tinkled.

Garrett said: "But we've *got* to find out about the ship! And get passenger lists and check——"

He broke off as White opened the door and admitted a neat, small person with an attaché case.

"Mr. Perry!" said White and held the door open for the departing maid and closed it behind them both.

"The answer," said Anthony, "to the Playwright's Prayer." He went across the room to where, just inside the door, there stood the subject of White's announcement. He said:

"Mr. Perry? Very good of you to come so promptly." He waved a hand. "Mr. Sheldon Garrett. Mr. Pike . . . Mr. Perry, of the Green Star Line. Have a drink, Mr. Perry?"

The firelight glinted upon Mr. Perry's pince-nez. "Thank you," said Mr. Perry with surprising promptness. "I will."

3

"You see, therefore, Colonel," said Mr. Perry neatly, "that it must be the Gigantic. It is true that the Cunarder also docked on the eleventh but *she* left"—a little cough of pride was tidily inserted in the speech—"a day earlier than our ship."

"Yes," said Anthony. "Got a passenger list?"

"Indeed, yes." Mr. Perry's capable little hands set down his tumbler, unlocked the attaché case and brought forth papers.

"Good!" said Anthony and gently eased away with his shoulder the crowding body of Garrett. "Now, could you tell us whether there were any children aboard? First class, of course."

Mr. Perry coughed, firmly but without any undue noise. "Let me see now . . . that *may* be possible, to an extent." He settled the pince-nez more firmly on his nose and flicked over the pages of a neat loose-leaf book.

Garrett started to say something but Anthony's elbow took him in the ribs. He was quiet.

"Abel, Mrs.," said Mr. Perry as if to himself. "Aaronson, Miss . . . Arden, Mr. and Mrs. . . . Axel, Herr." His white fingers travelled swiftly through the leaves of the book, their rustling making subdued accompaniment to the rapid murmuring of his voice. Every now and then both fingers and voice would stop as Mr. Perry neatly and swiftly jotted down certain names. Except for his voice and the flicking of the leaves there was no sound in the room.

". . . Witherspoon, Sir Guy," said Mr. Perry. ". . . Wessex, Mr., Mrs., and Miss . . ." Again Mr. Perry stopped to make a swift note upon the pad beside him. "Walters, Mr. . . . Wyatt, the Honorable Mrs. Jeffry . . . Yoland, Mr. and Mrs. . . . Yeomans, Miss . . . Yule, Miss . . . and," said Mr. Perry, shutting the loose-leaf book with a tidy little slam, "Prince Zeffatini."

He picked up the pad upon which at intervals he had been writing and studied it for a moment. He said:

"You'll at once see the major difficulty, Colonel Gethryn." He looked at Anthony over the rims of his pince-nez. "I can tell you definitely that there was one first-class passenger who was a child—namely, *Master* Kenneth G. Lester, travelling with Mr. and Mrs. Lester, presumably his father and mother. That was, obviously, the only boy on the ship in the first class. But when it comes to *girls*, we're in a different pair of shoes."

"Quite," said Anthony.

Mr. Perry regarded him with some signs of severity. "Because, in the case of girls, we can't tell whether 'Miss' indicates maturity or the reverse."

"Quite," said Anthony.

Mr. Perry pursed his lips and, picking up his half-emptied tumbler, set it precisely to his lips and drank.

"Look here . . ." said Garrett violently and was once more cut short by Anthony's elbow.

There was a small silence while Mr. Perry finished his whiskey and soda. He took the glass from his lips and set it down upon the tray. He said: "To ascertain speedily how many young *girls* were travelling first class on the ship, Colonel, there's only one thing we can do: Get in touch with some member of the ship's company who would be able to enlighten us."

"Quite," said Anthony. "Have another drink?"

"Thank you," said Mr. Perry firmly. "I will."

4

When Mr. Perry, having made much play with Anthony's telephone, finally left Stukeley Gardens the time was a quarter past six. He left behind him an empty decanter, a profoundly irritated American, a memory of one hundred per cent efficiency and the name and address of the chief steward of the *Gigantic*, who, it must be known, was on leave in London.

At ten minutes to seven Anthony's Voisin drew up outside Number 27 Elmview Crescent, Brixton. A thick, white mist, marked every here and there by the orange nimbus of a street lamp, hung over Elmview Crescent. Anthony got out of his car and shivered and turned up the collar of his overcoat and opened a small iron gate which dismally whined. He went up a narrow path flanked by sorry shrubs which loomed uncouth through the misty half-darkness. He came to a door and discovered to one side of it an iron bellpull at which he dragged. From somewhere inside the house came a ghostlike tinkling, almost immediately followed by the sound of footsteps and the illumination of a glass transom above the door.

The footsteps drew nearer and their maker opened the door. Immediately, as if destroyed by the wind of a Merlin, the ghoulish and decaying atmosphere of Elmview Crescent was dispersed. Standing in the doorway, her head thrust a little forward, the better to see her visitor, stood a tall plump woman whose smile and carriage seemed to Anthony, in this uncertain light, to tell her age as somewhere in the thirties.

Anthony raised his hat. "Is Mr. Lawes in?" he said. "Mr. Peter Lawes?"

The neat head was shaken and Anthony saw with surprise that its fairness was white and not blonde. "I'm sorry. He's out for the evening," said a round and reassuring voice.

Anthony said: "That's very disappointing. I'd some urgent business with him. They sent me here from the Green Star offices."

"I'm Mrs. Lawes—Peter's mother," said the woman. "Was it very important?"

"Very," said Anthony and gave the word full value.

Mrs. Lawes looked intently at her visitor with an eye which, for all its pleasantness, saw deep. She said at last:

"Well, Peter won't like it; but I'll tell you where you might reach him." She gave the name of the largest moving picture theatre south of the river. "He's taken a girl there. He's that fond of pictures you wouldn't believe!"

"Thank you!" Anthony smiled at her. "You're very kind."

He left a card upon the back of which he scribbled a message in case he did not find Peter. A clock somewhere in the house began to chime seven. The front door closed and the light behind its transom went out and once more the dankness of Elmview Crescent closed in upon him.

He went quickly down the path between the shrubs and out through the gate to his car.

5

A horde of Bedouin horsemen surged irresistibly up the slope. Captain Dick Gordon, his teeth bared in a grin of desperation, pulled his revolver from its holster and, turning back into the cave mouth, dropped to his knees and looked down at the golden head of the exhausted girl.

And then, cutting through the hoarse, feral shouts of the advancing Arabs, there came to his ear the high sweet notes of a trumpet playing "The Charge."

"The regiment!" whispered Dick Gordon—and gently lifted Alice to her feet. Below them, on the hillside, the charging lancers—gallant men of the 35th—took the Arabs on the flank, utterly routing them.

The girl's arms stole about Dick Gordon's neck and their lips met—just as, from somewhere close at hand, came the high sweet notes of a trumpet playing "The Rally."

To a sudden orgiastic blast of apparently divinely inspired music *Star of the Desert* reached its final fade-out, to be immediately replaced on the screen by a roughly printed notice which read:

"If Mr. Peter Lawes is in the theatre will he please communicate with the manager at the box office."

That was at a quarter to eight—and produced no result! It was repeated after the three short pictures which, with *Star of the Desert,* made up the program. It still produced no result. There was then another hour and a half to go before it could be shown again, and Anthony, leaving his card with the manager—a genial and helpful and courteous person happy in the name of Aaronson—set out for home.

As he drove away from the glittering portico of the Colossal Theatre the hands of the clock on his dashboard stood at eight-forty.

6

Lucia, deciding not to wait for Anthony, dined in gloomy triumvirate with Avis and Garrett—and then, on circumstantial pretext, left them in the library.

But to no purpose. She had been gone a bare five minutes when, descending from a nursery which, every night now, she was wont to visit an inordinate number of times, she went into her drawing room and found there half of the pair she had left downstairs.

Avis Bellingham was curled, a picture of beauty and apparent comfort, in a chair near the fire. There was an open book upon her knees in which she seemed engrossed.

"Hul*lo!*" Lucia was momentarily startled into surprise.

With some effort Mrs. Bellingham took her eyes from the book.

"Oh, hello!" she said vaguely and dropped her eyes to the book again.

Lucia perched upon the arm of another chair. She lighted a cigarette and studied her guest, who went on reading.

Lucia bent forward. "Try it this way," she said. "It's not so difficult!" She twitched the book from Avis' hands and turned it the right way up and gave it back.

"*Oh!*" said Mrs. Bellingham.

"Quite," said Lucia Gethryn, rather in the manner of her husband. "What's it all about?"

Avis closed the book with a slam. She said abruptly:

"I'm unchristian! I *cannot* suffer fools!"

Lucia repressed all trace of amusement. "Who's a fool?" she said.

"Mr. Thomas Sheldon Garrett!" Avis spoke without opening her teeth. "A *damn* fool! . . . If he'd mind his own business, instead of interfering with other people's and nearly getting killed and *still* going on being a busybody, pr'aps he *might* have the intelligence to realize the obvious and stop being so—so bloody noble!"

Mrs. Gethryn whistled; then broke into a laugh—which would not be denied.

"Anyone," said Mrs. Bellingham bitterly, "can laugh! . . . But I tell you——" She did not, however; before she could, the door opened upon the belated Anthony. . . .

7

Garrett was packed off to bed and Anthony, besieged by questions, ate a scratch meal.

"That's all there is to it," he said and set down a glass. "Lawes'll catch the message somewhere."

"Isn't there *anything* else we can do?" There was concern, even agitation, in Mrs. Bellingham's voice.

Lucia looked at her and smiled. "Busybody!" she said.

The door opened and White came in. He said to Anthony:

"There's a Mr. Lawes to see you, sir. Mr. Peter Lawes. He hadn't got a card."

8

Mr. Peter Lawes was young and ruddy faced and inclined towards social nervousness. He had, however, a well-developed sense of humour which made this rather naïve gaucherie amusing even to himself. He also had, very fortunately, an observing eye, a retentive memory and a quick intelligence.

He sat upon the extreme edge of one of the straighter chairs in the library and nursed a glass of whiskey and soda and replied quickly and clearly to questions. He frequently blushed and then laughed at his own embarrassment.

Anthony said, smiling at him:

"So you can say, definitely, that in the first class there were only two children?"

Mr. Lawes nodded his blond head. "That's right, sir. Mr. and Mrs. Van Renseler's little girl. And Mrs. Lester's boy."

On the couch Avis stirred. She seemed about to speak but was checked by the pressure of Lucia's fingers upon her knee.

Anthony said: "Good. Now, Mr. Lawes, how much d'you remember about the two families? Tell it any way you like. But everything."

Peter Lawes dared a sip from his glass. He swallowed and coughed and shifted still further forward upon his chair. He said:

"I had more to do with the Van Renselers, sir. So I'll start with them. Pr'aps you know the name, sir. Mr. Van Renseler's one of the richest men in New York. And Mrs. Van Renseler must have near as much money herself, being old Cresswell Graham's daughter. But they're a very nice lady and gentleman. Very nice indeed! Very quiet like and yet plenty of life and always with a civil word. And Mrs. Van Renseler's a very beautiful lady. The little girl—she's a sweet kid if ever there was one—would be about nine. Just like her mother. A real happy family. Kept themselves to themselves on the voyage but still very popular—you know the sort of people I mean."

"Exactly," said Anthony.

"That seems to be all about the Van Renselers," said Mr. Lawes slowly. "Unless you'd like to ask me some questions. Sort of draw it out of the witness." Mr. Lawes blushed and smiled.

Anthony smiled back. "Any nursemaid?" he said with an admirable appearance of casualness.

On the sofa Avis Bellingham sat upright with a sudden movement.

"Yes sir," said Peter Lawes. "Nice sort of quiet girl. English, I believe."

"Oh!" said Avis. "I——" She cut herself short at the renewed pressure of Lucia's hand.

Anthony said: "Happen to remember her name?"

Mr. Lawes, holding his glass with his left hand, scratched his head with his right. He said:

"I *should* . . . it's on the tip of my tongue. . . . Got it! It was Barnes. Mabel Barnes."

Avis sank back against the padded leather of the sofa.

Anthony looked at Mr. Lawes. "Sure?" he said.

"Quite sure. It only just slipped my mind for the moment."

Anthony said: "English, you said. What sort of a girl?"

Mr. Lawes pondered. "Just an ordinary sort of a girl," he said at last. "Pleasant faced; not ugly, but not much to look at. Any age between nineteen and twenty-four. Very nice and quiet, she was, with the little girl. Just a good nursemaid, you know."

"Was she tall?" said Anthony. "And slimmish, with a good figure?"

Mr. Lawes laughed; then blushed at the sound. "Oh, no sir!"

"I see," said Anthony slowly. "All right. Now what about the people with the boy. Lester, wasn't it?"

"Yes and no. The boy's name was something else. I'm afraid I don't know what. He was around ten years old and a nice little chap. His mother married this Mr. Lester about a couple of years ago. Least, that's what I'd put it at. They weren't such a pleasant family as the Van Renselers. Mr. Lester was very short tempered. Mrs. Lester was all right but seemed sort of crushed like. She and the little boy seemed real fond of each other, but—well, they both seemed sort of scared of Mr. Lester. Nothing out of the ordinary, you know, sir; but just a case of a bad-tempered man with what they call a strong personality."

Mr. Lawes took another swallow from his glass; coughed; found that he was unable to move further forward on his chair and so sat a little further back.

Anthony said: "The old stepfather story?"

Mr. Lawes nodded.

"Two questions," said Anthony. "Are they rich? And, if so, who had the money?"

Mr. Lawes pursed his lips. "They're rich, all right. At least they had that sort of way with 'em and I'm sure it was genuine. But as for who the money belonged to—well, I wouldn't like to say."

"Any nursemaid?" said Anthony.

Mr. Lawes nodded. "Oh yes. Nice sort of girl! Very superior!" There was a personal warmth in Mr. Lawes's tone. "She was English too."

"Name?" said Anthony.

"Matthews, sir. Jane Matthews." Mr. Lawes exhibited no hesitation whatsoever.

"I see," said Anthony slowly. He did not look towards the sofa. "D'you happen to know how long both these girls—Barnes and Matthews—had had their jobs?"

Mr. Lawes blushed. "Couldn't tell you about the Van Renselers' girl, sir," he said gallantly, "but Jane—Miss Matthews had only been with the Lesters a little while. She was talking about having done two trips across the Atlantic within a couple of months."

"I see," said Anthony again.

There was a little silence. A log in the fireplace crumpled and sent up a shower of sparks. Avis Bellingham, to whom a startling thought had obviously occurred, was breathing fast, her eyes flicking quick glances from Anthony to Lucia. Mr. Lawes shifted uncomfortably in his seat and finished his drink. He sat and nursed his empty glass in the manner of a small boy playing with his cap.

Anthony said at last: "What sort of a looking girl is Miss Matthews?"

Mr. Lawes hesitated. His face scarlet, he stared straight at Anthony with very blue eyes. He said:

"She was *good* looking, sir! Sort of dark with big brown eyes—almost black, they were—and one of the prettiest skins you ever saw!"

"Short?" said Anthony. "Or tall?"

"Tallish, sir. And sort of a slim figure." Mr. Lawes's tone became reminiscent. "She looked real nice in her uniform. *Real* nice!"

Anthony rose and took Mr. Lawes's glass and, not heeding murmured protest, refilled it and brought it back.

"Thank you, sir," said Mr. Lawes and then, carried away by desire to do the right thing, raised the tumbler in the direction of the sofa. "Ladies," said Mr. Lawes, "your very good health!"

He then blushed, vividly, and put the glass to his lips. Anthony said, looking down at him as he drank:

"Just one more question, and I won't bother you any more."

The visitor took his glass from his lips. "No trouble at all!" he said.

"I just want to know," said Anthony slowly, "whether *you* know where the two families were going from the boat?"

9

A desk lamp cast a bright circle of light upon the desk of Superintendent Arnold Pike. In the aureole was an open file and, just outside and above it, the long, lantern-shaped face of Pike himself. He was gazing down at the typewritten sheets; but his eyes were unseeing. He was thinking, not of the bloody business—so drily dealt with on the official paper—of the minor canon whose body had been discovered in the cistern of his own house, but of the strange and inverted case in which the American friend of Colonel Anthony Gethryn had so thoroughly enmeshed him.

It all went round in the shrewd brain behind the long face. Ye Tea Shoppe . . . the shopping list . . . KJB . . . Lady Ballister's suicide . . . the disappearance of Janet Murch . . . the trailing of the blackmailer . . . the messy death of Ada Brent . . . the sense of Evans being just out of reach . . . the portfolio at Dulwich station . . . Master James Widgery . . . the contents of the portfolio . . . the possibilities of the passenger list of the *Gigantic* . . . the narrow escapes of Sheldon Garrett . . . the strangling of the shadowy Mrs. Bellows . . .

A lot! The dickens of a lot! And yet, so far as it concerned what they were trying to do, nothing at all!

The proverb concerning the horse and the stable door came into Pike's mind for perhaps the fiftieth time this evening. He smiled a little wryly; he was remembering a recent interview with Sir Egbert Lucas. . . .

He was wrapped so many folds deep in thought that he started violently at the shrill pealing of one of the telephones beside him. He stretched out a hand for it and lifted its receiver and answered the voice of Anthony Gethryn.

"The chief steward of the *Gigantic's* just gone," said the voice. "We're getting somewhere. Ready?"

"Yes," said Pike and reached for pad and pencil.

"Two children only," said the telephone. "A girl—Van Renseler—with mother and father; rich; New York; believed to've come straight to London from Southampton. . . . Got it?"

Pike finished scribbling. "Yes," he said.

"The other kid's a boy," said the telephone. "Surname unknown at the moment, travelling with his mother and stepfather; name, Lester; American; rich. Believed to've come up to London, like the Van Renselers, direct from the boat."

Pike scribbled fast. "Anything more, sir?"

"There's little; but how much it *might* be, Pike! Both families had English nursemaids. The Van Renselers' was called Mable Barnes and seems nondescript. But the Lesters'—the Lesters', Pike—the Lesters' nursemaid bore the name Jane Matthews. Jane Matthews: you'll note the initials?"

"*Janet Murch,*" said Pike without knowing he had spoken.

"Exactly!" said the telephone. "And she was tall and slim and—according to the impressionable Mr. Lawes—of certain attractions. Also the Lester family—as compared with the Van Renselers anyhow—wasn't so happy! Stepfather's unpleasant! . . . And if you put that all in your pipe, how long before we get any smoke?"

Pike grinned. When he spoke there was in his voice a reflection of the excitement in Anthony's. He said:

"It's a matter of luck, sir. I'll get right onto it. I gather that you want the present whereabouts of both families with more particular attention paid to the Lesters."

"How right, Pike!" said the telephone.

"How late can I call you, sir?"

"At any time, Superintendent!" said the telephone. "At any time at all. And if you're waking call me early, call me early, Super dear, for tomorrow I *might* be Queen of the May!"

The click of a replaced receiver sounded in Pike's ear. He put down this telephone and reached for another and became, on the instant, very busy indeed.

CHAPTER XXIII

The bedside extension of Anthony's private telephone—the one which is listed nowhere—began to ring, its insistent trill cutting through sleep like a sharp sword.

He sat up, awake with that instantaneous awareness which has so often served him well. He made a long arm and took the receiver from its hook and spoke into the mouthpiece.

"Pike here, sir," said a voice harsh with fatigue. "The Van Renselers are at the Alsace Hotel, Suite 306. The nurse is with them and the little girl. That's easy enough. But the Lesters—well, they're a different matter, sir."

"Haven't you got onto 'em at all?" Anthony's tone was sharp.

"Only in a manner of speaking," said the weary voice. "They came up to town straight from the boat and stayed at the Milan. But they left yesterday morning."

"Where for?" Anthony's voice was still sharper.

"That's just it. We don't know—yet. All I can get from the hotel is the address of Lester's bank and the information that he told several people that he and Mrs. Lester and the boy—the boy's name is Barris, by the way; Kenneth Barris—were going on a motor tour."

Again Anthony interrupted. "Motor tour! At this time of year!"

"Yes sir; it does sound fishy. But I've got the number of the car. And I've sent out an all stations call. I should hear something within the next hour. . . ." He hesitated, then added: "Sorry, sir."

Anthony said with a cheerfulness which he was far from feeling: "Don't be an ass! Been to bed?"

"No," said the tired voice.

"Well, I have," said Anthony. "You ought to come round and kick me. But don't; go and have some breakfast instead. In the meantime I'll just do a little private check on the Van Renselers. We mustn't miss anything."

2

At twenty-two minutes past eight Pike, newly shaven and fed and with most traces of vigil gone from his face, re-entered his office.

Sitting upon a corner of his table, he reached for the telephone and spoke into it. It said in answer:

"No sir—nothing yet." And then: "Just a moment, sir, there's a call just coming in from York. . . . Hold on, please. . . . Here it is, sir."

3

At eight-thirty Anthony's private telephone was answered by White.

"Colonel Gethryn there?" said a familiar voice.

White said: "Colonel Gethryn's out, Mr. Pike. He said if you called I was to take a message and tell you he'd be back by nine-thirty."

"H'mm!" Sounds of cogitation were borne along the wire. "Tell him just this, will you: the Lester car's been seen in Yorkshire. Near Stagby. It was going north and—er—just say everything's all right, so far."

4

At twenty minutes to nine Miss Patricia Van Renseler came out of the bathroom of Suite 306 in the Alsace Hotel. Outside the window in the little lobby a pale winter sun shone with almost silvery brightness. Miss Van Renseler stood upon tiptoe and looked out of the lobby window at the river. There was a barge with a russet sail and the water glittered and cohorts of sea gulls changed formation against a hard blue sky.

An exclamation of pleasure escaped Miss Van Renseler—to be immediately replaced by one of surprise at a sound which had come from behind her. She turned to see that she was not alone. A long man in overalls lay upon the floor near the outer door. With tools he was doing something to the bell box of the telephone.

Miss Van Renseler, her hands deep in the pockets of a blue dressing gown the same colour as her eyes, walked towards him. He looked up, showing a lean, dark face—slightly grimy—which smiled at her.

Miss Van Renseler liked the smile. She smiled herself. She said:

"Who are you?" in an accent whose transatlanticism was only delightful.

"Telephone man, missy." The man in overalls was sharply Cockney; but he smiled again.

Miss Van Renseler chuckled. "You talk like Whosit in the movies," she said. "But I like you." She surveyed him with her head on one side. "Why've you got green eyes?"

The man on the floor opened the black box of the telephone bell. He said:

"So's I c'n spot the 'obgoblins!" He twisted his head and peered into the box in a manner which brought a bubble of laughter from Miss Van Renseler's throat.

A door opened and there was a rustling of starched skirts and a woman's voice, high pitched yet soft and pleasant. It said:

"Your mother wants you, Pat——" And then broke off the sentence suddenly. "Oh! Is there something wrong with the phone?"

The telephone man was tinkering with a screw driver. He looked round and up at a dumpy woman in the indoor uniform of a nursemaid of the higher sort.

"Fix it in a couple o' seconds, miss," he said.

From behind a door came another voice. A woman's.

"Pat!" it called. "Pat darling!"

"Bunchy!" said Miss Van Renseler to her nurse. "*You* talk to him! He's sort of nice!" She suddenly raised her voice and shouted "Com-ing!"

The man on the floor heard a thudding of running feet; a door opening; greetings in a deep woman's voice and a laughing man's; the sound of a small body leaping onto a bed; squeals of merriment from Miss Van Renseler mingling with the other voices.

The nurse shut the door. The telephone man got to his feet and picked up his tool bag and towered over the nurse and looked down at her pleasant, placid face.

"Nice little nipper," he said. "Pretty too!"

"Oh *yes!*" said the nurse. "Is the phone all right?"

"Yes miss," said the telephone man. "*Everything's* all right here!"

He went out of the suite, ran down the stairs and, out on the Embankment, took a taxi for 19A Stukeley Gardens, a bath and breakfast.

5

At nine-thirty Master Kenneth Barris came out of the ground-floor lavatory of the Bull and Bear in Cloughton and made his way into the coffee room.

It was cold in the coffee room, which somehow was like a roller-skating rink which has missed its vocation. At the far end was a fireplace in which a recently lighted fire fought against its draughtless construction and poured out into the room intermittent streams of greyish-black smoke.

Near the hearth, coughing at the smoke, Kenneth's mother and his stepfather sat at a table covered with the preliminary dishes of what the Bull and Bear considered breakfast.

His mother smiled at Kenneth cautiously—a thin woman of indeterminate age whose pleasant face bore traces of past beauty. Kenneth, with a glance of mingled defiance and apprehension at the paper behind which his stepfather was entrenched, returned the silent greeting. He approached the table and sat, making as little noise as possible.

But the paper rustled and was lowered. Over it appeared the heavy-featured face of John Lester. A thin but virulent jet of smoke shot from the fire and, it seemed, straight into his lungs. He coughed with rattling violence and glared at his stepson and spoke angrily. He was, it seemed, burdened beyond endurance by the inability of his stepson to come to meals in time. He told what he thought of his stepson, and what—if the stepson were not very careful—he would do to him. He switched attention to his wife at her almost whispered intervention, and then was himself interrupted in mid-speech by the appearance of a slatternly waitress.

John Lester stared at her. She should have been carrying a tray laden with the sorry best that the Bull and Bear could provide: instead she was empty-handed. John Lester glared his unbelief.

The waitress sniffed. "Some'un askin' see tha," she announced.

Her speech was North Country at its broadest, and therefore, to John Lester, completely incomprehensible. He said, between his teeth:

"Where is our breakfast? We've been waiting nearly an hour." He articulated every word clearly, in the manner of a tourist in a foreign land striving to make the aborigine brain find meaning in a strange tongue.

The waitress sniffed. "Some'un askin' see tha," she said again.

Kenneth Barris stared at his stepfather with uncowed eye. He said curtly: "She means someone wants to see you."

Mrs. Lester looked at her small son with an almost imperceptible shaking of her head.

John Lester looked at his stepson—but before he could speak the sound of a heavy, measured tread made him look towards the door.

A man was coming across the room. He was a burly, stolid person in tweed clothes of the pattern known as pepper-and-salt. His boots squeaked a little and he carried, in a hand of approximately the shape and almost the size of a leg of mutton, a hat which Kenneth would have called a derby.

The waitress sniffed. " 'Ere 'a be!" she said, and was gone.

The visitor loomed large over the table. John Lester stared at him. So, with varying expressions, did the woman and the small boy. Of their existence, however, the visitor seemed unaware. He said:

"Mr. Lester? Mr. John Lester?"

Lester nodded. He said with heavy sarcasm:

"You have the advantage of me, sir."

"My name's Bull," said the newcomer, his gaze fixed and oxlike. "Inspector Bull of the Yorkshire Constabulary."

6

At twenty minutes to eleven Anthony Gethryn, now in clothes of normal elegance, sat upon the edge of the bed in the largest spare room in 19A Stukeley Gardens and surveyed its occupant.

Sheldon Garrett had slept, and well. There was some colour in his face and last night's look of gauntness had lessened. He had eaten a large breakfast with pleasure and said so. His cigarette tasted of tobacco. He began upon expression of gratitude and was cut short.

"The Van Renselers," said Anthony, "are all right. I went to the Alsace myself. As a telephone man. Nice child; apparently pleasing parents. Excellent atmosphere. Nothing ominous."

"Nurse?" said Garrett.

"All right," said Anthony. "Nothing like your description. Kid's on very good terms with her."

Garrett crushed the cigarette in his saucer. "It must be the others, then—what's the name?—Lester."

Anthony nodded. "Definitely. But unfortunately, *they* aren't staying put. They're on a motor tour."

Garrett sat upright. "Odd time of year," he said.

"Exactly," said Anthony—and there was a silence broken by a knocking upon the door and a parlourmaid who said:

"Mr. Pike to see you, sir. He's in the library."

"I'll come down," said Anthony; then looked at Garrett. "No. Ask him to come up."

They waited, and Pike came, smiling. He said, after greetings:

"Well . . . we're on to the Lesters!" He looked at Garrett while he spoke. "They stopped for breakfast at an inn in Cloughton. Inspector Bull of the Yorkshire police interviewed the man *and* the nursemaid."

Garrett sat forward. "What's the setup?" he said.

Pike stared. "Beg pardon, sir. . . . Oh, I see . . . well, it seems they must be our people. I spoke to Bull on the phone and got the story direct from him. He's a good man; very sound. What he says, in brief, is that there's something odd, as you might say, about the whole—er . . ." He hesitated, groping for a word.

"Setup," said Garrett.

Anthony laughed. "Say it, Pike. Don't be insular!"

Pike grinned; then grew immediately serious. "It's this way, sir: Bull didn't know what he was looking for because my instructions carefully omitted anything definite; he simply knew, like the other officers all over who got the orders, that under some pretext he must interview the Lesters, if they stopped their journey in his district, and then communicate with me after he'd got all the information he could about where they were going and cetera—a general picture, as you might say, of the family *and* servants."

"And," said Anthony, "Bull no likee setup. Why?"

Pike, aware that he was being kept up into his bridle, repressed a fleeting smile. He said:

"Just coming to that, sir. Bull—and don't forget he knows nothing—didn't like the nursemaid!"

Garrett threw back the bedclothes and swung his legs to the floor.

"Passport?" said Anthony.

Pike looked at him. "Seemingly all correct in the name of Jane Matthews, sir. Bull got all the particulars and I've started a check."

"The little more," said Anthony, "and how Murch it is!"

Pike smiled dutifully. "But, as you can see, sir, the check's going to take time. Quite a time."

Garrett said: "You say this inspector didn't like the girl?"

Pike nodded. "After he'd finished with Lester, Bull made opportunity to talk to the girl and—well, he didn't cotton to her. Nothing definite, you know, but her manner wasn't right. He said she seemed a bit too quick to resent police inquiries."

"What *were* the inquiries?" said Garrett.

"Very tactful, you may be sure, sir." Pike looked slightly pained.

Garrett was putting on a dressing gown. "Why's tact necessary?"

"Well, really, sir!" Pike's tone was mildly astonished. "We've got to be careful. As it is, Bull had to trump up some question about Alien Registration even to have the right to speak to them. You see, there's nothing against these people: not yet."

Anthony said: "Pike: shake your sleeve!"

Pike laughed like a small boy, proud of an uncle's shrewdness. "Well, sir, there's a funny thing—Bull didn't like Lester any more than he did the nurse. Not so much, in fact. 'Superintendent,' he said to me, 'if there's anything rum about that lot, there's two of 'em in it—Lester himself and the nursegirl.'"

Garrett was lighting a cigarette from a box on the dressing table. He turned and walked across to Pike and stood facing him.

"And so what?" he said harshly.

Pike stared. "I don't quite follow you, I'm afraid, sir."

"Mr. Garrett," said Anthony, "is wondering what action the police are taking. What he'd like is to have these people detained."

"Yes," said Garrett. "Hold 'em—*and* give 'em the works!" He dropped into a chair.

Pike drew in his breath with a reproving little hiss. "We can't do anything like that here, sir." He shook his head slowly, in a movement of absolute negation.

Garrett stood up suddenly. A half-muffled groan of exasperation escaped him, but no words came.

"What we *have* done," said Pike, "is to issue general orders that the Lester car's to be watched for and reported on everywhere it goes. When the party stops for any reason, we shall know at once and a watch—though unobtrusive, as you might say—will be kept to see that nothing goes wrong. When they stop for the *night*——" He broke off and glanced towards Anthony, who now stood at the window. "Well, even if there's no *official* action, I'll wager that Colonel Gethryn and yourself will probably be at the place before morning."

"Very nice!" said Garrett savagely. "All very nice—unless something happens at some place along some road where there aren't any policemen! Which doesn't seem a bit unlikely!"

An angry light came into Pike's eyes and in his long face the mouth became a narrow line. He said stiffly:

"Mr. Garrett, this isn't the United States! Rightly or wrongly we've got what you might call a cast-iron legal system. . . ."

Garrett said harshly: "I know all about that! But don't you realize that if somebody doesn't *do* something——"

"Shut up!" said Anthony suddenly. He came from the window and stood looking from one angry face to the other. "Pike, Mr. Garrett's got some cause to be worried, and what's biting you is that you know it and can't do anything about it. Garrett, it's no good snapping at Pike; he's done everything that can be done—and a bit more! I'll do plenty of unofficial stuff—but we mustn't go chasing blindly all over the north of England when our people may be doubling back for all we know. So there's nothing for it but to wait until they're set for the night. And there are worse things to put your trust in than Scotland Yard. . . . Now, be good little men and make up!"

Garrett smiled, the angry light fading from his eyes. "Sorry!" he said.

Pike's mouth appeared again. "And me, sir."

"Bless you!" said Anthony and surveyed them benignantly. "Dear kiddies!"

7

The morning crept on and became noon—and still the sun, as if determined to make fools of the Air Ministry and those unsung necromancers, Zambra and Negretti, went on shining from a sky of impossible blue.

It shone, with what to Avis Bellingham seemed delightful partiality, through the french windows of Lucia Gethryn's drawing room and made of that charming chamber a place in which, thought Avis, a man could not be otherwise than happy—not even a man who, like the man with her now, was suffering from an idée fixe and a broken head.

She did not *think* this, she found; she *knew* it, although for ten minutes no word had passed between them and she could not, as she sat at Lucia's piano, even see her companion.

From her fingers—long slender fingers whose looks were so much at variance with the controlled strength of their touch upon a keyboard—flowed the last, rippling, sweet yet discordant notes of Ravel's "Fountain." She sat motionless for a moment—and then caught her breath as a man's hands fell upon her shoulders.

"Tom!" she said—and twisted from under the hands and turned and was caught up by arms whose strength appalled and delighted her.

She found herself upon her feet, but the arms were still around her. A voice said her name and lips fastened upon her own lips and the world went away.

Then the lips went away and the world came back and was focused in Garrett's eyes. She put her hands upon his shoulders and heard herself laugh—a little, shaky sound. She said, in a voice which sounded to her own ears far away:

"Mr. *Garrett!* This *is* sudden!" And was immediately horrified at the banality of the attempted jest.

He smiled down at her, the old smile which she had known when they first met; the smile which made his eyes almost disappear; the smile with which she had fallen in love—how many years ago was it?—and which she had been forced, until she had found its owner so improbably asleep in her London flat, to put out of her mind as completely as she might. He said:

"It's time I talked to you. Sit down!"

He put his hands upon her arms and she found herself again seated upon the piano stool. He said:

"I haven't been myself. I've been—well, you know how I've been. I ought to apologize—and I do! I——"

Avis interrupted him. "Of *course* I understand!" she said and smiled up at him and set a hand upon his arm.

"How could I help but understand!" she said—and got to her feet, closing the fingers of the hand.

"You see," she said, "I've something to tell you; something I ought to have told you weeks ago!"

She moved the hand from his arm to his shoulder. She stood very close to him. She said:

"You mustn't be angry with me. I——"

She broke off, abruptly. Her eyes clouded, losing their blueness behind a veil of steely grey. They had seen the thought of her and the bright gleaming of happiness go from the man's eyes. She said:

"You're not *listening!* You're not even thinking about—about us! You're——"

There was misery in Garrett's face, and a puzzled wonder. He strove with evil-shaped, misty thought and wrenched his mind back to this room and this woman whom he loved. He said:

"Darling, forgive me! I was . . . I suddenly had . . ." He struggled painfully for words. "Look here, I *know* there's something wrong with this business! There's a *mistake!* I—I feel it! It's something wrong and twisted. There's something, somewhere, going on *now,* that we ought to be stopping! I——"

He cut himself short. He was looking at a back which receded.

"*Avis!*" he said—and took a step in pursuit and found himself alone, the sound of the closing door ringing in his ears. . . .

The grandfather clock in the corner by the french windows came to life. It whirred and struck. Its hands showed the time as fifteen minutes past noon.

8

At thirty minutes past noon, a woman entered a sitting room on the seventh floor of the Alsace Hotel. She was laughing at something said to her in the bedroom which she had just left. She was neither short nor tall but most pleasingly in drawing; and of an age which might have been anything between twenty-eight and thirty-one. She walked to the high windows and stood looking out, over the green of gardens and the grey of the Embankment, at the sunlight playing upon the river. Stray rays of this light picked out gleams of gold in her neat dark head and bathed with hard radiance a face which had no reason to fear it.

A man came into the room and stood with an arm about her shoulder. He was tall and heavy and moved with the sure, easy smoothness which tells of conditioned muscles. His clothes looked like an Englishman's, but in his clean-shaven face was something pleasantly and essentially transatlantic. He held the woman close and they stood in silence, studying the river and the roofs beyond it.

"*This* isn't London!" said the woman at last. "Oughtn't it to be foggy? Or at least raining? This is a sort of New York day."

The man's arm tightened its grip about her shoulders. He said: "What time's Brat coming in?"—and would doubtless have been answered had not the bell of a telephone begun to ring.

The woman crossed the room and picked up the instrument. She said into the mouthpiece:

"Hello? Who is this?"

A man's voice came along the wire, but it did not answer her question. It was a flat, toneless voice with no accent in particular. It said:

"Mrs. Van Renseler?"

"Yes," said the woman. "Speaking."

"Mrs. Theodore Van Renseler?" The flat voice was insistent, an unpleasing sharpness somewhere concealed within it.

"Yes," said the woman. "Who *is* this talking?"

"Are you in the sitting room of the suite?" said the voice. "Or the bed-room?"

Helen Van Renseler looked up at her husband, who now stood close. Her face was screwed up in a deliberately comic—and extremely attractive—expression of histrionic bewilderment. Into the telephone she said icily:

"If you won't say who you are I shall hang up!" She winked at her husband.

"You'd better not," said the flat voice. "For your own sake!" It went on at some length, while Van Renseler studied his wife's changing expression at first with amusement, then with curiosity and finally with anger.

"Give me that!" he said at last and held out his hand for the telephone.

But the owner of the flat voice had rung off, and Van Renseler spoke into a dead instrument. His wife was frowning. She said:

"What an extraordinary . . ." and let her voice tail off into silence.

"What's it all *about?*" said Van Renseler angrily; then laughed at himself.

"Must've been *crazy!*" said his wife; but the frown was still etched into her forehead.

Van Renseler took her by the shoulders. "Shake the life out of you!" he said. "What—is—it—all—about?"

He was smiling; but the woman was not. She said:

"It was a man's voice. It was sort of—well, beastly! And he said there was a letter in the Railway Guide." She pointed to a small corner book-shelf. "What do they call the things? . . . Bradshaw."

She twisted away from her husband's hands and crossed the room.

"Some publicity stunt," said Van Renseler, and followed and stood beside her as she stooped and pulled the heavy Bradshaw, in its stiff leather case, from a shelf. She said, speaking as if to herself: "Page two-o-two-three . . ." and began, with fingers that seemed a little uncertain, to flip over the leaves.

Van Renseler said: "I tell you it's some advertising trick!"

Helen Van Renseler turned a page—and a piece of note paper, covered with typescript, fluttered to the floor.

She was upon it before her husband could move. She began to read as she was straightening her body—and as she read the colour drained from her face.

"My *God!*" said Van Renseler, watching her. He put an arm about her and felt her body sag against the support. Over her shoulder he read:

To Mr. and Mrs. Theodore Van Renseler:

At 12:15 P.M. today we took charge of your daughter Patricia. If you wish to have her returned to you unharmed, you are to carry out the following instructions *to the letter:*

    1. Make no communication whatsoever to the police—or to anyone—concerning the situation. (You may be sure that if you fail to observe this instruction you will not see your daughter again.)

    2. Obtain fifteen thousand pounds (£15,000) in one-pound currency notes.

3. Place this money (which must not be marked) *and* Mrs. Van Renseler's emerald necklace, earrings and pendant in a plain suitcase.

4. Mr. Van Renseler will bring the suitcase to Cromwell Road station at nine-thirty o'clock this evening.

5. He will then purchase a ticket and go down to the westbound platform by the *stairs*.

6. Someone will approach him within a few minutes of his arrival. This person will say, "Have you a safety match?" which is a signal for Mr. Van Renseler to hand over the suitcase.

7. The person taking the suitcase will then leave the platform. Mr. Van Renseler will stay where he is for five minutes.

If these instructions are fully and personally carried out, and the contents of the suitcase are found to be in order, Patricia Van Renseler will be returned to you before tomorrow evening.

CHAPTER XXIV

Within a stone's throw of Victoria underground station there is an underground cocktail bar. It is, perhaps, the most pleasant of its kind in London and known only to a sufficient clientele. It is open during the usual hours; it is never empty and desolate, nor full and discomfortable. It is always quiet, unfailingly cheerful and invariably soothing. The liquor it stocks is of the best and its staff are expert craftsmen.

Here, at seven o'clock in the evening, were some eight or nine regular customers who sat about at tables—and Sheldon Garrett, who stood at the bar.

He was doing what, out of respect to his battered skull, he should not have done—drinking his third martini. It was a good martini, but to Garrett it tasted like water tainted by the dissolution of a slate pencil.

The barman watched him with anxious eye. "How's that one, sir?"

Garrett sipped and essayed a smile of appreciation. He said the right things in a poor imitation of the right voice—and let his glance flicker towards the archway at the end of the bar.

Here, in the nearer of two telephone cubicles, Anthony Gethryn spoke urgently into a mouthpiece set immovably three inches too low for comfort. He said:

"Well, that's that. But they'll *have* to stop somewhere soon!"

"Yes sir," said Pike's voice. "And where shall I call you when they do?"

Anthony said: "If I'm not here—Victoria-84328—call the Buckingham Theatre. I might take Garrett there. Anything to get his mind off this hunch of his."

Pike's voice said: "You sound worried, sir."

"I am. Garrett's no fool, and hunches aren't always to be despised. He says there's something wrong—and *I'm* beginning to feel it. . . ." Anthony's voice tailed off into silence.

"It's very trying, sir, waiting like this." Pike's tone was soothing. "Especially when, as you might say, our hands are tied."

"Yes, Auntie; yes *indeed!*" An antidote for oil was noticeable in Anthony's voice. "Jet is black, and the clouds over the mountaintop are the purest white. . . . In other words, Pike, call me either here or at the theatre the minute you hear where the Lesters lodge."

"Yes sir," said the telephone.

Anthony went back to the bar and his unfinished drink. He said:

"Just spoken to Pike. Lesters last noticed as having tea in Burtonbury. Then drove on. Pretty soon they're bound to put up for the night. Then we'll fly up——"

Garrett drank more slate-pencil water. "God!" he said. "I wish they'd hurry."

"Yes," said Anthony, and concealed irritation behind his glass.

Garrett said: "I wish we could *do* something! . . . Pike going to call you here?"

Anthony set his glass down on the bar—so hard that he experienced relief that it did not break. He said:

"No. At the Buckingham."

"The what?"

"The Buckingham Theatre," said Anthony. "It calls itself a Palace of Variety. In your tongue—a vaudeville joint."

"Oh!" said Sheldon Garrett. "But I——"

"But nothing!" said Anthony. "We're going."

2

Patricia Van Renseler waked. Her head hurt badly, worse than it ever had in all her ten years. And something had happened to the sheets, so that the blanket was scratchy against her chin. And she ached all over the way she had when scarlet fever had made her so ill. There was a bad taste in her mouth, too, and she was so thirsty that she could not think of anything but water.

She opened her eyes upon darkness. She closed them again, quickly, because with the lids lifted a funny, burning pain shot through them.

She opened the parched lips. She tried to shout "Bunchy!" but only a croaking sound came from her mouth.

This frightened her—and, opening her eyes again in spite of the pain, she made as if to sit up.

But she could not. There was something around her body, outside the bedclothes, which pressed her down. And now she could see a little—and she did not know the room she saw!

Her aches were forgotten, and the funny pain behind her eyes, and her thirstiness, and the scratchiness of the blanket—all swallowed up in a great, unreasoning, comprehensive wave of terror.

"Mummy!" she screamed.

The sound, though roughly edged from the dryness of the small throat, was high and sharp and piercing.

A door opened, showing a rectangle of yellow light and a tall slim woman's figure, which advanced.

Patricia screamed again. But this was only half a scream, cut short by something soft which fell across her nose and mouth and was then pressed down by a hand whose weight made no concession to the youth of the face it crushed.

"Quiet!" said a voice which Sheldon Garrett would have recognized among thousands. "Quiet!"

It was a deep, harsh voice and had in it a definite ring of masculinity which accorded strangely with the ultrafeminine grace of the woman's body and movements as she sat upon the side of the bed, still pressing down upon the cloth and what was beneath it.

"Quiet!" she said again. "Understand me?"

Desperately Patricia's small head was nodded. Air, now, was her one desire; a necessity more vital even than water had seemed.

The pressure was eased; the cloth pulled away. Patricia drew in shuddering draughts of air. Her small body shook—but beyond the gasping of her breath no sound came from her.

"And *now,*" said the woman, the deep voice even deeper, "you'd better go to sleep again."

With one hand she took the child's right wrist, drawing the whole naked arm clear of the blankets.

Through Patricia's dry, bruised lips came a whisper of sound; a shaking whisper which was inadequate gauge of the terror which gripped her.

"Please!" said the whisper. "Please, I——"

"*Quiet!*" The deep voice was savage in its harshness.

The woman's free hand came from her side as she spoke. It held something which faintly glittered.

"*Oh!*" said Patricia on a high note of pain. Something had pricked her arm just above the elbow. It hurt.

She tried to pull the arm away, but the woman's hand about her wrist was like steel. . . .

"A-ah!" sighed Patricia on a low note of drowsiness. And then: "Theo . . . Helen . . . I . . ."

The voice died away—to be replaced by heavy, laboured breathing.

Once more Miss Patricia Van Renseler slept. . . .

3

The first performance at the Buckingham was in full swing.

There were two acrobats and a girl in tights who handed them things. There was a performing seal who applauded himself and his self-satisfied trainer. There were a "Whirlwind" dance team; a Lancashire comedian; a family on stilts called the Stargays Brothers, and a remarkable person who wrestled and fought with a dummy.

And then there was Eustace Vox—a name which minimized the surprise of finding that he was a ventriloquist and a good one. Billed as THE MAN WITH THREE FRIENDS, he presided at a dinner table for three, his two guests being life-size dummies.

The audience, held silent for nearly two minutes by the skill of the one human on the stage, began to titter, then to laugh uproariously. For the dialogue, said by many to be the work of Mr. Vox himself, was excellent.

And then the third friend of the title made her appearance. It was another life-size dummy, operated by ingenious mechanism. It wore the neat uniform of a parlourmaid.

It spoke—and somewhere in the middle of the third row of stalls a man stood up, clapped a hand to his head, and in no uncertain voice called upon a traditional power.

He was a tall man who, by accent, clothes and bearing, should have known better. And he did not improve upon his first inexplicable *gaffe* by his subsequent actions—which consisted of seizing the arm of the man sitting next to him and dragging this person—heedless of the shoes and knees and comfort of others—out of his seat and the auditorium.

4

Garrett blinked in the sudden light of the exit corridor. He was breathing hard and his head hurt him. Behind him the laughter from the packed house dwindled in volume as the door through which Anthony had dragged him swung shut. He said irritably:

"What's the big idea!" and then suppressed further speech as he saw his companion's face.

Anthony said: "The women in the teashop: there was a short square masculine one?"

Garrett nodded.

"And a tall, willowy, feminine one?"

Garrett nodded.

"And the short masculine one had a deep harsh masculine voice as she bullied the tall willowy one, who had a high soft feminine voice?"

Garrett nodded.

"How do you know," said Anthony slowly, "which voice belonged to which woman?"

Garrett stared. "Damn it! I was there and . . ." His voice tailed away, and he looked at Anthony with open mouth. He said in a whisper:

"My God! I *don't* know! I just assumed——"

"Come on!" said Anthony—and was gone.

CHAPTER XXV

In the sitting room of Suite 306 in the Alsace Hotel Helen Van Renseler sat in a straight-backed chair. She was motionless and rigid. Her face was blank and on her cheeks the dustings of rouge showed angry against the surrounding pallor. Every now and then the pupils of her eyes would narrow to pin points; then gradually widen until they well-nigh covered the irises.

She was trying, without success, to keep these eyes from looking towards the clock upon the mantel. Its hands stood at five minutes past nine. It seemed to her that they would never move. She wished passionately that they would and prayed desperately that they would not.

They did. They reached the sixth minute; then the seventh.

A soft knocking came upon the outer door of the suite. A scream welled up in Helen Van Renseler's throat, but she forced it back—and found herself standing.

The knock came again; a little louder—and she found herself just beside the outer door, her fingers on its handle. . . .

The fingers turned the handle, and their arm pulled back the door.

A tall man stood upon the threshold. Her eyes took in a picture of him which told her mind nothing. He said:

"Mrs. Van Renseler?"

Her head nodded. The man stepped over the threshold, taking the handle from her grasp and shutting the door.

Through the grey mist which seemed to swirl about her mind she was aware of his eyes. They were green eyes, hard with purpose.

"Mrs. Van Renseler," he said, "is your daughter with you?"

The grey fog was ripped apart. She said in a strange, shrill voice:

"Who are you? I——"

The man interrupted her. He said:

"Mrs. Van Renseler: Is your daughter here with you—*now?*"

She breathed through distended nostrils. She said:

"Of course. She's been asleep for hours. Who are you?"

For a moment the man looked at her; then moved quickly past her to the first of the inner doors and through it.

She stood bewildered—amazement and fear bemusing the exhausted mind. She clasped her hands and wrung them so that the physical pain made her gasp a little. She thought:

"What shall I *do?* What shall I *do?*"

The man came back. Helen stood where she was. Even if she had wanted to move she could not have done so. He opened the outer door and put his head out into the corridor and spoke to someone invisible. He said:

"Get over to the Yard. Tell Pike to drop the Lesters and stand by."

He pulled his head back and shut the door and turned once more to Helen. He said:

"My name's Gethryn—Anthony Gethryn. You can consider me a policeman." He moved closer. "When did you discover that your daughter had been stolen? And have you heard from anyone claiming to hold her?"

She said harshly:

"I don't know what you're talking about. I must ask you to go."

Anthony took her by the arm. Under his fingers the bare flesh was cold and the muscles beneath the soft skin set like iron. He said:

"I can help. Come in here." He moved towards the living room.

Helen Van Renseler swayed. The fog was back in her mind now . . . swirling . . .

She found herself in an armchair in the living room. Anthony stood over her, a glass in his hand. He held this to her lips in such a way that she was forced to sip. Brandy burned her tongue and throat, and she coughed and fought away from the glass and sat upright. She said, choking:

"Don't! Don't! . . . I'm all right!" Her eyes shot a glance towards the clock, whose hands stood now at twelve minutes after the hour.

Anthony watched her.

"So there's a time limit!" he said, and sat in a chair to face her and set the glass on a table beside him. He looked at her steadily. He said after a long moment:

"I think that a little while ago you engaged a nursemaid who crossed from England to America to work for you. I think that at some time today this woman took your daugther out—and did not return. I think that since then you've received some sort of message from the kidnappers. I think, as you're alone, that your husband has gone to get in touch with these people as a result of the message. Am I right?"

Her eyes were wide as they stared at him, and their whites were visible all round the irises. Her throat worked and her lips moved, but there was no sound.

Anthony stood up. He said:

"And I think you won't admit that all this is right because you've been threatened that any interference will mean that you won't see your daughter again. . . . *But*, Mrs. Van Renseler, you'd better tell me all about it."

She got to her feet with a sudden jerky movement which sent her chair crashing to the floor.

"I won't!" she said in a flat voice which cracked. "I don't care who you are!" Her words began to come fast and faster. "In this country you don't know about . . . about this sort of thing. We Americans do!" A sobbing gasp shook the voice again. "My God, how we do! After I've got Patricia again I'll tell you anything—*everything!* I'll spend every minute of my life with you until these devils are caught! But I won't say another word until she's back! If I did, you might make everything wrong, and then . . . and then——"

Her voice ceased abruptly. All numbness had gone from her now; all control. She was a distraught woman whose child was lost. Her face worked and her breath came in hard, irregular gasps. Her eyes flickered yet again towards the clock.

Behind an expressionless face Anthony's mind was racing. She must tell; must be forced to tell. But how, when her every instinct told her that to tell might cost her the child? How, when . . .

A sudden light came to his eyes. Into the racing mind words had flashed; a sentence from the report of Detective Inspector Andrews, C.I.D., upon Garrett's first visit to Scotland Yard: ". . . some criminal undertaking involving possibly the abduction of a child and the execution of bodily harm upon some other person. . . ."

In one long stride he was close to her. He took her by the shoulders with hands which were not gentle. He said:

"Tell me! Unless you want to lose your husband as well!"

She was very still under his hands. Her eyes stared up at him. She said: "Oh, God! I can't stand this! I——"

Anthony tightened his grip. "From the beginning of this case as we know it there's been this suggestion—that a child was going to be kidnapped *and* that someone else—a man—was going to be killed."

The shoulders twisted in his grip. Hands thrust vainly at his chest. She panted:

"Let me go! Let me go!"

Anthony said: "Tell me where your husband's gone!"

She struggled with desperate strength. The fingers upon her shoulders bit into her flesh. She shouted: "It's a trick! That's all I see! Let me *go!*"

Anthony said: "Listen to me! These people who have your daughter are going to hurt your husband—perhaps kill him. He's probably got ransom money with him; don't you see that if they take that and put him out of the way, they can still hold your daughter, for *more* money? Think, woman!"

She broke. The struggling fury became a limpness which needed his arms to uphold it.

He picked her up bodily. He set her upon the sofa by the long windows and stood over her. Tears rained from her eyes—helpless, hopeless tears which rolled unchecked. And sobs tore at her.

Anthony dropped to a knee beside her. He did not touch her, and he did not speak. . . .

The sobbing grew less.

"Tell me!" said Anthony—and suddenly she was on her feet.

Anthony rose to face her; and now it was she who touched him. Her hands gripped his arms, just below each shoulder. Her eyes fixed their gaze upon his eyes. Her face was ravaged, but the new fire in her burned bright and steady. She said:

"I'm going to tell you. If it turns out wrong, I shall kill myself. My husband has gone to see—these people. He has the money with him, and my emeralds. He has to wait for someone on the westbound platform of a subway station. Cromwell Road. He has to be there at nine-thirty."

Her eyes went to the clock. Its hands were at nine twenty-one.

She said in a sort of dead whisper:

"There's not time! There's not time!"

She swayed and fell. But Anthony did not catch her. He was already at the telephone.

CHAPTER XXVI

A taxi sped down the grey, interminable length of the Cromwell Road. In the back of it Theodore Van Renseler sat huddled. His face was a dull mask, but behind drooping lids his eyes were alive. Upon his knees was a large dispatch case of dark leather—and his hands gripped it with a strength in odd contrast to the limpness of his body.

Upon the right of the cab the tall ugly houses gave way, with a sort of sullen enmity, to a row of small bright shops which nestled about the glass-canopied, brick façade of an underground station.

The cab stopped. It had barely ceased to move when Van Renseler was out of it. He thrust a ten-shilling note into the driver's hand, muttered something and was gone.

In the station vestibule the clock over the lifts showed nine twenty-five. A ticket collector lounged and yawned, and, save for Van Renseler, was the only human visible. At this time and in this place there is always lack of life; the workers are at home, the pleasure seekers already carried to their goals.

Van Renseler's step was heavy; without elasticity. He walked like a man who has to give thought to the business of movement.

At the only open booking window he bought a ticket for Piccadilly Circus —the only station his aching mind could remember. The clerk looked curiously at the white, expressionless face of his customer and was a little slow with his giving of change.

Van Renseler forced himself to wait: nothing, *nothing* must be unusual in his behaviour.

He took his change and turned and glanced at the clock. Nine twenty-seven . . . Three minutes . . . Then, the ransom paid, a frightful, sick waiting. "Patricia Van Renseler," that letter had said, "will be returned to you before tomorrow evening." The wait—the nightmare, agonizing interval —might, then, be twenty hours!

He checked the groan that rose to his lips. The liftman threw open the grilled gate and stood aside.

Van Renseler shook his head. "No," he said between lips which barely moved. "Can't stand elevators. Where're the stairs?"

The liftman pointed. "Over there, sir. Past the bookstall."

"Thanks," Van Renseler said. He walked away—very erect, very deliberate in gait, the black dispatch case at the end of a long right arm.

The liftman looked after him, a flicker of puzzled interest momentarily lighting his bored young face. "Looks queer," he thought, and once more leaned and yawned and waited for his shift to end.

The stairs were iron and sharply spiralled. The sheer, tubular walls were unrelieved grey-white, harshly lit by shadeless electric bulbs. The iron was slippery and rang hollow as Van Renseler's feet descended.

He plodded down . . . around and down . . . around and down . . . around and down. . . . The shaft seemed endless. He looked up and saw nothing but the circular sheathlike wall and the awful regularity of the twisting iron. He looked down, still plodding, and saw the same pattern inverted.

Sick fear caught him by the stomach in a sharp, new wave. Jagged irrationalities flashed through his mind. Suppose "they" didn't keep the date! . . . Suppose this iron and this sheath *were* endless! . . . Suppose his mind had gone and this iron-lined shell had no existence and instead of saving his child he were useless to her!

He began to run. His feet made a great clattering. His breath came hard. Beads of icy sweat started out upon his white face. . . .

The stairs ended. There was a door. He went through it. He drew in a great breath and jerked back his left cuff and looked at his watch. It showed twenty-nine and a half minutes past the hour.

He was in a cross passage, blue-and-white tiled. The roar of a passing train shook the earth. He turned and went towards the sound and came out upon an empty, gaily-postered platform. Panic seized him as he realized that he did not know whether . . . Ah! he had seen a lighted sign which bore, among others, the word "Eastbound."

It was the other platform then. He turned sharply and went back down the cross passage, passing a uniformed porter as he did so.

He came out upon the westbound platform. There was no train nor anyone awaiting a train. And no official.

Again he looked at his watch. Half a minute past the time now. He walked with slow, heavy steps along the platform. He must wait; must wait; wait; wait. . . .

He had reached the extreme end of the long, echoing platform when, from the last of the cross passages, just behind him, came brisk footsteps.

He turned. His heart beat with terrific force. He saw a man coming towards him.

2

Anthony's black Voisin screamed down the Embankment, its horn sounding almost continuously. It slid in and out of the variegated traffic like a snake through undergrowth. It achieved, even in this crowded, tram-strewn thoroughfare, an average speed beyond belief. Unscathed, it reached the

Westminster Bridge corner, swung right and, writhing tortuous way between cars, drays, cabs and omnibuses, reached St. James's Park.

As it turned by Birdcage Walk a motorcyclist policeman leaned from his sidecar and gripped at the arm of his colleague astride the saddle. The Voisin, its horn playing an insistent, raucous fanfare, receded at terrific speed. . . .

The policeman in the saddle shook his head. He had seen the unobtrusive sign (not to be mentioned here or elsewhere) which tells guardians of the law that here is no speedster but a colleague upon vital business.

The clock upon the Voisin's dashboard read nine thirty-two.

3

Two dark blue limousines of sedate appearance made their way, at a speed far from sedate, down an astonished Knightsbridge. Their horns, like the Voisin's, blared without cessation. And no policeman looked more than once at them without knowing them—as no civilian could—for what they were.

In the back seat of the first were Pike and Garrett and two others—quiet and burly men who spoke not at all.

Garrett twisted in his seat. He said:

"Wonder if Gethryn's behind us?"

Pike smiled thinly. He shook his head. "Not *behind* us, sir!"

Garrett said: "D'you think your people have done that phoning yet?"

Pike lifted his square shoulders, very slightly. "If they're not through yet, sir, they will be at any minute."

The clock on the dashboard stood at nine thirty-three.

4

A through train—eight out of ten go through Cromwell Road between eight-thirty and eleven at night—came roaring out of its sheathlike tunnel, rocketed past the long platform and hurled itself into the black mouth of the interrupted tube.

Van Renseler stood, trying not to look at the man who had seemed to be about to speak to him until a porter in uniform had come onto the platform and, by means of a portable ladder, had mounted to the direction board and begun to tinker with it.

That had been, it seemed to Van Renseler, an endless time ago: actually it was three minutes, for the clock now said nine thirty-four.

The porter came down from his ladder, folded it up, lifted it and walked off through the centre cross passage, his footsteps echoing shrill and metallic in this empty man-made warren.

Van Renseler, his heart pounding until to draw breath was conscious effort, watched the other man.

It was, primarily, an *ordinary* man. Of medium height and build; of indeterminate clothing; of briskly inconspicuous gait.

The hollow reverberations of the porter's footsteps grew gradually less.

Van Renseler, unable to move, stared dumbly at the sauntering back of the other man.

The echoing footsteps died away.

The man turned—not sharply, not hurried; just the ordinary turn of a platform loiterer.

But now he was walking directly towards Van Renseler.

He came on and on. Van Renseler ceased to breathe. Now the man was close. Now he halted, less than a full pace away.

His face was, at first sight, as commonplace as the rest of him. Neither round nor oval, sanguine nor pale, it was a face which a man might look at every day for a moment and never remember. But Van Renseler looked for longer than a moment. Moreover, this face and its owner were to him of paramount importance. And he saw that between cheeks of indeterminate shape and brows of indeterminate hue were eyes the like of which he had never seen.

For they were without colour, iris and pupil blending into one another through indeterminate shades of drabness, and the whites not white but merely a grey lightening of the utterly indeterminate shade of the cores.

The man spoke. He said:

"Have you a safety match?"

Van Renseler tried to speak but did not succeed. He proffered the black dispatch case.

The man took it. He shifted a little as he did so. He now stood with his back to the wall of the platform and facing the rails. Van Renseler had waited at the extreme end of the platform, close to the tunnel mouth. Shifting in sympathy with the other's movement, he now had his back to the edge of the platform just where it merged into the horseshoe wall of the tunnel. He was some three feet from this edge.

The man snapped open the lock of the dispatch case, which he took by its handle in his left hand. He looked full at Van Renseler with his colourless eyes. He said, in a voice which was neither deep nor high pitched, round nor thin:

"I've got a message for you."

He put his right hand into the inner pocket of the inconspicuous overcoat. Van Renseler's tongue came out in a vain effort to moisten dry lips. The man was groping in the pocket. He said, after a glance down the empty length of the platform:

"Here it is!"

His right hand came out of his pocket. It came very fast. In it was something dully black, like a long pantomime sausage. . . .

Van Renseler jerked his head aside—but it caught him a heavy blow on the temple, glancing down to his shoulder.

A flare like that of a Verey light soared inside Van Renseler's head. . . . He was falling. . . .

As he began to crumple his assailant thrust out the hand with the sandbag in it and caught him in the chest.

There was nicely judged power in the thrust; enough power to jerk Van Renseler's buckling legs into three staggering backward paces.

The fourth pace carried his senseless body beyond the edge of the platform. He fell like a limp sack. His body was in the darkness of the tunnel mouth—and directly across the passive, deadly, shining riband of the live rail. . . .

Before the body had completed the bare four feet of its fall to certain cindered destruction by thousands of volts of electricity the man with the bag had turned and was walking—with brisk, unhurried, commonplace gait —towards the first of the cross passages. . . .

And the clock over the direction board showed a few seconds before nine thirty-five.

5

"Yes sir!" said the inspector in charge at Drayton Street police station. "Yes sir, I understand, sir. Right away, sir . . . five minutes at most."

He set back the receiver of the telephone and began to give curt, concise orders. Over his head the clock upon the wall showed nine thirty-five. He said finally:

"Got that, Sergeant?"

The sergeant stood rigid at attention. Out of a wooden face came sharp, metallic phrases. "Yes sir. Ten men. Surround Cromwell Road station, covering all hexits. Let no one enter or leave station till officers arrive from the Yard. Then take their orders."

The inspector nodded. "Get at it. Quick!"

6

"Yes, I will," said the little man in charge of the Cromwell Road tube station. "Yes, at once!"

His eyes were bright with excitement: here were happenings indeed.

He stood up and locked his desk: he was a neat little man. He started towards his office door, glancing at his watch as he went.

The time was nine thirty-six.

Some two seconds before he opened his office door a man carrying a black dispatch case crossed the vestibule from the direction of the stairs. An ordinary-seeming man, with a brisk yet unhurried walk. He went out into Cromwell Road and turned to his left.

7

The underground station faces Cromwell Road, but its eastern side is in a dismal Kensingtonian backwater called Illingham Street. At nine thirty-seven the black Voisin penetrated the gloom of Illingham Street like an angry bullet. . . .

Exactly at this moment the little stationmaster, accompanied by two uniformed porters, hurried onto the westbound platform.

The stationmaster looked up and down the platform.

"No one here," he said. "I——"

One of the porters drew in his breath with a sharp hiss. He was staring at the gleaming lines near the tunnel mouth at the far end. He shouted indistinguishably and began to run.

"What in the . . ." began the stationmaster; then himself saw and ran too.

At this moment, up above upon the surface of the earth, two blue limousines drew to a stop opposite the front of the station. Quiet men came from them and walked into the vestibule between the glowing windows of the shops. Pike was among them, and Garrett. To meet them, cutting through from the side entrance past the lifts, came the long form of Anthony Gethryn.

Across the wide straightness of Cromwell Road policemen in uniform—eleven of them, all at the double—came towards the station.

Pike saw them and glanced at his watch. "Not bad," he said, and turned to meet the sweating sergeant.

Anthony, who had merely nodded to Garrett, turned away again and went back towards the lifts. The movement gave Garrett a clear view of the roadway, and he saw, receding across it, a figure which had apparently come from one of the shops upon the same side of the street as the station, some twenty yards from the entrance.

It was a man's figure, of medium size and inconspicuously clad. It walked with brisk yet unhurried gait. And it carried a black bag in its right hand.

There was, in this figure, nothing at all out of the ordinary. Its movements were anything but furtive; it had not come directly from the station; in movement, stature, pace and appointment it had probably ten thousand counterparts in London.

Yet Garrett could not take his eyes from it. Perhaps it was the fact that the figure carried a bag; perhaps it was something far less simply explicable, but in the twentieth part of a second he made up his mind that he must know more of this man who was so calmly walking away. With a sudden feeling of breathless weakness in his stomach he turned to speak to Pike.

But Pike was not near, nor was anyone. They had all moved across towards the ticket office and lifts. . . .

8

Standing at the extreme edge of the platform, near the tunnel mouth, the stationmaster looked down and shook his head. His small face was pinched and white under the yellow radiance of the lights.

"Bad business!" he said, and made a ticking sound with his tongue. "Bad business! Must've died instantaneous."

The elder of the two porters was scratching his head and looking down in bewilderment at the sprawled body upon the gleaming rails. He was not perturbed like the stationmaster; he was not fixed in bovine curiosity like his mate; he was all bewilderment.

The stationmaster jerked himself into bustling semblance of activity.

"Come on, now!" he said busily. "Got to get him moved before the next train."

"Ah!" said the bovine porter.

But the other porter still stared. He said:

" 'E ain't dead!" He pointed with black-edged finger. "W'en they gets burned they goes all twisted like. An' there's a stink. An' . . . *look!* You c'n see 'im breave!"

"But—but the current," stammered the little stationmaster.

The bovine porter came to life. " 'E *is* breathin'!" he said firmly. "Cummon!"

9

A dark blue taxi, very new, very discreet and extremely shiny, sped westwards along Cromwell Road. One of a new fleet, it was a most superior taxi. It was smooth running, excellently sprung and admirably driven. It had —unusual for a London cab—shining bumpers at front and back. It also had, between the rear bumper and the body, a luggage grid.

Within it carried one passenger: a composed and ordinary-seeming man who held upon his knees a black bag.

The taxi slowed; then turned off Cromwell Road to the right. The turn completed, it was about to accelerate when there swerved in front of it a small boy upon a bicycle. Any onlooker would have given odds upon the boy's death—yet he was passed unscathed. The driver, as already has been said, was a good one. He braked, swerved, skidded, accelerated—and very nearly shook Garrett from his prone precarious perch between rear bumper and grid.

He felt himself going. His legs swung sideways and one foot actually scraped along the road surface. With a terrific effort he clenched his grip upon the bars of the grid. The muscles of his back and arms seemed to be tearing loose. And then, the swerve over, the taxi righted itself and he was once more safe. . . .

He put his head down upon his arm and wiped away the sweat which streamed from his forehead. He prayed—as he had been praying since that fantastic moment when, seeing the taxi begin to draw away with his uncertain quarry, he had run blindly after it and swung upon his perch like an oversized gamin—that somebody would see him. Surely, surely, they must soon—in this best-policed city in the world—pass a constable who would catch sight of him and stop the taxi. Surely, if they persisted in escaping the eyes of the law, another motorist would see him in his headlight beam and overtake the taxi and tell the driver. Surely, stopping at an intersection of streets, some curious loiterer would shout to the driver concerning his extra passenger. Surely something must happen to stop this cab before the end of its journey. Even a smash, he reflected, would be better than nothing. Once stopped by some outside agency, and he would at least—although under suspicion himself—be able to delay matters for long enough. . . .

But the cab went on unchecked, through these dark and frowning and

always deserted Kensingtonian streets. Not a policeman met Garrett's eye
. . . not an observant busybody of a passer-by . . . no overtaking car. . . .

10

The lift gate opened with a rattling clang. The stationmaster was kneeling by the body of Van Renseler. He was looking down into the still face
and shaking his head. He was talking to himself.

"No current," he was saying. "Can't understand it at all."

Brisk men came and tapped him on the shoulder and moved him aside.
And uniformed policemen bent and raised the unconscious man. In the back
of the lift the two porters, swelling with a delicious sense of importance,
began unanimously to talk to a burly person in the plainest of clothes.

The stationmaster, blinking, got to his feet and stepped out of the lift.
Now the inert body of the man who should have been dead was being
placed upon a stretcher held by more policemen. Over this bent a tall man
in clothes of easy elegance.

The stationmaster was drawn irresistibly towards the stretcher. He said
timidly:

"Is he—I can't understand how—he was lying right across the live rail.
. . . He——"

The tall man straightened and turned. He said brusquely:

"He's all right. Crack on the head. And the current was cut off from
Lot's Road."

The stationmaster's eyes were wide and wondering. "But I don't . . ."
His little bleat died in his throat as it became plain to him that he was
unnoticed.

The tall man had turned to another. "Where's Garrett?" he was saying.

11

The blue taxi, having threaded tortuous way through gloomy frowning
streets of shocking similarity, turned into another which, although no better
lit, was wider and longer and flanked by more portentous buildings.

There were lights in many windows of the tall brick houses, but they
were yellow, dismal lights which served not at all to relieve the dank atmosphere of disuse and decay. They were allies, it seemed, of the dirty-paned
and infrequent street lamps.

The taxi stopped.

Garrett, who had been wondering what he would do when this thing
happened, now made up his mind. He lay motionless. Thus he could not
see anything save the roadway. But he heard the door of the cab open . . .
feet alighting . . . a curt murmur of voices . . . the chinking of coins
passed from hand to hand . . . and then brisk feet crossing the pavement
and the whining of a rusty iron gate.

What he had not heard—because this man wore heels of rubber—was the
taxi driver's descent from his driving seat. So that, rolling himself with caution off the unkind iron, he was shocked to find himself, as he rose to his

feet and began painfully to ease his aching muscles, regarded by a burly person with arms akimbo and menacing stance. . . .

12

The two dark limousines from Scotland Yard sped westward down the Cromwell Road. Anthony sat beside the driver of the first and spoke to Pike over his shoulder.

"Five minutes start," he said. "Too much."

Pike said: "Maybe, sir." And then, uneasily: "And how do we know Mr. Garrett's on the right tack?"

Anthony exploded: "God damn it, man! Isn't it enough that he's on a tack at all! *We've* got nothing—except Van Renseler with his head bashed in and a broken collarbone!"

"That's all very well, sir." Pike was stubborn. "But I'm afraid it's a wild-goose chase, as you might say. Don't forget, Mr. Garrett had that crack on the head himself. And if he'd been—well, *normal*—why should he go running off and taking a whip-behind ride on some taxi without telling anyone? If that young constable hadn't happened to see him——"

Anthony interrupted. "Yes, yes! Quite, and all that! . . . But don't forget, his hunch was right and we were wrong. What he probably did was to see something that we didn't—and have no time to do anything except what he has done." He went on, half to himself: "Hope to God enough people've seen him."

Almost as he spoke the driver swung the car into the curb and pulled to an abrupt halt with a screeching of brakes. At the curb stood a tall and massive and helmeted policeman.

Pike was out of the car almost before it had stopped moving. He ran round the front of the car and talked to the policeman. He ran back again and got into his seat and snapped at the driver:

"First to the right. Cranbrook Street. Keep your eyes open for constables." He said to Anthony: "That man saw him. Said he couldn't believe his eyes. Only hope, sir, we can *keep* on the trail."

The police cars—for the second had halted beside the first—moved on, swinging to the right at the next corner. London—even off the Cromwell Road—is not so lawless as it had seemed to the Garrett who had clung to the back of a taxi.

13

"But I tell you," said Garrett between his teeth, "that it's a police matter! Scotland Yard——"

The driver interrupted. His hands had come away from his hips and turned themselves into fists. He said:

"P'lice matter, is it? Tell yer what, cock, that's the first bleedin' truth that's passed your bloody mouth." He came closer.

"Aw, the *hell* with it!" said the Sheldon Garrett, once the best light heavyweight his university had ever produced.

His right foot drew back; his left foot went forward. His right fist, moving not more than nine inches, met the chin of the driver with a crisp and smacking sound.

The man's knees buckled and he fell forward—a sure sign of complete unconsciousness.

Garrett jumped away from the falling bulk; and then, without so much as a glance at it, stepped onto the pavement. He glanced apprehensively up and down the length of the dismal street. But no one met his gaze and there was no sound of footsteps. He looked next up at the house into which the man with the bag must have gone. There was one light visible—from a small window on the second floor. There was no sound.

On tiptoe he crossed to the spear-shaped railings of rusty iron which bounded the patch of mildewed garden before the house. His eyes strained upwards at the lighted window. He tried to see whether or not it was open and could not. He was obsessed by the fear that his quarry had heard his altercation with the driver.

His heart beat fast, with irregular thumps. His head hurt him, but he did not know it. His mouth was dry—and in him was ever-increasing certainty. On tiptoe still he went along the railing to the gate whose hinges he had heard creaking. He set his hand upon this to open it; then changed his mind.

He thought: "If I go in and ring the bell and spin some sort of a yarn—well, I won't be any place. They'll either get me—or I won't find out anything. Maybe I ought to scare up a bobbie. But if I leave *he* may get out while I'm gone—and then where are we?"

He took his hand from the gate and once more looked up and down the road. One way it stretched on interminably; but a hundred yards away in the other direction was a turning with a lamppost at its corner.

With long, loping strides he ran silently towards this corner. As he went he counted the houses so that, when he was behind them in the next street, he could tell which one was his goal. . . .

14

The two quiet police cars surged in file up the dark, straight inevitability of Derby Street.

The leading car came to a crossroad and stopped. A street named Paignton ran off to the right; to the left there curved away into obscurity something called Biddlecombe Avenue.

Again Pike shot out. He ran back to the second car. He said: "Take the left. We're going right. Ask all constables."

15

In a drab, unfurnished, dirty room upon the second floor of Number 17 Paignton Street a man and a woman talked. The woman knelt. The man sat upon a carpetless floor with his back against the wall and fumbled over a black bag upon his knees.

The woman, looking into the bag, drew in her breath with a sharp and sensually gratified hiss. She said after a moment:

"So we've done it!"

The man nodded.

He closed the bag, snapping its locks. He looked up at the woman over his shoulder. His mouth smiled and he said:

"Yes. And we've only just begun." He got to his feet, the bag in his left hand. "But we're not taking any chances. We're going, *now!*"

The woman looked at him. "Chelsea?" she said.

The man nodded, turning away.

The woman put her hand upon his arm. She said with a backward jerk of her head to indicate a room behind her:

"How do we take it? Open or trunk?"

16

"Easy there!" said Anthony to the driver, and pointed.

The police car lights swung a little to the right—and in the white beam there showed clearly the back of a shining dark blue cab. And something else—the huddled figure of a man who lay upon the road behind the cab.

The light seemed to rouse him. He stirred. His eyes opened. Groaning, he struggled to a sitting posture and put a hand to his head. Like a sleepy, peevish child he turned his head away from the white glare of the lights. He mumbled to himself and set a hand upon the edge of his cab's bumper and tried to pull himself to his feet. He was aware of the car with the lights stopping, and men getting out of it. He tried to stand without support and his knees buckled.

He would have fallen had not the adequate arm of Superintendent Arnold Pike come about his shoulders. A voice said to him, seeming to come to his ear from far away:

"Take your time and tell us about it."

His strength coming back to him with every moment, the man began to talk. . . .

17

Roughly, efficiently, the woman pulled down the single garment which she had slipped upon the inert body of the child. Now she began to pull stockings onto the straight small legs. This done, she looked down for the shoes—and saw only one. She frowned and called over her shoulder in her deep, harsh voice:

"Bring in that other shoe, will you?"

She was answered immediately—but not in the way she had expected. The man to whom she had spoken came swiftly through the door. His movements were tight and quick and soundless. There was that about them which made her look suddenly into his face, the colour ebbing away from her own. She would have spoken, but he silenced her with a quick movement of the hand. His strange eyes, normally colourless, seemed now to have a reddish glow behind them. He said:

"Quick. Back way. There's a car in front. Looks like police."

The woman's hand flew to her mouth. She said hoarsely:

"But how . . . ?"

The man paid no attention. With an ease which told of a strength not promised by his build, he picked up the flaccid, stertorously breathing body of the child and hung it like a sack across his shoulder.

18

The street which runs parallel with Paignton Street, to the south, is called Beckford Place. It is like Paignton Street but, incredibly, yet more dismal.

The house which backed onto Number 17 Paignton Street was, by divine grace, untenanted. In its weed-choked patch of back garden Garrett stood beneath a seven-foot wall of brick which now was all that separated him from his goal.

At some time or another, for some reason quite possibly disreputable, someone had made a door in this wall. It was, as he stood, some few feet to the right of him. He had tried its handle but with no success. Now, crouching, he suddenly sprang upwards—and his crooked fingers caught the top of the wall. With an ease which would have been greater had he not for the past days been a sick man, he levered himself up to sit astride the rough brickwork.

It was very dark. Above, the black vault of the sky showed no moon; and such stars as were visible at all could only be seen through the high, dark grey pall which London so often throws around herself. In the gloom the twisted shapes of drab persistent trees seemed to Garrett's straining eyes to thrust themselves upward like ugly hands. In the windows of houses to his right and left showed occasional dingy lights—but the house which he watched was unrelieved black.

He swung his right leg over the top of the wall so that now both his feet hung over the terrain of 17 Paignton Street. He made ready to slip down; then suddenly checked.

He had heard a door—or perhaps it was a window—being softly opened. It seemed to him that the sound had come from the blank black face of the house he watched. But he could not be sure.

He lay now along the top of the wall, flat upon his belly. He made himself small. And he held his breath as he listened.

He heard the door again; definitely it was a door. It was, he saw with that inner eye which translates sound into pictures, being opened more widely than before. Something came through it. There were scraping foot-steps and a sort of soft, shuffling bump as if something heavy had struck against the doorjamb.

And then, waking thunderous and unexpected echoes, came the sound of a door knocker. It thundered against a door in Paignton Street; the door, it seemed, of Number 17.

The sound ceased, and Garrett heard other and nearer and softer sounds—footsteps which ran softly over the neglected garden; ran towards the wall.

Other footsteps followed. They were lighter yet less feline. They were short striding and quite definitely a woman's. He strained his eyes down into the darkness and saw indistinguishable shapes approaching, one some fifteen feet in advance of the second.

And then the knocking began again.

But he had no time for wonder. Below him the first running figure had arrived at the wall and was stooping beside the door. Even through the darkness, he could see that this figure was a man's; could see also that over its right shoulder another, far smaller figure hung limply. . . .

In one movement Garrett got to his knees and leapt downwards. He landed, as he had hoped, upon the left shoulder of the man.

They fell and rolled. And the small figure which had been over the man's other shoulder fell away from their struggling bodies. . . .

In the darkness, on the dank, dead soil, Garrett and his adversary fought in silence.

There was a strength entirely unexpected, Garrett found, in his enemy. But he himself was the heavier, and though his breath came in hard rasping gasps and there was searing pain in his head, he found himself at last astride of the other's body and caught the throat with his left hand while he drove short, heavy punches at the dimly seen face.

A savage flush of victory warmed him—and a pair of arms locked themselves about his neck from behind. They were soft arms, but there was a steely core to their softness. Garrett, choking, was forced to take his hands from the man beneath him. As he flung them up and backward in an attempt to snatch at this new assailant there was a violent heave beneath him and an upthrust knee came with sickening force into the pit of his stomach. He was flung backwards and sideways. He rolled in agony, fighting for air. . . . Two figures stood over him, and the small pointed toe of a woman's shoe cracked against his cheek.

The man was fumbling at his pockets. He said hoarsely:

"Take the kid and get out. Quick! I'll be with you!"

Like a guardsman the woman obeyed. In a stride she was beside the small, motionless bundle and had gathered it into her arms.

Garrett conquered the momentary paralysis of his lungs and drew in a whistling gasp of air and started to struggle to his feet.

The child in her arms, the woman reached the door and, after bending over its lock, swung it open.

Something shone with a dull gleam in the hand of the man who stood over Garrett. He raised his arm.

With her burden the woman ran through the door in the wall.

Garrett, sensing a descending and fatal blow, put up a weak arm—and from the other side of the wall came a high-pitched scream, long drawn out. In the darkness it was animal, filled with panic and rage and frustration.

The upraised weapon of Garrett's enemy was checked in its movement as the man turned involuntarily to look in the direction of the sound. Garrett flung himself with his last ounce of strength at his adversary's knees. . . .

And now came more sounds from the other side of the wall . . . men's voices . . . running footsteps. . . . And then the white, knifelike beams of electric torches as men came running through the door and threw themselves upon the struggling pair and tore away from Garrett a man who snarled at them and raved and fought—and was at last subdued.

Garrett felt a strong arm about his shoulders and found himself looking into the face of Anthony Gethryn. He giggled weakly.

"Attaboy!" he said and giggled again. "That you knocking?"

"Take it easy," Anthony said. "Take it easy. . . . Yes, knock at the front and you push 'em out at the back. . . . It's a rule of nature. . . . Here! Where're you going?"

For Garrett, with a sudden twist, had pulled himself away from the encircling arm and now, on legs which were a little unsteady, was moving at a shambling run towards a group who knelt beside something upon the ground.

He, too, threw himself upon his knees and found himself shoulder to shoulder with Pike. He tried to say something, but only a foolish little rattling noise came from his throat.

Pike said: "All right, sir. All right. Just doped, that's all."

Garrett shouldered him aside and, still on his knees, shuffled to the little body and raised its head and shoulders in his arms. He looked down at the small white face of Patricia Van Renseler.

Its eyes opened, very slowly. In them, even through the darkness, Garrett could see the sudden fire of panic, and against him the body stirred with a quick constriction of every muscle. He held it tightly, and words came from him.

The fear went out of the eyes and the tenseness from the limbs. The eyelids began to droop again and the head fell against his shoulder.

"Oh," said Patricia Van Renseler. "You're *nice!*"

EPILOGUE

Paignton Street by daylight is no less dismal than at night. Indeed, it is more so, as was apparent to Anthony as he stood in a bare room upon the ground floor of Number 17 and looked out at a street bathed in remorseless sunshine. He saw dusty pavements; squalid gardens whose untamed, soot-stained growths seemed more unnatural than any brick; blistered paint and peeling stucco and windows of grimy glass. . . .

He shuddered and turned to Pike, who sat at a table set in the middle of the room and pored over tidy little piles of such ill-assorted matters as ancient envelopes, tins of foodstuffs, cheap and dirty and unmarked handker-chiefs, an incongruous—and empty—magnum of Perrier Jouet '29, a heap of newspapers.

Pike looked at him. "Not much here, sir." His tone was dejected, and a corner of his mouth pulled down.

Anthony stood over the table, looking down at the heterogeneous mixture. He said after a moment:

"What did you expect? Pretty good worker, Evans. Not the sort to leave his card."

Heavy footsteps sounded overhead, and others upon the stairs. A large man in clothes of the plainest came into the room and set down upon the table a blanket and some shreds of sacking. Pike looked at them; then at their bearer.

"That all?" he said.

"From the bedroom, sir? Yes sir."

Pike grunted. "All right. Keep at it."

Anthony moved the magnum and sat upon the edge of the table. He said: "Anything new since yesterday?"

Pike shook his head. "Not a thing, sir. I don't mind admitting it's got me sort of baffled, as you might say. Over twenty years in the force and I've never struck anything like it." His tone was lugubrious.

Anthony said: "Clever man, Mr. Evans. Medium, you know." He looked at Pike and smiled. "Cheer up. You've got enough to hang him on. Twice."

"If we hadn't, sir, I'd—I'd *resign!* But it's not *that* that worries me, it's the sort of professional viewpoint, as you might say. Here we are, having laid our hands on the worst criminal I can remember, and yet it looks as if we're going to hang him without even knowing his real name. We go back and back, along every line we've got, and where do we end up? Nowhere! Why, even the KJB lot don't really know any more about him than we do. I questioned Hines myself and I know he's speaking the truth when he says that. Their blackmail business has apparently been going for years, and Evans must have horned in on them somehow."

"Poor Pike!" said Anthony. "What's his woman's name, by the way? You never told me."

Pike passed a hand across his forehead. "Believe it or not, sir, but he's even fixed her the same way. With the landlords of this place she passed as Mrs. Evans. And that's all the name we've got!"

Anthony lit a cigarette. "You know what Garrett'd say? 'Give 'em the works!' Sometimes, Pike, one sees the reason for the third degree."

For a moment a light flashed into Pike's brown eyes; then was officially repressed. He said:

"That's as may be, sir. But I do know this—once I get hold of this Janet Murch, *then* perhaps I'll get somewhere."

"King's evidence?" said Anthony.

"Yes sir." Pike's tone was more cheerful. "I got the commissioner's permission this morning."

Anthony surveyed him with sympathy. "So you're really back, my poor fellah, just where we started: where's Murch? Where is Janet, what is she, that we poor boobs can't find her?"

Pike's jaw was outthrust. "I'll find her," he said. "She left the Alsace Hotel with the child. She must've been seen by hundreds of people! And I've got a hundred lines out."

Outside the room four pairs of heavy feet could be heard descending the stairs, and the man who had brought in the blanket and sacking stood in the doorway.

"All through upstairs, sir," he said to Pike. "There's only the cellar left and Bruce and Piggott are going there now."

Pike got to his feet. "Well—that's that!" He looked at Anthony. "Coming, sir?" Together they strolled out into the bare hallway. At the far end of it two plain-clothes men were fiddling with the handle of a door beneath the stairs. One of them turned to Pike.

"Locked, sir," he said. "And there's no key. Break it in?"

Pike went towards him, Anthony lounging at his heels. Pike said: "Yes. And be quick about it."

The man who had spoken pushed his companion out of the way and kicked at the door, just below the lock, with the flat of his foot and tremendous force.

There was a crash of rending wood. . . . The kick was repeated. . . . Almost limply the door swung gently open, revealing a dark and cavernous little stairway.

The kicker pulled an electric torch from his pocket and stepped over the threshold. They heard his feet descending a little way; then come to an abrupt stop.

A muffled exclamation came up to them; then the man himself. He said to Pike:

"Look at that, sir!"

He swung the beam of his torch along cobwebbed walls and downwards. From the doorway Pike and Anthony could see, in the yellow pool of light, a figure which lay huddled upon the narrow stairs.

It was the figure of a woman. Her feet were towards them and her head upon the bottom step. She was, obviously and dreadfully, dead. The body was short and thick and square, and to its head there still adhered the long-veiled cap of the uniformed nursemaid.

"Meet Miss Murch!" said Anthony beneath his breath, and then, to Pike: "That's game and set to Mr. Evans! But we *still* get the match!"

2

Patricia Van Renseler left the room in merriment. From the other side of the slammed door the sound of her laughter came back, mingled with imperious summons for her mother.

Anthony looked at his host. "Yes. She *is* all right," he said.

Van Renseler laughed. "All right!" he said. The sling which supported his broken collarbone seemed to hurt him, and he adjusted it with an impatient twitch of his free hand. He said:

"She's so much all right that you wouldn't think anything had ever happened to her!" He looked at Anthony with eyes grown suddenly sombre. "And it's all due to you that she——"

Anthony interrupted. "Cut that out! I warned you."

Van Renseler said: "I never realized before that a man can *suffer* from gratitude." He smiled a little, but his eyes were grave. "I'm sorry if it annoys you, Gethryn, but I must——"

Anthony again interrupted. "Hold those horses! If you must bubble over, don't do it on me any more. Because there are plenty of others."

"Tom Garrett, of course! And Pike. But they aren't here, so you'll have to take it."

Anthony shook his head. "No. Plenty more yet. Very important, although some of 'em don't even know they had anything to do with it."

Van Renseler looked at him. "Don't get you," he said.

Anthony smiled. "I'll elucidate. First, Miss Letty Lamb. If it hadn't been for her we should never have had even the name Murch to follow."

"Lamb?" said Van Renseler. "Lamb? Oh yes. The girl on the shopping list."

Anthony nodded. "I'm giving you these in order of importance. Then there's the unfortunate Ballister woman. If it hadn't been for her we'd never have got onto the KJB Agency, which was the first string that attached us to Evans. You can't thank her, poor woman; but you might like to consider an extra gravestone or flowers or something. Then, of course, we sewed up KJB and got nearer still to Evans through Avis Bellingham——"

It was Van Renseler's turn to interrupt. "I've already talked to her. And so's Helen."

Anthony said: "Growing more important with every step, we now reach a junior member of the Criminal Investigation Department. One Detective Officer Frawley."

Van Renseler sat forward. "Who's he?"

"A boy with one year's detective service," Anthony said. "But if he hadn't used his brains and exceeded his orders by opening Evans' bag when that kid called for it at Dulwich station—well, I wouldn't be here now and Evans wouldn't be in jail . . . and you can finish all that for yourself."

"Frawley," said Van Renseler to himself. "Frawley. Frawley." He looked across at Anthony. "I won't forget that. . . . But all this doesn't get you out of anything, Gethryn. If it hadn't been that you were behind——"

"Wait!" said Anthony. "Moving on, we come to the still more important case of Mr. Vox, the ventriloquist."

Van Renseler stared.

Anthony grinned. "I mean it. He's nothing to do with this business—*and* everything. Entirely everything! If it hadn't been for him, Garrett and I would still be chasing over the north of England after an unpleasant fellah called Lester."

Van Renseler fiddled irritably with the knot of his sling. "I suppose," he said, "that you'll eventually tell me what you're talking about."

Anthony said: "We were after this man Lester. Garrett had a hunch we were wrong. To keep him quiet I took him to a music hall. This man Vox had three dummies—and one of 'em was in cap and apron. The combination of the voice-throwing and the uniform jerked my mind back onto the voices Garrett had heard in the teashop, *plus* the fact that one of these voices was a nursemaid—Janet Murch. I suddenly saw that Garrett might have made a mistake in ascribing the voices to the figures. And he had. And in ten minutes I was talking to your wife."

"God!" said Van Renseler—and fell silent. His face grew grim, and much of the colour left it as memory took him.

Anthony said quickly: "Then there's Harold Mattock. He's chief engineer of the tube railways. If he wasn't what I believe is known in your country as a 'right guy', he'd never have taken my word—over the telephone and at two minutes notice, mark you!—that he might be responsible for a death if he didn't have the power current cut off." He looked at his host and found that the colour was coming back to his face. "Incidentally, it was Evans himself who gave me the idea which saved you. You see, he'd tried that push-you-onto-the-live-rail-trick on Garrett already."

"There you are!" Van Renseler said. "It's you again!"

"And, last but not least," said Anthony without pausing, "is Mr. John Bodie. It was on the back of his taxi that Garrett got to Paignton Street. If Bodie didn't make a practice of getting out of his cab to take his money, he'd never have seen Garrett. Then Garrett wouldn't have hit him—and Pike and I wouldn't have found him there and consequently wouldn't have known what house—or even what street—Garrett had tracked Evans to."

Van Renseler was about to speak, but his wife came in and Patricia with her, and there was laughter and talk of other things and a drink for Anthony.

"By the way," said Helen Van Renseler as she poured this, "where *is* Mr. Garrett?"

Anthony smiled. "In the country," he said.

3

To Avis Bellingham, who had loved the Greyne country ever since she first knew it, the hamlet of Ford-under-Stapleton had always epitomized quietness and deep peace and a way of life which made the outer world seem hysterical and not of real account.

Which must serve to explain how it came that she had been staying, alone, at the inn called the Spanish Guardsman for two days.

For the first day she had done nothing but think. For the first night she had thought. And so it had been until now—when she sat at the writing table in the Spanish Guardsman's one sitting room and began upon a letter.

After two false starts and one cigarette she got going. Her pen scratched busily, and four sheets brought her to the end of the little she meant to write and the much more she had to imply.

She sat back and put the sheets together and began to read what she had written.

She did not get far; for there came footsteps in the corridor and the sound of an opening door—and the voice of Sheldon Garrett.

She did not hear what it said. She jumped to her feet and her chair fell behind her to lie unheeded. She said at last:

"Is this accident or treachery?" and gave him both her hands.

He took them and did not let them go. He said:

"I found out from Lucia Gethryn. She didn't exactly *tell* me you were here, but I saw an envelope." His voice, though he did not know it, was unsteady.

"I was writing a letter," said Avis. She had, she found, to keep her eyes from his. "To T. S. Garrett, Esquire." She made a little movement with her head towards the desk.

"To hell with letters!" said Garrett and released her hands and put his arms about her. "I've something to say and I'm going to say it without letting you go. When I've said it you can throw me out."

She was very still in his arms, and they tightened their clasp.

He said: "I'm a boor and a fool. But I love you. I *think* I can exist without you, but I don't want to try!"

She lifted her head, but her eyes did not meet his. She said:

"I was the fool. You had something big to do—and because I wanted you to tell me you loved me, I——"

He cut her short. He said unsteadily:

"Do you mean that you—that I—that you're not going to tell me to get out?"

She did look at him now. "Just *try* and go!" she said, and was prevented by his lips from saying more.

He released her at last and held her at arm's length while his eyes searched her. She smiled at him and he caught his breath. She grew grave on a sudden; very grave.

"What is it?" he said. "What's the matter?"

She looked down. She said, it seemed with difficulty:

"Tom—what shall we do about—about George?"

Garrett's arms closed about her once more. She found herself crushed against him so that breath was difficult.

"The hell with George!" he said between his teeth—and was amazed by her laughter.

He let her go. He stepped back and stared at her. She laughed still. She put out her hands and caught at him.

She said: "You should read your social news, my darling. *And* realize that women want to be loved for themselves alone!"

He took her shoulders in a grip which hurt. He said:

"What are you talking about? Tell me!"

Her eyes were full of laughter still, a tender laughter which played havoc with him.

"Divorce," she said. "I was unmarried from George two years ago!"

"My *God!*" said Sheldon Garrett.

ESCAPE

CHAPTER I

I've read somewhere that it's not the thing to write a story in the first person, but I can't help that. I'm the only one that could possibly tell this story, and I want to tell it. But I must tell it my own way.

I'll start by saying that my name is Peter Craven; that at the time I am writing of I was thirty-five years old, and that to look at I'm well enough when you've got used to my face. I am fully developed and semi-educated. I was a lance corporal of P.B.I. for the first two years of the war; a subaltern of cavalry for the third year, and a full-blown captain for the last. I stand six foot and three quarters of an inch, and weigh, fit, one hundred and eighty-five pounds. I have always been fond of horses, women, dogs, whisky, and Peter Craven. I have managed to dodge death and at various times to make some sort of living—as a sailor, a secretary-chauffeur, a chucker-out, a hack reporter, a second-rate actor, a first-rate (very temporary) civil servant, a paid organizer of sweepstakes, a bad reviewer of worse novels, and for a little while, in Australia, a professional boxer. Once I made quite a lot of money. That was in Australia too—out of horses. One of the biggest breeders and dealers took a fancy to me and made me a junior partner. When he died he left most of the money to his wife and the business to me. I lost my share trying to carry on with insufficient capital. I am a Roman Catholic and wear nines in everything except hats. I got blond hair from my father, blue eyes from my mother, and a sense of humour from my nurse.

A year before this story begins I came back from Montreal to London. I'd saved a bit of money, though not much. I was looking for a job. I hitched up with a fellow called Pearson. He'd invented a patent pencil sharpener and eraser combined. After he'd protected it, his idea was to sell it by mail order until he got enough money to deal with it and some other gadgets in a bigger way. I put my savings in and we started. It looked like going very well, until another bird brought out something else of the same kind which was a good deal better. We went down the drain.

I moved, in a month, from West Kensington to the Fulham Road, from the Fulham Road to Chelsea purlieus, from Chelsea to Lambeth. If you don't know Lambeth—don't. I couldn't get any sort of job. I hadn't got any sort of money. I was just going to go down to the docks to look up an old friend of mine who was purser on one of the small Green Star boats when I went down with 'flu. Whenever I get anything like that it always becomes complicated with malaria. This time the combination nearly did for me.

When I had substituted in place of a longing for death an even more passionate one for beefsteak, I found, first, that I was expected to clear out of my filthy lodging and, second, that my amiable landlord, to cover as much of his rent as he could squeeze, had sold all my clothes except a vest and pants, a pair of patent shoes, one dress shirt and collar and tie, a dinner jacket, trousers and waistcoat, and three studs. He didn't sell all these although they were the most valuable. Maybe he thought I'd pinched 'em and he'd catch it for selling. He wanted me to put the things on and clear out then and there—this was after I'd asked him for more food and he could see I wasn't going to die. His wife was a bit better sort, however, and I managed to stay in the hole nearly another week and get some sort of nourishment. Then the woman fell sick herself and to avoid a row I had to clear out.

I'm telling all this so that you can get some idea of how I was feeling. If it hadn't been for the incongruity of my clothes; if it hadn't been for the black and vicious mood induced by semi-starvation; if it hadn't been for the fact that I hadn't a single coin, or any way of getting one, I'm certain I'd never have had this story to tell. Perhaps I shouldn't even if the weather had been different.

I left No. 132 Palmer's Rents, Lambeth, S.E.—which thoroughfare is a final argument against civilization—at half-past five in the evening of the 29th of May. Oh, to be out of Lambeth now that spring is here! Especially when there's a northeast wind with an edge to it, and a coppery-looking sky which promises snow or hail or sleet, or all three. Oh, more particularly, to be out of Lambeth on such an evening, when one is clad for the other side of Westminster Bridge, has no hat, no overcoat, and no money.

I remember every yard of the walk from Palmer's Rents to Lambeth Bridge. I won't go into its details here. It was this walk which put the final touches to my definitely anti-social mood. By the time I'd crossed the bridge and was making my way along Grosvenor Road towards the Houses of Parliament, I was in a fit mental condition to stand on a plinth in Trafalgar Square and harangue the masses. I could have proved beyond doubt that wealth should be evenly distributed. I could have swayed any mob into immediate application of the theory, but I wasn't worrying about mobs. I was worrying about Peter Craven. I wasn't cold any more, because of the walk. But I was damned hungry.

It's lucky for me that I have always had good recuperative powers, for I think that lots of men, after such a three weeks as I'd been through, wouldn't have been able to walk at all, let alone walk hard and fast. Except, however, for the feeling that the lining of my stomach was rubbing against my backbone, I felt pretty fit. In body that is; in mind I was definitely sick.

People must have looked at me. I was walking at somewhere between four and five miles an hour. Sleet had begun to fall as I turned into Birdcage Walk, and a hatless, overcoatless, dinner-jacketed man walking like that, on that evening, with taxis all round him, buses behind him, and Rolls-Royces on either side, must look odd to say the least. Odder still if he is frowning all over his ugly face, hasn't even troubled to turn up his collar to save the silk of his lapels, and is muttering away to himself nineteen to the dozen.

I went straight down Birdcage Walk towards the Barracks and Victoria. It is a queer thing that I don't remember once being in any hesitation about my direction. I just walked and went on walking. Crossing the little snicket which leads up to Queen Anne Mansions and the Underground building, I had a very narrow squeak of it with a car just coming out into the park. There was a hoot and a yell and I jumped about ten feet. I felt the wind of the thing flap my coat. But I didn't take any notice; just pounded on. All I remember thinking is what the driver would have thought if he'd killed me, and what the police would have thought when they'd tried to identify me. No marks on underlinen; indecipherable initials on shirt; nothing whatsoever in pockets save two flat parcels wrapped up in dirty newspaper, containing, between them, a safety razor, a comb, a shaving brush, a toothbrush, and—treasure—the remains of a cake of soap. Nothing else. Not even a handkerchief.

As I came out of the gates into the Buckingham Palace Road a sudden scurry of snow brought me to my senses. For the first time I thought seriously about how odd I must look. I couldn't go on walking like this in a snowstorm without somebody asking me what I was at. And I didn't want to be asked anything. Because, although I hadn't got any definite plan in my mind, my anti-social complex was so active that I knew that before the night got much older I was going to do something which, if I wasn't very careful about it, might get me into trouble.

I turned up the collar of my coat, crossed the mouth of Buckingham Gate, and sprinted for the first shop doorway. Luckily there was no one else to share it. I shook the snow off myself as well as I could. I was glowing with heat and light-headed with hunger. Two steady streams of cars and taxis flowed up and down Buckingham Palace Road. I treated myself to a five-minute hate of their occupants. An old match seller shuffled past. He was apathetic and probably half tight. But I felt as much friendship towards him as I did hatred towards the occupants of the cabs and cars. Buses, somehow, I didn't notice. I suppose my anti-social bug didn't know what class to put the bus riders in, and so ignored them. A bobby came up and looked at me. For a moment I thought he was going to speak, and my heart seemed to drop into the base of my tummy. But apparently my clothes reassured him, and he walked on.

The snow stopped as suddenly as it had begun. For a few minutes I stood where I was, leaning against the glass of what must have been the back door of the shop. I think I was in a state which, although it definitely was not sleep, was nearly as unconscious as sleep. What brought me round was the altered sound of the traffic. Have you ever noticed what a difference lying snow makes to the sound of a town?

I pushed my hands into my empty pockets and walked out again into the Buckingham Palace Road. I turned left and walked up towards Victoria. Opposite the little alley which leads into Victoria Square my mind suddenly changed, and I turned sharp right and crossed the road and entered the square. I crossed it and came out by the corresponding snicket at the other side. Within a few minutes I was pounding down the long straight stretch which leads from Grosvenor Place, through Eaton Square and the others, to Sloane Square. With one of the sudden changes which London is always showing you, the sky had cleared and now, so far from being overcast, was a bright, hard, dark blue as full of stars as a good pudding is of raisins. The wind had dropped and I got so hot that I had to slacken my pace. I went through Sloane Square and wriggled by side streets into Pelham Crescent.

It's queer, but the journey which I must have made between South Kensington Station and Royalty Gardens—a journey which must be the best part of a mile—seems, with all its incidents, to have gone completely from my memory. All I know is that people—I suppose because the weather was all right—didn't stare at me any more. Or if they did I didn't notice it. I do remember quite distinctly, though, turning into the quiet backwater of Royalty Gardens. I remember it because I suddenly got a pain in my head. It was so bad that I had to stop walking and lean against the railings and hang onto my scalp with both hands. It passed off in a minute, and I went on. I was warmer than ever, but feeling queerer than ever. The lack of food must have been the cause. I remember I had an odd feeling that my feet weren't touching the pavement at all. They seemed to tread on a sort of cushion of air between my soles and the pavement. My head felt very large and light, but my body felt strong enough for six.

And then, halfway down Royalty Gardens, I began to slow down. I had found out why my legs had brought me here. I heard, from just ahead of me, the sound of a basement door being slammed. I came abreast of the railings of the area from which the noise had come. I stopped and began to fumble in my pockets as if in search of a match. From just below me there came the sound of chattering voices. My mind, foggy enough in some ways, seemed preternaturally clear in others. There were three voices—all women's. They were plainly servants. They were, equally plainly, all going out for the evening. I took a pace forward and looked into the area. There was a light over the basement door. I could see the women. One was short and round; one was tall and skinny; the other well made enough. I couldn't hear much of their words because of the singing in my head, but I did see what the short, fat one did. She stooped and pushed something, which clinked against the stone, under the mat which lay just outside the door. My legs started to carry me backwards. After four paces I turned and walked face forward. I halted after twenty steps and turned again. I heard feet coming up the stone steps from my area and saw the three come out. My heart began to knock against my ribs. I saw with immense relief that they were going away from me. I waited until they must have been at least a hundred yards towards the other end of the street. My legs began to carry me forward again. I halted outside the area gate. And now I knew what I was going to do. I was going to go down the steps, lift the mat, take out the key, open the door, and get inside the house. Quite what I was going to do when I had got in I wasn't certain.

The job sounds, the way I have written it down, simple enough. But I can assure you that it wasn't. It's one thing to write about feloniously

entering somebody else's house. It's quite another to do it. If I looked once
behind me and before me and across at the other side of the street, I must
have done these things twenty times. But luck was with me.

There wasn't visible, in the whole length of Royalty Gardens, a single
human being. At the far western end was a dark red blur which must have
been the lamp of a stationary taxi, but otherwise there was nothing.

At last I put a hand to the area gate and gently shoved it wide enough
to let me through. It screamed like a child. I hung onto the middle spear of
its bars and had another look up and down the street. But still, to my huge
relief, there wasn't a sound or sight or smell of any other human being. I
didn't dare to close the thing. Its squeaking, probably quite ordinary, had
seemed like a dozen sirens. I tiptoed down the steps. My heart seemed to be
trying to dislocate my tonsils.

It was dark down in the area. I groped my way along by feeling the wall
with my fingers. I got to the mat long before I expected. I tripped over the
damned thing and hit my head against the door. I felt the bang must have
sounded as far as Scotland Yard. I tried to make myself small in the darkest
corner and listen. But no heavy measured footsteps came. Nor any sound
from inside. I made my way to the mat again. I knelt in a puddle and lifted
the edge of the thing—I can remember how it scratched my palm—and
groped underneath it with my free hand for the key. I found it at the first
sweep.

CHAPTER II

There was a roaring fire in the kitchen. The cook had damped it down with
slack, but I'd given it a few stirs with a poker and pulled out a damper.
It was a comfortable kitchen and a house which did not stint food. I had
had, my confidence increasing with every moment, a good third of a pigeon
pie, ham and pickles, half the crusty top of a new cottage loaf, a wedge of
gooseberry tart, and—thank God for the lack of cellar space—two bottles of
beer.

One never knows when one is well off. My belly distended with good
food, I felt a craving, to my mind now just as bad as the craving for food had
been, for a smoke. My luck was in. On my second aimless circling of the
overwarm kitchen, I saw a packet of Gold Flake tucked away behind a pot
of sorry-looking flowers on the dresser. There were four cigarettes in it. I
smoked one, inhaling every mouthful down to my heels, threw away the
stub, and lit another. I padded luxuriously round to the Windsor chair
drawn up to one side of the range. The last trace of wet had steamed off me
long ago, my shoes were drying in the fender, my stomach was full of food
and my lungs of tobacco. I sat in the Windsor chair and put my legs up on
another small chair.

The last thing I remember thinking was that I couldn't afford more than ten minutes of this. Cooks and housemaids and parlourmaids don't often go out together, and certainly they don't stay out on a winter's evening until after midnight. And I had other things to do. The house had given me food and shelter so far; now it must give me the possibility of more. . . . And then, of course, I went to sleep, though I wouldn't so much call it going to sleep as temporarily dying.

I knew afterwards that I had slept for three hours, but it might just as well have been three minutes for all I knew about it. I waked with a frightful jerk. Funnily enough, I didn't have to grope about in my mind for memory of where I was and how I happened to be there. One minute I was dead asleep, and the next I was broad awake. And I was afraid. My scalp was prickling and my tongue was sticking to the roof of my mouth.

The fire was low, but the kitchen was still warm. The light was on. It hurt my eyes as I opened them. For a full minute I didn't move. I just stared. I knew there was someone—or something—in the room with me. From my chair I could see the whole of the kitchen except the corner immediately behind where I was sitting. In the part I could see there was nothing. And nothing was changed. The door to the passage, which I had carefully shut behind me, was still shut. The other door, which led to the service stairs, was shut too.

And yet I was certain there was something. I held my breath and listened. From behind me I heard—or was it felt?—a movement. I shot out of my chair as if somebody had stuck the first quarter-inch of a sharp knife into the back of my neck. I landed at the other side of the fireplace. I remember thinking, even as I was turning to face whatever it was, that it was a pity I hadn't put my shoes on before I slept. I turned and, half-crouching, ready for anything, saw a girl.

Perhaps it wasn't a girl, though. I never quite know when they stop calling themselves girls. This one, as I judged then and found out later, was somewhere in her later twenties. She was small, but she had a shape. Not an aggressive one, but a good one. Everything about her was in proportion. I didn't, in that first moment, take in her features. All I saw, consciously, were two very large eyes in a chalk-white and terrified face, and a funny little mop of smooth black hair, not quite as short as a boy's, which somehow looked both neat and untidy. She must have been, before she came down to the kitchen, either in bed or just going to get there. She'd got on pyjamas —I could see the lower part of their legs—and a thin sort of dressing gown which was held tight round her. The pyjamas were yellow, the dressing gown blue. They were very good colours.

We stood—or rather she stood upright as an arrow and I crouched like something out of Barnum's—and stared at each other. I gradually straightened myself. The nearest I can get to explaining my state of mind is to say that I felt a damned fool. I certainly must have looked odd. Hair all over the place. Shirt all crooked. No links in my cuffs which, after my sleep, were sticking about a yard out of my sleeves. No shoes, and the remains of a tie somewhere round my left ear. Neither a gentleman nor a burglar, but a waiter on strike.

The silence went on. When she saw that I wasn't at any rate going to be violent, some of the strain went out of her face and a faint colour began to creep back to her cheeks and mouth. She ought to have spoken first, but actually, as I remember it, I did. I said:

"I'd better put my shoes on."

That was silly enough in the circumstances, wasn't it? Sillier still, I actually bent down and pulled them out of the fender where they were lying like a couple of over-roasted chestnuts and, somehow or other crammed my swollen feet into them. She watched me. I stood up again. And then she did speak. She said:

"Exactly what are you doing?" Her voice was surprisingly deep. It was also at that moment a bit breathless. You can't blame her for that, poor kid!

I stammered something. I don't remember what. She said:

"You've broken in here!"

I nodded. I was getting a bit of courage back. I saw two things quite clearly and they were—first, that if it was a question of being handed over to the police, she couldn't do it and wouldn't do it! Second, that she was frightened of something which was not me. Something else altogether. She said:

"I—I can't make this out. I don't understand." She looked at me with bewilderment taking some of the fear out of her eyes. I knew I had to say something. I felt a ghastly fool.

"Look here," I said. "It may sound nonsense, but I was pretty near starving, although I haven't got a wife and six children. I'm just broke. Flat broke. The owner of the house where I was lodging sold all my other clothes to meet his bill. I had to get out. I happened to walk along this street here. I saw your servants go out and one of them put the key under the mat. . . . So here I am. I'm afraid I've had a lot of food. And pinched a couple of cigarettes. And some beer."

Her eyes wandered away from me round the room, then came back to me again. There was something else in them now besides fear and bewilderment. She said, in a new sort of voice:

"It must feel beastly not to have anywhere to go, and no money. Awful!"

I gaped at her. "Good God!" I said. "Do you really believe all that?"

Her mouth twitched a little. "All what?"

"That story I was telling you."

"Of course. Wasn't it true?"

"Absolutely."

"Well, why shouldn't I believe it then?"

I still stared at her. "A lot of people wouldn't," I said.

From behind me there came a sudden creak. I turned as if I'd been stung. But quick though the movement was, I hadn't made it before my eyes had seen and registered what had happened to the girl's face. The colour which had been creeping back to it was wiped away in that quarter-second. And everything went out of the wide eyes except fear.

What I saw when I turned was that the door to the service stairs stood ajar. It had been pushed open. But all it had been pushed open by was a large black cat—the fattest cat I've ever seen in my life. I felt nearly sick with relief. I turned back to the girl. I saw that she'd seen the cat too. The horror had gone out of her face, but one hand still clutched at her left side beneath her breast. She managed a little laugh. It didn't sound as if she were finding life very funny. She said:

"Oh! . . . It's only James."

She stooped and clicked her fingers, and the cat slid under the table and came and rubbed itself against them.

"What is it, James?" she said. "What's the matter?"

I could hear, more distinctly now, the well-controlled but definite shaking of her voice. I said suddenly, the words seeming to come out of my mouth before I knew what they were going to be:

"Look here, what's the matter?"

She didn't look up. She went on scratching the cat's ears. "Nothing," she said.

I got insistent. "That's nonsense. What is it?"

"Nothing, I told you."

"I *know* there's something. You're scared and it isn't of me. You ought to be scared of me, but you're not."

She stood up at that. She looked straight at me. One corner of her mouth twitched. "Afraid of you? Why should I be?"

I felt a fool. I couldn't answer that one. I mumbled something about having to go if she'd let me.

"Let you!" Her eyebrows went up. "*Let* you! I suppose if you want to go I can't stop you. Even if I was a man, I shouldn't be up to your weight, should I?"

I grinned at that. There was something new and odd and sort of comically attractive about her tone. I said:

"You're very kind."

She looked at me, raising an eyebrow. "Tell me something. If you hadn't gone to sleep, what were you going to do?"

"Before I went to sleep, I meant going upstairs and seeing if there was anything . . . if there was anything——"

"Quite. Don't bother to go on. And now what are you going to do?"

I felt awkward. "Not that, anyhow," I said. "Look here, I'm sure I'd better go."

She said: "Has it struck you that we aren't playing our parts very well?"

I said it had struck me, very forcibly, but that I didn't think anybody ever lived true to the drama.

The cat was rubbing against her legs. She bent down and began to fondle it again.

"I think you're right," she said slowly, without looking up. There was something odd in her tone. It brought back to me the fact that she was frightened.

I tried once more, using a new tack. I said:

"If you're kind enough to want to make me feel better, tell me what's the matter. Perhaps I could do something. See here, you're frightened of something in this house. And I know it isn't me. What is it?"

She stood up. Once more she was as white as a sheet. She looked at me for a long time. I felt as if her big eyes could see right to the back of my head. A queer girl. She said, after a long pause:

"All right. I'll tell you. I believe you mean that about helping me. But you might not mean it when you . . . when you . . . Here, just follow me. It's all right. You needn't worry about not making a noise."

She pulled the blue dressing gown more closely about her and crossed to the door which the cat had pushed open, and went through it. I followed. She led the way up the steep stairs and opened a baize door at the top of them, and I found myself standing on the soft carpet of a warm and very comfortably furnished hall. She walked across this to the foot of the main stairs. She didn't once look back. I kept in her wake, about three paces behind her. She went up the stairs. The carpet on them was very thick and our feet didn't make any sound. It was dark on the stairs themselves, but from the landing above came enough light. We got up onto the landing. There were three doors on it—one facing the head of the stairs, one to the left and one to the right.

She halted opposite the door on the right. The light was just above her. She turned for me to come up, and I saw that if she'd been pale downstairs, that pallor was a weak imitation of what her face could do in the way of whiteness. She was controlling herself well, but I could see that under the blue dressing gown she was shaking. She didn't say anything. I waited. I saw her shoulders stiffen, and then she turned the handle and threw the door open. When I say "threw," I mean *threw*. It swung back and hit the wall inside the room with the devil of a crack.

I looked into the room. It seemed to be a sort of library. The light was on—a big bowl hanging from the middle of the high ceiling. There were bookshelves round all the three walls I could see, reaching from the picture rail to the floor. In the bay window opposite the door was a big writing table. There were also a cabinet with china in it, two big armchairs, and a huge sofa. A standard lamp stood to one side of the fireplace which was big and open and had some red embers in the bottom of it. From behind my shoulder came a small voice.

"Go in," it said. "Go in. And look!"

I went in. I wasn't more than two paces over the threshold before I knew what was the matter. I had been thinking there was no one in the room. But there was. The door had hidden it from me as I stood on the threshold. Just to the left of the door was another writing table, or perhaps I should say a bureau. Its flap was down. There was a chair in front of it and on the chair was sitting a man. He was slouched forward right on top of the flap.

His head was resting on a blotting pad. His arms hung straight down beside him. The way he was slumped made his fingers just brush the floor.

I had seen enough dead men in my time, but here, quite plainly, was another.

CHAPTER III

I was stooping over the thing in the chair when I heard a sound behind me. The girl had crept in at last. There came a queer little noise from her throat. I saw that her eyes were closed and that she was rocking as she stood. I caught her just in time. I picked her up and crossed the room with her and put her down on the sofa. I shoved all the cushions under her feet. The blood began to drain back to her head. She'd got a lot of pluck. She was round again almost at once. Before I could stop her she'd swung her legs to the floor. The only sign she gave of having passed out was that every now and then she took hold of her head with both hands and held it down over her knees. But in between these spasms she talked. She said:

"Sorry. . . . Didn't mean to do that. . . . Ridiculous! . . . Don't mind me. Go and . . . go and . . ." Her hand made a weak gesture in the direction of the bureau and the huddled thing on the chair.

I did as I was told and left her, and went back again to the dead man. I didn't touch him, but I looked at him very closely.

It wasn't hard to find how he'd died. Just above the edge of his low, stiff collar—he was in dark day clothes—and in the centre of the little dip between the two tendons which run down the back of the scalp to the neck, was a small round hole about a sixteenth of an inch in diameter. It hadn't bled much, probably owing to his position, but the edges of it were nasty enough.

I looked about for any sort of weapon which could have made it, but couldn't see any. I went round him and knelt down, and looked at what I could see of his face.

I made him out to be a man of anywhere between fifty and sixty. He had a seamed, leathery-looking skin, and a grey and bristly and untidy moustache which hid most of his mouth. His eyes were wide and staring. They were of a muddy blue, with bloodshot whites. I couldn't tell anything from their expression. Gingerly I took up one of his arms and looked at the hand. It was a long, fine, thin-fingered hand. The nails were well kept and the skin was soft. His clothes were of expensive material but dull enough pattern—a black coat and most respectably striped trousers.

I looked at the desk and saw that to one side of the blotter was a sheet of paper headed—in a neat, black die—"48 Royalty Gardens, Kensington Gore, S.W."

Right in front of his head, pushed up against the middle cupboard of the back of the bureau, was a double silver inkstand. The lid of the right-hand pot stood open. At the extreme right-hand edge of the flap was a pen. It must have rolled there. I bent down and looked at its nib. It had obviously been dipped in ink recently, for a sticky gleam came from it as I moved my point of view this way and that to catch the light. I touched his cheek with my fingertips. He couldn't have been dead very long. The skin was not warm, but it hadn't any of the chill of death. I went back to the couch.

She was sitting upright now, and there was a sparkle in her eyes and more colour—too much colour—in her face. I said, looking down at her:

"Who is he?"

She looked straight in front of her. "My stepfather."

I went on looking down at her. "Know anything about it?"

She shook her head. "Nothing. That's the point."

"What's the point?"

She shot to her feet at that. She stamped her foot and opened her eyes at me, and said:

"Can't you *see*? I don't know anything about it, but they'll say that I do! They'll say that I know *all* about it. They'll say that I did it. They're bound to!"

I made a mistake. I tried to humour her. I believe I put out a hand and patted her shoulder. I know I said:

"Why should anyone think that? Pull yourself together."

She blazed at me. "Damn you," she said. "I didn't ask you to be a Nanny. I asked you to help. I can't waste time now telling you why I know they'll think I did it. You've got to take my word for it. . . . Look here! You offered to help and I accepted your offer. If you want to withdraw it, get out."

I mumbled some sort of apology. I must have looked pretty sheepish, but at the same time I must, by my attitude, have conveyed that the offer held good, because she said:

"Sorry! Didn't mean to go for you like that."

She came closer and her right hand came up, and her fingers caught hold of my arm. They had an astonishing strength to their grip. I'd a sort of idea that I could feel them burning right through my sleeve, but that may be just nonsense. She said:

"Look here! This is dead earnest. Deader earnest than anything that's ever happened in my life." She kept on looking straight at me, but she made a little gesture in the direction of the bureau. "That is my stepfather. Everybody'll think I did it. We—we—we hated—we didn't get on. Everybody'll have very good reason for thinking I did it, but I didn't! . . . Now I've only got one chance, and if you want to help me it's your chance too. *Do* you want to help me? There's no reason why you should——"

"There's every reason why I should," I said, "and even if there wasn't, I would."

She kept her eyes on mine. "If you want to help me, there's just one thing you can do. We can't discuss it. We can't argue about it. There's no time. I've worked it all out. There's just one thing to do and that's"—for a moment she covered her eyes with both hands—"that's to take him . . . it . . . away. I don't know how he was killed. But they can't *help* saying I did it, unless—unless——"

I helped her out. "Unless he was found somewhere else; somewhere away from here. Then they mightn't be *able* to hitch it up with you, even if they wanted to. Right?"

She nodded. She said, and I could see that, to keep her mouth from trembling, she was talking without opening her teeth:

"That's exactly it. Now look here. I'll give you anything. You're hungry and you haven't anywhere to go, and you haven't any money. I'll give you money, and then you can go somewhere and feed yourself, and clothe yourself and keep yourself decent until you can get something to do . . . if you'll do this for me. I don't know how you're going to do it, or where you'll put——"

I said: "That doesn't matter."

I thought hard for a minute. "I'll do it," I said at last.

All at once she crumpled. Her legs wouldn't support her. She flopped back onto the sofa. She said in a different voice; a weak voice:

"Thank God!" She closed her eyes. She was very pale again.

I said: "What about the servants?" I'd just looked at the clock on the mantelpiece, and it said eleven. "They'll be back any minute now."

She did not open her eyes, but her head began to nod from side to side. "No, they won't," she said. "They're not coming back till Monday."

CHAPTER IV

Some things stick in one's memory. Some don't. I remember, for instance, the first time I ever tasted rock candy. I also remember my first cigar and the first time I got tight. I also remember suddenly coming to an understanding of why my mother thought sunsets were beautiful, and why my father thought Presbyterians should go to hell. I remember seeing my first dead man and my first live woman. But all these memories have got to fade into the meanest sort of insignificance compared with my memory of the hours between 11:10 P.M. on the night of the 29th of May, and 5:15 A.M. on the morning of the 30th.

Between these times my memory is as clear as a good cinematograph film. At the first time I have mentioned I was standing in the hall of No. 48 Royalty Gardens. The girl was in front of me, with her hand on the latch of the front door. I was three paces behind her. I had on a raincoat two sizes too small for me and a hat half a size too big; otherwise, I was as I had been. But I had something with me. I had, held up by my right arm—which is pretty strong, anyhow, but which now seemed strong enough to tear a hole in the walls of Buckingham Palace—a companion. In life I suppose he weighed about a hundred and forty pounds—that is, clothes and boots and everything. In death he seemed to weigh three times as much. He, too, had on a raincoat and a soft hat. It was a pretty gruesome job even for a hard case like me to put them on him, but I'd had to do it. I can see myself now, standing there in that hall, right under the light, and thinking that at any moment I'd wake up, sweating, in my filthy bed at No. 132 Palmer's Rents.

The girl opened the front door about three inches. She looked out. She pushed it to again and turned to me. She said:

"There's no one." She kept her gaze away from us.

Somehow I got my companion onto my back—piggy-back fashion. I moved towards the door.

I often wonder whether I'd have done this job at all if it hadn't been for what she told me about him, a story which you may or may not hear in due course. . . .

Anyhow, there he was on my back. I staggered down the three shallow steps outside the porch. I hoped—though I was afraid we didn't—that we looked like the jocose tail end of a drinking party.

I had a vague plan in my mind, but I didn't know whether I could pull it off. We had discussed several, but at last I'd insisted that she should leave it to me. I was certain that any plan we did make might have to be completely altered by circumstances.

I turned to the left at the bottom of the steps. I glanced up once at the doorway and saw that she hadn't yet closed the door. She was looking after me. We purposely hadn't switched on the porch light, and I could only see her face as a dim white blur.

I looked at the houses across the street and on each side of the one I'd just left. All the windows were curtained. No doors were open. There seemed no sign of life except light.

If you can imagine a worse job than this one that I had, you're free to do so. I can't. Except for a vague plan of what I would do with my burden if I could get him to a certain place, I hadn't an idea in my head. My brain seemed taken up entirely with fear. I was bound to pass people. People were bound to look at me. You can't carry a man piggy-back round London at eleven o'clock at night without people being curious if they see you. And how in hell could they avoid seeing me! The one idea I clung to was that when I did see anyone, I must be drunk. I must lurch and stagger, and even—ye gods!—sing. I wondered what my voice would sound like if I did have to sing. The thought of singing put me into such a cold sweat of horror and fear that it did me good, in a way. I mean it excluded from my mind other—and much worse—possibilities. Also it made me impervious to fatigue. The weight on my back was nothing to the weight on my mind. . . .

For a bit I had almost unbelievable luck. From No. 48 to the end of

Royalty Gardens is about four hundred yards. The night was fine now and such snow as had lain on the pavements had melted and dried. And yet, in three quarters of the distance, I saw no one and, much more, felt reasonably certain that no one saw me. Then, suddenly, when I was about twenty yards from the point where Royalty Gardens ends and Viceroy Road runs across it, I had my first shock.

A car with headlights on came down Viceroy Road across the end of the gardens. The headlights showed me what I should never have seen without them. Standing at the junction of Viceroy Road and the pavement upon which I was walking was a bobby. I saw his shape distinctly and I hoped I saw that he was looking, not down Royalty Gardens, but across Viceroy Road at Hallam Gardens. But I couldn't be sure.

I stopped dead. The weight on my back was suddenly unbearable. I let my burden slip off my back and caught its weight with my left arm, and managed to lean with it against the railings of the house I was outside. I took in great whooping breaths. Now, straining my eyes, I could see the tall, helmeted figure without the help of any lights. But I still couldn't be sure whether he was looking directly towards me or directly away from me.

My mind was a blank. I couldn't think of anything to do. If he *had* heard me, the sudden cessation of footsteps might lead him to come down this way. If he hadn't, he might go on standing where he was for an hour. And at any moment *any* door in Royalty Gardens might open and someone come out—perhaps even the door of the house we were outside! Or anyone might walk along our pavement. Or Royalty Gardens might be part of the bobby's beat and he might come down it. . . .

There *was* nothing to do. Crazily for a moment I thought of a cigarette, and then gasped with fear at the thought of how near I'd been to striking a match. The one thing—and this sounds mad—that I didn't think of was leaving the job where it was. I suppose I could have done that and just beat it myself. Looking back, I can only assure you that it never even crossed my mind. Mark you, I don't know what it was that stopped me from thinking that. I can only tell you I didn't so much as think of it. I'm not setting up as something out of the *Morte d'Arthur*. Not a bit of it. I expect that if, at this stage of the affair, it had occurred to me that I could just leave him and skate off, I'd have done it, although it would have been a pretty lousy sort of trick because the thing wasn't far away enough from No. 48 to do Frances any good. . . .

All I did do was to stand there like a fool, holding up my charge with both hands against the railings and nearly sending my eyes out of my head trying to see what the bobby was doing. Sometimes it seemed to me that he was looking straight at me, and even soundlessly moving towards me. At other times I was dead sure that he was looking away from me.

I don't know to this day how long I stood like that. I can only tell you it seemed a good hour. I expect it was really about a couple of minutes.

And then the taxi came! It swung round from Viceroy Road and came straight towards me. I felt that it was going to stop immediately by us; and then I tried to laugh at myself for being so determined that I was in for bad luck. I divided my attention between its approach and the still motionless figure of the bobby at the corner.

I was just beginning to congratulate myself that it was going right past me, when it suddenly swerved into the curb about twenty yards ahead. The shock I'd got when I'd first seen the policeman was nothing to the one I got now. I'd been right after all. It was bringing someone to the very house outside which I was standing. I tried to summon the strength to pick up my burden and walk on, even if it was towards the bobby. I tried, but I couldn't. If I had been doubly strong before, I was trebly weak now. I just stood. I could feel cold sweat trickling down between my shoulder blades. Then came relief. The taxi stopped about the third house from where we were standing, directly in line with the bobby. I breathed again, if you can call it breathing when your lungs are labouring like a beaten horse's and your heart's beating so fast that you can hardly see. The porch light of the house suddenly came on. It gave me another fright at first, but, when I could think, I realized that I was in luck. The more light there was there, the less chance there was of anyone coming out of the house or into it seeing properly beyond its field. The bad part of it was that I couldn't see across the light to make out whether the bobby was moving or not. I was obsessed by him. It was due to the fact that I was straining my eyes to try to see him that I only heard the slamming of the taxi door and the clink of silver, and feet going across the pavement and up the steps of the house. Luckily, however, I *saw*—suddenly—the taxi driver, in a white mackintosh and flat-topped cap, leave his cab and go along the beam of light and up the steps, carrying a heavy trunk.

My head cleared. It had been a puddingy mess of panic; in a flash it became a well-oiled, smooth-working machine. I thought:

If the driver's carrying the trunk up the steps, it probably means that there isn't a manservant. Trunks must go upstairs. If there isn't a manservant, it's at least five to one that they'll get the driver to take the trunk up and finish the job. If he finishes the job he's bound to take at least two minutes. In about a minute and three quarters I could get myself, and *this*, into the cab.

It takes a long time to write, but it took an infinitesimal time to think. My strength came back to me twofold. I did not attempt, this time, to get my burden onto my back. I took hold of its right arm and put it round my neck and held its wrist with my right hand. I put my left hand round its body and half lifted, half dragged it along the pavement. I rolled in my walk and tried to sing. But that was too much for me. I believe I achieved a maudlin sort of whistle, but I'm not sure.

We got into the beam of light. The door of the house—I think it was No. 14—was still open. I could see right into the hall. Thank God there was nobody looking out. There wasn't anyone, in fact, to be seen anywhere. I freed my right hand and, keeping the weight supported entirely by my left arm, I wrenched open the door of the taxi, and was instantly seized by the

worst fear up to now. I might just as well have been on a stage in the full
beam of the limelight as far as the bobby was concerned. *If* he was looking
my way. But I was here now and I had to go through with it. I picked the
body up. With a heave, I got it half through the narrow door of the old cab;
with another, I finished the job. I climbed into the cab myself and shifted
the thing—with what seemed my last ounce of strength—along the seat to
the other corner. I reached out a hand and slammed the door.

Then, for the moment, I closed my eyes. I felt sick and faint and worse
than at any time so far on this extraordinary night. Above me at the head of
the steps I heard the slamming of the door. And the porch light went out. I
shot out of the seat and thrust my head and shoulders out of the window,
throwing my borrowed raincoat open to show that I was in evening kit. The
taxi driver was coming down the steps. I had hoped for one of the old Bill
type. I saw that, unluckily, this one was young and alert. He was also, and
this was unlucky too, a cheery and probably helpful fellow. He was whistling "Mademoiselle from Armentières." He stopped on the bottom step and
stared at me. The whistling stopped. I said, over-loudly and, I felt as soon as
the words were out of my mouth, over-drunkenly:

"I shay, I shay. . . . You there. . . . Ish thish your cab?"

He came and stood close by the door. He grinned.

" 'Smy cab all right, sir. Want to go 'ome?"

I moderated the drunkenness a bit and said I did want to go home. Or,
rather, I wanted to take my friend home. "Driver," I said solemnly, "you
may think I'm drunk, but I'm nothing of the sort. But my friend *is* drunk.
He'sh so damned drunk I had to lift him into your cab!"

My tongue seemed thick and swollen. It was certainly very dry. I didn't
like the feel of it but, looking back, I see that it must have helped the impression. The man seemed to pause for a minute before answering. I felt
sick. But it was all right. Perhaps it had been just imagination on my part.
He grinned and said:

"Rye-char, sir. Where yer want to gow?"

I didn't hesitate. I suppose I must have been thinking things out without
knowing. I said, speaking now with the over-deliberation of the tight playing sober:

"I want to proceed to the corner of Aberdeen Gardens. Do you know
Aberdeen Gardens?"

He'd got his foot on the step and he said, grinning: "I know it awright,
sir. But which corner jer want? There's four."

"The corner, driver, which is next to the Hammer—Hammer—Hammersmith Road."

He put a finger to his cap. He was still grinning.

"O. K., chief!" he said.

He climbed into the driving seat. I was on the point of letting myself
down into my seat when I saw something which made me change my mind.
While I'd been talking, I'd been looking at the driver, exclusively of everything else, I suppose, in a desperate attempt to convince. I hadn't heard and

I hadn't seen that the bobby was standing not more than a yard away. How long he'd been there I couldn't tell. That was what shook me. My God, how it shook me!

I still maintain that I did the wrong thing. If I'd just sat down, I don't suppose he'd have said anything. But I felt that I'd *got* to know. I said:

" 'Evenin', constable. Lovely evening." Again, to my own ears, my voice sounded far too drunk.

He didn't speak from where he stood. He came towards me, as I leant out of the cab window trying to make myself twice as broad as I really am, with three ponderous but silent steps. He said—and I couldn't tell whether his voice was genial or suspicious, or a bit of both:

"And what may be the matter with *you*, sir?"

I had to make about three shots before I could speak at all. I said at last:

"Nothing, officer! Absolutely nothing, Sergeant! Jus' a little party . . . a little party . . ."

I couldn't see his face properly. All I could tell was that he had a big moustache. He put his head on one side and stared at me. He said, with disapproval:

"I should say it had been a big party, sir. Much too big!"

At last the engine responded to the driver's efforts and began to chug. That was relief one. Relief two was that a man, walking fast, passed by. He was coming the way I had come. Idly the policeman turned to look at him; he was a big, broad-shouldered, rather slouching fellow in a whitish mackintosh with its collar turned up. He had a soft hat pulled down over his eyes.

The cab started with a jerk. I hit my head on the top of the window. It hurt. The policeman gave me the best send-off he could have done. No doubt relenting from his perhaps over-official attitude, he called:

"Good-night, sir."

I sank back into my seat. We chugged up Royalty Gardens and swung, right-handed, into Viceroy Road. I'd got my eyes closed and was breathing fast. I heard what sounded like a biggish car scream past us on second gear. It must have taken the corner pretty wide to go by us the way it did. Anyhow, my driver had to swerve. I was brought back to my senses pretty sharp. A heavy, limp weight lurched against my right shoulder.

Up till now I'd been entirely preoccupied with danger, but now, in the momentary safety of the cab, I began to feel the macabre side of the business. There was something indecent in the limpness of the weight which had fallen against me. I could hardly bring myself to push the thing upright and into its corner again, but I had to do it, *and* I had to sit with my right hand forced against its shoulder to keep it in position.

I must have seen—I believe I've said this before—as many dead men as most. I've been in charge of, and even worked on, burial parties in France. But that was somehow different. Death was the order of the day. It was what you expected and it was what you got. It's very different when you meet it in the middle of so-called civilization—particularly when you know what the said civilization will do to you if it catches you interfering.

The distance from Royalty Gardens up Viceroy Road, out across by Princes Road and down to the Hammersmith entrance to Aberdeen Gardens is, I suppose, a little over a couple of miles. The taxi, old and slow though it was, can't have taken more than ten minutes to do the journey. It seemed to me, alternately, as if we were hurtling at Grand Prix speed and crawling like anæmic snails. There's a clock just before you turn the corner into Aberdeen Gardens where I had told the cabby to stop. When we got there I looked at it and saw—with a shock because I was in one of my snail fits— that the time was only 11:28.

The cab pulled up with a jerk, about ten yards round the right-hand corner of the gardens. My most difficult time was coming. I hadn't realized until we were stationary what an obstacle the driver was. It wasn't as if he'd been one of the lethargic, cantankerous kind. He was young and keen and obliging, and probably would want to help. Somehow or other I'd got to stop that at least. I stuck my head out of the window. I give you my word that I had no idea what I was going to say until I said it. The words were, when they came:

"Drive on about fifty yards, will you? Stop just short of the next lamp-post."

As soon as I'd said them I realized that I'd forgotten to be drunk. I peered apprehensively through the glass at the driver's back. He wasn't looking round, and I hoped he hadn't noticed anything. Of course, I might have sobered up. On the other hand, I'd been so very drunk when I got into his cab . . . I determined that when I did get out—if I ever got out—I'd be just a bit on the tight side still.

The cab crawled up the right-hand curb to the place I had said. I did more thinking in the few seconds of the little journey than I'd ever before got into a similar time. When we stopped again I had a scheme. It wasn't a very good one. But it seemed the only one in the circumstances.

Directly the cab stopped I stepped over the legs of my charge, whipped open the door, and got out onto the pavement. I leaned confidentially towards the driver, picking at the sleeve of his coat. I said:

"Driver, my frien'—he livesh here! Now, you can see I'm sober ash a judge. . . ."

Even in the half-dark I could see his eyes twinkling under the peak of his cap. "Yes, sir," he said.

"Sober ash a judge. . . . But my frien'—well, he'sh *drunk!* I might shay, driver, he'sh dead drunk. He can't stand. He can't see. He can't even feel." Here I tried to giggle weakly, as if the humour of the thing were too much for me; it must have been a curious noise. "Now, thish house jush in front of us, driver, that'sh his house an' hish wife'sh very, very particular. . . . Oh, terribly particular! . . . Now, what I'm goin' to do, driver, is to—is to——"

The man moved as if he were about to get out of the cab. He said:

"That's awrigh', guv'nor, I'll give you a nand. Married meself!"

This didn't give me such a shock as it might, because I'd not only been ready for it, but I'd been playing for it. I said:

"You siddown! No offensh; but siddown. 'Slike thish, driver. Any noise and that woman will be awake!" I snapped my fingers very loudly in his ear. "Jus' like that . . . she'sh—well, she'sh like that." I fumbled in my pocket for some of the loose silver which the girl had given me before I left. I pulled out three half-crowns. I said: "Don' know what your fare is, but— here sheven and a tanner. That's a little presen' if you'll help me by doing what I want."

He held out a palm and I dropped the three coins into it. They vanished. He said:

"Much obliged, I'm sure, sir. Anythink I can do——"

I explained that what I wanted him to do was quietly to reverse for about twenty yards, then turn and go off, also quietly, as quickly as he could. I pointed out that I didn't want to run the risk of the taxi being heard opposite the house or any lights being seen opposite the house. If I was left alone, and in darkness, I might get my friend in through the back door—he had the key—without being heard. Once I'd got him into the house I could manage the rest. I felt at the time that I alternated, none too well, extreme thickness of speech with perfect clarity. But he seemed to notice nothing. He touched his cap. He said:

"Righ-char, sir. . . . Give you a nand to get 'im aht, will I?"

I shook my head. "That'll be all right," I said. "When I've got him out and shut the door, you jus' back and get out . . . the way I said."

He put his fingers to his cap again. I opened the door and got hold of my burden by taking him with either hand under each arm. With one heave—I still look back at that as a miracle of strength and neatness which I couldn't have performed except under some dire compulsion—I got it out onto the pavement. I managed to slew round so that my back was to the driver, in case he was looking, and my charge was clasped against my chest. Somehow or other I slid my left arm round his waist and, with my right hand round his right wrist, got his arm round my neck. I held my breath and waited to see whether the five-bob tip had been enough to make the cabby obey instructions implicitly.

Thank God, it had! He hadn't switched off his engine and, even as I kicked the door shut with a slam, he was backing. So far as I could tell, all his eyes were on his job.

I started off. Beside me my charge dragged scraping toes along the pavement. After four or five steps I slipped and lurched, and a soft felt hat fell to the pavement with a flop. If it had been mine I wouldn't have worried; but we were just underneath a street lamp and it wasn't.

With the hat on, drawn well down over the eyes, my companion might pass. With it off he couldn't. I seemed to hear not one but a dozen sets of footfalls. Somehow bending down, I picked the hat up and put it on again. The footfalls seemed all round me. When I got my breath again, and my sight was beginning to behave properly, I realized that the sounds had been only in my mind. There wasn't—and surely this must have been the biggest stroke of luck of all the strokes of luck I'd had—a sight or sound of anyone.

I went on thanking my stars I'd got some sort of a plan. It was this: about a hundred yards ahead of me was the little high-walled alley—they call it Holly Walk—which is a short cut from Aberdeen Gardens to Carlisle Square. Just beside the Carlisle Square entrance to the alley is a telephone box. I knew it because before our crash, Pearson had lived in Carlisle Square and I'd sometimes used it. I'd often remarked on the idiocy of the Post Office in putting a box in such an unlikely place. I don't suppose more than a dozen people a week used the thing. . . . My scheme was to put my charge inside it and shut the door, and leave him. Not a very good place, you may say. But, if you do, my answer's—find a better.

I ploughed on with a desperate lack of caution. I was so near my goal that I felt I'd got to put all my trust in my luck.

It held. My only bad moment was when I heard—really heard this time—footsteps. It was just before I got to the mouth of Holly Walk. They sounded to me as if they were on the pavement just behind me. But they weren't. They were on the far side of the road. There was no lamp near and, Aberdeen Gardens being as wide as they are, there wasn't any danger of anyone on the other pavement being able to see me.

I went up Holly Walk faster than you would believe possible. I came to the telephone box. It was empty. There was no one about. I freed my right hand, holding my charge up with my left. I opened the door of the box and wriggled into it and pulled him after me.

CHAPTER V

As I closed the door of the telephone box behind me and began to walk across Carlisle Square, I felt as if someone had left me a couple of hundred thousand. The feeling should have kept on, but it didn't. I can't tell you why, but I hadn't gone more than a quarter of a mile before I was sweating with a new and quite different fear. Now—whether it was because of the time, although this isn't likely, or because of luck, which seems the only explanation—I kept on meeting people. I passed at least four bobbies and what seemed to me like half-dozen upon half-dozen of ordinary citizens, and each one, I thought, looked at me with dirty looks. While I'd been on the job, so to speak, I'd been so terrified that I was numb. But now, the job done, I'd got nothing to take my mind off myself. I ought to be ashamed to admit it, but at one point—it was after the third bobby and while I was going through some square or other in the region between High Street, Kensington, and Notting Hill—I broke into a run. Not a jog trot, but an honest-to-God run.

It was while I was running that I passed the fourth bobby. I shot round a corner and cannoned into him and that, for the moment, made me worse. I'd been running like a rabbit. I ran now like a hare and a good one. I'd startled the Law. Through the thudding of the blood in my ears I heard him stop and shout, and heard—or thought I heard, which was just as bad— heavy feet pounding after me.

I took the first turn to my left, the first to my right, the first to my left again and came out into the safety of High Street, Kensington. I say safety because here there were, allowing for the hour, more than a few people. Just before I actually turned into High Street, coming out of one of those snickets opposite Ponting's, I pulled myself together. I walked instead of running and I stripped off the raincoat and carried it over my arm. I took off my hat and carried that too.

I walked on. For a bit I thought I heard behind me shouts and whistles and pounding feet, but, taking hold of myself, I was soon able to distinguish sounds *inside* my head from the real sounds going on about me. The bobby I'd cannoned had either given up the chase or had lost the trail.

I found that I was drenched with sweat and that my face, on what was after all a very sharp night, looked as if I'd just been playing tennis. I groped for a handkerchief and remembered. I hadn't got one. I managed to mop my face surreptitiously with my sleeve. I walked on slowly and went past Kensington Church, and at last was opposite the mouth of Viceroy Road. I paused. My first idea was to go back, now, to Royalty Gardens and report. My second was to do nothing of the sort. I was feeling, alternately, that I'd been noted and that I hadn't been noted. If the first were the truth, then to lead a trail, however vague, straight back to Royalty Gardens wouldn't do me, or Frances, any good. On the other hand, if the second were right, it would still do no harm if I did a bit of doubling and got back later.

So I went straight on, keeping the railings of Kensington Gardens on my left. I didn't walk fast, although, every now and then, my inclination was to burst into another mad spurt. I kept hearing people following me. All the way I had that cold feeling in between my shoulder blades which you get when somebody's after you, and you don't want to turn round and show 'em you've got wind up.

I stuck it, and no heavy hand dropped on my shoulder. By the time, walking slow, I'd reached Knightsbridge Barracks, and after that, walking slower still, the coffee stall at Hyde Park corner, I was honestly believing I'd got right away with it.

I was going straight by the stall, but the sudden scent of tobacco and hot liquid and some sort of cooking hit me in the stomach. I realized that I wasn't only nearly played out but also damned hungry again. I slewed sharp left and went up to the high counter. There were three other men at it—two taxi drivers and a pimpled youth with buff-coloured spats and a blue suit which must have belonged to his father. They took no notice of me. At that coffee stall—I believe they sometimes call it the "Junior Turf"—any and every sort of evening kit is more the rule than the exception. I felt in my pocket. There was still a good deal of silver there—about twelve and sixpence worth. I had a cup of coffee, two ham sandwiches, and a sausage roll. I then had another cup of coffee and bought a packet of cigarettes and a box of matches.

I felt better; a whole hell of a lot better. I took a long time over the second cup of so-called coffee and smoked three cigarettes. I leaned on the sloppy counter. I felt, momentarily, that I didn't care if it snowed blood. I asked the man behind the counter the time. I was flabbergasted to hear that it was "close on two," but I wasn't displeased. The walk had taken longer than I'd thought. I said good-night and went on with it. My feet were pretty sore and I should have liked a bed, even a wooden one. But I kept on, very slowly, until I'd got halfway down Piccadilly—to be exact, opposite the end of St. James's Street. The time must have been about half-past two. A taxi drew up beside me invitingly. I fell. I felt I couldn't foot-slog any more. I told the driver to go to Viceroy Road—No. 38, which was the first number that came into my head. I said:

"Got a bad head. No hurry. Go as slow as you like."

He went slow all right; so slow that the last thing I remember before his opening the door was the corner of Park Lane. I remember the drive, but because of the dreams I had. You can imagine the sort of thing. Not pleasant. . . .

I was jerked forward and waked. The taxi had stopped. The driver was out and was opening the door. He didn't say anything, just waited until I got out. I gave him a shilling over his fare. He held it on the palm of his hand and looked at it. He grunted and turned away back into the cab.

I suddenly got the wind up again. He didn't seem to be starting. I felt he was waiting for me to go up the steps to No. 38. I didn't want to go up the steps to No. 38. Desperately I slid my hand into my pocket and flicked one of the remaining coins out onto the pavement, and began to look for it. I judged that I shouldn't have any help. I didn't. In a minute I saw the coin in the gutter, but pretended not to. After what seemed about three or four minutes, but, I suppose, was really only about half a minute, the cab chugged off. Luckily it didn't turn, but went straight ahead. I waited for it to get about fifty yards and then I scooped the half-crown up, pushed it into my pocket, and set out for Royalty Gardens. On this journey I didn't pass anyone—not even a bobby. Going down the right-hand pavement of the gardens I suddenly knew that I wasn't scared any longer. Or, rather, that I was too tired to have any emotions at all. I lurched up the steps of No. 48 and put my thumb on the bell, and held it there. I could hear a muffled pealing from the basement.

Nothing happened. I stopped ringing and waited. I sat down on the stone arm of the porch balustrade. I waited five minutes, which, mixed up as they were with snatches of sleep, seemed any time. I then heaved myself up and rang again. This time I kept my thumb on the bell twice as long, but still nothing happened. I looked at the knocker. I considered beating it, but then thought I'd better not. I staggered down the steps and had a look round. There was still nobody about. I looked up at the windows, hoping to see a gleam of light, but they were all squares of darkness and so was the basement window. I went up to the porch again and had another try at the bell. I could hear it ringing, but still nothing happened. I sat down on the balustrade again and lit a cigarette.

I don't suppose I'd had more than three draws at it when I went right off. The next thing I remember is waking with a jerk. My shoulder was being shaken and my head was lolloping about like a pumpkin on the end of a rope. The girl's deep voice was whispering:

"It's you! Thank *God!*"

I didn't seem able to get my eyes open properly. I rubbed at them and even hit myself on the face. I managed to see her. She was still in the dressing gown and pyjamas. It was very cold on the porch. I realized what it must be like with next to nothing on, and I got up and stumbled into the house. She followed, shutting the door behind her. I remember hearing the soft click of the bolts going home.

In the dark I felt a hand on my arm and I heard her voice saying: "This way." She led me through the first door on the right. She switched on the light. I was standing in what I suppose—although I don't really know to this day—was the drawing room.

She pulled up a chair. "Sit down," she said.

She gave me a little push as she spoke. My feet were together and it was enough. I dropped into the big chair. I realized that my left hand was still clutching the borrowed hat and that over my arm was the raincoat. I let them slide to the floor. I managed to keep my eyes half open. I looked at her and said:

"Don't you worry. It's all right." I'd seen the grey-white pallor of her face and the dark rings under her eyes, and the lines round her mouth that had no business to be there. She said, coming very close and looking at me:

"How did you . . . what did you . . . where . . . ?"

I believe I raised a hand and wagged it at her for silence. I said:

"Telephone box. . . . Other side of Kensington. All right there. No one ever uses it. Won't be found till midday to-morrow at least—I mean to-day."

She put out a hand. I couldn't keep my eyes open properly, but I thought I saw that she lurched a bit as she stood. My eyes closed, and when they opened again she was sitting on a chair to face mine. There was some colour in her face, and some of the strained look had left it. Even through my fatigue I realized that I liked looking at her. She was very easy to look at. She said:

"It's so silly to say thank you. . . . But I . . . but I . . . I can't do it properly, so I won't do it at all. I hope you understand."

I was feeling better now. Sleepy, but able to keep my mind from skating. I said:

"I'd much rather you didn't. . . . What I want is . . ."

She seemed to recoil a little, but she spoke at once. "I'll get it for you," she said. "We didn't talk about exact amounts, but . . ."

But I bit that. I bit it hard. I said something rude, I don't remember what, but it was to the effect that I wasn't thinking about her something money.

My eyes were wide open. They must have been glaring at her. I saw her face slowly flush and then pale again, but with a different kind of pallor from any I'd seen before. She shot out of her chair as if something had released a big spring underneath her. When she spoke her voice was thick and harsh; it was like a clever man mimic trying to imitate her real voice. Her lips opened as if they were going to speak. Underneath them I could see that her teeth were tight clenched. I could have sworn that she was going to speak, but she didn't. A small tremor seemed to run all over her. I realized, as I watched, that when she had shot out of the chair like that her body had been like a wire spring, but now the rigidity softened. It was as if something—I hope you won't think I'm too fanciful or trying to write fine, but it's the only way I can describe it—it was as if something had been what they call "in possession" of her and had as suddenly been thrown out by her *self*. She took two small and rather wavering steps backwards and sank back into her chair. She put hands to her face, and spoke from behind them.

"I—I'm sorry." Her voice was shaking; but it was her own voice. "I'm very sorry. I see you didn't mean that." She laughed—a queer shaky sound. "Not that there's any reason why you shouldn't have. . . . What did you mean?"

I was staring at her. I found my mouth was open, and shut it. I said, trying not to stare:

"What I was going to say was that I could do with an hour's sleep."

She looked at me. Her eyes seemed to grow larger and larger. They were soft now, very soft, and seemed to shine with a light which was behind them.

Then I went to sleep. What I remember is her eyes. I said they grew larger. They seemed to grow larger and larger until they filled the world.

And then I didn't remember any more until, for the second time, I waked to find her shaking me by the shoulder.

I must have been far gone that time. For the first minute of waking I didn't know anything about anything. I didn't know the room, I didn't know her, I didn't know myself. I did know that something had happened, but what it was I had to dig desperately down in my mind to find out. Perhaps I should have come at once to remembering everything if she hadn't looked different, but now, instead of the dressing gown and pyjamas, which were the only things I knew her in, she was dressed. A tweedy sort of dress, very smart. I remember that the first thing I noticed was that it had a high collar. I like women in high collars. She was saying something. She kept on saying something. About the fourth time I heard it properly; that was when I'd remembered. She was saying:

"I'm sorry, but you *must* wake. It's seven o'clock!"

I got out of the chair. I was very stiff and ached. I felt as uncomfortable as one does when one's slept in a chair not only with clothes on, but with evening clothes on. I must have looked pretty ghastly. A dirty stubble of beard, a crumpled shirt front, a wreck of a collar and, once more, my cuffs sticking out of my sleeves about a yard and a half, with no links in them. I tried to straighten myself a bit, but I don't think it was much good. I said, for something to say:

"Why didn't you wake me before?"

She looked at me. "I hadn't," she said, "got the heart."

"Seven," I said. "Seven!" I kept on mumbling the word over like an old woman. I'd got my ideas straight, but I wasn't reacting properly yet. I felt sure that I ought to get out of here, and get out of here quick. And then, as I moved a little, the few remaining coins clinked in my pocket. That was all that was wanted to bring me fully round. I looked at her.

"I'm sorry," I said. "I shall want . . . some money."

She cut me short. "Of course," she said. "Now, I've got a suggestion to make—about all that. . . ." A faint tinge of extra colour crept into her face, but her eyes went on looking straight into mine. "I want to suggest that we don't—how shall I put it?—just—er, arrange matters so that you—so that I— so that you get a little money now and—then that's over. What I want to suggest is that you take some now—enough to get you some food and some clothes, and somewhere to—some sort of anchorage. . . . I want to suggest that—that after you've done that you come back here, and we have another talk."

I began to say something, but once more she cut me short. She held up her hand. "Please listen to me," she said. And now there was more colour in her face still. "You've done something for me which I can't imagine any other person would have done . . . certainly no one who'd—who'd . . ." She boggled at finishing that sentence and changed it to another. "As you have done this for me," she said, "I *can't*, I *won't* just pay for it as if it were a pound of tea or something." She came a little closer to me. "Please, will you just take some money now, there's plenty upstairs, and then promise me that you'll come back?"

I nodded. After all, to come back, I discovered, was just what I wanted to do. It wasn't that I wanted to come back to 48 Royalty Gardens. It was that I definitely wanted to see this girl again. And again. And again. I said:

"That's all right. That's all right."

She dropped her eyes. For a moment we stood in one of those silences which grow increasingly awkward with every second, and with every second are harder to break. At last she moved towards the door. She said, without looking round:

"If you wouldn't mind coming upstairs. The money's in the library."

Once more I followed her through the house. This time I didn't look at my surroundings at all. I was looking at her back. I felt queer, as if I were still dreaming.

Up the stairs we went and stopped, as we'd stopped the night before, outside the right-hand door on the first landing. This time she didn't have to pull herself together to open the door. She put her fingers boldly on the handle and turned it, and pushed the door gently open. She stood aside and waved me in.

I crossed the threshold. I crossed the threshold and entered the room knowing that I was sane. I was no more than a couple of paces inside the room when I felt—*believed*—that I was mad.

The little bureau was still against the wall. The chair was still before it. And on the chair, with its arms and head upon the bureau exactly as they had been, was *still* the body which, seven hours ago, I had taken a good three miles across London and left!

CHAPTER VI

I sat on the bottom step of the second flight of stairs and held my head in my hands. It wanted steadying, badly. Facing me was the open door of the library. The light in there was still on. I could see a great part of the room, but I couldn't see the incredible occupant of the chair at the small writing table. I was glad I couldn't.

The girl was leaning against the wall, to my left, close up to the jamb of the library door. Her hands were behind her, pressed close between her body and the wall. Her head was thrown back so that her chin was pointing almost directly up to the ceiling. This may sound as if she were at ease; I can only assure you that she was nothing of the sort. From neck to heels her body was rigid, and it trembled a little with every breath that she took.

I don't know how long we were there like that. Inside the room we had hardly spoken. The incredibility of the thing had taken away our capacity for speech. How we'd got out on the landing I couldn't tell you, because my memory's blank regarding the time between my first sight of the returned and the time when I found myself sitting on the stairs. But I do know who broke the silence at last. I did. I said something like this:

"It's *impossible,* but it's happened. . . . We've got to face up to that. . . . We can't get away from it! . . ."

There was a pause. I wondered whether she was going to answer. She said, at last:

"I suppose you *did* . . . did . . . take him away?"

Her voice was different again, I remember thinking, even in the middle of my funk and bewilderment, that I'd never heard a woman, or a man for that matter, with so many different voices. And then what she had said sunk in, and I jumped up and began to shout at her. I suppose I was a bit wrought up.

"Damn it all!" I said—or I hope I said that; I've a feeling it was a good deal worse. "You *know* I took him out. Didn't I have to risk my neck at every street corner and put about eighty years onto my life taking him halfway across London! And after that didn't I get the wind up so badly that I had to walk the legs off my trunk! And didn't you see me start! Of course you did . . . so what the devil d'you mean?"

As soon as the words were out I began to cool off. But she spoke before I'd had time to get out an apology. She didn't, even then, bring her chin down; I've an idea that she didn't want me to see her face. I've another idea that she felt that, if she moved as much as half an inch, she might collapse. She said:

"Sorry. Sorry. Of course I know. Of course I saw you. You ought to have known that what I said didn't *mean* anything. I—I suppose—I was just talking to make sure that we hadn't both gone mad. . . . But what are we going to *do?*"

Her voice was still the dead, different voice. I put my head back in my hands again and spoke down at the carpet. I said that she could search me; for it was well past dawn, and further, when I'd touched the thing just now inside the room, I'd felt that rigour was well on the way. Any possibility of moving it again was gone.

Suddenly she thrust herself away from the wall. She took a step forward and looked down at me. I glanced up at her face. All I can say about it is that it gave me a shock. She looked a good ten years older. Of course her face was white; but it was also—and I mean this quite literally—*thinner*. And the lines round her mouth looked as if they'd been cut in with an etching tool. And the rings under her eyes might have been put in with black chalk. If ever I saw fear, I saw it then. And if ever any man saw fear controlled with more courage, I'll eat my hat *and* a pair of trousers.

I got up. I did my best to look purposeful—as if I were in charge of the situation and had a plan, and all she had to do was to leave it to me. I succeeded in getting hold of her arm and taking her down the stairs without any resistance. I asked her where the dining room was. She jerked her head towards the centre door in the right-hand wall as you come in. I led her to it and through it, and turned on one of the three switches just inside the door. Four corner lights came on. I pulled one of the armchairs away from the dining table and pushed her into it. She went down stiffly, with a bit of a bump. She was like a badly jointed wooden doll.

I looked about the room. There was a big mahogany sideboard—pretty old, I should think—across the far left-hand corner, and on it I could see decanters. I went across and opened one of the cupboard doors and found some tumblers. I smelt at the decanters and found brandy. To nearly a quarter of a tumblerful, I splashed as much soda. I took the glass back to the chair. I held it out to her, but she didn't make any move. She wasn't looking at me. Her eyes were wide open but they weren't looking at anything. I took hold of her chin with my right hand and put the glass to her lips with my left. She was very stiff but she was docile. In sips she swallowed nearly a third of what I'd put in the glass and then she did move and speak. She waved the glass away and rested her head against the high back of the chair and looked up at me. She said:

"Thank you. . . . I'm better. . . . I don't want any more."

I sat on the edge of the table and drank what she'd left. An idea struck me as I put the glass down. I said:

"I want to go back upstairs. . . . Be all right here?"

She nodded, once, and the lids closed over her eyes as if they were too heavy to hold up any longer. I didn't like leaving her but I had to.

I went back to the library. I thought I'd found the explanation. We'd only just looked at the body in the chair. It was dressed the same and it was in the same position, but it *couldn't* be the same man. It was impossible that it could be the same man. If it was the same man, then two and two didn't equal four.

But it was the same man. There was no possible doubt. I crossed the room to the sofa and sat down on it and once more got hold of my head. I was trying to think *exactly* what his position had been the first time I'd seen him. I tried to make a picture in the front of my head and got it at last. I got up and compared it with the unbelievable reality. But there was no difference—or none that I could see. I then verified my impression about rigour. It wasn't setting in, it was pretty nearly set.

I looked desperately, even going down on my hands and knees, and crawling round the carpet like a bad imitation of Sherlock Holmes, for signs of *anything* different in the room. But I couldn't find any. Unfortunately, I hadn't done the Sherlock the first time, but I don't suppose that even if I had I'd have seen any difference. It's my firm belief there wasn't any. Even the dents in the thick pile of the carpet made by the legs of the chair he was sitting in hadn't been blurred or thickened. And the desk was the same, with the pen in the same place, and the ink pot open, and the piece of notepaper.

From a pigeonhole I took another piece of paper and, from one of the drawers, a pencil. I went back to the sofa and put down some notes. I've still got the piece of paper. I read it over and wasn't impressed, but I took it downstairs. I'd got to do something.

In the dining room she was sitting exactly as I'd left her: relaxed and with eyes closed. I said:

"Look here, I've got some questions. I can't do anything till you've answered them."

She opened her eyes. "Ask them," she said.

"First, did you kill him?"

Her eyes opened wider. For an infinitesimal bit of time I thought they were going to blaze the way they'd blazed when she'd had that queer fit in the drawing room just after I'd got back. But the odd light died away as soon as it had come. She said dully:

"I've told you I didn't. I thought you knew I didn't. If you think I did, why did you help?"

"Whether you did or not, after the story you told me, doesn't make much difference, but if it's any consolation I believe you. I don't believe I thought much about it before."

"Thank you," she said, with a sarcastic flash.

I got a bit rough. "We haven't got time for that. That was question number one. Number two is: Any idea what it could have been done with?"

She shook her head.

"Right. Question three: Unless we're going to go gaga and think this is black magic, someone brought him back. That's to say, someone followed me and, the minute I'd gone away from that telephone box, somehow reversed my process. We've got to face up to that. The question that leads out of that is this: how the devil did they get into the house, and upstairs, without your hearing?"

She was beginning to show signs of life. The first shock and fear seemed to have worn off. Once more there was a little colour in her face, and her eyes looked at me almost normally.

"That's easy," she said. "I was asleep. I wonder you didn't realize. I expect you had to ring several times before I found you, didn't you? I woke up sort of knowing the bell had been ringing, and yet not actually having heard it . . . you know . . ."

I nodded, but I was curious. "Sleep?" I said. "How the devil did you manage that?"

She lifted her shoulders. Off the right one a sort of long end of the high collar slipped down and she threw it back again with a definite, determined sort of flick which showed me she really was better. Ten minutes ago, or even three, she wouldn't have cared what had happened to any of her clothes. She said:

"I can't tell you. When you'd gone, I felt as if everything would be all right. You—you—you seemed to be so *safe*. . . . I know it sounds odd—but I just went to sleep."

I was pleased; I don't think I could have helped being pleased. I said:

"Where did you sleep? What room, I mean?"

She lifted her head a little. I saw, as her face came into the dimmish light, that she was looking better yet.

"I went upstairs. To my own room. It's just above the library. I hadn't meant to go to sleep. I sat on the edge of the bed—and that's the last thing I remember until I waked, as I told you, and *knew* the bell had been ringing."

She looked full at me for the first time since we'd started this conversation. I thought more of her than ever. She'd pulled herself round as no other woman I've ever met could have done. There was actually some sort of smile behind the big eyes.

"I'm sorry!" she said, after a pause. "If I hadn't gone to sleep, we should have known where we were, shouldn't we?"

I thought it was a good thing she had slept; and I said so. Anyone hard-boiled enough to do what must have been done with the thing upstairs wouldn't be nice for a girl to meet alone in the house, especially when he was on the job.

She nodded. She put her hands up to her breasts with a sudden movement as if her heart had jumped. She said, in a hushed little voice:

"That—that's what frightens me! *Who—who—*could . . ."

"That," I said, "is another of my questions. I hadn't got it written down, but I saw it as we were talking . . . 'fraid I'm not very good at this . . . been most things, but never a sleuth. It seems to me, though, that you've *got* to have . . . wait a minute!" I got excited. "Who's got a latchkey to this house, besides you and—and . . . ?"

It's funny how obvious things like that miss the ordinary person when the ordinary person's rattled. It had missed me up till now and it had missed her. It hit her though. She was out of her chair so quickly that the movement made me blink. The next thing I knew was that she had got hold of my arm with both her hands and was shaking it. If I'd been excited, she was twenty times more so. She almost shouted:

"There is someone. Someone who's got a key, I mean. A great friend of —of—my stepfather's. His name's Marriott, Edgar Marriott."

"A *friend?*" I said.

She shook my arm harder than ever. "When I said friend I only meant that he seemed to be a friend. Everyone thought so. My stepfather thought so." Her eyes were very wide. Looking at them, I knew what novelists mean when they say that eyes "blaze." She went on shaking my arm; she almost pulled me off the table. For a little bit of a thing like that, she was amazingly strong. She said: "But suppose—*suppose*—he wasn't *really* a friend." Suddenly her excitement seemed to ooze out of her. She dropped my arm. She took a step backwards and sank back into the chair again. She looked smaller. She said:

"But I know he was. He was about the only person who ever saw anything good in . . . Oh! I ought not to talk like that!"

"We've got no time for bilge," I said. "And we ought to be in an asylum. Both of us. Here we sit gabbing away about How and Why and Who, when we ought to be thinking—and damn hard—what we're going to *do!*"

She opened her eyes wide. There was a long pause before she spoke. When she did, she said, very slowly:

"You're right. But only half right. You ought to have said that *I* ought to be thinking about what *I'm* going to do." With a quick little movement she put both her hands to her face. I could see that the middle finger of each hand was pressing hard into a temple as if to stop some sort of pain. "What *I'm* going to do," she said again. And then, talking much louder: "This isn't any of your affair. You've done more than anyone had got any right to ask you to do. You've finished. What you've got to do is to *go.* This is *my* affair, not yours."

This is a point in my story where I'm going to find it very difficult to show you, properly, my state of mind. I'm not a Galahad, and I've never pretended to be one. But, if I go on the way I'm going, you'll think I'm one of the worst sorts of Galahad—the sort that says he isn't and really is. I'm not that either. I'm perfectly well aware that what I ought to have done, having some common sense, was to have taken a tenner for my efforts and said I was very sorry and she must let me know if there was anything I could do—and then just floated off. I am also perfectly well aware that this didn't occur to me at all. It didn't occur to me enough to make me wonder why I said what I did say. The best fist I can make of it is to write that this was a young woman who'd had the most peculiar effect upon me—a more peculiar effect than any I'd ever experienced; which is saying a good bit. I could no more have walked out on her than I could have cut her throat. Mark you, it wasn't unselfishness that prompted me. Much the reverse: I suppose what they call my "subconscious" had been telling me, since the beginning of this nightmare, that if I didn't help her, I shouldn't see her again. And even my conscious knew that to see her again—lots of her, at many different times —was a necessity.

Anyhow, even when she'd said her piece about my clearing out, I didn't stop to consider it. I said:

"Look here! You've forgotten that I did a Sykes into this house. You've forgotten that I'm broke. You've forgotten that I want a job. You'd better give me this one. In fact, I appoint myself. Now, *will* you put your mind to thinking what our next move's going to be?"

She played up. We didn't have any more nonsense. She got down to business. She stood up and said:

"If it's as you say, what we've got to do first is to have something to eat. What I must do second is to get hold of the car. What we must do third is to take you out, with some money, so that you can get some clothes. After that, we'll think. There can't be any danger"—here her voice faded—"for a bit. The servants aren't here and won't be to-day. There's only me. If any-one comes, they can't get in and that's that . . ."

It was here that I interrupted her. I'd been staring at her like something out of a bowl. I said:

"Did you say '*get the car*'?"

She looked at me. "Yes. Why shouldn't I?"

"D'you mean to tell me that you've got a car?"

She nodded; her eyes looked astonishment. I took a step nearer to her. I was angry. I said:

"I suppose you'll tell me now that it's a closed car?"

She went on staring at me. "As a matter of fact, it is."

I grabbed at my hair with both hands and began to walk up and down. I could have beaten her. She said: "What's the matter?" And that started me off. I said that if she'd only had a minimum of brains she'd have thought of the car last night. I pointed out that if she had I should have been spared four very unpleasant hours; should consequently have been more useful this morning, and, above all, would have probably bamboozled her secret enemy. I didn't say all this gently; in fact, I was rude.

She told me so. A pink patch showed on each of her cheek bones. She glared at me—not with the queer glare of that funny spasm of hers—but with the honest-to-God glare of a resentful woman who isn't frightened. She said:

"You've no control over a very bad temper! . . . If you'd waited, I'd have told you that the car couldn't have been used last night. It was in for repairs. I wanted it for to-day and they were going to work all night on it. They said it would be ready at seven this morning. *That* was why I didn't mention it. If you remember, we hadn't a great deal of time to talk uselessly."

She paused there, and I thought she'd finished. But she hadn't. She said: "Will you please wait here." And I was left staring at a closed door.

She hadn't banged the door. She'd done worse—shut it with an exaggerated noiselessness. I managed to feel, at the same time, a fool, a boor, and an injured party. I sat in the chair which she'd been sitting in and cursed myself and her and the whole rotten business. For the first time I began to wonder whether I was mad to be in the house still, but that mood didn't last. It was kicked out of my mind by more urgent stuff. Where had she gone? What was she doing?

I stuck it for a bit, but not long. I tiptoed out into the hall and stood and listened. Through the panes of the ground glass of the front door came grey morning light. The place, in spite of its comfort, seemed cold and empty and very dangerous. I couldn't hear a sound. I went upstairs, slowly. The library door was still open and the lights were still on. There was no grey daylight here because there were heavy curtains across all the windows. I'm not squeamish as a rule, but I've got to confess that I switched off the light and shut the door without looking inside the room. I stood on the landing and listened some more. I still heard nothing. I began to get wind up. I ran up the next flight and opened all the doors I could see. I found one man's big bedroom, one woman's big bedroom, what seemed a spare room, a bathroom, and a little sort of sewing room. There was no sign of her anywhere. I went up the next flight and found more bedrooms, and a box room and some cupboards. She wasn't anywhere. I went down the stairs four at a time. I stood in the hall again. I didn't feel tired any more, I felt sick.

And then I heard a sound which changed my state of mind—the clinking rattle of china. It didn't take me long to get to the service stairs and down them.

She was in the kitchen. There was a smell of coffee and frying bacon. She'd got a sort of overall on. The sleeves of it were rolled up and her short black hair was rumpled. I didn't make much of a noise coming in, and she either didn't hear me or pretended not to. Her back was towards me. I shut the door and said:

"Look here . . . sorry I lost my temper. I'm . . ."

She whipped round. Her face was flushed with her work and, what with this and the overall and the rumpled hair, she was a different person. And then she smiled; the first full smile I'd seen. And she was a different person again. She seemed to have as many personalities as she had voices. You never, so to speak, knew what was coming next. She said:

"Oh, *that's* all right! Shall I bring this tray up? Or shall we eat down here?"

We ate down there. I still remember that breakfast. I enjoyed it more than any meal I've ever had before or since. We both ate well. I daresay it sounds queer, but the fact remains. We didn't talk much, but we certainly weren't strained. We were just a man and a woman having breakfast which the woman had cooked.

She was the first to come back to business. There was a little watch on her left wrist and she looked at it. I saw her eyebrows go up.

"It's getting on," she said. "Quarter to nine." As she spoke, I could *see* the situation get up and hit her in the face. Her colour ebbed away and her lips tightened. I knew what she felt like; I'd got a sickish feeling myself—a sort of Monday-morning-back-to-the-office sensation multiplied by a thousand. I said:

"What about that car? What've you got to do? Telephone?"

She lifted her shoulders. She pushed her chair back and got up, and began to strip off the overall.

"I've been thinking about that," she said. "Normally I'd phone, but do you think I ought to? Hadn't I better just go round . . . it isn't far."

I could see what was in her mind. She was thinking that if she telephoned it would be a sure sign that she'd been in the house. I agreed that she'd better not. She said:

"All right. You can't come with me, can you? . . . No, of course you can't. You wait here. I'll go up and put on a hat. I'll be about—ten minutes." She drew herself up to the full of her five feet and a scrap. I wanted to say that I'd go with her, but managed not to. It was obviously wrong. With her fingers on the handle of the door, she turned. She said, with a little catch in her voice:

"I say! You won't—you won't . . . You're going to stay here, aren't you?"

I thought the best thing to do was to pretend to be angry. I must have done it pretty well. When I'd finished, she half smiled.

"All right," she said. "Sorry." And then she was gone.

I walked about the kitchen for a bit. I heard her come down the main stairs and then heard the bolts of the front door being pulled back and the sound of the door slamming. I wanted to rush after her and say I'd come after all; but I found the sense to stay put.

I suddenly found that I wanted a cigarette. I'd finished the cook's Gold Flake, so I had to go upstairs. I wondered whether I'd have to go into the study. Fortunately, I didn't. I found a box in the dining room.

She'd said she'd be away ten minutes. She was actually away fifteen. In that time I must have smoked ten cigarettes. I remember looking at the litter in the ashtray as I heard a car pull up outside. And I remember having the sense to find a piece of paper and tip the stubs into it, and screw it up and push it into my pocket. I left the dining room to go along the passage to the front door, just as there came the sound of a latchkey being put into the lock.

CHAPTER VII

The car was a Jamieson—a big blue sedan. Having driven a lot myself I'm scared with other drivers unless they're good. I wasn't scared now. She drove like an angel. I sat beside her with the borrowed hat pulled down over my eyes and the collar of the borrowed raincoat turned up. From between collar and hat brim I spent most of the journey looking at her profile. A small severe hat made her look different again. Her face was set. It was stern and mature and, as I've said, different. But it was none the less attractive.

There wasn't much traffic in the heart of Kensington, but as soon as we got out into the Hammersmith Road the usual nine o'clock rabble was there. We'd arranged, in the few minutes we'd spent in the hall after she'd come back, that I should go to the Regent Street branch of Creed's. There, under the same roof, I could get fitted out from top to toe. I'd wanted to shave before I left the house, but had been overruled—very wisely, I think. My yarn was to be that I'd been at one hell of a party and hadn't been able to get back to the country to my clothes—and after parties like that one doesn't shave oneself.

She swung the car through Princes Gate and into the park. We were held up at the cross turning just inside. She stared at the policeman who was stopping us, and I saw that her teeth were biting into her lower lip. I felt a bit pale myself. The bobby was facing us. He wasn't looking at us really, but it seemed to me—and I'm sure it did to her—that he was peering at our faces. The stream from the park to the gardens thinned and ended. He waved us on. She swung the car right-handed and shot off down the road towards Hyde Park Corner much too fast. The needle on the speedometer was at forty-five when I reminded her of the twenty limit. We certainly didn't want to rush ourselves into a police court. She said:

"I'm sorry. Nerve went for a minute. I didn't like that policeman at the corner."

I grunted. And then I put the question which had been worrying me ever since we'd started.

"Seems odd about your servants," I said.

"Odd?" she said.

She gave me a quick glance out of the corner of her eye.

I nodded. "Damn odd. House of that size doesn't generally send all the staff away for the week-end. Tell me this. . . . How did it come about? What I'm wondering is—could this 'X' of ours have worked it? Could this Marriott have?"

She was driving very slowly now, but she slowed still further as she thought. The car crawled along at something under fifteen. I told her to speed up—too slow is as conspicuous as too fast. She got the needle back to twenty and said:

"I know it seems funny." She spoke very slowly. "But I don't think it really is. You see, they're all one family. The mother's the cook, the elder girl's the parlourmaid, and the younger's the housemaid. . . . We ought to have four really, but never mind that. We've a woman in sometimes when there's any turning out. . . . No . . . I don't see how it *could* have been arranged unless they'd known about it. And that's absurd, utterly absurd!"

I egged her on with a "Why?" She explained that it was absurd because of the women's characters. They were "dears." All of them. Their name was Prescott. The mother had been the first to come. She'd been there altogether nearly five years. The elder girl had come along about a year later and the younger two years ago. The reason for their all having the week-end together was the death of the mother's brother. The funeral was in Yorkshire on the Sunday. By going on the Friday night, they could get back at midday on Monday. Being the sort of servants they were, she'd agreed. She'd had trouble with her stepfather, but that was inevitable. She'd won. No . . . summing it all up, she was certain that their going away was coincidence.

We were held up again at Hyde Park Corner, but this time we were in the middle of a line of cars and couldn't see the bobby. I thought about what she had told me. I said, just as we started moving again:

"Might not be coincidence at that. I mean our X—or Marriott—they might have known . . ." A good idea hit me. I said: "Look here! Who but you and your stepfather *could* have known that the servants were going to be away from last night until Monday morning?"

She sat very still for a moment and then slowly turned her face towards me. Her eyes were wide with excitement. She said in a whisper:

"Marriott *did* know."

In front of us the block moved. Fortunately I saw the bobby waving at us angrily. I nudged her and she slipped into first gear and was off. We didn't speak again until, having wormed through Piccadilly, Bond Street, and Vigo Street, we pulled up on the wrong side of the road just outside Creed's. I'd been thinking a good deal. If Marriott had known about the servants and he had a latchkey, it looked at least as if he ought to be seen. As the car came to a standstill, she said:

"Hurry, now, hurry! Here take this. I'll wait round the corner in Sackville Street." She pushed a thick roll of notes into my hand. I stuffed them into my pocket, opened the door, and shot across the pavement. I was overconscious that what with my filthy patent shoes, my dress trousers, the obviously borrowed raincoat, and a hat not quite big enough, I must have looked both damned silly and—much worse!—easy to remember.

Fortunately I'd been in Creed's before. I walked straight from the door across the black-and-white marble floor to the lift. On the third floor I buttonholed something which looked like a sub-manager. He was very tall and very thin, and a bit overdressed. I told him my yarn. Still playing nervous, I pulled out the roll of notes. There were two or three fivers and a good thick wad of ordinary currencies. Without seeming to, he looked at that. His manner changed. I must say that, unpleasant though he was, he lived up to Creed's motto of "Service, Service, and More Service." In fact, I'm willing at any time to write a special advertisement for Creed's. Inside forty minutes I'd washed, been shaved, chosen and put on underclothes, shirt, socks, shoes, suit, and hat; had paid for them and got in exchange for my money a receipt and a neat flat parcel containing the stuff I'd discarded. I felt better. A hell of a lot better. It's amazing what clothes will do for you. And I wouldn't like you to think that Creed's reach-me-downs looked like reach-me-downs. They didn't. Except for one or two very minor faults not noticeable in their newness, the clothes might have been made for me in the shop in Sackville Street, outside which I saw the car as soon as I turned the corner.

But I saw something else as well as the car. Beside it was the largest bobby I'd ever seen. And he wasn't beside it accidentally, because he was bending down so that he could speak through the window. I didn't feel better any more. I felt worse. I stood in the middle of the pavement, holding onto my parcel as if it were a cork jacket. My heart seemed to be missing on three cylinders. I don't know how long I should have gone on standing there if somebody hadn't run into me, given me a dirty look, muttered and passed on. That brought me to myself. I tried to put what they call a bold face on it and walked towards the car. Each step I took was a bigger effort but I got there. The policeman straightened himself, looked at me—I thought searchingly—and turned back to the car again. He stooped once more and touched his helmet. He said:

"Here you are, miss. There needn't be any trouble."

What that meant I don't know. He opened the door and smiled at me. Somehow or other I got into the car beside the driving seat and sank down, pitching my parcel into the back. I managed to say:

"Thanks very much." My voice sounded all wrong to me. Whether the bobby noticed I couldn't say. I didn't look to find out. He shut the door. I didn't dare look at the driver. I half closed my eyes. I heard the self-starter go and then felt the car move slowly off.

We were nearly at the Piccadilly end of Sackville Street before I turned my head and looked at her. I felt pale myself but I'll guarantee she was paler. Her eyes weren't closed because she was driving, but they gave me the impression that, if she hadn't been driving, they would have been tight shut. She was breathing very quickly. Her lips were apart, but her teeth were clenched. I said, in a voice like a consumptive crow's:

"What the devil was that?"

She let out her breath in a long, hissing gasp. She said, with an effort at a laugh:

"Nothing. Absolutely nothing. Car been standing too long. Wanted me to move along. You came up just in time."

I gasped too. "My God! I was scared."

We'd just got to the corner of Piccadilly and she had to stop the car. She turned and looked full at me.

"What about me?" she said. "*Scared!* I thought I was going to die!"

She started the car again and began to edge out into Piccadilly.

"Where to?" I said, trying to speak normally. She shot in front of a slow-moving lorry and turned right, round the taxi rank, into the stream going westwards. She said, very low:

"There's only one place, isn't there, where we can go? We've got to go there . . . for a little, anyhow."

After a long pause she spoke again. She said, not looking at me:

"Haven't we?"

I was doubtful. "What I'd like to do," I said, "is Marriott."

"Oh!" She looked at me for a second. "Ye-s. But how? And if it comes to that, where?"

"Don't you know where he lives?"

She shook her head. "It isn't far from us. I think it's in Empress Gardens . . . but I'll have to go home, anyhow—to find out. I know the phone number, but not the address." She was quiet for a moment, then added, very softly, as if she were talking to herself: "You see, I wasn't very fond of Mr. Marriott."

When she said this we were halfway along the railings of the Green Park. We didn't speak again until we were actually entering the southern end of Royalty Gardens. Then she said, quite suddenly and as if there hadn't been any pause in our conversation:

"You're right. We've *got* to do something, and the sooner we do it the better. You stay in the car. I'll go in and get the address and we'll go there, shall we? And see what happens and just——"

I hadn't time to answer. We came to a jerky stop in front of No. 48 and she was out in the road before I could even reach over and open the door. I stayed where I was. I didn't look at the house. I fumbled in my pockets for a cigarette which wasn't there. That was the one thing I'd forgotten at Creed's. When I did look to my left and up the steps and towards the door, I saw that it was standing open. There was no sign of Frances. I began trying to think how we were going to get at this Marriott.

But I didn't have much time to do any thinking in. It seemed to me that she hadn't been in the house more than a hundred and twenty seconds when she came out of it again.

I was looking idly at the door when, suddenly, it framed her. I knew the second I saw her, I can't tell you how, that something was badly wrong. And then, as she half stumbled over the door sill, slamming the door behind her, recovered, and jumped—literally jumped—clean from the top step to the pavement, I half guessed. I can't tell you exactly what I thought, but I can tell you that I give myself full marks for quickness. I opened the door against which I was sitting and shot myself along the seat until I was opposite the wheel. Before she'd got more than one foot on the running board, I'd started the engine and had engaged first gear without letting in the clutch. She made a mess of getting in and I had to lean over, still keeping my foot on the clutch, and grab at her and haul. I saw, with the tail of my eye as I actually got her inside, that the front door was open again. And I saw, as we started with a bump that sent her head against the wind-screen, that in the doorway was a man in dark uniform which had shiny silver buttons. I gave one look back just before I changed into second—one fleeting look— and saw that on the pavement was a bareheaded policeman. He was gaping after us.

CHAPTER VIII

I screamed in second gear up to the northern end of Royalty Gardens and swung left. I didn't change up until I was practically at the junction of Viceroy Road with the Old Brompton Road. I took appalling chances at the other cross-roads, but was lucky. I took a worse chance still by shooting into the Old Brompton Road itself at something close to fifty. Again I was lucky. Neither of us said anything. I couldn't look anywhere except on the road at the pace I was going, but I don't think she was in any condition to speak. I've often wondered how long it would have been before she spoke if I hadn't asked her a question as we shot over the steep railway bridge at West Brompton.

"What's up?" I said. I still had to keep my eyes on the road. I'd been lucky so far, but now there was more traffic.

When her answer came, it was in the voice I'd first heard her use when she'd surprised what she must have thought was Raffles in the kitchen. She said:

"Policemen. They were in the house. *And* Marriott. There was one in plain clothes. It was—awful! I went in and everything seemed the same. I ran upstairs. I wasn't thinking about anything except getting that address. I got to the top of the stairs. You know you can see right into the library. The first thing I saw was two policemen. One hadn't got a hat on, the other had one of those flat caps I think inspectors wear. Mr. Marriott was with them. And the plain-clothes one. They were all sort of grouped together; they weren't looking at the stairs, so they didn't see me. I can't tell you what I felt like. I wanted to turn round and run away, and I wanted just as badly to go in and ask them what they were doing. But I couldn't do either. All I could do was just stand still and hang onto the banister. My head was singing and, though I could hear their voices, at first I didn't hear what they were saying. Then my head went clear. I could see better and I could hear again . . ."

She had to break off here as we got into a close bit of traffic. We were just turning out of the end of Lillie Road, and I'd got to negotiate a lot of street barrows before getting to the Fulham Road. As I went by the church and turned right, it was fairly clear. I said, going back into top gear again:

"Go on."

She obeyed. Her voice was still flat and level, but, every now and then, there was a little shake in it. She said:

"They were looking at something. How it was they never turned away from it and looked at me standing there only a few feet away from them, I can't think! But they didn't. I wondered what it was they were looking at. When I found out, I nearly fainted. It was something of mine and, as soon as I saw it, I knew why they were looking at it. It was a thing my mother gave me which I've always used for cutting books. It's a little brass dagger nearly round and very sharp at the point. For its size it's very heavy. It was the man in plain clothes who was holding it up. He was pointing to the end of it and, from where I stood, I could see there was a mark on it. It wasn't bright all the way down, the way it generally is. It was . . . sort of dark . . . and sticky at the end. He was saying: 'If you look at that through the glass, the way I've just done, you'll see that the thumbprint on that powder bowl's reproduced here exactly! No need for any photos, though we'll get some.' . . . I tell you these were his exact words. I don't think I shall ever forget them. I knew what they meant. They meant that whatever . . . devil . . . did *that* has made sure that they'll think I did it. . . . It's no good shaking your head. I *know*. . . . You listen to me. After that the man said—he had a *horrible* voice: 'Here, borrow my glass. There's a scar that runs right across the ball of the thumb. It's got a sort of pothook on it and . . .'

"It was then that I found out how scared I was. I only knew one thing, I *had* to get out of the house. You understand that, don't you? I *had* to! I turned and just *flew* down the stairs. Just as I was turning, I half stumbled and, as I caught hold of the banisters, they gave a sort of squeak. If only I'd just backed down quietly I don't suppose they'd ever have known I was there. As it was, they did know. They stopped talking and I heard a sort of shout and, just as I got into the hall, somebody running down the stairs. I–I . . ."

She broke off. The shaking in her voice had got past her control now.

I wanted to look at her badly, but couldn't. We were just turning round that tricky bend before the beginning of Putney Bridge. There's always a jam there and it seemed worse than ever to-day. I dropped into second and swung out a bit and shaved in between a lorry and a tram and just made a gap about seven cars ahead. We were then on the first rise of the bridge and I kept in second. I had to shout to be heard. I said:

"Why did you think they were talking about you?"

It was a damn silly thing to say. If I'd known her better I don't suppose I'd have said it, but I might. Anyhow, the minute the words were out of my mouth they were answered. Something was thrust right under my nose. It was a small thumb, ball upwards.

I saw that, reaching from the very top of the ball down almost to the base of the thumb, was the thin white thread of a scar.

The thumb was withdrawn. While I did two flagrant cut-ins down the far slope of the bridge and eventually swung round up the first road to the right, towards Barnes, we didn't speak. But, when I was out of the press and doing forty up that road which leads to the new arterial bit to Roehampton Corner, she broke the silence. She said:

"Now perhaps you see! Now perhaps you'll stop looking like—like . . ." She fell silent as suddenly as she'd begun. There had been a queer, harsh note in her voice—something between laughing and crying.

The road was clear and I had a look at her. Instead of being pale, her face had more colour in it than I'd seen. Too much. Whether it was because she was angry or for some other reason, I couldn't tell. I kept my mouth shut. The silence lasted until we'd passed the bobby on the crossroads at the corner of Roehampton Lane and were halfway to Sheen. Down that wide bit I got sixty-five out of the Jamieson, and knew that she'd do a good deal more. A good sort of car. I'd never driven one before and, in a queer sort of way, I was enjoying it. And then she spoke suddenly.

"Where are we going?" she said.

"God knows!" I said. "Richmond, anyhow."

"I suppose," she said, "that's as good as anywhere else." Her voice was another new one—a tired, hopeless monotone.

"What d'you mean?"

"Simply that they're bound to get us. One of those policemen ran out of the door after me."

"I know. What's that got to do with it?"

"Are you being stupid on purpose?"

"You mean that very soon they'll be having all the roads watched for this car?"

"I looked back," she said, "just as we turned out of the gardens into Viceroy Road. He was staring after us and he'd got a notebook out. Of course he got the number."

When she said this, we were going into Mortlake. I looked at the speedometer and saw that we were doing nearly sixty. Too fast, much too fast—at least for a man who didn't want to draw attention. I slowed to a family forty. After what we'd been doing it seemed a crawl. I knew this part well, fortunately. I suddenly turned left by the Black Horse. Once off the highroad and in the broad stretch of Queen's Road, I was up at *The Star and Garter* in an incredibly short time. The Jamieson made nothing of hills. The more I drove it, the better I liked it. At the top I slowed, swung round and went into the park. For the first time since early morning I noticed the weather. When we'd started on my shopping expedition, it had been a grey, misty morning with a sort of feeling that there might be more snow. Now—at any rate, here in Richmond—the mist had gone, the nip in the air was only pleasant, and the sun was strong. Everything was very green and through the open windows of the saloon came fresh, cool air smelling of spring.

I hope no one will ever ask me why I changed my mind on the Mortlake Road and went up into the park because I don't know the answer. Whether I'd got some dim idea of doubling back, I don't know. Perhaps I wanted just to pull up in solitude so that we could talk properly and I could look at her. Perhaps this, perhaps that, perhaps the other. I just don't know. But, mind you, I probably should have known in a few minutes if it hadn't been for the sight of something which put everything else out of my head.

After getting into the park at *The Star and Garter* gate, I'd taken the right-hand road—the one which is signposted to Kingston Gate, although it's the longest way round. I'd just crested the hill and was trying the Jamieson free-wheel business for the first time down the other side of it, when we passed a car pulled right off the road and onto the grass. I must have noted it at the time, but we'd gone a good quarter of a mile before what I'd better call the notation connected properly. I stopped with a jerk which sent Frances's head nearly through the wind-screen and my own stomach much too hard against the wheel. She said:

"What on earth——?"

I didn't answer. I was too busy turning the car. I drove slowly back up the long slope. The car I'd passed was a Kubelik convertible coupé, with the hood and windows up. It was also empty. *And* it had, wired over the real number plates, red trade plates.

I stopped the Jamieson about fifty yards before we got to the Kubelik. My mouth was dry with excitement and I wanted a cigarette more than I'd ever wanted anything else. In fact, I said:

"Got a cigarette? Must smoke." I didn't look at her, but I know that she'd looked suddenly at me. But she didn't ask a question! She opened the door on her side and then opened the rear door, and from the flap pocket on that took a large box of cigarettes. Without a word she came back again and opened this, and held it out to me. In the top of the box were matches.

I grabbed a cigarette and lit it. I took about three mouthfuls of smoke right straight down to the bottom of my lungs before I spoke. While I was inhaling she took a few cigarettes out of the box and slid them into my side pocket with the matches.

When I was ready to speak she was beside me again and all the doors were shut. I turned half sideways and looked at her fully for the first time for what seemed hours. I said:

"You're right about this car business. They'll be after us all right. I should say we've got about another hour to travel in this car before we're stopped somewhere or other. Right, then. What have we got to do?"

She looked at me harder than ever. "Leave it?"

"Yes, but what else?"

"Get another car?" She spoke slowly, with long pauses between each word.

"Yes. And get it quick."

She looked away from me and straight up the road to the Kubelik.

"That—that one?" she said.

I nodded. "They're even faster than this. And that one's got trade plates. We can do an hour's worth on the trade plates and then take them off and do another hour's worth on the real numbers. We can leave this car for the fellow we're robbing. By the time he's complained, or they've stopped him, we'll be two or three hundred miles off."

"And then what?"

I shrugged. "God knows. Swop again, perhaps. Anyhow, what's that to do with it? What we've got to do is cover some distance or blind the trail or both."

She wasn't looking at the Kubelik now. She was very quick. She was looking across the grass to the left and then across the grass to the right. On our right there was a good hundred yards of grass before the trees started. On our left even more. I'd looked already, but I looked again. Nowhere was there a man or woman in sight. The only living things in fact, beyond birds, were a few fallow deer. She said:

"Ignition lock?"

I opened the door on my side and got out. I said, through the window: "I'll see if he's taken the key. If he hasn't . . ." I left that unfinished and strolled, puffing at the remains of my cigarette as casually as I could, towards the Kubelik.

Luck was with us. The fool hadn't taken the key. He must have been so keen on his girl that his brains were addled, or else he thought—as he very well might, poor blighter—that Richmond Park was as safe as St. James's Square. I strolled on a bit to give an impression of casualness—I suppose to the deer—but I'm afraid my walk back to the Jamieson was a good deal quicker than it ought to have been for really good acting.

I opened the door on the near side of the Jamieson. Without a word she got out. She was very white, but steady as a rock. I remember that she looked up at me and tried to smile. I shut the door and looked at the clock on the dashboard. Its hands stood at 10:40.

At 10:43 by the clock on the dashboard of the Kubelik we passed out of Kingston Gate. On the straight bit, away from the Jamieson, Frances had knelt on the seat and looked back through the talc window of the coupé hood. She'd seen nothing.

Through Kingston we drove very quietly. I calculated that for two hours at least, and four hours with luck, we weren't likely to be stopped on our own account. My desire was to drive all the time like the flames of hell, but my sense told me to drive in towns like the milk of heaven.

Until we got to Esher I don't remember doing any constructive thinking. All I'd thought about till then was just putting distance between ourselves and London. But after Esher, calming down with the monotony of driving perhaps, I began to try to make plans. I said:

"I don't know where we're going. Where shall we?"

I got no answer. I turned my head and looked. My partner was fast asleep. Her right cheek was resting on the leather cushion only about half an inch from my left shoulder. As we took a bend in the road, it slipped further down and actually rested on my shoulder. I drove on, keeping the Kubelik at her best and smoothest pace—a steady sixty-five.

CHAPTER IX

After Esher the Kubelik's speedometer showed a mileage of 1584. Frances didn't wake until it stood at 1629, when we were just outside a village called Lesser Fanning, about twelve miles from Deyning Water. I hadn't tried to get there. I'd just turned off after Liphook and kept going on the principle of keeping west and avoiding main roads. I know that part of the country well; and I know that it sounds as if it ought to be more than fifty miles from the middle of Surrey, but actually it isn't.

I don't suppose she would have waked even then if I hadn't suddenly seen that the needle of the heat indicator was right over onto the "danger" mark. I couldn't afford to be stranded with a damaged car, and pulled up dead. The stop shook her face off my shoulder. She gave a squeak and shook her head and sat upright. She looked about her, puzzled and half frightened. I didn't say anything. I know what it's like to be waked up suddenly, especially to a situation more unpleasant than your worst dream.

She suddenly sat bolt upright and put the backs of her hands against her cheeks. She stared around. It can't have done her much good. There were high hedges on each side of the lane. She said:

"What've you stopped for?"

I told her.

"What's the time?" she said.

I pointed to the clock on the dash. Its hands stood at five minutes to one. She said:

"Has anyone . . . have you seen . . . have they tried . . . ?"

I told her I hadn't seen, heard, or felt anything out of the way. I pointed out that it was a bit early for the news to have got round. I added, lying, that if all patrols, or whatever they call them, had been warned to look out for a car, it would still be the Jamieson. And then I had an idea. As it turned out, a pretty good one. I said:

"All the same we might do a bit of quick change."

I slipped out of the car on the driving side and found—just between the side of the door and above the running board—the handle which converts the Kubelik coupé. After a minute and a half she was an open two-seater. I then went and looked at the trade plates and saw they were just hitched over the real numbers with bits of wire. I got them off inside a couple of minutes. And then, as a finishing touch, I took off the radiator cap and managed to unscrew the greyhound mascot, and put the cap back without it. Where we'd been in a closed car with trade plates and a glittering, twelve-inches long, futuristic mascot, we were now in a plain, open two-seater with ordinary registered numbers, white on black, and a plain radiator cap.

The roof gone and the windows down, she seemed to cringe into her corner. She said:

"Won't they . . . won't people *see* us better?"

I leant over the door and looked at her. "It doesn't matter if they do. What they're looking for is a closed coupé with trade plates and a mascot. What they can see now——" I left the sentence unfinished. "You stay here while I get some water."

She nodded and I trudged off. The cottage was about a hundred and fifty yards ahead of me, showing through a break in the right-hand hedge. But I hadn't got more than fifty yards before I heard the car door slam and whipped round. She was out of the car and running after me. I waited. When she came up her face had lost all the flush her sleep had given it and was white again. It was pinched and drawn, and her lower lip, although it was clenched by her teeth, was trembling. She came rushing up to me and grabbed hold of my arm with both hands. She said, without opening her teeth:

"Let me go with you! I don't want to stay! I want to go with you!"

Her eyes were very big. There came from her, as she stood there close, looking up at me, the faintest suggestion of scent. I'd noticed it before when I was driving. It was a good scent. I've smelt a lot of scents in my time, from Jockey Club to Morny, but this was better than Morny. My inclination was to say, "Of course you can. Grab my arm." But what I had to say was—and not very kindly because I thought kindness wouldn't pay:

"Don't be a damn fool! Go back to the car. Suppose you were my sister or my wife, or something. Would you trudge a quarter of a mile because I wanted water?"

She let go my arm and stood back from me a couple of paces. For a moment there came into her eyes the odd sort of glare I'd seen in them when she'd had that queer fit in the drawing room in Royalty Gardens. And then it died away, and she turned suddenly and began to walk back towards the car.

I went on, not feeling too good. Her back had looked so forlorn. I had a bit of a job proving to myself on the way to the cottage that I was right.

The cottage was just the sort I'd expected. But the woman who answered the door to my knock was more genial than I'd expected. She was willing to give me water and more willing to talk. Not wanting to make myself conspicuous by being surly, I hovered while she let me have it. Here's some of what she said:

". . . Fine hot day considerin' it's so cold for the time o' year . . . but then they always say 'Snow in May, Year's good hay.' . . . So your motor car's run out o' water . . . that's one thing to be said for the 'osses. That's never the trouble with them. . . . You'd think not many motors 'ud use this lane, but you'd be wrong. . . . You wouldn't believe as you're the *third* as asked me for water to-day. The last one, he was one of them immobile policemen. He was chasin' some of these car thieves, he was, so he told me. . . ."

And a lot more of it. I told myself that motor cars were stolen every day. I told myself that the police were after motor cars as often as they were stolen.

But that didn't help me. Reason doesn't help fear. I stood there with the big tin jug in my hand and some of the water slopped over onto the path. I put a question which I wanted to sound casual, but which didn't sound like it to me.

But no, they hadn't said what car it was or what sort. "But there, then," she said, and the long brown hair which stuck straight out of the third mole from the left on her chin seemed to point at me like an accusing finger, "it's as like as not he was tellin' me a yarn. Nice-lookin' young feller he was and all. Thank ye, sir, if you'll just drop the jug on this 'ere side of the gate as you come by in the motor, I'll be very grateful. . . . Well, sir, there's no charge . . . but thank you very much, I'm sure, sir. . . ."

I spilt some more of the water on my way, but by the time I was back at the Kubelik I'd got myself in hand. I didn't look at Frances. I took off the radiator cap and filled up as carefully as I could.

We slid up the lane in third and stopped opposite the cottage, and, without getting out, I managed to lean over and drop the jug into the cottage garden. We went on. We didn't talk, but as I drove, I found I wanted badly to look at her. I stuck it for about a mile and then, just as we turned into a second-class road which went one way to Deyning—which I took—and the other to Stoke-in-Martins, I fell.

But she wasn't looking at me, although I could have sworn that I'd felt her glance on my face. She was looking straight ahead. Her mouth was set and her eyes seemed half closed. I kept going as fast as I could although the road was so twisting that thirty-five was about the highest average you could hope for.

We pulled into Deyning at twenty-five past one. We came round by *The Hand and Flower* with the big pond on our left. Just on the corner there was a large, white-sleeved policeman standing plumb in the middle of the road. He was facing us and had his hand held up.

I stopped. I saw, when my heart had stopped thumping, that he was holding us up because a hay wagon was coming out of the narrow street they call Water Alley. My relief to find that he didn't want *us* made me speak to him. I crawled on in first when he waved us on and stopped opposite him. He leaned towards me like a bishop with lumbago. I said:

"Is this Deyning, constable?" I felt like betting myself a fiver this was the first time I'd ever said that word.

He grunted that it was Deyning *Water*.

I kept on at him. "I wonder whether you could tell me, constable, what's the best place to have lunch here?"

He said that *The Three Bears* was good or *The Hand and Flower*, or, of course, as every motorist should know, *The Compasses*. Motorists from all over the world knew *The Compasses*. I felt that, beside me, my partner was stiff with funk and indignation but I didn't care. I'd produced the effect that we were ordinary, decent motorists and I was going to keep it up. I could see the sign of *The Three Bears*, freshly painted, swinging across the narrow seventeenth-century street about a hundred yards ahead of us on the left. I drove straight up to it and turned the Kubelik slowly, and drove through the old archway into the yard.

And so we had lunch just like two everyday, fairly prosperous, sight-seeing motorists. I remember the meal well. I was very brotherly. I had a hell of a job to get her out of the car and into the inn, but I won. As she wouldn't talk and looked really ill, I was very solicitous in front of the waitress. My sister wasn't feeling at all well. My sister would want a really "nice" light lunch. My sister this, my sister that, my sister the other.

My sister had a glass of sherry—forced down her throat by a hypnotic glare from brother; some fairly decent sole; some apple tart and cream, and a cup of coffee. Her brother had two glasses of sherry, a pint of beer, a plate of soup, cold beef and potato salad, a lot of cheese and bread and butter, and two cups of coffee.

Brother paid—and then, under the table, counted the wad of notes. He looked across at sister, but she shook her head to show him that she hadn't any.

So here we were, having paid for lunch, with twenty-nine pounds, ten shillings, and eightpence. Not bad. But also not good.

We met in the yard at the Kubelik. I found that we were nearly out of petrol and wanted more oil. I asked the old ostler, who looked at the car as if Satan had made it, for a garage. We followed his mumbled directions and found one. The proprietor served us. He was a quick little cockney like a sparrow. He talked even more than the woman in the cottage. And, if she'd begun to put the wind up me, he finished the process. It was while I was watching him draw oil. He said, at the end of what the press must mean by a "long, rambling statement":

"Got a pop'lar make of car there, guv'nor. These 'ere Kubeliks; why, they are pop'lar. I've 'ad the p'lice round about one of 'em. . . ."

I made a noise in my throat.

He didn't seem to notice it. "That's right," he said, "very pop'lar. Why, Sergeant Moss, 'e came round 'ere only about a hour and a narf ago; about a Kubelik that had been stole—somewheres up London way. Richmond, I think. . . . I says to 'im, says I, 'Wot's the game? Lot of fuss about a stolen car. Why, the boys there knock off one car after another as fast as they can.' . . . It's a fact, they do, sir. One after t'other. I don't suppose there's a minute of the day but what a car's being pinched—especially in London. . . . Wot d'you say she'll want, sir? . . . A quart? . . . She'd take a couple."

"Make it a couple," I said. Again he didn't seem to notice anything wrong with my voice.

He drew off another quart. He bent over the open bonnet and poured it into the sump. He seemed, suddenly, to have lost his talkativeness. I said:

"Kubelik stolen, eh?" And then I got wind up. Why draw attention? And then I thought as I'd started I'd better finish. I said, coughing to hide my voice tricks:

"Goodish car to pinch. I haven't had this one long, but it's O.K. What type's the stolen one?"

The can was empty and he stood up and looked at me. He said:

"One of these 'ere coops. Trade car, too. Trade plates on."

"Trade plates?" I said. Having got into the pond, I thought I'd better swim.

He turned round and set the can down on the top of the drum. He turned back. "Well, y'know; red numbers, like."

I nodded. I said I did know. I said I'd never realized what they were before. He worked his head up and down like a cross between an owl and an East End tough.

"There's lots of folks," he said, "don't know trade plates when they see 'em. Yes, this 'ere Kubelik was a coop. Trade number, 8134 RH. . . . That'll be fourteen an' nine altogether, sir. Thank 'ee, sir."

I shoved another florin into his hand. "And have a drink," I said. I started the car and began to slip away from his pumps and his tanks. He called after me:

"And don't you let anyone go pinching yours, guv'nor."

The laugh that followed his joke seemed to stick in my ears for the next two or three miles.

Once out of Deyning I didn't go straight on as I'd meant. I took a right-hand fork on a road I didn't know which was signposted to Borsted Abbotts. It was narrow, but it had a good surface. There were high hedges on each side, uncut, which got in the way of one's view at every bend. And there were at least two bends to every quarter-mile. After a bit of this I felt a tug at my left sleeve, and heard a small, harsh voice which said:

"Stop a minute, will you?"

I pulled up. Without a word she got out of the car and went to the back. I sat staring straight in front of me, but I heard her open the dickey and then I heard the rattling of metal and then the dickey closing again and then a pause. And then footsteps on the macadamed road. And then she was beside me again. I didn't look at her. She said:

"I suppose you think I didn't hear or hadn't got any brains or something. But I did and I have."

I put my thumb on the self-starter, but a small hand, a lot stronger than you'd give it credit for to see it, closed round my wrist and jerked it away. She said:

"Stop! It's time we faced this. . . . You're always saying 'We've got to face it!' But you don't do it. Now I'm going to do it. . . . And don't look away from me like that! Look at me!"

I looked at her. Again, unbelievably, she looked different—quite different.

"This," she said, "is my business! Isn't it?"

"Partly," I said, a bit grudgingly. I felt that it had got to be quite half my business. I'd certainly done half the work so far. I was, to tell the truth, more than a bit peeved at her tone. You see, I didn't know what she was driving at.

"Partly be damned!" Her voice was almost like a man's. "Wholly! It's my business and I'm taking charge of it."

I suppose we were both a bit worked up. We'd had enough to make us, anyhow. I began to behave like a girl out of the sixth form at St. Winifred's. I opened the door on my side and wriggled out and slammed it, and stood in the road and leant over. I thought she was angry and I'd better be angry too. It didn't take much pretense to make me.

She didn't move towards the wheel, but she put one hand on it and turned herself sideways and looked straight at me. I thought there was something funny about her look, but I couldn't read it. She said:

"I see you think the same as I do. But why get out here?"

"I don't know what you mean."

"You know very well what I mean. I mean, if you must make me say it, that this is where you finish. This is my business and I'm in it, and I'm not going to drag anyone else in."

I stared at her. I'm sure my mouth opened. She said:

"Don't stand there gaping. Get in and drive to the nearest village. Or to just outside it and then drop off. Understand?"

I didn't say anything. I shut my mouth and got into the car. I took the wheel again and started the Kubelik. I think I've said before that, round these Deyning lanes, forty was a very high average and a bit too fast, but I did the next few miles at something like sixty. I took chances at every bend and got away with it. We didn't pass anything except the village of Borsted Abbotts. That has one street. It's about four hundred yards long. I should think it took us something under two seconds to get through it. When we were well on the other side of it, I felt a touch on my arm. Not hard—she was too good a driver to risk that—but enough to draw my attention.

"I thought I told you to stop outside the first village," she said. Still her voice was almost like a man's.

I shook my head. I felt, for the minute, as if there were a sporting side to all this. I said:

"Shut your mouth and don't talk damn nonsense!" And then I didn't look at her. The hand stayed on my arm for a minute. I thought that its fingers, before they let go, pressed ever so slightly, but I'm not sure. All I know is that I drove on.

I went slick through all the Abbotts, passing Fearing Abbotts at about half-past three. At half-past four we were on the other side of the county, skirting Grayborough. I'd managed to keep off main roads, but I was now in a country I didn't know at all. And then, halfway between Grayborough and the small town of Horchester, we had a bit of luck. It didn't come any too soon for my feelings, I can tell you. I was right down again before it happened and feeling sick and weak with funk, telling myself it couldn't be more than a couple of hours at the best before they got us. And more on those lines.

We were on a narrow road, but there was more traffic than I liked. By that, I mean that we were either overtaking or meeting cars every other hundred yards. I suddenly saw just ahead of me a lane opening onto the road. I checked and swung into it. It went along, straight and narrow, for about half a mile and then broadened out into a good road, gravel-surfaced. On our left I saw the beginnings of a line of bungalows. I began to slow up. I thought we should come to a dead end and I'd better be ready to turn and go back to the main road again in spite of the traffic. There was quite a space between the bungalows, and I was just getting ready to turn opposite the first one when I noticed two things. First, there was a garage beside it with its doors not quite closed and a gleam showing through them, and second, all the windows were shut and the curtains drawn.

Instead of turning I stopped the Kubelik and shot out of her, jumping over the door instead of waiting to open it. I marched through the gate of the bungalow and up to the front door and began to hammer with the knocker. There was no reply. To make sure, I walked round to the back and beat on the back door. Still no answer. It was empty all right. I then came down to the gate again and looked up the road. There were some trees at the end of the garden which hid me and the Kubelik from anyone in the next house who happened to be looking. I didn't go out into the road, but went up the driveway which led to the garage. I pulled open the garage doors. There, sure enough, was a brand-new Ford cabriolet. What's more— our luck was certainly in—I found the ignition key. It wasn't in the lock, but in the pocket of the near side door.

She started like a bird. I left the engine running and opened the doors fully and opened the gates. I then backed her slowly out, turning her head the way we had come. I stopped her and left the engine running and got out. In the Kubelik, Frances was kneeling on the seat and looking at me. She didn't look surprised. She was too quick for that. I made a sweeping sign with my arm and she understood at once. She backed the Kubelik a few yards until it was nearly touching the Ford and then swung her left and drove her very quietly into the garage. I went to help her with the doors and we shut them. We then ran down the driveway and shut the gates. As I slipped the Ford into first gear and started back by the way we'd come, I could have hooted with a childish sort of excitement. I think she felt the same. I had a quick look at her just before we got back into the main road and saw that there was colour in her cheeks once more. And her eyes were shining and her lips, a little bit parted, showed her teeth white between them.

CHAPTER X

It was at five o'clock that I began to realize that I couldn't keep awake any longer. At quarter-past, when we were about fourteen miles along the secondary road from Grayborough to Learmouth, I had to stop the car and get out and run round it. My eyes felt as if they were full of grit and had plummets hanging onto every third eyelash. My whole face felt stiff and drawn, my legs were too heavy, and my arms seemed to work independently of the rest of me.

I went back to the driving side of the car again. I found that Frances was already sitting at the wheel. I gaped at her. She looked at me and said:

"Get in the other side."

I went round like a lamb and climbed in. I remember hearing her voice, mixed with the grinding roar of the self-starter, saying:

". . . I'm a pig! You go to sleep, but tell me something first; were you going somewhere or just anywhere?"

"Just . . . anywhere," I said. Sleep was on me like a bucket of chloroform.

I don't remember anything else until I came to and found that she was shaking at both my shoulders. The car was pulled up by the side of a road. It was more than half dark—dark just turning into real night. My head was wobbling about like a pumpkin on the end of a beanstalk.

"Ease-o!" I said. "Be all right in a minute."

It seemed to me that she sat back in her seat again with something like a sob. She said:

"I thought . . . I thought you were . . . I thought there was something the matter with you."

"I'm not dead if that's what you mean." I sat up and rubbed at my eyes. I didn't feel too good but I was awake. I said: "Where are we?"

"The last signpost said, 'Learmouth four miles.' I should think we've been about one since then."

I found a cigarette and lit it. I asked her the time and she looked at the watch on her wrist and told me half-past six. She said:

"I know I haven't got very far, but I've done it all on side roads until a mile back."

Inside the car it was very dark. I couldn't see anything except that she'd got her face towards me, but I swear I could feel her eyes.

"Sorry I went off like that," I said. I felt a bit ashamed and then, at once, very sorry for myself.

She seemed to read what I was thinking. "We keep apologizing," she said. "But I'm sorry too. I had to wake you there. First, because I was frightened something had—happened to you. Second, because I wanted to know what . . . what . . ."

"What we're going to do?"

"Yes. Wouldn't we be less . . . conspicuous . . . if we got off the main track somewhere and found some little inn—and put up for the night?"

I thought that was a good idea and said so.

"But then," she said, "we haven't any luggage. And how . . . ? And what . . . ?"

I helped her out. "I know Learmouth. And the country on the other side." A sudden memory hit me and I began to feel better. "*And* I know just the place we're looking for." Through the darkness I grinned at her. "What we are is brother and sister. Easy. We'll go on into Learmouth, do a bit of shopping, and then go on to Widdeley Green."

"You know," she said, "I think you're incredible! You've always got something up your sleeve."

She drove on. We got to Learmouth just before the big shops shut. We
parked the car in the Market Square opposite the town hall. I can't say I
liked leaving it, but there was nothing else for it. After all, as I said, with
any luck the people in the bungalow might not be back yet. Or, if they
were, they might not have looked in the garage yet. Or, if they had looked,
they might not have been able to get at the police yet.

We got through the shopping, each of us, in under twenty minutes.
She'd bought a fibre suitcase, and I'd got something made of American
cloth and papier-mâché. There was enough inside each of the things. Total
expenditure, fifty-four shillings.

I was feeling less like warmed-up death and took the wheel again. From
Learmouth to Widdeley Green, if you use the coast road, is only about
seven miles. It's rough going, but I did it in creditable time. That Ford
went well.

Widdeley Green stands a bit inland from the Foreland Cliff—about three
miles. I don't know why it's there. The road to it certainly comes from
Learmouth, but the road from it doesn't go anywhere. It doesn't seem to be
an agricultural spot and it certainly isn't marine. It's got a population of
about a hundred and seventy-two; one post-office-cum-general shop selling
anything from bull's-eyes and beef to bathing suits and bolony; a cluster
of cottages; one old rectory, untenanted; three walls and half the roof of a
Norman church; and *The Green Man*.

Nothing in Widdeley Green had changed except the landlord of *The
Green Man*. I was glad about this. Strangers, at the moment, were the people
I liked best.

Without any trouble we got garage for the car and adjoining bedrooms
under the eaves. In the little parlour room there was a fire of apple logs.
At ten to eight we were sitting in front of this drinking brown sherry
which wasn't half bad. At eight o'clock our supper was ready and we went
into the dining room. There was someone else there already—a sight-seeing
German who wasn't staying the night. He was inoffensive, but his presence
stopped us from talking. If we'd been able to talk over the meal a lot of
trouble might have been spared us. But as it was, we could only try to
make conversation. We made a poor fist of it. We must have sounded like a
foreigner's phrase book.

We got out as soon as we could. The same thought was in both our
minds: we *must* get alone and talk. And also we were scared right through
the meal. The dining room was twice as big as the parlour. And there wasn't
a fire and the light was bad. I had my back to the door and Frances had
her right shoulder. Every time it opened we both had to stop ourselves from
jumping and staring. Every time I heard a footfall outside, I thought it
sounded as if it were made by a No. 9 police boot.

But when we got back to the parlour, that was occupied too. The landlord was there with a friend. They were playing backgammon. I expect

they didn't know they were fashionable. We had a cup of vile coffee, and I had another glass of the good brown sherry. Frances leaned over to me, and whispered:

"We ought to talk."

"Walk?" I suggested.

She shook her head. "I'm sorry. I . . . I . . . I *couldn't!*"

She was going to say some more but I stopped her. I didn't want any more whispering. And I knew what she felt. She felt, wrongly, that being inside four walls was a bit safer than being outside them. I felt the same myself.

We were silent for a long time. All we heard was the subdued chatter of the landlord and his friend and the rattle of their blasted dice. After a bit it began to get on my nerves. I said, as naturally as I could:

"I'm for bed. We've got a long drive to-morrow."

She backed me up well. Within five minutes I was in my room and could hear her moving about in hers next door. On the stairs we hadn't been able to say anything, because the landlady had been with us. She was a good soul, but one of the bustling sort. She'd get this for us and that for us and the other for us if we wanted it. She hoped we'd be comfortable-like. She got me over pretty quickly but I should think I'd smoked the best part of two cigarettes before she left the other room, and I heard her clatter downstairs.

I threw half a cigarette away, out of the window, and immediately lit another. I wanted to walk up and down, but thought I'd better not because of the noise. I sat on the edge of the bed and waited. I thought I'd let a quarter of an hour go by and then knock on Frances's door and see if we couldn't manage to talk somehow. The waiting wasn't pleasant. Every minute seemed a good ten. I was beginning to feel dead beat again and, without anyone to talk to, I didn't seem able to think. The more I tried to put my mind on the problem, the more it filled up with other things which all led in the same unpleasant direction. By the time what seemed like an hour had gone—although I expect it was only five minutes of my fifteen—I was nearly ready to commit suicide. I felt that it would be better to break my neck chucking myself over Foreland Cliff than to have somebody else break it for me down a much smaller drop. I thought what a fool I'd been to end up like this. I thought what a fool I'd been ever to go into this damn silly, impossible job. I thought what a fool I'd been to help Frances to run away when there wasn't an earthly chance of our keeping away. I felt that what I ought to have done was to refuse to let her bolt for it; to have made her, instead, go back to the house and the policemen—even go into a cell for a bit —but to stick to her guns that she didn't do it.

I've said all this to show you why it was that, when I heard—having heard nothing else before it, mind you—a couple of sharp raps on my door, I shot up as if somebody had stuck a knife into my stern and backed into the farthest corner of the small room.

The knock came again. Harder this time. My eyes went to the window, but I knew it was no good. It was a tiny casement and, even if I could have wriggled out of it, there was no way of getting down except dropping, and underneath were the big cobbles of the yard.

There was another knock, a single one. And then the handle turned and the door opened. I was jammed up against the washstand and the fingers of my left hand closed round the neck of the heavy water bottle. What I was going to do with it I don't know—throw it, I suppose. It's a good job I didn't because, as soon as the door was open properly, I saw that it was Frances who'd been knocking. I hadn't heard her step because she had taken her shoes off. She closed the door and stood against it looking at me. I suppose I must have looked either silly or dangerous or both. I came out from my corner. It wasn't until I was in the middle of the room that I found that the water bottle was still in my hand. She pointed at it and said:

"What's that for?"

I stared at it and turned and put it down again. I mumbled something, I don't remember what. There was one chair in the room opposite the dressing table. She twisted it round with her foot and sat on it. She sat heavily as if she were fagged out. She looked smaller. Her eyes seemed huge in her white face. She said:

"Got a cigarette? You left me without any."

I was pretty glad of the question. It gave me something to do and a chance of hiding what my state of mind had been. I fumbled about and got one for her and gave it to her and looked for a match. I waited till she'd got the thing well lit. I said then:

"I was coming in to you, you know."

She looked at me. Her voice was very low. "I couldn't wait. It seemed . . . *hours!*"

I nodded. "I felt like that too."

There was a silence. We both wanted to talk, but neither of us knew where to begin. She said at last:

"I suppose it's all right? If we talk here, I mean . . . I mean, they won't think it odd and get interested in us or anything, will they?"

I'd got hold of myself now. I'd felt better the moment she came into the room and now I was feeling, all things considered, pretty good. I said:

"It doesn't matter a damn if they do. Talk, we've got to."

She nodded at that. "Yes," she said. "But . . . but . . . it seems so difficult to know where to begin."

"I know. It is. Still, we've got to make a start somewhere. You see, we've been so damn busy doing things to-day we haven't had time even to think about where to start thinking. But I should think—Marriott."

She looked at me. She opened her eyes wide. She took the cigarette out of her mouth and said:

"I don't see . . . Never mind, you know best."

I felt better still at that. I said: "Suppose I ask you a few questions. Just to get started. First: Who *is* Marriott? Tell me all you know about him."

"His Christian name—the only one I know—is Edgar. He's something to do with the Stock Exchange. He's a man of about fifty. He's known my stepfather since they were both at school. He's a bachelor. I've always understood he had plenty of money—not rich, you know, but very comfortably off—especially being a bachelor. My stepfather always treated him as his greatest friend. From what I've seen of Marriott, I should think he replied in kind—outwardly, anyhow." She got up from her chair and went across to the window and pushed it wider open and threw her cigarette stub out into the yard. I didn't turn round. From behind me she said:

"That do?" She went back to her chair and sat down again. She didn't seem so tired now. I couldn't see her very well because the oil lamp was in the far corner on top of the chest of drawers and was flickering a bit. The shadows kept moving uncertainly so that I couldn't really tell what expression there was on her face. I said:

"What's he look like?"

She thought for a moment. "He's thin. And tall. He looks . . . well, about your height. But perhaps he'd be even taller if he stood up straight. But he can't do that." Her voice was acid. It was quieter even than when she'd started speaking. But somehow every word, with her dislike of this Marriott, was so distinct from the other words that it was as if she were talking very loud. "He dresses very badly. He's got black, greasy hair, but there isn't much of it. His head's shaped like a turkey's egg. He's quite bald on top. He's got a thin grey moustache and hair grows out of his ears. He's got a beastly habit of rubbing his hands all round each other when he's talking to you. His eyes are very small and are very close to his nose. His nose is big and thin like a beastly bird's. I hate him. . . . That do?"

"I can see him. It will. Now. Give me the same sort of thing about your stepfather. You needn't describe *him*, though." As soon as I'd said them, I wished I hadn't said the last five words. If I hadn't been a blundering fool, I'd have seen that it wasn't necessary to remind her that I knew exactly what her stepfather looked like.

I'm not sure whether she winced a bit. If she did, she hid it up very well. There was a bit of a pause and then she said:

"He was older than Marriott. To be exact, he would have been fifty-six next month. He married my mother nine years ago; when I was seventeen. But I told you all that. Anyhow, before he married Mother, he was a stockbroker of some kind. After he married Mother, he sold out his shares of the business. All he's done ever since is to write articles and pamphlets—and even one or two books—on coins. I believe he's considered one of the greatest numismatists—or whatever they call them—in England." Her tone was different again. It wasn't less clear, but where, while she'd been talking about Marriott, it had been sort of acid, it was now something much more than that. It was round and deep, and full of . . . I can't find the right word for it. But I suppose *loathing* will come pretty near.

"That business of his," I said. "Did he sell out for much?"

In the flickering light I thought I saw a shrugging movement of her shoulders but I couldn't be sure. The colour of the tweed frock seemed to melt into the black and gold of the darkness and lamplight. She said slowly:

"I don't know. I was at school at the time. I've got a very strong idea that he didn't get much. Not more than two thousand. But I can't answer that accurately."

"Do you know whether he was ever mixed up with Marriott? In business, I mean."

She shook her head. "I don't know. I don't think so. Of course, they may have been before . . . before he married Mother."

Now I'd started, questions were crowding into my mind one on top of another so fast that I didn't know which to get out next. I was quiet for a minute. She didn't get my reasons for silence right. She said:

"You needn't mind what you ask me, you know. I can't be particular."

"It wasn't that," I said. "My trouble is there's so many things I want to ask I don't quite know what order to put 'em in. Try this, though: what do you know about the relations between Marriott and your stepfather more than you've told me?" Again she shook her head. Her eyes were closed. I don't think from sleep, though. At any rate, her voice wasn't sleepy. She said:

"Nothing. I hated Marriott and I . . . well, you know what I felt about my stepfather. I knew they were great friends—or seemed to be—that's all." She opened her eyes and I found them staring straight at mine. "I suppose," she said, "that what you're trying to get at is how on earth it could have benefited Marriott to kill my stepfather? . . . If you are, there's nothing doing. I've been wondering that myself."

I was disappointed and I expect my tone showed it. "I've read enough detective stories to know that the first thing you have to look for is motive. But as you're the only person I've got to ask and you don't know . . . well, there we are!"

Another silence. I didn't like it. I felt all right while we were talking, but the minute we stopped the room seemed to get darker and the lamp seemed to flicker more and the empty feeling in my stomach—the sort of feeling you have when you're a kid and you're waiting for a good hiding—grew worse every minute. I said, at last, a bit desperately:

"If we can't find motive, we can at least have a shot at method. Tell me this: was Marriott a powerful sort?"

She pondered. "He didn't look it," she said slowly. "I've told you what he looked like. . . ." Her voice seemed to tail off into silence. It gave the impression that there was something else she wanted to say, but was trying to remember what it was.

I waited. I got it in a minute. She suddenly sat forward. She said, in a new, excited sort of voice:

"Wait though! I remember something. About a year ago it was. There was something my stepfather wanted moved in our box room. I don't know what it was, I only heard them talking about it. I heard him say he'd have to get a porter or someone. Marriott was at dinner that night. He said something like: 'Never mind. I'll do it for you.' After dinner I went out. When

I got back, Marriott was just going and I remember my stepfather making some joke about Sandow and I gathered that, after all, Marriott had done whatever the job was."

I sat up too. This was better. At any rate it wasn't a dead end. If Marriott was a strong-arm, besides having had the latchkey and known that the servants were going to be away for the week-end, he *could* have reversed my process with the body. I said as much. I said too:

"And you're sure—*dead sure*—that Marriott was the only other person that had a latchkey? What about the servants? Have any of the keys been lost ever? Any relatives have one?"

But she was firm. "There wasn't *anybody!* My stepfather was very particular about keys. I had a fight with him before I could even get one for myself. I remember him giving Marriott his but I know very well he didn't give one to anyone else."

"And *you* never have?"

She flared at that. "What d'you mean? If I'd given anyone else a key or lost a key, d'you think I wouldn't have told you? Don't you think this is serious enough for me to be truthful? Can't you *see* that I'm trusting *you?*"

I stooped and began to take off my shoes. I *had*, for some reason or other, to walk about. I said, when the shoes were off:

"I'm very sorry! Damn silly question!"

Another silence.

"I'm sorry too," she said, in a small voice.

But I'd been struck by an idea, or rather a memory. It was so important, and yet so ludicrous, that I didn't know whether to swear or laugh. I went and stood in front of her. I looked down at her, and said:

"There's another question. Very important. What's *your* name?"

I'll swear her lower jaw dropped half an inch. Certainly my packet of cigarettes which she was still holding did drop. It fell to the floor with a little clap. She ignored it and stared up at me. And then an odd thing happened. She put her hands over her face and dropped her head forward. I saw her shoulders shaking. I thought—and you can't blame me—that she was crying. What I felt was that she'd been on the edge of tears for a long time—and God knows she very well might have been!—and that she was due for any stupid thing to send her over the edge.

She was very quiet, but I heard a sound like a sob. I couldn't stand it. I took a half-pace nearer and bent down and put my hand on her shoulder. She dropped her hands from her face and pushed me away. I saw that she wasn't crying at all. She was laughing!

She pushed me away. She said, controlling her laughter:

"I'm—sorry! But when I think—when I think that we're *here* like this—when I think of all we've done to-day and—and—everything . . . ! And then—*then*—you suddenly remind me that you don't know my name and I don't know yours. Well, all I can say is, it's—funny!"

It ought to have done me good to see her laugh. I can't say "hear" her laugh because, through it all, she remembered that we mustn't kick up a din. But it didn't do me good. There was something ghastly about it. It made me feel that she didn't realize what she was very probably in for within the next few hours. Instead of sending my spirits up, it sent them right down. I said gloomily:

"Look here, my girl, you've got hell-all to laugh about. You're in the soup. You may as well know it."

She stopped laughing as suddenly as she'd begun. She sat bolt upright and looked at me hard. I couldn't read her expression because of the light. She said:

"I know that! But isn't the best time to laugh the time when there isn't really anything to laugh at? What's the matter with you? . . . You're not . . . what I . . ."

I cut in. I said angrily: "That's all very well! I daresay you're right. But I don't like laughing when *I* don't feel like it."

I sat down on the edge of the bed and started groping about in my pocket for a cigarette which wasn't there. I'd forgotten that the packet was on the floor. I didn't look at her. The next thing I knew was that she'd got up and got the packet, and was pushing a cigarette into my hand. As she stood looking down at me her whole face was in shadow. But I could tell what it was looking like from the tone of her voice. I wanted to see it all the same. She said:

"Here they are. And I absolutely refuse to say the two words I've been saying all day to-day any more. '*I'm sorry.*' How silly it sounds! . . . Let's get on, shall we?"

And then she sat down beside me on the edge of the bed. There were about six inches between us, but it seemed to me as if there were six miles. But across the six miles there still came to me a suggestion of delicious scent which, on and off, I'd been noticing all day. I found myself looking down at the cigarette stuck in between the first and second fingers of my right hand. I said at last:

"I'm going to say it, anyhow. *I'm* sorry! Why the hell shouldn't you laugh if you want to? If I'd got any guts at all I'd laugh too. I know what you mean. Anyhow, my name's Craven—Peter Craven. I'm a knockabout, but not a comedian. I've done a lot of different things none too well. Age, thirty-five. Parentage doubtful. Antecedents nil. Undesirable character. Birthmark just under left shoulder blade."

She said: "Mine's Brandon. Frances Brandon. In full, Frances Mary Brandon. Oh! And my stepfather's name was Armitage—Philip Armitage."

I'd come back to myself. I saw the time had come to put the most important of my questions. It was too disturbing to sit like this so I got up. Once more I began to walk up and down the room. I found a match before I spoke and lit the twisted cigarette. I said:

"Here's another question. There's something you haven't told me——"
She interrupted violently. She said:

"That's unfair. There isn't anything I haven't told you! It's more than unfair, it's rude! Only a few minutes ago I told you that I wasn't keeping anything back!"

I didn't look at her, but I stuck it. I said:

"There *is* something. You've got to tell me why you're so damn *certain* that they're going to say it's you."

From the corner of my eye I watched the effect of this. She jumped up from the edge of the bed. For a moment I thought she was going to come at me. But she sat down again. She opened her mouth as if she were going to speak. And then she didn't speak. She just shut it again. There was a long silence. When she spoke she said in a very different sort of voice from the one I'd expected—a small, quiet voice:

"There's that knife. And the print of my thumb with the . . . with the scar on it. . . . I showed it to you. . . ."

I still couldn't look at her, but I shook my head. I said:

"That won't do. I can't prove it, but there's something else. Something underneath." I suddenly wheeled round to face her. I believe I was actually so melodramatic as to point at her. I know I said: "You know there's something else. There *is*. Why the hell don't you out with it? How can we get anywhere unless you do?"

For the second time she covered her face with her hands. This time she wasn't laughing. She wasn't crying either. When she spoke it was still with the hands in front of her face, and her voice came out muffled but clear enough. There was a long silence first, but when she did speak she said:

"They've only got to look back at my . . . at my . . . They'd find things in what they'd call my *history!*"

I couldn't make out what she was driving at. I was so interested that I lost the odd sort of fear I'd had of her. I went back to the bed once more and sat on the edge close beside her, this time on her right side.

"You tell me!" I said. "You can't do any harm by telling me and you might do a lot by not."

She dropped her hands at that. They lay in her lap with their fingers interlocked. They looked still enough, but I happened to glance down at them and could see, even in the bad light, that her knuckles were white with the strain she'd got on them. And her wrists and arms were trembling a little. She said, looking straight in front of her and in a dull, monotonous sort of voice:

"There's something *wrong* with me! I think, perhaps, I might say there *was* something wrong with me. When I was a child I used to have fits of rage—I don't mean 'bad temper,' I mean *rage*. I usen't to know what I was doing or even what I'd done. Mother thought I was cured of it when I was about twelve, and sent me to school. It didn't sort of *happen* until I'd been there about a year, and then I—I—well, I nearly killed another girl. I don't know anything about it except what was told me afterwards—after I'd been taken away from the school! There was something about throwing scissors. . . . I never understood it much. . . . And then, when I'd been at home about three years—that was for two years after my father died—Mother took a chance and sent me to school again. Everything was all right until I was almost grown up and then, just before I left, it all happened all over again— only worse . . . !"

I can't hope to describe to you what her voice was like. It was, as I've said, monotonous. But it had something else in its tone which held me put. I couldn't have moved if I'd wanted to. I wanted her to finish and at the same time I felt that she could go on for ever. . . .

I just waited. After a bit she went on again. She said:

"That time . . . that second time—was—was . . . I'm sorry, I'm afraid I can't talk about it. But I still don't know anything about it except what they told me afterwards. I don't know what Mother did—Father had been dead some time then—but I do know that I was taken away again. Mother took me abroad. While we were abroad she met my stepfather. They were married after we got back—but what I'm trying to tell you is this: *all* these things are known—easy to find out. And what's more—much more—is that they wouldn't find it difficult to find out that in the morning of yesterday, I had a violent row with—with my stepfather. *They* can't tell that I've got my temper in hand now, after years of—of *fighting!* They wouldn't wait to if they could. The *history* would be enough for them—especially on top of— of—everything else. . . ."

All the time she had been talking it was as if she'd been a statue with a voice. This is the only way I can think of putting it. But now, suddenly, she moved. It wasn't much of a movement, but it was so startling after the absolute stillness she had been in that it gave me a shock. She half-turned towards me and looked at me. But I got the feeling that she wasn't really looking *at* me at all. She said:

"I needn't tell you any more, need I?" Her voice had changed. There was a queer sort of note in it which took all the guts out of me. I couldn't sit still any longer and I got up again. I mumbled something in my throat and began padding up and down the room again until the silence got too much for me.

Then I looked at the bed. She wasn't sitting on it any longer. She was lying or, rather, half lying on it. Her feet were still on the floor, but her body was flat and her head was pillowed on her arms.

We'd had, as you know, several silences. And they'd all been uncomfortable. But they were nothing to this. For a bit I went on walking up and down. Then I started stopping beside the bed and trying to say something and failing and starting to walk again. Nothing happened.

The oil in the lamp must have been low. The light grew dimmer and a thin thread of black smoke started to crawl up towards the ceiling. The shadows in the room thickened. It was so quiet that, through the open window, I could hear the sea washing against the shore miles away, or thought I could. I stood stock still in the middle of the room and listened. For a moment I thought I'd heard a footstep on the stairs, and voices. But I found I was wrong. I remembered that the landlord and his wife and such servants as there were slept on the other side of the house. I grabbed hold of my courage and went over to the bed and put my hand on her shoulder. Her body felt, somehow, as if there weren't any life in it. In the bad light I couldn't see her shoulders or any part of her rise and fall to her breathing. And, when I had my hand on her, I couldn't feel her breathing either. I took a sudden scare—rather like the one she'd taken when I'd been so dead off in the car just outside Learmouth. Hardly knowing what I was doing I tightened my grip on her shoulder and began to shake her. I even put my other hand on the other shoulder to help.

Suddenly she moved under my hands, and I dropped them and stood away, and she sat up. The lamp was flickering. I couldn't see anything because the light was changing its strength every minute, and the shadows were going mad. But I could *feel* that she was staring straight at me. And I could just see that she had her elbows on her knees and her chin in her hands. I waited. At last her voice came. She said:

"I don't know whether I've worried you. But if I have, you oughtn't to let me. That's not very clear, is it? What I mean is: that . . . I suppose I've got to call it 'temper'—well, I've got it under control." She gave a little sound which, I suppose, she meant to be a laugh, but it was a sound which made even a hard case like me want to. . . . I don't know what it made me want to do. . . . It was a sound which I can't analyze.

She said: "I mean I don't want you to think that I'm—I'm—insane or anything like that. I'm not! I don't want you to think that perhaps I might have—I might have—killed my stepfather and then forgotten all about it."

She got suddenly to her feet on her last word. She came across to me and reached up and put one small hand on each of my shoulders. I could feel her fingers—little slim things though they were—biting into my flesh right through my clothes. She said, in a tone which I can't hope to describe:

"You *don't* think that! You don't, do you? Do you? Answer! *You don't think that, do you?*"

This was getting too much for me. I didn't know whether I was standing or sitting. I felt as if the real, solid world I'd known had suddenly melted underneath my feet and I was in some other sort of place altogether. All I did know was that I was sorry for her—and a good deal more. I said quite truthfully:

"Of course I don't! There's no question of that!"

She still kept hold of my shoulders but her fingers had eased their grip. I could feel them, but they weren't digging in any more and she wasn't trying to shake me. She said:

"As long as you don't believe *that*, I don't mind. I'll tell you why I'm asking you. You can't see me in this light, otherwise I don't suppose I should have the courage. But *this* is why I'm asking you: I sort of feel that you'd be doing all this you're doing whether you thought I'd done—I'd done *that* or not. You would, wouldn't you?"

I tried to speak, but couldn't. That sounds funny, but it's quite true. Whether I made any sort of blah sound out of my throat or not I don't know. But I went on nodding just the same. She must have seen the nod. She said:

"Thank God!" She fell silent for a moment and then added, dropping her hands from my shoulders as she spoke: "That's all I wanted to know. But you knew I'd got the—the—*possibility* of—of—a vile temper? Didn't you?"

I didn't try to speak this time. I just nodded again. She said:

"I knew you had. That time—how long ago was it?—in Royalty Gardens. When you thought that I thought that you wanted money, when you really wanted to go to sleep. And then another time—I suppose it was this afternoon, but it seems years ago . . ." She cut off her speech abruptly. It was as if someone had clapped a hand over her mouth. Her hands, which had been sort of half stretched forward, dropped to her sides and she turned away from me towards the bed and slumped down to sit on the edge of it again. She suddenly looked inexpressibly tired.

I found my voice again. I said:

"Don't you worry. I *know* you didn't do it. But you're right. Even if I thought you had I'd still want to get you out of it!"

It's a funny thing, I felt as if I *could* get her out of it while these words were coming out of my mouth. But as soon as they were out I felt that I knew I couldn't; felt it so suddenly that I had to say:

"I thought I could, you know! But—though maybe I feel like that because I'm so darned tired—at the moment I'm certain I can't. I don't want you to think that I'm a mixture of Houdini and the archangel Gabriel, because I'm not. What we've had to-day is luck. Luck at the beginning, luck in the middle and luck at the end. Big luck we've had. We can't expect to go on having it. And what we've got to sweat over now is what we're going to do!"

She said, and her voice seemed to come from a long way away: "Well, what *are* we going to do? I suppose you're going to tell me in a minute that what I ought to do—in fact, what I ought to have done right from the beginning—is to go and what they call 'give myself up.' I know that would have been the sensible thing to do. I've known it ever since I ran away from the house. But I also know—know, know, *know*—that it would've been wrong! There's some beastly, foul, unearthly thing against me. It's too clever to be caught that way!" Again her speech seemed to be cut off in midsentence, and then she lifted her head wearily—or it seemed as if she did in the flickering light—and looked at me, and added: "You *do* think that way, don't you? Please!"

I wasn't sure whether I did or not, but I made the right answer.

"Thank you," she said. And then: "What *are* we going to do?"

My legs were tired; moreover I'd got a splinter in the sole of one of my feet from walking up and down. I went back to the chair and sat on it. I said:

"So far as I can see it, there's just one way out." Before I'd spoken I don't believe I'd known what the way was, but it seemed to come to me with the words, so I suppose I must have been doing a bit of subconscious thinking. I said, half to myself:

"If we could get to Tilbury before they're on to us . . ."

She stood up. I didn't see the movement; I was only aware that she was beside me again. She didn't speak. I went on, but to her as well as myself this time:

"It's only that I know a cove who's a big bug on the Fort Line. They're South African boats. He's a good friend of mine. We've done each other a lot of good turns. We might——"

She clapped her hands together. She seemed suddenly full of life again. "Yes!" she said. And I can't hope to tell you what she put into that ordinary word.

"But we've got to get there," I said. I suddenly found myself—I suppose her enthusiasm was catching—feeling a hell of a lot better. "Dammit!" I said. "We *can* do it! Or, at any rate, we can have a stab at it. We'll start early. And once we're away . . ."

She finished it for me. It was wonderful how she seemed to see, all the time, what I was thinking. She said:

"We can really *think!* We can work out how we could get them to see that it *must* be Marriott."

I had a moment's doubt and, like a fool, put it into words. "If," I said, "it *is* Marriott."

She didn't like that. She said: "*If!* It must be! If you don't think it's Marriott, there's only one other person you can think it could be!" She stood suddenly away from me. My temper got a bit short. I told her not to be a fool. I said:

"Because Marriott's the only person you can think of, it doesn't mean he's the only person in the world. There's nearly eight million people in London, you know."

She came closer again. "I know," she said. She laughed a little. "I suppose I've got to say 'I'm sorry' just once more! I *am*, though. But you've got such a queer, direct way of saying things." She suddenly leaned back without moving her feet and looked at me—rather in the way I've seen people look at a picture. Though what sort of an oil painting I could have looked like, after that day and in that light, makes me shiver to think! She said:

"All I can really say before we both do what we ought to have done hours ago—go to sleep—is: thank you!" Her voice was very deep suddenly. "And I do say that. Believe me, I do!"

She held out a hand with a quick movement rather like a shy boy's. She said:

"Thank you! And will you please shake hands?"

I've hesitated over writing this next bit for a long time. But I've come to the conclusion that, if I'm going to tell this whole story at all, I've got to be honest. What comes next is about the eighth version and seems to me to be —taking always into account that a man will always try to whitewash himself—as near the truth as I can get. When she held out her hand like that, I put my own in it and shook it. I'm perfectly certain that, before our hands touched, I hadn't got any idea of doing anything but shaking it and saying good-night. I'm also equally sure that, as soon as our hands did meet, I realized that shaking hands wasn't any good to me. It was as if somebody had got up and told me, inside my head, what I'd really known since the early morning. . . .

My memory's a bit confused. You must remember—and perhaps this will serve to excuse me a bit as well—that I was only three quarters fit, very scared, more than very tired, and considerably in love. You must also remember that I'm not, never was, and am never likely to be, a gentleman.

Anyhow, our hands met. We shook hands. But I didn't let her hand go. Something else took charge of me. I kept hold of her hand, and with a sudden jerk, pulled her towards me. I let go of her hand and put my arms round her shoulders and bent down and, before she knew what I was doing, had kissed her. I held her very tight. My head was full of coloured lights. . . . I can't tell you my state of mind. I seemed to have two at the same time—one which knew that I was doing the silliest thing I could do and another which said, "If you don't do it now, you may never have the chance."

I remember feeling her mouth under mine. For a moment it was passive—I suppose with shock—and then, for a fraction of the hundredth part of a second, I thought I felt an answering pressure.

And then—then—well, the balloon went up. And it didn't go up slowly. I thought I'd got hold of a small and very lovely woman. I found out that I'd got hold of a cat as wild as they make 'em and as strong as a couple of devils. She tore herself from me. And, when I say that, it isn't a lady novelist's phrase—I mean *tore*. Remember that both my arms were round her and that she was very close. In the next second she wasn't very close, and something had hit me in the face—not once, but three times. They were small hands, but they were very hard. I got one in the eye and one on the ear, and one on the lip. The one on the lip drew blood.

She said something—I didn't catch what it was. And then she was gone. My door slammed and then, close beside it, her door.

CHAPTER XI

I

You see that figure 1 at the top there? That's technique. In other words, I'm dividing this chapter into sub-sections like a real novelist. I've just had the idea that it will save me a good deal of trouble. Because, anyway, the part I'm covering is a bit disjointed.

After the slamming of the door I sat on the edge of the bed. If you want to know what I felt you'll have to go on wanting because I don't know. I got up and took the packet of cigarettes from the chair and lit one. And then the lamp went out.

In the dark I took off the new Creed's suit and folded it quite tidily. When I'd got it off I was quite certain, as I sat on the edge of the bed, that I wasn't going to sleep.

2

There were four policemen. One had a red uniform but the other three were in white. They did physical stunts at the end of the bed. They didn't say anything to me, but they kept on whispering and looking at one another, and then at me.

The walls of the house fell in and my bed was in the yard. It was very awkward. I kept trying to get to sleep, but every time I was nearly off a car drove up and the lights shone in my eyes. I got up in a rage. I found a man and said to him:

"What the hell's all this? Why the blank can't you blank well keep those blankety cars out of here? There's a poor blank trying to get some blank sleep. And he's me!"

"Don't be a convict!" the fellow said. "Don't you know there's a grand rally here to-night? A great four million miles test from Land's End to John o' Groats; a great test between Jamiesons, Fords, and Kubeliks."

I couldn't stand any more of him. I kicked him in the belly and he disappeared. And all the cars went away too, all together.

I got back into the bed. It was very funny but it seemed full already. There was someone else in it. He'd got all his clothes on. It was very dark, but somehow I could see what they were. They were a black coat and waistcoat, and grey striped trousers. He had a grey moustache. I kept trying to push him over to the right-hand side so that I could get a scrap to lie on, but it was no good. Just as I was going to tilt the bed up and roll him out onto the ground, he spoke. He said:

"It's no use trying to shift me. You're only wasting your time. They'll bring me back!"

I didn't like that and went away. I had a sort of feeling there must be another bed round the corner, but there wasn't. I found a car instead. The gears were on the wrong side and so was the wheel, and all the forward gears made it go back and the only way I could get on was to go into reverse. I got tired of this after a while and pulled up. I found myself outside a shop. I went in. It was bung full of clothes. There was a man there. I asked him whether I could take some of the clothes down and put them on the counter, and sleep on them. He didn't seem to mind, and so I did.

It wasn't a very nice sleep. I hadn't had more than a quarter of an hour when I felt somebody shaking my shoulders and looked and saw Frances.

"You're a nice sort of thing!" she said. "Call yourself a man! There am I in the next room and here are you snoring like a hog!"

I got very angry. I said: "Well, why did you . . . ?" But before I could get out any more she was gone, and where she'd been standing there was another bobby. This one had a green uniform, but there was something familiar about his face.

"You've seen me before!" he said. "Remember Palmer's Rents, Lambeth?"

I remembered him. It was my old landlord. He must have joined the force.

Everybody seemed to have joined it. The place suddenly got full of policemen. I got fed up with the whole lot and told them so. I jumped on the counter. I said:

"You're a pretty smart-looking lot of blanks, but you can't catch me."

I gave the nearest one a kick on the face, jumped on the shoulders of the next, and shot out of the shop like a rabbit.

I found myself in a telephone box. I was trying to get to the telephone. It was very urgent that I should ring up Frances. I had to tell her not to be so damn silly. I'd got my money all ready and everything.

I couldn't get to the telephone because there was somebody else there. A middle-aged man. He had a soft hat on, a bit too small, and a black coat and striped trousers. He didn't take any notice when I pulled at his arm. I suddenly realized that the hat he'd got on was mine.

"What the hell do you think you're doing?" I said. "That's my hat!"

I tried to pull it off his head, but it seemed stuck tight, or else it was very heavy. He turned slowly round and I knew his face. He said:

"It's no good trying to move me. If you do they'll bring me back again!"

I said: "I must telephone."

He said: "You can't telephone. You want to telephone to Frances. She won't answer. I've just telephoned to her. I've told her not to speak to you."

I said: "If you don't get away from that telephone, I'll smash you!"

He said: "You can't smash me. Rigour's setting in. You can't even bend me, Bo!"

3

I waked up in a hell of a sweat. I've only given you a mild idea of the dreams I had. If I wrote down the worst of them I should never be allowed to go into print.

It was light but I didn't know what the time was. My mouth was like the bottom of a very old canary's cage. I'd got a headache and a backache and all my joints seemed stiff.

But I couldn't stay in bed. I got up and found a cigarette and lit it. It tasted vile but seemed to pull me together. I had a long drink of water out of the jug. It tasted as if it had been there for a week and it probably had.

I wandered to the window and looked out. I stared at what I could see of Widdeley Green. It was fast asleep. I suppose the time must have been about half-past six.

The first thing I saw was an old labourer who walked slowly across my field of sight. He had a clay in his mouth and the smoke from it hung all round his head as he walked. It was one of those heavy, half-misty mornings, when the air's as still as the Mediterranean in midsummer.

I don't know how long I stood at the window, but I do know that the next thing I saw came just after I'd thrown away the stub of my cigarette. It came into my field of sight from the opposite way—that is, from left to right. It was a boy on a bicycle. And he had one of those canvas satchels on his back that are always worn by newspaper carriers in the country. At first I looked at him idly. I knew what he was, but the connection between what he was and what I was didn't strike me at first.

And then he turned in from the roadway to the yard of *The Green Man* and dismounted. He was just underneath my window. He pulled his satchel round to his middle and groped in it and pulled out some papers and put them on the step which led up to the front porch. I drew back a bit. The significance of what he was doing had struck me. From deeper in the room I watched him get onto his bicycle again and turn round and go back the way he'd come. I thought, with a return of the empty, sickish feeling in my stomach, that I must go and look at those papers.

I don't suppose I'd ever have written this story if I hadn't obeyed that impulse. I pulled on my trousers and opened my door very quietly and stole down the stairs. I went through the public bar and got to the porch door. It was bolted top and bottom and the key had been turned.

Thank God the lock and the bolts had been oiled. I managed to free the door without making noise enough to wake anyone. Mind you, the noise I did make seemed to me enough to raise a graveyard, but I realized afterwards that it couldn't have been much.

On the top step was a bundle of papers. I took them up and shut the door, relocking and rebolting it with my heart in my mouth. I stole back up the stairs and shut my own door, and sat on the bed, listening, with the papers clutched under my arm.

After what seemed like hours of silence, I felt better. I unrolled the papers. There was a *Daily Courier,* a *Morning Clarion* and a *Telegram.* I looked at the *Telegram* first, at the middle page. I saw nothing at first glance, nor did I on the front page of the *Courier.* I felt better.

I picked up the *Clarion* and stopped feeling better. Spreading right across the front page were headlines and, occupying nearly two thirds of the front page, a photograph.

The headlines said:

KENSINGTON MURDER
Where Is Frances Brandon?
WEALTHY SAVANT FOUND MURDERED
Stepdaughter Flees
WHO IS THE MAN WITH FRANCES BRANDON?

The photograph was a three-quarter face portrait of Frances. Unlike most newspaper reproductions it was good. It was inevitable that anyone seeing it would immediately recognize her.

CHAPTER XII

Before this I'd had an idea that some of the staff of a country pub must be up and about before seven. Since, I know at least one where they aren't.

It was five minutes past seven by Frances's watch when, having got the Ford out of the garage after smashing the flimsy padlock, we saw our last of Widdeley Green. So far as we knew, no one had seen or heard us go, though they'd had plenty of chances.

Behind us we'd left, on purpose, two one-pound notes. Also, by accident, my American cloth case.

I'd no sooner seen the photograph than I was in Frances's room. Thank the Lord she hadn't locked the door! I'd shaken her by the shoulder and cut short all her talk. One sight of the front page of the *Clarion* had done more than ever I could have done that morning. She was up and dressed in an incredible time. When she got downstairs and through the front door—which I'd opened—I'd already broken the lock of the garage door.

Until we were through Learmouth I actually hadn't had time even to guess at her mood. But once back on the secondary road from Learmouth to Grayborough I'd had time to think. It struck me—pretty forcibly—that I couldn't be popular. On the first straight bit, about three miles out of Learmouth, I chanced a good look at her. I got no change. The papers were on her knee. She was looking straight ahead of her. Her face was very white, but then it might well have been. Her mouth was very set, but that was nothing either. You might say, and tell yourself the truth, that I got nothing from her appearance. But if you said that I got nothing from herself, you'd be wrong. I knew that, in spite of other things—and surely to God they were important enough!—I was still in trouble and bad trouble.

I made a remark, I forget what. It didn't get an answer. A mile farther on I tried another one, louder. That didn't get an answer either. I stopped the car, and said:

"It isn't a bit of good going on like this. Be sensible."

"Sensible!" she said.

"Read the papers . . . do something useful!"

A little sound came from her. It was an angry sound, but it was at least human. I started the Ford again and drove on. Out of the corner of my eye I saw that she was huddled up in the corner pressing her back against the inner side of the hood and reading the *Clarion*. I couldn't see her face.

I took the same road that we must have come down the night before, but a couple of miles before we got to Grayborough I took a turning on the right which, by the grace of God, wriggled right round the town and came out on the Horchester–Deyning road again. I went up this for perhaps five miles and then, at the big crossroad where the first A.A. box is, I turned right instead of left, and bumped the Ford up to fifty-five and held her there. We were heading then for Mulchester.

It was a broad and straight road with a good surface. Several times I got the Ford up to a point well over sixty. Beside me, Frances held herself as steady as she could and went on with her reading. Round her feet—and mine—lay the *Clarion* and the *Courier*. She'd got to the middle pages of the *Telegram*.

About ten miles on we passed an A.A. patrol and, immediately after that, a couple of mobile policemen in a small car. They gave me a fright. They were going fast in the opposite direction and they didn't so much as look at us. But that was pure luck and I decided that main roads wouldn't do for us. I began to look for a turning and took the next but one on the left. There was a signpost on its corner which said: "To High Whitfield, Low Whitfield, and Whitfield-in-the-Martins." I took it, trusting to luck. About a mile down it, I suddenly got a scare that we hadn't got enough petrol to get us more than a couple of miles on. There was no visible gauge, so I stopped the car. I was just going to get out when I felt a clutch on my arm.

"What's the matter?" said a low voice.

I looked at her. "Worried about petrol." I was a bit surly.

"What you said just now was right," she said. "It isn't a bit of good."

"What's not a bit of good?"

"Going on like this. I suppose I ought to . . ." She hesitated. "But I'm damned if I'm going to. . . . Whatever made you get up and find the papers?"

I shrugged. I didn't know and said so. I added that I supposed that it was luck.

I wasn't looking at her because I found it difficult somehow, but I could tell by the change in her voice when she spoke again that the weather was clearing, at least as far as Peter Craven personally was concerned. She said:

"Where are you making for?"

I said I didn't know.

She said: "I asked because I thought . . . I remembered what you said—last night—about Tilbury and your friend on the Fort Line."

I still couldn't look at her. "What about it?"

"Nothing. Only—I was going to say . . . Did you read these papers?"

"No. Didn't have time. Saw the headlines in the *Clarion* and the photograph. That was enough." I broke off there and waited for her to say something, but, as she didn't speak, I said angrily: "Wouldn't *you* have thought that was enough?" I put my hand to the door on my side and opened it. I was just going to get out when she said gently:

"I thought you hadn't. If you had, you'd realize that Tilbury's no good. You'd even realize that nothing's any good!"

At that I did look at her. She was very white, but she was very game. Her mouth wasn't set. She seemed resigned. I admired her courage more than I'd ever admired it before and that's saying something. I said:

"Want me to read the papers?" And then I looked at her. "Or will you tell me?" I felt, for the first time, really sorry about the night before. I hadn't got time to say so and I shouldn't have known how to say it properly if I'd had time, but I tried to put it all in underneath.

I think I must have managed it all right because, when she spoke, she was just as she'd been before the bother. She said:

"I'll tell you. They've got it all. They know about the Jamieson. . . . They know about the Kubelik——" She caught her breath a little. "And they know about this car." She tapped the *Telegram.* It's all in here—and in the others. They know everything! So far, the *Clarion's* the only one with a photograph of me, but what with the description they've got and the one of the car, there's not a hope. Not a hope at all! And there's something else. Something much worse! All we've been pinning our hopes on is knocked on the head. Marriott can't have had anything to do with it. It's all in the papers. He's apparently a more important person than I thought he was. The night before last he was at the big steel dinner which the Prince of Wales was at. He was even one of the speakers. And after the dinner—it says it in the papers—he spent the night at the house of an old friend of his —Sir Herbert Lawrence, the motor man. He got back to his house just after nine in the morning and found that my—my stepfather—had rung him up the night before and told him to come round early in the morning as he wanted to see him urgently. He had his key and let himself in. When he saw . . . you know . . . he rang up the police at once." She tapped the paper on her knee. "It's all down here. There's not a chance it could have been him. And that's our last hope gone."

She said all this in a dead flat voice. Quite matter-of-fact, but so much without any sort of yeast in it that it was worse than if she'd been sobbing. I said, a bit desperately I've no doubt:

"Right! What we've got to do is to think of something else . . ."

She cut me short. "But what else? It's a funny thing, Peter, but my mind's as clear to-day as it was muddled yesterday. I can save you the trouble of thinking. There *isn't* anything else."

I stared at her. "Did you call me Peter?" I said.

She nodded. Her eyes were heavy-lidded this morning—and small wonder, poor kid!—but she opened them and looked straight into mine for a moment. A little colour seemed to splash suddenly into each cheek, just beneath her eyes.

I didn't know what to do. I didn't know what to say. I knew what I wanted to do, but that was impossible. I wanted to kiss her. Not the way I'd tried to kiss her last night, but another way. I said instead:

"There must be something we can do." I had to fight with myself, after that look she'd given me, to keep even a bit of my mind on the problem. That may sound ludicrous, but it's true. I went on: "I admit *I* can't think of anything, but then I'm a second-class mind. You've got to help me. You're a first. Think, girl, think!"

She didn't look at me any more, but she shook her head very slowly from side to side. She seemed to have shrunk. Her shoulders were right forward and she was limp.

I didn't know what to do, so I went round the car until I found the tank at the back. We'd got plenty of petrol. I went back to my door again and got in, and slammed it after me. I leaned my head out of the window and looked up and down the road. There wasn't a sign of anyone. I looked at Frances and tried another tack. I said, roughly:

"If you can't think for yourself, think for me! Don't forget that I've got into this with you. *I'm* not content just to walk into the nearest clink and drop on my knees in front of the sergeant in charge, and ask him to forgive me. I want to *do* something! I've done all the thinking so far. Now *you* do a bit!"

I didn't know what that would produce. But if I'd been given a hundred years to guess, I'd never have guessed right. She wasn't silent, she wasn't angry, she wasn't hopeless. She laughed! Actually laughed! "You!" she said. "You're . . ." She stopped; and I never knew what she'd been going to say. She said: "Of course there's Uncle Ned! Why didn't I think . . . oh, but I couldn't . . ."

"Who's Uncle Ned?" I said quickly, starting the car again.

"He isn't an uncle really. He's my stepfather's brother."

That disheartened me. I must have looked my thoughts, because she said, at once:

"Oh, but he's not—he's not a bit . . . You ought to have guessed by my calling him uncle. He happens to be the very nicest man in the whole of the human race. He and I have been friends for years and years." She stopped, and then added with the queer note which came into her voice whenever she so much as mentioned her stepfather: "If you want to know, Uncle Ned and my stepfather never spoke to each other. Or hardly ever. I've never been able to understand how they managed to be brothers . . ." She hesitated again. "But . . . I *couldn't* go to Uncle Ned! He'd be . . ."

"What?" I said, as she paused.

"What I meant to say is—I should be putting him into the wrong. He'd help me. I know he'd help me. But I should be—might be—getting him into trouble. Wouldn't I?"

"What about me?" I said. "More important—what about yourself? Somebody else has got *you* into trouble, haven't they?"

She stiffened. I saw it out of the corner of my eye. I thought she was going to flare up, but she didn't. She said, instead, very low but distinctly enough:

"You're right. We'll try him. Where are we?" She was all business now.

I told her that, as near as I could say, we were in the middle of Grain-shire, about fourteen miles from Grayborough and ten from Mulchester.

She smiled. She said: "Your luck still holds, Peter. Uncle Ned lives about three miles out of Hamton. I know Hamton's not more than fifteen miles from Grayborough. . . . If we can only get there before—before . . ." She stopped.

I said—I suppose it was that second "Peter" that had done it:

"We bloody well *will* get there!"

I started the car. I didn't know the way at all, but I thought the best thing to do was to go on the way we were going. We came out, after a lot of winding about, onto another main road. We were at a signposted crossroad which actually said, on its eastern arm, "Hamton 9½."

There was an A.A. box here too, but there weren't, praise God, any mobile policemen, nor, for the moment, was there even an A.A. man. I turned into the Hamton Road. We hadn't gone more than a mile before Frances nudged me. She said, shouting a bit, because the Ford's engine made the devil of a row over sixty:

"I know another way. Take the second on the left. We can get off this main road."

I slowed. I took the second on the left, which was about half a mile from where she'd spoken. It wasn't a bad road at all but, like most of the roads we seemed to have been running along for the last twenty-five years, it didn't seem able to go straight for more than a couple of hundred yards at a time. She said:

"This way we go through Upford and Cressham, and then there's nothing at all until we get to Monk's Chase."

I looked at her. "Monk's Chase?"

"Uncle Ned's house."

In the look I'd had I'd seen that, now she'd made up her mind to go to this wonderful uncle, she was a hundred times better than she'd been ever since I'd known her. She was flushed and almost smiling, and certainly excited. She got her fingers on my arm and pressed it. She said, in a voice which was more than a bit breathless:

"Surely, *surely* we can get there all right!"

I said that surely we would. Myself, I wasn't so sure. It seemed so damned easy that I felt it must be too good to be true. But I couldn't think of anything better. I just drove on and gave the road all my attention.

We'd just passed through the two villages she'd spoken of without a sign of anyone even taking any interest in us. We hadn't even seen a bobby. We'd come to a particularly winding bit of the road, which here was a good deal narrower than it had been and ran between high hedges which didn't even grow level with the road, but were on the top of five-foot banks. I was getting more windy with every moment which seemed to bring us nearer to what might be safety. Consequently I was going a good deal too fast for the sort of road we were on. I came round a corner—I should think the eight hundred and fourth that morning—and nearly ran over a child. I had to jam on my brakes and go into a really first-class dry skid. I was helped by the loose upper surface of the road. If I hadn't had all my attention on my driving I should have probably hit the child *and* turned the car over. As it was, I just missed hitting her and brought the car to a standstill with her bonnet facing where her tail had been a second before.

I'd seen nothing but the kid. I'd had a vague notion there was a dog

about somewhere, but that was all. It wasn't until I felt Frances's hand on
my arm and saw her staring, white-faced again, through the window on
my side of the car that I looked. What I saw gave me a shock which, for a
few seconds at least, put all thought of our own dirty position right out of
my mind. We were up against it, but we weren't as much up against it for
the moment as that kid.

We'd stopped opposite a little, isolated house—two cottages it turned out
to be—which had been knocked into one. By the first of the two white
gates a man lay sprawled out like a dummy. Backed up against the middle
of the hedge which stretched from one gate to the other was the kid. She
was a girl of about seven. She had a red print frock on and no hat. She had
bare legs. In her right hand was a bit of a stick. Facing her, snarling, was
one hell of a big dog; some sort of cross, with a lot of Alsatian in it.

I've always liked dogs. I've often wished people were more like them.
But, just like people, there are good ones and bad ones. This was a bad one.
Really bad.

Even as I first looked, I saw him jump and slash at her and she, in her
turn, made a futile swipe at him with the stick. When he jumped back there
was a dark splodge on her left arm. It made me feel sick. And I saw, even
as I was opening the door and plunging out, that there were other marks
of the same sort on her legs and on her other arm and even one on her neck.

I bundled myself out of the car so darned quick that I tripped on the
step and met the road with a considerable smack which knocked half the
wind out of me. I got myself up pretty quickly and found my mouth full of
dust. I spat it out as I was running. Just as I got across the road—this all
takes the devil of a long time to tell, but I suppose actually from the moment of our stopping the car to the moment of my getting at that blasted dog
not more than about half a minute had gone by—just as I got across the road,
he'd made another jump at the kid and this time, in trying to press away
from him, she'd stumbled and tripped, and was down.

I just got him in time. I tried a trick on him I'd once seen done with a
yellow dog in Karachi. I didn't know whether I could do it myself, but I
didn't stop to think. If I had, I might have tried something else and not
been so successful. . . .

He was the devil of a big dog. Much bigger than any yellow dog. But I
didn't realize that until I'd begun. I ducked a slash and stooped and gripped
him by the hind legs just below the hocks. I straightened myself suddenly.
Being tall and shooting my arms up as I rose, I got him off the ground. I
realized, even as I did it, that if I couldn't pull the thing off I'd been more
than damned stupid in trying the trick at all.

But it worked. I took a half-turn with my arms above my head and then
bent again and straightened my arms at the same time, and he came down
as if he'd been a sack of wet tripe.

He didn't even move after he was down. His skull had split. He wasn't a
pleasant sight. The whole thing hadn't taken more than a couple of seconds,
but before I could get to the kid, Frances was with her. I thought too many

cooks might spoil the job and, looking round, saw the man by the gate. He was a fellow just over middle height and absolutely ordinary-looking. He'd got one of those cycling suits on with silly little knickers and a coat all over pleats and belts.

He was just pulling himself up. He'd obviously taken a nasty toss. He was white with dust all down his right side. Even that side of his face was white. There was a smear of blood on his head. I went up to him.

"What's the trouble?" I said.

He didn't take any notice of me. He pushed past as if I weren't there. I turned and saw him holding out his hands for the kid. She was standing up. She seemed all right, but a bit dusty. Frances was on her knees beside her.

The fellow picked the child up. She put her arms round his neck and said something which I couldn't catch. He brought her along the path towards the house. He said something to Frances in a low voice, and they came along together. Neither of them took any notice of me. I found myself walking behind them up the flagged path to the door of the house. Their voices came back to me, but I don't remember what they said, if I heard it at the time. All I do remember, looking back now, is that for the first time in the most crowded twenty-four hours of my life I actually forgot my own position. And Frances's. I seemed to have got into another sort of world altogether. I remember looking about me as I walked up the path and thinking that the little garden in front of the house was just what it ought to be. Not too formal; not too untidy. It was full of spring flowers and there was a sun dial. I like sun dials. The door was open and the man and the child and Frances disappeared through it. I followed them slowly and found myself in a long low room which must once have been the two front rooms of the two cottages. At any rate, it ran the whole length of the house. There were leaded windows. It was oak-beamed and whitewashed. The ceiling was very low. To get through the door I had to stoop quite a bit. It was furnished well. I can't tell you how because I'm not much of a hand at describing that sort of thing, but I can say that there wasn't anything in it which seemed wrong. There wasn't much furniture, but it seemed enough. And I should say, quite ignorantly, that what there was was good of its kind. At any rate, I had, the minute I got into the room, a definite feeling of comfort and *pleasantness*. At each corner of the wall opposite the one through which we'd come in was a door. The right-hand one of these stood open and I just saw Frances's back as she went through it. I didn't follow but I stood looking about me. I heard, from somewhere in the back of the house, the sound of running water and knew they were washing the kid's wounds. There was a gate-legged table in the middle of the room and on it I saw what looked like a cigarette box. I wandered up to it. I was going to pinch a cigarette, but I didn't get that far.

There was something else on the table; something which took my attention right off cigarettes. It was a copy of the *Clarion*. And it wasn't folded. The unmistakable photograph of Frances stared out of it.

I went close to the table and stood looking down at it. I give you my word that I didn't hear a sound until a voice spoke just beside my shoulder. And then I jumped—literally. I went about three feet and turned as I came down. Standing to face me, looking at me from under a pair of shaggy eyebrows like prawns, was the fellow who was presumably the owner of the house and the kid's father. He was looking straight at me. He had odd sort of eyes. They weren't any colour you could put a name to. Very pale they were, with a sort of yellow look about them. Otherwise there wasn't anything out of the ordinary about his face. In fact, the most extraordinary thing about it was its ordinariness. I mean it was the sort of face—if it hadn't been for the eyes—that you might see twenty times a day and yet never remember. I took him all in in one glare. He was a bit over medium height and lean. He might have been any age between forty-five and fifty-five. He must have washed his face, because the dust and blood weren't on it any longer. He'd got black hair, straight and lank, and brushed back to try and cover a big bald spot on the top of his head. I noticed that he'd got very big hands. They seemed out of proportion to the rest of him.

I didn't know what to do. And it wasn't any good saying anything. He stared at me and I stared at him. And then he did an odd thing. He was standing just by the table, on the other side of it from me. He took a step round it and, without looking down at all, but keeping his eyes fixed on me, he put out a hand and took up the *Clarion* quietly and folded it and chucked it onto a chair by the window. He said:

"I'm afraid I haven't thanked you, sir." He'd got an odd, flat sort of voice. There didn't seem any change of tone in it. It wasn't unpleasant, just blank. Or, perhaps, not blank but deliberately hiding any meaning except the top meaning—if I can say that—of the words themselves that he used.

I didn't say anything. My tongue had gone dry. It seemed as if everything were worse for my having forgotten it for a couple of minutes.

He didn't take any notice of my silence. He said:

"Words aren't much use on occasions like this. All I can say is that you saved my daughter in a way I think very few men could have done. . . . I was in here. I heard the dog, and then heard Doris calling me." He pointed to the open window. "I went out through there and ran down the path. The gate sticks and I thought I would save time by jumping it. But I slipped as I jumped and my foot caught the top bar. I nearly knocked all the sense out of myself—as you saw. If you hadn't come up when you did, I don't like to think of what would have happened."

He didn't smile and he didn't frown. His face, in fact, was as expressionless as his odd voice. "I must apologize if I appear ungrateful," he said. "I can assure you that I'm nothing of the sort. . . . Now, sir, can I offer you any refreshment?"

I found my voice again. What he'd done with the paper seemed to me a good sign. Although he was such a queer sort of cove that I couldn't be sure. Anyhow, I said:

"If you've got such a thing as a whisky and soda . . ."

He went to an old press in the corner and took from it a bottle and a siphon and two glasses. He poured a small one for himself and then a very large one for me. I had to put a lot of soda in it. We stood side by side and looked at each other and drank.

The silence grew until it became uncomfortable. He never took his eyes off me and I began to get uneasy. I began to think, even, that he was doing the cat-and-mouse on me. I said, walking away from him and pretending to look out of the window at his garden:

"How's the little girl?" I didn't turn round for his answer but, suddenly, again without a sound, he was beside me. He said:

"Quite all right, sir. Thanks to you and to the—to your—to Miss . . ."

It seemed to me that the hesitations weren't genuine. I took the bull by the horns and turned and looked straight at him. I said, reaching out without looking and putting my empty glass down on the window ledge:

"You mean my sister. Yes, she's got a way with children."

"She has indeed," he said. I began to hate his voice. I wanted to get out of this place. The room didn't seem friendly the way it had when I'd come in. I said:

"Time's getting on. My sister and I are in a hurry. I wonder if you'd mind calling her?"

He looked at me for a moment in silence. He said at last:

"She'll be along in a minute, I'm sure. When I left them to come and look after you, she'd just succeeded in doing what I should never have been able to do. She was inducing my daughter to submit to iodine."

I liked his face less and less. I liked his manner even less than that. I didn't take much pains to hide it now. For two pins I'd have treated him the way I'd treated the dog. I must have looked as much, for he suddenly took a step backwards and a rum expression came into his eyes. It wasn't, mark you, that he looked scared. He just seemed very much on the lookout. *Wary*, I think, would describe it. He also looked—and it gave me quite a shock to find that he could—a pretty useful customer. I said:

"I'd thank you, all the same, to go and find her and tell her that we'd better be getting on."

We stood for a moment looking at each other. The air got a bit electric. I've never been so near trouble, I think, without having it. But at last he turned on his heel and went back towards the other door.

But he didn't get there. Halfway to it he stopped and turned.

"Mr. Brandon," he said, and then paused. If he wanted an effect, he got it. For a second, the significance of the name didn't catch me, but when it did, it caught me properly. I made a couple of jumps at him and caught him with my right hand by the lapel of his coat. I said:

"So it wasn't an accident your folding that paper?"

He shook his head. He didn't move. I hadn't done anything except catch hold of his coat, but I once more got the impression that he was a more dangerous sort in a row than you'd have thought to look at him. He looked straight at me and said:

"Don't you worry, Mr. Brandon. I'll say your name to your face but, as far as I'm concerned, you're just a passing motorist." He was speaking very slowly and repeating himself. "Just a passing motorist," he said, "who saw my girl in trouble and very kindly—very kindly in the circumstances—got her out of it."

Suddenly, for the first time, he smiled. There was something funny about his smile. Smiles always change faces, but I've never seen one make such a great difference. I suddenly felt as different as his smile made him look. I dropped my hand from his coat. I said:

"I'm sorry. But you've got my name wrong. And I'm funny that way! I don't like having the wrong name used."

He said: "But I thought you were Miss Brandon's brother?"

I couldn't make him out at all. He'd stopped smiling again. He looked more dangerous than before. I took a half-step towards him and then checked myself. I said:

"Look here; I don't know your name and I haven't asked for it, have I? My name is *not* Brandon. Nor is that lady's who is looking after your child. She is Miss Smith, and I'm Jack Smith. Got that?"

His mouth twisted. He said: "Yes, Mr. Smith."

What I should have said then I don't know, but through the open door behind him there came the kid, piebald with iodine. She had Frances by the hand. They were both laughing. She was a pretty kid. I looked at Frances and marvelled. She looked as if she hadn't a care in the world. She came straight up to us and she said to the father:

"I'm sorry, Mr. Allwright, but I'm afraid we must be going." She looked at me, and added: "Mustn't we, Joe?"

I said that we must. I was very firm. We all went to the door. Frances and the kid went down the path first. I was just going to follow them when I felt a little jerk at my sleeve. I turned and he was looking at me from under his bushy eyebrows. He said, dropping his voice until he was almost whispering:

"Don't you worry, Mr. *Joe* Smith. I'm all right." He suddenly held out his hand. "If you wouldn't mind?" he said.

I began almost to like him. I hesitated a minute and then shook the hand. He didn't come down the path. He stood in the doorway and watched me go down it and join Frances and the kid at the gate. I could feel his eyes on my back for the whole of the distance. We left the kid inside the gate. Frances kissed her and I gave her half a crown for her money box. We walked straight across to the Ford. The dog still lay in a nasty heap in the middle of the road, but I hadn't got time or inclination to move it. We sat in the car and I started her. Just before we moved, I looked at the cottage and saw that the front door was shut. Neither the kid nor Allwright was visible.

CHAPTER XIII

The gates of Monk's Chase were under a mile from Allwright's cottage. They were big iron things which stood open and led to a rough driveway which went along between two fir copses. Even when you were inside them, you couldn't see the house which lay, Frances said, about a quarter of a mile away. I said, as I turned the Ford through the gates:

"Must be a millionaire, Uncle Ned!"

She shook her head. "Not a bit. The drive's long and he's got about seven acres of fir trees, and some bits of paddock. But that's all. It's a nice house, but it isn't big. It isn't his, either. It belongs to Lord Cranfield. Used to be a lodge to the estate when the Cranfields had some money."

The drive went twisting this way and that, still between fir copses up the hill. I know it's hard to believe, but we hadn't passed—or hadn't seen—a human being since we'd left Allwright's cottage.

We were so near to what might be safety, or a reasonable imitation of it, that every yard seemed a mile. I remember saying, after the fourth twist in the driveway:

"Is there a house at all?"

She laughed at me. The sound did me good. She said:

"Of course there is!" And then, "Oh! . . . Stop!"

It shows what my nerves were like that I stopped absolutely dead. I plonked my foot on the brake and conked the engine. We both jerked forward in our seats. She said:

"I'm sorry. I didn't mean to sound so urgent. I was just thinking, though, that perhaps it would be better . . ." She paused, and I said for her:

"If I didn't come all the way to the house."

She nodded. "Very quick, aren't you? . . . But do you think I'm right? You see, what I was thinking was: this is going . . . well, it won't exactly tickle Uncle Ned to death, will it?"

"No. You're right. What you mean is, you'd better break it to him gently. And it'll be gentler if you go by yourself without dragging in a hired thug."

She looked at me solemn-eyed for a moment. I don't think she was quite sure whether I was trying to be bitter or not. She must have seen that I wasn't because she said:

"What shall we do, then?"

I looked at her. "What we won't do is leave Peter Craven in this car in this driveway." I looked about me. "There's too much uninterrupted air. And you can read these number plates half a mile away."

I wouldn't have said so, or shown it for anything, but the last thing I wanted was to be left alone, at any rate, with the car. I knew I was going to feel like a kid who's lost his mother in the middle of the zoo. I looked about me again and saw that, on the left-hand side of the road at least, the grass that led to the beginning of the copse was level enough. Also, just opposite where we'd stopped, there was a great gap in the first two or three ranks of firs. I pointed to it.

"If I drove her in there," I said, "I might let you go. . . ."

What I'd thought I was going to feel like was nothing to what I felt when she'd gone. The grass was all right and the Ford took it well. The gap in the trees was all right, and I felt pretty sure that I was hidden from anything except a search party. But I didn't like it. I watched her as far as I could, but that wasn't far. The trees hid my view and, anyhow, there was another twist in the drive twenty yards ahead. I smoked half a cigarette and threw it away and then wished I hadn't. I lit another and got out of the car and walked round it. I hadn't got a watch or I expect I'd have sat with my eyes on the second hand.

Time seemed to obsess me. I actually began, after God knows how long at trying to pretend that I didn't care two hoots, to count. Every time I got to sixty I shut down one finger. When I'd used them all up, I began using my toes. Then, after I'd counted seven minutes—and I can tell you that each seemed like seventy—I suddenly remembered that some fool had once told me that it's no good counting time unless you allow enough for each second by saying "one bloody second, two bloody seconds," and so on. I had to start all over again. When I'd done another four minutes I got fed up with it. I calculated that, allowing for mistakes in the first lot of counting, I'd already been waiting for something like a quarter of an hour. And a quarter of an hour in the circumstances in which I was is just fourteen and a half minutes too long.

I did one of the silliest things—knowing it was silly—that I've ever done in my life. I left the car and went into the drive, and even walked up to the corner. I felt that, as long as I was doing something to see where Frances had gone, I didn't care whether the whole world and the archangel Gabriel saw me or not. And before you criticize that, just really try and think yourself into my shoes. I was lucky. I certainly didn't see her but, equally certainly, nobody else saw me.

When I got to the bend I could see the house, or rather, one corner of it. It was, as she'd said, a good sort of house. It was built of those reddish bricks which have got a sort of mellow, golden top gleam to them. From one of the chimneys, a thin trail of grey smoke was going softly up into the still air.

The sight of the house did me good. I didn't make a further fool of myself, but slid back into the trees and sat in the car. I didn't feel good, mark you, but I felt better. I felt that I might possibly stand another ten minutes without going cuckoo altogether.

Talking about the smoke going up into the still air as I did just now reminds me that I don't believe I've told you what sort of a day it was. I don't know why I should, but I suppose that you won't get the right feel if I don't. One of our fool turns of weather had changed winter into summer overnight. Yesterday morning, at this time, it had been cold. But this morning it was promising to be really hot. I suppose the time must have been somewhere between ten and eleven. Until just now there'd been a top mist between the sun and the earth; but now this was clearing and the sun was beating through the remains of it. The air was absolutely still, and the sky was just beginning to show really blue as the mist cleared. In the copse there were stirs and rustles, and twitterings of the kind which you only hear in good weather. There was that sharp, sweet smell which the sun brings out of fir trees.

There wasn't, in fact, anything the matter with the day. Even I knew it was a good sort of day. I tried to buck myself up by thinking how much worse I'd be feeling if there'd been cold and rain.

I smoked another cigarette, this time down to the last fraction of an inch. I only spat it out when it started to burn my lips. And then I saw something move at the bend of the road. I was out of the car like a shot. It was Frances.

There was something wrong. She was walking fast and every now and then breaking into a run. I stood at the edge of the trees and watched. She got across the grass and came straight to me. She was as white as a bit of paper. Her teeth were set and her lips stretched back from them. She got almost up to me and then she stumbled. I jumped away from my tree and grabbed hold of her arm. Her breathing was very heavy. Underneath the tweed frock I could see her breasts rising and falling.

I kept hold of her arm. I believe I even shook her a bit. I said:

"Take your time! Don't try to talk till you can."

She stared at me. Her mouth moved, but only a queer little sound came from her throat. I shifted my grip and slid my right hand under her shoulders and my left under her knees and lifted her to the car. The door of the driving seat was open and I sat on the floor, still holding her. I said:

"Easy, now! Easy!"

For a moment her head dropped on my shoulder. When she lifted her head again, the tight little hat was pushed a bit to one side. At any other time, the effect would have made me laugh. It didn't then, although I noticed it. It's queer, but I said:

"Your hat's crooked!" And it's queerer still—or isn't it?—that, although she'd got hold of herself and her breath would let her speak, she didn't speak until she'd put the hat straight and asked me:

"Is that all right?"

I said: "Yes. . . . Now, what is it?" She lifted her shoulders and spread out her hands in an odd little movement which was a good deal more French than English. She said:

"He's not there! He's away for the day! We missed him by half an hour."

She suddenly twisted away from me and stood up. I'd never known before what was meant by a person "wringing their hands!" I knew then. She did it. She said:

"What shall we *do*?"

I got up too. I suppose it was disappointment, having been so near to what might have been temporary safety, anyhow, and then so far from it again, which sent something off inside my head. I get like that when I'm really up against it. Everything which has been a hashed-up muddle gets suddenly hard and clear. Instead of seeing two or more ways of acting I see one, and one only, and do it whether it's right or wrong.

I bent down and took her by the elbows and lifted her into the car and dropped her down into the seat next the wheel. I said:

"Pull yourself together! Who told you he was away? We can't waste time. Answer short!"

"His servant," she said.

"Man?"

She nodded.

"Know him?"

She nodded again.

"How long?"

"As long as I've known Uncle Ned."

"Trust him?"

She nodded.

"Absolutely?"

She nodded again.

"What did he do when he saw you? Did he know?"

"Yes. Obviously. He was frightened. I didn't ask him to let me into the house. But he wouldn't have if I had. I . . ."

I cut in. "Will he split?"

She shook her head emphatically. "No. Smith would never do me any harm. We're great friends."

"Why the hell didn't he let you in, then?"

She flared. "I couldn't expect him to, could I? If you were somebody's servant and your employer's niece came to you and you knew she was wanted for—murder . . . and your master wasn't there to give you authority . . . would you let her in? No; of course you wouldn't. . . . I can't imagine why . . ."

"Shut up! Did he say when this uncle of yours would be back?"

"Yes. This evening. To-night, rather."

"Where is he?"

"I don't know. Smith didn't say."

"Why didn't you ask?"

The colour seemed to rush back into her face at that. I saw it even staining her neck just above the high collar of the tweed frock. She closed her mouth in a hard line.

I said: "You're sure this Smith isn't ringing up the police?"

She didn't answer.

I leant over the door of the car and grabbed her by the shoulders and shook her until she must have thought her head was coming off. I said:

"We can't fool about now! We're not in the conservatory after waltz number four. You answer my question!"

I let go of her shoulders. She didn't look at me, but she said:

"I've told you. Of course he isn't."

I walked round the car to the driving seat and started her through the gap and swung her round and bumped her over the grass as fast as she'd go. We shot up onto the drive and I went round the bends to the iron gates at something pretty near fifty. I hardly slackened for them, but swung out left-handed and went back the way we'd come. I knew what I was going to do.

I'd marked the road very carefully from Allwright's cottage to the gates. It had been all uphill and halfway there'd been a sudden break in the hedgerows on my left side as I'd been driving, and I'd seen a bit of wild common land with a path which led up to the lip of what looked like a disused chalk pit.

I was back at this point in, I should say, one third of the time that the same distance had taken before. Still our luck had held. We'd only passed one thing—a sleepy farm labourer with a shire mare pulling a hay wain. The man had been at the near side of the horse and hadn't so much as looked at us.

I backed up to the break in the hedge and suddenly swung the car onto the path which led up through the gorse and heather.

The lip of the chalk pit was perhaps thirty yards from the road and, also perhaps, fifteen feet above it. Fifteen yards from the pit I stopped the car. I said:

"Get out."

She got out. I did too. I hared up the path and stood on the edge of the pit and saw that we were in for another bit of luck. It was one of those pits which had been abandoned because of springs being tapped and water seeping into the bottom of it. This pit, which I was willing to bet was sixty feet deep, actually was chalk for only about twenty feet. Then there was water—green, scummy, weed-covered water; black as ink underneath the vivid slime. To make sure, I took up a lump of loose chalk and chucked it down. The splash it made was a good sounding one. There was plenty of depth. I went back to the car. I vaulted over the door, hit my knee on the wheel, and had her started in a second. I drove her slowly up the path. Her width was too much for it and her off wheel lifted and bumped all the way along the heather roots. I stopped her about fifteen feet from the edge. I got out again and turned to shout to Frances, but found she was beside me. I said:

"Go back to the road. Look up and down it. If you see anyone wave once. If you don't, wave twice."

I climbed onto the top of the hood and stood there and looked in front of me, to my left and to my right. I saw heather, heather, and more heather. I didn't see a sign of life except, about four miles away straight ahead of me, a thin spiral of smoke from some moor fire or cottage chimney.

We were in luck all right. When I turned round to look for Frances she was standing at the foot of the slope just by the road. She was facing me. She waved her arm twice. And then she ran up the slope towards me again.

I jumped down, leant over the door of the car, made sure she was in neutral, pressed the self-starter, and fiddled about with the hand throttle. She started like a bird. I opened the door and leant in and put down the clutch with my right hand while I pulled the gear lever back into first with my left. I kept the clutch down and levered myself up and let off the hand brake. I reached up with my left hand and, with a bit of a struggle, pushed the hand throttle hard over. I then jumped back—only just in time. She shot forward, and then, looking as if she were trying to stand on her hind legs, hit the edge of the pit, seemed to waver for a moment, and then went.

CHAPTER XIV

The hut was eleven feet by six. It was made of creosoted match boarding. Its floor was beaten earth. Down the inside of the eastern wall hung the sort of tools a keeper—or poacher, for that matter—might need. In one corner were spades, a fork, and an old, double-barrelled, hammer-lock shotgun. There was a rough table in the middle, a bench just beside the door, and a three-legged stool close to the table. The door of the hut faced due east and there was a small window in the western wall—a square hole about two feet wide covered on the inside with wire netting.

When we'd first gone into the hut the sun had been streaming in through the doorway. Now, it was just beginning to edge through the corner of the window. You'll gather that we'd been there some hours. We had. After that colossal splash—drops of water hit me in the face as I stood on the lip of the chalk pit looking down—when the Ford had gone and, by the grace of God, had been covered by the slimy water, I'd turned to find Frances about four feet behind me. She was staring at me with wide eyes. I went to her. I said:

"That had got to be done. It'll be better if you agree."

"I do agree," she said. And then she looked at me. "But . . . but . . ."

"But what?" I said. I was feeling pretty good; pretty good in the way you feel, I mean, when you've made up your mind to do something difficult or that you thought was going to be difficult, and have put the job through all right.

"But," she said, "where are we going?"

I said: "I don't know. But we've got to hide till dark. You know the country, I don't. But if you can't think of anywhere, it'll have to be the heather."

She stood for a moment thinking, her eyes looking straight down at the ground. And then she lifted her head and smiled. I suddenly felt that I'd been too rough on her all this time. I began to say something, but she cut me short.

"Listen!" she said. "I know just the place. *If* you think we're going to go on being lucky."

"We've got to!" I said. "Why?"

And then she told me about the hut. It was on the edge of the Monk's Chase grounds. It was pretty well hidden in a clearing in the eastern fir copse. It was a sort of a keeper's hut. But there wasn't a keeper. Not a regular one, anyhow. Monk's Chase had a biggish garden and there was a permanent gardener and an under-lad. Between them they did all the keeper's work there was. But there wasn't much and they only used the hut intermittently. She'd known the hut for years. For days no one went near it. And then, perhaps, it might be used for two or three days at a time. That's what she'd meant by wondering whether our luck was still in. If we were lucky, this wasn't a day when they'd be using it. If we weren't—well, there we were.

We'd chanced it and our luck had held. No one had come near us. We hadn't so much as heard another human being. And we'd been there now, when the sun had crept round to come through the window instead of the door, six hours and more.

We were very hungry and thirsty. We hadn't had anything, you'll remember, since nine o'clock the night before, and we'd been through enough since then to make food and drink seem even more important than they would have in the ordinary way.

Thank God I'd got ten cigarettes left. I wanted to split them fifty-fifty, but she said three would do for her, so I kept seven. We had a watch and so we could at least know the time. I'm inclined to think, really, that perhaps we'd have been better off if we hadn't. . . .

I'm finding this bit extraordinarily difficult to do. Up to now it's all been plain sailing enough. I've got a photographic memory, and what we did and what we said up to this—though I've very often had to fill in with my own imagination as regards the latter—are easy. But when I come to *this* time it's not easy at all. In the first place, we didn't *do* anything. In the second, our states of mind—mine I can swear to, and Frances's, I think, was as bad—kept changing so often and so completely that the whole of that seven or eight hours seems, looking back, sometimes a week and sometimes only a few minutes. In fact, it's all so odd that it's impossible for me to describe it, and so I'm not going even to try to give a full description; I'm just going to give disjointed bits as I remember them.

Every now and then we talked for long periods. The first time I think was after some disjointed remarks about whether the hut was safe or not, ending in an agreement that, as we couldn't tell, we must try and forget that side of the matter. Then we started on Marriott.

"I can't," said Frances, putting her elbows on the table and resting her head in her hands, "understand! I can't understand at all! Marriott seemed to fit so well, Peter! He's the only one that does fit, and yet what it says in the papers seems to make it *impossible* that he could have done it after all. . . . Oh, it's all so muddled and horrible. . . . I think we're in a dream or something . . . !"

I told her it wasn't a dream. Not a bit of it. I also said, trying to be very clever:

"The only really bad dreams I've ever had weren't dreams at all."

She raised her head and dropped her hands from her face and clenched them into fists and began to pound on the table with them. She said:

"It *must* be Marriott! It must! It must! . . . But it can't be. Oh! why, why didn't I bring the papers with me out of the car? Then we could have read what they said again, here, when we had time to think."

"You didn't bring the papers out of the car," I said, "because I didn't give you the chance. They wouldn't have done you any good, anyhow!"

She looked at me and the frown went from between her eyes, and she suddenly smiled. She said:

"I suppose you'll tell me to shut up again in a minute. You know, you're the most completely rude man, when you want to be, that I've ever met."

"You probably met them," I said, "only you haven't had any truck with them." I looked at her very hard. "You see, you can't very well get rid of *me!* First, we're in a mess, and second, I'm no gentleman."

She dropped her eyes. She seemed to be looking at her hands and not finding their state desirable. She said, still looking at them and speaking softly:

"Would you go so far as to say that? . . . Of course, you're a bit—a bit—shall we say, 'harsh' at times——" She broke off. She went on looking at her hands, but the corners of her mouth were twitching.

But I didn't feel like smiling with her. There suddenly came over me, here in the quiet of this place, the memory of how I had behaved to her. I knew it had been essential for me to behave like that. I knew, too, that if I hadn't behaved like that, we shouldn't, once or twice, have got things done as quickly as it was necessary for them to be done. I knew all that, but I felt, for the first time, very bad about it all. I said, not looking at her:

"Look here, you've got an apology coming. I've got to say 'I'm sorry' again. I mean it. But—but . . ."

I still wasn't looking at her. I couldn't, therefore, have seen her raise her head and look at me. I didn't. But I knew, all the same, that this was just what she'd done. I can't tell you how.

"Listen," she said, and went on speaking very slowly with long pauses between her words. "If," she said, "I *ever* hear you talking nonsense like that again I shall—I shan't—well, I don't know what I shall do, but it'll be something very unpleasant." Her words came quick again. She said: "Do you think I don't know what you've done? Do you think I don't realize that, if you hadn't behaved in *exactly* the way you have, we shouldn't be here now, but—but—somewhere—unpleasant. D'you think I don't realize that? If you don't, you ought to. Because I do. I realize it fully. So please don't be silly any more, will you . . . ? And you might have manners enough to look at me when I'm being so nice!"

It took all the guts I've got to do what she asked. But I did it. I mumbled something—I don't know what—and lit a cigarette which I'd meant to keep for at least another hour. It gave me something to do. I said:

"What's the time?"

She looked at her watch and told me. I don't remember what it was. And then there was another of the silences. She sat where she was. Sometimes she rested her head on her hands, sometimes she put it down on her arms. She'd taken off her hat, and her black hair was tousled like a boy's. I got up and walked about. Then I sat down on the stool again. Then I walked about some more.

I kept looking out through the door like a scared rabbit. But, as you know, I never saw anyone—not that that kept me from being scared. If I don't keep telling you how many times we looked out of the window and the door, or how many times we got scares thinking we heard someone walking towards the hut, it's simply because, if I did, I should fill nine books and you'd be bored stiff.

I believe it was nearly an hour before either of us spoke again. And it was either then, or at some other time so like it that it makes no odds, that Frances, who'd had her head on her hands and had seemed asleep, suddenly lifted her head, and said:

"I can't stand it!"

She looked at me with her eyes very dark in a white, lined face. I came and put both hands on the table, and leaned on them and looked down at her. I said:

"Can't stand what?"

"I'm so thirsty," she said. And then repeated in a whisper I hardly caught: "I'm thirsty! So thirsty!"

By this time I'd lost all the flaring decision which had got rid of the car. And, too, I felt different towards her. Something had happened to me. When she whispered like that, it seemed as if a great hand had got hold of my entrails and twisted them round. But I tried not to show any feeling. I said, as shortly as I could:

"What shall I do? Tell me where I can get some water and I'll have a stab at it."

She got angry then. She was so tired, poor kid, and so uncomfortable, that she wasn't responsible. She said:

"Don't be stupid! How can you get water? There's only one place to get water and that's at the house. You can't go there! Please, please don't be silly!"

I didn't say anything. There wasn't anything to say.

There was another of the silences.

I broke it at last by asking her the time again. She told me. I don't remember it exactly, but I think it was somewhere in the early afternoon between half-past three and four.

And then she suddenly got to her feet. I can't tell you what a shock it gave me. I suppose in the odd state of mind I was in, it had seemed to me that she'd been sitting there for ever and would go on sitting there for ever.

Anyhow, when she suddenly got up and the chair fell over behind her, I jumped. I stared at her. She was standing straight and rigid. Her arms were stretched down at her sides and her hands were clenched into fists. She trembled all over. She spoke again and, when she did, I noticed that, for about the third time since I'd known her, she was speaking without opening her teeth. She said:

"I can't stand it!" Her voice was hard and flat. "I can't stand it!" she said again. "I'm too *tired!* And it's all so *useless!* We're just fools!" Her voice rose. She was looking straight at me, but I don't think she saw me. She said: "Why don't we just go—go and—what do they call it?—*give ourselves up?* They're bound to get us! They can't help getting us! Why do we waste time and harrow ourselves if they're going to do that? They'll at least give us something to drink and we shan't have to stay here like this, like a couple of rats in a hole." She took two steps towards me. Her feet seemed to waver.

I said something—I don't know what. I took a step nearer to her and it's a good job I did. I think she'd have fallen if I hadn't grabbed at her. I sat on the table and held her. She was shaking all over. Her teeth began to chatter although she seemed to have them tight clenched.

The next quarter, half, or full hour—I haven't any idea what it was, but it couldn't have been more than an hour—I spent in just holding her. It didn't seem to me any good to say anything. I don't know what I'd have said if I'd tried. But I didn't even try. I just held her. She kept on talking it doesn't matter what. And then, by very slow degrees, she began to calm down. At last—and a very long last it was—she said, in quite a different voice—almost her ordinary voice although it was very faint:

"I'm sorry. . . . There! I've said it again. . . . Please, I think if I sat down . . ."

I let go of her and picked up the chair and set it for her. She sat in it. At first she put her arms on the table again and rested her head on them in the old position. Then something seemed to catch hold of her and she sat upright. She looked at me. She opened her mouth as if she were going to speak and then shut it again and shook her head.

I went round to the other side of the table. I felt that I'd be better for the width of it between us. I'd a damned odd mixture of feelings going on inside me. I couldn't place them and I tried to push them to one side. I said, at last:

"I know the time seems pretty long, but it'll get dark some day and then we'll go."

"Go?" she said. "Go? Where to? That's just it. We can't—we can't go *anywhere.* Unless—unless you're going to wait until Uncle Ned gets back. Is that it?"

I cut her short. I said: "I'm not. We're going as soon as it's dark. Seven forty-five will see us out of here and on the way to the cottage."

She stared at me. "What cottage?"

"The cottage where we were this morning. What's the fellow's name? Allwright? I'm going back there."

She stood up very slowly. "You're not!" she said incredulously.

"I am!" I said. "He can't kill us. At first I didn't like him, then I did. Now I don't care whether I do or not. After what we did for him this morning he won't——"

"Give us away?" she said. "Are you sure? *Dead* sure, as *you* say?"

I nodded. I wasn't sure, but I thought it was a good seventy-thirty chance.

She sat down again, suddenly. She put her chin on her hands and spoke without looking at me. She said:

"I'm *so* thirsty!" And that was in the whisper again. And then she braced herself and dropped her hands into her lap and sat upright. She looked at me and forced a smile. "Daddy knows best!" she said.

I wanted to put one hand on the table and vault over it and just make a grab at her. I had to shove my hands into my pockets and look right away from her and begin to walk up and down to stop myself. I didn't say anything and another of those timeless periods began again. I remember that this one seemed longer than any of the others. I think it's easy to see why.

When, at last, I let myself look at her again, I was going to ask her the eternal question: "What's the time?" but I didn't. Her head was down on her arms once more and so far as I could see she was asleep. For a moment I was enough of my ordinary self to wonder how the hell she dared go to sleep when I was awake. And then—and this may show you how much I'd changed—I thought better of it. I thought:

If she's asleep, poor kid, so much the better for her.

But with all my new-found Galahad stuff, I still managed to feel martyred. I was so certain that she was asleep that it gave me a shock when, without raising her head, she spoke.

"I've just looked at my watch," she said.

My back was to her and I whipped round. She still had her head on her arms. She was talking without raising it. She said: "It's a quarter to six. We've been here—do you realize it?—something like half a day! And it seems either two or three years, or a minute or two, whichever way you look at it." Her voice wasn't hard and flat any more. It was soft and sounded almost as if she were half asleep and didn't know she was talking. "You know," she said, "that just now—or was it months ago?—I said to you that this was all like a bad dream? And you said that the worst dreams were never dreams, but realities? I've just had another idea. . . . It seems to me as if, perhaps, we weren't real people at all. . . ." Her voice seemed to die away and she was silent for what was, to me at any rate, too long a time.

"What d'you mean?" I said sharply. I was scared. That, again, will go to show you what the state of our nerves was like. Just having her say some fool thing like that got me all warmed up.

She didn't, even then, raise her head and look at me. She just went on in the same dreamy sort of voice. She said:

"I just had a silly thought. That's all. I'd the sort of idea that perhaps we weren't real at all. That, perhaps, we were somebody else's invention. . . ." Again her voice died away.

Again I couldn't stick the silence. I didn't like this. I wondered whether she was going off her rocker. I tried to keep the irritation out of my voice.

"Don't know what you mean," I said.

"I didn't," she said slowly, "mean anything. Not anything much, anyhow. I was only thinking," she said, still without raising her head or changing her voice, "of all we've been through in the last day and a half. It's incredible! I don't think we're real. I think we're in a cheap novel. No *real* people would behave and talk the way we're behaving and talking. No *real* people would be even on speaking terms by this time."

She suddenly raised her head. She didn't look at me, but she laughed. It wasn't a real laugh and I didn't like it at all. Even as I write about it I can hear it. I didn't know what to do. And then she put her head down on her arms again and went on in the same sort of voice.

"We *aren't* real!" she said. "This"—she raised her head and looked about her—"this place isn't really in the world. It's just in print. We're not in life! We're in bad print in a daily newspaper. We're going to be . . . going to be . . . '*continued in our next.*'"

Her voice stopped again. I stood staring at her. She didn't raise her head or move, or show by any sign except a slight movement of her shoulders that she was alive. I've got to admit I was worried. I couldn't understand all this. I knew, mind you, what she was feeling. She was describing my own feelings almost exactly, only a good deal better than I could have myself. But I didn't like it. I didn't know what to do. I thought it would be bad if I left her to herself and her own thoughts. But I thought it would be worse if I tried to do anything.

There was another silence. The sun was coming in through the window now, just in the way I told you at the beginning of this chapter. But it wasn't coming in straight. It had worked across the window and was coming in slantwise. Instead of being a blazing yellow, it was turning to a deep orange and the noises outside in the copse had stopped. Night time was beginning. Soon it would be dark and, as soon as it was dark, I was going. And she'd got to come with me. Therefore, she must be got out of this mood. But how was I to get her out of it?

I suppose I ought to have done something, but I didn't. My motto with women is: when in doubt, do nothing. I'd a hard job to stick to it with this one, but managed it somehow. She'd got to make the first move unless I was sure it was essential for me to make it.

Again I can't tell you how long it was before anyone spoke again. It might have been five minutes or it might have been an hour. I don't know. I do know there was still some sun coming through the window, but not much. There were shadows in all the corners, and the light was very low.

Part of the time I walked about. Part of the time I sat on the stool. Part of the time I sat on the table. Part of the time I got up, as I'd been doing at intervals through the hours we'd spent there, and looked and listened.

Actually, when she spoke next, I was sitting sideways to her on the far side of the table from her. She said, suddenly:

"I'm tired!" She raised her head and sat right back in her chair, letting her arms hang down over the sides of it. I got the impression that she wasn't looking at me, but past me.

She stood up and, for the second time, her chair fell over and crashed onto the floor. She stood to face me and now she looked at me. It was getting darker every moment and I could only see her face as a dim white blur. She said:

"I'm so tired that if I don't lie down—I think—I think I shall be sick!"

As I've said, the floor of the hut was just stamped earth. And all the furniture it had was the table, the chair, and the stool. But there was, in a corner—I think I've forgotten to tell you about them—a pile of empty sacks. I went over to them. I found there were six. Not enough to do much good, but I did what I could. I put three crosswise and then three doubled on top of them. I said:

"You can try that. Or shall I put them on the table?" She didn't answer me. She just walked over, stiffly and automatically like a marionette, to the corner and went down. I say "went" because I can't think of any other way of describing it. She didn't sit, or lie, or fall. She just—went.

I stood by the table still and watched her. At first she was still. And then she kept shifting, trying to get her body comfortable. I knew this was impossible. If it had been any good, I'd have taken off all my clothes and added them to the sacks, but I couldn't do that. Nor could I think of anything else. I had wild ideas—like going out and cutting gorse and fir twigs to make a bed—but I knew that, the moment I left the hut, she'd be worse.

Another silence. More walking up and down by Peter Craven. More looking out of the door like a startled rabbit by Peter Craven. More time going without seeming to and yet dragging.

The sun slid away from the window. It was dark in the hut when she spoke again. She said:

"I can't get comfortable. It's hard!" She sat up. I could see the movement dimly, but I could tell more from her voice.

I went to the corner and stood over her. "We can't go yet," I said.

"Thank God!" she said. "I couldn't move. I'm tired. I'm sorry, but I'm *so* tired!"

I had a sudden idea. I bent down and groped about in the dimness and found her wrists.

"Get up a minute," I said, and pulled. She got up. Not lightly, but with an effort which made her half a dead weight. I kicked the sacks up until all but one of them lay in a bunch in the corner. The one left I spread out. I sat just beside the bundle. I said: "Get down here."

She was docile like a child. She knelt down on the one sack spread out. I put my arm round her and, with a jerk which must have been rough, lifted her back until she sat upon the pile with her legs stretched out on the open sack. I kept my arm round her and pulled her down towards me.

It wasn't necessary to say anything more. Most of her body lay at ease.

Her shoulders were supported by my arm and her head came down onto my right shoulder.

I think she was asleep in something under a minute.

I sat there, looking alternately at the door and the window. Although it was dark, almost pitch dark, inside the hut, I could see that it was still twilight outside. We mustn't go until it was really dark, and it wouldn't be for another hour at least. And the longer we left it, in a way, the better off we should be.

Her head was a weight on my shoulder. She didn't move. It was all right for her because she was asleep—dead asleep. It was all right for me, but in a different way.

I went on watching the door and the window and tried to go over everything in my head. The incredible return of the stiff. The chase. The old woman at the cottage. The ostler at *The Three Bears*. The man at the garage. Stealing the Ford. My sleep in the car. The shops in Learmouth. Widdeley Green. . . .

It was on Widdeley Green that my thoughts centered. I remembered the kiss I'd taken. I knew what I'd felt like then, and I knew that, with the slightest provocation, I could feel like that again—but with a difference. Because something—as I believe I've told you before—had happened to me since the morning.

It got darker and darker. I shifted a little and managed to get hold of her left wrist and lift it up and pull back the peaked sleeve of the tweed frock. The figures on her watch dial were luminous. It was a very small watch to fit a very small woman, but I could see it all right. The hands stood at ten to eight; and I'd thought they were going to say at least ten past nine.

Time—although I believe it's the newest thing to say that it doesn't exist —kept going on. I began to wonder how I should wake her up.

She saved me the trouble. Her head suddenly moved on my shoulder and her whole body moved too. She was waking. She murmured something which I didn't catch. I began to speak, but, before I'd got out more than a word, she moved again and said, this time quite audibly:

"Peter!"

I said: "We'll soon be able to go now. Feeling better?"

She pulled away from me and sat up. She said:

"I . . . I don't know . . . I . . . where . . . oh, yes!"

On the last word her voice dropped to a sort of hopeless note. I hadn't pulled my arm away from round her and now, to reassure her, I tightened its grip.

I've said "to reassure her"! It was reassurance I meant to start with, but the intention of the action changed—quickly and beyond my control.

I said something; I don't know what.

And then a thing happened which I've never been able to understand. She moved once more in the darkness. She sat quite upright. She made no effort to get rid of my arm. She came, instead, closer still to me. I felt an arm come round me as mine was round her—just below my shoulders.

And then she turned. And her other arm and another hand fell on my left shoulder.

I couldn't understand it. I sat there like a dummy. And then she moved again. She pressed against me. In the darkness—it was very dark now—I felt that her head was close to mine.

And then I felt her mouth on my mouth.

After a time she drew her head back about an inch. She said, in a little whisper which I seemed to hear inside my head instead of through my ears:

"I'm sorry, Peter!"

I said, stupidly, because something in my head was buzzing round and round like a sawmill:

"I don't understand."

She said: "I just said that, I suppose, because I've been saying it all the time I've known you." She laughed a little. She managed, somehow, to laugh in a whisper.

I couldn't say anything. I turned as I sat and put my left arm round her as well as my right. I said:

"Don't say anything."

The hut had been dark and got darker, but there wasn't any darkness inside my head.

I didn't care any more what had happened. Or what was going to happen.

It had been, when I'd looked at her watch, ten minutes to eight. It was at a quarter-past nine that we left the hut and began to thread our way through the fir trees to the edge of the road.

CHAPTER XV

There was no moon that night and it was lucky that Frances knew the country so well. She managed to get us within a couple of hundred yards of Allwright's cottage without hitting the road at all. By the time we had to come down onto it, it was unlikely there'd be anyone about.

We could see, just as we turned the corner, that there was a light in the room which I had stood in this morning. The curtains weren't drawn.

Our feet made a devil of a noise on the hard road and Frances suddenly pulled at my left arm. She drew me into the side and, after a stumble, I found myself on a grass bank wide enough for the two of us to walk on. We came right along past the hedge on this and at last stood by the gate through which we'd come out in the morning. I said, bending down so that she could catch my whisper:

"Any servants?"

"No," she said. "At least I didn't see any. He probably has a woman who comes in by the day. She'd be gone by now." She dropped her hand from my arm, and I saw her bend her head back and try to look up at me through the darkness. She said:

"What're you going to do? Please, *please* be careful!"

"You stay here," I said, and went through the gate. I stopped halfway up the path and tiptoed back. I gave a little whistle between my teeth and she came in through the gate after me. I said: "Stay *inside,* by the hedge. If you hear anyone, lie low. I'll be as quick as I can. If you hear me whistle three times, clear out and go back to Uncle's and wait till he comes back."

She whispered something, but I didn't wait to hear what it was. I knew she wouldn't follow me. I went up the path on my toes. I flatter myself I didn't make a sound. I could see into the windows of the long room as I went, but it was quite certain that anyone sitting in there couldn't see me. There was only one person in the room—its owner. He had his back to the window. I could see his head over the top of a chair. He was holding a big book so that the light fell on its pages.

I thought quickly. When I got into the porch I tried the handle, quietly, to see whether the door would open. But it didn't, so I had to put my second plan into operation. You must remember that I didn't know how this fellow would take me. It's one thing deliberately not to recognize someone who's wanted by the police when they're just going to leave you after having done you a service. It's another thing to keep that attitude up. But I had to do something. And I'd quite definitely got a hunch that, if I could get over the first five minutes, this fellow Allwright would be useful.

There wasn't a knocker on the door, so I thumped on it as hard as I could with my fist. I made a decent sort of a row. I put my ear to the door and listened. I heard him get up, pause, and then, as I knocked again, cross the room. I whipped out of the porch, bent double, and ran along to the open window. I was glad he liked fresh air. He'd got a big fire inside but both of the windows to the right of the door were wide open. I waited, crouching under the low sill—doing a bit of damage to some of his flowers— until I heard the door open. The minute I heard that I straightened, put my hand on the sill, and scrambled into the room.

The whole job can't have taken, from my first knock, as much as a minute. I stood stock still after getting into the room and waited. He didn't waste long at the door. I hadn't made much noise getting through the window and would have been prepared to bet that he hadn't heard me.

But he had. I could see his back at the door, but, as he shut it and turned round to face the other end of the room—the end that I was standing at—I knew from his movements that he'd heard. He came forward, slowly but deliberately. He halted again when he was a few paces from me. He stood looking at me without saying a word.

The silence was definitely awkward. Someone had to break it, and so I did. I said:

"Sorry to come in like that, Mr. Allwright."

"That's all right, Mr.—John Smith," he said slowly. "Or is it Joseph?"

I said, a bit lamely: "I thought if you saw me at the door you mightn't let me in. And I didn't want to . . ."

"Be rough?" he said. "No, I think you were right."

In the lamplight the eyes that I'd noticed that morning seemed queerer than ever. They were quite plainly yellow now—and it isn't very often that you see yellow eyes in a human head. He said:

"Well? . . . And what can I do for you, Mr. Brandon?"

I grinned at that. I knew, somehow, that he was going to be as good as his name. I said:

"You've got that wrong too. My name isn't Brandon any more than it's Smith. The lady I was with is called Brandon. But I'm not her brother. I'm not any—relation."

His eyebrows went up. "Indeed!" he said. And that was all. He seemed determined that I should do all the talking.

"You asked what you could do for me," I said. "You can help me. Or, rather, you can let me tell you what I've got to tell you, and then decide whether you'll help me or not. Of course, you may decide not to." I looked at him hard. "But somehow I don't think you'll do that."

"Don't you?" he said. His tone was odd because it was even more expressionless than usual—and that's saying something. He seemed to be deliberately trying to tell me that he wasn't sure himself what he'd do.

But I'd burned about six of my boats already, so I decided to let them go on blazing. I said:

"The first thing I'd like you to do would be to have Miss Brandon in."

That did move him a bit. He looked almost astonished. And, for a moment, his face, which I've told you was absolutely ordinary, was definitely unordinary. He said:

"Where is she?" And then: "Yes. Bring her in. Use the door this time."

I went to it and opened it, and went a bit down the path, and called "Frances!" in a voice just loud enough to reach her.

She came running. She caught hold of my arm with both hands, and whispered:

"Is it all right?"

"I don't know," I said loudly. I wanted the fellow to hear. "I think so. We can only try. Come in."

I put my right hand round her left arm just above the elbow. Even from that slight touch I could feel that she was shaking all over. I squeezed the arm as reassuringly as I could.

We went in. Allwright was standing where I'd left him, down at the other end of the table where I'd seen, that morning, the telltale copy of the *Clarion*. I shut the door behind me. I'd thought that Frances would wait for me and that we'd go together and that I should start talking to Allwright. But you never knew what that girl was going to do. She went on and went straight across to Allwright. She came to a stop not more than a foot from him. She said, in a voice which was steady enough but which showed, all the same, what a strain she was under:

"I don't know what he's told you, Mr. Allwright. But I know that you know. I'm Frances Brandon. You've read the papers. You know that I'm wanted by the police. They think I killed my stepfather . . ." I think she was going to say some more, but Allwright didn't let her. He interrupted.

"They haven't said that," he said. His voice wasn't so dead-seeming as it had been when he talked to me.

I was close behind her and I was standing just at her shoulder. She didn't take any notice of me. She went on looking straight at Allwright. She said:

"But that's what they mean! And you know it as well as I do. We're doing the meanest trick on you that anybody could on anyone else. My—Mr. Cra—Peter . . . happened to do you a service to-day. It was a service which anyone would have tried to do—though I've never known anyone else who could have done it so adequately—so that doesn't really put you under any obligation. But you were very nice this morning. You knew this morning. But you didn't say anything. And I don't believe you've said anything since. And I don't believe that you ever will. Am I right?"

Allwright smiled. I noticed again, as I'd noticed in the morning, what an amazing difference it made to his face. He said:

"I've got to have notice of that question, Miss Brandon. That's what they say in the House of Commons. And a very useful phrase too!"

Frances stood stock still. I couldn't see her face, but I knew that she was looking at him. And I felt that I knew just the sort of look that was on her face. After a long silence—so long that I was just about to chip in myself to break it—she spoke again. I'll wager that her eyes had never left All-wright's. And I'm certain, because I could see him, that his had never left hers. It was as if they were kids who'd been playing a game of Stare You Out and found that neither could win.

"That's all right!" Frances said at last. She turned to me. She said: "Peter, would you get me a chair?" And then, at once, she turned back to Allwright. "I'm sorry," she said. "I ought to have asked you."

I'd got a chair already. I glanced at Allwright and saw that he was smiling again. I set the chair down and Frances sat in it. It was a high-backed one with a rush seat—one of the sort that look very uncomfortable but aren't.

"In for a penny," said Allwright, "in for a pound."

That's a silly enough phrase, isn't it? The sort of thing that everyone's old nurse used to say. But, somehow, when this fellow said it, it sounded like good sense. He looked across at me, and said:

"Mr. . . . Peter . . . Joseph John Smith, would you like a drink?" And then—he'd got his back to Frances—he whipped round to her suddenly. "I'm so sorry, Miss Brandon. May I offer you anything? I'm afraid my cellar is limited, but I've got some port wine. And I believe it isn't bad. And I've got some whisky and I believe that somewhere, upstairs, is some brandy. Or I could make you a cup of cocoa."

Frances shook her head. I was on the verge of saying, "Don't let's be so damned civil. Let's get at something!" when I found that Allwright wasn't, as I'd expected, looking at me. Frances, after shaking her head, had dropped her eyes and was looking steadfastly at her feet. And Allwright was looking as steadfastly at her face, or what he could see of it. He said, with an effect of suddenness:

"Miss Brandon! Have you had anything to eat to-day at all? Or anything to drink?"

Frances didn't raise her head. She just shook it again.

Allwright looked at me. I shook my head too. With this sudden raising of the subject I suddenly found out that I was so hungry that if I spoke it would be to roar, and so thirsty that I couldn't speak at all.

He said something under his breath—I think it was an apology—and left the room. He didn't seem to walk very quickly, but I noticed that he didn't take long.

Afterwards I learned that Frances had been right when she said that the only servant Allwright probably had was a char who'd gone by the time we got there. But when he came back in under twenty minutes and I saw the tray he carried and what was on it, I felt—not that I minded because all my heart and soul were with that tray—that he must have a staff of at least three. There were two plates and on each were rashers of bacon and fried eggs. And there was a pot of tea, and cups and saucers, and spoons and milk and sugar. And a loaf of bread, and butter.

I may have said once before in this book—in the casual way that one does —that some meal was the best I'd ever tasted. If I did, I take it back. *This* meal was—and I mean it—the best in my life. Not counting all the times I'd got food during my life when I'd been much nearer starving than I was then.

It wasn't so much the food and drink. It was the feeling of . . . of . . . *sanctuary* that did it. The word isn't mine, but it fits the situation exactly. It was given me by Frances. It came in something she murmured to Allwright after the meal; something I only half heard. . . .

While we ate, he moved quietly about the room. He closed one of the windows. He drew the curtains over them all. He went out of the room and we heard him going upstairs—I suppose to look at his daughter—and then came down again and put some logs on the fire.

When we'd finished he made us sit in two big chairs, one on each side of the fireplace. Himself, he sat on a stiff, high-backed thing in the middle. He gave us cigarettes. He seemed determined that, now he'd burned his boats, he'd burn them properly. He said at last:

"First of all I'll tell you, Miss Brandon—and you Mr. John Joseph—that all I know about you is what I've seen—by an extraordinary coincidence— and what I read in the papers this morning. That is, that you are a young man and a young woman—you tell me unrelated—and that the night before last your stepfather, Miss Brandon, was murdered—by the thrust of a knife or some sharp thing like a knife which severed the spinal column just below the base of the skull. I know that, and I know that the murder was discovered at somewhere round ten o'clock yesterday morning, by a friend of the deceased—Mr. Edgar Marriott. Mr. Marriott had called at the house in answer to a telephone message which had been received at his house the night before from the deceased. Mr. Marriott had a latchkey and was able to let himself in. He found the house without servants and, walking about, discovered the body. He immediately notified the police. At somewhere between ten and ten-thirty you, Miss Brandon, returned to the house. You went up the stairs, and, apparently, saw the police officers with Mr. Marriott standing round the body. You didn't speak to them, but turned and fled. A police officer pursued you down the stairs, but you were sufficiently ahead of him to jump into your car—a Jamieson sedan—which was standing outside the house. The policeman obtained the number but couldn't catch you. They saw that you weren't driving, but were driven by a man." He stared at me. "I suppose that was you, Mr. John Joseph. Immediately police warnings were sent out to apprehend the Jamieson, but this was found, at about one o'clock in the afternoon of yesterday, to be in the possession of a motor salesman belonging to Messrs. Walgrave. His story is that he was driving a Kubelik car with trade plates on it in Richmond Park and got out to stretch his legs. When he returned after stretching his legs—they seemed to have needed a lot of stretching, I must say—he found that his Kubelik had gone and that he was left with the Jamieson. So soon as his notification was received at all stations—which was effected very quickly—the police warning was sent out to look for the Kubelik. The Kubelik was found about half-past five yesterday afternoon in the garage of Mr. and Mrs. Walters who live at Abbott's Wood, near Grayborough. Beyond this, all I know is that—and you can't blame them for it—the police are extremely anxious to ascertain the whereabouts, first, of Miss Brandon, and second—though not so urgently—of the man who was driving the Jamieson and who, presumably, has been driving with Miss Brandon during her somewhat foolish escapade."

"Foolish!" said Frances. She was sitting bolt upright. Her eyes were sparkling. The fire and the food and the sense of sanctuary had made her nearer, in outward appearance, to her real self than I'd ever seen her. "Foolish!" she said again. And then she started. She said:

"Mr. Allwright, now Peter and I will tell you the story of what *really* happened. It's so incredible that you won't believe it. . . ."

"Why shan't I?" Allwright's tone was almost plaintive.

"Listen," said Frances, "and perhaps you will understand." And then she told him the story. I only had to chip in twice and then I found that I needn't have after all. The points that I thought she'd missed were coming later.

I watched her face and Allwright's alternately. Naturally, it was hers that my eyes were on most. But I gave Allwright the once-over quite often enough to see that he was interested to the top of his form.

". . . And I can tell you," said Frances, "that I honestly and seriously, Mr. Allwright, thought that I was going mad. I'd thought that everything was going all right. I hadn't known Peter long, but from what I'd seen I'd got a sort of trust in him." She turned to me for a moment. "As I very well might have," she added. "Then we got up to the library and I was going to give him some money and tell him to go and get some clothes and come back . . . and inside it we found that . . ."

She broke off. Not because she wanted to—she was going strong—but because Allwright had suddenly sat up with his yellow eyes blazing like a cat's. He said incredulously:

"You're not going to tell me . . ."

Frances interrupted *him*. She said:

"But I am! My . . . he . . . *it* was there! Back again! In exactly the same position as it had been before! Mr. Allwright, I know . . ."

He cut in again. He said:

"It's unbelievable!"

I thought it was time to put my oar in. I said:

"Of course it is. That's why it's so . . . so . . . *unbelievable!*"

Frances laughed.

The sound seemed to do us all good. For a moment, though, Allwright looked at her with a sudden, half-suspicious opening of his eyes as if he'd begun to doubt for a moment. Then he changed again. He had—thank the Lord—a sense of humour. He said, after a pause:

"One to you, Mr. John Joseph Cray—— By the way, what *is* your name?"

I looked at him. I made up my mind in a couple of seconds to take a chance. I said shortly:

"Craven. Peter Craven."

He kept on looking at me. "Where do you hail from?"

"Everywhere."

"Meaning?"

I shrugged my shoulders. "Exactly what I say—everywhere."

"Where were you born?"

"I've forgotten."

He didn't like that. His tone changed. He said:

"If you're going to be *funny* . . ."

"I couldn't," I said, "if I tried."

Frances said: "It's because there isn't anything funny about it, Mr. All-wright, that one's got to try at least to see . . ."

Yet again he interrupted her.

"I'm sorry," he said. "In for a penny, in for a pound!"

He settled himself in his chair and looked across at me. He said:

"I'd like to know, Miss Brandon and Mr. Craven, exactly why you happened to come to this part of the world. I'd also like to know where your car is—or rather Mr. Walters' car."

I answered first. I told him where the car was, but I left the rest to Frances. She said:

"We came here because the only friend I've got in the world—except a girl who lives in South America now—and Peter—lives near here. I went to try and see him this morning. He wasn't there. And his servant had been reading the papers and was frightened and wouldn't let me in. So then we hid. And then Peter said we must come back to you."

Allwright nodded. His eyes were half closed. He said:

"I'm not going to bother Mr. Craven by asking him why he said that. I'll take it as a compliment, though perhaps I should take it as the reverse. What I *will* do, Miss Brandon, is to ask you what you intend to do to-night?"

Frances said, after a glance at me: "I . . . think—I'm sure—that I should go to Uncle Ned's. They said he'd be back to-night. But . . ."

"But," Allwright finished for her, "it wouldn't be advisable for Mr. Craven to go there too. While an uncle might do something for a favourite niece, he isn't so likely, by any means, to do something for a man that the favourite niece has . . ."

"Picked up," said Frances.

Allwright smiled. He said:

"Miss Brandon, I don't know whether you realize that you're in a very bad position. You've succeeded in putting yourself so much in the wrong that it'll take a good deal of right to get you out of it. What you should have done, yesterday morning——"

I cut in. I couldn't stand that. I'd said all that to the poor kid long ago. I said:

"Before you say that, you ought to wait until you've heard her story. Whoever killed her stepfather was the man, or thing, that brought him back to the house after I'd moved him. Whoever killed her stepfather had a knife of hers all ready to show to the police—but that knife wasn't there at all when we were in the house." I looked at Frances. "Was it?" I said.

She shook her head.

"I hadn't seen it," she said, "for at least a week."

Allwright looked as if he were going to speak, but I got in first. I said:

"*And* that knife had her fingerprints on it. She heard those policemen talking about it. She's got a scar on the ball of her right thumb. And she heard them. They'd noticed it. They'd got her prints from something else and were comparing them. You can't blame her for running away when that suddenly came on the top of everything else."

Allwright got up. He seemed to have smooth, quick movements like a cat's. He stood in front of Frances.

"Miss Brandon," he said, "may I look at your thumb?"

She held it out for him to see. He bent over it for a moment. He straightened himself and made a stiff, jerky little bow. It was as if he were apologizing for having touched her fingers. He went back to his chair.

"Yes, yes, that scar's unmistakable. There aren't many people with scars across the ball of the thumb. H'm." He began to stroke his chin with the fingers of his right hand. I noticed that the fingers were very long and oddly square-tipped.

The silence seemed to go on for half an hour. I could hear the fire crackling and the clock ticking and Frances breathing. And my own heart bumping. But all these sounds were as if they were behind some sort of curtain. On the other side of this curtain—our side, I mean—there was a silence which got more uncomfortable with every second. Just when I felt I couldn't bear it and was going to get up and say something, Allwright spoke again.

"Miss Brandon," he said, and got to his feet, "I think you're right. You must go to your uncle's. I suppose your uncle is the Mr. Armitage who lives at Monk's Chase?"

Frances nodded her head. Allwright stood over her.

"If you will let me," he said, "I'll take you there. Mr.—Craven had better stay here."

"Oh!" said Frances, and looked round at me.

"Mr. Craven," said Allwright again, "had better stay here." He hadn't appeared to change his voice, but this repetition seemed to carry a lot of weight. Frances looked at me again and I nodded. She got up. She put her right hand on Allwright's arm. She said, looking up at him:

"I don't know what to say, Mr. Allwright. There's nothing I can say to you—yet. I can only show you what I feel about you. I'll do exactly what you say."

Allwright turned to me. "Mr. Craven," he said, "there's whisky and soda there. And a glass. There are books there. You *may* find them interesting. And there are tobacco and cigarettes. I shall be gone about—about three quarters of an hour."

I didn't get a chance to say good-night to Frances. Perhaps that was just as well. I think if we'd been alone for more than a minute, we should have decided that we couldn't be parted. As it was I just stood while they went out of the room and the house, and then sat down in front of the fire and stared into it and smoked Allwright's cigarettes.

After ten minutes by the clock I got up and helped myself to a whisky and soda. Trying to keep my mind off Frances and myself, I went over to his bookshelves.

I took down a book and read perhaps the first ten words of the first paragraph of the first page. And then my mind wandered. But I suppose it helped, because time seemed to go quicker. Actually the clock showed that he'd been gone an hour when I heard a step coming up the path and the door opened to let Allwright in. He'd have looked almost normal if it hadn't been for the hat he had on. It was a confection in green velours turned up all round. Thank God he took it off and put it down, with his stick, in a corner. The stick, too, was a bit odd. It was the first stick I'd ever seen that made me realize what the lady novelists mean when they talk about their hero carrying a "stout ash-plant."

I stood up, shutting the book and putting it on the table. I said, trying to keep the anxiety out of my voice:

"Was she all right?"

He nodded. "I didn't go up to the house," he said. "You can't blame me, Mr. Craven. I've decided against my better judgment to help you and Miss Brandon. But I don't see any reason why I should take trouble to implicate myself by showing myself in your company to other people. Do you?"

I'm afraid I was rude. "Never mind that," I said. "Was she all right?"

He looked at me for a long minute. And then he smiled.

"I've told you," he said. "Quite all right. I stood in the dark and watched her go to the door. It was opened by a servant. But just as she was speaking to the servant a gentleman came to the door and drew Miss Brandon inside and the door shut."

There was a silence.

I didn't mean to say it, but I did.

"Was . . . did she . . . I mean is . . . ?"

Allwright nodded. "Yes. She sent a message. She said that she would see you in the hut at ten to-morrow morning. She said that you would know the way to go there without touching the road. She said would you please be sure and not be late."

I nodded. I was standing up, but at a sign from Allwright I went back to my chair. It was one of the big chairs by the hearth. He came round the table and sat in the one to face me. He sat on the extreme edge of the chair and squeezed his hands between his knees, like a parson at a party. He said, looking at me with his queer-coloured eyes:

"I want you to tell me, Mr. . . ."

"Craven," I said, half grinning.

"Craven," he repeated solemnly. "I want you to tell me, Mr. Craven, in your own words the story Miss Brandon told me this evening, here, in your presence."

I didn't know what he was getting at. But I had a feeling that he meant something. I weighed him up for a minute but got no forrader. It took me a good few seconds to make up my mind, but when I did it was in his favour. I told him. I started before Frances had started. At an earlier point, that is. I started with the reason for my being in Palmer's Rents. The reason for my leaving it, and the condition of mind I left it in. I suppose the story took me quite a while. But I can assure you that during the whole of it he didn't move as much as an eyelid. I've never seen a man sit so long and stare so long without blinking. His eyes didn't drop once.

I came to an end at last.

"Don't you see she was right?" And then a thought struck me, and I added: "Or else you think we've rehearsed it very well."

I expected a negative answer to this. I was disappointed. He didn't say anything at all. He went on staring at me and through me. It wasn't very comfortable. I got up and began to shift about the room, stretching my legs. He suddenly said, in a mildish sort of voice:

"Have another drink."

I took him at his word and helped myself. I went back to my chair. I thought I might as well brazenly face out this uncomfortable situation. I sipped at his whisky out of his glass and over the rim of the glass stared at him. It seemed to be a very long time before anything happened. There wasn't a sound in the place. I was determined that I shouldn't break the silence. I don't know whether he was trying to make me, but if he was, he didn't succeed. He said at last—and a very long last it was:

"I had a long talk with Miss Brandon on the way up. She told me a lot. I must say that young lady would make an ideal witness . . ."

I couldn't stick that.

"If it was only a witness she was likely to be . . ." I began, but he cut me short. He seemed to open his eyes wider, although they were wide enough already. He lifted a hand like an old schoolmarm. He said:

"Never mind that. I was saying I had a long talk with Miss Brandon. So far as I can see she is telling me the truth. . . . Now, don't go getting excited. This is no time for heroics. . . . If what Miss Brandon tells me is true, Mr. Craven, there is no one except herself—and a possible brother of the—er—deceased, who lives in Australia—who would benefit by the death of the deceased."

I was getting sleepy. I had a struggle with that one, but I got it at last. I said nothing, and after a moment he went on:

"Which makes our task, Mr. Craven, a good deal more difficult."

I liked the sound of that "our." I had, somehow, a queer sort of faith in this odd being.

"Miss Brandon, therefore," said Allwright, looking at me with an unwinking stare like a cat's, "is at the moment the only person with a possible motive for destroying Mr. Armitage. And she has a double motive. She has the motive of getting control of her own money. And she has the further motive of hatred. She hated her stepfather, and, as you know, with good reason too. She has also, so she tells me, a past history which, while doubtless innocent enough in itself, would not assist in proving that it was unlikely that she had killed her stepfather in temper." He paused a minute there. I imagine he was thinking that he had put that rather neatly. I thought he had too, but again I did not say anything. I just waited. If he was trying to draw me, he did not succeed. There was another long pause, and again he had to break it. He said:

"In this case, however, we have got to start from a different point of view from the ordinary, or police, detective."

For the first time since he had come in, his eyes left mine. For an instant his gaze flickered towards the bookcase. I thought it lingered lovingly on the tall volumes on crime which I had noticed. He said: "We have to start, I say, in this case, from an entirely different angle from that in which the real, or police, detective would start. We have to start by being *prejudiced*. In other words, we must say to ourselves—as we believe it, or think we believe it—that Miss Brandon is innocent. There must therefore be someone who will benefit in some way or other by the death."

For the first time I chipped in. I said, trying to look at him as steadily as he was looking at me:

"I don't see why it might not be one of those sudden jobs. The feller says something annoying and the other chap happens to have a sticker in his hand and sticks him and then is sorry afterwards."

I knew I was talking rot, but I wanted to draw an opinion from him. I got what I wanted. He said:

"Not at all, Mr. Craven. You must not forget there are two things you must keep in your mind. First, that this murder must have been committed by someone fully conversant with the ways of the household of No. 48 Royalty Gardens. Also, by someone who had access to that household. In other words, a key. Second, you must remember that this person—or persons —must have been in or about No. 48 Royalty Gardens for the whole night. Otherwise they could not have performed this seemingly incredible business of bringing the body back after you had moved it . . ." He broke off suddenly there. He jumped out of his chair like a jack-in-the-box. He took a step towards me. He suddenly shot out an arm and his forefinger pointed straight at me. It was so near to my face that by leaning forward I could have bitten it. I had a childish desire to do so. But I just waited. He said:

"Now then, Mr. Craven, did you or did you not move that body?"

I leant back in the chair so that I could look straight up into his yellow eyes.

"I did move it," I said. "I did exactly what she told you I did, and what I have just told you I did. I moved the body and it . . . it came back!"

He went back to his chair as quickly as he had left it.

"Right," he said. And as he said it I realized that for a moment or two his voice had been quite different from the tone he had used during the whole time I had known him. It had been a rasping sort of voice; a voice which reminded me of something which I couldn't place; something with some unpleasant association. I placed it long afterwards, but I couldn't then. He said, going back to his own voice again:

"I've got to take that. I suppose I'm foolish, but there it is."

"You aren't," I said.

He took no notice. He just went on:

"There you are then. As we know, the murderer is a person who knows all the ways of Royalty Gardens, even down to the fact that the servants were going away for the week-end. Second, we know that he has a key to Royalty Gardens. Third, we know that he was about Royalty Gardens when you were moving the body. For if he hadn't been, he couldn't have followed you. And if he hadn't followed you, he couldn't have got it back."

"He?" I said.

He frowned. He didn't seem to like being pulled up.

"Or they," he said impatiently. "In fact, it must certainly be they. What you did that night is a thing very few men could do. It's not likely that there were any more like you about that night. So we'll say 'them.' But it's easier to talk in the singular. . . . I don't know if you realize what we've got. We've got a murderer, most probably with an accomplice, who lets himself into Royalty Gardens when Miss Brandon is out, kills Mr. Armitage just before Miss Brandon returns, waits—either *in* the house or near the house, in order, presumably, to see that his plan has carried all right. And then, when he sees that it has not, and that Miss Brandon has procured help to move the body, follows you and brings the body back, having the great *luck* not to disturb Miss Brandon when he gets back to the house again."

I didn't like the way he said "great luck," and I said so with a good deal of force. For the third time since I'd seen him, he smiled, and I felt better at once. He said:

"By that emphasis, Mr. Craven, I was trying to show you how bad a superficial case Miss Brandon's got."

"You needn't try to show *me* that," I said. "What's next?"

He was some time before he answered. He said then:

"There's another thing. We've got all these things I've mentioned, and we've also got a murderer who *wants* to do another murder via the law, if I can put it that way. In other words, he wants to kill both Mr. Armitage and Miss Brandon."

"Yes," I said. "I suppose you're right. Mind you, though, the way he's trying to put it onto Miss Brandon may be just because to push it onto her is the easiest way to push it off himself."

I wanted him to disagree with this and he did. He shook his head.

"No," he said. "The trouble he must have gone to to show that it was Miss Brandon's job makes it definitely a case of his trying to *plant* it on her."

He looked at me queerly for a moment. He said, with an odd sound in his voice:

"I hope you will forgive my criminal vocabulary—'job,' 'plant'—I get all these sort of words from my reading. No . . . you have got to agree with me. If Miss Brandon didn't do the murder, as we are supposing she did not . . ."

"And believing," I said.

He bowed. "If she did not do the murder, then the person that did it most definitely wanted to plant it on her. We know this, because otherwise he would never have taken the trouble to bring the body back the way he did!"

I thought that one over. I saw that it was right and said so. He smiled again. "Thank you," he said. "Very well then, this intense desire of the murderer—if I can put it that way—to murder Miss Brandon as well as Mr. Armitage gives us motivation. It can't be mere hatred of Armitage. If the motive was hatred only, it must have been a hatred which covered not only Armitage, but also Miss Brandon. This, as the two were inimical, is extremely unlikely. So unlikely that I think we may pass it over—for the time being at least. What are we left with then? If it is not hatred of the two, it must be that the *death* of the two will prove of benefit to the murderer. . . ."

"Money?" I said.

He lifted his shoulders. "Presumably. I'm afraid, Mr. Craven, that presumption comes a good deal into my preliminary survey of this case. But I can't help that. I'm only an amateur, you see, and this is the first time that I've ever tried to put my theories into practice. The very first time. And now, here I am, starting off from an angle from which no detective would even so much as attempt to start—a prejudiced angle. However, as I've begun that way, I've got to finish that way. . . . You say, was the motivation caused by the desire for money? I say yes. The motivation must have been gain. It cannot be gain of a man or a woman so far as we can see; it cannot be gain of land or property, and therefore, again, so far as we can see, it must be money. And here, Mr. Craven, we come to easier ground. I think it possible that I may know a little more about Miss Brandon's money affairs than you do. . . ."

"If you don't," I said, "you don't know anything."

He nodded without smiling. He said:

"Exactly. I've had a chance to ask her questions and I knew in what direction my questions must tend. Briefly, what Miss Brandon told me was this: It was her mother (formerly, of course, Mrs. Brandon) who was the wealthier of the two by a considerable sum. When Mrs. Brandon died, she left all her money—so far as Miss Brandon can tell me the sum seems to be something in the neighbourhood of £100,000—in rather a peculiar way. She left £50,000 to her husband—under whose thumb, it seems, she was—and £50,000 to Miss Brandon. But Miss Brandon's £50,000 was to remain under the control, so far as the capital was concerned, of Mr. Armitage, until Mr. Armitage's death. Now, anyone who knew himself to be the heir, either by testament or relationship of Mr. Armitage, could be certain that, if he could kill Mr. Armitage, and also, by finding Miss Brandon guilty of Mr. Armitage's murder, kill Miss Brandon he would come into not only Mr. Armitage's £50,000, but also Miss Brandon's £50,000. There was no trust, and it is extremely unlikely that so young a lady as Miss Brandon—especially when her money was not under her own control and she has very few relatives—would have made a will."

He paused. Once more he got up. But this time he didn't jump up like a jack-in-the-box. He got up slowly. He stood with his back to the fire and with his hands in the pockets of his Norfolk jacket. He stared at me with an odd gleam in his eyes. He said slowly:

"Now, Mr. Craven, do you see what I'm getting at?"

I'd followed what he'd been saying, but I'd also found that, what with the exertions and emotions of the last twenty-four hours, his whisky, his fire, and his comfortable chair, I was in danger of going to sleep. I daresay this sounds silly for a man in my position, but perhaps it isn't so silly as it sounds. Anyhow, it's true. I said, trying to keep my eyes wide:

"I see what you mean all right. You mean that whoever did it is some relation."

He shrugged. "Not necessarily. But, if not, a friend who knew that Mr. Armitage intended to leave him everything."

Sleepy as I was, I wouldn't have that. I said:

"If it was only a friend there would be no chance of his getting the £50,000 of Miss Brandon's, therefore . . ."

He wouldn't let me finish.

"I'm not so sure of that," he said. "After all, Miss Brandon's money has got to go to someone. If it was proved that she killed Armitage, it would go to his estate. If he had left the whole of his estate to this friend, then he would get the whole £100,000. You see that, don't you?"

The drowsiness was growing on me. I had to fight to keep my eyes open at all. I looked under my eyelids at him. He said:

"I grant you, though"—his voice was a bit more pleasant now—"that it is more likely to be a relative. But possibility as well as probability must be regarded in this sort of work. We have now the probability—always supposing that Miss Brandon, the obvious author of the crime, was not the author of the crime—that the criminal was the next heir, by blood relation. We have also the *possibility* that the author of the crime was a close friend of the dead man, who knew that the dead man's estate was to pass to him."

"What we want to know now, then," I said, "is, who is—what d'you call it?—the blood heir, because . . ."

He cut me short.

"Because, you were going to say," he said, "we know who the friend was —Marriott. Yes, yes." He was annoyed again; an odd customer. "I thought all that out long before I began to speak to you, Mr. Craven. We know who the friend was—Marriott. But I know, having talked to Miss Brandon, who the blood heir, as you call it, is. It is Mr. Armitage's elder brother."

"Uncle Ned," I said, speaking more to keep myself awake than for any other reason.

"No, no, no," he said peevishly. "Edward Armitage, the one that lives up the road there, is a younger brother. Lionel Armitage is the elder brother. He lives in Australia." To my ears, his voice, though it went on, seemed to get farther and farther away. It was as if he were walking away from me down a tunnel. I fought, but it wasn't any good.

The next thing I remember is him shaking me by the shoulder. I pulled myself together with a jerk. I mumbled something like:

". . . *Lives* in Australia. I wonder if he's here on a visit—"

I was cut short by Allwright laughing. I'd seen him smile, as I've told you. But this was the first time I'd heard him laugh. He had an odd laugh. It was rather like a bray, but there was nothing silly about it. It had a good deal of humour in it, too, and that was funny, because I'd suspected all the time that there wasn't a spark of humour in the man. I remember quite distinctly what he said. He said:

"You're dead beat. You come along with me. I always was one to talk too much."

And then I remember stumbling out through the door and up some narrow, twisting stairs—making a hell of a racket—and being pushed into a little bedroom under the eaves. Whether I took off my own clothes or not, I don't know. But there was a pair of pyjamas, and somehow my carcass was in them. The bed was a bit short for me, but how I liked it!

CHAPTER XVI

I don't know what time it was when I went to bed; somewhere, I suppose, around midnight. But I do know that I waked up sharp at eight-fifteen. The sun was streaming in through the little window right onto my face. If it hadn't been, I don't know whether I should have come to at all. I lay in bed and stretched myself and fumbled about on a chair by the bedside to see whether I could find a cigarette. It was a good three minutes at least before I remembered. For these three minutes I was in a state of being definitely awake but equally definitely not conscious so far as memory goes. When I did remember, my first thought was the time, because there were two figures that were right in front of my mind—a 1 and an o. It was at ten o'clock that I had to be at the hut and be there I should. I shot out of bed and pushed the little window wider and looked at the sun. I made it out to be, with due allowance for summer time, between eight and nine.

I found a cigarette in the pocket of my coat and lit it. I smoked and thought. My thoughts, at the back, were a hotch-potch of this amazing, incredible, muddled affair that I was going through. But this was only a fraction of my real thoughts. You can guess what they were about. They were so exclusively about *her* that I believe I even forgot whose house I was in and how much I owed to him.

I hadn't finished the cigarette before there was a tap on the door. I was so used to jumping at sounds that I jumped at this one. I pulled myself together and called "Come in."

It was Allwright. He was dressed in the same suit—a Norfolk jacket and the ludicrous cycling "knickers." But, as I believe I've said before, on him they seemed just clothes. He looked different, though. He had a different coloured shirt and a different tie, but that wasn't it altogether. He seemed thinner in the face. I rubbed my eyes and looked at him again and saw that he had the thin, drawn look a man gets when he hasn't slept at all.

He didn't say much, but he was pleasant. He lent me a razor and showed me the bathroom—a little box of a place but useful enough. He also lent me a shirt, but when it came to the time of putting it on it wasn't any good. I put on the dirty one and turned the collar and managed to make a job of it. When I got downstairs I could smell breakfast. I went into the long living room and saw it was ten past nine. I worked out that the walk, using the cover Frances had shown me the night before, would take me ten minutes, so I'd got nearly three quarters of an hour to play about with. All the same I was fidgety. One minute I wanted to be off and wait there; the next I thought that it would be dangerous. One minute I thought I wasn't hungry; the next I felt I could eat a horse.

There was no sign of Allwright. I could hear someone moving about in the kitchen. I didn't know whether it was he or not. I began to get a bit windy. I got out of the way of the windows and sat in the big chair and tried to make myself small. I didn't know what would happen if the woman came in and saw me. I wondered, too, about the kid and how it was I hadn't heard her already.

At twenty past nine the door opened. I shrank farther into my chair, but it was only Allwright. He was carrying a tray. He put it down on the table and began to clatter about with plates. I got up and began to help him lay two places. There was good stuff on the tray. I said:

"Look here. I ought to be saying 'thank you' all the time, but it isn't much good saying that. Will you take it for granted?"

He looked at me and I noticed that there were black rings under his eyes. I was more certain than ever that he hadn't slept at all. I wondered what he had been doing. He didn't say anything. I said:

"Look here. What about this woman of yours? And what about your daughter? And what about people passing or calling?"

He smiled with one side of his mouth.

"That's all right," he said. "I've been busy, Mr. Craven. While you were asleep I took my little car out and I took my daughter over to her aunt's at the other side of Mallow. And on the way back I called in at the woman's cottage and told her she wouldn't be wanted to-day. As for people seeing you from the road, they can't. And as for callers, there aren't any. The milkman's been; the baker's been; the groceries and other things don't come till much later. You sit down and have some breakfast, and then you get off and keep your appointment."

He was busy dividing a dish of eggs and bacon as he talked. "But for God's sake . . ." He spoke with a sudden desperate sort of earnestness and looked at me with a queer look. "For God's sake don't go and get yourself seen."

He stood upright with a knife and fork hanging from his hand as if he didn't know they were there. He went on staring at me and there was a bit of a pause. Rather an uncomfortable one. He said at last:

"This, Mr. Craven, is a very grave business! Very grave indeed. I want to make sure that you know that."

I looked at him. I'd been grinning when he started, but I wasn't grinning when he finished. I wanted him to see that I did know it. I got a bit hot under the collar. I said, not too politely:

"Don't be damn silly! If you'd been through what I've been through, you'd know that nobody but a half-wit would think it wasn't serious."

He took that all right. Very soberly, though. He got down to work on his dividing job again. He said, without looking at me:

"That's all right. I just wanted to make sure."

We sat down. He didn't eat much, but I made up for his slackness. I ate like a tiger and drank about six cups of coffee. He was a good cook. While I was eating, and thinking about Frances, and what I was going to say to her, and how we were going to get out of this mess if we ever did, I was thinking, somewhere at the back of my mind, of what an odd fellow this was. We didn't talk at all, or if we did, I don't remember a word of it. I kept looking at the clock. When the hands stood at twenty to ten I'd finished. I got up and pushed back my chair. I said:

"I'd better be pushing along."

"Wait," he said. He got up too. "Wait here. I'll go and have a look round."

He went out by the front door and I heard his steps on the path to the gate. Then he came back and I saw him pass the window going round the garden. Presently he came in by the back door of the cottage. He stood in front of me and said:

"It's all clear. Now, look here, Mr. Craven. Be careful. Be very, very careful. This is a grave business. If I hadn't promised Miss Brandon, I would try to persuade you not to go, but I did promise her. When you've done, get back here. But again, be careful!"

"You needn't worry," I said. "When I leave the hut, if there's any chance of being seen, I won't come back here."

He looked at me without speaking. An odd look was in his yellowish eyes again. I couldn't make out whether it was sarcastic or sympathetic.

I don't like not understanding looks, but obviously I'd got to put up with anything from him. I mumbled something and went. I went out of the front door, down the path, and out into the road. The morning was misty and warm. I had a queer feeling as I stood in that road. Suddenly the black side of the business came into my mind. I felt for a second or two just as I'd felt when I thought we were going to be hunted down without anyone giving us a hand. I had a nasty sort of feeling down my back. I felt sort of naked. The whole world seemed to be one great eye staring at me. . . . I shook off the feeling and got on with the job of getting to the hut. If it hadn't been that Frances was there, I'd never have got farther than the roadway. I'd have been back into that cottage like a rabbit into a hole when it gets wind of a greyhound.

I remember every inch of the way. I've got a good memory for that sort of thing. The walk took me perhaps three minutes under the ten I had allowed. I came out from the thick of the western fir copse and saw the hut a hundred yards in front of me. Quite unconsciously I broke into a run. I then had the idiotic thought that this was a bit undignified. I stopped and looked all round me. Just as it had been the whole way, the landscape was empty of human beings. My luck was holding still. I began to whistle under my breath and sauntered round the corner of the hut and made for the door. It stood open. There was bright sunshine outside and the doorway looked like a square black hole. I knew that I'd been quick and I wondered whether she was there yet.

I stopped just outside the door. I whistled. There was no answer. But I heard—or thought I heard—a little movement inside. I grinned to myself, took my mental hat off, bent my head, and went through the door.

I stood blinking in the darkness. It was really dark in there. There was a shade, or something that hadn't been there yesterday, over the window.

"Frances," I said.

I was sure she was there. I could either feel, or hear, or see with some part of my eye which didn't register, a movement.

A pair of arms came round me.

But they weren't Frances's arms. They weren't a woman's arms at all. There was a faint smell of beer and broadcloth, and a hoarse voice shouted close to my ear:

"Gottim! C'mon, Joe!"

This all takes a long time to write. I suppose, though, that it wasn't more than a second—or two seconds at the most—after I entered the hut that I had felt the arms round me and known them for a bobby's.

I heard what the one who was holding me said, and at the sound a sudden blaze of light as "Joe" pulled the cover from over the window.

What follows may also take me a lot of words to describe, even in brief, but that too didn't take nearly so long as you might think.

He'd got me half sideways and half from behind. He was a big fellow. Pretty near my own build but much stouter and not so used, thank God, to a bit of roughhouse. I did an old one on him. I wriggled, pretending I couldn't move, until my back was squeezed against his silver-buttoned belly. I then suddenly straightened myself, using the whole of my force, and, stretching my arms upwards, got him by the back of the neck. I could feel the harsh blue cloth of his collar. I bent suddenly.

Although I says it as shouldn't, it was a good throw. He turned right over and slid a bit and his head hit the raised bit round the bottom of the boarding with a click.

I'd only just got right back in time though, because Joe was at me. He was at the other side of the table which still stood where it had yesterday. He put out a hand like a ham and pulled it aside. He came for me a bit more cautiously. He didn't run or jump. He just came. And he had a whistle out and between his teeth. If I hadn't jumped, I think he'd have got out two or three blasts before I got to him. As it was, there was only a faint cheep as I grabbed at it. The whistle came out and the cord broke. He grunted and let out. He was a bigger fellow than the one I'd just dealt with, but considerably clumsier. He threatened me with a punch. I saw it starting somewhere round his waist line. Naturally enough I wasn't there when it finished. But I was just inside it. And I dropped him a couple of short ones on the chin—explosive ones, with a bit of a twist to the wrist as my fist caught his jaw. All my force and a good deal more was in those blows. . . .

And then there I was, the most wanted man in England, in a hut with two officers of the law with whom I had just dealt well and faithfully.

CHAPTER XVII

I didn't know whether to get out of the trap or stay in it. I decided I'd better get out. And as I was going to do it, to do it quickly. It was no good trying to take cover from anyone watching, or reinforcements coming up, or anything. I just shot out of the door, turned left, and bolted for the little copse. I was in the middle of it when I heard, from away behind me, the shrill blast of a police whistle. Either there were more men than I thought, or quite probably one of the two in the hut had come round. Of the two I was prepared to bet it wasn't the chap I'd hit. I ran along among the small boles of the firs. I ran well. It was astonishing how fit I felt. And then a thought stopped me and I didn't feel fit any longer. Frances!

I'd been thinking, or rather I *hadn't* been thinking at all, that she was all right up at the house with her uncle. Now I saw myself for the fool I was. That hut job there had been a trap obviously. If it was a trap laid in that place, they must know about Frances. If they knew about Frances, then they'd got her. I sat down and leant my back against a young fir and felt sick. All the snap seemed to have gone out of me and my head was a nest of half-baked ideas rushing round and round trying to find the other bits of themselves. . . .

I didn't care a damn whether anyone saw me or not—until I heard again, a good deal closer, the police whistle. That did bring me to my senses. I scrambled up, slipping a bit on the carpet of needles. I went cautiously nearer to the edge of the wood and got behind a thick clump and looked out. I saw, so near that it brought my heart into my mouth, a policeman and two fellows in shirts and corduroys, one carrying a stick and the other a spade. The policeman hadn't any helmet on. He was running and blowing as well as he could while he ran. It was the one I had given the "Flying Pony" to. They weren't more than a couple of hundred yards away. They were running roughly in my direction but it was obvious that they hadn't seen me—yet. I crouched down and shot back into the depth of the copse as fast as I could, running doubled up. I kept alongside the hedge which divided this land from the road leading to Allwright's cottage. All the time I kept thinking of Frances. At one moment I felt that it would be better, if they'd got her, to get myself taken, and then I thought: No! I must do anything—*any damn thing*—to keep free. If I didn't keep free there would be nobody to go on working for her . . . wouldn't be anybody? Perhaps that was wrong. Perhaps Allwright would go on. . . . On the other hand, once the spur of having us to help had left him he might just shrug and tell himself he had been a damn fool and keep clear to see whether we split on him. . . .

The trees began to thin. Presently I should be out in the open. I stopped and dropped on my knees and crawled to the outer edge of this thin end of the wood. I had gained another hundred yards. The two labourers were walking in front now and the bobby was coming behind, holding his head. He wasn't whistling any more. I thought that if I could get back to the road edge of the copse before coming out of it, and then down the dip and so onto the road before they got more than another hundred yards, I should never cross their line of vision—if I moved fast enough.

I used to be considered a good runner, but I'll bet a hundred quid to a glass of clear cold water that I never ran so fast as I ran then. I just did it. I crossed a bit of open and got down into the dip. Just before I hurtled down I looked over my shoulder and saw that they weren't in sight. If I couldn't see them, they couldn't have seen me. I went down the dip, which was a sort of grassy bowl, so fast that I fell over at the bottom. I was up again and at the other side and through the hedge and onto the road in about three seconds. With these three at the back of me I couldn't stop to consider whether there was anyone on the road or not. I thought, my luck being out, that there probably would be. But there wasn't; not a soul. I ran up the path and got to Allwright's garden gate. I looked quickly about but I couldn't see any sign of him. The door was shut. I couldn't make up my mind whether to go into his cottage or not. I had promised him that if anything went wrong I wouldn't go back. But then there was Frances. Everything else went by the board. I shot up the path and tried the door, but it was locked. I looked at the windows but they were shut on the inside. I ran round to the back of the house. There I had better luck. The back door was open. I went inside and shut it behind me and stood a minute and got my breath. I hadn't realized until I was inside how puffed I was. Then I shouted. My voice went rolling all round the cottage but it didn't get any answer. I didn't know what to do. They might come in here or they might not. . . . Almost certainly they would, though. I went upstairs. I remembered that just by the bathroom, which was a little cubbyhole practically in the centre of the building, I'd thought I'd seen a trap door.

I was right. I had seen a trap door. I jumped for it and pushed at it. There was nothing on top of the lid and it swung back at my second jump. I sprang at the hole and managed to pull myself through it. I'm not much of a gymnast as a rule, but it's wonderful what a bit of fear will do for you. I went through that as well as any Fairbanks.

A minute later the trap door lid was down again and I was lying along the top of some dusty packing cases with a lump on the back of my head the size of an egg. But it didn't matter about that. I felt, compared with what I'd felt just now at least, pretty good. It was a tiny place; just a hole under the eaves really, but there was a little window to it, a thing about four inches square, where somebody had taken a brick out and inserted a little bit of thick, coarse glass. It was so gloomy there that I didn't notice it for some time. But when my senses began to come back to me, I found that there was a bit of light in the place which couldn't be explained by anything else but a window. It was covered with dirt and dust. I took out a handkerchief and spat on it, and rubbed the window and found I could see out into the road. I lay there looking out of this peephole.

I hadn't got a watch, and I shall never know how long it was I lay up there before anything happened. It may have been five minutes but it seemed like an hour. Just as I was beginning to think that nothing ever would happen, it all happened at once. And how!—as Englishmen think Americans say. I heard the shrilling of that blasted whistle. It came up to my little hole a good deal muffled, of course, but it must have been loud. Round the corner, into my narrow field of vision, came the three that had been chasing me. Again the bobby was in the lead. They were running. The two labourers, tagging behind, seemed a bit sheepish. I figured the first flush of excitement had worn off and they were feeling ridiculous. There was nobody underneath, but I remember thinking that if there had been, he would surely have been able to hear my heart beating against the boards. It sounded to me like somebody hitting a tree trunk with the back of an axe. . . . Would they come into the cottage or would they not? If they did, had I left any sign of the trapdoor having been opened? Would they come up? Would they this; would they that; would they the other? . . .

And then there came into my field of sight from the other way a motor-car. It was an open four-seater Morris, not too new. There were four people in it: the driver who seemed to be a bobby with a flat hat; an obvious inspector of police; a bobby complete with ordinary helmet—and Frances!

She was sitting very close to the bobby. Her knees were covered with a rug. I couldn't see very well, but I had a damned awful feeling that she might be handcuffed underneath the rug. I wanted to get out and pull the house down and jump out and murder the lot of them.

It shows you how worked up I was that I actually got up and began to fumble at the lid of the trap door before common sense returned to me and I crawled back to my peephole. Now my bobby, without the helmet, was standing by the car talking to the inspector. After a few minutes the inspector got up and got out of the car. He was a tall fellow but looked more like a sergeant-major of cavalry than a policeman. He seemed to be giving my poor unfortunate fellow hell. They looked this way and that and then they looked at the cottage. I thought:

Now for it.

But not a bit. From round the corner came another car. A small, ancient, ramshackle De Dion. Sitting very upright behind its perpendicular steering wheel was Allwright. I didn't know whether to be pleased or sorry. I kept taking my eyes off Frances and looking at him as he drew up. I wondered what he would say and what they would say. I wondered what he would do with Frances. It was like watching a play in which you knew all the principal characters and were one yourself. The whole thing seen from above, as I was looking at it, looked as if the people were behaving not like real people but rather bad actors. They all seemed stiff in their movements. . . . But that's enough of that nonsense. Now for some facts.

Something happened right away which puzzled me. It didn't seem to be the first time Allwright had spoken to those policemen. The way they spoke to each other, their general attitude, told me that.

Where had he been? Had he been putting up a bluff on us all the time and trying to get the reward? I looked at Frances. Allwright was standing close beside her, talking to the inspector. She didn't so much as turn her head to look at him, and as for him—well, she mightn't have been there at all. There was a long confab during which the bobby without the helmet— my bobby—began to point to all quarters of the compass. The inspector turned round on him suddenly and said something I couldn't hear. I could see all the bounce go out of him. Then a funny thing happened. Allwright turned and looked at his own house. He pointed to it and the inspector laughed. And that was all, if you can believe it. I can hardly believe it myself. They never came near the cottage. The two labourers went sheepishly off the way they had come. The bobby without the helmet stood on the step of the police car, and it disappeared going towards Monk's Chase. I couldn't make that out for a minute and then I realized that they were going back to see whether the fellow I'd hit was seriously injured. I almost broke my neck trying to see the last of the car from my little window. Frances had been sitting so still. She'd been so calm all the time. I hadn't had a good look at her face but I knew just what it was looking like. And then I got the horrors. They'd got her and they would damn soon have me. Allwright was a traitor. I'd perhaps killed the bobby up in the hut. . . . There was no doubt about it, I was done. I put my head in my arms and thought—or rather I didn't think. I just gave myself up to a good wallow in gloom. And I can tell you I was damn frightened. No man wants to see his girl hanged. No man wants to hang himself. I thought if the worst came to the worst I'd do the job before they got me. I actually got as bad as that.

After a bit I pulled myself together. I wriggled up and had another look out of my peephole. Allwright's car was gone.

The next thing that happened was that I heard, below me in the house, someone opening a door. I guessed it was the back door. I heard feet coming upstairs. They came right up and stopped directly below my hiding place.

Someone tapped on the lid of the trap door. I supposed it was Allwright but I didn't know. I didn't much care, anyhow.

It was Allwright. "You'd better come down out of that, hadn't you?" he said.

I came down out of it. I must have looked pretty odd. It was filthy up there. He looked at me, and his mouth twitched. I glared at him. I said:

"Before either of us moves from this spot, you're going to tell me what your game really is." I must have looked a bit grim, for that odd look came into his face that I'd seen the night before when I broke in—a look that made me think he might, in spite of his appearance, be a tough sort of blighter to handle. But he might have been a hundred Jack Dempseys for all I cared at the moment. And even if he had been, probably I could have dealt with him. It's a funny thing, I don't remember making a move, but I do remember suddenly having my fingers clamped onto the front of his coat holding him. He didn't move. He looked at me. I couldn't read his face. He said:

"Don't be a fool, Mr. Craven. I know what you're thinking. You're thinking that it's something to do with me that led to Miss Brandon's arrest. And your narrow escape. I tell you here and now that it was nothing of the sort. I tell you also that I'm trying to help you, but I can't help you if you take this attitude. Why do you think the police never came and looked into this cottage? Because I happen to know them, and they happen to know me. So that it never occurred to them when I told them that the house was locked that you could be in here. It's a good thing for me that they didn't come in, because you'd left traces of your entry into the box room that a baby could have read. . . . Now, if you will let me go, we'll just fix you up. They've seen you now, but I want you. You've got to be able to move about and you can't move about looking like Peter Craven."

During the whole of this speech his voice had been level and calm, but yet there had been something in it which made me—rather against my inclination—believe every word he said. I dropped my hand and stood gaping at him. I must have looked a pretty sight with my face half black and half white and my mouth open and my clothes filthy and all anyhow. Once more the corner of his mouth twitched in the beginning of a smile. And then he turned. He took me down the narrow and uneven passage and opened the door of what was his own room, the biggest room upstairs. He said:

"Get your clothes off. All of them."

I got them off. I'd made up my mind that, for a bit anyhow, I'd do what this fellow said. When I'd stripped I went and had a cold bath—again his instructions. When I'd finished with that I felt a lot better. I went back to the bedroom in his dressing gown. My arms stuck out of it about twelve inches and it came somewhere about halfway down my legs. I wondered how on earth he was going to rig me up if he'd only got his own clothes and I wasn't to wear mine. I said as much in the bedroom. He pursed up his lips and nodded.

"It's awkward. Very awkward. But I think we can manage. You can wear a pair of my trousers—let them right down. And downstairs I have an old raincoat which is a good deal too big for me."

He gave an appraising look at my head.

"My hats will fit you, anyhow," he said. "We'll have to do something about the shirt."

He got out some underclothes and I forced myself into them. He then took one of his shirts and cut the stud holes and the collar. I pulled it over my head and managed, by using a big knot in my tie, to make it wearable. I stood there feeling like a small boy. I turned round and found him looking at me. He had his head on one side. He was looking rather like a bird. He had his eyes half shut in the way people have when they're looking at a picture. Just when I thought he was never going to, he suddenly moved.

He took the wooden chair by the dressing table and planked it down in the middle of the floor.

"Sit on that," he said. "No, not in that way. Turn your face to the light."

Little Peter Craven did as he was told.

"Now hold your chin up a bit. That's right. Now when I say 'Get back to that position' you get back to it, Mr. Craven. I'm going to work on you."

He knelt down and pulled out a box from under the bed. He took some keys from his pocket. He opened the box with its lid towards me. I wondered what he was going to bring out of it. What he did bring out were four things. A little safety razor; a small bottle full of some dark stuff; a little bottle of spirit gum, and a thin strip of crêpe hair. I said:

"Good Lord! Surely you don't think people can get away with amateur theatricals in broad daylight! What are you going to do?"

He seemed to get huffy. He was a funny devil. You never knew which way to take him. He didn't answer. He came over to me and he put the bottles and the hair down on the dressing table. But he kept the razor in his hand. He said:

"Now, put your head back in that position."

I got as near to it as I could. I wondered what he was going to do. What he did was to begin shaving the corners of my eyebrows. It hurt like sin but he didn't take long. He said:

"Sit just as you are." And put the razor down and brought a towel from the washstand and wrapped it round my neck. I began to crane round to have a look at myself in the looking glass but caught his eye and didn't try it on. He was just like an old schoolmarm. He went to the dressing table and got the small bottle. He said:

"Shut your eyes now, and keep them shut. If you get this in them it'll hurt."

He began rubbing the stuff all over my scalp. It took him about five minutes. Then I heard him put the bottle down again. My scalp was tingling and smarting. He said:

"Now, keep your eyes tighter shut than ever."

I felt something like a little brush rubbing over my eyebrows up and down. This job, whatever it was, seemed to take longer than the scalp job. But it finished at last.

"Keep your eyes shut still, Mr. Craven. You'd better keep them shut for two or three minutes more, just in case. Now tilt your face back a bit."

I felt his fingers under my chin and he pushed my head back; and then I felt the sticky sort of feeling of spirit gum over my upper lip. Not all over my upper lip; just in a thin line above the edge of the fleshy part of the lip itself. Immediately after, I felt something pressed on. I knew the feeling of crêpe hair—did I tell you that I'd once been a second-rate actor?— but this felt a little different.

It seemed that he had finally finished with me. He said:

"All right. You can open your eyes in a minute. When you've got the brush and comb and brushed your hair, part it on the other side lower down by your ear, and brush the rest straight back."

I felt like saying, "Very good, sir," but instead I said nothing. I looked in the glass and got the shock of my life. I think I've mentioned that I'm not distinguished for beauty of feature, but I've got used to that. What I've never been used to, and what I should never get used to as long as I live, is to look in the glass and see the worst-looking sort of foreigner. My hair was jet black; my eyebrows were black too and seemed to go a different way. Across my upper lip was one of those thin-line moustaches.

"Good God!" I said.

CHAPTER XVIII

We stood in the living room and looked at each other. Allwright had a glass of beer in his hand and I had a whisky and soda. The time was a quarter-past twelve. He was looking at me in the self-satisfied way that you sometimes see an old woman looking at a picture she has just painted of the ducks on the Round Pond.

"I must admit," he said, "I've made a good job."

"I'd got a fawn-coloured raincoat which fitted me near enough. All that showed was a collar and tie at the top and a pair of clean grey flannels underneath. The trousers were let down to their very lowest and just managed to look as if they were my own. On the table was a brown soft hat, pretty new. With this, and my black hair and my filthy moustache and my black eyebrows, I don't think anyone that knew me, even well, would have got me the first time. Certainly not a couple of bobbies who'd only seen me for a couple of minutes' rough-housing in which they'd got the worst of it. I wanted that drink badly. I'd begun, after the process of being disguised by Allwright, to think of Frances again, and every time I thought of Frances I got a sick feeling in my stomach. I said, more to drive these thoughts away than anything else:

"You've made a good job of me, I must say. Where did you get all your knowledge?"

He looked at me abstractedly still, as if I were a work of art and not a human being, but he said:

"That's my business, isn't it, Mr. Craven?"

He paused. "But if you must know, I'm very fond of amateur theatricals."

I saw I'd dropped another brick. I said, to cover it up:

"Where are you taking me?"

He put his glass up and finished his beer.

"If you'll drink that up," he said, "I'll show you. We are going to pay a call quite close. We are going, in fact, to visit Mr. Edward Armitage of Monk's Chase."

I stared at him. I began to speak, but he cut me short.

"We shall start, Mr. Craven, in about two minutes. I propose to employ these two minutes in telling you what your part is. I'm a journalist staying in the neighbourhood. You're another journalist friend of mine who has come to see me. Your name is—let me see—Trantor. And all you do is to keep quiet except when it's obvious that I want you to speak."

His eyes had lost their abstracted look. They were looking keenly into mine.

"I've enough faith, Mr. Craven, in your intelligence to leave it at that. I think we'd better start now."

Without a word he went in front of me to the door. He was dressed this morning in a fairly decent suit of grey tweed. It made him look much taller. It made him, in fact, seem quite different. He even seemed to be walking differently. He had rather a jerky self-assertive strut.

In silence we left the house and turned left out of the gate and round to the old shed where he kept the De Dion. He started her and in silence we sat side by side. We passed, this time—it's funny how luck runs—three or four people before we'd been half a mile. If any one of them had seen me as Peter Craven rather than Mr. Gigolo Trantor it might have been awkward. As it was, they never so much as gave a look at me. The car chugged up the last bit of the hill and Allwright swung her round through the iron gates into the driveway of Monk's Chase. Here, just inside, he surprised me by pulling into the side, almost on to the grass, and stopping his engine. However, I waited. I'd been thinking of Frances and welcomed any sort of talk or action. I didn't look at him while he was talking. He said:

"Mr. Craven, Miss Brandon is in a very serious situation. It's the view of the police—you saw me talking to Inspector Brown this morning—that the case is absolutely a cold certainty. You and I—you certainly and I with certain reservations—believe that this case is what Americans call a frame-up. What we've got to do, therefore, is to find out the author of the crime, who will, I think we shall find, prove to be the perpetrator of the frame-up. I know you are . . . now please don't get impatient with me, Mr. Craven; I have my own way of putting things, and I want to clear the air before going up to the house . . . I know that you are about to say that this was the position last night. But it's now far more urgent. If Miss Brandon is, as we believe, innocent, it's absolutely essential that she should not be subjected to more of the mental suffering she must be enduring than is necessary. Now last night I think we proved to our own satisfaction that the person who did, so to speak, plant this crime on Miss Brandon must be either a close friend of the deceased, or a relative. You, perhaps correctly, held that it must be a relative. I kept a more open mind. The events of this morning, however, have completely satisfied me that the author of the crime is a relative."

Here he broke off, leant over and tapped me on the arm. I looked at him. "Or, Mr. Craven," he said slowly, "relatives in the plural. I ascertained from Inspector Brown that the information which led to the capture of Miss Brandon this morning, and the subsequent attempt to trap you in the hut, emanated from this house. Actually the gardener laid the information. Personally, as the hut was used, it is quite clear to me that the information must have come from someone in the house who knew about the rendezvous. That person can only have been, in all probability, the master of the house or his confidential manservant. Which, being boiled down, if I may use the expression, means the master of the house in any case. Now it's just possible that this Mr. Armitage . . ."

His voice held a note so almost savage that I looked at him startled. "This Mr. Armitage may merely have wished to get his niece arrested without wanting to have the unpleasantness of informing her of what he was doing. In other words, that he is entirely unconnected with the crime, but just happens to be the sort of man who has not the courage to shield someone in trouble or to expose them openly. That may be so, Mr. Craven, but I think not. Mr. Armitage fills one of the requisites of the X we are looking for. He is a relation. He has an elder brother, Lionel Armitage, who lives in Australia. But, Mr. Craven, who may not be in Australia at this moment. What I have to do first is to find out where Mr. Armitage is. . . ." His voice broke off suddenly. He lifted his shoulders and in silence started the old car again. We went round the long twisting drive and came in front of the house.

As I've said before it was a nice house. In other circumstances I should have spent quite a time looking at it. Now all I did was to get out of the car and follow Allwright up the steps. I began, even through my dismal gloom, to be intensely interested in Allwright. What an amazing bloke he was! For all his dry precision and his books on crime and his make-up boxes, he was as unordinary as these things ought to have made him seem ordinary. Now, for instance, I saw, more definitely than I had before, the change in his walk. A little later I was to hear a change in his voice and that was to give me a shock too. He was not a quiet, restrained, middle-aged Englishman any longer. He was a bouncing, strutting, midway successful journalist.

He rang the bell, a heavy affair of chain with an iron handle. From somewhere inside the house came a muffled clang and then, a few minutes later, the door was opened.

I saw, for the first time, the Smith that Frances had told me had been this Armitage's sort of faithful old retainer for such a long time; sort of secretary, friend, and butler. I wanted to get at his throat. In spite of what I knew—or what I thought I knew—of course I couldn't. All I could do was to stand at Allwright's shoulder and try not to look amazed at the man Smith's appearance.

I don't know why, but I'd expected something quite different—tall and thin and pale, with a hatchet face and small, shifty eyes. What I saw was a soldierly looking fellow of between forty and fifty, with a round, red, almost cherubic look about his face, and blue eyes which seemed as honest and kindly as you could find in a day's walk. He stood in the doorway in the proper attitude of a manservant not quite certain of his callers.

And then I got the shock of hearing Allwright speak in his new voice. It was a loud, brassy sort of affair, fitting his walk to a T. I stole a look at his face.

"Mr. Armitage in?" he said.

Smith looked at him. "Your name, sir?" he said cautiously.

Allwright burst into a loud laugh. "You know who I am, all right. I've been living in the cottage down the road for the last couple of months. I've seen you often about. I've never spoken to Mr. Armitage or you before, but you know me all right."

Smith's face expressed just the right amount of surprise and recognition. "It's Mr. Allwright," he said.

He backed a little pace. "I'm not sure," he said, "whether Mr. Armitage is at home. If you will step inside for a moment, I will ascertain."

We stepped inside and found ourselves in a little hall. There was some oak panelling which I should think was very good; some comfortable chairs, and two or three pieces of what I should think again were very good oak. Smith left us. He walked very quietly. After he'd gone I went close to Allwright and whispered:

"Different sort of guy from what I thought."

He looked at me, not with the expression which I knew, but with the expression which suited this new personality he seemed to have put on as easily as a man puts on a glove. He said:

"Don't know what you're talking about, Trantor."

There was a good deal of emphasis on the Trantor. I took my cue. I was to think Trantor and to be Trantor. I went over to the fireplace and stood looking down into the small log fire which was burning in an iron basket.

Smith came back. He said to Allwright:

"Mr. Armitage is in, sir. If you'll step this way he'll see you."

Allwright said then: "This is Mr. Stephen Trantor, a friend of mine, another newspaperman."

At the word "newspaperman" I thought I saw Smith stiffen ever so slightly. And there seemed to be a trifle of hesitation in the way he turned and led us to his master. But if there was he got over it quickly. We followed him across the hall and down a passage at the back of the small western wing. At the end of the passage was a door. He opened this and, holding it open for us, said loudly:

"Mr. Allwright and Mr. Trantor."

A man came forward to meet us. Again I got a shock. I'd expected him to be like his brother. And although I had never seen his brother alive, I'd got a good idea of what he must have looked like. This man was as different from Mr. Philip Armitage as coal from cheese. In the first place he wasn't tall. He was short and very stoutly built. In the second place he hadn't a white complexion, but a rich and red and very expensive one. In the third place he was what I can only describe as nattily dressed. In fact, he was too natty for words. A suit of plus fours in a brown check; stockings to tone; handkerchief to tone; silk shirt and heavy silk tie; three rings and a chin which gave the air of being too closely shaved. He was also quite bald. His eyes were dark and set rather close to a fleshy but high-bridged nose. Altogether in appearance a prosperous retired stockbroker trying to play the country squire.

He was very affable. He shook hands with Allwright and apologized, in a rich, hearty voice which matched his clothes and complexion exactly, for never having called upon him. He shook hands with me and expressed himself as being delighted to know me. He asked us whether we would like whisky, sherry, or gin and bitters. Allwright, in his press reporter's voice, said that for the moment he was on "the wagon." Dumbly Mr. Trantor shook his head.

"Well," said Armitage, waving us into two comfortable chairs. He looked at Allwright. "Now then, Mr. Allwright, what can I do for you? You must forgive me if I'm a little distraught this morning. . . ." He'd shown no signs of this complaint, but I suppose thought he'd better mention it. "I don't know whether you have heard of the very, very grave trouble in my family—and the—a—excitement round this quarter this morning. Most distressing! Most distressing!"

Mr. Trantor said nothing. He just waited while Mr. Allwright got back out of his chair and went and stood in a confidential attitude with his hands supporting him on Mr. Armitage's desk, on which lay a pile of letters and papers.

"Have we heard?" said Allwright, his press voice ringing round the room. "Have we heard? Look you here, Mr. Armitage, it's just that that we've come to see you about. Now I've been on holiday here, and I've kept myself to myself, and I don't suppose there's a soul that knows what my profession is. But I'll tell you. My profession, sir, is the press. I'm what is called a free-lance journalist. And though I say it myself"—he straightened himself and put his fingers on Armitage's arm—"I'm one of the leading lights in my profession. This is my friend, Mr. Trantor. He, too, is a journalist although he comes from the north of England. He is a star reporter with the Birmingham *Standard*. That's why he's here. Now, sir, you know what we newspapermen are. A holiday means nothing to us."

Mr. Armitage rose, stealing a glance at me. I thought I could see a fading of the expensive complexion, but I couldn't be sure.

"Really, sir, this is painful. You can't realize how painful. Do you realize that my niece has been arrested for the murder of my brother?"

Mr. Allwright turned to me. "Do we realize it, eh, Trantor?" Mr. Trantor murmured something inaudible. Allwright turned back to answer it. "We had realized it, sir. And while we are genuinely sorry for you in your terrible trouble, we are also newspapermen—first, last, and all the time! . . . Now, Mr. Armitage, please don't misunderstand me. I don't want to trouble you at all, sir. I must confess that Trantor here wanted to see you right away and get an interview, but I managed to dissuade him. We simply want to get hold of your servant and get him to show us round, and particularly to get him to show us the hut where this man seems to have half killed a couple of policemen. That's all we want, sir; and that's the last you'll see of us. Don't forget, sir, that you will be inundated with the press before the day's out. You can't dodge them. You might just as well let us in now, especially as we're not going to worry you, and you can bet your life the others will."

He looked down at Armitage, still leaning on the edge of his desk, with one of his hands on a pile of letters and the other close to the inkwell and smiled winningly. I think he knew that he'd won. Personally I was wondering what he was driving at, but I'd promised to leave it to him and leave it to him I must. I was getting faith in this queer bloke. Armitage was some time before he spoke and then he sat back in his chair and looked up at Allwright.

"Very well, Mr. Allwright. I must say that I dislike your profession intensely, but I can see that you're behaving in what might seem to members of your profession a considerate manner. . . ."

He seemed suddenly to me to be anxious to get rid of us and in a way relieved. He touched a bell on the desk, and, in a time so short as to make me suspicious, Mr. Manservant Smith was beside him.

And in another two minutes Smith and Allwright and I were walking through the garden towards the paddock. Smith led. Allwright and I walked behind. I tried to fit my walk to look like what I imagined Mr. Trantor's to be—a slinky sort of Latin slouch. I admired immensely, even in the midst of my chaotic thoughts, Allwright's jaunty lurch.

Smith was some yards ahead of us. I wanted to get close to this new Allwright and ask him what the hell we were playing at, but, remembering the ticking off I'd had in the hall for not "keeping" Trantor, I kept my distance and slid along with my Latin stroll. We crossed the paddock, passed through the gate, and there, just fifty yards ahead of us, at the edge of the fir copse, was the hut. Allwright checked his pace. Smith, not looking round, led at a good four miles per hour. Allwright slid closer to me. He began to talk a lot of rubbish in his new voice. In between the nonsense his old voice came out. It said in a whisper:

"Get him in the hut. Lay him out. Properly. Do you understand? He's got to be, in fact, right out. Don't speak. I'll be outside."

I didn't speak. I walked on. I felt better. I couldn't think what we were playing at but I liked the notion, especially my part in the programme. We walked faster, Allwright still jabbering reporter's nonsense at the top of his assumed voice. At the doorway of the hut Smith turned and waited for us to come up. He said, looking at Allwright:

"This is the place, sir."

"Hah," said Allwright. He put his hands in his pockets and strolled round, looking at the hut from all angles. From his left-hand pocket he took a little camera and began to fiddle about with it.

"Say, Trantor," he said, "get him to show you inside. I want to take a few photographs of the outside."

Smith looked at me for the first time. He said:

"Would you care to see the inside of the hut, sir?"

He turned and went in. It was not so dark now with the blanket down, but it was dim enough after the bright sunshine outside. He stood just inside the door, a little to the left. I faced him. I looked past him into the corner. I said:

"What's that over there?"

He turned to look and then, as I thought he would, he turned his head over his shoulder to look at me and said:

"I can't see anything, sir."

Or at least that was what he was going to say.

He didn't get past the first part of the "anything."

I got him a real punch. All my feelings were behind it and even when I'm good-tempered I've got a decent sort of wallop. This one got him just below the left ear, on the carotid. It sounded like a wet bathing dress being smacked against a stone wall.

I heard a little gasp from outside. I could feel the tingle of the punch right down to my waist. I got the fellow just before he fell straight onto his knees. If you hit them there and in that position they always fall forward, because they crumple at the knees. I stretched him out nice and flat and went to the door and whistled. I needn't have. Allwright was just outside. He looked at me with a gleam in his yellow eyes. He said, half seriously, half humorously:

"Have you killed him?"

"Not him," I said.

Allwright smiled. "That," he said, "was a real punch." He looked for a moment more human than I'd ever seen him. He said: "How long will that last?"

I shrugged. I said: "Five minutes, anyhow."

"That'll do," he said. "Come outside. Just listen." There was a new and urgent quality in his voice, and he spoke very quickly and with far less than his usual finicking precision. "Look here, Mr. Craven. I'm not going to be in this. I'm helping you, but you've got the work to do. Understand? But you've got to do what I tell you."

I nodded. I was quite willing to, especially if it involved any more of this. I said: "Shoot!"

Allwright poured brief and, I must say, absolutely lucid instructions into my ears. He also slipped into my pocket a notebook, pencil, and a length of cord. I took 'em all in. He took about two minutes. I went back into the hut and lifted Mr. Manservant Smith up until he was leaning against the door. I then rubbed his neck and patted his cheeks and at last, as I couldn't get any sense out of him, did the old second's trick of biting his ear. He was round in under five minutes. I said:

"Stand up." He didn't move, so I got him by the collar and helped him up and propped him against the wall. I put my hand on his shoulder and said: "I arrest you, William Smith, on the charge of being concerned in the wilful murder of Philip Armitage! I have to warn you that anything you say is liable to be taken down and used in evidence."

He kept dumb. I expect his head was singing a goodish bit. I said: "Do you hear me?"

He kept still, gaping like a fish. The colour slowly ebbed away from his face and I saw that it was only his complexion that had made him look like an Honest John. The first thing he said was:

"Who the —— —— are you?"

I said my piece as directed. "Detective-Inspector Copley of the Criminal Investigation Department."

"My God!" he said, and collapsed.

I helped him up again and got the chair and propped him on it. I sat down on the table and took the notebook and pencil that Allwright had given me and got a statement from him. It's an interesting little document. They let me keep the original. But before I took it—and the reason I got it was that I said my next piece so well—I put my hand on his shoulder, and I said:

"Smith, you are not the prime mover in this. It's your boss back in the house there." He glared at me dumbly. The shock coming on top of that wallop had got him really groggy. "You are under his thumb. That's how I see it. Now, listen. I can't promise, but I think there's a reasonable chance that if you give me a statement here and now, you might escape that nine o'clock walk. You know what that means, don't you? You may get off with penal servitude. You don't want to die, do you?"

At the time I didn't mind, but in retrospect it's rather a painful business. Anyhow, at last he talked. I got it down very short. The document was in my writing and signed by Smith. It reads:

"The charge is quite right. I was concerned with the murder of Philip Armitage. A week before the night of the murder, Mr. Edward Armitage approached me and put a scheme before me. He had the idea that if he killed his brother, whom he hated, and made it look as if Miss Frances had done it, he was bound to come in for the money. It was a lot of money he told me—nearly half a million pounds. He trusted me absolutely, he said. He wouldn't have put the scheme up to me but it wanted two men. To cut a long story short, I accepted as he promised to give me twenty thousand, and I thought that he would have to do this because, after I went in with him, I'd got him where I wanted him. It was arranged that we were to *appear* to spend the night at Monk's Chase as usual. That was easy because I could get my wife, who is the only servant living in, to swear to it. Lights were to be left on and everything. My wife carried out this part of the scheme although she did not know what it was for. She's frightened of me and will do whatever I tell her. At seven o'clock we got the Chrysler out and went by the back way through Hangman's Park to Dorford and from there on the Portsmouth Road up to London. We got to Royalty Gardens.

Somehow Mr. Edward Armitage knew that the servants in Philip Armitage's house would be away for the week-end. I suppose Miss Frances or someone must have told him. I can't say about that. He also knew that Miss Frances would be out and that Mr. Philip Armitage would be alone. He opened the door with a key. I don't know where he got the key, but I think that a goodish while ago he had got hold of Miss Frances's key for half an hour and had taken an impression and had one made for himself. I don't really know anything about that. We parked the Chrysler, which I'd been driving, on the other side of Royalty Gardens a good deal farther down—I think opposite No. 109. I sat in the car and Mr. Edward Armitage went into the house. I watched him go across the road and let himself in. Presently he came back to the car—after about three minutes, I think it was. He said to me that he could not go into the house alone. He wanted me to go with him and listen in case anyone came. I went into the house with him. The hall was dark. We tiptoed in. Mr. Edward Armitage started to go upstairs, but he hadn't got more than halfway when he came down and got hold of me, hustling me along with him. When we got to the first landing we saw a light shining under the door of the library. Mr. Armitage told me to wait at the top of the stairs. He pushed the door open quietly and I moved round to the left so that I could see into the room. I could see Mr. Philip Armitage seated at a desk writing. He did not hear the door open and he didn't look up. Mr. Edward Armitage took something out of his pocket and crept into the room. He stood behind Mr. Philip Armitage. I watched. I did not like the job, but I could not do anything but stand where I was. It was queer like. Mr. Philip must have heard something behind him, because he started and dropped his pen and began to turn round. But he had not quite turned round before I saw Mr. Edward lift what he had in his hand and strike at Mr. Philip's neck. Mr. Philip collapsed, doubled up. I saw blood. Mr. Edward looked down at him and said something I did not properly hear. Then he came out to me. He was wrapping something up in a handkerchief—a little sort of knife. He said to me—in a very queer voice: 'Wait here, Smith.' And he ran up the stairs. I wanted to go after him, or down the stairs and out of the house, but I could not move. I was sort of rooted. Presently Mr. Edward came down the stairs again holding something in his hand. I went to him and said: 'For God's sake, sir, let's get out of this!' He said to me: 'We will be out in five minutes. It's all right.' I remember the words as if he had just said them. I saw what he had in his hand. It was a sort of paper knife. He was holding it in his fingers, in a handkerchief, by the very end. It was not the same knife that he had struck Mr. Philip Armitage with. While I was speaking, he shifted his grip, still under the handkerchief, to the top of the handle. He went back into the library, I looked to see what he was doing. It made me feel fair sick. He was putting this new knife into the wound. I guessed it must be Miss Frances's knife. Presently he came out and ran upstairs again. 'I've just got to plant this,' he said. When he came down we went down to the hall together. He told me to go out first and see if there was anyone about. There wasn't and we went back to the car. I was getting ready to start, but he said, 'We must wait and see the girl get back.' After about half an hour she did come and we saw her go into the house. I was for driving off again, but still he said as we'd got to wait. He said we had to be *sure*. After about another hour, we suddenly saw the door of No. 48 open again. And then—it gave us the turn of our lives—a man comes out. It looked like he was carrying another man. We could not understand it. We had been watching the house and no one but Miss Frances had gone in. We could easy guess what this man was carrying, but we could not understand the man himself. Somehow or other, he must have been in the house the whole time. It fair shook Mr. Edward. He says to me: 'Follow him and see where he goes.' I did not like the job, but I had a go at it. Just as I got abreast of the door of No. 48—I was walking, you see, and the governor had stayed with the car—I heard it shut. I could see the man ahead of me. He still had I knew what on his back. I slackened down. Presently the man stops and puts down what he's carrying against the railings and a taxi draws up pretty near opposite him. The fare goes into a house and the driver follows with a trunk. The bloke I was after lifted Mr. Philip's body into the cab as quick as light. He was a big bloke and must have been as strong as a lion. I walked on, and just as I passed the cab the driver came out and got back into the cab. There was a policeman too, but he didn't seem to notice anything unusual or out of order, because in a minute the taxi drives off, passing me and turning right into Viceroy Road. I kept going and then the governor comes tearing up with the Chrysler, picks me up, and we pass the taxi on the first corner. We pulled down a side street and let it go on, came out again, and followed it. It went to the corner house of some gardens off the Hammersmith Road. The big fellow got the body out somehow without the driver seeing anything funny was up and the cab went off. We stayed where we were, a lot lower down, on the other side of the road. The governor got out of the car and followed the bloke. After a bit he came back and told me Mr. Philip's body had been left in some telephone box. I said: 'For God's sake let's leave it there.' He said we could not do that, because if the body wasn't found in the house Miss Frances would not be had for the job and then there would only be half the dough coming. We drove round into some square. The governor got out again at the corner, and he pulled Mr. Philip's body out of a phone box. I got out and helped him. There wasn't anybody about and we got it back into the car easy enough and shot straight back to Royalty Gardens. I said to the governor what were we going to do about getting it back, because Miss Frances would be sure to hear us. He let off at me like some wild animal and said we had something well got to chance it, and that if the something girl did get in our way she would have to go through it the way her stepfather had, only worse. Fair beside himself, he seemed. I was scared of him. I said I would do what he said. We took the body out of the car and got it back into the house again somehow. We did not make any noise, but having to be so quiet made us take a long time. All the while I was sure Miss Frances would hear us if she was in the house. But nothing happened, so I guess she must have gone out again before we got back. Anyway, we got it back upstairs and into the library and in exactly the same position as it had been in before. It was a terrible sort of job. When it was done the governor had to help me down the stairs. I was shaking that bad I could not walk. He got me back to the car and drives all the way back himself. And that is all I have got to say.

"WILLIAM HAVILAND SMITH."

I got this all down. I read it out to him in the approved manner. He sat with his head in his arms. When I got to the end, he signed. I said:

"You won't take this back, Smith? It won't be to your advantage if you do."

He shook his head. "I'm glad to get it off of my mind," he said.

I said my next piece. I didn't know how it would go down, because even to me it sounded unprofessional. But I had to go on doing what Allwright had told me; he'd been right all along the line so far. I felt like singing. I felt sorry for the poor blackguard sitting there hunched up like a sack of wet oats. I said to him:

"Smith, I'm going back to arrest Armitage. I've no men with me, and so I shall have to leave you here. Therefore, I'll have to make sure you can't get away. I'm sorry."

He didn't give any trouble, poor devil. He submitted like a lamb. I tied his arms and ankles, using Allwright's cord.

I put the notebook into my breast pocket. It was bulky, but you can imagine I liked it. I found Allwright just outside. He said:

"Very good! I've been listening. Everything is working out well. You did your part well, too—if I may say so."

He started to walk towards the house with long, quick strides. I lengthened my own stride to keep up with him. I said, as we walked:

"It was all your idea. You'd have done it a hell of a sight better than me. Why did you keep out of it like that?"

He said: "Mr. Craven, if I am to help you, I must be allowed to do it in my own way. There are certain matters—well, anyhow, do as I say, and we may get you through."

"What are we going to work on Armitage?" I said.

He didn't look at me, but he said:

"We? . . . I cannot appear, Mr. Craven, in this business. You have the work to do. Now, listen to me."

We were halfway across the paddock by this time. I said, before he could speak again:

"Just a minute! There's something I can't get squared up in my mind. Why did this Edward Armitage do this when he's not the heir at all? D'you mean to tell me the elder brother in Australia gave him the job? On a fifty-fifty basis or something?"

Allwright shook his head. "That may very well puzzle you, Mr. Craven."

This time he looked at me as he spoke. He even slackened his pace a bit. "But I think, when I have told you what I'm going to tell you now, you will find that Lionel Armitage isn't alive. You saw me leaning over Mr. Edward Armitage's desk? Well, there was a letter there on the top of the pile which had an Australian stamp on it. It had also a black edge. You can call me a fool if you like, but I'm willing to wager that Lionel is as dead as the proverbial doornail. And that leads me to the instructions that I am going to give you. Don't walk so fast. Slacken down and we'll just have time."

Well, I listened to more lucid instructions—this time given to me without any sort of paraphernalia.

CHAPTER XIX

The front door wasn't open. I didn't know what to do. Suddenly Allwright appeared at my shoulder. He said:

"If you walk a little way down the west wing there's a side door into the lobby. Go through that lobby and you'll find yourself in the passage to the study where we were before."

I did as he told me. He was, of course, quite right. It crossed my mind that he must be a most annoying man to live with. I got down to the end of the corridor. I tapped on the door and then, following instructions, didn't wait for an answer but opened the door and went right in.

Edward Armitage was still sitting at his desk. He was working on some figures on a slip of paper. He heard the door open. He looked up. When he saw me the colour flooded away from his red face and then immediately came back again. A scowl creased his heavy forehead. He pushed the slip of paper under his blotting pad and glared at me. He got up and said:

"I'm sorry, sir. I'm very busy. I understood from Mr. Allwright that neither he nor you would bother me any more on this very—a—tragic morning for me."

I slid, with my best gigolo walk, up the middle of the big room and stood in front of the table. I said, in the oiliest voice I could summon up:

"I'm very sorry indeed, Mr. Armitage, but Mr. Allwright and I separated. He was taking some photographs and I'm afraid I've—ha!—mislaid both him and your servant. I came back really to see whether he was here." I must have remembered a bit more of the art of acting than I'd thought, because he took it quite well.

"Quite all right, Mr.—er——"

"Trantor," I said.

"Quite all right, Mr. Trantor. Don't apologize. No, I'm afraid I haven't seen him. Perhaps you would care to sit down. Would you take a glass of sherry?"

I sat down, but I refused the sherry. I got on with my job. I said, after we'd murmured some foolish phrases about the weather and the state of the country and so on:

"By the by, Mr. Armitage, troubles seem to be coming on you thick and fast. I hope I may express my condolences, not only about this tragic affair of Mr. Philip Armitage, but also about the sad death of your elder brother, Mr. Lionel Armitage."

I've often read about people's lower jaw dropping, but I've never known what the lady writers meant by it till that moment. He gaped at me just like a codfish. The colour ebbed and flowed in his fleshy face. He said, trying to control himself:

"How the hell . . . I beg your pardon, Mr. Trantor, I have only had the sad news of my brother's death myself for a few . . . er . . . a few . . . a few hours."

"Your brother," I said, going a little closer to the table, "was a very well-known person in Australia. I, too, am an Australian and I heard the news from an Australian friend. I think you're mistaken, Mr. Armitage, in saying that the news of your brother's death only came a few hours ago." That was a bit of my own, but it seemed to work. He shot to his feet and the heavy chair crashed over behind him. He put his hands on the table and leaned over and glared at me. He said, in an almost unrecognizable voice:

"What the hell d'you mean by that?"

I came back to Mr. Allwright's programme. I said, drawing myself up and changing my voice to the one I'd used to poor Smith in the hut:

"Edward Armitage, I am here to arrest you for the wilful murder of Philip Armitage upon the night of the 29th of May. I have to warn you that anything you say is liable to be taken down and used in evidence against you."

He didn't move. He just swayed a bit and I saw that his hands were holding onto the edge of the table. An odd sort of noise came from his throat. I said:

"I am Detective-Inspector Copley of the Criminal Investigation Department. I should also inform you, before you make any statement, that I have here"—I produced the notebook with a flourish—"a signed statement by William Haviland Smith, your manservant, which gives his account of all the details of what took place upon the night of Philip Armitage's death."

I don't know what reaction I expected, but it certainly wasn't what I got. Because he didn't do anything except stare at me. There was an odd look in his eyes though—as if he wasn't seeing me at all. He said:

"So you know I killed Philip . . . and tried to put it on Frances . . . everything . . ." His voice was odder than his eyes. So help me, it was *conversational!* And sort of tired.

But there was nothing tired about the way he suddenly moved—bending over the desk, and yanking at a drawer, and coming up with something that glittered in his hand.

Now I've knocked about the world for long enough to know how to take care of myself. I don't jump at people who produce guns. I make for the nearest cover. Actually, what I did then was to drop down behind the writing table.

Have you ever heard a revolver fired in a room? If you haven't, I shouldn't advise you to court the experience! It makes one hell of a noise!

I got up. I felt a bit shamefaced. I'd thought he was going to pull his gun on me and he'd pulled it on himself! He was lying across the table. His right hand, still holding the gun, was hanging down over the side of the table. In his right temple there was an unpleasing, blue-edged hole. He was extremely dead.

I could have kicked myself. Here I'd gone and let the guy shoot himself, and I was the only one who had heard his confession. I began to get frightened. I even saw pictures of me being accused of having killed him and then trying to make it look like suicide. I'd been so happy I hadn't known what to do. But now gloom came right down on me again. You can imagine my feelings when, through the low-framed, wide-open window at the far end of the long room, I heard a shrill little whistle. I was round the table like a cat. Allwright was standing with his head and shoulders right into the room. He looked at me and, by gosh, he winked. He said:

"It's all right! I heard everything. And everything, Mr. Craven, is what the Americans call O.K." He turned and made as if to go away. I made one dash at the window and got hold of his coat.

"Here! What am I to do? Where are you off to?"

He turned back. He was once more the old Allwright—the brassy-voiced, journalistic Allwright had gone. He said, quietly, with his yellowish eyes fixed on me:

"Stay just where you are. I don't mean in the room—I mean in the house. Presently the police will come. Say as little as you can to the inspector." He twisted his coat out of my hand and was gone. I was left staring after him. I sat down on a chair by the window. I tried to think it all out, but I couldn't.

The inspector, in the same blue Morris car, drove up to the house—I was in the hall then—within half an hour. It had been a long thirty minutes in going, but it seemed short enough as soon as I heard the sound of the car. The inspector spoke to me and was civil, but there seemed a certain restraint about his attitude.

"Mr. Trantor, I believe?" he said.

I nodded.

"I've heard all about this. I'll send a man over to the hut to secure Smith. Now, if you'll show me the study where . . ."

I showed him the study. Other men came in and made notes and took photographs and measured things. And they took away from me my notebook with Smith's signed statement in it. And then, after nearly two hours, I was alone with the inspector again. He said, still with that odd constraint:

"I should suggest, Mr. Trantor, that you come down to the station in Mallow with me. I'm just returning. I think you may probably be of some assistance to Miss Brandon who is, I've had orders over the telephone, to be released immediately."

That shook me. I forgot all about the Trantor business. I said:

"Has Allwright fixed this?" I wanted to shake everybody by the hand and kick everybody's behind and generally behave like a kid. He looked away from me. The waxed points of his moustache seemed to droop disapprovingly.

"Allwright? . . . Allwright? . . . I'm afraid I don't understand." And that was the last word I got out of him—not that I cared.

EPILOGUE

Thirty-six hours after we had said good-bye to the police station in Mallow we were married. The police court case came up the same day and we had, of course, to attend. But there was nothing except formal identification —both there, at the trial of Smith and later at the inquest on Edward Armitage.

We had nothing further to do for at least ten days, so we went on a honeymoon. I don't know much about them, but this seemed to me to be about the best sort of one there could be.

We couldn't understand Allwright. We'd gone back, straight from the police station, to his cottage. We'd found it shut, bolted and barred. We'd asked everyone about him and received nothing but blank looks. At last we couldn't waste any more time and got away on our own.

Two days after our marriage we received a parcel addressed correctly to our hotel. It was addressed to Mr. and Mrs. Peter Craven. It was a small but very heavy parcel. We opened it. Inside it, under many layers of tissue paper and cotton wool, was a beautiful wrought thing in gold. It was the figure of a dog—perhaps the best thing of its kind I've ever seen. Frances went into ecstasies over it. There was nothing in the parcel to say where it came from, but, after a few minutes, we picked it up and glanced at the base. And there, engraved, was the following: "To Peter Craven with all gratitude from a father." That, with the date, was all.

. . . .

There's only one thing more to be added to this story. A few days after we received the statuette we were at breakfast. I was doing nothing except look out over the sea. Frances was looking at one of those morning papers which are full of pictures. I suddenly heard a little cluck of astonishment. I said:

"What's up?"

She got up from her place and showed me the paper. Her forefinger pointed to a small picture at the bottom left-hand corner of the page. It was of the head and shoulders of a man. It was a face which we both knew well. And underneath there was what I believe they call a "caption":

"SUPERINTENDENT DUDLEY ALLWRIGHT

Superintendent Allwright—perhaps the most famous of Scotland Yard chiefs—returned to work to-day. After serious injuries received during his amazingly skilful tracking down of the Burbage murderer, Superintendent Allwright was ordered a complete holiday for four months. Although this time is not quite up yet, we understand that Superintendent Allwright has returned to duty. It is further understood in certain circles that Superintendent Allwright will give sensational evidence at the forthcoming Royalty Gardens murder trial."

"Well, blow me down!" I said. And then: "I ought to have guessed."

THE POLFERRY RIDDLE

CHAPTER I

"Shut it, man! Shut it!" said Trenchard. His heavy, swarthy face screwed itself up almost ludicrously. He pulled a handkerchief from his breast pocket and mopped at his neck and his left cheek. The storm-driven rain, as Banner had opened the window, had come clear across the long room; drops had spattered into the fire, other drops were the cause of the handkerchief.

Banner shut the window. He had some difficulty, but managed it at last.

"Dirty night!" he said.

Hale-Storford laughed; a joyous sound. He was at a side table, fiddling with decanter and glasses. He said:

"It's a good night. If one's inside. . . . Have another, Banner? And you, Trenchard?"

Banner brought his bulk back to the fire, walking with the heavy-seeming but light-sounding waddle of the old sailor. He let himself down into his chair with a grunt. The sound was at once affirmative answer to his host's question and an expression of pleasure—almost delight—at once more being seated.

"Thanks," said Trenchard.

Hale-Storford gave them their glasses; came to them with a siphon. "Say when."

They said it. Banner, with an impatient-seeming twist of his neat iron-gray beard, almost before the siphon had begun to hiss; Trenchard when the whisky was noticeably paler.

Hale-Storford mixed his own. He said, glass in right hand, broad shoulders leaning against the corner of the oak mantel:

"Yes, a damn *good* night if one's inside. . . . D'you know, Banner, that's why I took this place?"

Banner grunted.

Hale-Storford laughed. "Dare say it wouldn't appeal to you. Though I'm not so sure of that. But it does appeal to me. It's nights like this—in this sort of place—that make a house a thing to take joy in and not just a place to use. What do you say?" He looked at Trenchard with the last words. Trenchard shrugged; a half smile lit up faintly his heavy face, which most of the time seemed to express, unwillingly, its owner's anger with the world and the ways of the world. Banner grunted again; his oversolid body seemed to be straining his clothes of gray flannel almost beyond endurance. He said:

"Always the way with you fellows that've lived in a town. Good God! I've seen enough dirty weather in my time to last me forever. What *I* really ought to have is a nice little house called 'Mon Repos,' with trams running by the door every other minute. Some place like Palmer's Green." He grunted again. "Instead . . ."

Hale-Storford put his fair head back and laughed again. "Instead you potter about inside and outside the estuary all day, every day, in a little one-ton ketch that ought to've drowned you long ago. You can't fool me!"

Trenchard laughed now. "Got him there! Though I must say he didn't want to go out this evening. I made him."

"Made hell!" Banner grunted. "Only reason I went out is because I couldn't trust a hog-walloping lubber like you not to drown yourself. And see where your damned trip landed us! If Hale-Storford hadn't just taken this house, where'd we've been? I'll tell you—wet through and through and then through from the back again, and trudging four miles up the estuary to get to the coastguard's place. And I'll tell you what would've happened then, Ralph, my boy! Instead of having a nice sissy silk shirt and a pair of striped flannel bags and a nice chair and more whisky-and-sodas than're good for you—an' a lot of charmin' women to talk to until half an hour ago—you'd have been sitting in front of a fire that belched out smoke at you at every other breath, drinking brown tea out of a cup as thick as that bookcase, and wearing a pair of reach-me-down trousers over your lower parts and a scrubby guernsey next your chest!"

Trenchard grinned. "But our host *had* taken the house; *was* here; *did* happen to see our bit of bad luck."

Banner tossed his bulk about in his chair. "Bit of bad luck! Bit of blasted landlubberly sailing!" His grunts were a crescendo. "The only place you ought to handle a boat, Ralph, is on the Serpentine on Sunday afternoons. *With* braces."

"You finish that whisky," said Hale-Storford, "and shut up grumbling. As Trenchard said, I was here; I had just taken the house, and there you are. And I expect you'd have done just the same thing with that boat yourself. Looks a sow of a thing, anyhow!" He paused for a moment; surveyed his unexpected guests.

Trenchard cut in. "All the same," he said, "luck or no luck, it's damn decent of you to put up with us like this."

"Decent nothing," said Hale-Storford. "I'm no good at pretence. Too busy generally, I suppose; got out of the habit. Damn pleased to see you. . . . I say, you know, most extraordinary coincidence, you knowing Eve."

Trenchard nodded. He did not speak.

"Damn funny, really," Hale-Storford went on. For a moment his usual eager, curt incisiveness had changed to a slower, wondering tone. "To pick up a couple of fellows on one's own beach and find that you'd known one of 'em for twenty years'd be odd enough, but when you find the other's known your wife for—well, I suppose it must be nearly as long, according to what you were saying—then it's *damn* funny!"

Trenchard spoke now. "Oh, it's not twenty years! Steady on a bit! I first knew Eve when she was ten, and that can't be more than fourteen years ago. . . . But it *is* queer. . . . I don't mind what happens, though. So long as nobody says, 'It shows what a small place this world is.'"

"Nobody's likely to here," said Hale-Storford, "except Uncle Percy there. I'll brain him if he does."

"Give me another shot of that whisky," Banner said, "and you can do what you like. How long've you been married? Never read the papers."

Hale-Storford took the empty glass held out to him; crossed to the tray-laden table. He said, pouring whisky:

"Six months. If I'd had my way it'd have been eighteen. But six months it is."

"And after six months you come down to a benighted, God-forsaken, devil-blistered part of the world like this!"

Hale-Storford brought back the glass, filled again. "Take this," he said. "And anyhow, you live here, don't you?"

Banner grunted assent. "But I hog it in a cottage, and nobody takes any notice of me, and I don't take any notice of them. But what do you think you swagger people are going to do . . ." He paused; held up a hand for silence. "Listen to that!" A wild scurry of rain which sounded against the leaded windows like handfuls of grapeshot thrown by angry gods broke the small silence into a thousand pieces. And then, as the rain squall died down, there came again the monotonous howling screech of the wind, below and beneath it the steady, unsubdued "hish-hish" of the sea.

Once more Hale-Storford laughed—a big, alert, trim man. Happiness and well-being irradiated him. "But I've told you I like it. Eve likes it. That's why we took the house. If we hadn't liked it we shouldn't be here. Eve found it; Eve wanted it; and as soon as I saw it I wanted it too. . . ."

"Accommodating husband!" said Banner.

"Accommodating nothing! Eve and I don't always agree, thank God! . . . Fancy living with someone who always agreed with you! . . . but we do over this. . . . She's going to be happy here and so am I."

Trenchard interrupted. "There's one thing, though, you won't get any servants."

Hale-Storford raised his eyebrows. "Think so? We've got two, anyhow. Man and wife. They're coming on Monday. And then there's Mrs. Graye —you met her—she's our sort of housekeeper, you know. That ought to be enough for this place; Eve's arranged for what I think they call 'daily help' from the village."

Banner set down his glass upon the floor beside him with a little thump. His neat beard twitched to a tremendous yawn. His bulk stirred lethargically. He said:

"Bed soon, if you don't mind."

"Have a nightcap?" said Hale-Storford.

"We-ell . . ." The gray beard twitched again. "If you make me. . . ."

Once more the trip to the little table. At it Hale-Storford turned. "You, Trenchard?"

Trenchard shook his head. His dark face had relapsed once more into its usual expression of heavy gloom. He said abruptly:

"Who's that kid? Boy at dinner? He staying here?"

Hale-Storford squirted soda into the glass he was manipulating. "Yes. Young cousin of mine. Just left Ripton. Going to Caius just after Christmas. Nice kid." He came back with the glass; handed it to Banner; received in return for the glass a grunt almost ecstatic; went back to rest his shoulders once more against the mantel. He looked down at Trenchard asprawl in his chair. He said:

"I say! I'm very sorry, I probably made a muck of the introductions. Generally do. If you'd like to get straight before to-morrow . . . Well, there's Eve. You know her, of course. Ha! You've known her longer than I have. Then the tall, dark, handsome woman's her sister. You must know her, by the way."

Trenchard shook his head. "So that's Eve's sister, is it?"

"Yes. And the little fair, silent person—she's not nearly so silent when you know her—that's Susan Kerr, friend of Eve's. And the tall, dignified one, that's Dorothy Graye, our housekeeper. She's had rotten luck. First husband killed in the war; second husband a rotter. He was drowned last year in the *Megantic*, and a good job too, I should say. But he had all her money. . . ."

"Interesting bunch!" Trenchard's smile, lighting up the gloom of his face as he spoke, robbed the words of any incivility. Hale-Storford's quick smile came in answer; the quick smile which made his gravely perfect face into a good-looking boy's. He said:

"Glad you think so."

Banner interrupted. Once more he put down an empty glass with a little thump. He said, looking at Trenchard:

"And he's left out the most interesting one. That's himself. Not often you're such a big bug in the bug world as Dick here. Not at his age, any-how. What are you, son? Thirty-six?"

"Eight," said Hale-Storford. With one of those quick, somehow ultra-decisive movements he turned, took his own empty glass from the mantel-piece behind him, walked across the room, and set it down upon the tray. He said, from the table:

"Still feel like bed, uncle?"

"Uncle yourself! But you're right." Banner heaved his heaviness out of his chair. "Come on, Ralph!"

Trenchard rose. Hale-Storford opened the door. It led out onto the great high hall of the old house. A lamp burnt dimly on a table in the far corner. It sent flickering shadows over the black immensity. As the door opened a gust of wind shook the house from end to end. There were a thousand rattles, a thousand groans; wailings from the eaves and chimneys as the wind eddied round and down them. Banner said into the darkness:

"If this is the sort of night you like, you can keep it!"

"Ssh!" said Hale-Storford. And then, in a whisper: "Sorry! But those girls are tired out. We've only had Mrs. Graye and they've been doing all the work. . . . If you wouldn't mind coming up as quietly as you can . . . There's no carpet yet."

He led them silently into the half light. They saw him at the table with the lamp, and then the lamp's flickering paleness blaze up to a steady yellow light. He picked it up and came back toward them.

"Come along after me," he said.

They followed. At the foot of the stairs Trenchard stopped. They stood in a little group. Trenchard said:

"I say! Where're those dogs of yours?"

Hale-Storford raised his eyebrows. In the lamplight his face looked almost unreasonably boyish. He said:

"They're about. Don't you worry. I've introduced you."

Trenchard grinned and shrugged. "If you say so," he said. "But they're not little 'uns. I was just wondering if they'd resent a stranger answering a call in the middle of the night." He dropped his voice at the end of the sentence to a whisper. "Sorry!" he said. "Didn't mean to make a row."

"That's all right," said Hale-Storford. But his voice also was a whisper. He began to lead the way upstairs. He said over his shoulder:

"Eve was terribly tired to-night."

They went up the wide uncarpeted oak staircase. They trod like cats, but under their feet the creakings seemed like pistol shots. Banner grunted. Trenchard swore beneath his breath. Hale-Storford kept on. He said at the top:

"Damn place sounds like a barrage."

Banner whispered, looking about him in the shadows of the three-sided gallery which was the house's upper floor.

"That noise won't wake anyone. Not if they can sleep through the blow. Just listen to it! Will you listen!"

The wind seemed to have doubled its strength. It tore at the house. It shook the house. It seemed to howl and shriek with fury at the failure of its efforts upon the house.

"God!" said Hale-Storford. Then: "Come on, you fellows!" He spoke in a low voice less carrying than any whisper. "First door's my sister-in-law's. . . . This one's Susan Kerr's. . . . This next one's Eve's and mine." He halted. "There're your two, next each other."

He held the lamp over his head; he looked at his two guests. The soft yellow light made a bright pool in which they all stood. They were just outside the door he had pointed as his own. He said:

"Don't know how you'll fix it. One's a big room, t'other's small. Luckily we got the beds up to-day." He looked at Banner. "You'd better have the big one, hadn't you, uncle?"

"Uncle yourself!" said Banner. And then, staring at Trenchard: "Lord, man! What's up?"

Hale-Storford swung round. . . . The pool of light widened in a flickering circle.

Trenchard was staring at the floor. Not at that part of the floor immediately beneath his feet or his comrades', but at the boards which were just inside the circle of the lamp's light, outside the bedroom door of his host. In the yellow glow his face showed as a pallid blotch. As he stared, his right arm rose to point a rigid finger.

"What's that?" His voice was a harsh, strident whisper.

Banner drew in his breath with a sharp hiss. He said roughly:

"Water. Don't be a damn fool! Water, I said. Somebody spilt some water."

Suddenly they stood, he and Trenchard, in the darkness. . . . But the door and the sluggish, barely glistening streak which seemed to come out from beneath it were bathed in the soft flood of light.

Hale-Storford was at the door. Hale-Storford set his fingers to the door and flung it open. . . .

They heard his voice. "Eve darling! . . . Eve! . . ."

Then, more dreadful than any sound, dead silence. . . .

In the darkness old Banner felt fingers clutch his arm, digging painfully into his biceps. He could see into the room a little; the door was wide. He could see, reflected from the white ceiling, the yellow flood of the lamp.

And then a sound. A sound indescribable. A sound half stifled shout, half sob. The yellow flood of light swayed back, rushed through the doorway; sent flying the darkness between the doorway and the waiting men. . . .

Hale-Storford stood in that doorway. He was steady and still. Too steady, too still. . . .

Banner, with an impatient twitch of his arm, threw off the gripping fingers; took three steps forward.

"What's up, boy?" he said. "What's up?"

Hale-Storford spoke. He said:

"Trenchard, go downstairs. Telephone in the hall. On the table. Ring Polferry Police Station." And then dreadfully his voice seemed to go. His lips were moving, but no sound came.

Banner was close to him now, touching him, gripping his coat and shaking him, saying still:

"What's up, boy? What's up?"

Hale-Storford's voice came back. It was not the same voice. It was a dead, flat sound. It said:

"Eve. Look!"

He turned; took two steps back into the room. Banner followed. In three strides Trenchard was behind them.

Hale-Storford stood motionless, holding the lamp unnaturally high above his head. . . .

"Oh, my God!" said Banner.

From behind him came a stifled gasp, and from beneath the lamp, a voice that should have been Hale-Storford's. It said:

"Trenchard! Telephone!"

Trenchard went.

"Oh, my God!" said Banner again.

CHAPTER II

Superintendent (late Chief Detective Inspector) Arnold Pike of the Criminal Investigation Department sat with his feet upon his desk—feet clad in black boots of an abnormal polish—and gazed out at the four square yards of Thames which was his view. He was trying to think of those poisoned sweetmeats which had been sent to Jacqueline Roget. His thoughts —as he had known they would when he began them—got him nowhere along this line. They persisted most obstinately in staying upon another. He whistled lugubriously and flatly between his teeth, switched his gaze from the bit of river to the glistening toes of his boots, from the toes of his boots to the river again. Nothing happened. . . .

The telephone upon his table rang shrill. He took his feet from the desk and the telephone into his hands in one movement. He listened. He said, "Very good, sir. Right away, sir!" and put back the receiver upon its hook.

He stood up. He straightened his tie. He made one last, and unsuccessful, effort to clear his mind of the line of thought along which it had been running, and left his room. He went along the bare stone-floored corridor, and down one flight of stairs. He turned to his right and knocked on the third door on his left. He was, within two minutes, then in the presence of Assistant Commissioner Egbert Lucas.

Lucas was standing, hands in his pockets, by his window; a window which looked out upon much more river than Pike's. He turned. He said:

"Morning, Pike! Sit down."

Pike sat. Lucas, a tall figure of early middle-aged immaculateness, lounged from the window to sit opposite. Lucas said, tilting back his swivel chair:

"Well, I've read it."

Pike waited.

"I've read it," Lucas said again. "Damn it, I've read it three times!"

"Yes, sir?" Pike was politely inquiring. "Which one, sir?"

"Don't be a fathead, Pike. Have a cigarette."

"Thank you, sir. You speaking like that, I suppose I'm to take you as meaning the Polferry job."

"Suppose be damned! You know perfectly well, Pike, that I meant the Polferry job." Lucas twisted uneasily in his chair, took a cigarette, lit it, threw it away after two puffs; said at last and irritably:

"Well, say something!"

Pike shrugged. "Nothing to say, sir."

"I know that. I've just read your report, haven't I? But I want to hear you say it. All over again."

It was Pike's turn to shift uneasily in his chair. He began to speak but was cut short by the burring of the telephone. Lucas picked it up.

"What's that? . . . Yes, Lucas speaking. Who? . . . Of course I can. Send him up at once. And you needn't ask another time. You ought to know that by now."

He put down the receiver and looked at Pike. A slow smile lightened the gloom. Pike smiled too, dutifully.

"That," Lucas said, "was to say that Colonel Gethryn wanted to see me."

Pike's smile changed from one of duty to one of reality.

They waited.

The door opened and there entered to them, in clothes of an easy elegance putting Lucas's studied effects to shame, the person of Anthony Ruthven Gethryn.

They made much of him. A little too much, he thought. He sat—his favourite place in this room—on the broad, low window sill. He smoked and waited.

Lucas said: "Pike's just come down. We were talking about that Polferry business. Heard about it?"

Anthony grinned. "Not so much as I'm going to hear. . . . Know what I've come for, Lucas?"

Lucas shook his head. "Not unless it's just to pass the time of day with the police."

"I have come," said Anthony, "to say good-bye. Good-bye, anyhow, for six or seven months. We're going away. There seems to be an idea prevalent in the medical profession that Mrs. Anthony Gethryn and Master Alan Gethryn would do better for themselves if they stopped filling their lungs with a mixture of soot and carbon monoxide. Air, sir, and pure air! is the doctor's cry. I must say I'm rather with 'em."

Lucas made unsuccessful effort to hide dismay. But he was brave. "Where is it, this air?"

"Switzerland," said Anthony. He smiled suddenly at Pike. "Now shoot! What were you saying—Polferry? Polferry? Where is it? Country? Let me see, that's where . . . doctors . . . I've got you! That young cancer fellow. Inquest still on. Wife had her head cut off."

Lucas tried to make hay while the sun still shone. "Read it up at all?" he said.

"Nary word. Never read the papers."

Lucas got up and began to wander about the room. "Pike," he said, "has been down there. I will say *that* for the Wessex Police: they asked us to help at once. They didn't wait until they'd mucked everything up."

Anthony looked at him, then at Pike. He said, to the air between them:

"Which worries us most? Getting nowhere or having to tell the Wessex Police that we've got nowhere?"

"Both, sir." Pike was glum.

"Yes, damn it!" Lucas agreed. "And it's so crazy, the whole thing."

"Is it now?" Anthony stood up and pitched his cigarette into the fire. "Bear to let Pike tell me?"

Lucas went back to his chair and sat down. "Could I *bear!*" he said. "Carry on, Pike!"

Pike looked glumly at his shining boots. Pike collected his thoughts. Pike said:

"Don't know whether you know that end of Wessex, sir. Polferry. Practically Cornwall. . . . This house is called the Watch House. It's right on the mouth of the river Starr. There's very high cliffs just where the sea begins, and this house—well, it's right up on top of the westmost cliff. And when I say right on top, sir, I mean right on top. Why, there's a drop outside the drawing-room window of hundreds of feet. . . . Well, Dr. Hale-Storford—you know about him, sir; he's the young doctor that's made such a stir in this cancer research—well, sir, he took the Watch House matter of a month ago. Seems they wanted a quiet place in the country for himself and his wife. He's only been married about six months. Married a young lady called Rossiter—Eve Rossiter. Very happy couple, according to all accounts. Well, sir, they had to keep their London house on, so they'd left their regular servants up in London and got a man and wife who were going to come in in about three days after they took over the house. Dr. and Mrs. Hale-Storford took down with them Miss Miriam Rossiter—that's Mrs. Hale-Storford's sister; a young gentleman called Anstruther—George Anstruther, a cousin of Dr. Hale-Storford's; and Miss Susan Kerr—she's a friend of Mrs. Hale-Storford's; was at school with her; and a Mrs. Graye—Dorothy Graye. She's a lady, sir, who's apparently been unfortunate in her choice of partners and lost all her money. She's been housekeeper for Dr. and Mrs. Hale-Storford ever since they were married. I think it was Mrs. Hale-Storford's mother who got her the job.

"Well, sir, they took over the house on the seventeenth of November. By the morning of the eighteenth they'd got a bit straight. And then, on the second night, Mrs. Hale-Storford gets found by her husband with a great gash in her throat that's bled her to death.

"All very nice, sir. All very straightforward, *up* to there. Where it begins to get what you might call complicated is here. That house, sir, the Watch House, that's absolutely cut off, as you might say, from civilization. And Dr. Hale-Storford's got two big dogs—Great Danes, they are—very fine house dogs. They're in the hall and won't let even a black beetle come into the house without letting everybody know it. The house is locked. All windows, except in one room which was occupied, are latched. All the doors are bolted. The dogs are inside."

Pike paused here, partly, perhaps, for breath; partly, certainly, to order his story.

Anthony lit another cigarette. "Other two men?" he said.

"Right, sir. May as well go on from there as well as from anywhere. On this second night, sir, about seven-thirty, Dr. Hale-Storford's outside the house in the garden. That's on the southeast side of the house, away from that cliff drop I told you about. He looks down at the beach—there's a twisty path leads down from the garden—and he sees a light bobbing about and hears people talking. He goes down and sees a boat, half stove in, on the beach. A private boat, sort of little yacht, I make it. This boat, sir, belongs to a retired naval captain of the name of Banner—Percy Banner —and it turns out that he's an old friend of Dr. Hale-Storford's. He's got with him a man much younger, of the name of Trenchard—Ralph Trenchard. These gentlemen are soaked through and have got nowhere to go, being about five miles from their home port, which is Fraxton, where Captain Banner lives and this Mr. Trenchard is staying with him.

"Naturally, Dr. Hale-Storford, who, as you may know, sir, is a very friendly, open-hearted sort of a man, takes his old friend Captain Banner and Captain Banner's friend Mr. Trenchard up to the house. They have a hot bath and change of clothes and are asked to stay the night, which they do. After dinner—seems to've been a sort of scratch meal, as you might say, got up by this lady housekeeper, Mrs. Graye—after dinner the whole party sit around for a bit in the drawing room, and then—you must remember, sir, that they've been sort of camping out in this big house and moving furniture here and there and doing all the thousand and one odd jobs there are to do on a big sort of a move like that—the whole party, except Dr. Hale-Storford himself and the two what you might call castaways are so tired that they go to bed. That's about half-past ten, sir."

Anthony interrupted. "Half a minute, Pike! Half a minute! That gives us—let me see—Mrs. Doctor, the Rossiter woman who's Mrs. Doctor's sister; the Andrews—no, Anstruther—boy who's Doctor's cousin; the girl Kerr, who's Mrs. Doctor's friend; and the decayed gentlewoman Graye. They're all in bed by ten-thirty. Hale-Storford, Banner, and Trenchard are downstairs. Right?"

"Yes, sir."

"No one else in the house at all?"

"No, sir."

"No one else been in the house at all that day?"

Pike smiled. "No, sir."

"Sure?"

"Yes, sir."

"And the two dogs. Really loose or shut up in rooms?"

"Really loose, sir. Their beds're in the hall. Right at the back of the hall in a little recess under the stairs. They can hear anything from there. It's been proved."

"And they were all right?"

"Yes, sir."

"That night?"

"Yes, sir."

"Next morning?"

"Yes, sir."

Anthony took out his cigarette case again. "A. R. Gethryn now goes to the foot of the class. Carry on, Pike."

"Well, sir, as you say, the whole party, except those three gentlemen, go upstairs to bed at half-past ten. The three gentlemen stay downstairs. Not in the drawing room now, but in the room that's going to be Dr. Hale-Storford's study. They sit there, smoking and chatting and having a glass of whisky or two, for about an hour and a half. The only one who's any good as to actual time is Captain Banner, and he says that about five minutes before they went upstairs he looked at his watch and saw that it was twenty to twelve. When they do go, Dr. Hale-Storford takes the lamp out of the hall and leads the way upstairs. Everything's quiet upstairs, all doors shut. Leastways, sir, that's according to all three of the gentlemen's stories. Dr. Hale-Storford leads the way until he gets outside the door of his own room. He stops there and points out to the gentlemen their two doors just close by. While he's talking, Mr. Trenchard suddenly sees what he called 'a dark trickle' coming out from under Dr. Hale-Storford's door. Gave him an awful turn; and Captain Banner, when *he* saw it. Dr. Hale-Storford takes the lamp, opens the door, goes in, and finds Mrs. Hale-Storford, as I told you, sir, on the edge of the bed with her throat cut halfway round. Stone dead. She was half lying on the edge of the bed with her head hanging down so that her hair—only short hair, sir—was on the floor. The blood from her throat had run out, and owing to the lay of the floor—it's a very old house, as I told you—had run right under the door."

Again Anthony interrupted. "Just a minute, Pike. More fathead questions by Carlton Howe. Ready?"

Pike's lantern-shaped and normally lugubrious face split in an enormous grin. "Aye, ready, sir!" he said. "You'll never forget that Carlton Howe, will you?"

"Don't mock, Pike! A great investigator. Probably at his best in the *Case of the Darts of Death*. However, what I want to know is something about these bedrooms. All on the same floor?"

"Yes, sir. Two-storied house. Upstairs, sir, is just what you might call a big gallery round the staircase. Three sides."

"How many rooms?"

Pike did rapid and silent but lip-moving calculations. "Nine bedrooms, sir; one bath; one w. c.; one big storeroom; one what they call stillroom; one big linen cupboard, and another they call a cupboard, but which looks more like a spare room to me. That makes fifteen."

"H'm. Give us the order?"

"Easy, sir." Pike took paper and pencil from Lucas's desk and sketched rapidly.

Anthony rose. He looked over Pike's shoulder. When the drawing was done, he took it back to his window seat. He studied it for a moment in silence. He said at last:

"Right. Carry on."

Pike shifted in his chair. He seemed to have become uneasy. Lucas too grew restless. Pike said:

"That's what happened, sir. Now for the trouble about it! Dr. Hale-Storford, Captain Banner, and Mr. Trenchard say good-night to all the others—Mrs. Hale-Storford included—at half-past ten. And after that *they stay in the study all the time*. Not one of them went out of that room, *at any time for anything*, until they went upstairs and made the discovery. Upstairs, if we leave out the poor lady that was killed, we've got four people. *And nobody else, sir*. And nobody else *could* have got in! And there was no one in that house besides those mentioned. *But Mrs. Hale-Storford was killed, sir. Murdered*. There's no chance of suicide."

"No knife, I suppose?"

"Exactly, sir. And not a trace of one. I've been over that house and over it. And, as you might say, down through it and up through it. I've been into every corner, over every shelf, up every chimney, into every bit of luggage, through every drawer. . . . Everywhere, sir. And when I say everywhere, I mean everywhere. I've been through all the possible places, and then I thought of you, sir"—here for a moment a faint smile illumined Pike's gloom—"and I looked in all the impossible ones. Still nothing doing." He leaned forward in his chair. He looked first across at Lucas and then up at Anthony. He said very slowly:

"That weapon isn't in that house, sir."

"What sort of a cut?" said Anthony.

"Very, very clean, sir. Very sharp tool did it."

"So, Pike, when you say that tool isn't in that house, you mean that that tool, dirty, isn't in that house."

For perhaps half a second Pike stared, then nodded. "Yes, sir, of course. It could have been one of the razors—but then where are you? . . . Want me to go on, sir?"

"In a minute. Let's see whether I'm up to you. Your trouble, you must be going to tell me, is this: you have got a killing which *must* have been done by someone in that house, and yet you have no evidence against anyone in that house. That right?"

Pike nodded, dolefully grim.

"And of the people in that house it looks more probable that the upstairs bunch contained the killer?"

Pike remonstrated. "More probable, sir? Dead certain, you mean. . . . Unless—unless—oh, gosh! sir, you're not going to say those three gentlemen was all in it together?"

Anthony shrugged. "I'm not saying anything. I'm just trying to take an intelligent interest."

Lucas stared. "What were you thinking of, then?"

"My Creator," said Anthony, "may know. I don't. Just groping, I am. All zeal, Mr. Easy, all zeal! You get me up here, you know, and expect me to listen to these stories and be intelligent. I've got to put up some sort of a show!"

"Oh, shut up!" said Lucas. "Go on, Pike."

Pike looked faint bewilderment. "Where, sir? I mean, what to?"

"You tell *me* something, Pike!" said Anthony. "Let's get rid of facts for a bit. I should say you've had your belly full of 'em. Nasty tricky things, anyhow. Hardly ever spell the truth. Let's have some conjecture."

"Yes, sir." Pike was alert.

"Let's take the case seriatim. Upstairs is more probable. We will start with upstairs. Let's look at this plan of yours a minute. . . . We'll start with Miriam Rossiter."

"Yes, sir."

"What's her age?"

"Forty, sir."

"Look it?"

"No, sir." Pike's head-shake was decisive.

"Good looker?"

Pike was doubtful over this. He said slowly:

"Yes, sir. Has been, very. Dignified type. Tall, very dark. Very reserved kind of lady. One of the sort you think's cold but probably isn't. Just her manner."

"Take this hard?"

"Difficult to say with that type, sir. If you follow me, sir, she's all control, if I can put it that way."

"You can. Relations with Hale-Storford?"

"Very good, I should say, sir. Very good indeed."

"Work? Profession? Hobby?"

"Private means, sir. Seem a fairly well-to-do lot, all of 'em. All of 'em. Don't know about Miss Rossiter's hobbies—not yet, anyhow. Seems to spend seven months out of the year in the south of France and the other five sort of visiting. She's got a little place of her own, sir. Surrey, near Hindhead."

"Right. Next orders, please?"

"Miss Kerr, sir." Pike's previously heavy tone was noticeably lightened, though his face still wore semiofficial immobility. "Young lady, twenty-six. Very neat, sir, very little. What I think you call peteet. Very pretty young lady. Very charming. Lot of pluck too, sir. She seems to have been very fond indeed of the dead lady. They were at school together, and all that. Lot of pluck too, sir. Took it all very quiet."

"Profession? Hobby?"

"Young lady's very well-to-do, sir. Father's Sir David Kerr. Shipping. The young lady, so I gather, is very what you might call horsey. Hunts most of the winter. Got a lot of horses; goes to all race meetings and that."

"Horsey?" Anthony asked. "Huntin', shootin', ridin'—that sort?"

Pike shook his head, firmly. "No, sir, not at all. Know exactly what you mean, but not at all."

"Right. Next, please? That'd be, going right round the corner, the Anstruther boy."

"Quite an ordinary type of lad, sir. Public school, just going to Cambridge." Pike seemed inclined to dismiss Mr. Anstruther.

Anthony did not. "Know anything about him, Pike?"

"Everything, sir."

"What's he look like?"

"Biggish. Heavy built but quick on his feet. Very good at games. Played for Somerset, sir, all last season while he was still at school. Captain of football as well. School was Ripton, sir."

"Face?"

Pike stroked his long jaw. "Ordinary sort of face, sir. Not bad-looking; certainly not handsome."

"Any brains?"

"Oh, yes, sir. Two scholarships to the University, which I take it he didn't want from the money point of view." Pike's voice held a subtle shade of indignation. "Two scholarships at Kyus college, sir."

"H'm! Dressy?"

"Fairly, sir. Not unusually for the age."

"Reactions?"

"Just what you'd expect, sir. Bit dazed at first, then sort of horrified— nearly broke down at the inquest—then, well, I'm not saying anything against the boy, but a bit bored, sort of."

"Quite. Who does he get about with most?"

Pike smiled a small smile. "From what I saw while I was down there, the matter of a week or ten days, he was always *trying* to be with Miss Kerr, and generally *was* with Miss Rossiter."

"H'm! Miss Kerr unkind?"

"No, sir. Not at all, sir. What I mean, though, she naturally didn't want to have this young lad hitched onto her all the time, and Miss Rossiter didn't mind: she's an older lady. . . . She was very nice to the boy, I must say that."

"Right. Let's leave George. Now we come to our decayed gentlewoman. Is she?"

Again Pike's head-shake was emphatic. "No, sir, not at all. Very quiet lady, but not the type you're thinking of. Gives her age as thirty-seven, but I must say that was a surprise."

"Which way?"

"Right way, sir. Thought she was five or six years younger than that."

"Reactions?"

"Great shock, sir. Doesn't seem to have quite the nerves of the other ladies." Pike cut himself short here. His eyes, deliberately blank, searched Anthony's.

"How great a shock? Prostrate? Bed of sickness? Or walk about tremble-tremble?"

"Both, sir. First two days abed. Tried to get up, collapsed, and had to go back again."

"Doctor?"

"Dr. Hale-Storford himself, sir. He just gave her a tonic or some sort of a pick-me-up and told her to keep in bed. She did, for another day, and then she got up. Didn't seem to me that she ought to have."

"Relations with the others?"

"Very good, sir. They treat her well, she returns it. If you know what I mean, sir, she don't seem to let her—well, it's a sort of servant's work, especially in that house—she don't seem to let it knock her pride about at all. And yet she isn't stiff-necked. . . . Afraid I'm not being very clear on this, sir."

"Lucid, my dear fellow! I could draw you a picture of her. What's she look like?"

"Tall, sir, nearly as tall as Miss Rossiter. Fair colouring. Very—how d'you say?—attractive."

"H'm! Friendly with the boy Anstruther?"

Pike shrugged. "Couldn't say, sir."

There was a long silence. Anthony seemed—as so often he had seemed in this room—rapt in contemplation, apparently painful, of Lucas's steel engravings. Lucas tilted back his chair and lay back, staring at the ceiling. Pike, his head cocked on one side, his long face longer even than its wont, gazed at his boots.

Lucas brought his chair forward with a little crash. He said savagely: "Well, we're wasting time!"

Anthony looked at him. "My dear fellow! Yes, I see the trouble. Damned nasty case. Somebody must have done it, but who *could* have done it? . . . Coroner's inquest get anywhere?"

"Get anywhere!" Lucas still was savage. "Get anywhere!! Round and round the mulberry bush!"

"Anyone's fault?"

"Oh, damn it! I suppose not! We're doing just the same thing, or Pike has been. No, that's not fair! Sorry, everybody, this thing's got my nerves on edge. Seems so damn ridiculous! Here we've got four possible people who could have done what was done. One or more of 'em must've done it, and yet we can't lay a finger on anybody! . . ."

He got up suddenly and began to walk about the room. Pike and Anthony gazed at him compassionately. As he walked he went on talking. He said:

"D'you mean to tell me, Gethryn, that, though we *know* we've got the people who did it, we can't get anyone?"

"Haven't told you anything," Anthony was smiling. "But if you'd asked me, that's what I might have said. Assuming the continued lack of evidence, what else can you do but nothing? It's only a microcosm of every case."

"How?" The word came from Lucas like a bark.

Anthony shrugged. "Well, I ask you! If, when we go out to that lunch I'm going to take you to presently, we find a fat man lying in the middle of the road ripped up the belly, what do we know? We know that his belly's been ripped up by somebody in London. But if you couldn't find that somebody, you wouldn't go about saying it was ridiculous. You'd take it as quite normal. And yet, Lucas, you've got the same position as in this Polferry job. Only in the Polferry job your possibles happen to be four. . . . Or I'd rather call it seven, you know. . . . And in the fat man case you've got somewhere around seven million."

Pike laughed; then immediately controlled himself, darting a look of apology at Lucas.

Lucas glared at Anthony. "All very well! Damn clever and all that, and I see what you mean. But you're not being helpful, exactly, are you?"

"My dear fellow! Helpful? You tell me here's a case that nobody can help in, and then you accuse me of not being helpful. . . . There's just two courses for you to follow, Lucas. The first is: Take a fresh piece of paper and do it all over again. That's long and difficult and may get you the same answer. The second and wisest is to call it a miss."

Lucas exploded. "Call it a miss! How the hell can we call it a miss? There's a woman killed. There's four people, one of whom must have done it. Four people and we can't get one. Call it a miss!"

Anthony stood up. "Thinking of Justice, are you? Or a second leader in the *Daily Express?*"

"Both! Both!" Lucas stopped in his walk. He faced Anthony. He said, after a pause:

"Look here, Gethryn! . . ." There was a note of excitement in his voice.

Anthony shook his head. "No. No. Sorry. But the Gethryn family really is off to look for air . . . and anyhow, you know, I shouldn't make any better fist of it than Pike."

For a moment a smile twisted Pike's long face, but it was gone as soon as it had come. He shook his head. "No, sir. That won't do. Remember the Hoode case. Remember the Lines-Bower case. Remember Bronson. . . . You can't remember all those, sir, and then think that you mightn't be able to . . ."

Anthony raised a hand. "It's no good, Pike. I'll say the same to you as I did to Mr. Lucas. The Gethryn family are going for air. You've told me all about it, with the result that I, just like you, know nothing. . . . Leave it alone, Lucas. Leave it alone!"

Lucas stood leaning his arms upon the back of his chair. He said: "My good Gethryn! How the devil *can* we leave it alone? There you've got——"

"Oh! Please!" Anthony's tone was compelling. "Come out to lunch now. Come to Marvel's. I'll give you something to put in your tummy that'll make you forget all about it. Not your tummy, the Polferry riddle. Good title that! Come on out!"

Lucas stood irresolute. Pike rose. Pike went to Anthony. Pike said, in a low and penetrating whisper:

"All very well, sir, but Mr. Lucas is right. Here we are. The C. I. D. We've been called in to make something out of this tangle and we've *got* to make something out of it." His lean face was doleful, but there was a great eagerness in his eyes. "It's like this: It wouldn't matter so much if this could possibly've been an outside job. If it could've been, we might've been able to cook up the usual stuff and nobody could say much to us if we didn't get any forrader. But it couldn't have been an outside job, and the public *knows* it couldn't have been an outside job, and the public *knows* —you may not read the papers, sir, but I assure you there's been a great deal about this case in 'em—and the public *knows* that not only was it an inside job but that there were only four people who could be expected to include the murderer. . . . Now, if you . . ."

Anthony shook his head. "It's no good, Pike. Not a bit. The Gethryn family, as I seem to have remarked somewhere before, are departing from this island at once."

Lucas straightened himself; walked to his cupboard and took out coat and hat and stick. With these in his arms he turned. He said to Anthony: "Mean that?"

Anthony nodded. "Every word of it. . . . Sorry. The best thing you can do with that job is to put it on one side. . . . It's not a murder, you know. Not at all. More like a penny-in-the-slot 'Spot the Winner.' "

Lucas struggled slowly into his coat. He said:

"Did you say anything about lunch?"

Again Anthony nodded. "I did, but I'm double damned if I'll take you if you're going to talk Polferry all the time. Hands off Polferry! Coming?"

Lucas picked up his stick. "Oh, I suppose so. . . . All right, Pike. Let's forget it."

"Forget it, sir?" Pike was incredulous.

"Until," said Lucas, "half-past four this afternoon. You'd better come and see me again then, and we'll both go along to the Commissioner."

Pike's lower jaw thrust itself out until it became almost a deformity. He looked at Anthony. He said:

"Isn't there a chance, sir?"

Anthony shook his head, smiling. "Nary a chance, Pike. Nary a chance. As I've told you once, this sort of job is your sort of job. There's no man anywhere who can touch you at it. You carry on with it. Sooner or later you'll get something. If anyone can, *you* can."

Pike smiled without noticeably lessening his gloom. "Butter's all very well, sir. Very nice on bread and all that."

Anthony grinned. "I know. I know. But I meant what I said. Carry on. Good-bye, Pike, and good luck! Drop me a line and let me know how the show goes on. Funny business. . . . Come on, Lucas!"

Lucas went, and the door closed behind them.

Pike was left staring at its inner side. His lips moved soundlessly.

Anthony was eating marrons glacés. He was also, most unusually, reading an English newspaper. The sky was impossibly blue. The snow upon the slopes of the Roche Menon across the valley was incredibly white. Into the revolving wooden sun house in which he sat the sun streamed; the Swiss sun whose heat is so often in such paradoxical contrast to the thermometer. He turned over the pages of the paper idly. It was an *Evening Planet,* three weeks old. Up the steep narrow path from the chalet came Lucia Gethryn—a white-clad figure of grace and beauty and health. She sat beside him on the wooden bench. She looked at the half-empty box of chestnuts. She said:

"Pig! Oh, pig! One, two, three . . ."

"More, probably," said her husband. "Have one?"

Lucia nibbled. She glanced down at the paper on his knees. She said: "Aren't you well, dear?"

Anthony began to fold the paper. "Eminently. What's fit for you to read . . . Great Scott!"

Lucia turned to stare at him. She knew that tone. He had unfolded the paper again and now read in silence. It seemed many minutes before he set the sheets down upon the bench beside him and rose. He stretched himself then. He murmured something and was gone. After him Lucia called:

"Where're you going?"

He turned in the path. "Telephone. Back in a moment."

Lucia sat looking out across the valley at the dazzling whiteness of the snow slopes. The glare hurt her eyes; she turned her head away, and her glance fell upon the folded paper. She picked it up. There was the paragraph which he had been reading. She read too. She read:

BOY CRICKETER DROWNED
Tragic Fate of George Anstruther
DOCTOR'S GALLANT ATTEMPT FRUITLESS
Chain of Tragedy
(From the PLANET'S *special correspondent)*

Polferry, Wessex.

AT THREE o'clock yesterday afternoon a boating tragedy occurred here, when Mr. George Anstruther, the well known young cricketer, was drowned within sight of the beach jetty.

A most gallant attempt to rescue his young cousin was made by Dr. Richard Hale-Storford, the famous cancer research surgeon. When the accident which led to his death occurred Mr. Anstruther was sailing Dr. Storford's yawl *Bluebird.* He was alone in the boat and had just set out from the jetty. Fishermen and others on the jetty suddenly noticed that the boat was about to founder; it was labouring and apparently half filled with water. They could see young Mr. Anstruther bailing desperately. By an evil chance there were no other craft of any kind available. Two fishermen, Bert Dawling and Albert Tresidder, immediately set off for the next point about a mile along the shore to where a boat could be obtained. The *Bluebird* suddenly keeled over, and the remaining horrified spectators saw Mr. Anstruther disappear. He came up again, however, and started to strike out for the shore, being then nearly a quarter of a mile out. Unfortunately the tide was against him.

Dr. Hale-Storford, with whom Mr. Anstruther had been staying, had in the meantime arrived upon the scene. Seeing that there was no boat yet available in which to go out to help and knowing that his young cousin was far from being a strong swimmer, he stripped off his outer clothing immediately and dived from the jetty. Dr. Hale-Storford himself is a very strong swimmer. Helped by the tide, he made rapid progress, but the onlookers were horrified to see that, when quite a distance still separated the two, Mr. Anstruther was visibly weakening. He then, when Dr. Hale-Storford was about fifty yards from him, sank, but came up again to continue his battling when the doctor was twenty-five yards nearer. Just before he sank for the second time, Dr. Hale-Storford came up with him and clutched at him. The spectators were greatly heartened at this, as they thought that Mr. Anstruther was allowing Dr. Hale-Storford to tow him in the approved manner, and further hope was given to them when a motor launch was seen some way off hurrying toward the swimmers. Dr. Hale-Storford did not at first see the motorboat. He struggled gamely on. When he did sight it, he slackened his efforts and contented himself with supporting his cousin. When the motorboat drew level with the swimmers and dragged them aboard, however, it was found that Mr. Anstruther was beyond recall.

GREAT LOSS

Cricket enthusiasts will be particularly aghast at the tragedy. Mr. Anstruther, who played all last season, when he was still at Ripton School, for his county, was one of the most promising young bats in the country. He was to proceed after Christmas to Cambridge University, where he was certain of getting his Blue. Besides being an all-round sportsman, he was a young man of brains, and his loss will be felt deeply by his many friends. He had few relations, his father and mother, Sir William Anstruther and Lady Anstruther, having died ten years ago. Mr. George Anstruther lived with a guardian, Mr. Hastings Pollock, of The Grange, Bury-St.-Wilfred, Kent. He was spending a long vacation, however, with his cousin, Dr. Hale-Storford.

DOCTOR'S OUTBURST

"Fate must owe me a grudge." These words, spoken in a tone of controlled but indescribable bitterness and pain, burst from Dr. Hale-Storford when he found that, despite all his gallant efforts, his young cousin was dead. Readers will remember that it is less than seven months since Dr. Hale-Storford lost his wife under the most mysterious and astonishing circumstances, and that less than two months ago, Miss Miriam Rossiter, his sister-in-law, was killed in a motoring accident on Polferry Hill.

Lucia finished her reading. There came to her ears the sound of her husband's step, and then his entrance, momentarily blocking the flood of sunshine. She set the paper down. He came and sat beside her. She slipped her hand through his arm and said:

"What's all the telephoning?"

"Just a craving for journalism." Anthony was vague. "All I did was to ring up Stein at the hotel. Asked him whether he could rake up some old papers for me. He could. What're you doing this afternoon?"

Lucia's eyes travelled from her husband's face to the discarded paper, then back again. She opened her mouth to speak, but changed her mind. She got up.

"Tennis, I suppose," she said. "Will you?"

He shook his head. "Not if you can do without me. . . . Let's go and see Alan. Where is he?"

"Out at the back of the chalet with Nannie. Let's."

Arm in arm they went down the narrow path. At the bottom, just as they were turning into the wider sweep which ran round the chalet to the terraced garden at its rear, Lucia halted. Anthony, checked by the hand through his arm, halted too. She looked up at him. His gaze was abstract. He was looking out across the valley to the Roche Menon, but it was plain he saw neither snow nor mountains nor valley. The fingers squeezed his arm.

"Oyster!" said Lucia. "You *might* talk, but I suppose you won't, not until you're . . ."

"Talk!" Anthony, without moving, gave the impression of a man who has just shaken himself. "Talk! You wait, my woman! Come on, where's this kid?"

2

The large and flat and orange-coloured envelope addressed in the angular writing of his good friend M. Stein lay beside Anthony's breakfast plate three mornings later. He made no parade of his interest in it, but it is to be noted that well within an hour he was once more in the little sun house, and once more reading a paper and an English paper. This time it was *The Courier*; date, November 21st of the previous year. He did not have far to look for what he wanted. It was splashed about the front page. The headlines were in even more excitable type than that common to *Courier* headlines.

He read once, and then again. After the second reading he let the paper slip from his hands. It sprawled untidy and unheeded by his feet. He smoked one pipe and then another. He did not seem to hear Lucia's approach. She was, before he looked up, actually within the hut. She sat down beside him, stooped, and picked up the crumpled sheets. She straightened them, smoothed out the front one, and glanced at the headlines. She said:

"I thought so. But why's it worry you?"

Anthony looked at her. "Who's worried?"

"Don't be silly! *You* are. At least, something's on your mind. Ever since you were reading that paper in here the other day—that other paper—you've been miles away somewhere. You haven't written a word. You haven't played any tennis. You *have* been fit to speak to, because, strangely enough, you nearly always are, but to try and sit there and tell me there's nothing on your mind—that's just silly. Especially as I know what it is."

"You know, do you?" He looked at her again. A little smile twisted one corner of his mouth. "Yes, I s'pose you do. What is it?"

Lucia tapped the paper impatiently. "This, of course!"

"What? Lord Otterbourn?"

"Don't be *exasperating!* No, this—*this!* This—what's the man's name?—Hale-Storford business. What I want to know is, *why?*"

Anthony's smile became a grin. "So do I. We must've both got to the same stage."

He became aware that Lucia was, with calculating wrath, eyeing him up and down. He shifted nervously. He said:

"All right! All right! I'll be good! What d'you want me to do?"

"Tell me all about it."

"That, my dear, is not at all a sensible thing to say. If I knew all about it I shouldn't be what you call worried. It's because I know nothing at all about it that I'm what you call worried."

"Just one more bit of rubbish like that," Lucia said, "and I shall fall upon you. I know you're cursing me for being a nuisance, but I don't mind."

Anthony grinned. "All right, all right! I don't think I told you, but just before we left I saw Lucas. Now, he was worried, very. About the Hale-Storford case. And I must say with some reason."

"You mean because it looked as if they must be able to find out who killed the poor man's wife and yet they couldn't?"

"Exactly, Lecoq! I pointed out to him that logically he oughtn't to be worried over that more than any——"

"You would! I don't suppose that made him stop worrying, but I do suppose he asked you to stay and help."

Anthony nodded. "I couldn't, though. Anyhow, what could I have done? Pike had been on the job, and Pike, as you know, is a very good man. . . . No, I forgot all about it, except in the way of an occasional and very passing thought. But I remembered all about it when I was reading that paper the other day. Did you see that paper? Did you see that the boy Anstruther—who was one of the people staying in the house when the Hale-Storford woman was killed—had been drowned?"

It was Lucia's turn to nod.

"And did you see at the end of the account of that drowning that this was the second death, within about six months, of members of that original house party?"

Lucia stared. "No, I didn't." She glanced down at the paper she still held. "Oh, I see. . . ."

"Exactly. Three months before Mr. Anstruther gets drowned, Miss Rossiter gets broken to pieces. Hence all this chain-of-tragedy, Fate's-hand sort of thing. . . . What're you doing?"

Lucia's head was bent over the paper. "Reading." She read. She lifted her head again at last. She said:

"You may not like the way they put it, but surely 'Fate takes a hand' is about right. . . . What did they say at the end of the inquest, by the way?—about poor Mrs. Hale-Storford?"

"What they said at the end of the inquest about poor Mrs. Hale-Storford was that poor Mrs. Hale-Storford had been killed by a person or persons unknown. Not very original."

Lucia pondered. "But surely—surely there was something about a tramp?"

"My dear child, when a coroner or a coroner's jury don't know what to say they always say something about a tramp. Here you have what amounted to an impossibility of the woman's death having been caused by anyone *outside* the house. But they couldn't prove that death had been caused by anyone *inside* the house. Hence your tramp . . ." His voice died away. He bent down to knock the ashes from his pipe.

The sun was streaming fully into the hut, but Lucia suddenly shivered.

"Cold, dear?" said her husband.

"N-no. Somebody walking over my grave. . . . I was just thinking, how terrible for the husband."

Anthony shrugged. "What about the other people who were in the house and who *didn't* do it?"

Lucia held out her hand. "Give me a cigarette, will you? And then start at the beginning."

Anthony gave her the cigarette, held a match to it, said, when it was glowing:

"P'r'aps you're right. . . . On the fifteenth of September, Hale-Storford, his wife, his wife's sister, his wife's friend, his own young male cousin, and his housekeeper move into the Watch House, which overlooks the mouth of the Starr estuary. There are these six people only in the house. There are no servants, and will not be any until the following week. On the sixteenth of September, tired after a day's furniture shifting, the young male cousin, the wife, the wife's sister, wife's friend, and the housekeeper go to bed at 10:30 P.M. Each has a different room. Downstairs Hale-Storford and two stranded friends, a retired naval captain named Banner, and an indeterminate fellow named Trenchard, stay to smoke and drink and talk. The house is locked up. There are two enormous dogs loose in the house, very good watchdogs. It is a foul night. The house is inaccessible except on one side. Probably—almost certainly—no outsider could have got into the house, killed the woman, and got out of the house again.

"Hale-Storford and his two friends go up to bed at about a quarter to twelve. They've been in that room, together. No one of them, say the other two, has left that room since ten-thirty, when the first party went bedward. On getting upstairs they find that Eve Hale-Storford has had her throat cut and has bled to death. The doctors fix the death as having taken place somewhere between ten-thirty and eleven forty-five, which is very, very clever of them. Immediately after the discovery Hale-Storford sends Trenchard downstairs to telephone for the police, and, with Banner, goes round to each of the other occupied rooms. In every case the occupant is either asleep or pretending to be asleep and has to be roused. All are aghast. At the subsequent inquest not even the more nosey questioning nor the concurrent efforts of the police can unearth the slightest reason for any of those persons within the house—including even the apparently impossible suspects, Hale-Storford himself, Banner and Trenchard—wishing to kill Mrs. Hale-Storford. Mrs. Hale-Storford can't have killed herself, for no trace can be found of the weapon which killed her. Verdict of coroner's jury—person or persons unknown, which equals one convenient tramp.

"We are left, then, with four unarrestable possibles—the boy Anstruther, the housekeeper Mrs. Graye, the sister Miriam Rossiter, the friend Susan Kerr. We also have three unarrestable unlikelys—Hale-Storford himself, Banner, and Trenchard."

"But they aren't unlikelys, surely? They must be impossibles."

Anthony looked at her with large grave eyes of sorrow. "Oh, my dear— and oh!"

"But you said just now that those three people were downstairs together all the time and that none of them left the room. Therefore they——"

"My dear Lucia, you're losing your grip, your touch! Those three can't qualify for the impossible class. We've only their word for it that none of them left the room."

"You mean that they might all . . ." Lucia's face had grown suddenly white.

"Exactly. Unlikely, but not impossible."

"Well, I don't care what you say. I think it's impossible."

"What you really mean," Anthony said, "is that it is very, very improbable. . . . Now don't speak, I'm going on. We get left with—let me see— five distinct possibilities. I'll write them down." He took a notebook from his pocket, tore out several pages, and wrote rapidly.

Lucia's eyes followed the flying pencil. She read:

POSSIBILITIES

UPSTAIRS PARTY	1	That the murder was done by one of the upstairs party *with the knowledge of no one else at all.*	100.
	2	That the murder was done by one of the upstairs party *with the knowledge of some other person or persons within the house.*	50.
DOWNSTAIRS PARTY	3	That the murder was done by one of the downstairs party with the knowledge at least of both the others in that party.	25.
OUTSIDE	4	That the murder was done by an outsider entering and leaving the house *without the knowledge of anyone within the house.*	NIL.
DOWNSTAIRS, UPSTAIRS, OUTSIDE PARTIES	5	That the murder was done by an outsider entering and leaving the house *with the connivance of someone or ones inside the house.*	10.
SUICIDE	6	That the killing was done by Eve Hale-Storford herself and that an outsider removed the weapon.	NIL.
	7	That the killing was done by Eve Hale-Storford herself and that someone within the house removed the weapon.	25.

Underneath the seventh point, the pencil drew a flourish of finality. Anthony held out the small sheets of paper. Lucia took them and read again. When she raised her head it was to find her husband looking at her with the small smile which she knew so well. She said, giving back the paper:

"Yes. But aren't some of these—well—almost impossibilities?"

Anthony nodded. "Observe the figures against each point. They're probability marks on a percentage basis. First we have murder being done by one of the upstairs party entirely on his or her own, 100. (2), The murder being done by one of the upstairs party not on his or her own, 50. I think we can assume that the likelihood of a job of that kind being worked out by two people of that kind is only half. Now, (3), that the murder was done by one of the downstairs lot, who *must* have had—because they all backed each other up in their alibis—the knowledge of the other two. Well, I don't think that's worth more than 25. (4), The "lonehand" outsider. No marks at all. The inaccessibility of the house; the presence of the dogs; the intense improbability of premeditation, and the reputed locking up of the house —all these together fairly reduce this fellow's marks to nothing. Then (5), The outsider helped by the insider. I have given him 10. Then (6), Suicide plus an outsider. I've put down nil, but I think I ought to have put minus nil. (7), though, is a different matter. You may think 25 is too much. But I think it must be 25 until we know, if ever we do, a great deal more about the dramatis personæ. . . . Have you got all this? Don't forget you asked me for it. . . . Right. . . . We will pass on to a survey of the events of the next seven months. Now, seven months is not a long time, whichever way you look at it. Yet in seven months there die violent deaths no fewer than two of our unarrestable possibles. The first is Miriam Rossiter, the murdered woman's sister. She is driving down from the top of Polferry Hill, which is by hundreds of feet the highest part of that part of the Wessex coast. Her car swerves or skids or—something, and she goes over the edge, and that's that. It's at night, there's no one about, and she's not found until next morning. That's on the twenty-first of November.

"Four months later, an even shorter time you will notice, Watson, than the seven months I spoke of just now, young Anstruther gets drowned. He is out sailing when——"

Lucia laid her hand on his shoulder. "Yes, yes. I read all that in that paper. What I *don't* see, what I *can't* see, is how it joins on, *really*, to Mrs. Hale-Storford. The poor woman gets killed and nobody knows who did it. That's beastly, but it's not absolutely unusual, is it? And then two of the people who might have been the people who did it get killed too. But they're killed in the way hundreds of people are killed every day. Horrible, I know, but as I see it—— Anthony! You're not going to tell me that you think they're the people who did it and that they—that they——"

She broke off. She seemed at a loss for words, but her eyes searched her husband's face. Anthony smiled.

"Surely! Who's getting mixed now? What are *you* trying to say?"

There came an answering smile, but the dark eyes were troubled still. "I don't know," she said. "You tell me!"

"At the moment you're just being another of the 'chain-of-tragedy, hand-of-faters'; in fact, you looked quite scared at the sudden thought that a Conan-Doyle Nemesis may have overtaken two villains. That's what you're thinking. I'm not . . ."

Silence. Lucia waited. Still silence. She was looking down at the old copy of *The Courier,* now twisted into a tight roll between her fingers. When she did look at her husband she saw that he was once more placidly smoking. She threw the paper down. She said with a little rush of words: "You *are* irritating! Go on! Go on!"

Anthony took the pipe out of his mouth and smiled at her. "Sorry, dear! You know I don't mean to get like this, but I can't help it. What you want me to tell you is what I'm thinking, but I can't, because I don't know. Now, now, that's not clever, it's purely a statement of fact. We've been married quite long enough for you to know me by this time, but you never seem to have understood properly what a tidy mind I've got. That, you know, is really why I'm always getting mixed up in this 'finding-out' business. When I see a thing all unreasonable and all at loose ends, I just have to see whether I can't straighten it out, and it's the same with my own thinking. When my own thinking's just a mess, it isn't tidy, and therefore I won't let it release its untidiness onto the world. I have to get it nicely rearranged and sorted before I can really talk."

Lucia smiled at him. She shifted a little closer along the seat and slid her hand through his arm.

"Even to me?" she said.

Anthony laughed. "Damn you!" he said. "Oh, damn you! I can't tell you what I'm thinking. I don't know what I'm thinking. . . . Look here. The farthest I'll go is to say this. The whole Hale-Storford job's so messy that there must be something wrong with it. There's an original murder. That, because it's been impossible to fix upon anybody, has got eight loose ends to it; if you found one the right one and put a rope round it and pulled it, all the others would jump back properly into their places. But as it is, they're just—eight of 'em—all waving about messily in the breeze. Or all *were* waving messily about in the breeze. Now, two of those loose ends have been cut off. They haven't been cut off tidily. They've been cut off clumsily, so that their jagged remains are untidier than ever. Get me?"

"Yes! Yes! Go on."

"I won't go on because I can't. . . . Tell you what I'll do, though. To-morrow, no, the next day, when I get an answer to a letter I wrote the day before yesterday, I'll talk to you some more. That talk may be to say that there's nothing more doing on the subject, or it may be to say that there is. I can't tell. If I promise that, will you shut up? Can we go and play tennis or something?"

The arm linked in his arm pressed gently. "Yes, I'll agree to that, dear. If . . ."

"If what?"

He tried to look down at her face but could see only the top of her dark head.

"If," said a small voice, "you'll tell me just two more things." The words were slightly muffled. She was laughing.

"Go on, then. P'r'aps I will, p'r'aps I won't. What are they?"

"First, d'you know how Dr. Hale-Storford took this horrible tragedy of his wife's death? Second—I haven't read all that—was that motor accident that killed Miss What's-her-name—Rossiter—a likely motor accident?"

Anthony disengaged his arm. He stood up, looking at his watch. He said:

"It's now two minutes to eleven. After eleven this subject is closed until that letter. First answer, Hale-Storford was as near broken as a good man can be. Second answer, couldn't say until after that letter. Come on, now!"

CHAPTER IV

The long blue Bentley coupé of Miss Susan Kerr pulled up at that corner of the Row which faces the gates at Hyde Park Corner. An impressive car. The loiterers looked at it with mouths slightly more open even than usual. They also gaped, when she got down, at Miss Kerr herself.

Miss Kerr was very small and extremely neat. Her face, when one was near enough properly to see it, more than bore out the promises made by the rest of her. It, too, was small; it, too, was neat; but there was about its very neatness a certain most charming irregularity which had always saved it from the stigma of prettiness.

Miss Kerr, this morning, as upon every morning anywhere, was about to ride. She left the Bentley to its own immovable and superior devices and with neat, swift, strides crossed the gravel path and came onto the tan itself. By the railing which divides the tan from the footpath, was an old and saturnine groom, holding a big bay mare whose every restless but utterly graceful movement, whose every line and every vein told of her breeding.

Miss Kerr smiled at her groom. Her groom saluted Miss Kerr. She walked round the mare, surveying her. She gave a little nod of approval.

"Looks well, doesn't she?" she said.

The old groom's words, when he spoke, came out as mere part and parcel of a steady hissing. He said:

"Looks well enough. 'Orrible 'andful this mornin', though, Miss. Fair rattled me old bones up gettin' 'er 'ere."

"Don't be a pessimist, George." Miss Kerr took the reins in her left hand, a grip of saddle with her right, and lifted the left of her admirable boots.

George, with deftness, put her up. The bay mare snorted; danced; made those little ominous back-to-front rocking movements which are often the prelude to real "standing-up." George caught at her head.

"Stand!" said George. He also said, fortunately not quite audibly, a great deal more.

Susan laughed. "You let go of her head, George. Go on. Do as I tell you."

George, with reluctance, did as he was bid. George also made a remark which apparently had to do with the highly qualified foolishness of some people in bringing such even more highly qualified horses to such an inaudibly unpleasant place as London.

Susan's hands with a horse were the envy of a great part of Leicestershire and many, many show rings. She checked a tendency for biped progression. She put the mare to a walk. She called over her shoulder:

"George, sit in the car and smoke yourself into a good temper. I'm only going twice round."

She did not go once round.

She started down the Row, toward Knightsbridge barracks. First, while the mare showed tendency to dance which must be repressed, at a walk; then, when the mare settled down, at a trot.

About fifty yards before that break in the railings which is opposite the first gate after Hyde Park Corner, a small car backfired. Any excuse, thought the bay, is better than none. She put her ears flat and flung up her heels. She tried—very hard she tried—to get that pretty, wicked-eyed head right down, but she couldn't. Those hands which seemed like feathers could also be strong as iron. Susan laughed. To her a horse wasn't much good if it didn't need riding. There was a little scurry while the argument went on. Tan flew. And then the plunging attempts to start a tear-away gallop were subdued. The mare pranced, but she pranced straightforward and orderly. Susan, her cheeks a shade pinker, her smile serene, looked about. She was now abreast of the break in the railings and consequently the gate across the road. She waved to a girl of her acquaintance and received an answering wave. She began to cross the gap. There was a little line of cars abreast of her, held up by the traffic policeman. The exhaust of one was roaring. The mare's ears began to flatten. Susan bent forward to gentle the arched neck—and then it happened.

There is a great difference in feeling—any horseman will tell you—between that of a horse who *may* catch hold and go with you and that of a horse who *has* caught hold and *is* going with you. Susan had the second of these two feelings, and it is a feeling whose unpleasantness increases in direct ratio with the rider's skill and experience. Susan didn't like it at all. Susan, quite frankly, was scared. The mare had both bits well between her teeth; her neck and head were straight out in one continuous line; she was moving like the wind. By the wild, uncontrolled speed it was plain that for the while, at least, she ran without sense. Something—something quite unusual—had startled her. She had gone off almost as if she had been struck unexpectedly. . . . But Susan was not thinking of any of these things. Susan was occupied with wondering solely what was going to happen to Susan. She did what she could, which was practically nothing. The wind of their going caught at her. It seemed to pour itself down her throat until it was impossible almost for her to breathe. . . .

Vaguely she heard shoutings. Vaguely she saw, streaming past, the roadway and the trees and white-faced scurrying people.

She was almost at the curve at the Serpentine end. . . . She was round the curve. . . . Her breath was almost gone; her arms one throbbing ache. . . .

And then that heaven-sent riding master—Mr. James Tunkin—with his own gray cob and no fewer than four empty-saddled ponies, whose riders were now on their way home. Mr. Tunkin saw her coming. Mr. Tunkin saw what he might do, with a bit of luck. And, like the good fellow he was, he promptly tried to do it. Tried and succeeded. He spurred the old cob into the very centre of the way, and the ponies, as Mr. Tunkin had hoped they might, fanned out in a jiffling, terrorized fan. He managed—quite how, he doesn't know to this day—to keep his hold on their leading reins. And for just the one necessary moment, he, his cob, and the four ponies blocked the Row from rail to rail.

No more than any other horse would Susan's bay mare override either another horse or a man, but up to the very last moment she maintained her stampede. Then at the last moment she checked.

Susan, her legs without power to grip, her head whirling, her breath gone, tumbled forward and over. She landed sitting. She was right between the forefeet of Mr. Tunkin's gray. She said afterward that the first thing she really remembered after the start of that bolt was sitting there and looking up at two faces. One a frightened gray equine face, and the other an astonished brown human face.

"Gord save us all!" said Mr. Tunkin.

Susan fought for her breath. Before she had quite got it she smiled at the two faces. She said:

"He seems . . . to have . . . had . . . a pretty good . . . try." And then she began to laugh.

"Gord stiffen me!" said Mr. Tunkin.

Somehow he scrambled off the cob. Somehow collected all those myriad reins into one hand. Somehow stretched out his other hand and pulled Susan to her feet.

At that moment Mr. Tunkin's fortune was made. Within three years he had almost forgotten those lean times when he had been merely a struggling Bayswater jobmaster. Susan never forgot her friends any more than they forgot Susan.

She did not say much to Mr. Tunkin then. Still holding his hand, she stood up, struggling for breath. And then, with a heart-catching banging of clutch and screaming of brakes, the Bentley drew up beside the rails. It was not on the road. It was on the path.

"*George!*" cried Susan.

George, despite his sixty years, was already out of the car and over the rails. As he came there issued from his lips a sound like many kettles, all boiling.

"George," said Susan, "I didn't know you could drive the car."

George hissed. "Can't," said George, "and 'ow many times 'ave I told you that it's sheer bloody foolery to bring a bloody horse like this to a bloody place like bloody London. That's the worst of you bloody kids. You never know when to bloody well stop. The bloody thing might 'a' broke your bloody neck *and* 'er own—not but what that last wouldn't 'ave been a good job. Look at her now, standing there looking as though butter wouldn't melt in her bloody mouth."

"Now then," said Mr. Tunkin at last, "language."

Susan reeled; clutched at the railings. George leaped for her, but checked his leap when he saw that the stagger's cause was laughter.

He walked off to where the bay mare, now placid, was nearly staking herself in an endeavor to reach the rhododendron leaves.

2

Bird, who was the butler of Sir David Kerr, closed the door of the library behind him with even more than his usual softness. A small frown of bewilderment creased the expansive and usually placid brow. At the foot of the stairs he saw coming down them Hewson, who was Sir David Kerr's valet. When their heads were level Hewson said:

"Get anything?" His voice was the trained non-carrying subtone of the experienced servant.

Bird shook his bald head. The frown increased. "Don't know what's up with him. Walking about up and down in there like a caged animal. Really wild, Hewson, white of the eye and all that. Hardly seemed to know I was there, if you know what I mean. And when I did cough and ask him whether he'd like a drink and then tried to get the usual out of him, all I got was: 'Don't talk to me about *horses.*' It wasn't the words so much as the way he said 'em. You'd have thought, m' lad, that instead of horses being, so to say, his religion and his work, they were his anthemma."

"Who's that?" said Hewson.

"A word, Hewson"—Bird was all benevolent superiority—"meaning a thing that you can't abide more than anything else."

Hewson whistled. "Said that about 'orses, did he? . . . Oh! *I* know! Did he go round to the mews before he came here?"

Bird nodded gravely. "Why?"

"He's been talkin' to George, that's what it is. I saw George for a minute just now when he brought the horse back. That new one. 'E muttered something about her having 'ad a spill or something."

"That's it, then." Bird's tone was no longer bewildered. "I'll try to catch 'im before he goes out. He'll be all right after a couple of hours, when *she's* down. I did want to know about that Guiding Star. If you look at the weight, Hewson, that horse has got to carry, and him only the age he is, I don't see——"

"Bill-oh!" said Hewson out of the corner of his mouth.

Bird bill-ohed. He proceeded up the stairs with massive dignity. On the landing he stood aside with grave humility while Susan brushed by. He must have caught something of her smile, for he, too, was smiling when he went on his way.

Trevor Heath, once a Squadron Leader in the Black Huzzars, now the second most successful trainer and steeplechase rider in England, was still prowling up and down the library of his future father-in-law's house.

The hearth was littered with cigarettes which he had lighted only to throw them away as soon as he found them in his mouth. His thin, clean-shaven face was of a curious gray pallor; a deep frown pulled together the fair brows over the deep-set blue eyes.

The door burst open; was slammed again. Inside it stood Susan. Susan very small, and Susan very neat. A Susan, in fact, against whom it seemed impossible to harden one's heart.

Generally, on these rare mornings when Trevor got up to town so early, their meeting place in this room was less than three feet from the door. But to-day Trevor stood his ground and Susan checked her advance.

"Trevor!" said Susan.

He threw away the fourteenth untasted cigarette, and looked at her. "Trevor!" said Susan again. She came forward slowly.

He stood his ground. She came up to him. He had his back to the room's one window, and his face was in shadow. She peered at it.

"*Trevor!*" she said for the third time. Then: "What's the matter, dear?"

He moved now. He took her by the shoulders and thrust her into a chair;

went back to the fireplace; stood, his hands behind his back, still staring at her. He said:

"I've been talking to George."

Susan was out of her chair and close to him in one movement. She put up her hands and took between the fingers and thumb of each a lapel of his coat. She said:

"Trevor darling! . . . That's what it was! You are a devil, you frightened me! I thought it was something really wrong."

He exploded at that. "Really wrong!" he said without opening his teeth. "Susan, will you go and sit down!"

She went back to her chair. She sat in it very straight and prim, her hands folded in her lap. She looked like a patient schoolgirl waiting for a necessary but harmless lecture from a doting parent.

There was silence. Heath, his face still set, and with none of the colour back in it, looked at her. Susan waited. Still silence. At last she said, in a voice very small:

"I've sat down, Trevor. Can't we get it over?"

"You little devil!" he said, and then: "For the last time, Susan, will you give me your word that when you're in London you'll only hack reasonable horses? This must be the fiftieth time I've asked you! You keep buying these damned show young 'uns that ought never to have left their damn grass country and start——"

"Trevor!" A very small voice indeed. "Trevor, nothing's ever happened before, and it *does* do them good. I'm not quite a fool, you know, and I can do more with that sort of horse after three months in London than——"

"Be quiet! There's only one issue at present, and that is, will you or will you not promise me now that you'll stop it?"

"But, darling——"

"Will you or will you not give me your word now that you'll stop it?"

"I—Trevor—I wish you wouldn't look like that. I don't like it. I think it rather frightens me. *Please*, Trevor!"

"Will you or will you not give me your word?"

Again a silence, and then a smaller voice than any yet:

"Well, I s'pose I must." She stood up. "That's on one condition, dear, and a very important condition."

"Which is?" The man's voice had changed now. Once more she was close to him. Once more her hands were on his coat. She said:

"On the one condition—that you never look like that again. *Never!*"

His arms came out and closed round her. . . .

"And that," said Bird to Hewson, after coffee had been taken into the dining room one and three quarter hours later, "is that. All clear now. I'll catch him before he goes out. Anything you want to know?"

"Only what I told you. Guiding Light."

Bird nodded; moved off with pontifical dignity. Inside the dining room talk had come back, pleasantly enough now, to Susan's adventure of the morning. Heath was saying:

"Wonder what sent her off like that? Some damn-fool kid, I suppose, with a handkerchief or something."

Susan shook her small head of smooth gold. "She's not that sort. Besides, I'd just passed about a dozen handkerchiefs and about a hundred and twenty cars all with their cutouts open, and she'd never taken what you could really call any notice at all. . . . No, it was very funny, Trevor. Just as we got opposite that opening near the Hyde Park Hotel gates—you know; just as we got there she seemed to fly-jump about thirty feet, and then she was off. It was just as if somebody had hit her. Most extraordinary thing. . . . Trevor! What *is* the matter now?"

At a quarter to three there was a tap on the door of Bird's pantry. Bird knew that tap. He did not worry himself to conceal the port. He called, and Hewson came in, a look of eager inquiry on his sharp face.

But Bird shook a bald head. "Not our lucky day, m' lad."

Hewson sat down. "Damn it! Miss him or something? Or hasn't 'e gone yet?"

Bird drew down the corners of his mouth. "Oh, he's gone all right, blight him! And there *she* is, bless her, crying her eyes out in the libery! *I* don't know what's up to-day!"

Hewson scratched his head. "Thought you said they were all right at lunch?"

"And so they were. As all right as all right may be. No, something else happened. Just after I'd taken in the coffee, they were all right then. Bit later, though, not more than five minutes, just as I was going by the dining room I could hear his voice: very angry, it was. I couldn't catch his words, but he was angry all right. I've never heard 'im like it, not even this morning. And then, just as I got past, the door flies open and out 'e comes. Doesn't wait for me nor nobody. Just grabs his hat and stick then, biff! the door's open, and bang! the door's shut. Exit Captain Trevor Heath and our chance of a few bob next week."

Hewson continued to scratch his head. "Fair knockout!" he said.

Bird nodded dolefully. "It is that! . . . Glass of port, son?"

"To tell you the truth," said Hewson, "I don't mind if I do. What's this? The 1901?"

"'o8," said Bird. "It's better."

3

The room of Superintendent Pike was noiseless save for the heavy ticking of his clock and the busy scratching of his pen. He was finishing his final and confidential report on what the evening papers had been calling "The Great Contango Mystery." It was a good report, and he was pleased with it. He threw down his pen and with a sigh stretched and searched about in his pockets for pipe and tobacco.

His door opened to admit Jordan. Jordan was one of the Big Four and looked it. He was big enough, as people had often said, to be all of them.

"Finished?" he asked, and sat himself down upon a corner of Pike's table. The table creaked. Pike nodded. He clipped together the seven buff sheets and handed them over.

"There it is, only don't read it in here. Study it by yourself to spare my blushes. It's all right, though."

Jordan folded the papers and slid them into his breast pocket. "Who's that," he said, "in your waiting room? Walking about like a tiger or something."

Pike started; pursed his lips into a silent whistle. "Gosh!" he said. "He's been waiting a bit longer than I meant." He reached out for a card that lay on the desk.

"Who is it?" said Jordan again. "I had a snoop at him through the transom. Face looks familiar somehow."

Pike read from the card. " 'Trevor Heath, The Uplands, Newmarket, Bucks Club' . . . Isn't that that . . ."

"That's it!" Jordan said. "Good bloke, I think. He's the lad that trained Whisky for the National last year, *and* rode him *and* won. Going to marry that Kerr girl, isn't he?"

Pike shrugged. "Not a racing man myself. You float off, and I'll see what he wants. Insisted on seeing *me,* for some reason."

Jordan went. Pike pressed a bell upon his desk. Within two minutes Trevor Heath was in the room. Pike rose to meet him. His long face was now gravely, lengthily official. After a murmured greeting he set a chair; sat down again himself. He said:

"I'm very sorry, sir. Afraid I've kept you waiting rather a long time. What can I do for you?"

From behind the official mask he studied his visitor. Sound man, he thought; straight, I'd say; angry or frightened. Or both. . . . Yes, probably both. . . .

Trevor Heath put hat and stick down upon the floor beside him. He sat upon the edge of his chair and leaned forward, staring at Pike. He said, without preamble:

"It's about my fiancée, Miss Susan Kerr. . . ."

Pike repressed a start. He remembered the name now, Susan Kerr . . . Susan Kerr . . . He knew her—one of those people who had been in that house at Polferry; that very odd house party at Polferry; that house party at Polferry which Pike, for Scotland Yard's sake and his own, would rather forget. He said, with a polite resignation he was far from feeling:

"Miss Kerr, sir? Is that the daughter of Sir David and Lady Kerr?"

Heath nodded. "Yes. And I think you know it, Superintendent. They wanted me outside to see somebody else, but I wouldn't see anybody else because I happen to know—I know from Susan, as a matter of fact—that you're the man who went down to Polferry from the Yard about the murder of Mrs. Hale-Storford. That's right, isn't it?"

Pike nodded. It was a cautious movement but definite assent.

"Right! . . . Forgive me—I can't tell you this sitting down. I must get up and walk about." He jerked himself out of his chair and began to stride about the room. Pike sat still, following him with his eyes.

"Don't quite know where to begin," Heath was saying. He spoke savagely. Pike's gaze noted his pallor, his jerkiness; saw that some great force was moving the man. Pike said gently:

"Try the beginning, sir. From what you say I gather it's got some connection with the Polferry murder."

"Some connection! By God, it has!" Heath was at the table now. He stood leaning his hands upon it, gazing down at Pike with eyes that seemed afire. He said:

"All right, I'll try it. You know that Polferry case. You know—whether you say so officially or not—you know yourself that the Hale-Storford woman was killed by someone in that house. Don't you?"

Pike's long face did not change its expression. He said quietly:

"Answered your own question, haven't you, sir? Please go on. Wouldn't it be better if you sat down?"

"Sat down!" said Heath. "Sat down! That's what everybody's been doing, especially you people up here. Just sitting doing nothing, while there's some damn fiend about who's killing—yes, man, *killing* I said—and after he's killed, just laughing at you up his foul sleeve."

"Try sitting down, sir." Pike's woodenness seemed, paradoxically, to have a soothing effect. Heath sat down. He was silent a moment, fighting obviously for self-control. He said at last:

"Sorry! Been making a bit of a fool of myself. But this thing's beginning to shake me up. . . . Look here, Superintendent, has it ever occurred to you to wonder at all about those other two deaths?"

Pike's expression was a mild question. Heath jerked himself about in his chair. He said:

"Yes, yes! I suppose you can't answer leading questions like that. I won't ask any more. I'll say this, though. It *has* occurred to me to wonder about them. First the Hale-Storford woman, and though it's murder nobody can find out who did it. Then her sister, and that *looks* like an accident. And then that kid Anstruther, and *that* looks like an accident too."

"One moment, sir!" Pike had weighed up his man. He had decided to become human. He said:

"You must realize, sir, that whatever the papers and the writers of detective stories say, we're not all fools up here. I admit that the Hale-Storford death got us guessing, but then as you might say, there must be cases every now and then which would get the Archangel Gabriel guessing. In regard to these two subsequent deaths, sir—well, not being fools, as I've said, and the coincidence being what it was, we naturally looked into those very, very carefully. A lot more carefully than they would have been looked into, I might tell you, in the ordinary course. And the result was——"

"Yes?" said Heath eagerly, leaning forward until he almost slipped off his chair.

"The result, sir, was that we found there was no occasion whatsoever for supposing that the deaths were due to anything but bona fide accidents. In the second case it was found that the plug in the boat which Mr. Anstruther was sailing was faulty—and that happens to many boats at many times; in the first case—well, I don't know whether you know Polferry Hill, sir, but it's a very dangerous road indeed for anyone, let alone a lady, to drive down at night. As a matter of fact, the Council have been considering doing something to make it safer for the last two years. Unfortunately they've only been considering. It's only a twenty-six-foot road, and along parts of it there's practically a sheer drop on the off side. It was at one of those points that Miss Rossiter swerved and tipped over. What led her to swerve it's impossible to tell, but it's also impossible to say that such a thing couldn't be an accident. In fact, such accidents happen practically all day, as you might say, and every day. . . . Now, sir, you go on."

Heath seemed more at ease now. He sat back in his chair and crossed one long horseman's leg over the other. He even looked at Pike with the beginnings of a smile. He said:

"You're being very decent to me, aren't you? . . . Right, I'll go on. What would you say, Superintendent, if I were to tell you that unless somebody does something and does something quickly and thoroughly there's going to be *another* accident?"

Pike pursed his lips. It was the only movement in the long face, but his small brown eyes were very keen. He said, after a pause:

"P'r'aps you'd go on, sir. You haven't told me much yet, you know. When you've given me your grounds for saying what you said just now, then perhaps I'll tell you what my views would be."

Heath, now that he had been drawing near to his real point, became restless again. He grunted apology; got up from his chair; once more began to pace about the room. Pike sat solid, only his eyes moving as they followed the figure of his visitor.

"The accident," said Heath, in a tone so savage that momentarily Pike almost lost his mask of composure, "the *accident, if* someone doesn't do something, is going to be to Miss Kerr. This morning, while Miss Kerr was riding in the Row, somebody did something to her mount which made it bolt. Miss Kerr might easily have been killed.

"About three weeks ago, when Miss Kerr was driving back at night from Ranelagh, a big car, going very fast indeed, came straight at her as she turned into the main road out of Ferrier's Lane. Miss Kerr was alone in the car. Because she's a very fine driver indeed, and because she's got the nerve of about ten men, she got away with her life. Instead of braking, as ninety-nine out of a hundred women would have done, she slammed her foot down on the accelerator. As it was, this car smashed into the rear of hers and actually took off her spare wheel. She stopped her car and hopped out, but she wasn't quick enough. The other one had gone. She couldn't read the number; there was no rearlight. That's *One!*"

Heath fell silent for a moment. He walked round until once more he was standing by his chair. Pike saw that his pallor had increased. He said, leaning his hands upon Pike's table:

"That's One! Now Two: Ten days ago Miss Kerr and I were coming out of the Diplomat's Theatre, again at night. You know the sort of scrum there is there as a rule. It's a very small place, and the exits are very wide, and the crowd simply surges out. I left Miss Kerr on the curb while I went for a taxi. I was very lucky, I got one quick. I perched on the running board and came back with him—coming down, that is, from the corner of Shaftesbury Avenue. I suppose we were about twenty-five yards from her—I could see her quite plainly—when there seemed to be a sudden lurch forward of the mob behind her. . . ."

Pike, who had been listening intently, but with his eyes fixed upon his blotter, looked up in surprise at the sudden silence. Heath had covered his eyes with his hand, but almost immediately he straightened himself, dropped the hand, and went on. But now his voice was the level flat voice of the man who is determined at all costs to be unemotional. He said:

"We were, as I say, about twenty-five yards away when I saw this sudden surge of the crowd. There was a bus coming up the road, coming up, that is, on the same side as the theatre. This what I have called lurch of the crowd seemed to shoot Miss Kerr forward. She fell sprawling into the road right in front of the bus. Again through good driving—this time the bus driver's—Miss Kerr was saved. How that man stopped the bus as he did I don't know. He had to skid her to do it. When it was finished Miss Kerr's head was lying about two inches off his near-hind wheel. She wasn't hurt at all. By the time I'd got up and seen her all right and thanked the bus driver and answered the damn fool questions some officious bobby was asking, it was too late to *do* anything. I didn't say anything to the bobby, but I went about among the people who'd stayed to look. All they could tell me was that somebody coming down the steps of the theatre behind the press on the pavement had seemed to stumble. A man, they thought it was, but even that they weren't sure of. Anyhow, they said that this stumble seemed to push everybody forward on top of everybody else, and Miss Kerr was the last one, and not being ready—well, I've told you what happened. . . . That's two, Superintendent, *two*. Two of your *accidents* in under three weeks. But that wasn't enough. To-day we got Number Three. I've told you about that."

He seemed about to say more; then closed his mouth. He sat down. He waited.

Pike raised his eyes from the picture he had been drawing on his blotting pad. His voice was devoid of expression; now even his eyes seemed guarded. He said:

"Yes, sir. This third one you talk about—the horse accident, I take it you mean—can you tell me anything more about that?"

Heath hitched up his chair. He rested an elbow upon the table and his chin upon his hand. He seemed suddenly tired. He said:

"I can. This afternoon, with the groom, I examined that mare. The groom showed me something that he had found, not at once when he brought the mare home, but later, when he was dressing her. What he had found was a little, very deep puncture in the near quarter. When he first found it, it'd had a drop of blood congealed on the top. When he removed this scab fresh blood had welled up at once. Even when *I* saw the mare, less than two hours ago, fresh blood would well up each time the scab was taken away."

"I know nothing of horses, sir," said Pike's quiet voice. "Have you ever seen a small wound of this description before on a horse?"

Heath shrugged; an impatient movement. He said:

"How the devil can I tell you? It's the sort of place which might be made by any sharp thing which had been jabbed into the animal. I may have seen a hundred. If I had, I should never've remembered them enough to have noticed 'em. . . . Tell you what, this was about the kind of place a horsefly would make, but multiplied by about twenty."

"And it couldn't have been a horsefly, sir?"

"My dear feller! . . ."

"I see, sir. And it's impossible to account for this mark on the horse in any ordinary way. It couldn't have got it in the stable?"

"Absolutely impossible."

"And you think that whatever caused this mark . . ."

"Made the mare bolt? Yes, I do. I don't think, I *know!* What Miss Kerr told me of the way she started off is proof."

"Are you trying to tell me, sir"—Pike's voice was still a level, official monotone—"that you think this wound was caused by someone deliberately, with the intention of making the horse bolt?"

"Damn it, man! That's what I'm saying, isn't it?"

"All right, sir. Don't let's get heated. I'm only trying to get to the bottom of this. Now, if you think that, will you also tell me how you think the wound was caused?"

Heath shook his head wearily. "You've got me there. Can't have been done by anyone else mounted, because Miss Kerr knows there was no one near her. Anyhow, you can't very well lean over and jab a spike into another feller's horse without being spotted. And I don't see how it could possibly have been caused by anyone on foot. You can't get near enough to the other side of the railings, for one thing, and anyhow, Miss Kerr says she was quite twelve feet from the edge of the tan."

For a moment Pike's eyes looked straight into his visitor's. Pike said very slowly:

"So you have no idea at all, sir, how this could have been done? . . . No idea at all?"

Heath laughed. A surprising sound, but it was a laugh which had no mirth in it. He said:

"Well, I've got a damn-fool idea, but it's not the sort of idea you could say in cold blood at Scotland Yard."

Again Pike looked at him. "*Is* your blood cold, sir?" he said.

Heath stared for a moment. Then: "By God, it's not!" he said. "You're right. Well, I'll tell you: laugh if you like. I think that place on that horse was made by a large-sized slug from a large-sized air pistol."

"And that the air pistol," Pike broke in, "was fired from a motorcar, either stationary or moving slowly along that side of the road nearest to Miss Kerr?"

Again Heath stared. "By God! That's exactly what I do think!" he said. "You don't mean to tell me you agree?"

Pike shrugged. "Can't go as far as that, sir, but certainly the idea had occurred to me while you were talking."

Heath leaned forward in his chair and took out a cigarette case from his hip pocket. "Have a smoke," he said, and held out the case. Suddenly Pike sloughed officialdom completely. His lantern face cracked into one of his disarming grins. He said:

"Very kind of you. I will."

There was silence while two cigarettes were lighted, and while, in part, at least, they were smoked. It was Heath who spoke first. He flicked ash into Pike's ash tray and said:

"Well? What are you going to do?"

Pike looked at him. "I'll be frank with you, sir. I don't know. After what you've told me I've got to talk the matter over with my superiors." He looked at his watch. It was four o'clock. "If you'll give me a telephone number, I'll ring you up at, let me see, half-past five. Will that do?"

Heath got to his feet. He bent down and picked up hat and stick. He said, straightening himself:

"Thank you. It will."

He held out his hand; he smiled. "You must forgive my madness," he said. "But this isn't exactly . . ."

Pike shook the hand. "I quite see, sir, and if I may say so, I sympathize. Very difficult position."

4

Heath, now in a dinner jacket, for it was seven o'clock and more, sat where he had sat in the afternoon. Across the table he stared at Pike, in his blue eyes a sort of baffled, hopeless anger which knows itself unreasonable. He was saying:

"That's final, is it?"

Pike nodded gravely. "I'm sorry, it is. After all, Captain Heath, you must, as a man of intelligence, see the chief's point of view. In spite of the very flimsy evidence—now, don't fly at me, sir, because, if you look at it from our point of view, flimsy it is—in spite of that, the chief said he would be prepared to give Miss Kerr police protection for a reasonable period *if* she herself were to apply for it. You say that you've tried Miss Kerr and that Miss Kerr won't hear of such a thing."

Miserably Heath nodded. "That's right. I didn't tell you before, but we've had God Almighty's own row about it."

Pike shrugged. "Exactly, sir. Well, what can we do? Miss Kerr won't apply; she's the party concerned . . ." His voice trailed off into silence.

Heath got up. "Well, I suppose there's nothing for it. I shall have to knock off work and do the job myself."

"Look here, sir." Pike rose with his visitor. He was entirely human now; nothing about him of the policeman. "Look here, sir," he said again, "if you take my advice you'll patch up that quarrel with Miss Kerr. I hope you don't think I'm being impertinent, sir, but I've a reason for it. Patch it up, and then you can keep next to her. And if you see anything which seems to you corroborative of what you've seen to-day, you get onto the nearest telephone and let me know. And then—well, I can't promise—but *I'll* do my level best to help you."

Heath endeavoured to smile, failing rather wretchedly. "Right-ho, I'll do that. You've been very decent to me, you know, Superintendent. . . . I say! Is it any good, any good at all, my getting her people to—— Oh, damn! They're away, but I expect I could cable 'em."

Pike considered. "Miss Kerr—is she a minor, sir?"

"Good Lord, no! She's twenty-five."

Pike shook his head gloomily. "Sorry, sir, afraid that wouldn't be much good. The chief was very definite."

"All right." Heath's tone was blackly despondent. He picked up his hat. "I must do the whole blasted job myself. I suppose you're right and we must patch up the quarrel. But of all the blasted silly ways——" He cut himself short. He snapped open the hat and turned round, holding out his hand. "Good-night, Superintendent. I won't forget what you've told me. As soon as I hear anything, you bet I'll telephone you."

Pike shook the hand and opened the door. But as soon as he had opened it he shut it again. He said:

"Half a minute, sir. Half a minute!" He seemed excited. He also seemed as if he were trying to make up his mind. Apparently he made it up for he said:

"Look here, sir. If I give you a bit of advice, a sort of tip, *as a purely private person*, will you take it as coming from a purely private person? Even keep my name out of it?"

Heath looked at him and nodded. A nod which Pike found, looking at him, as decisive and satisfactory as many a man's oath. Pike said, dropping his voice:

"It's this, sir. D'you happen to know Colonel Gethryn by any chance?"

"Gethryn?" Heath's voice showed rather incredulous surprise. "Yes, I know him, but where did you get the 'Colonel' from?"

Pike smiled. "I know he doesn't like having the rank used, sir."

"But he isn't a colonel, man! Lord, Sam Gethryn hasn't even got enough brains to ride a horse properly, although he does try."

Pike shook his head. "Oh, no, sir, no! I think you must be meaning some other gentleman of the same name. Colonel Anthony Gethryn, I mean, sir. You must have heard——"

"Oh, that one!" Heath's tone showed signs of excitement. "And now I come to think of it he's some sort of cousin of Sam's. Why?"

"Well, if you could get hold of him in some way or other and put your trouble to him, I believe you might do yourself and me—everybody, in fact —a good turn. I wanted Colonel Gethryn to come in on this Hale-Storford case right from the beginning, but he couldn't at the time. Knowing him as I do, I should think he'd been away quite long enough, even for him. If you could get him, sir . . . what I mean, if he *did* take an interest in this, I think something might begin to happen. I can't ask him myself, even unofficially."

"I see." Again Heath held out his hand. Again they shook. "You're a good fellow, you know. Wait and see whether you hear anything from me."

The door closed behind him. Pike crossed over to his table, sat upon it, and began to fill a pipe. A slow grin wreathed his face. He began to whistle to himself, a semitone flat: "Won't you come home, Bill Bailey?"

CHAPTER V

At half-past seven in the evening of June sixteenth—two days, that is, after Trevor Heath's interview with Pike—these two men met again. They did not know until meet they did that meet they were going to. All, in fact, that each knew until that time, was that he was to dine with and at the house of a suddenly returned Anthony Gethryn.

Pike was early; Heath, late. Pike and Anthony were, indeed, having their second glass of sherry when Heath arrived. He shook hands with his host, but even while he was shaking hands he was staring not at his host but at his fellow guest.

"Exactly!" Anthony surveyed them with something of benevolence in his look. "Exactly. I said a small party, and a small party it is. You can see it all. All boys together. I'd like to suggest that for the first part of dinner, at any rate, we talk fluff. When I say, 'Go!' then we will go. Agreed?"

So it was not until White had left the room and the port was on the table that business began. Then it was Anthony who started it. He said:

"You know, Heath, you ought to congratulate yourself. On being, I mean, the most persuasive letter writer in my experience."

Heath smiled, wryly. "I've got something," he said, "to be persuasive about. In fact, I'm not sure I oughtn't to be somewhere near it now instead of here . . ."

Pike filled his glass from the decanter and pushed the decanter farther on its travel. He said, looking at Heath:

"By the way, sir, I suppose nothing else has turned up?"

Heath shook his head. "No, damn it! I suppose I ought to be glad, but I'm sorry."

"Nothing at all?" said Pike.

"Absolutely nothing at all."

"This," said Anthony, "is cryptic. I suppose I'm right in inferring that this something is a further *accident* involving or nearly involving Miss Susan Kerr?"

Heath nodded. And Pike said:

"That's quite right, sir." He looked at Anthony with his head tilted. He added:

"And if I might, sir, I should like to take a small bet with you."

"It is, Pike?"

"It is, sir, that even before Captain Heath's letter to you, you'd thought of putting a finger into this pie."

Anthony grinned. "Bet's off, Pike. You've won." His grin faded as quickly as it had come. "Only *thought* though, mind you. You see, until you wrote to me, Heath, I hadn't got, really, a decent excuse for butting in. But now I have. Look here! I'll tell you what I'd like to do. I'd like to give you my idea—made up from what I've heard, what I've read in the papers and what you've told me in your letter—of the situation as it affects you and everyone to-day. Where I'm wrong, you fellows can put me right. That suit?"

Heath nodded.

"I should say so," said Pike.

"Right. On the sixteenth of September Mrs. Hale-Storford died as the result of a wound in the throat. On the twentieth of November, Miss Miriam Rossiter, Mrs. Hale-Storford's sister, died as the result of a motor accident. On April thirtieth, George Anstruther was drowned as the result of a boating accident. On the twentieth of May Miss Susan Kerr has a narrow escape from almost certain death in a motoring accident. On the first of June she has a narrow escape from being run over by an omnibus. On the tenth of June, six days ago, she has a narrow escape from death or serious injury by reason of her horse bolting. Your contention, Heath, is that these three misadventures were not chance misadventures; were, in other words, not accidents at all, but the results of deliberate intentions on the part of some person or persons. You go farther than this, I think, and say that the cause of these misadventures is or are the same person or persons who caused the death of George Anstruther and Miriam Rossiter.

"You've endeavoured to persuade Miss Kerr of what you consider her danger but have failed entirely. Because you've failed, it's impossible for you to obtain protection for Miss Kerr. You want, therefore, something done to prove, first, that the *accidents* causing the deaths of Miriam Rossiter and George Anstruther were not, in fact, accidents at all but murders; consequently and secondly, you want the person or persons responsible for these murders caught before they can carry out any fresh schemes in regard to Miss Kerr. . . . How many marks do I get for that?"

"So far as I'm concerned," said Heath, "a hundred per cent."

Pike nodded agreement.

"My next move, then . . ." Anthony began.

But he was interrupted. Heath cut him short. "I say—I say!" said Heath, "just a minute! Not a hundred after all. Didn't you say just now, that I thought that whoever it was who'd been trying these tricks on Susan was the same person who'd tried 'em successfully on Anstruther and the Rossiter woman?"

"I did."

"Well, didn't you leave something out, if that was all you said?"

Anthony shook his head. "Don't think so. How?"

Heath, seeming to labour under some great excitement, flung out an arm. He knocked over his glass, and the port made a dark stain upon the white cloth. He did not notice it. He pointed a finger at Anthony. He said:

"What about the first death? What about the Hale-Storford woman herself?"

"My dear chap," said Anthony. "What do you say to that, Pike?"

Pike shook his head. Pike was not committing himself. Pike said with a half smile:

"You go on, sir. This is your party."

"But my dear feller," Heath began.

Anthony pushed the decanter toward him. "You pick up that glass and fill it. Also, give me a chance. You think that the killer of Eve Hale-Storford is going on with his killing. I don't. Look what you're saying. You're saying, in effect, that the killer of Eve Hale-Storford was either Hale-Storford himself, or Dorothy Graye, his housekeeper, or Banner (R.N. retired) or Trenchard (God knows what!). You *are* saying that. You must be saying that, because, of the other four people who were in the house on the night of Eve Hale-Storford's death, that woman herself, Miriam Rossiter, and George Anstruther are dead, and Miss Kerr (I am speaking all the time from this point of view of yours) has been the subject of attempts at her death. Now examine the four you have left. You are saying, in effect, that either Dorothy Graye alone; or the triumvirate of men without Dorothy Graye; or the whole quartette composed of that triumvirate *and* Dorothy Graye are your murderers. I submit that that theory is pure. . . . I should say that that theory won't hold water. Or not enough water, at any rate. Look at it!

"I can't believe that Hale-Storford, a noted doctor; Banner, a retired naval man of the usual respectability of naval men; and Trenchard could together be this murder club or even part of it. This sort of crime isn't committed by such a chance assortment of hitherto ordinarily peaceable men. I don't know, but I'm going to chance the guess that Pike, when we ask him, will tell us that at least two of this trio had never met before the night of Eve Hale-Storford's death; that all their pasts have been rigorously examined and are as blameless as may be; that there is no apparently possible or probable link which would bind them into a sort of Sudden Death Unlimited Combine. . . . Go on, Pike, blast me out of the water, if you can."

Pike beamed benevolence over his glass. His eyes, although the smile had touched them, were bright and very shrewd. He said:

"You know I can't, sir. You're quite right. That three have been under the microscope, so to say. And it's no mere probability that they weren't together, sir; it's as near a cast-iron certainty as you'll get in a month of leap years."

Anthony raised his glass and drank. "Thank you, Pike. . . . Now, Heath, it's no more likely that any one of those three men is by himself the author of these three deaths than that they all were. For if one of them was the original murderer of Eve Hale-Storford, he must have been such murderer with the knowledge of the other two, or they wouldn't have backed up his alibi by swearing that on the night that Eve Hale-Storford was killed he didn't leave the room between the time when the upstairs party went to bed and the time when they themselves went upstairs and discovered her body. . . . Follow me, Heath?"

Heath nodded slowly. "Go on, will you?" he said. There was a frown of concentration between his brows; he was chewing a cigar as yet unlighted.

Pike, looking at him covertly from the other side of the table, was shocked to see the change which only four days had wrought in the man. The thin face was yet thinner. It was now, indeed, almost gaunt and the blue eyes had black rings of sleeplessness beneath them.

Anthony went on:

"Right. We've done away with Hale-Storford plus Banner plus Trenchard, and we've done away with Hale-Storford *or* Banner *or* Trenchard. We have left Dorothy Graye, and that—yes, I can see you grinning, Pike —is absurd. I'm going to have another guess. I'm going to chance my arm —a bit more risky this time—I bet you ten to one that Pike, when I ask him, will tell us truthfully that Dorothy Graye hasn't left the Watch House. That Dorothy Graye couldn't have been the author of the two successful *accidents* nor the author of the three unsuccessful attempts on Miss Kerr. . . . Look at him, Heath, and you'll see that I'm right without waiting for him to speak. . . . So, Heath, we're without Dorothy Graye as well. Now what?"

Heath put his head in his hands. He ran his fingers through his sleek fair hair until it stood up in tufts. He said from under those hands:

"I'm with you, of course. Very clear and perfectly logical and all that. But what's it come to? Nonsense. Nonsense or magic! And I don't believe in either of those, Gethryn. Don't know about you." His blue eyes blazed suddenly. He raised a hand and turned it into a fist and thumped the table with it until the glasses rang. "For God's sake, man, let's have some sense, not theorizing—however clever it is!"

"Easy, man, easy!" Anthony's tone was as compelling as it was sympathetic. "Don't take it so hard. And don't let your troubles run away with your reasoning. Perhaps I've been annoying. I'm always being told I am. But I think you've missed something. All I was doing was to show you, in effect, that in all probability—in so much probability that we must, at least at this stage, take it as certainty—the murderer of Eve Hale-Storford did *not* cause the *accidents*."

Once more Heath put his head in his hands. The other two men were silent. When he raised his head it was to show them a face so ravaged with a miserable hopelessness that both the watchers, despite their utter innocence, felt immediately a sense of personal guilt. At this face Anthony stared a moment. He said contritely:

"My dear fellow! You've got me wrong again. I see now that you think I am trying to say that your accidents aren't real ones. In other words, that you're wrong about them. I'm not saying that I don't believe you about those accidents. I'd begun to believe you before I knew of your existence. Now, listen to this and grip onto it. All I told you, boiled down, comes to this: *that the murderer of Eve Hale-Storford was not the author of the accidents.* That, in other words, one person or set of persons killed Eve Hale-Storford, and another person or set of persons has killed Anstruther and the woman Rossiter and is trying to kill Miss Kerr. Get that?"

The relief that Heath felt was shown by his first broad smile of the evening.

"I always was a bloody fool," he said. "Yes, I've got you now. Go on, will you? I don't understand where you're getting to, but I do understand up to now. Go on, will you?"

Anthony smiled. "Now, we can assume, first, that the murderer of Eve Hale-Storford was someone within the house. Secondly, we can assume that the author of the accidents is some other person (in each case I am using the singular number for convenience) within the house; in each case, again, I am using the expression 'within the house' to mean someone who was in the Watch House on the night of Eve Hale-Storford's death. Now, to take a primary view of this business—and let me tell you that the primary view is often the sanest and best—which person within the house would you say was the most injured by the act of the original murder?"

"Husband," said Heath.

"Exactly. Hale-Storford. I think Pike will tell you, as indeed he may have already, that Hale-Storford had the reputation of being utterly devoted to his wife; that he was as nearly knocked over by her death as a man can be. Will you, Pike?"

"I will, sir." Pike was emphatic. "I should say beyond all possibility of play-acting."

Anthony nodded. "Right. Hale-Storford is the most genuinely injured person and also therefore a genuinely innocent person. Therefore, again, both Banner and Trenchard are innocent persons. Witness my previous remarks this evening. Therefore, and here once again we come back to the primary view, the guilty person was one of the upstairs party which was composed, besides the murdered woman herself, of Susan Kerr, Miriam Rossiter, Dorothy Graye, and George Anstruther. Now, Heath, Miss Kerr belonged to that upstairs party. Accidents, unsuccessful so far, have happened to her. Miriam Rossiter belonged to that upstairs party, but a successful accident happened to her. George Anstruther belonged to that upstairs party, and a successful accident happened to him.

"If, before we break up *this* party to-night, we ask Pike, officially or unofficially, to find out for us exactly where Hale-Storford was and what he was doing on the days when these unsuccessful accidents happened to Miss Kerr, what shall we have?"

Once more Heath struck the table with his fist, but this time not in despair. He said:

"Good God! I've got you." He looked at Pike. "Have you? Do *you* see what he's at?"

Pike nodded. "I've worked with Colonel Gethryn before, and if I hadn't I think I should."

The words were barely out of his mouth before Heath was talking again. Heath was saying, almost shouting: "But, look here, man, why don't you ask him this too?—why don't you ask him what Hale-Storford was doing at the times of the two successful *accidents.*"

Anthony smiled. "Easy, easy, Heath. I shan't ask him that because, knowing the man, I bet he's done it already and, knowing him, I bet he'd have told us already if there was something there to get hold of. Is that so, Pike?"

"It is, sir. Very much so."

"I see," said Heath. "I see. But, look here, Gethryn, what can you do even if Pike *can* tell us that Hale-Storford was in the neighbourhood of Susan's accidents every time she had them? Hale-Storford can't be a fool—in fact, by God! he must be as clever as Satan—and just the mere fact of his being near doesn't give you anything you can catch hold of him with, does it? . . . And if you can't catch hold of him you're still . . . My God! all I want out of this job's to make sure that Susan's safe. Feller must be mad —mad!"

"Of course he is, my dear fellow! Mad as a March hare!" Anthony's tone in its everydayness was soothing.

"Good Losh, sir!" Pike burst out, "I think I must have been wandering or something. I've only just got to the full meaning of what you're giving us. D'you mean to say that this young doctor, this decent man that was so knocked over when his wife was dead, that he's been so knocked off his balance by not knowing how his wife died that he's—that he's—that he's——" Pike felt at a loss for words.

"Exactly what I do mean. It's the one explanation, the one reasonable explanation. There's a fellow, brilliant, possibly—who can tell?—a little unbalanced always, probably by reason of that very brilliancy aided by overwork. He falls in love, desperately in love. He gets married, he's happy, he's married for six months, and then, snap!—just like that, his wife's killed. And he *knows*—as all the world knows, Pike, but as all the world can do nothing about—he *knows* that someone in that house—that someone of that upstairs lot I've been talking about—did it. The Law fumbles about (I'm putting this from his point of view, mind you)—the Law fumbles about and gets nowhere. By letting the four *who must contain the killer* go free, the Law refuses him even the satisfaction of civilized revenge. So, being a man who can think for himself—and he does, in fact, think too much for himself—he decides to exact punishment himself. As I see it, he probably works like this: He thinks and thinks. He thinks round the subject and round it. Brooding, half insane, and half coldly calculating, he makes up his mind. He says to himself: *'That's the one!'* and he points the finger in his mind at his wife's sister. And so, somehow, he brings about the death, in such a way that it won't incriminate himself at all, of that sister.

"But where is he after the first thrill of having carried out this execution has died away? Nowhere. Or, rather, he's back where he started from. He finds that what he had held in his turgid, unresting mind as a certainty now seems only the wildest of guesses, and like all guesses, possibly wrong. He looks round. There are still three left. He begins all over again. Soon he has persuaded himself that his first execution was wrong. That, in the state he is in, is no matter. What he must do is to make another execution; this time the right one. He thinks round and about the remaining three. He chooses, at last, the boy Anstruther, and so the boy Anstruther dies too. And then, very soon, the whole vicious circle again. Once more that finger in his brain points round, settles on . . . Well, you see what I'm driving at." Anthony cut himself short here. He looked sidelong at Heath.

Heath, his elbows upon the table, his chin upon his fist, was staring into nothingness. He said in a toneless voice:

"My God, man! That's awful! Awful! And we must sit here in this room all comfortable and warm and talk about it. Just talk, talk, talk!" His voice began to rise. "Why don't we stop talking? Why don't we *do* something? Why don't we get hold of this mad devil and kill him or put him somewhere where he can't . . ."

His voice died away. Anthony was anxious and looked it. He said:

"My dear fellow, you mustn't pay much attention to me. I know I've been talking a lot, but, after all, I've only been talking conjecture. I'm afraid I've been a bit too——"

Heath cut in. "You haven't been too anything! You're right, you're right. Any fool could see you're right."

He suddenly straightened in his chair. He shot out an arm and pointed at Pike. "Tell him, tell him and his lot it's up to them. They're the people we pay to look after us. Isn't it up to them? . . ."

"Easy, man, easy!" Anthony said. "You can't accept impossibilities. Suppose the police were to listen to every silly, self-satisfied ass like myself, where should we be then? None of us'd be safe."

Pike rose. He said, leaning his hands upon the table and looking straight at Heath:

"Look here, sir, don't you worry too much. It's me, you remember, who put you on to getting Colonel Gethryn to come home. And I'm as thankful as you are that come home he has. Just at the moment what Colonel Gethryn says about the police not being able to do anything is right. But it's only right just for the moment. Because I know Colonel Gethryn, sir, and I know myself. And with those two bits of knowledge put together I know this: that, having got where we are in what Colonel Gethryn calls 'pure conjecture' but which I call something else a good deal better, we'll very soon get on to a point when we *can* do what we want—act. It's quite true that officially I can't do anything, yet, but it's also true that neither Colonel Gethryn nor I am going to just leave things at pure talk. We're going to get on with it. You bear that in mind, sir. We'll all play our cards properly, and no harm will come to your lady."

With a hand which showed its shaking by the rattling of the decanter against his glass, Heath poured himself wine. He drank it at a gulp. He straightened himself in his chair. He said, looking round:

"I'm sorry, you fellows! Seem to be always making a fool of myself nowadays. What's to do, then? You two talk, I'll shut up."

Over Heath's head Anthony looked at Pike. He said:

"Mean to tell me, Pike, that you've swallowed my stuff too?"

"Lock, stock, and barrel," said Pike. "I wonder why the blink I didn't see it before."

Suddenly Anthony grinned. He said:

"If you go on like this I'll begin to believe it myself. . . . Well, Pike, Heath said it. What's to do?"

"Ask me that, sir, and I'll ask you. I'm official; you're not. What are *you* going to do? Captain Heath's got *his* job."

"I," said Anthony, "am going to ring the bell, thus, and when White comes in, as he does, within forty-five seconds—thus—I'm going to say to him, 'White, in the morning just see that the car's ready for a long trip. Pack enough stuff for me for three days. If you've got any spare time after that you can spend it with a map, looking out the best route to Polferry on the Wessex coast.'"

CHAPTER VI

Trewarth Arms Hotel,
Morlock,
Wessex.

17th June.

Dear Heath:

Important. Please get Miss Kerr—or do it yourself—to put in all the Social Columns a statement to the effect that she is leaving for Scotland to-morrow. Then let her stay in London, you sticking by her as close as usual, if not closer.

Explanations later.

Yours sincerely,
A. R. Gethryn.

2

Trewarth Arms Hotel,
Morlock,
Wessex.

17th June.

Dear Pike:

Something for you. As you see, I am staying some way from Polferry, but I was over there all the morning. So was White. I had no luck, but White did. He got hold of the boatman who had sold the yawl *Bluebird* to Hale-Storford. There is the permanent bad time on for boatmen, and old Tresillian had no objection to drinking beer so long as White went on paying for it. White, on instructions and enough money, did go on paying for it. He did not, being a man of some experience, start upon his real subject until the old man was on his seventh pint. But when he did start, he seems to have worked fast. Result: Tresillian grew boozily critical of 'the doctor's' care, before 'the young gentleman' met his death, of the *Bluebird*. Hale-Storford, as you are sure to know, bought the *Bluebird* about a month after his wife's death; *but*—and here's something you don't know because it never came out at the Anstruther inquest, and until he met White the old man never breathed the words—Tresillian was, for about ten days preceding Anstruther's fatal trip, telling Hale-Storford that the seams of *Bluebird* wanted repitching and the plug replacing. At the inquest, you will remember, Hale-Storford said that he had put in a new plug; that he supposed that it was something to do with this plug's newness which caused it to be driven out and so let the boat fill. That plug, you will also remember, was never found. Now, Tresillian told White this morning that he didn't believe this plug story; that he was sure no new plug had ever, in fact, been put in. The old man, mind you, wasn't suggesting or even trying to suggest that there was anything deliberate about Hale-Storford's omission, but he holds that 'the doctor' had never replaced the old plug.

I know there's nothing in all this which the official mind (all right! I'm not getting at you personally) will be able to allow itself to take hold of enough to warrant any action. I give it to you as just one further stick to place upon the pile of confirmation.

You'll hear from me again to-morrow. I'm going to be busy this afternoon. Have you sounded Lucas about this matter? If so, give him this letter to read at once. If not, pass it on to him after you've told him the tale.

Yours,

A. R. G.

3

(Telegram handed in at Morlock at 1 p.m. 18th June. Received Kensington Gore at 2:5 p.m.)

LUCAS 112 VERE MANSIONS

 HAVE YOU SEEN PIKE STOP IF NOT DO SO STOP BOTH COME DOWN
HERE TOMORROW MIDDAY EXPRESS STOP FISHING SUCCESSFUL STOP GARDEN
LOVELY

             GETHRYN

4

"Which shows," said Lucas, "just what we do think of you."

Anthony grinned. "I know. A damn nuisance, but better take some notice of him."

"That is," Lucas agreed, "roughly what I mean. And now, perhaps, after
wasting this hour—well, perhaps not wasting, it was a good meal—perhaps
you will tell us exactly why we're here. Eh, Pike?"

Pike shrugged. Pike permitted himself a joke. Pike said:

"Perhaps he will, sir, perhaps he won't. Either way, nothing we can say
will alter it."

"You are here," said Anthony, "to be persuaded. To be persuaded that
you have grounds for, if not the immediate arrest, at least the watching of
Hale-Storford while you rake up a case against him."

"Are we indeed?" said Lucas. He strove to keep his tone calm and toler-
antly disbelieving. He did not notably succeed; too much of his real interest,
almost excitement, showed through.

Pike did not attempt to dissemble; he leaned across the table. He said
eagerly:

"Where is he, sir?"

Anthony smiled, shaking his head. "I don't know, Pike. If I were to make
a guess, I should say somewhere between St. Pancras and Carlisle."

Pike started as if he had been stung. "Somewhere between—— What are
you talking about, sir? . . . Isn't he here? Isn't he over at Polferry?"

Anthony shook his head. "No. He left rather hurriedly last night. He
had, so I found out from his man when I called this morning, been sum-
moned upon urgent business."

Lucas knocked the long ash from his cigar. "Urgent business, eh? Any
idea what it is, Gethryn?"

Anthony allowed himself a smile. "I know exactly what it was. Dr. Hale-
Storford left in a hurry because Dr. Hale-Storford had read in his London
papers that Miss Susan Kerr was going to Scotland. Dr. Hale-Storford suddenly discovered that he, too, wanted to go to Scotland. And so he's gone."

Pike stared. "But—good Lord, sir! Oughtn't we——"

"No necessity. Miss Kerr's not really gone, Pike. The first day I got here,
I wrote and told Heath to get the notice put in. I wanted to see whether
it would have an effect on Hale-Storford and also get Hale-Storford out of
the way. It did both."

"You can't prove that!" Lucas put in quickly. "And I don't suppose, if
it comes to that, that you actually _know_ he's gone to Scotland."

"My dear Lucas, of course I can't prove it; of course I don't _know_ it! I can't

prove *anything* in this damn hotch-potch of a business. Even what I'm going to show you to-night—" he looked out of the coffee-room window at the
gathering dusk—"you'll tell me isn't proof. And it isn't. But it's such a circumstantial backing to conjecture that even the official mind will have to
take notice of it."

And that was all they could get out of him just then. He would talk—and
did—upon any subject other than this one nearest their minds. They gave
it up after a bit, having to be satisfied with the one reasonable statement
they had had from him.

"I am going," he had said, "to take you for a nice drive in my new car . . .
when it's dark. Everything looks so weird and nice, don't you think, under
the headlights. . . ."

5

"Old Nick's Corner," said Anthony over his shoulder. The big car
checked; swung round a bend so acute that when once more it ran straight
it was going back almost parallel with the way it had come.

Lucas clutched at the top of the door. "Old Nick's driving!" he muttered
to Pike. "Damn it, man, d'you like this?" He turned his head, peering at his
companion through the soft, thick darkness.

Pike's shrug Lucas felt rather than saw. Pike's voice said:

"Well, sir, he never *has* had a smash!" There was an undercurrent in the
tone which suggested little faith in the continuance of this clean sheet.

Lucas leant forward. He said into Anthony's ear:

"Easy, Gethryn. Go easy!"

Anthony did not turn his head. But his voice showed surprise. "My dear
chap! Not going very fast."

The head lamps cut a path of impossible whiteness. But on each side
of the swath of brilliance was darkness blacker, thought Anthony's passengers, than darkness has any right to be. The near side obscurity was
nothing to them. They knew, from the glimpses the lamps gave them at
the many curving corners, that on this side lay the comparative safety of rock
and bramble. . . . But the other side! Of that side, because of the angles
of the turns, they had only had two glimpses. But these had been enough
and more than enough. Upon their right was nothing . . .

"Nothing!" Lucas muttered. "And a great deal of it, going down the devil
of a long way!"

The car purred on. And up. Its hundreds of horsepower made light of
the twisting, ever-steepening ascent. Always Anthony's passengers felt on
their right that blankness, that void.

"Where the hell's he taking us?" Lucas's voice hid perturbation beneath
assumed ill-patience.

Again Pike's half felt shrug. "This is the west road up to the Tor top, sir.
The Long Road they call it . . . and rightly, I'd say! We come out just
above Polferry itself, sir."

"If . . ." said Lucas. "God! Easy, Gethryn!" The car, to take a particularly sharp left-hand bend, had swung its great nose first outward to the right. The white shadow-pitted ribbon of road had for an instant become part of the blackness. The lights' beam had gone out, a full quarter mile, into—void.

"Right!" came Anthony's voice. The car swung left. The road came back again, and the rock and bramble. The night air, almost cold now at this height, fanned Lucas's face. He sighed and put up an unsteady hand to a forehead which was frigidly damp.

Pike let out pent breath in a little hissing whistle. He said:

"*Think* we're at the top now, sir."

The car slackened, drew smoothly to a standstill. Anthony turned in his seat. They saw his face as a faint blur. It said:

"We are." He made a gesture. "You are now, gentlemen, upon the plateau of Polferry Hill. Or Tor. If you could see, you could see for miles in any direction." Another half-seen gesture. "You could see, for instance—over there—the main Exeter—London road. It joins this road about a quarter of a mile ahead of us. And about another two hundred yards on, past the join, a steep hill, a very steep hill, runs down to Polferry and the sea. At the end of that steep hill is the Watch House."

"I wish I knew——" Lucas never finished this sentence. The car started, not with a jerk but with a smooth, enormously accelerating rush, which left him actually without breath and imaginatively without insides.

It slowed, and Anthony spoke from the driving seat:

"There, just to your left, that's where the London—Exeter road joins on. Along it, some months ago, came Miriam Rossiter driving her own car alone. She was going down to see her dead sister's husband. She was late. She was always a fast driver." The car slowed still further. Now it could not have been doing more than fifteen miles an hour. Anthony turned to end this speech. He said over his shoulder: "*We* are now Miriam Rossiter. Get me?"

He did not wait for answer. He turned, settled himself back in his seat, and put his right foot down. When the needle on the speedometer dial touched 55 he held the car at that pace.

The headlights now showed the road as a broad white river. The big engine was so silent that only the scream of new tires on the macadam surface spoilt the silence. Anthony said suddenly:

"Three hundred yards ahead on the road is the beginning of Polferry Hill." His voice carried faintly to the back seat.

Lucas turned to say something to Pike; thought better of it; held his tongue.

Pike said: "He's going to go past it!"

But Anthony did not. Fifty yards from the turn, he began to brake; had slowed the car at the turn sufficiently to take the turn. As the front wheels came straight again, his voice came to the passengers' ears once more. It said:

"Don't forget. *We are Miriam Rossiter.* We are alone. We are a fast woman driver, and we know this hill. Hang on a bit."

"Oh, my *God!*" said Lucas.

The car, at first, seemed to drop like a plummet. This was a hill—and a steep one—and its steepness after the first two hundred yards was not straight but winding. Hugging the left of the road, Anthony put out a hand and turned out the switch which lit the dashboard. Pike sank back with a grunt. He found himself clutching the door on the off side just as Lucas was clutching the door on the near. The car swayed a little at the turns; otherwise it held magically to the bumpy road.

Lucas had not been down this road before. Pike had. It is to be guessed that Pike suffered the more. For while Lucas's fear came atop of and after each hazard, Pike's fears were constant both for hazard past and hazard to come.

There is, halfway down Polferry Hill, a sharp bend to the left followed by a slow curved bend to the right—a most dangerous piece of road. On the left a bank topped by curious little stunted trees rears up to a height of thirty feet or more. On the right, a ridiculously fragile single post and rail fence—rotten with age—is the only barrier between the road and an almost sheer drop to the coombe below.

Anthony slowed for this, but he did not slow much. Not enough for Lucas. Lucas abandoned, for one instant, his grip upon the door, leaned forward and touched the driver on the shoulder.

"Gethryn! . . . Gethryn! . . ." he said, "for God's sake, man, slow down!"

But Anthony did not slow down. His voice came:

"Shut up! *We are Miriam Rossiter.*" He went on.

The slope increased, and he had to brake. He changed up into third gear. The speed, as well indeed it might, decreased. Still the bank towered upon their left. Still the rotting fence marked the drop on the other side of the road. The lights cut a white highway through the darkness. In the back seat Pike was breathing heavily, Lucas cursing softly between his teeth. . . .

Another turn. Another steeper drop. Another turn. A noticeable decrease of steepness once more. The car in top gear again. Then Anthony's voice, louder this time:

"Two turns now and then the Watch House wall. As soon as it begins, think 'Rossiter'."

Between his curses, Lucas found time to speak to his companion. He said in a whisper:

"What's he playing at?"

No answer: and with a sudden swerve, first to the right, then once more to the left, they were running under the lee of the wall of which they had been warned. The wall of the garden of the Watch House. It ran parallel with the road, grimly replacing the bank which had been upon their left until now. Part of the hard-cut flood of light from the lamps showed it to them along its length. They saw suddenly, only a few yards ahead of them, yet another bend. The wall swung left, and with it, following round it at a more obtuse angle, the road. A blind corner, if ever there was one.

"Rossiter," said Anthony.

He slackened the car's speed, but only a little. He hugged the left, nosed out a little for the turn, then, with a hard wrench of his wheel, took it. . . .

"*Oh, God! . . . .*"

Lucas's voice was a shout. Pike rose in his seat, then fell back. His breath left him in a gasp. . . .

Rushing toward them was another car; the blaze of its headlights blinded them. They could not see. They felt already the beginnings of that lurch with which, if their driver did the only thing a driver could do and swung out right-handed, they would crash through the single rail and go over and down into the coombe.

Lucas flung up an arm to cover his eyes. Pike's hands were over his face.

Anthony's voice: "I said '*Think Rossiter*'."

The car came to a halt so abruptly that both its passengers found themselves on their knees.

"I said *Rossiter*," came Anthony's voice again. "Don't you trust me?"

Pike, the first of the pair to regain full control, got to his feet. He stood, his mouth open in amazement, clutching the back of Anthony's seat. Over Anthony's head, over the windscreen, he stared at the car which had nearly been their death. It had stopped not more than two feet from them. Still its headlights blazed into his eyes. It was a big car. A big black open car foreshortened by his end-on view of it. There was a man in the driving seat—and something in the back. What was it? A man standing just as he was standing looking over his head at him just as he was looking over Anthony's head at the man. . . .

Suddenly he realized the truth.

"Well, I'm goshed!" he said. He bent down. He shook Lucas by the shoulder. "Have you seen, sir? Have you seen?"

Lucas, peering out as he sat, nodded feebly. "Yes! What is it? What the hell is it?"

"Us, sir!" Pike's nerves found relief in a hoarse cackling little laugh. "Us, sir. It's a blooming mirror!"

"Well, I'm——!" Lucas said what he was: it is to be doubted whether anyone had ever heard him more Chaucerian.

Now Anthony was out of the car and standing in the road. He was saying, impatience in his tone: "Come on! Come on! I want you to look at this."

They came on. Pike, fully recovered, with agility; Lucas with not even pretence at speed. When he came up to them, some nine feet in front of the car, he found them examining a great mirror in which the glare of the car's lights was now obliterated by their own bodies.

In an oaken frame, the mirror seemed, at first sight, to be standing upright without support. Lucas blinked; looked again; found it propped from above. Its left-hand edge, as he faced it, was almost against the wall, and at that point in the wall was a gap; a gap some two feet wide and five in depth, reducing the head of the wall from eleven feet to six. Through this gap, out into the road, at a height of six feet from the ground, was thrust a limb of ash. And it was to this limb that the top edge of the mirror was fixed, so that the mirror was held four inches off the ground and more than half-way across the narrow road.

Lucas frowned. Anthony and Pike were talking, but he was not yet in mood to join them. He was trying, instead, to puzzle things out for himself. He had not got far when he was made to join the conversation. Anthony turned. He drew a torch from his pocket; shone the beam across the narrow road toward the rickety fence which guarded the precipice. He said:

"Look there! That's where she went. Lucas, have a look at this."

Lucas joined them. Looking along the white beam of the torch, he saw that immediately opposite where he was standing, almost directly facing the gap in the wall, was a section of fencing whose newness was in glaring contrast to the rest.

"That," said Anthony, "they did a fortnight after the Rossiter woman went over. Straight there, she went, and straight down. The car must have turned over about six times, but she was still inside it. Come over here and look." He took three strides and was at the rail. He bent over it, shining his torch downward. They followed him slowly. They stood one on each side of him, craning over. The torch was a powerful torch, but its beam did not show them, they could tell, the half nor the quarter of the drop. Not quite a sheer drop, but perhaps all the worse for that. Anthony sent the beam casting this way and that. It flickered; came to a stand which showed, twenty feet down the steepness below them, a broken sapling with half its root in air, the other half precariously clinging to earth. He said:

"She hit that and then went on." He snapped off the torch beam and turned.

Lucas was himself again. He said:

"What's all this, Gethryn? Do I get what you seem to be trying to tell us? Or am I dreaming?"

"You'll see soon enough." Anthony's voice was pitched low. "Quiet now, and just follow me. Not much of a climb."

Lucas groaned. "My *God!* What are we in for now?" He thought he was making this remark to Pike, but found that he was not. Pike, on Anthony's heels, was already at the gap. Through it went Anthony. Then Pike. Lucas struggled after; found himself, after a painful, hand-scraping descent, standing ankle deep in leaf mould and loam. He looked about him, blowing on his scorched palms. He became aware, with the shock a man will get when he realizes that there has been something near him for many moments that he has not seen, that he was standing almost immediately beneath a gaunt and darkly towering mass. He craned his neck to peer up at it. It seemed to his jolted and disordered mind like a giant's tripod camera. The legs of the tripod he could see, but the mass atop of them he could only guess at. He moved instinctively closer to his companions. He said, in a voice whose steadiness did him credit:

"Where are we, Gethryn? Pinch me, will you? I think I must be asleep."

"Quiet!" came Anthony's voice. "Don't want the Great Danes at us, do you? I don't."

Lucas dropped his voice to a whisper. "What *is* this? Where are we?"

"Watch House grounds. That—" in the darkness Anthony's arm made a gesture— "that's what they call the Tower. We're going up there. Now quiet, for God's sake!"

He turned from them. He put a hand up to his mouth. A plaintive whistle like the sound of a bird disturbed made a soft hole in the silence.

Beside him Lucas felt Pike suddenly stiffen.

"What's that?" he said.

Anthony turned on them. "Quiet, will you! Only White." A shape came out from between the legs of the giant's tripod. Its feet made soft rustlings on the mouldering carpet. It came close to them, a stocky, thickset figure. A dim gesture in the darkness showed it to be touching its cap. It did not speak.

"Good work, White," said Anthony. "Now we'll get the props back. Bear a hand, Pike, will you?"

Lucas was left standing. The three went from him back toward the gap in the wall. He barely heard them. After a small pause he did hear them. They were coming back. They were carrying between them something large and flat which, catching such light as there was, sent out faint gleams. They came level with him and set down the mirror upon its back.

"Get that bough off again, White." Anthony's voice was very low, almost a whisper.

White, taking something from his pocket, knelt. There came, separated at thirty second intervals, three separate creakings. Then White's voice: "What will I do with the bough, sir?"

"Where you found it," said Anthony, "and then stay down here. We're going up. If you hear anything, whistle. . . . Come on, you two."

He led them straight into the blackness encompassed by the tripod's legs; out again the other side and there turned sharp to his right. They were now at the end of a flight of wooden steps. Anthony led the way. He quoted, his foot on the first stair:

"'Ush, 'ush, I will 'ave 'ush."

They followed after him, treading like cats. They came up, after a precarious climb which took much of Lucas's recovered breath, onto a wooden platform. Before them loomed a bulk like an enormous beehive. Lucas could see now, but only dimly, what the giant's camera really was. Opposite Anthony there was a door. He set his fingers to the handle. There came the click-click of a lock giving, and then his whisper to their ear. They followed.

The beam of his torch shone out again; went flickering round.

"Just a minute!" he said. Then the splutter of a match and after it the faint, increasing light of an oil lamp.

Lucas and Pike, now beyond all amazement, looked around them. They were in a big hexagonal room. The heavy shutters lining five of the six sections of wall were over windows; the sixth section was wooden wall distempered over. They stood upon a plain thick piled carpet which stretched over the whole of the floor space. They saw a desk and armchair before it; other chairs; a table or two; bookshelves. Anthony went to the centre table and picked up the lamp. Held it above his head.

"Yes," he said, "the workroom, study—call it what you like—the place, anyhow, of Dr. Hale-Storford. Moved his things here to work after his wife's death. Couldn't, quite reasonably, stand his own study in the house. Likes this. View's good. Which isn't surprising; this place is built on the site of the old Watch Tower. . . . Now look!" He went, still carrying the lamp above his head, across to the one section of wall. They followed after him, Pike with two eager strides, Lucas more slowly. They stood at his shoulder. With his free hand he pointed.

"See that? See that discoloured square there? Those two hooks? That's where the mirror hangs. It's been up here ever since Hale-Storford had the room furnished. Three weeks after he'd had the room furnished, that is, about five weeks after his wife's death, there was a gale. A big ash, which you may or may not have seen lying there as you came through the gap, was blown down and smashed the wall. Hale-Storford, sitting up here every day, brooding, must've seen the gap every time he looked out of *that* window. I can feel the idea coming to him, can't you? Lonely road. . . . His suspect driving down it, as she always did, a little too fast. . . . Dark night. . . . What would happen if, just as she comes round the corner before that gap, hugging the wall because of the narrowness of the road, she was suddenly to see what looked like another car rushing at her? What would she do? First she'd brake. Then see that braking was useless. Then, when she saw that the other car was still hugging the wall, she would, almost at the last moment, desperately wrench her wheel over to the right in the dim hope of passing the oncoming car on the outside. But the road is so narrow that the hope doesn't come off. She hits that rotten bit of fencing and down she goes. . . ."

A long low whistle came from Pike. "That could be it, sir. But how, in the name of Jing, did you hit on it?"

Anthony walked back to the table and set down the lamp. He said: "Not so difficult. You see, following my normal practice, I was prejudiced to begin with. I believe—you could almost say I knew—that Hale-Storford had been the author of this accident. Therefore I'd only got to say to myself *how* was he the author of this accident? I drove slowly down that road in the daytime. As soon as I saw the gap in the wall, which is almost dead opposite the place where the Rossiter woman went over, I naturally connected gap with smash. I thought, at first, that through that gap he'd done something to scare her—flashed a great light; made a faked obstruction —anything like that. A dozen ideas or more. But I found that none of them was really sure enough. I thought: What would make an experienced driver take the awful risk of swerving out there? The answer, the most satisfactory answer, was another car going the other way on its wrong side. I began to make inquiries about other cars as best I could. I found first, through the servants via White, that neither Hale-Storford's own big car nor what had been his wife's small car had left the garage on the night that Miriam Rossiter was killed. I also found that all that day Hale-Storford had been at home. He hadn't left the house, or at least he hadn't left the grounds. This car, this possible car to frighten Miriam Rossiter off the road, was therefore, not one of his cars and couldn't have been any other car driven by him. Therefore, again, it was probable that Miriam Rossiter's death wasn't caused by another car. Yet another car was the best solution. . . . I got a bit gummed up there, I must say. But then I discovered that this place we're standing in now wasn't derelict but used. On principle, I sneaked up here, very late one night. And the first thing I saw when I got in here was that mirror. . . . I looked at it. I looked at it for a long time. Then in my mind I saw the gap, and after I'd seen the gap, I saw the whole thing.

"I took the mirror down. Through the top of the frame I found recent nail holes. I also found, sticking to the rough wood at the back of the frame, fragments of fibre which turned out to be bark. I remembered all those great ash boughs lying about just below. I saw the whole thing." He broke off suddenly and turned to Lucas.

"Sorry about that drive," he said.

"How," asked Lucas sourly, "do you look when you're pleased?"

Anthony grinned. "It was the best way to convince you. It *did* convince you, didn't it?"

Lucas nodded without speaking.

"And now," said Anthony, "what about Hale-Storford? Will you or will you not have him officially watched? I know this isn't really evidence, but is it enough to make you look for real evidence? It *must* be, Lucas!"

Lucas nodded. "It is." He stood in the centre of the room looking about him. He said slowly:

"One thing. How the devil did he get that great glass down and then up again. Not a one-man job."

Anthony contradicted. "It is a one-man job. It's been done by one man to-night. In a moment I'm going to whistle, and you'll find that within three minutes White's back again with the glass and inside another two has it up again. You see, it's a three-leaf thing, hinged.

"Specially made, sir?" Pike put in.

Anthony shook his head. "Not a bit of it. I should say it's a fairly old mirror made for a very large dressing table. It's quite solid work. And Pike, I don't think the desirability of killing Miriam Rossiter made Hale-Storford think of the mirror but that the mirror made him think of the best way of getting rid of Miriam Rossiter. That's sure, Pike."

He stopped abruptly and with four strides was at the door. He opened the door. A little breeze came coolly in. In the lamplight, Pike and Lucas looked at each other. From just outside there came to their ears once more the sound of the plaintive triple-note whistle.

CHAPTER VII

Lucas's telephone buzzed angrily. Lucas, standing by the window looking out over the sunlit Thames, nodded toward the instrument. "See who that is, Pike."

Pike was at the table in a long stride; picked up the telephone. "Yes? . . . Yes." He looked up and said: "Colonel Gethryn, sir. Tell them to send him up?"

"Of course! Of course!" Lucas's tone was impatient. "I've told them about that before."

There was silence until the opening of the door. Anthony was with them. He was gay this morning; he gave gay greetings. Lucas surveyed his smartness with a jaundiced eye.

"Pleased with life, aren't you?" he said. "Why, exactly?"

Anthony grinned. He sat himself on his favourite window sill and lit a cigarette.

"Well, Police." he said, "what's doing?"

Pike looked at Lucas; had his unspoken question answered with a nod. He went to Lucas's table, took from it an envelope and from the envelope folded buff sheets of foolscap. He gave these to Anthony.

"I think, sir," he said, "you'd best read that for a start."

Anthony read:

"RICHARD HALE-STORFORD

"Accordance with instructions, proceeded Edinboro by train 20th inst. Discovered at station Edinboro sleeper booked Hale-Storford's name by midnight train returning London. Waited station, found subject on train. Followed, picking up subject again at St. Pancras morning 21st inst.

"Subject proceeded Doulton's Hotel, Norfolk Street, S.W. Booked single room with bath, stated was staying two or three days, booking in own name.

"4 P.M. same day (21st inst.) subject left hotel, chartering taxicab. Followed in another cab. Subject drove to offices of the Thameside-Carringspey Steamship Company. Stayed outside offices while subject was within, subsequently followed subject back to Doulton's Hotel. Reported Inspector Fox and accordingly handed over outside Doulton's Hotel to D. O. Bryce. Self proceeded back to steamship offices. Inquiries elicited that subject had booked passage to Carringspey for night sailing of 22d inst. on S. S. *Sheila McNab*. Booking was for two, with adjoining cabins. Subject gave name John Garratt. Subject stated to shipping clerk that he was taking invalid daughter to Scotland for health. Must have adjoining cabins, as daughter required constant attention. Booking was made and fee paid by subject in Bank of England £1 notes.

"S. S. *Sheila McNab* sails from Grafton Docks 8:15 P.M. 22d inst.

"Returning to Doulton Hotel relieved D. O. Bryce. Booked room in Hotel for self on same landing as subject. Subject had been in room since return from shipping offices and continued in room until 6:30, when descended and sat in lounge reading.

"(Regret to report that owing to possibility of telephone in subject's room having escaped my notice, did not check up on telephone calls. Discovered later that subject had telephoned; call having been put through to Polferry 10. Unable obtain any information in regard purport of call.)

"Subject did not leave hotel at all, retiring to bed at 10:30. Kept subject's room under observation throughout night; subject did not leave.

"Telephoned Inspector Fox this morning and at 9:30 handed over again to D. O. Bryce, returning to make report herewith.

P. *Strangways,*

D. O. (C. I. D.) 342.

June 22."

Anthony folded up the buff sheets. He said, looking first at Lucas, then at Pike:

"So Mr. Garratt and his invalid daughter are going to Scotland. Well, well! What about the invalid daughter, Lucas?"

Lucas frowned. He was plainly disturbed this morning. He said, after a pause:

"Point Pike and I were discussing when you came in. So far we haven't had Miss Kerr watched. Heath's been doing that himself. But now . . ."

Anthony nodded. "Exactly! Well, we don't want, do we, to frighten the doctor off altogether?"

Pike brightened at this. "Just what I was saying, sir." He looked at Lucas apologetically, then back at Anthony. "If I may say so, sir, what Mr. Lucas and I were suggesting was to leave Miss Kerr as she is, only to warn Captain Heath and herself that she's not to leave the house to-day. After all, clever as he may be and mad as he may be, this Hale-Storford can't go into a house and pull her out of it, can he?"

Lucas turned from blank-eyed contemplation of the river. He said:

"I don't like this case. It's a mess." His tone was petulant.

"I think," said Anthony, "what Pike said is right. If we scare Hale-Storford off, we may never get him. We've got nothing yet that would go against him in court, you know, Lucas."

"Do I *know!*" Lucas was almost shrill. "That's the devil of it. . . . All right! Pike, can you get onto Captain Heath?" Pike nodded. "Do it, then, and do it now. Just tell him that Miss Kerr's not to go out of the house to-day. You can tell him also that his job of looking after her will be taken over by us from seven o'clock to-night."

He stopped here to look at Anthony. "We'd better do that, Gethryn. If he's going to try and get her, it'll be before that, won't it?"

Anthony nodded. "Yes, sound move. After seven put a man on, if you like. Plain clothes. Obvious or not. Up to seven, leave it alone."

Pike nodded; was gone. The door shut softly behind him. Lucas walked from the window back to his chair; sat and stared at Anthony.

"There's a thing," he said, "I meant to ask you when we were down at Morlock. Who's in that house of Hale-Storford's now? You said something about servants."

Anthony nodded. "Yes. Two servants—man and wife. And of course Dorothy Graye, housekeeper."

Lucas frowned, twisting uneasily in his chair. "Yes, I thought you'd say that. That Graye woman. . . . Look here, Gethryn, has another possible solution of this business occurred to you?"

Anthony smiled. "Yes. The one you're just going to put forward."

For a moment Lucas lost his frown. "You say it first, then," he said; "otherwise glory's easy."

"After all these years," said Anthony sadly, "you still don't trust me! Listen, what you were going to suggest was that Dorothy Graye was the killer of Eve Hale-Storford, and that she was the killer of Eve Hale-Storford with Richard Hale-Storford's knowledge. That right?"

Lucas smiled; a little wryly. "Blast you!" he said, "it is. What's the matter with it, anyhow?"

It was Anthony's turn to frown. "Tell you the truth, I don't know, but it's not right. Don't fit. For one thing, if Graye killed Mrs. Hale-Storford with Hale-Storford's knowledge, why this elimination holocaust?"

"Accidents," said Lucas. His voice was very low, almost ashamed. "Pure coincidental accidents."

"My *dear* chap! What about Mr. John Garratt and his invalid daughter and their nice little holiday in Scotland?"

"Easy," said Lucas, but he did not sound it. "Doctor Hale-Storford has a lady friend, and that'd be a nice quiet way of getting his lady friend up to a nice quiet country for a pleasant week or so."

Anthony nodded. "Ingenious . . . but it won't wash, Lucas, and you know it won't. You're uncomfortable about it. You don't believe it yourself. Do you, now?"

With an impatient gesture Lucas threw down the pencil he had been holding. He got up, thrusting his chair back. He said:

"No, I don't. If you want to know, I don't believe anything in this business. And one of the things I find it hardest of all to believe is that we've had three deliberate murders and haven't got one scrap of evidence that'd be a ha-porth of good in court. Look here, Gethryn, suppose we do find that Hale-Storford is mad, as you say; that he's what you call eliminating possible murderers of his wife; suppose, in other words, we catch him to-day trying to make Miss Kerr into John Garratt's invalid daughter. . . . Then we know and he knows. But how the devil are we going to *prove* it?"

"Ask me," said Anthony, "another! But once get your hooks into him and you may at least be able to prove he's mad, and in any case, you could get him several years for abduction."

Lucas snorted. "Several years for abduction! When the man ought to be hanged twice! What's the good of that?"

Anthony's smile was sympathetic. "Unsatisfactory, I know, but the good of it is, Lucas, that we take a young and very charming girl out of danger. That we put an end to the possibility of there being other 'accidents.'"

"Oh, I know all that!" Lucas was pacing up and down his carpet. "I know all that, but it's all so . . ."

"The official mind," said Anthony, "*in excelsis!* You know, Lucas, what you'd really like would be to get the Kerr girl nicely killed and have Scotland Yard officers taking photographs of Hale-Storford while he killed her. You'd then have a nice tidy case against him. It seems to be a rooted idea that policemen are for shutting stable doors. I think they ought to be for seeing that the horses are tied up properly."

Lucas stopped in his walking. Lucas glared at Anthony.

"If you think," he said, "that I——"

Anthony's smile cut him short. Anthony said, looking at his watch:

"It's half-past twelve. A bit early, but still . . . You come out with me and have some lunch. That's what you need, largely liquid."

2

Once more Lucas and Pike and Anthony were in Lucas's room. The swift-dropping sun cut a gilt path across the dull carpet. The clock upon Lucas's desk stood at five minutes before seven. They were silent; Lucas and Anthony smoking, Pike looking reflectively at the shining toecaps of his boots.

Lucas stirred. "What time was it we start, Pike?"

Pike looked up quickly. "Half an hour, sir. Just about twenty past seven. I've ordered the car for then. I'm taking two men and you and Colonel Gethryn. We go straight to the Docks." His tone showed a barely controlled eagerness. The prospect of action, even after years of service in this most active of professions, always excited him.

Anthony stood up; flung a cigarette stub across the room and into the empty grate. "To meet," he said, "John Garratt and daughter. Well, well!"

The telephone buzzed. Lucas tilted forward his chair, reached forward a long arm; spoke:

"Yes? Who? . . . He's what? . . . *What!* Send him up at once, man, at once!"

He stared, the receiver still in his hand, at his companions. He put the receiver back. He said slowly:

"Heath's downstairs. Murphy says 'in a state.' Something about Miss Kerr."

Anthony's eyebrows went up. Pike jumped to his feet, and crossed with long strides to the door. He left it wide behind him. They heard his quick footsteps crossing the outer office, and then, as he reached that door and opened it, the sound of other footsteps in the corridor outside, and voices. . . .

And then he was with them again. Behind him there came Heath, whose white, drawn face and blazing eyes brought Lucas and Anthony simultaneously to their feet. It was to Anthony that Heath spoke. He said, his voice low and straining for steadiness:

"She's gone!"

No sound from Pike. From Lucas:

"What! What's that you say?"

From Anthony:

"Here, man, sit down!"

He pushed a chair forward with his words. Its edge took Heath behind the knees and he sat abruptly. Anthony said, looking at him:

"When?"

From his breast pocket Heath pulled a handkerchief, passed it across his forehead. "Somewhere," he said, "between five and six-thirty."

"How?"

"God knows!" Heath's voice was beginning to rise. His teeth bit his underlip. He said:

"I'd made her see reason. She wasn't going out. I went out, bloody fool that I am! Went out at quarter to five; said I'd be back in another two hours. She wasn't to move. I went to my father's house. I was just leaving there——"

"Time?" said Anthony.

"About six. I was just going when the phone bell went. It's in the hall. My father's man answered it. The call was for me. It was from St. Adrian's Hospital. . . ."

"Hammersmith?" asked Anthony.

"Yes. The house surgeon was speaking. Doctor something—I didn't catch his name. He said there'd been a motor accident in Hammersmith Broadway, that a Miss Susan Kerr had been very seriously injured and kept asking for me. . . ."

The handkerchief again. This time the man wiped his lips as well as his brow. He said jerkily, gasping:

"She was barely conscious, they said, but kept asking for me. Could I please arrange to go there at once. I should—I should, of course, have rung you first, but I don't know why—except I'm a damn fool not fit to be trusted —it never entered my head—nothing entered my head except Susan. My father's car was just outside the door. I just bolted out of the house, jumped into the car, and drove to Hammersmith."

He broke off again. Once more the handkerchief. He said, after a fight for composure:

"Of course, when I got to the hospital they knew nothing about it. Nothing at all. . . . I saw what had happened. I got back into the car and went to Susan's house quicker even than I had driven to the hospital. When I got there . . . You can guess, I suppose."

"Mean she'd gone?" said Lucas.

"Shut up!" Anthony was savage. "What did they know, Heath? At the house, I mean."

Heath shook his head. Rather a painful sight; he forgot to stop shaking it. He said:

"Nothing. Only one of the servants had seen her go. A telephone message had come for her, and she'd answered the telephone. After that she'd said nothing to anyone, but they saw her go upstairs and come down a few moments later dressed for the street. She seemed, they said, very white. There was no one in the hall actually when she came down. She must have let herself out. All they could tell me was that a parlourmaid who happened to be in the dining room saw Susan go down the steps, saw her look this way and that, saw a taxi pull up and Susan get into it."

He swallowed twice and endeavoured to clear his throat. "That's all," he said hoarsely. The whole man seemed to slump with these last words. Huddled in the big chair, he looked half his size. Pike looked at Lucas; got an answering nod; was gone from the room.

Anthony put a hand on the sagging shoulder. He said:

"It's all right, man. It's all *right!* We know where. We're going soon. At once. You can come too."

Into Heath's body life seemed to flow back visibly. He stood erect. His shoulders squared themselves.

"You *know?*" he said. "Tell me! Tell me!"

Anthony told him. At the end of the telling Pike was in the room again. He had in his right hand a glass. He held it out to Heath.

"Drink that, sir," he said.

Heath stood up. He took the glass and swallowed the contents at a single gulp. "Thanks," he said.

They were all standing now.

"Car right, Pike?" came Lucas's voice.

"Yes, sir."

"Men there?"

"Yes, sir."

Lucas looked at Anthony. "All set, Gethryn?"

Anthony nodded.

They filed out. The room was empty.

3

The closed blue police car shot along the Embankment at speed. Behind it always, almost as if an invisible chain were coupling the two, was Anthony's Voisin-Maxwell. In the police car were Lucas and Pike and two plain-clothes men. In Anthony's car were its owner and Trevor Heath.

Out of the Embankment they went, and then plunged into the thoroughfares of the City. In the police car there was silence but at Anthony's side, Heath talked incessantly. His speech did not require answer. Anthony let him talk.

As they came into the Minories from Fenchurch Street Heath looked at his watch.

"Seven-thirty," he said. "Are we in time, man? Are we in time?"

Anthony nodded. "Plenty. Sailing's not until eight-fifteen."

Ahead of them the police car took a sharp left turn into East Smithfield. The Voisin-Maxwell swung round on its tail. A few hundred yards, and then sharp right into Nightingale Lane. Then more twists and turns. . . .

Heath, with this approach to the end of their journey, grew almost silent. Only every now and then, for an instant or so, when the police car was out of sight, did he speak. Then a halt. Anthony shut off his engine and brought his car to a standstill with its nose almost touching the tail light of the blue saloon. Already Pike and the two plain-clothes men were on the pavement, and Lucas was following. Heath swung his legs over the Maxwell's low side, and rushed to join them. Anthony came after. Pike was saying to the driver of the police car:

"Stay here till we're back, Richards, and look after Colonel Gethryn's car as well as this one."

The man touched his cap.

Pike said to Anthony: "Thought we'd best stop here, sir. Less conspicuous, as it were, if we walk. Only a step." He turned to the two plainclothes men. "You two drop behind," he said, "until we're on the berth."

The little procession moved off. First Pike and Lucas; then, a yard or two behind them, Heath and Anthony; then, at a greater interval, the two detectives.

Pike, who knew the dock district as well as his own house, led them by a twisting short-cut which seemed, as Heath said, to be never coming to an end. But it did end, and suddenly. They came out opposite the big main wooden gates of Grafton Dock. At the wicket Pike spoke softly to its guardian. The party passed through.

Anthony was silent. Heath, beside him, kept hitching up his sleeve to look at his watch. Once he began a sort of stumbling run. In two strides Anthony was up with him; had laid a restraining hand on his arm. "Steady there, man!" he said.

Heath passed a hand across his forehead. It came away glistening. He said:

"Sorry! But they're so *bloody* slow!"

Past berth after berth Pike led unerring way. Everywhere were soot and coal dust and grayness. Everywhere, towering to their right and to their left and to their front, were the masts and funnels of shipping. Every now and then, mournfully, a siren hooted. Every now and then, from everywhere came shrill whistles.

The party trudged on. Once more Anthony had to lay a steadying hand on Heath's arm. And then, at last, the halt.

"What's up?" said Heath. "What's the matter? Why are they stopping?"

Anthony pointed. Heath followed the finger's direction; saw in great black letters upon a board of grimy white the figures 18. At the moorings was a small, sturdy little passenger-tramp. Upon her bows, seen mistily through an oily veil of coal dust, were the words *Sheila McNab*.

It was Anthony's turn to look at his watch. The hands showed him that the time was ten minutes to eight. A foul, rickety gangway still stretched from the waist of the ship to the berth-side. Pike and Lucas spoke together in whispers. Lucas stood his ground, barring the way of the others. Pike ran up the gangway. Heath started forward, to be jerked to a standstill by Anthony's clutch at his coat. To Anthony he turned a face almost unrecognizable.

"Damn you!" he said. "*Damn* you! Let me go."

"Easy, man!" Anthony's tone was curt. There was something in it which brought Heath back to sanity. He muttered something and was still.

Pike, now at the top of the gangway, was talking to a head which appeared to rest upon the bulwarks; a head fringed with gray beard and hair; a head surmounted by a dirty peaked cap several sizes too small for it. They saw the head shaking decisively, and then saw Pike put hand to pocket and bring out something over which the gray head pored; saw Pike, after this, turn toward them and beckon them on.

They went up the gangway: Lucas first, then Anthony with Heath hard upon his heels, then, at decent orderly distance, the two plain-clothes men. As the last of the party put foot upon the deck the gray beard was wagging at Lucas. From somewhere behind it came a bass and grumbling voice which said:

"Aye, twull be yon pairr. They're but now gone below. Fife's the cabin." A huge, spatulate thumb was jerked at the deck. "Wull I be showin' you?" said its owner.

The square bulk of the *Sheila McNab's* skipper went down the companion immediately before them. They stood, at last, in a group about him. He said, dropping his voice to a sibilant whisper of well-nigh incredible loudness: "Doorr yonder!" Once more the thumb was jerked. "That's the chiel. Lassie's next beyond."

Lucas muttered something. The old man stood aside. Pike pushed past him. Anthony kept firm grip on Heath's arm. At the first door Pike knocked. No answer. He knocked again, louder. No answer. He tried the handle. He turned to look at them standing there in a huddled group behind him, a face from which the usual dark tan seemed to have paled. He said, looking at Lucas:

"Break it in, sir?"

Lucas nodded.

There was a violent wrench at Anthony's hand—and Heath, thrusting himself off from the other side of the companionway wall, hurled himself at the door. It shivered and groaned but held.

Pike made a grab at him. "Back there a minute, sir, I'll do it."

But the man was beyond restraint. He thrust Pike away and leaped again. With a splintering crash the door gave. Headlong into the cabin he shot. They poured in after him. . . .

It was Pike and Anthony who, with their combined force, managed to lever the fingers of Heath from the throat of Hale-Storford.

Hale-Storford was flat on his back on the floor with Heath kneeling over him. In the one bunk, on a heap of bed linen, disordered and not too clean, a woman lay face downward and motionless. . . .

The little cabin was full of men. Pike, backing Heath into a corner, left him under Anthony's charge; turned to the two plain-clothes men. He pointed to the limp figure of Hale-Storford on the floor. "Take him outside," he said.

The taller of the two took the unconscious man's shoulders; the other the feet. They shuffled out with their burden.

Lucas was bending over the woman in the bunk. He had turned her to lie upon her back. He said now, over his shoulder:

"She's alive all right but I don't know what to make of her. Have a look, Gethryn."

With the last words he stood up and away from the bunk. The three men in the corner, Pike and Anthony with Heath between them, could not see the bunk. With a wrench Heath was free. He took half a step forward—then checked. With Lucas's words, "She's alive," a sudden flood of colour had come back to the ashen face, but now, once more, as if by an invisible sponge, the colour was wiped away. He stared. His mouth dropped open. He seemed to be trying to speak but could not. It was Pike who said, in a dazed whisper:

"*That's* not Miss Kerr!" He took two rapid steps and was at the bunk side. He looked down at the limpness, then turned. He said:

"That's Mrs. Graye!"

"My *God!*" said Heath. He sat down heavily upon the cabin's one chair. He put his elbows on his knees and buried his head in his hands.

Lucas, bewildered, looked at Anthony. The little place, so recently a shell of pandemonium, was filled now with utter silence.

Anthony broke it. He crossed with one long stride to the bunk, bent over the woman's limp body. Like Lucas, he felt the action of her heart. His fingers then sought her wrist and found the pulse, slow and perhaps a little faint, but regular. He bent above her face, his own close to it. He straightened, shaking his head. He said to Lucas:

"Some drug I don't know. Can't smell anything. I should say she's all right."

"Can't bring a doctor here," said Lucas. "We must move her. This boat's sailing in ten minutes. Pike, slip along to that Old Man of the Sea and ask whether he's got a stretcher. As you go, tell Stenson and Coker to get their man off. . . ."

Five minutes later they were on the quay. From the rail of the *Sheila McNab* a row of grimy, curious heads looked down. The dockyard policeman came hurrying up; saluted. Pike took him aside. After talk Pike came back. He said:

"Ambulance coming, sir. That'll take the lady. Hale-Storford can walk."

Lucas looked round. "Where've they taken him?" he said.

"Behind that shed, sir. Think you'd better come and see him. And you too, sir." He looked at Anthony. "It's on our way out."

"What are we *talking* for? God man, can't we hurry? Can't we hurry?" Heath, ever since his entry to the cabin, had been alternating silence with wild outbursts of speech.

Fifty yards away, round a corner of a long shed, appeared an ambulance. From it there came hurrying a round and bustling little figure with a black bag. Pike went to meet him; was back again after hurried speech. "This way, sir!" he said. "They'll look after the lady now."

He began to lead, almost running, back along the way they had come; when he reached the first long shed he stopped. They came up to him, Heath first, then Anthony, then Lucas. At the other side of the shed, seated on an upturned barrel, was Hale-Storford. Beside him, still stolid, still uninterested, were the two plain-clothes men.

"Look at that, just look at that!" Pike was saying.

A little faint whistle came from Anthony. Lucas was silent.

"My—*God!*" said Heath.

They had put handcuffs on Hale-Storford. He was hatless, and his blond hair was ruffled like an untidy child's. From under its thatch there peeped out upon the world two eyes which were overbright, overjoyful, overrestless. Like an animal's but not so sane.

Hale-Storford was pleased with his handcuffs. He held up his wrists, looking at the bright things round them this way and that. He shook his wrists so that the bright things jingled. And every time they jingled there came from his throat little chuckles of delight. The taller of the two guardians touched him on the shoulder. "Come on, now!" he said.

The bright eyes looked up at him; a bright smile lit the face. The blond tousled head was shaken mischievously. Once more the wrists were held in air and shaken. Again the jingling; again the chuckle. . . .

Lucas turned to Anthony. "Come on!" he said. "If I look at that I shall be sick."

Pike gave rapid orders. The taller of the two detectives nodded.

Heath jerked savagely at Anthony's arm. "Come *on*, man! For God's sake!" They went on. Pike, running now, led the way.

CHAPTER VIII

Once more Lucas's room was full and Lucas back again by his window. Anthony stood before the fireplace. Up and down the other side of the room paced Heath. Heath was saying:

"But who? Who? In the name of God, who?"

"For your own sake, Heath—" Anthony's tone was very even—"for your own sake take it quieter. We're not wasting time. Pike'll be back in a minute."

With the words, Pike was. Before him he ushered a neatly dressed and more than neatly pretty girl of twenty. She was plainly nervous; equally plainly she had recently been weeping. Heath stared at her. "Good Lord!" he said. "Aren't you—aren't you . . . ?"

"Yes, sir." The girl's voice was quivering still. "It was me that happened to see poor Miss Susan running out of the house this evening."

Pike brought a chair for the girl. He cut her short. "Now, now!" he said. "I've told you you're not to worry. You've got to help us, not cry." He was firm and benign.

"Y-y-y-yess, sir!"

"You just sit quietly there and keep hold of yourself. No need for you to talk just yet." He turned to Lucas and said:

"This is one of the parlourmaids at Lady Kerr's house, sir. The one that saw Miss Kerr leave this afternoon. She's already given me one very important piece of evidence. I brought her along here in case she might be wanted. She just saw Miss Kerr run out of the house, look up and down the road—you correct me if I say anything wrong, my dear—and then run toward a taxi which was on the wrong side of the road, making straight for her. She looked through the window of the taxi, seemed to say something, and then wrenched open the door and got in. Miss Polton—that's this young lady's name—wasn't taking much notice, but she did happen to see all this. And then the taxi turned round and was off. What I've done is to put out a comb for all the taxi drivers round Brooke Square and district. If it's one of the regulars, we'll have him in and find out what he knows within an hour or two. If it's one—" he glanced at Heath, seemed about to stop, and then went on—"if it's one from outside—floaters, we call them, Captain Heath—then it'll be a longer job. But you must remember that being a taxi makes it a help. If it had been one of two million private cars, then things wouldn't be so easy."

"Easy!" said Heath in a sort of barking laugh. "*Easy!*" He flung himself into a chair and lay back, one hand pressed across his eyes.

Pike turned to Anthony. He said:

"Now for your line, sir. I've had Jackson ring up the Station at Morlock. He's had his answer already. Captain Banner's very well known down there. Hasn't left the town for more than six hours—and that in his boat—for the last six years. Still there."

Anthony nodded. "Thought so. Trenchard?"

Pike shrugged. "Jackson asked about that too, sir. This Mr. Trenchard was just staying for a week with Captain Banner at the time that Mrs. Hale-Storford was killed. Owing to the crime and his being in the house and having to wait for the inquest, he was there over two months. He left there, to be exact, on the thirtieth November last. Since when, sir—"

"—they've heard no other," Anthony finished.

"Exactly, sir."

"Pike— Lucas, can we ask Pike to get lines on Trenchard?"

Lucas stared. "Yes, yes. Anything. Pike, do what Colonel Gethryn asks."

"Yes, sir." Pike turned to Anthony.

Anthony, his eyes half closed, spoke quickly. He said:

"Get all Trenchard's particulars. You must have 'em from the inquest papers. Get onto every address and every possible address. Find out where he's been over these intervening six months or so. Find out his last known address. Get onto it. . . . You've got me, Pike? Anything and everything, and more than everything, about Trenchard. Keep Trenchard in your mind like a flag."

With long strides Pike was gone from the room. The door banged behind him. In his chair Heath, striving for control, writhed his body about. In the middle of the room, upright upon a straight-backed chair, sat the girl Polton. Her eyes went this way and that. Her hands in their cheap, neat cotton gloves, twisted one about the other. Lucas sat upon the edge of his table and beat a little tattoo upon his teeth with the nail of his forefinger. Anthony stood where he was, back leaning against the mantelpiece, hands in his pockets.

Silence.

Suddenly Lucas swung to his feet, crossed to Anthony, said in a low voice:

"Why all this Trenchard, Trenchard, Trenchard? I see what you're driving at, but are you *sure?*"

Anthony shrugged. He said in a voice lower even than his questioners:

"What's sure in this world, Lucas? Nothing. But here's a thing that'll pass for sure. Take a life like Susan Kerr's. Is she likely to have been mixed up in a *lot* of things which would lead to attempts being made upon her life? What's the answer? She isn't. But she *has* been mixed up in one thing, and out of that one thing we know that the 'accidents' sprang. Therefore it is—most *probably*, Lucas—out of the same thing that this abduction springs. Another separate thing would be stretching coincidence too far. I don't say it's impossible, because it isn't. Nothing's impossible. But we've got to deal with probabilities, Lucas. We're in a hurry. And out of that grisly house party—it *was* grisly, if you come to think of it—there's only one *possible* left, and that's Trenchard, if we except Banner working through understudies, which for our present purpose won't wash. It *must* be Trenchard we're after. Damn it, man, it's got to be!" He dropped his voice still lower. "Look at that poor devil in the chair there! Think of what he's going through. We've got to do something." Despite its lowness, his voice carried urgency greater than any Lucas had ever heard in it before.

Lucas nodded. "Yes, you're right. Damn you, man, you're always right!"

Anthony—his first sign of perturbation—bit at his thumbnail. "I wish that was right."

"What?" asked Lucas.

"What you said."

Lucas drifted back to the table again, once more sat, once more began to beat out that barely audible devil's tattoo on his teeth. The girl Polton still sat rigidly upright. Still her dark eyes darted their gaze from that face to this, from this face to the other. Her hands were still folded in her lap. In the armchair, almost facing her, lay Heath. His eyes were closed. His face showed dead-white against the dark leather of the chair. He was motionless, with a sort of explosive stillness.

Moments passed, turned into minutes. Minutes became a quarter hour. Lucas, crushing out his fourth untasted cigarette, came back once more to the fireplace and Anthony. He said:

"Shall I ring for Pike? Been the devil of a time."

Anthony shook his head. "No, leave him. I would."

Now Lucas's left shoulder was brushing Anthony's right. They leaned, side by side, against the mantelshelf. Lucas turned his body. He said in a tone so low that it was really a whisper:

"What do you think? Has Trenchard been in it with that madman all the time?"

"God knows!" Anthony shrugged. "I don't know what to think. And when I don't know what to think, I don't think. I'm not thinking."

"Where the hell," said Lucas, "has Pike got to?"

He was answered by the man himself. But Pike did not enter the room. Only his head came round the door. He looked at Lucas. "Just a minute, sir," he said. He looked at Anthony. "And you too, sir, if you would."

With one movement they left the fireplace and crossed to the door; passed through it. Pike said, very low:

"Nothing doing at all, sir. Can't get anything. This Trenchard—well, he seems like a ship without an anchor. Got plenty of strings on him, but they don't any of 'em lead anywhere. After he left Captain Banner he went back to his rooms at the Albany. He was there for eight or nine weeks, then he gave them up. Then he pops up in a new flat—he still rents it—in Vere Court, Westminster. He's there for another couple of months. Seems to have plenty of money. There's a man of his still there, but the man don't know where he is, or says not. Since then, nothing. Told the man he was going to Norway; all letters to be sent care of his bank."

Lucas said sharply:

"This man, what is he? Valet?"

Pike nodded. "I should say so, sir. I've sent Bryce round there. Maybe he'll have something when he comes back, but—" he shook his head, slowly this time— "somehow I don't feel he will."

"Anything in the taxi line, Pike?" This from Anthony.

Once more Pike's head was shaken. "No, sir. Nothing. Mind you, I never had much hope of that. What I said I said to try and cheer Captain Heath up. I'm not saying we shan't get anything, but we shan't get it all in a hurry like this."

Lucas made a little helpless gesture with shoulders and arms. He laughed; a sound with no mirth in it. He said:

"Looks like a stalemate."

Anthony began to walk up and down. "Stalemate hell!" he said.

"London—" said Pike— "well, London's a biggish place, sir."

"Scotland Yard," said Anthony, "is a biggish institution."

Lucas took fire. They were all on edge. Lucas said:

"And Scotland Yard's full of bloody fools! I know what you're thinking, Gethryn. Well, A. R. Gethryn's supposed to have a biggish brain. Suppose he does something about it!"

Pike looked from one to the other. His lean face, on top of its real distress, showed surface awkwardness at this bickering. Suddenly Anthony smiled.

"Sorry, Lucas, sorry! I asked for it!"

"Apologies," said Lucas, also with a smile, "returned. My fault! But what do we *do?*"

Anthony resumed his pacing. His footsteps sounded somehow slow and ominous. They watched him in silence. At last he came to a halt. He said:

"Let's try this girl. Let me try her. Send her out here. You two, if you don't mind, go back into the other room or somewhere else. Willing?"

"Aye, willing," said Lucas, and was gone. Pike went after him. The door of Lucas's room closed behind them.

2

The girl came in, shyly.

Anthony settled her in the room's one comfortable chair, stood back from her and sat upon the table's corner. He said:

"Now, look here, Miss Polton . . ." then smiled. "That's a bit stiff, isn't it? What's your name?"

His tone was the right tone; a cunning blend of paternity, interest, and friendliness. There came immediate signs of returning self-confidence. The dark eyes—in their way rather fine dark eyes—met Anthony's green ones fully. She said:

"Elsie, sir," and then: "Oh, isn't this dreadful about poor Miss Susan? If you only knew, sir, how——"

"I do, Elsie. I do. That's why I've asked to have this talk with you. Now, looking at you and talking to you, I know you'd do anything for Miss Kerr, wouldn't you?"

"Oh, I would, sir!"

"And you don't dislike Captain Heath, do you?"

"No, sir. We've— I've always thought the Captain and Miss Susan——"

"Exactly," said Anthony. "Exactly." His smile and his tone were more than sufficient excuse for the interruption. He said:

"It seems to me, Elsie, that you're just the one person in the world who *might* be able to help us find Miss Kerr, and find her quickly. Mind you, find her we shall, sometime or another, whether you can help us or not, but what we want to do, Elsie, for Miss Kerr's sake and for Captain Heath's sake and for our own sakes, is to find Miss Kerr now."

"But sir!" The girl's voice was eager, yet despairing. "But, sir," she said again, "that other gentleman, what's his name, the police gentleman, the one that came to the house, he asked me, and I told him everything. Everything. You see, it wasn't as if I knew that Miss Susan oughtn't to 've gone out of the house. If I had, I might've looked. I mean, I might have looked more specially like. As it was, well, I wasn't thinking, and it was just luck like that made me see anything at all. You see what I mean, sir?"

Anthony's smile was sympathetic. Very sympathetic. He pulled out a cigarette case. He said:

"Don't you find that thinking's easier when you're smoking? . . . Have one of these."

He slid off the table, held out his case, and, when she had taken a cigarette, lit a match for her. He said:

"We know you told Superintendent Pike all that you could. Don't think I'm not absolutely sure of that. What I'm trying to do is to get you to try and remember *more* than you remembered when you were talking to Superintendent Pike. After all—" his tone again was most carefully blended: it had in it something of the deliberately flattering appeal of man to woman; something of the deliberate clarity of doctor explaining to patient; something of essential friendliness; something of all these but not too much of any—"after all, Elsie, you know as well as I do, that when something has happened you didn't take much notice of, and then someone jumps up and tells you that thing is very, very important, you get flustered—at least I know I do. So then you say all you remember, quite truthfully, only to find afterwards that other things have come back to you. You see what I mean?"

The girl was leaning forward in her chair now. She nodded. "Yes, sir, I do. I know exactly."

"Right. Now then: all this business has been a great shock to you, must have been. Therefore, it's quite probable, isn't it, that what you *think* is all you remember isn't *really* all you remember." He laughed a little; a friendly laugh. "You see what I mean, don't you?"

"Oh, yes, sir. I do indeed. You mean sometime, say next Sunday like, I might sort of wake up and remember something I didn't tell the detective gentleman."

Anthony nodded. "Exactly, Elsie." Another smile; very friendly, perhaps a little more. "But what I want you to do now—what I want you to *try* and do, is to make that extra remembering come *now* instead of that next Sunday of yours."

"Yes, sir. But I don't see—" a worried frown had come between the brown eyes—"I don't see how to start about it."

Anthony laughed. He said:

"You've nearly finished that cigarette. Throw it away and have another and I'll try and help you. I've done a bit of helping people like this before."

The frown persisted but the mouth smiled. "Yes, sir," she said. But there was doubt in her tone.

Anthony kept hold upon himself. It was essential that he should seem to go slowly while really he worked fast. He said:

"Oh, it's not hypnotism or anything. Nothing like that about me, you know."

Elsie laughed, but a pink flush mounted to her cheeks. She said, "Oh, no, sir. Of course not."

Anthony cut her short. "All I meant, Elsie, was this: Instead of making you think and think, just going round in circles inside your head, how would it be if I helped you by asking a few questions. You wouldn't mind that, would you?"

"Of course I shouldn't." Elsie's tone was sharp. "Don't you know I want to help?"

Anthony rejoiced both at the tone and the omission of the "sir". They were the first signs that his efforts at making Elsie Polton into Elsie Polton instead of the parlourmaid who "knew her place" were meeting with success. He said:

"Right. Now you take this cigarette . . . and this light . . . and we'll begin. All right with you?"

Elsie nodded firmly. Now, definitely, she was Elsie Polton. She said crisply: "Course it is. Go right on."

Anthony went right on. He said:

"You were in the dining room at Brooke Square at somewhere between five o'clock and half-past six, when you saw Miss Susan run down the steps?"

"Yes."

"Can you tell me—just forget anything you said to Superintendent Pike —can you give me any more exact time than this?"

"Yes." Elsie was entering whole-heartedly into this game; this game that meant so much.

"What time was it?"

"Can't say exactly, but it was nearer six than five and nearer half-past six than six."

"Right. Did you notice anything unusual about Miss Susan? Did she seem herself?"

"No. She seemed, well, very upset like."

"I see. She *ran* down the steps?"

"Yes."

"Did she turn left or right?"

"Left."

"Did she walk or run straight on after she had turned left. As if, I mean, she had got somewhere to go and knew where it was?"

"No. She seemed hesitating like. She was looking about the road. I thought perhaps she was looking for the Captain's car."

"Then a taxi came along, didn't it?"

"Yes."

"Where was the taxi when you first saw it?"

"Just coming round the corner out of Pool Street and turning down towards our house."

"And then it crossed over the road? Onto its wrong side—onto the side Miss Susan was walking along?"

"Yes."

"Did it just wander over, or did it cross over as if it was going to drop a fare at a house? Or did it——"

Elsie leant forward in her chair, raising a reproving finger. Elsie said: "Now, not so many questions. Not all at once. Give me a chance and I'll tell. . . . I'm remembering now. The taxi, when it swung out of Pool Street, well, it just made straight—sort of slantwise straight, if you know what I mean—straight at Miss Susan. And it stopped opposite her and she stopped when it stopped."

"And what did she do then? Did the driver do anything?"

"No. Miss Susan looked in the window. She seemed to be talking to somebody. She was waving her arm a bit. Seemed like as if she was excited."

"And then?"

"And then she stopped waving her arm and sort of pulled open the door in a hurry like and jumped in. And then the taxi turned round."

"To its left, would that be?"

"Don't be silly. Of course he had to turn round left, otherwise he'd've gone over the pavement. . . . Well, anyway, it turned round and was gone. I don't suppose I was watching more than a couple of minutes at the outside."

Anthony got up from the table. He began to walk about. He let Elsie cool for a moment. He said at last:

"Now, Elsie. I think that's where you stopped with the superintendent. Is that so?"

Once more Elsie was almost the parlourmaid. But not quite. She said: "Yes, sir. After all, that's all I can remember. After I saw the taxi turn round —well, Miss Susan was gone, and there was nothing for me to watch and never is in that street. Nothing but page boys and cats, and I don't like either of 'em."

Anthony came and stood before her, looking down at her. When he spoke his voice was different; grave and very deep. It impressed Elsie. "It went," said Elsie afterward to her friends, "sort of through a girl." He said:

"That, Elsie, is where you *think* you stop remembering. Now, it's up to us, between us, to find out whether there's something else you remember."

"Yes, sir," said Elsie.

"You saw that taxi turn round, didn't you? I mean, you didn't go away from the window until after it *had* turned round?"

"No, sir."

"So you saw the back of the taxi?"

"Yes, sir."

"Elsie, shut your eyes."

"Yes, sir." Elsie, obedient, closed her eyes.

Now Anthony's voice was very low and his words came slow. "Think of what you saw of that taxi. What colour was it?"

Silence. And then:

"Red. A sort of dirty red."

"The top was shut?"

"Yes."

"The top was shut. The taxi, or the back of it at least, was red. Was the back clean or dusty?"

Silence. And then:

"Dusty. Sort of whity over the red, if you know what I mean." Elsie's hands were clenched in her lap, each cotton glove stretched tight over a small fist.

"The taxi was red, had its top closed, and was dusty. . . . Now keep those eyes shut, Elsie, and *think*. Think of that taxi. Make a picture of it inside your head. Look at it going away from you. Look at it going toward Pool Street. Look at it, Elsie! . . . And tell me something else about it—anything."

The girl's eyes screwed up with the concentration of her effort. Anthony watched her; leant forward, bending down over her, trying to see with his mind into hers.

Silence. Then a sigh. Then:

"No. It's no good. I can't see anything else." Very slow these words; hopeless.

"Don't open your eyes. Think, girl, think! This isn't a party game. D'you know what may be happening to Miss Susan? D'you know that if we can't find her soon you may never see her again? D'you know that, Elsie? Think of that. . . . Think. . . . Think of that taxi. *Make* yourself think of it. *Now!*"

Silence.

The girl dropped her head into her hands; rocked to and fro with the violence of her effort.

Anthony watched her, his eyes blazing down at her unseeing head.

And then, slowly, she began to speak. "No. . . . it's no good. . . . OH! A bit of string. . . . *A bit of string!*"

Silence. A silence which Anthony left as long as he dared. He had to say at last:

"A bit of string? Where? On the taxi?"

"On the bottom of the back of the taxi." The words were coming very slowly. "A bit of string. . . . Untidy. . . . Tied round something. . . ."

Silence again. Then, at last, Anthony's voice; low, barely audible yet perfectly audible.

"That bit of string, Elsie. That bit of string. It's tying something on, isn't it?"

"Oh!" A shrill little squeal. The girl sat up. Her hands dropped from her face. Her eyes opened. "Yes, yes! I can see it all now. How I came to forget, I don't know. It was his number plate. It was all sort of hanging loose on the skew-dab, if you know what I mean. And he'd got it tied up with string and round and round. However I came to forget that I just don't know——"

She found herself speaking to empty air. The door by which she had come in, the door of the room where the Captain and those other gentlemen were, this door was open again. . . .

3

Into the heavy, taut silence of that other room Anthony entered like a gale. The three men at the moment of his entrance were seated, but he had barely crossed the threshold before all were on their feet.

"Got it!" he said. "Pike—forgive me, Lucas—put every damn man you've got onto this. A red taxi, top up, with a broken number plate tied up with string which brought a fare from farther west to Brooke Square and in Brooke Square picked up a lady at a quarter-past six this evening. Jump!"

Pike jumped. Heath's face was working. He said:

"What's this?"

"You sit down," said Anthony. "We're all right. We're onto something now. You wait."

"How long?"

Anthony was silent. "How long?" said Heath again, this time looking at Lucas. "Tell me!"

Lucas said, a little heavily:

"I'll be honest with you. It's something—it's a great deal. We can get that taxi. We might get it in an hour or we might get it in seven. Those are the limits."

Heath turned his back and walked away. He stared out of the window into the darkness. Lucas looked at Anthony.

"Gad, man! You look worn out! What you been doing? Third degree?"

Anthony mopped his face. "Third degree nothing! Svengali. What about a drink?"

"Alcoholic liquor," said Lucas, "is not allowed upon these premises." He went to a big cupboard, unlocked it with a key from his chain, produced a bottle, a siphon and two glasses. "Say when," he said, and then, "Heath!"

Heath turned. "Have one?" said Lucas.

"Thanks!" Heath almost snatched at the glass, poured himself a peg which came near to halfway, splashed in a little soda, put the glass to his lips and drank. "Thanks!" he said again. And then: "Tell me, is there a chance? Is there?"

"I don't know," said Anthony. "But I do know we're nearer something than we were twenty minutes ago. Here, let's have that glass. My subject wants one, I should think."

He took the glass, and the bottle and siphon, opened the door with two fingers, pushed it wide with his foot, went through it.

Elsie Polton was sitting where he had left her. Her eyes were closed, but at his approach they opened. She smiled at him; not quite the smile of the real Elsie Polton, but certainly not quite the smile of Elsie Polton, parlourmaid. He said: "What the doctor ordered."

He poured out a drink, splashed soda into it, and gave her the glass. "It should be taken with tobacco." He opened his case and held it out.

"Thank you, sir," said Elsie. She took both glass and cigarette. She said, looking up at him:

"Don't know why, but I feel real tired. Sort of like all the strings had been pulled out of me, if you know what I mean." There were darker shadows under the dark eyes.

"You drink that," Anthony said. "Back in a minute."

He was halfway to the door when she called him back. He heard her half-swallowed words and turned. She was standing up now, the cigarette dangling unheeded from her fingers, the glass in the other hand at such an angle that it was in danger of spilling its contents. She said:

"Could you tell me, sir—have I—is it—has there been any good like in what you made me remember?"

"Any good!" said Anthony. He came back toward her. He said: "You sit down again, and drink that and then see if you can't have a nap. If we get to Miss Kerr, as I think we shall, it'll all be due to you."

He held out his hand, and she took it. And then he was gone into the inner room again. As he entered, the telephone buzzed. Lucas was at it in one stride. Heath turned from the window. He stood tense; his face was impassive now, but with an impassivity somehow shocking.

"Yes?" said Lucas. "Yes. . . . Yes. . . . You've what? . . . You *haven't!* . . . Good God! All right. . . . Yes, yes, take *all* the cars if you want 'em. . . . Hurry, man. Hurry! . . ."

He put down the receiver on its hook. He got up slowly. Still his eyes were astonished. He said very quietly:

"That was Pike. They've found that taxi already!"

"Hallelujah!" said Anthony.

Heath took half a step forward; opened his mouth and then shut it again.

"Yes," said Lucas. He looked at Heath. "Luck's beginning to be with us now. That's the quickest find I've ever known in years. It's a Kensington taxi, in Baron's Garage. The driver's off duty, but they've got his address. Pike's going round there now." He looked at his watch. "Let's see, the streets are clear, Ross is driving. . . . They'll get there in seven minutes. They ought to be back here nearly within twenty."

They were, in fact, within twenty-two. Pike and a short, fat, untidy and bewildered being whose name, it appeared, was Periwinkle. Mr. Periwinkle, having been dragged from an early bed, was not only frightened but cross. But Mr. Periwinkle was handled—handled firmly and yet kindly. It was Anthony who gave him a drink. After the drink Mr. Periwinkle's seeming reluctance to part with information became miraculously changed to an overweening desire to help.

Mr. Periwinkle put down the glass with a smack upon Lucas's mantel-piece. "Ar, yerss!" said Mr. Periwinkle. "Corst I remembers. I'm a man as never fergits nothink. Wonderful mem'ry I've got! Yerss! These fares you're talkin' about. The first one, 'e picks me up round the back of Queen's Club there. 'E sez, 'Got a long job fer you, cabby.' I sez, 'Yerss, hop in.' An' 'e 'opped in. Told me to drive direck to Jook Square: when I gets there 'e'd direck me again. Just as we turns the corner into Jook Square from Pool Street, 'e 'ollers down my speakin'-choob—an' I'd 'ave you know, gentlemen, as my speakin'-choob is a speakin'-choob that you *can* speak froo. It's not just a lump o' rubber wiv a nozzle on the end to misguide folks. It's a speakin'-choob!—Well, my fare, 'e 'ollers down the speakin'-choob so stutterin' loud 'e nearly wrecks my eardrum. 'E sez: 'See that lady just come out of that 'ouse? I want to pick 'er up.' So I slews across, sir, an' we picks up a little piece, sir—a very smart young lady wot 'ad just come out of one of the 'ouses. I think it was number firteen."

"Half a minute, Periwinkle." This from Lucas. "Did the lady seem to be expecting a car or taxi?"

"Oh, yerss! At least, it looked that way to me. Not as I was takin' much notice like, me bein' a man as just does his job and takes no notice of nuffink. But, yerss, now you come to mention it, it did seem as if the lady was expectin' somethink. But, anyways, I drove up alongside of 'er, on the right-'and side that is, that's my wrong side, if you foller me, sir, accordin' to the instructions down my choob. Then the lady, she looks in at my fare froo the winder and she lets out some sort of a little squeak. Well, I thinks, that's a bit funny, but I starts to turn round, and then I thinks, 'Well, t'ain't none o' Bert Periwinkle's business, and that's that.' I just sits there, and as long as the clock's tickin' I'm 'appy."

"*But where did you go, man?*" Heath had come forward now. His hands were clenched into fists, his whole body stiff.

"Shut up, blast you!" said Anthony into his ear. And Heath muttered in his throat and was quiet.

Mr. Periwinkle rolled a watery eye in his interrupter's direction.

"Comin' to that," said Mr. Periwinkle, "in joo course. I tells the story in me own way or not at all, an' I'm not frightened of no man, bein' honest meself. Not even if I *am* in Scotland Yard!"

"Now, then, Periwinkle, cut all that out!" Pike's voice, crisp and official. Then, in the man's ear, Anthony's whisper:

"Ten bob if you keep your shirt in, Periwinkle. Stick it!"

Periwinkle stuck it. He picked on Lucas to talk to. He said:

"Shall I go on, sir, or do I jest answer questions like?"

"Go on! Go on!" said Lucas. "Did the lady get in?"

"Yerss, sir, just what I was a-comin' to before all these interruptions. An' we should 'a' bin there a sight quicker if it 'adn't bin for all these interruptions. . . ."

"Go on, man. Go on!"

"Well, the lady gets in me cab, sir, seeming to 'ave recovered from that sort of shock like what made 'er give that little squeak. And then my fare —the bloke—'e picks up the choob again and yells froo it, 'Victoria.'"

A gasp—Heath's—from the background.

"Yerss," said Mr. Periwinkle. "Victoria, 'e shouts, and nearly splits me eerole agen. The fact is, it's still buzzin'." He put a tentative finger into his left ear, probed gently with a gentle look of inquiry upon his face, shook his head, and resumed.

"So to Victoria I goes, sir. And at Victoria out gets my fares, and the bloke pays me, and off I goes, and that's all, sir, as I c'n tell you, thankin' you kindly for the same!"

Pike cut in: "Now, Periwinkle, did you get a look at your fares at all?"

"Oh, yerss! I've told you wot the young lady looked like, and anyway you all seems to know——"

"What was the man like?"

"Tallish," said Mr. Periwinkle. "Stiffish build; toff. 'Drave me lake L to Jook Squaw.'"

"Clean shaven?" It was Anthony's turn.

"Oh, yerss!"

"Whereabouts at Victoria did you drop them? Station yard?" Pike.

"I said Victoria and I meant Victoria. W'ere else at Victoria would you drop a fare that arst to go to Victoria excep' the station yard? Yerss, station yard, it was."

"You see where they went? In which direction?" Lucas.

"So far as I can rec'leck, sir—" Mr. Periwinkle knew the difference between his commissioner and his superintendent of police—"so far as I can rec'leck, sir," said Mr. Periwinkle again, "into the station they did go. Under the canopy and down what you might call the first alleyway."

"What time did they get to Victoria?" Anthony.

"As near as I can say, sir—" Mr. Periwinkle did not know who this other tall gentleman might be, but he kept upon the safe side—"as near as I can say, sir, somewhere around fifteen minutes of seven."

"I see." This from Lucas. "Pike, this man can go. Got that car downstairs?"

"Yes, sir."

"Got any men by it?"

"Three, sir."

"Right." Lucas looked at Anthony. "Victoria, I think, don't you, Gethryn?"

Anthony nodded. He had his wallet in his hand. From it he had abstracted a ten-shilling note which, cosily folded, found its way a moment later into Mr. Periwinkle's receptive hand.

4

Once more the blue police car and the black Voisin-Maxwell were parked tail to nose. They were in the fore court of Victoria Station. By them were four men: the driver of the police car and three plain-clothes detectives. At the other side of the station, in an austere, barely furnished, but cleanly room which yet smelt of a thousand engines, were Lucas and Pike, Heath and Anthony. They sat stiffly on stiff wooden chairs, rigidly arranged to face the station master's table. Behind the table was the station master himself, pompous, kindly, perturbed, and efficient. To the right of the table stood, not at all at ease, the third of the ticket collectors who had appeared before this conclave.

"Very well, Briggs," said the station master. "You can go. Tell the next man to come in."

Heath, sitting beside Anthony, shifted uneasily.

"Wait," said Anthony.

The fourth man came in. Younger than his predecessors, pleasanter to the eye, more self-assertive.

"Travers," said the station master, "you were on number six gate on second shift?"

"Yes, sir." Travers's voice was as smart as his appearance.

"I think you are an observant man, Travers. Now, you must have passed in on your shift hundreds of young couples of whom the man was dark and tall and the young woman short and fair?"

"Thousands, more like, sir."

"Exactly. Now these gentlemen, Travers, are from Scotland Yard."

"Yes, sir," said Travers. He strived, not very successfully, to keep his eye from dwelling on the sleuths.

"They want, Travers, to trace the destination of a tall, dark, clean-shaven, well dressed young man, probably giving first-class tickets, who had with him a short, fair, smartly dressed and very charming young lady."

"Yes, sir."

"*Very* smartly dressed," Anthony put in quietly. "*Very* charming."

"Think of that, Travers."

"Yes, sir," said Travers.

"These gentlemen think," said the station master, "that it is possible that the young lady was appearing ill. That's their theory, you see. . . . Yes, Travers?"

"Seen 'em, sir," said Travers. His tone was even crisper, his words even quicker than before. Under his trim exterior he plainly seethed with the excitement of the chase and the prominent part he might play in it.

"When, Travers?" The station master again. "Don't answer too quickly. Think before you speak."

"Yes, sir." It was plain that Travers knew; equally plain that he was obeying instructions and thinking, albeit quite unnecessarily, before he spoke. "Yes, sir. . . . They went by the seven fifty-three Marsham–Hailsbury fast, sir."

The station master held up a finger for silence. He looked at Lucas. "Now, sir, I think perhaps we have found our man. Perhaps you would like to take on the questioning of this collector? Travers, just answer as briefly as you can all the questions this gentleman likes to put to you."

"Yes, sir."

"Travers," said Lucas, "give us your description of this couple, will you?"

"Yes, sir. Tall gentleman, very well dressed, sort of half-country, half-London clothes. Tweeds, if you know what I mean, sir. Age anywhere between thirty and forty, sir. Dark complexion, clean-shaven, heavy build, full face, sir. Young lady, much younger, very small, sir, *very* pretty like. Young lady didn't seem to be well, sir. Gentleman had his arm round her. Her eyes were half closed. She didn't seem to know where she was, like. While I was clipping the tickets, sir, the gentleman kept saying, 'It's all right. It's all right. You'll be all right as soon as I can get you sitting down in the train.' The gentleman apologized for holding the tickets awkward. Said the lady had been taken queer but would be all right in a minute."

Lucas bent forward in his chair. Into his official monotone there crept an easily discernible anxiety. "Travers," he said slowly, "you don't, I suppose, happen to remember the destination on the tickets this man gave you?"

Travers smiled; a brief smile, eminently respectful, of self-esteem. "Oh, yes, but I do, sir!"

"What?" Lucas was startled out of his calm.

"I remember quite well, sir. Owing to the way he was standing, holding the young lady and all, the gentleman dropped the tickets. I bent down and picked them up. That's what fixed the destination in my mind. The tickets were for Chasing Bury."

"Where's that?"

The station master answered this one. "It's a small station about forty miles down the line between Horfield and Clissop."

Heath half rose from his chair, but Anthony's hand forced him down again. Lucas was saying:

"Does that train stop at this place?"

"Yes, sir," said Travers before the station master could speak. "After Horfield it stops at Chasing Bury, Little Benders, and Ockleton. Then there's no stop till Marsham itself."

Lucas rose. He said to the station master:

"We're much obliged, sir. What's the next train?"

"To Chasing Bury?" The station master thought a moment. "Let me see, is there one?"

"Excuse me, sir." The self-complacent Travers once more. "Excuse me, sir, if these gentlemen was to move, sir, they could catch the eleven twenty-one and change at Bramingham Junction. There'll be a wait there of ten minutes, and they could catch the branch mail to Chasing Bury."

The gentlemen moved.

5

But they did not go down to Chasing Bury by rail. Upon a table in the long room of the Victoria refreshment bar they spread maps; pored over them; found their route.

The police car was the first to start. But the police car only held its lead for some two hundred yards down the Vauxhall Bridge Road. Then the Voisin-Maxwell drew abreast. From the seat beside the driver Heath leaned out and shouted. The police car pulled up. From the offside window was thrust Lucas's head. Anthony called:

"Lucas! Let me have a policeman?"

The head nodded; was withdrawn. The door upon the far side of the saloon opened and shut, and presently, with them, climbing into the back seat, was a smiling Pike. The two cars moved off. Once more Lucas leaned out of the window. This time he shouted:

"You may be there first. If you get anything, leave word at the station."

Anthony raised his left hand in salute and acknowledgment; and then his left hand came down to the wheel again. The big car shot forward. In the back seat Pike gasped. In the seat beside the driver's Heath leant forward. The faster they went, the faster he wished they would go. . . .

The driver of the police car—the best and at the same time the most notoriously speed-thirsty driver in the police force—did his best. But after that salute of Anthony's the others did not see, upon the forty-mile run down the Portsmouth Road, even so much as the flicker of his tail light. It was not a journey that Pike cares to remember. He is, when asked about it, very reticent. Heath remembers nothing because he was noting nothing. Heath, for this time, was an Idea.

They were near the end of their journey before anyone in the Voisin-Maxwell spoke. And that was when Anthony pulled up at a crossroad, and a hillock with a signpost sticking up out of it like a finger. He switched on his spotlight, and Pike spoke from behind him.

"Right-hand fork, sir," he said. "Chasing Bury, three miles."

Heath twisted in his seat, his first movement since the beginning of this rush through the night. He muttered something they couldn't catch and was silent again.

The car started, swung slowly right; gathered speed.

They were driving down a narrow Surrey lane. Upon either side of them were green banks. Along the tops of the banks were great trees whose green arms met above their heads. A tunnel of green and black; a tunnel whose floor turned into a blazing river under the lights. . . .

The clock on the dashboard stood at ten minutes past twelve. Over his shoulder Anthony spoke to Pike:

"Station first, I think."

"Yes, sir."

They found it easily enough, for they came, after passing the straggling outskirts of the village, down a hill and under a railway bridge. The station stood at the top of the hill on the other side. It was in darkness. It was locked. They stood on the pavement and looked about them. Anthony went back to the car; swivelled his spotlight; shone its beam this way and that.

"There!" said Heath. "There! Isn't that a cottage?"

"That's it, sir." Beside him Pike ran. Together they followed the white palings leading to the station master's garden. Anthony stayed by the car. Pike found a door, beat on its knocker. No answer.

Heath shouldered him aside; took the knocker and hammered with it. . . .

Success. Above their heads a window was thrown open. From it came a stream of abuse—and Pike, nudging Heath, stated who he was and why. Within two and a half minutes he and Heath were standing in the passage of the station master's cottage. The station master, an old overcoat over his nightshirt, his feet tucked into wool-lined slippers several sizes too small for him, strove to atone for the abuse. Yes, it *was* part of his duty to collect

tickets for the night trains. . . . Yes, he did start these duties before eight.
. . . Yes, he had done so to-night. . . . Yes, he did, now the gentleman came
to ask him, think he remembered a strange lady and gentleman getting off
the eight-forty. But then there was quite a crowd on that train always, and
it was a bit hard, with only one's self to take the tickets and all, to remember.
One didn't seem to have much time for looking at faces.

Heath seized his arm and shook it. "You *must* have seen them! You must!"

Pike said: "It's this gentleman whose wife has been abducted."

The station master clicked a sympathetic tongue.

"So you see," said Pike, "how very important it is that you try and
remember."

The station master strove. He seemed unable to think without grunting.
Judging by the number of his grunts, he was thinking hard. He spoke just
as they had despaired of hearing his voice again.

"Would the party you was looking for be a stout, elderly man and a
stoutish lady not quite so old?"

There came a muttered oath, and the banging of the door. Heath was
gone.

"Tck-tck!" said the station master. And then:

"That'd be all. Except of course, a young leddy and gennlemun, but they
wouldn't be——"

"Young lady and gentleman? What sort of young lady and gentleman?"

"First class. Tallish, stiffish-built, youngish gentleman; smallish leddy."
The station master cackled suddenly. "If that's them you're lookin' for, I
think him that's just gone out had best save himself. Very lovin' an' all this
lot were. Had his arm round her. An' on the public platform! *And* she was
leanin' 'gainst him! Where's your 'duction there? Eh?"

"You didn't," said Pike, "notice where they went, I suppose? Which way?"

The head was shaken again. "Couldn't tell you nought. They took one
o' Stevens's cabs."

"Where does *he* live?" Pike was growing curt. "Stevens, I mean?"

"Stevens? Would it be Joe or young Jim you be meanin'?"

"The one," said Pike, "that runs the cabs."

"Ah! That's Charlie. Charlie, he lives over t'other side of the yard. Over
yonder. Over his mother's 'baccy shop. But if you think that Charlie Stevens
—— Hi, mister!"

But now the station master stood alone. His front door was open, and a
chill night breeze played about his bony ancient ankles. He muttered. He
shut the door, muttering still. He went up to bed and to sleep. He waked in
the morning uncertain as to whether the whole affair had been dream or
reality. . . .

6

Now there were two cars in the station yard at Chasing Bury. The police
car had caught up. Over the road, outside the newspaper shop which bore
over its single window the name L. WIDDIMAN, stood a little group of

five. Inside the room, immediately above the Widdiman window, were Pike and Anthony. They were talking to Mr. Charles Stevens who "ran the cabs."

Mr. Charles Stevens was a red-faced and burly man. He was also, though his looks belied him, a man of ready intelligence. Also he was helpful. He said:

"No trouble at all, gentlemen. I 'aven't got to think, becos I drove the pair meself. Can't be mistaken, 'cause they were strangers!"

"You can't tell us where the house is?" said Pike. "Where they went?"

"It's a sure thing I can, mister. It's that new two-storied cottage Cockerinn put up last year. 'Bout three or four mile out along the Harling road."

Mr. Stevens was thanked quickly. Mr. Stevens was left even more quickly. With the slamming of the door the group upon the pavement sprang to life. Pike spoke hurriedly with Lucas; with the driver of the police car. The party split as before. By the signpost at the corner of the station yard they saw that Harling lay four miles to the east.

The police car was off first. But once more the Voisin-Maxwell in two hundred yards passed it with a roaring boom.

7

"Good!" said Anthony. "Follow along, will you?"

They were working—he and Pike and Heath—round to the back of the two-storied cottage called appropriately "The Firs." They were in a copse of firs. They had struck off from the road a hundred yards before the cottage. In front, at the other side of the house, were Lucas and the others.

Anthony led the way out of the trees, crossed a small paddock of rough pasture, wriggled through a wire fence, and was in the cottage garden. . . .

In one of the four ground-floor windows of the cottage a light was burning. Anthony halted; then went on again. Pike drew level. Behind them kept Heath. They crossed a small lawn. On the dew-drenched grass they moved without sound. The lawn came to an abrupt end, and they were on a small flagged walk which separated for the whole of its length the house from the grass. The pink glow from behind the curtained French window to their left still shone softly. Toward this window, moving now upon tiptoe, they went in single file.

It was as Anthony set careful fingers to the window latch that, from the other side of the house, came the sound of knocking. To Pike at his elbow Anthony whispered approval. The knocking ceased, but only for a moment; it began again with redoubled clamour. A thunderous noise.

Pike pressed his ear to the window; suddenly stiffened; suddenly held up a finger for silence.

The knocking went on. The three outside the window held their breath. Against his shoulder Anthony could fell Heath's fingers pressing, digging into the flesh. Pike whispered:

"Somebody's just gone out of this room."

The knocking ceased. The silence which followed it was broken by the rattle of chain and bolt.

"*Now!*" said Anthony. Together he and Pike threw their shoulders against the centre struts of the window frame. With a little tearing, rending noise it gave. Pike staggered, caught his foot on the inch-high sill, and fell headlong into the room. After him Anthony reeled; with a wrench recovered himself. As he stood, now firmly upright, something brushed violently past him—Heath.

But the room was otherwise empty. Anthony's eyes, in one swift circular glance, took in this room and its furnishings. A small room but pleasant, with trappings and fitments pleasing enough in their way.

Heath was at the door now. Suddenly, with a wrench, he had it open. . . .

From the floor Pike picked himself up; was on Anthony's heels at the door through which Heath had just now gone. Just across the threshold Anthony checked. Into his back, unable to stop, Pike crashed. "Sorry, sir!" he grunted. "Now, where the *Jing* . . . !

"Ssh . . . !" Anthony's warning was savage. "Listen!"

They listened. They were standing at one end of a long and narrow hall. At the other end was the front door, and the front door was open. And from just inside it there came a voice. Lucas's. Anthony's fingers groped the wall opposite him; pressed the switch. Light flooded the place. The first thing that these two saw was Heath. He stood three feet in front of them. He was motionless, but his body was bent forward from the hips. His arms were crooked, their hands reaching out a little way before him. He looked like an animal checked in midspring.

At the other end of the hall, just within the half-open door, Lucas stood facing them. But Lucas had not seen them. Lucas's head and gaze were downbent as he talked to someone—a woman, with her back to them. A small, slight figure—very neat. Under the lamp the head glinted with a sheen of coppery gold.

It seemed to Anthony as if neither he nor any of this group moved for quite an appreciable time. They were, he thought, like a suddenly arrested moving picture. It seemed to him, as indeed it must have seemed to them all, incredible that here was Susan, and a Susan—even just by that one glimpse of her back—utterly unfrightened, quite unhurt, completely and happily herself. . . .

For another long wavering moment the tableau seemed to hold. Then it was shattered by Heath. It was as if an image in a pool had been broken by the plumping of a rock.

Heath moved—and the little figure at the far end of the passage whipped round.

"*Trevor!*" she said. Her arms came out; she took half a step forward, but not more than half a step. Before that half step could be a whole one Heath was upon her.

Past these two, interlocked and oblivious, Lucas picked delicate way. Pike and Anthony came to meet him. They stood, the three of them, silent. Lucas spoke first.

"If somebody," he said, "will tell me that I'm still awake I'd be obliged."
Pike scratched his head. He said:

"Well, it won't be me, sir. I can't get the feel of this!"

Anthony grinned. "You know what's the matter with you, Police, is that
you're disappointed. You came rushing through the night hoping to find
dismembered parts of the lady packed away behind the bath, and when
you do find her, she's all in one and apparently not needing your assistance.
And you just can't bear it!"

But Pike was taking no chaff. He was too puzzled. He repeated: "I can't
get the *feel* of this, sir! I haven't spoken to her, but I'll take my oath that
young lady's not even worried!"

"She isn't," said Lucas. He stood a moment, then turned on his heel;
walked back purposefully to the lovers. Pike followed. Anthony, content
with the onlooker's part, sat down upon a table and began to feel for his
cigarette case. He heard Lucas's voice.

"Miss Kerr," it was saying. "Miss Kerr, I'm sorry, but I must ask you to
give me your attention. . . ."

Anthony's smile widened into a grin.

"Course she will, Lucas! Course she will!" This was Heath, but this,
thought Anthony, was the real Heath. This was a Heath with a different
voice, a Heath who seemed fifteen years younger and a stone or two heavier
than the man who had been with them throughout the night. Heath and
Susan stood now, arm locked in arm. Susan's golden head was not quite
level with her lover's shoulder.

Lucas was saying: "How did you get here? *Why* did you get here? If it
comes to that, Miss Kerr, *who* brought you here? Was it Trenchard?"

Susan nodded brightly. "Yes, poor man. He's very, very tired. He's upstairs, sleeping. Think how tired he must have been when your knocking
didn't wake him up."

Lucas put a hand to his forehead in bewilderment. Heath stiffened. For
a moment there came a return to his face of that pinched and bleak and
ravaged seaming. Susan looked up, laid a hand on his arm.

"Trevor!" she said. That was all. But it was enough.

"But Trenchard . . . Trenchard . . . He . . . Did you come . . . How
did he . . ." Lucas was battling bravely with his reeling mind.

Anthony, through the smoke of his cigarette, looked at Lucas's face and
then at Pike's. And if Lucas's face made him smile, Pike's made him put his
head back and laugh aloud. That laugh seemed to be the quick-match for
Lucas's temper. He turned; he glared. He took two steps forward and said:

"Yes, you can laugh, Gethryn! But if you're so blasted clever, perhaps
you'll explain to-night for me."

Anthony got to his feet. "My dear fellow, I wouldn't even try. I'm just
as much at sea as you are. But I'm not a disappointed policeman! I'm merely
a pleased civilian. You wait, my lad, you'll hear!"

He looked over toward the lovers. "Miss Kerr will tell you." He raised his
voice. "Miss Kerr!"

She looked up questioningly.

Anthony, still smiling, went toward her. "Miss Kerr," he said again, "I wonder whether you realize what a shock you've given us?" He looked at her. "Yes, I expect you do. I'd like to suggest that we find somewhere in this house to sit down and then hear from you exactly how you come to be here. What, in other words, the whole business is about."

"I think," said a voice—a new voice from behind and above them—"I think that ought to be my job."

Five pairs of eyes went to the stairhead. In the third stair, coming down toward them, was Trenchard. He was dressed still in the "tweedy clothes" described by the ticket collector Travers at Victoria Station, but they were no longer very smart seeming. They were rucked and rumpled and creased, and his black hair—wiry, kinky black hair—stood up now in wild disorder. There was about the whole man the appearance of one just roused from sleep. He blinked at the light. His heavy face was dead white. He looked first at Susan and then from Susan to the four men. There was in that look a certain sort of apologetic defiance.

For an appreciable moment nobody moved; no one spoke. Anthony was silent from choice, the other men because—although a moment ago they had thought they would, when see Trenchard they did, have plenty to say—they found themselves now without a word. When you have been rushing over a quarter of England in search of a man who has, most blackguardly, stolen away a young woman, and then you find the young woman is no more perturbed than was Susan Kerr, your mind, to whatever class it belongs, cries out for readjustment. It was Anthony who broke the silence. He looked at Trenchard and said:

"I was suggesting to Miss Kerr, as you heard, that we find somewhere to sit down and hear all about it. This your house?"

Trenchard nodded; a wry, rather bitter smile crossed for a moment his heavy white face. "Yes," he said. He pushed through the little group. He threw open a door. After him the party filed. They stood in a small dining room. Round the oak table Trenchard set chairs. "If you'd all sit down," he said.

They sat down. Lucas found his voice. Lucas said:

"I think it only fair to tell you, sir, that I'm not yet certain whether a charge lies against you or not. If we find eventually that it does, then anything you tell us now——"

"I know! I know!" said Trenchard, "'may be taken down and used as evidence against me.' That doesn't matter, and I rather fancy, you know, that there won't be a charge." He looked at Susan. "Miss Kerr," he said, "has already told me that she won't charge me, and I don't see that anyone else can in these circumstances. The worst I've been is a damn fool."

He stood at the end of the table, looking round upon the seated five. There was a chair beside him, but he did not sit. He rested his hands upon the table. He said, in a flat, heavy voice:

"Just damn' foolishness, that's all it's been. . . . I take it you want the truth without embroideries and in as few words as possible?"

Lucas nodded and Pike said: "Certainly."

Trenchard looked down at the table. He spoke lower now, almost as if he were speaking to himself. He said:

"From the time she was sixteen, until she—died—I was in love—very much in love—with Eve. When she was eighteen I began asking her to marry me. For a time it looked as if she would. I had to wait because her parents thought she wasn't old enough to decide. That waiting—did me in. Three years ago she met Hale-Storford. He fell in love with her and she with him. They married within eighteen months. I never met Hale-Storford before they were married—I didn't want to. I was away when the engagement was announced, and I stayed away. Then I went down—not knowing, mind you, anything about Hale-Storford having taken the house in the neighbourhood—to stay with old Banner in Wessex. We went out for a sail one evening and got driven ashore just below Hale-Storford's house. He saw us and came down and was very decent, I must say. We went in, stayed to dinner, and stayed the night. . . ."

Here Trenchard raised his head. He looked once more round at the seated party; looked, in fact, at each in turn, but each pair of eyes that met his were meeting, and knew they were meeting, eyes which did not really see them. Trenchard moistened dry lips with his tongue. He went on. He was now speaking more slowly; it was as if each word and the production of each word were an effort to him. He said:

"I can tell you, I got a pretty nasty jolt when I found whose house I was in. There was Eve, looking more beautiful, I think, than ever I'd seen her before. She was, as always, delightful to me. I kept telling myself that she must be happy, but somehow, I can't tell you when or how, something seemed to me to be wrong. . . . Perhaps that was only a premonition. I don't know much about those things. Can't say I've ever believed in them before. Anyhow, I'm not going to tell you the rest of what happened that night. You know for yourselves, all of you. I can only say—" very slowly his words were coming now; he seemed to stumble over some of them—"I can only say," he repeated, "that when Hale-Storford and Banner and I went upstairs and found—and found what you know we found, I thought for the rest of that night that I was going to lose my reason. . . ."

He stopped. He squared his shoulders, put back his head, and gave a little sound which was meant, it seemed, to be a laugh. A distressing sound.

"But I didn't!" he said. "Not on your life I didn't. Nothing so pleasant as *that* happened to me. I just went on being sane and suffering and hoping against hope that they'd find out whichever devil had done that—that—whichever devil it was and hang him. Or her. Though hanging, I thought, was a damn sight too good. . . ."

He put out a hand behind him and groped with it; found the chair, pulled it toward him, and sat heavily and quickly—almost as if his legs had betrayed him. "That's all," he said, and now his voice had in it so queer a deadness that the eyes of Susan came round to him, big with pity. "All, I mean, that it's necessary to say to lead up to to-night. What happened to me was this: I *knew* that either that woman Graye, that boy Anstruther, or her sister, had killed Eve. *Knew* it, I tell you! Knew it because as I was down there all that time with Hale-Storford himself and Banner—neither of them could have done it—and no one, whatever the puling fools at the inquest said, could have got into that house and done it and got out again without being found out."

Across the table Pike's small and now very bright brown eyes sought Anthony's. Anthony nodded.

". . . knew it, I tell you!" Trenchard was saying. His fist banged down on the table. A glass bowl which stood in centre of the table rang softly. "Knew it! And I had to sit there day after day after damnable day, watching whichever devil it was get away with it. And then—you all know this—the Rossiter woman ran her car over that cliff and was blotted out. And then the Anstruther boy was drowned. Those were supposed to be *accidents.*"

Again across the table Pike and Anthony exchanged a glance.

"But," said Trenchard, "I couldn't see them as accidents. I *wouldn't* see them as accidents! Four people, and one of them guilty of the foulest crime, and two of them suddenly to die *accidentally!* I didn't believe, and by God!"—again his fist hit the table—"I don't believe it now! . . . What I believed—what I *believe*, is that the devil who killed Eve turned into a frightened devil; thought that—perhaps going a little mad—one of the four must have seen or heard something dangerous which at sometime would come out. . . ."

He looked round the room again at his audience, this time with eyes which saw them, and in his eyes—dark eyes with a fire behind their darkness—was something of appeal.

"Don't you see," he said, "don't you see that I'm right? You must! You're not fools like those damn country bobbies and that doddering coroner! You must see! I'm not mad, I know that! Sometimes I wish to God I were! . . . Four people, one guilty, and two of them gone. Who were the two that were left? The woman Graye and—and Miss Kerr. Now, I haven't been down in Wessex all the time. I left as soon as I could, but I've kept abreast of Polferry news through Banner, and I knew, or thought I knew, the woman Graye hadn't been in a position to cause these accidents. Who then was left? Miss Kerr." Across the dead white pallor of his face an ironic smile of self-derision flashed momentarily. "I didn't, you see, know Miss Kerr so well as I do now. I thought—perhaps I didn't reason enough, but I thought it *must* be Miss Kerr, and I thought—damn it, I almost knew!—that the police were doing nothing. Was I to watch what I thought was the devil who killed Eve make itself safe by killing all those who might possibly be dangerous to it? I couldn't. I tried to stick it out; I even went away; but I couldn't. I kept coming back to—to——"

He suddenly put his elbows on the table and into his cupped hands dropped his forehead, but his voice went on. "I saw her, you know. Eve, I mean. None of *you* did! P'r'aps if you had you would—— Well, that's no matter. I've done what I've done. I began to look out for a chance to get Miss Kerr, thinking that she was the devil I was looking for, where I could make her—" words now were coming through barely opening lips—"make her," he repeated, "confess. I took to watching her. I think I was good at it. And I found that she was always with you." He said these words straight at Heath. "And I had to get rid of you, so I did that hospital story. I sent you off to that hospital for Miss Kerr, and I got Miss Kerr away by the same dodge about you. I came in that taxi. I told her I was from the hospital. When she saw me, of course, she knew who I was. But I told her some damn lie, and got her into the cab."

"It was a very good lie," said Susan.

"Once I'd got her in the cab, I——" He seemed to choke. He raised his head; he said slowly: "I drugged her—I'll give you all details of that afterward if you want to take me—and got her down here by train, pretending she was ill. I brought her into this room; waited until she came round. . . . When she came round I began to talk to her. I told her what I've told you, only more. I told her——"

Susan's voice interrupted; said very clearly and very kindly:

"Mr. Trenchard, I don't think it's necessary, you know, to tell too much. I've forgotten, you see. So . . ."

Trenchard smiled at her, a real smile this time which lit quite magically the saturnine mask of his heavy face. He said, looking now at Lucas:

"You hear that? That's the sort of woman Susan Kerr is. I've told you I'm not mad, and so it didn't take me long to find out that I'd made a mistake, and a ghastly mistake. You see, I didn't know Miss Kerr well—not at all, in fact. We had been together in the house at Polferry, we had been together a little during those weeks of the inquest, but we had never known each other. If we had, I'd never have made—never have been such a fool. . . . After Miss Kerr had talked to me, I saw . . ."

"That's all, I think." His big body slumped as he sat. He seemed, suddenly, to have lost all force. He sat staring straight across the table at Lucas.

There was silence; heavy and uncomfortable silence.

"Miss Kerr," said Lucas at last. His voice was tersely and monotonously official. "Have you no charge to make against this man?"

Susan smiled, a smile which robbed the words which came after it of much of their sting. "Isn't that rather silly?" said Susan. "I should have thought you'd have gathered that by this time."

"In that case," said Lucas, looking now at Pike, "the matter stays where it is. Miss Kerr, if you'd like to get back to London we can take you in the police car."

"I say," said Anthony mildly, "if nobody minds, I think I'd like to ask Mr. Trenchard a question or so."

Trenchard lifted his heavy head.

"I'd like to ask," said Anthony, "whether, Trenchard, you've given up your idea that it was one of those four who killed Mrs. Hale-Storford."

Trenchard stiffened. "No!" he said, and then again, "No!"

"Meaning . . . ?" said Anthony.

"Graye," said Trenchard. Once more he was erect in his chair. Once more his eyes had that fire behind their darkness.

Anthony looked at him. "If," he said, "I were to tell you, or rather get Superintendent Pike here to tell you, that it's quite impossible—and I'm using the word in its real and fullest sense—for Mrs. Graye to have been the author of these *accidents,* what would you say?"

Trenchard looked at him for a long moment before speaking.

"I don't," he said, "know who you are, but you look as if you're talking the truth as you know it. What I'd say is that perhaps after all I'm wrong in thinking myself sane."

Anthony leaned his arms upon the table. He gazed steadily at Trenchard. They looked at each other, these two, as if they were alone. Anthony said:

"And what would you say if I were to tell you, Trenchard, that less than six hours ago Hale-Storford—Hale-Storford, Trenchard—was stopped from killing Dorothy Graye? What would you say if I were to tell you, too, that there is no doubt now in the minds of Scotland Yard that it was Hale-Storford who was the author of all the *accidents?*"

Trenchard shot to his feet. His chair, thrust so suddenly back, fell to the carpet with a soft crash. His eyes, wide and staring, blazed into Anthony's. He put up a hand to his head.

"Hale-Storford," he said. "What are you telling me, man?"

"That Hale-Storford," said Anthony quietly, "sent Miriam Rossiter to her death, and that Hale-Storford drowned young Anstruther while pretending to save him; that Hale-Storford tried to kill Miss Kerr upon three or four occasions and failed, and that Hale-Storford to-night was only just prevented from killing Dorothy Graye."

Trenchard put out a hand behind him, groping for his chair. Not finding it, the hand came back to rest heavily upon the table, supporting his weight. Still he stared at Anthony. He said in a harsh whisper:

"But you're talking madness, man! *He* couldn't have killed Eve. I know it! I know it! I was there, wasn't I? I was there just behind him when he found her. . . ."

Anthony shook his head. "I'm not saying that Hale-Storford killed his wife. No. What I'm telling you is that Hale-Storford has killed Miriam Rossiter and George Anstruther and has tried to kill Dorothy Graye and Miss Kerr."

Trenchard gave a curious little shaking movement of his head, like a man who is trying to clear his sight. He said:

"Where—where do we get, then?"

Anthony shrugged. "Nowhere. That's the trouble. Nowhere, I mean, toward the original question: who killed Eve Hale-Storford? Hale-Storford has been insane since the death of his wife. And, being insane, he has tried to punish the killer of his wife. But, never being quite certain that his last victim was the real criminal, he has gone on killing. He would, I'm quite certain, have eliminated all four if he hadn't been stopped."

Trenchard raised from the table one of those hands which supported him; drew its back across his eyes. He said:

"But what do you want, man? Where do we get? Good God! . . ." A sudden excitement seemed to shake his thick body. "Good God! don't you see? We're just where we started. That Graye woman!"

Anthony shook his head. "I don't believe it. No, Trenchard, I don't believe it. . . . You said, what did I want—I'll tell you what I want. I want you; I want your help." Suddenly he switched his gaze to Lucas and from Lucas to Pike. "Look here," he said, "I want us to go down to that house, taking Trenchard. Trenchard can reconstruct for us. Don't you see, Lucas —don't you see, Pike—if there's an answer to this damned riddle anywhere —and there's always an answer to any riddle—it's in that house?"

Trenchard sat heavily upon the edge of the table. "I'm game," he said. . . .

8

Susan smiled. "I feel, you know," said Susan, "rather frighteningly unimportant. I mean, I'm not a bit used to being an anticlimax."

"You aren't," said Heath with controlled fervour.

They stood, Heath and Susan and Anthony, in the library of Susan's house. They had come up from Little Ockleton in Anthony's car. Somewhere, still on the road, was the police car, in it an extra passenger, Ralph Trenchard.

Anthony set down his glass. He smiled. To Susan he said:

"He's quite right, you know. You aren't."

"But," said Susan, "I am. Here have I, with *my* accidents, and *my* kidnapping, been keeping everybody—all the really big noises, I mean—frightfully excited, and now, just because they've 'cleared me up,' they go and get all bothered about something else. You know, Colonel Gethryn, you're being very polite, but you're not a bit interested in me now, are you?"

Anthony smiled again. "Personally, how could I possibly help it? Problematically, not in the least."

Susan grew suddenly grave. "I'm being rather a pig, you know, only this business—well, it's so somehow awful—isn't it?—that it makes you feel you've got to joke about it for fear of doing something else."

Anthony nodded. "Exactly."

"And you are—" now Susan was serious and eager—"and you are going down to—" she shivered a little—"to that house?"

"The day after to-morrow," said Anthony. "By that time we ought to be able to take Mrs. Graye with us as well as Trenchard. I wonder . . ." He looked at Susan. Susan shivered again, but she nodded.

"Certainly," said Susan. "Of course I will."

Anthony left then. They came to the front door and saw him off. Just as his car started he turned. They stood very close. Susan lifted an arm and waved. Anthony raised a hand in salute. His big black car shot forward. They watched the red eye of its rear light until, turning right into Pool Street, it vanished.

Susan slipped her arm through Heath's. In silence they turned and went back into the house.

CHAPTER IX

Lucas and Pike sat in the two chairs which faced each other across the hearth. Between them, facing the fire itself, were Trenchard and Susan. The three oil lamps lit the room with a hard yet yellow light. There was silence and uncomfortable silence. Pike looked at his watch.

"They've been a long time," he said.

Lucas nodded. "Yes, and we sit here like—— Well, never mind."

He stood up, a long and perhaps a little too elegant a figure. "Miss Kerr," he said. He looked toward the side table. "There's whisky there. Would you like a drink? Because I would, and I've no doubt Pike would, too. And you, Trenchard?"

Pike nodded. Trenchard—a silent and somehow ominous figure—shook his head.

Susan said:

"I'm afraid I would. I hate the stuff really, because they used to give me castor oil in it, but somehow—" she shivered; her small self seemed to be lost in the big chair— "somehow this room . . . Where *are* they?"

Pike jerked his head upwards. "Next floor," he said.

"I suppose," said Susan, her eyes very large. "I suppose I'm a fool to feel the way—to feel——"

Pike shook his head. He was by this time another slave of Susan's.

"Not a bit you're not, Miss Kerr," he said. "Not one little bit. I ought to be hardened enough, but I don't like this place."

Lucas came back with a tumbler for Susan. "Now, Pike!" he said.

Pike grinned. "Well, sir, I'll ask you the same question. Do you like this place? Honestly, now?"

Lucas shook his head. "I don't," he said. "But what worries me is why I don't. Perhaps it's the light."

"It's not," said Susan, "the *light*."

They fell silent again; uneasily silent. . . .

Upstairs, in the small bedroom which, with its large window, seemed like a box from which to look at the gray immensity of the sea; the room which had been hers for these past nine months which seemed twice that number of years, was Dorothy Graye. The window was open, the door was shut. She lay as she had been told, upon the bed. She listened. Listened, as also she had been told, with all her mind, all herself. She heard—nothing.

At last there came a tap upon her door. She swung her legs to the floor and sat up upon the edge of the bed. "Come in!" she said.

Anthony entered. There was a lamp—an old-fashioned white-globed, brass-standard oil lamp—in his right hand. Its yellow glow was soft and yet clear edged. "That's the last trial," he said. "Hear it?"

She shook her head. "I heard nothing again. Absolutely nothing."

Anthony considered this. The consideration did not seem to please him. He said after a moment:

"Right! We'll go down, then. Sure you're feeling fit for this, Mrs. Graye?"

Dorothy Graye nodded her head. "Quite," she said. Her tone was emphatic, but her looks gave the lie to what she had said. She was paler than even her usual pallor. Under her eyes were deeply impressed, black half circles.

They went downstairs.

"At last!" said Lucas. "Well?"

From a corner Anthony brought a chair for his companion. He said:

"Mrs. Graye has been in her room. She has been lying down and listening. While she listened I went from every one of those other bedrooms as quietly as I could into the bedroom which was Mrs. Hale-Storford's. I stayed there for as long as need be and went back to the room from which I had come. Not in any case did Mrs. Graye hear me. Pike, you and I tried it all, every other way round, this afternoon, and you heard nothing either."

Pike nodded. "That's right, sir."

Anthony, who had not sat down, went to the side table; poured whisky into a glass, splashed soda; brought the glass to Dorothy Graye. "Drink that," he said. "It doesn't matter if you don't like it. Drink it."

She smiled up at him wanly. She sipped; shuddered; sipped again. A little colour began to creep back into her face.

"What's next?" said Lucas.

Anthony exhibited irritation. "Damn it, man, I'm thinking of that! Let's wait, shall we?"

Lucas smiled. "All right! All right! D'you know, Gethryn, if this house hadn't got the feeling it has, I'd almost be inclined to like this. You're generally so certain, you know. It's refreshing to ordinary people like Pike and me to watch you when you aren't."

Anthony grinned. "Generally so certain!" he said. "I've been telling you for about twenty years that I'm never certain until just after I am." He fell grave again. He said suddenly:

"Mrs. Graye—I want to go over in my own words our conversation of this morning. I want you to listen. If I say anything wrong, pull me up, will you?"

The woman nodded. "Yes, I will."

"You have been a member of this household ever since it has been a household. You were housekeeper from the beginning to Dr. Hale-Storford and his wife. You therefore knew Dr. Hale-Storford and his wife very well. You knew, also well, Miriam Rossiter, Mrs. Hale-Storford's sister, and, not quite so well, the boy Anstruther. You must see, Mrs. Graye—we have had all this out—that if any member of the household murdered Mrs. Hale-Storford it must have been—because Banner and Trenchard and Hale-Storford were certainly out of it—either Miss Kerr, Miss Rossiter, young Anstruther, or yourself. We know Miss Kerr didn't do it; we know you didn't do it. . . ."

Dorothy Graye looked at him. "How?" she said.

Anthony returned the look. "I don't mean," he said, "that we can prove that either Miss Kerr or yourself didn't do it any more than we can prove that anyone else did. But we are—" he slid a glance out of the corner of his eye at Lucas, who had once more assumed the official mask—"prepared to back our judgment that if you or Miss Kerr had wished to get rid of Eve Hale-Storford you couldn't—and when I say couldn't I mean it—you couldn't have got rid of her in that way. Since you yourself have raised the question, I think it may be as well to answer it fully. I say that Miss Kerr, if she had wished to get rid of Eve Hale-Storford, would have done so openly and in an honest rage amounting to temporary madness. . . . Sorry, Miss Kerr, but I think I'm right. I don't say you do have rages like that, but if you did kill anyone it would be because you did have a rage like that. . . . You, Mrs. Graye, if you had wanted to get rid of Eve Hale-Storford—don't forget my additional clause—you would do it in a far more subtle way. You couldn't take a knife or a razor and cut someone's throat."

Anthony was speaking very slowly. The last four words of the last sentence came out separately and heavy; they dropped into the silence of the room like stones into a pool. He said:

"Also, Mrs. Graye—" his green eyes were staring down into the woman's —"also, Mrs. Graye, I have no reason for saying this except my judgment, but I think that you are afraid of blood. . . ."

The woman in the chair straightened her long body. She sat rigid, bracing her back against the chair. Her left hand clutched the chair's arm until the knuckles showed dead white against her skin. Her right hand, palm outward, covered her eyes. "Don't!" she said. "Don't!"

"Thought so," said Anthony. His words were now normal both in tone and speed. "We are left then with Miriam Rossiter and George Anstruther as possibles. Going over our conversation of this morning, I think that you, as the person out of all of us who knew these other persons best, cannot adduce any reason for either of these two persons wishing to get rid of Eve Hale-Storford, or for either of these two persons—even if have a reason they did—to do so in such a manner. Is that right?"

Still with the hand pressed against her eyes Dorothy Graye nodded.

"We are therefore," Anthony went on, "exactly where we started months ago. We have four possibles; four only. We know that it can't have been either Hale-Storford himself or Trenchard or Banner, and we can assume that it was not under any circumstances an outsider. The probabilities are so dead against any other assumption. There is only one thing left. . . ."

Trenchard started in his chair and spoke. It was the first movement and the first sound, almost, which he had made since their entry into the room more than an hour before. His heavy face showed shockingly white. He said:

"There's *nothing* left, you mean. Nothing!"

His eyes, which had been on Anthony at the beginning of his speech, flickered sideways, rested their glance for one almost unappreciable second on the woman Graye.

Anthony shook his head. "No, one thing left, Trenchard, and when every other possible thing's exhausted, the one thing left must be the right answer. You know that. . . . Child's Guide to Logic. . . . There were five persons that night upstairs, and if none of the other four killed Eve Hale-Storford, Eve Hale-Storford *must* have killed herself."

Another silence, broken this time by Lucas. And Lucas said, losing for the moment his officialdom and becoming an ordinary, intelligent, but much puzzled man:

"I've been saying that to myself, Gethryn—and I expect everybody else has —at the end of every sequence of thought about this business, right from the beginning. But—" he levered himself from his chair and crossed the room to face Anthony before the fireplace—"but, Gethryn, when you've said that, it's no more sense than any of the rest of this business. No human being can cut his own throat in the way that throat was cut and then hide the instrument with which the wound was made. And hide it, mind you, so that not even the most extensive search can find it. Have you read the description of the wound? The description of how the body was lying when it was found?"

Trenchard, stirring uneasily in his chair, had taken a handkerchief from his pocket and was passing it across his forehead. From Dorothy Graye there came a moan: "Don't! Please don't!"

"Sorry," said Lucas, "sorry! But I suppose you people knew what you were likely to have to go through when you consented to come down here." He was not sympathetic.

Anthony looked at him. "My dear Lucas! It appears obviously impossible for Eve Hale-Storford, if kill herself she did, to have hidden her weapon. But it does not, at least not yet, appear impossible that *someone else should have done so.* . . ."

The silence which followed these last words of Anthony's was broken by Pike. Pike, who jumped to his feet and said:

"My Gosh, sir!" and then lost immediately all elation. But he went on: "I've been all over this house myself, sir, and before that—on the very night of the death, in fact—the local police had been all over it themselves. That's so, isn't it, sir?" He looked at Trenchard.

Trenchard nodded. The laugh he gave was like the laugh he had given in his own house three nights before; a sound most distressing to hear. "All over it! Short of setting fire to the place and raking about in the ashes, they did everything."

Once more his eyes which had had, it seemed, meant to fix themselves upon Pike's, slid sideways to the form, half sitting, half lying in the chair next his own, of Dorothy Graye. He added, before anyone else could speak:

"But razors have been cleaned, you know. And there is running water."

Anthony spoke. His words came hard upon the heels of Trenchard's, but they seemed to have no relation to Trenchard's. They were:

"I want you to tell me, Mrs. Graye—and this is a question I haven't asked you before—whether you know of any reason why Eve Hale-Storford should have wanted to kill herself. I'm sorry if this is painful, but it can't be helped."

The woman let the hand which had been covering her eyes drop into her lap. It dropped like a dead weight. "None," she said. "None."

"There's one person," said Lucas, "who might answer that question, but he can't. He can't answer any question."

Anthony nodded. "Yes. Hale-Storford's madness holds us up. . . . Or not, Lucas. Or not." He turned again to Dorothy Graye. He said:

"Mrs. Graye, did you notice anything—I know you've been asked these questions before, and I know your answer to them, but I'm asking them again—did you notice anything about Eve Hale-Storford on the day preceding the night of her death which might show that she was in an abnormal condition of mind?"

Once more the head was shaken. "No, nothing."

Anthony sat himself down upon the edge of the padded fender. Now his eyes were more nearly on a level with the woman's. "Nothing?" he said. *"Nothing at all?"*

She met the gaze, raising her head proudly. "Nothing," she said deliberately. "Nothing at——" and then checked. Like a flash Anthony pounced.

"There *was* something, then? All right, Mrs. Graye, I'm not trying to 'catch you out,' I'm trying to help you. You've just—it's no good trying to say you haven't—remembered some little thing which until now you'd either forgotten altogether or thought unworthy of mention. That right?"

Once more the right hand of Dorothy Graye pressed its back against her eyes. From under the hand she spoke. She said:

"I don't know. . . ."

"Tell me," said Anthony slowly, "what you don't know."

The woman's left hand came up to join her right. Both the hands pressed themselves against her forehead. She said:

"It's only that that morning at breakfast I thought Eve had been crying."

Lucas swung round on her. "You've never said that before, Mrs. Graye." His tone was sharp, almost menacing. He looked at Anthony; met so ferocious a glare from Anthony's eyes that he fell silent. Anthony said quickly:

"Never mind that, Mrs. Graye. Tell me."

"I never thought of it before. I never thought of it before. It was so—I think it was a silly idea of mine. Because—because—well, no sooner had I noticed it—it's all coming back to me now—no sooner had I noticed it than Eve seemed to become her usual very happy self again. I thought perhaps

I'd made a silly mistake. In fact, I didn't think I'd made a silly mistake, I knew I had, or thought I knew."

Anthony, who had risen, sat himself down upon the fender. Again he looked steadily into the woman's eyes. Her hands once more were in her lap. Once more she seemed to steel herself to meet his glance.

"Mrs. Graye," said Anthony, "was there, to your knowledge, any woman member of this household besides his wife who was in love with Hale-Storford?"

"Yes," said Dorothy Graye. At this answer the eyes of the others in that room came round to her. She went on staring at Anthony. She was rigid.

"Miriam Rossiter?" said Anthony.

The woman shook her head. "No. Myself."

"And," said Anthony, his tone as emotionless as his face, "was any person in the house other than yourself aware of this?"

"No," said the woman.

Now Anthony's level voice cut the silence like a sharp but gently wielded knife. "So that, Mrs. Graye, the reason for the possible unhappiness of Mrs. Hale-Storford could not have been yourself?"

"No," said the woman. No part of her moved save her hands. These clenched and unclenched their long fingers as they lay in her lap.

"And did you, Mrs. Graye, know anything of the death of Eve Hale-Storford before that death was discovered by Eve Hale-Storford's husband?"

"No," said the woman. Her pallor was now so ghastly that Susan leaned forward, anguished, her eyes fixed upon that ashen face.

"You did not, then," the calm, cold voice went on, "find by some accident that Eve Hale-Storford had killed herself? You did not, having thus found, remove the weapon and hide it with the idea of saving some pain at least to the dead woman's husband who was also the man you loved?"

"No," said the woman.

Anthony's eyes remained on hers during the silence which followed. Then, suddenly, with a change somehow in the whole of his aspect he got to his feet.

"Thank you," he said. "I have been no doubt insulting. I will go on being insulting to this extent, that I will say that I believe every word you've said."

He turned his back on her. He said to Lucas:

"There's only one thing we can do. And if that fails, as it probably will fail, I for one give this thing up."

2

"You will *please*," said Anthony twenty minutes later, "stay here. Are you all right, Mrs. Graye? Miss Kerr, look after her, won't you?"

Susan nodded. "But will you," said Susan, her eyes enormous in a pale face, "will you, please, shut the door?"

Anthony smiled at her. "Of course we will. And we'll all be just upstairs, you know."

He opened the door. He went out into the pitch black and thick-seeming darkness of the hall. He called:

"Ready, Lucas?" and then waited. No answer came.

He went to the foot of the stairs and called again louder:

"Ready, Lucas?" Again no answer. Pike appeared at his shoulder. "Good Lord, sir," said Pike. "What——"

"*Ready Lucas?*" Anthony's voice was now a shout.

An answer came. At Anthony's shoulder Pike sighed relief.

"Ready," came Lucas's voice, very faint.

"Well, hold it till we get there." Anthony turned to Pike. "Come back now."

They went back, not into the drawing room, but into the room which had been, until he had begun to use the Watch Tower, Hale-Storford's study. In this room, pacing up and down before the cold blank hearth, was Trenchard. Anthony shut the door behind himself and Pike. The three men looked at each other in silence. The wide window of the room stood open, and faintly through the darkness there came to their ears the soft hiss-hissing of the sea against the rocks below.

"Ready, Trenchard?" said Anthony at last.

Trenchard nodded. He said, moistening his lips with his tongue:

"Nasty job!"

"Come on," said Anthony, "and don't forget—I'm Hale-Storford, you're yourself, Pike's Banner. We go out, me first, you second, Pike third. I take the lamp. . . . Oh, by the way, Pike, go and light that lamp on the hall table."

Pike went.

"I take the lamp," said Anthony again, "and I go upstairs. I am going to show you and Banner to your rooms."

Trenchard nodded.

"We walk as quietly as we can down the corridor, still in the same order. As Hale-Storford I stop outside my own door. I say something to you; you see what you saw. I dash into the room. . . ."

Again Trenchard nodded. He said:

"What then?"

"Lucas," said Anthony, "is lying on the bed as nearly as possible in the position of Eve Hale-Storford. . . . Sorry, Trenchard, but you said you'd do this."

"Go on!" said Trenchard between his teeth. "I'm all right!"

"Lucas has got in his hand a bit of firewood about the size of an ordinary razor. What we're going to try is this. I'm going to see if I can take that out of his hand, which is clenched tight, and put it into my pocket, hidden, within the time which Hale-Storford had at his disposal. That's to say, before he came back to the door again. You've got to use your judgment, Trenchard. So soon as you want me as Hale-Storford back at the door to make things right—or half a second before that—you must say, 'Now!' When you've said, 'Now,' I shall stop trying, whether I've succeeded or not, and come back to the door. Got that?"

Trenchard nodded. Pike came back into the room.

"We will go," said Anthony. "You know, don't you, Pike? You're Banner and you keep behind."

Pike nodded.

Anthony, the lamp held shoulder high, mounted the stairs, behind him Trenchard, behind Trenchard, Pike. The old house, except for sudden creakings and raps and the sound of their footfalls, was deadly quiet. The lamp's yellow flood—now circular, now elliptic, now distorted by contact with this wall and that corner—mounted steadily. . . . The three stood at the top of the stairs. Anthony turned left. He said, speaking his lines:

"First door's my sister-in-law's. . . . This one's Susan Kerr's. . . . This next one's Eve's and mine."

Outside the third door on the right he halted. He said:

"There are your two, next each other."

Into Pike's ribs Trenchard's elbow was driven. Pike did his part; said: "Gosh man! What's up?"

Anthony swung round. The pool of light widened in a flickering circle. Trenchard was staring at the floor. Not at that part of the floor immediately beneath his feet or his comrades', but at the boards which were, just inside the circle of the lamp's light, outside the bedroom door of Eve Hale-Storford. In the yellow glow his face showed as a pallid blotch. As he stared his right arm rose—slowly, seemingly without volition—to point a rigid finger.

"What's up?" His voice was a harsh, strident whisper.

Pike drew in his breath. "Water," he said. "It's water. Somebody's spilt some water."

Anthony left them. They stood there in the darkness. Anthony was at the door, and with him was the light. The doorway was bathed in the soft flood. Anthony set his fingers to the door handle; flung open the door. The others heard his voice: "Eve!" he said. "Eve!"

Then there was silence. . . .

Just as upon that night nine months ago Trenchard had grasped the arm of old Banner with fingers of iron, so now he gripped Pike's. He stared into the room. Pike stared too. They could see a little; the door was open. They could see, reflected from the white ceiling, the yellow flood of the lamp.

Softly to himself, with his breath coming hard and fast, Trenchard began to count. "One" . . . he said—"Two . . . three . . . four . . . five . . . Now, Gethryn!"

. . . And then Anthony was at the door again. They went to him. He shrugged.

"Did you get it?" said Trenchard hoarsely.

Anthony shook his head. "No," he said. "Could have in another couple of seconds. I was allowing time, of course, for being pulled up by the shock of the first sight."

Now out of the darkness came Lucas, straightening a rumpled coat. In his hand was a piece of wood about the size of a single-blade razor of the old-fashioned kind. Anthony handed the lamp to Pike.

"We'll go down now," he said.

They went down again and presently stood once more before the blank dismal hearth in the study.

"And that," said Anthony, "is that."

"I thought," said Lucas despondently, "that it would be. We'll never get anywhere on this, Gethryn. Never! Damn it, it's a sort of *Marie Céleste* business!"

"Here's a thing, sir," said Pike. He looked with some diffidence at Anthony. He thought that Colonel Gethryn had probably already seen this point, but bravely he put it.

"If Mrs. Hale-Storford had dropped the thing she killed herself with, then Hale-Storford would have had time to hide it."

"Yes, Pike," Anthony nodded. "But if Mrs. Hale-Storford killed herself with a razor or a knife, something that she could get a grip on, that grip wouldn't loosen. And if it didn't loosen, it would tighten. You know that."

Pike nodded, rather despondently. "Yes, there's that, sir. And, by Gosh! there's something I'd forgotten. There's the fact that if he had shoved this razor or whatever it was into his pocket, there'd have been blood, wouldn't there? And I think Mr. Trenchard will bear me out that the local police included clothes in their search."

Trenchard had walked over to the window. He stood now with his broad back toward them, hands in his pockets, staring out into the darkness. Without turning round he said:

"Yes, that's quite right. All our clothes."

"And I think," said Anthony, "that the number of old-fashioned razors in this house is just two. That right, Pike?"

Pike nodded. "Yes, sir. One of the boy Anstruther's—queer thing, a lot of boys seem to like the old type; makes 'em feel more manly, I suppose —and one of Hale-Storford's himself. Both tidy, both clean, both in the bathroom."

"And they," said Anthony, "were the only suitable weapons in the house?"

Pike nodded. "No knives of the right type, sir. No nothing. Dr. Hale-Storford had another razor, but it was one of those little Sambak safeties, and that was all tidy, all neat, and in the bathroom. Not that it could have been used, anyhow."

Lucas stretched his arms. "This thing will drive us all mad!" he said.

Trenchard spoke from the window, still without turning. "Perhaps we all are!" he said. His voice was higher than usual, and there was a harsh, strident sound about it.

Anthony began to pace the room, up and down the square of carpet in its centre. He said, pacing:

"Let's just see that we *have* got nowhere. We've shown that it's almost impossible, if Eve Hale-Storford killed herself, for her husband to have concealed her weapon. So, like the original problem of *murder*, we're back again with those four upstairs people—Dorothy Graye, Anstruther, Susan Kerr, and Miriam Rossiter."

"And," Lucas interrupted, "we can't tell, any more than we could when we were thinking of murder, about Anstruther or the Rossiter woman. Your experiments with Pike and Mrs. Graye show that anyone could have gone from any one of the rooms to Eve Hale-Storford's room and back again without being heard. Anstruther and Rossiter are dead. Susan Kerr and Dorothy Graye are alive. We say that we believe Susan Kerr and Dorothy Graye, and so we are left with the possibility—the utterly unprovable possibility —that either Anstruther or Rossiter discovered Eve Hale-Storford's suicide and hid the proof of it. . . . It's no good, Gethryn, you can try and make us think it's suicide, or we can think it's murder. Whichever way we look at it, we're no forrader."

Anthony was still pacing the carpet. His head was downbent, his shoulders hunched; a frown carved deep lines into his forehead. He said, stopping suddenly in his walk:

"I say, Trenchard!"

Trenchard turned. He leaned back now against the wall beside the window. He looked, and was, a man utterly weary. He said in a dead voice: "Yes? What do you want?"

"Just one thing," said Anthony. "Did we do that reconstruction without any mistakes at all? Think before you answer. Without any mistakes at all?"

Trenchard thought, closing heavy-lidded eyes. His white face against the dark wall looked like a death mask. He said at last, opening his eyes:

"Nothing. Nothing that I can remember."

Anthony drew closer to him. "Sure?" he said.

Trenchard nodded. "Sure!"

"And there was nothing in any way different about the proceeding? Think please! Think like all hell!"

Once more Trenchard closed his eyes and thought.

Lucas came to Anthony's side. "What're you after now?" he said in a whisper.

Anthony, not taking his eyes off Trenchard, shrugged. "God knows!" he said. "But I'm on the only line left to us. Not much of a one. . . ."

Trenchard's eyes opened. He shook his head. "Nothing," he said. . . . "Wait though! . . . Oh, but that's trivial!"

"What's trivial?" said Anthony quietly. "Better say."

Trenchard shrugged weary shoulders. "Just that it was all so much *quieter*. But that's because of the carpets being down now. *That* night there was no stair carpet and no carpet in Hale-Storford's room. Nothing else different —not that my mind registers, anyhow. Sorry!"

"Thanks," said Anthony. He threw himself angrily into a chair. He looked up at Lucas and then at Pike. He said:

"Well, we're beat, aren't we? . . . D'you know what's frightening me?"

He spoke in a low voice. He seemed not to want his words to carry to Trenchard.

Lucas said nothing. Pike looked enquiry.

"What's frightening me," said Anthony, still low, "is the thought of how this damned thing, just as a problem, is going to nag at my mind and nag at it and never give me any peace. Blast it!"

"We've got to forget it, I suppose," said Lucas. "If we do that something will perhaps go and turn up some day." His tone was far from hopeful.

Pike shook his head gloomily, looking at his boots. "Not in this case it won't, sir. You mark my words——"

He broke off suddenly, staring at Anthony. Anthony was leaning forward in his chair. His lips were a little parted, his green eyes blazing fire.

"My God!" he said under his breath.

"What's that, sir? What's that?" Lucas took a step forward. "What's up, Gethryn?" He got no answer, save the crash of the suddenly opened door as it swung back against the wall. . . . Anthony was gone.

On quick feet Pike was at the door, saw Anthony's tall figure at the table by the lamp, saw him raise the lamp and go upstairs running. He turned an eager face to Lucas. "He's onto something, sir. Come on!"

They went up the stairs, but they could not run. The lamp was gone, and they had to feel their way. It seemed suddenly cold upon the stairs. Quite cold and very dark. The darkness seemed to be pushing at them. Each man could hear the other's laboured breathing as he reached the top. They looked down the corridor. From the door of the room which had been the dead woman's a light gleamed. They walked toward it. As they reached the threshold Anthony came out.

"Pike!" he said, and his voice sent Pike running, in spite of the darkness. "Nip downstairs and find something like a cold chisel. Anything that will do for a lever, strong and with a thin edge. Hurry, man!"

He turned back into the room. Lucas followed him. Lucas saw that the carpet, the big, thick pile carpet, had been rolled back. The bed, too—the bed upon which Lucas just now in rather dreadful imitation had lain—was pulled aside. The old dark floor boards gave back faint reflection of lamplight. By the bed Anthony dropped on his knees.

"What the devil——" Lucas began.

"Shut up!" said Anthony from the floor. "Here, get that light and put it down here, will you?"

Lucas obeyed. Anthony, with a sudden lithe twist, was no longer kneeling but flat upon his face. "Light a bit nearer," he grunted. "Bit to the right . . . Bit to the left . . . there, hold it!"

"What the devil——" said Lucas. He was kneeling now. He heard Anthony murmuring to himself beneath his breath but could catch no words. There came the sound of feet in the corridor outside, and then Pike was in the room again. In his hand he held a cold chisel and a mallet. "These do, sir?" he said.

Anthony rolled over to one side and climbed to his knees. "That'll do. Here, have this board up. This one here."

Pike stooped to look, saw that the floor board indicated was the one which ran alongside the bed's normal position, and saw, too, a board whose aged edge, cracked and chipped, was gaping along nearly a foot of its length nearly an inch away from its fellow. Moved by an excitement but not quite knowing himself its cause, he set to work. . . .

With a little crashing screech the board came up.

"Lamp!" said Anthony. "Lamp!" Once more he lay upon his face. They pushed the lamp toward him along the floor. He peered into the yawning slit, his face level with the floor. "Well, well!" he said. He laughed, a hard sound. He thrust down into the pit a long arm; he groped. Presently, almost in one movement, he levered himself to his feet.

Lucas lifted the lamp. He and Pike gazed open mouthed, understanding flooding slowly into their minds. Upon Anthony's outstretched hand—a hand covered with gray-black dust and strands of ancient cobweb—lay something which dully and rustily reflected a few specks of golden light from the lamp. A small something. A something an inch in length by an inch and a half in breadth.

"See it?" said Anthony in a voice unlike his own. "See it? Know what it is, don't you? . . . That's a Sambak razor blade. Look!"

They pored over his hand.

"Great Jing!" said Pike. "Mean to say, sir——"

"Yes, Gethryn, what exactly do you mean?" Lucas's tone was impatient. He knew, or thought he knew, but wanted confirmation.

"Take this," said Anthony. He thrust the fouled hand forward and tipped the blade into Lucas's palm. "Got it, haven't you? The explanation, I mean? It was just that one thing Trenchard said just now that gave it to me. . . . Well, not gave it to me, but put me for the first time onto the extraordinary possibility. He said there was a carpet here now—this carpet—which wasn't there when the woman died. A few minutes before he said that Pike said something about a Sambak razor. Now, I know Sambaks, I've used one. They're not English, but they're good. They've only got, Lucas, *one edge*. That's to say, you can hold them and do things with them without cutting yourself with them the way you would with an ordinary double-edged blade. . . .

"Eve Hale-Storford did kill herself! . . . Look where that crack was, man. That crack an inch wide. She killed herself; she slumped forward as she had made the wound in her throat. . . ." He sat himself down upon the bed and went through a mummery ghastly in its accuracy of the actions he was describing.

"See, like that across her throat . . . like this tumbling forward; like this, right hand forward. . . . Then, because this blade isn't a thing you could grip but have to hold between finger and thumb, it falls out of her hand and down into that crack in the floor."

From Pike's pursed lips there came a long and almost soundless whistle. "That's it, sir!" he said. "That's it!"

Lucas, bending near the lamp, was looking at the blade. "They can tell us," he was saying, "whether this is blood or not."

"They will," said Anthony. "That's all right, Lucas."

Lucas looked up. "By God!" he said. "I believe you're right. But why, man, why? What on earth does a girl like that want to go and cut her throat for?"

Anthony shrugged. "That's a thing I'll never know. But I'll make a guess for you, if you like."

Lucas looked at him. "Which is?"

Anthony rose from the bed's edge. "Which is this, Lucas. You've heard the Graye woman—the woman you've never until now quite ceased to suspect—you have heard her tell about that instance when she thought the happy young wife had been crying? Haven't you?"

Lucas nodded.

"And you heard her say that so far as she knew there was no cause for jealousy on that young wife's part?"

Again Lucas nodded, slowly this time, as a man will nod who thinks he has seen the point but may not be quite sure.

"And you saw," said Anthony, "three days ago, Hale-Storford sitting on the quay side, a gibbering, witless thing, didn't you?"

Lucas nodded, decisively this time.

"It seems," said Anthony slowly, "to me that when a rather neurotic girl whose life is made up of her love for a man suddenly finds that that man, although he has hidden it from the world, is insane and will do nothing in life except to grow more insane——"

He broke off suddenly. "Not much good theorizing, is it? But it is a theory, and a possible one."

"And, sir," said Pike, "I should think the right one."

Lucas shrugged. He always strove not to show Pike's faith. He said: "Well, anyhow, we'll never know."

He looked round the room. "Let's go down, shall we?" he said.

Anthony nodded. "Yes. Not so pleasant up here, is it?"

In single file, Pike leading, holding the lamp above his head, they left the room.

3

Susan, her face white, her eyes big lakes of horror, stared at Anthony. They stood, alone, just within the drawing-room door. From the hall came the sound of voices as Lucas and Pike, Trenchard helping, carried the other woman out to the waiting car.

Anthony nodded. He said:

"Yes. *She's* the tragedy, you know."

Susan shuddered. "Oh, but it's all so awful and so—so——"

"Unnecessary," said Anthony.

She nodded the golden head. "Yes. Think of that poor boy and poor Miriam, dead for—for—it would be horrible anyhow, but dead for—for—a mistake."

"And think," said Anthony gravely, "of Hale-Storford himself. It's difficult, I know, but he's to be pitied."

Susan hid her face in her hands. She seemed to be shaking her head.

"I know," said Anthony. "It is difficult."

Susan raised her face again. "If only one could—could *do* something," she said.

Anthony smiled at her. "One can," he said. "Especially you."

"You mean?" Susan stared up at him.

Anthony nodded. "Exactly. Dorothy Graye. I said just now she's the pitiful one, because, you know, she's loved Hale-Storford all this time. Now, you can do something about her, can't you?"

He led the way out into the darkness of the hall and through the studded oaken door into the night. On the threshold he turned, caught the loop of iron in the door and slammed it shut. Susan shuddered; pressed herself against his side. He put a hand on her arm and guided her up the steep gravel path to the gate which led onto the road. . . .

The Watch House, empty and alone, stared out, as it had stared out for three hundred years, across the sea.